NATT

To my favor

There is such a thing as Grace. I love you so much —

Dad

August 10, 2013
The day before

BRAMBLEMAN

Also by Jonathan Grant

Fiction

Chain Gang Elementary
Party to a Crime (Fall 2012)

Nonfiction

The Way it Was in the South:
The Black Experience in Georgia
(with Donald L. Grant)

BRAMBLEMAN

A novel by

JONATHAN GRANT

Thornbriar Press
Atlanta

This is a work of fiction. Names, characters, places and incidents appearing in it are the result of the author's imagination or are used fictitiously. Any resemblance to actual persons, living or dead, events, or locales is purely coincidental.

Published in the United States of America by Thornbriar Press, Atlanta, Georgia. www.thornbriarpress.com.

Publisher's Cataloging-in-Publication
Grant, Jonathan, 1955-
Brambleman : a novel / by Jonathan Grant. –1st ed.
p. cm.
LCCN 2012931583
ISBN 978-0-9834921-2-2
ISBN 978-0-9834921-3-9 (ebook)

1. Authors–Fiction. 2. African Americans–Fiction.
3. Georgia History–Fiction. 4. Landowners–Georgia–Atlanta–History–20th century–Fiction.
5. Atlanta (Ga.)–Race relations–Fiction.
6. Forsyth County (Ga.)–Race relations–Fiction.
7. Lynching–Fiction 8. Suspense fiction, American.
9. Fantasy fiction, American. I. Title.

PS3607.R36292B73 2012
813'.6 QBI12-600019

Printed in the United States of America

Cover photo by Matthew King
Cover design by Jerry Dorris at AuthorSupport.com

Books are available at quantity discounts. For more information, contact Marketing Department, Thornbriar Press, 3522 Ashford Dunwoody Road Suite 187, Atlanta GA 30319.

In memory of my parents,
Don and Jeanne Grant

There was a man in our town, and he was wondrous wise;
He jumped into a bramble-bush, and scratched out both his eyes.
But when he saw his eyes were out, with all his might and main,
He jumped into another bush, and scratched them in again.

—Mother Goose

Prologue

Very early on the gray, drizzly morning of January 24, 1987, Thurwood Talton put on his blue suit and ambled into the bathroom of his brick bungalow in Atlanta's Virginia-Highland neighborhood. He trimmed his silver goatee and taped a gauze bandage over the gash on his forehead, which had required six stitches to close. He was rather proud of his wound—his "badge of courage," an admiring colleague had called it.

The retired Georgia State University history professor was preparing for the second Forsyth County Anti-Intimidation March, a follow-up to the previous Saturday's disaster. On that day, Talton and seventy-five others, led by fiery civil rights leader Redeemer Wilson, had been driven from the county by a pack of rock- and bottle-throwing thugs. Klansmen, neo-Nazis, and their Rebel-flag waving sympathizers had screamed at the marchers: "Get out of town, niggers!" "Praise God for AIDS!" "Forsyth County's always been white, and it'll always be white!"

Talton had heard someone shout "nigger lover" just before a beer bottle smashed his head. Although dazed and bleeding, he'd stayed on his feet—barely. The photo of a sheriff's deputy helping him back to the bus had run in hundreds of newspapers. After viewing several pictures of the mob, Talton had pointed out a hulking youth in a tan coat as his assailant. There had been no arrest. No surprise there. Forsyth County folks stuck together, he knew.

Redeemer, a fearless man, had responded to the violence by calling for a bigger protest. Now, nervous local and state officials were bracing for a march on the Forsyth County Courthouse in Cumming by an estimated 20,000 marchers from all over the world. Talton, one of the few Southern whites who had participated in the 1960s civil rights movement, would have an honored front-row spot.

This was, in many ways, the last hurrah for the old guard. Although the King Holiday had recently been established in Georgia, the movement was facing its twilight during the Reagan years. Talton had written in his journal of his hope that the march would begin a revival. He was sure some good would come of the fact that Forsyth's nasty secret was finally out: Blacks were not allowed there to live, work, play—or even breathe. Needless to say, the attention was overdue. Long a sleepy rural enclave, Forsyth had first been awakened by the impoundment of Lake Lanier, the state's favorite playground. Now, three decades later, it was a fast-growing suburb, thanks to Atlanta's boomtown growth next door. That it was only a racist's stone's throw away from America's black Mecca made Forsyth County's outright bigotry not only ironic, but bizarre. Contrary to the catcalls, Forsyth had not always been white. And no one better understood Forsyth's peculiar demographics than Dr. Talton.

At first, reporters wanted to talk to him only about his head wound, but coverage shifted when they found out he'd spent several years researching and writing a hefty manuscript entitled *Flight from Forsyth*. After a dozen interviews, he'd boiled the story down to a sound bite: In 1912, a sensational rape-murder trial and lynching fueled the twentieth century's worst outbreak of nightriding, and more than a thousand black residents were driven from Forsyth, never to return. Journalists misquoted him, reporting that *all* had fled. There was more to it than that. Talton had recently learned some horrible and fascinating new information, but he wouldn't share it just yet.

Unfortunately, his manuscript was *too* hefty. University Press had rejected it "primarily for reasons of length" although the acquisitions editor had noted other problems as well. But surely *Flight*'s prospects had improved in the last week, given the publicity surrounding the marches. Believing a book deal to be a sure thing, Talton planned to find an agent and cut a deal with a major publisher. He'd already promised to use part of the advance he would receive to take Kathleen on a cruise. To Alaska, maybe. Or Norway.

Alas, none of these things would happen.

As he looked in the bathroom mirror and adjusted the knot on his silver-and-red tie, Talton felt an overwhelming pain in his chest. He cried out in alarm and lurched into the narrow hall, bouncing off the wall, knocking down photographs, and stumbling into the front bedroom, where he died in his loving wife's arms. His last words were "not done." He was 68 years old.

The cause of death was an embolism of the left pulmonary artery: a blood clot. Kathleen Talton was certain that the man who threw the bottle had caused her husband's death, but no one listened to her pleas for justice. She grieved with her daughter Angela and a few friends. After the Unitarian funeral, she grieved alone.

Kathleen was certain that Talton had been talking about his book when he died, and she considered it her duty to see his work published. She tried to interest editors in *Flight from Forsyth*, to no avail. It needed extensive editing, she was told. Unfortunately, no one was willing to dedicate the time and effort necessary to fix it.

Many years passed. The manuscript gathered dust on the handsome walnut desk in Talton's study. Kathleen retired from her job as a high school English teacher in Decatur. Dementia crept into her life with the onset of Alzheimer's disease, and her world grew darker and lonelier. She feared becoming dependent on unreliable people. When unfamiliar faces showed up at her door, there was always a debate in her mind: Did she know them? Should she let them in?

One winter night nearly two decades after her husband's death, she wandered into the study and sat down at the desk, struggling to remember why she had come there. She was lonely—and angry at Angela for spending Christmas in Florida with her young girlfriend.

The manuscript sat where Thurwood had left it long ago. With a trembling hand, she lifted the title page, then put it back in place atop the pile of paper. She sobbed when she realized she'd let the book die and had failed in her duty to the man she'd loved for so many years. It would take nothing less than a miracle to get Thurwood's life's work published now. And what about justice? What about the man who'd killed him? She looked up at the faded newspaper clipping and its picture of that young punk, captured in an enduring grimace of hatred.

She wanted her late husband's work to be completed and published.

She wanted his killer to be brought to justice.

And it would be nice to have someone to talk to on desolate winter nights.

With the weight of loss and loneliness bearing down on her soul, she did something she hadn't done since she was a little girl who wanted a pony. She bowed her head and prayed. This time, she asked for vengeance, justice, companionship, completion, and closure.

It was a careless and jumbled-up prayer, but a most interesting one.

Chapter One

In the silence between the clatter of dishes and the waitress's barked order, Charlie Sherman heard himself dripping. He counted tiny splashes on the laminated menu: one, two, three. Waving to get the server's attention accelerated the patter. Interesting.

It was late on the night after Christmas, and less than an hour before, Charlie had been a semi-respectable stay-at-home suburban father, failing novelist, and not-so-loving husband. Now he was homeless, and he looked the part, in a torn blue nylon bomber jacket, tattered beige Henley shirt, paint-spattered gray sweat pants, and holey black basketball shoes. To top off his grungy appearance, he wore basketball goggles—a necessity after he'd broken his tortoise-shell frames during a Christmas Eve wrestling match with his four-year-old son, Ben. Not only did they make him look like a devolved alien, but the prescription was ten years old, so they gave him a headache, too.

He'd been thrown out of the house following an ugly domestic dispute that was not, at this fragile time, resolvable. Upon bitter reflection during the driving rainstorm, Charlie had concluded that Susan had wanted him out for months. Still, the eviction had come as a surprise. A shock, actually.

He'd been in the garage minding his own business, plunking bolts into a can, straightening up his workshop in preparation for his next home improvement project—just two days after he'd finished renovating the master bath. When he heard Susan hollering, Charlie thought his wife was being assaulted. Armed with a mini-sledgehammer, he'd rushed to her side, only to learn that *he* was the problem—one she'd decided she could do without.

She was standing in his office, pointing at his computer screen. Dumbfounded, Charlie stared at it. Honestly, he had no idea how that picture had become his screensaver. Due to the vagaries of Microsoft Windows, he had unwittingly turned a photo of a mournful-looking young blonde being gangbanged by a basketball team into his desktop background. An anti-virus icon covered her left nipple, but she was otherwise completely exposed. *Damn you, Bill Gates.*

Meanwhile, Susan let loose. "You fucking asshole," she said. "Get out of my house."

That was just her opening statement. When she unloaded, she could carry on for days on end, just like her mother. Before Charlie could properly formulate a response to her rapid-fire accusations, the cops arrived. Almost instantly, it seemed. Of course, she invited them inside.

While Charlie never swung the mini-sledge at anyone, hit anything, or even threatened Susan with it, he was still holding it when the cops came in, and they didn't like that very much. One of them drew his gun, and they ordered Charlie to put it on the floor—and his hands on his head. Her face pinched and flush, dark eyes throwing daggers in her husband's direction, blonde hair flying as she wagged her head and shook her fist, Susan then accused her husband of threatening her with the hammer, or more precisely, wielding it in a menacing way. "He acts like he wants to use it on something, maybe me," she said. Then she launched into her longstanding complaint: "It would take a miracle for him to get a real job instead of writing books no one will ever read." She delivered this pronouncement in that hateful North Georgia twang that was the hallmark of her family.

Charlie was left sputtering by the attack. "Hey. Just ... wait a minute—"

"Cool down," said the white cop, laying a hand on Charlie's shoulder.

"Chill out," said the black cop, pushing him toward the door.

"Just go," Susan said. "Porn freak."

So there he was, down and out. With his van blocked in by two squad cars in the driveway, Charlie stomped off into the jaws of a winter thunderstorm. After walking a mile in the rain, he came to the Hanover Drive overpass at Interstate 285. Consumed by both rage and despair, Charlie had a George Bailey moment as he stopped on the bridge and stared out through the rain into traffic. Yes, this seemed a fitting end, since his suicidal father had, on a lonely evening long ago in Missouri, embraced his own *Goodnight, Irene* moment and jumped in the river to drown—or at least to disappear forever.

And then something strange happened. As he stuck his left leg over the tubular guard rail and gazed out through the rain at the oncoming traffic, he saw a transit bus nearly sideswipe a gasoline tanker. An instant later, the tanker spun out of control at sixty miles per hour on the rain-slick Interstate beneath him. In cart-before-horse fashion, the eastbound tractor-trailer became a trailer-tractor. Its headlights flashed on the median wall, then swept across the windshields of the vehicles behind it, then spotlighted the noise barrier beyond the right shoulder, and finally returned to illuminate the highway ahead as the rig regained its proper configuration, having narrowly avoided crashing into the swerving bus and several other vehicles.

Not only had the truck spun out without wrecking and miraculously come back under control, but Charlie would swear he'd seen someone riding on the outside of the truck. For an instant, he'd glimpsed a man standing on the truck chassis between the back of the short-haul cab and the front of the tanker trailer.

Fascinated, Charlie removed his leg from the rail and ran across the bridge to see what would happen next. He put his hands on the cold, wet rail and leaned over to watch as the vehicle pulled to the shoulder and shuddered to a stop, air brakes squealing and gasping. A few seconds later, the driver jumped from the cab. Through the hum and whiz of traffic, Charlie thought he heard the man retching. But there was no sign of the truck-surfer.

Suddenly he realized that if he killed himself, he wouldn't be able to see weird stuff like that anymore, which would be tragic. Also, shame crept into his heart. After all, jumping off a highway bridge into traffic was one of the most socially irresponsible methods of suicide imaginable. At the very least, he could come up with a way to do it that didn't snarl traffic for hours. So he decided to mull things over instead.

Having temporarily given up on giving up, he hiked through the rain up the hill to Pancake Hut, where the waitress—Lil Bit, according to her nametag—refused to acknowledge his existence and pour him a cup of coffee. Usually he wouldn't set foot in the place. Pancake Huts were notorious for discriminating against gays and blacks, and Charlie was a liberal, of sorts. However, at the moment, he needed shelter from the storm, not political correctness. Anyway, he was white, so what was up with Lil Bit's cold shoulder? It was just a diner, damn it! With a "74" on its inspection certificate!

Perhaps the restaurant sensed his disrespect, for the place had turned against him the instant he walked in the door. One of the young drunks in the booth behind him called Charlie "'tarded" when he took his seat. The other muttered, "homeless fuck." Obviously, these were not his people: One wore a camouflage hunting outfit and the other a red baseball cap adorned with a Rebel battle flag and the words "Fergit, Hell!" And they'd been cooing insults at him ever since. Of the four other people in the place, only the cook had failed to show his contempt for the soggy newcomer. (Then again, his back had been turned the whole time, so maybe he had.) In any case, having just survived and escaped his own worst impulses, Charlie now felt trapped in this Pancake Hut of Hate.

The rain quickened, pattering on the roof like a manic drummer. Charlie lowered his hand and raised it. The dripping had slowed, so he waved to get the water molecules in his cuff moving again. Lil Bit, standing behind the counter just a few feet away, continued to give him the alert indifference only the best truly bad servers have mastered. She'd wait on him, all right—to leave. When he recalled a news story about a homeless man who'd been fed cleaning fluid by a Pancake Hut cook, Charlie thought that maybe it was better if they didn't serve him after all.

Well, she was stuck with him, since Charlie had nowhere else to go. He didn't even have his wallet, just a ten-spot he'd stuffed in the pocket of his sweat pants weeks ago. Enough to pay for food, if Lil Bit would notice him.

The drunks escalated their insults. Apparently, having failed to charm any women at the topless bar across the street, they were now intent on kicking some ass before they called it a night. "Come on, turdface, step outside," the Rebel said. "Just you and me. We'll go a few."

Charlie was big, six feet four inches, but he was in his forties, overweight, and relatively nonviolent, so he ignored the invitation. He just wanted some coffee. He didn't even care if it was good, so long as it was hot and not laced with ammonia or bleach. After that, he'd figure out how to survive the night. Or maybe, if he got a chance, he'd make a run for it.

Right then, he decided that no matter what, he wasn't going home, not until Susan got down on her knees, apologized for what she'd done, and begged him to come back. Which might not happen for a while. Or ever.

His thought was punctuated by a flash that lit up the sky. As the lights went out, a loud boom rocked the diner. The guy in camouflage drawled, "What the hell?"

As the diner's occupants murmured in concern, another bolt landed just behind the building with a blinding flash. A few seconds later, Charlie noticed a greenish-yellow glow through the rearmost side window—like some kind of radioactive fire.

The lights flickered back on. The rain let up.

His antagonists, apparently having short attention spans, refocused on their ham, eggs, and grits, so Charlie decided to take the opportunity to slip outside, check out the fire, and mosey off into the night, thereby avoiding the whupping he'd been promised. He slipped off his stool unnoticed as his antagonists grumbled and chewed.

Charlie stepped outside. He walked around the diner and saw something on fire behind the building. Whoa. Make that *someone*. Fighting panic, he ripped off his soaking wet bomber jacket and tossed it over the prone figure, putting out the flames and raising a cloud of acrid, funky-smelling smoke and steam. *Whew*.

The poor wretch lay motionless. Charlie picked up his coat and saw a six-inch-wide hole in the back of the victim's black leather jacket. Sure that nobody could survive a direct hit like that, Charlie reached for his cellphone ... which he'd left at the house. Damn it. He'd have to go back inside and use the pay phone to call 911, which meant facing those assholes.

He debated the issue for a moment, looking back at the diner, then into the night. Out of the corner of his eye, he saw signs of life. The victim's fingers drummed the concrete. *Shave and a haircut, two bits.* The body folded in on itself, fetus-like, and then jackknifed open with alarming speed. Charlie watched in amazement as the once-dead creature rolled over on his back and started to rise, yawning and stretching as he did so. His eyes fluttered open, showing rolled-up whites. Charlie yelped in horror at the zombie-thing, now standing in a crouch.

"Do not be afraid. I'm here to help," the fellow said in a raspy voice crackling with static.

"I'm not afraid," Charlie claimed as a deep chill swept through his body. "Just curious."

The guy he'd given up for dead held out his arms as if to suppress applause, then coughed out smoke. Shaking his head, he wavered unsteadily on his feet. He was short, with long, unkempt, iron-gray hair, and looked old beyond his time, like a wizened drug freak, scrawny old biker—or jazz trumpeter Chet Baker near the end of his days. He removed his jacket and examined the hole, which was bordered by a circular scorch mark. He sniffed it, said a rueful goodbye, and tossed the garment over his back into the Dumpster.

The stranger staggered around briefly but wouldn't let Charlie touch him, contorting to avoid a helping hand—as if he was an extraordinarily clumsy Neo dodging bullets in *The Matrix*. "You do *not* want a piece of me," he warned. "Not when I'm fully charged."

Charlie caught a whiff of the fellow and nearly gagged at the stink of homelessness—and something worse. The lightning must have triggered multiple excretory functions, yielding a horribly vile stench that could knock out a skunk at thirty paces.

As he stood with mouth agape, the stranger stared at Charlie with coal-black eyes. "What do you want, a friggin' wish for saving me?" He broke out cackling. "Go ahead. Make my day."

Charlie, nonplussed, managed to say, "I should call 911 and get help."

The stranger waved off the idea. "No cops. We'll handle this ourselves. That's the rule."

Obviously, the guy's brain was fried. Charlie shook his head. "I'm confused. Didn't you—"

"Walk here? Yeah." He pointed toward the Interstate. "From there. Nearly had a wreck. Truck driver saw some fool asshole about to jump off the bridge and lost control of his vehicle. My job to come in and save the guy. Trucker, that is. Used all my power."

He looked at Charlie knowingly, but the fool asshole had no response to that.

"So I was looking for food," the stranger continued. "But it takes days to build up energy that way. Mighty inefficient. Just when I'm feeling low—voltage, that is—I get myself a charge, and I'm good to go. Circuit breaker boxes work too, but you rarely get useful instructions from 'em. Less natural, I guess you'd say. Plus, you don't want to do what the power company tells you, do you?" He studied Charlie's blank face. "Well, maybe *you* do. I don't."

The rain started coming down harder. Charlie shook his head and said, "Let's get you out of the weather."

"Let's get me out of this weather," the stranger agreed.

"What I can't get over is, is ... how the hell did you survive?"

"Two things. Survival is never the issue for me."

Charlie waited, but there was no second thing coming. "OK," he said. "I'll buy you a cup of coffee. If they'll serve us, that is." He bent down and picked up his jacket, which now smelled of smoke and homelessness in addition to already being tattered, with a busted zipper. He tossed it in the Dumpster to keep the other jacket company and gestured for the stranger to follow. The old fellow started walking. It appeared to be a new experience for him—he looked like a tightrope walker with cerebral palsy. Horrible to behold. Charlie stepped toward him, but the stranger waved off his helping hand, causing Charlie's hair to stand on end. By the time they reached the diner entrance, the stranger had adapted to this mode of transportation, more or less.

If Lil Bit was unhappy to see Charlie return, she was horrified to see—and smell—his friend. She acknowledged the newcomer's arrival with a loud groan.

The Rebel laughed and punched his buddy. "Retard got hisself a spaz for a pet."

Charlie turned to address the men in the booth: "This guy just got hit by lightning! Cut him some slack." He hoped that this strange news would break the ice and relieve the antagonism that had been building up.

No such luck.

"You'll think you been hit with lightning when I'm through with you, bitch," the Rebel said.

Charlie whispered behind his hand to his new companion: "They're looking for trouble."

"Well then, today's their lucky day." The old man regarded the drunks disdainfully, drawing murderous looks in return.

Charlie shook his head at the stringy-haired bantam's bravado and slipped onto a counter seat. The stranger did likewise. "Two coffees, please," Charlie said, hoping this time that Lil Bit would acknowledge his order.

Feeling a static charge in the air, Charlie snuck a sidelong glance at his companion. Under the fluorescent light, the guy appeared to be not just old, but also terribly weathered—and abused. Veins threatened to break through the old man's paper-thin skin, which was darker than white and lighter than black. His grubby, uneven facial stubble looked like he'd hacked at it with an old knife, and he had the bloodshot, color-drained eyes of an ancient alcoholic. And he smelled worse inside than out—rotting teeth, with a hint of carrion. When Charlie leaned back, he noticed long bumps—or ridges—under a tight, wet, and remarkably unburned T-shirt that proclaimed *It's Better in the Bahamas*. Were those welts? Was this guy so old he'd spent time on a chain gang? What kind of hellhole had the poor guy been in where they flogged people? North Vietnam?

"What's your name?" Charlie asked.

"I've got a better question," the stranger said. "Who are you?"

"Who am I? Charles Sherman."

The stranger laughed. "Are you going to settle for that?"

That was rude. "Well, people call me Charlie. How about you?"

"I'm not from around here," the stranger said. "And I've been places you'll never want to go. Unless you're even stupider than you look."

Charlie grimaced at the insult. After a moment, curiosity overcame resentment. OK, the guy wasn't going to say who he was. He'd try a different tack. "Where are you from?"

"I just told you."

"Not exactly. Uh, how old are you?"

"What year is it?"

Charlie told him.

The stranger nodded and said, "Sounds about right."

"Huh? Never mind. Forget I asked." Obviously, the guy's brain was cooked.

Lil Bit, who had been staring at them with a curled lip, pointed to a sign above the grill: *Pancake Hut IS Home of the Sausage Cake*. She blinked in surprise and yelled, "Harley! Where's the sign?"

The middle-aged white man working the grill wiped his hands on his apron and looked up, then turned to Charlie and said, "Supposed to be a sign says, '*We Reserve the Right to Refuse Service to You.*'" Gray hair tufted over the top of his T-shirt.

"The one you had to take down after Pancake Hut got sued for discrimination?" Charlie asked.

"They didn't say squat about stink," Lil Bit countered.

"Just serve us some coffee and we'll be on our way," Charlie said. "*Ways*, actually."

The stranger beamed impishly at Lil Bit. "That's right. A cup of joe would go down good right about now, yes ma'am." She responded by moving to the far end of the counter and fanning her face with a rag.

"That reminds me," the stranger said. In a wire rack on the wall, there was an *Atlanta Journal-Constitution*, already read several times. He reached over and grabbed the Metro section, then leafed through it. "Hmm." He handed it to Charlie, pointing to a local brief:

Raccoon Gets Revenge

> Georgia Department of Natural Resources officials report that Forsyth County woodsman Phil McRae got more than he bargained for last week when he went raccoon hunting. After his hound treed the animal on a private farm near Lake Lanier, McRae shot the raccoon, which then toppled from the limb and struck the hunter on the head, chipping three vertebrae and sending McRae to the hospital. Currently recuperating at home, McRae was unavailable for comment.

Charlie shook his head. "Unbelievable." He jabbed the page. "That's my brother-in-law."

His companion, wearing a wistful expression, nodded. "That was some of my best work."

Charlie looked at him skeptically. "Are you a reporter?"

"No. I was the raccoon. And he's a liar. He missed me. Do I look like I got shot?"

If Charlie had been drinking coffee right then, he would have sprayed it over half the restaurant. Instead, he shook his head and tried not to laugh. Recovering, he said, "Now I know why Phil didn't show up for Christmas dinner. The varmints never tell me anything."

"Varmints?"

"My in-laws, from Forsyth County. The Cutchinses, more specifically—my mother-in-law's family. Phil married my wife's older sister, Sheila. I married Susan. Their maiden name is Powell, but take my word for it, they're Cutchinses. And Cutchins is as Cutchins does."

"Ahh … I wondered why I was out in the woods. Now I know. That explains a lot." The stranger nodded thoughtfully. "Now it's coming to me. You're the one."

"The one?" Charlie asked. "The one what?"

The stranger cleared his junk-filled throat and said, "So what do you do for a living?"

"I'm a writer." Charlie caught the waitress's eye and stirred a nonexistent cup of coffee with an invisible spoon. She scowled and turned away.

"Earn a living at it?" The stranger started mimicking Charlie's act, pouring imaginary sugar into a phantom cup—then spilling it and rubbing make-believe crystals around on the counter with his palm.

"Not right now. Got some things going on, though." This was true only if he counted as a prospect the one literary agent who hadn't bothered to write him a rejection letter. (Agents tended to promptly decline to represent his work, so the fact that Barbara Asher hadn't responded gave him hope, even though she'd held his query for nearly a year.)

"So you're looking for work."

"I will be in the morning."

"I know of a job you can start tonight."

Their steadfast refusal to admit they hadn't been served seemed to be getting on Lil Bit's nerves. "Get out," she snapped.

"You can't tell us to get out! That's illegal!" Charlie protested.

Harley stepped over to stand by her, arms folded across his chest, fists clenched. "No it ain't," he said. "You ain't a—ain't a minority."

"I sure am," said the stranger.

"This chain discriminates against nearly everyone," Charlie grumbled. "Why bother to open the doors?"

The Rebel spoke up. "That's why I come here. They keep it clean. At least until you two came in here. I don't know what's worse, nigs or homeless assholes."

Grinning, Charlie's companion swiveled to face the guy.

"That's right," the young man said, jabbing his finger at his cap so hard he looked like he was mimicking a suicide. "This here means I stand for somethin'. And you two can get the hell out of here so I don't have to look at you. Or smell you, you filthy fucks."

The stranger turned to Charlie. "What do you think of his hat?"

Charlie bit his lip. He'd nearly gotten killed on the Fourth of July over a Rebel flag—at a family get-together, of all places. This guy was just like the varmints, and he saw no point in arguing with such people.

The cook chimed in: "We told you to git. You're stinkin' up the place. Now git."

"We should leave," Charlie said. The stranger spun and hit the tiled floor with both feet. With blinding speed, he grabbed the Rebel cap by the bill. Flicking his wrist, he tossed it like a Frisbee over the counter. It landed on a burner and erupted in flames.

Arching out of his seat like a hunting bow, the Rebel yelped, "The sumbitch tased me!"

The stranger strode to the door, calling out over his shoulder to Charlie, "Come on. Let's go."

"I'm gonna kill both of you!" the Rebel shouted, flopping around as he tried to exit the booth.

Charlie slid off his stool and sprinted outside, shouting, "We gotta move, man! You know he's got a gun!"

The stranger kept his back to Charlie as he walked at a leisurely pace to the MARTA bus stop on Hanover Drive. Charlie caught up with him and looked at him in alarm. "You've got to be kidding! This is your idea of a getaway?"

The Rebel, moving slowly, struggled with the restaurant door on his way out, then stomped over to a Chevy pickup and opened the passenger door.

"He meant what he said!" Charlie cried out. "He's going to kill us!"

"Ha! That would be doing you a favor." Charlie's companion eyed their adversary in the distance. "He recovered quicker than I expected. Too bad."

"Too bad?" Charlie face was contorted in worried disbelief.

The Rebel bolted toward them, but when he saw they were just standing around at the bus stop, he slowed to a leisurely saunter and laughed contemptuously. As he neared, Charlie saw the silver glint of the man's pistol under the light from a streetlamp.

Charlie gulped, his throat bone-dry.

Just then, a bus appeared on the overpass, barreling toward them at highway speed. Its wheels left the pavement when it hit a bump, and for an instant, Charlie thought it was flying. The Rebel was in shooting range when the vehicle slid to a screeching stop right in front of the stranger. "Don't look back," he told Charlie.

The bus door opened. The stranger climbed aboard and Charlie followed, scrambling up the steps, shouting, "Get us out of here! Get us out of here!"

The driver, a plump black woman wearing shades, looked down at Charlie and said, "So loud. Tsk, tsk."

Before she could close the door, a shot rang out. Charlie grabbed his companion's arm and felt a sharp pain. Then there was only darkness.

* * *

A kick to the shin awakened Charlie, who was lying in the aisle on the bus. He blinked and looked up at the stranger. "Did I get shot? In the arm. Shoulder." He ran his right hand up his left arm seeking points of pain but found none.

"No such luck," his companion said. "You touched me."

Charlie shook his head. He didn't feel right. He must be crashing after the adrenaline bender he'd gone through. Reminding himself that he was lucky to be alive, he looked around. They were the only passengers on the bus, which was squealing to a stop. It was past twelve o'clock. Did that make it a new day, or a long night? "Where are we?"

"End of the line," said the driver, standing up and stretching. "Bayard Terrace. Close to it, anyway."

Charlie's eyes widened at the unfamiliar name. "Can I ride back?" he asked the driver.

"Why you wanna do that?" She opened the door. "People shootin' at you back there. Get real. Get out."

The stranger stood and stretched, popping several body joints. "This is the job."

"What job?" Charlie asked.

His traveling companion was already climbing down the steps. Charlie got off the bus and looked at its lighted route sign above the windshield: Out of Service. The rain had stopped. To their right, just ahead, stood Bay Street Coffeehouse, famous for the fact that there was no Bay Street within ten miles of it. They were in the Virginia-Highland section of Atlanta, many miles from where they'd started. What a screwed-up route. Charlie watched the bus pull away; he was unable to shake the feeling that a door had closed behind him.

The stranger walked a few paces to Bayard Terrace, a narrow side street, then turned and beckoned for his confused companion to follow. "Come on."

Seeing no choice, Charlie fell in step behind the stranger. They hiked up the hill on the cracked sidewalk beside Bayard Terrace. Rain-spattered cars glistened in their parking spots on the street in front of close-set homes. After passing ten houses, the stranger turned up the sidewalk of a bungalow with a glowing porch light. He called to Charlie: "Forward or back, which way do you choose?"

Charlie stopped. *This is absurd*, he thought. *Insane.*

The rain started falling again, pushing Charlie toward the house just as the door opened and a birdlike woman with snowy white hair stood bathed in light, gazing out past both men, calling, "Bounce! Bounce! Where are you?" She wore an old burgundy cardigan along with black stretch pants, and she seemed trim except for a little pot belly. Charlie thought she'd take one look at them and slam the door. She didn't. "My cat's been gone a week," she declared to the stranger. "I think my daughter had her executed. Maybe not, but I don't like the odds." She shook her head sadly.

"Do not be afraid," the stranger told her. "We're here to help."

The old woman, showing no sign of fear, gazed at them expectantly.

"Do you always say that?" Charlie cried out in exasperation as he stood halfway between street and porch. "It's guaranteed to make people suspect you, which they should. You almost got us killed."

"You wish." The stranger turned to the woman, who seemed not to mind his aroma. "He's the one. Charlie Sherman—or is it Charles?—"

"Charlie's fine."

"—meet Kathleen Talton." He neglected to introduce himself.

"The one what?" Kathleen asked.

"The one who's going to finish your husband's work." He turned to Charlie and said, "You're going to finish Thurwood's work, right?"

"Thurwood?"

"Her late husband. The history professor I told you so much about."

Charlie shook his head. "The professor you told me *nothing* about."

"Who are you?" Kathleen asked the stranger.

"Ask him," he said, pointing at Charlie.

"I don't know who you are," Charlie said, perplexed. "I'm sorry, ma'am. We—"

"That man found me," the stranger said. "And you were looking for him, and I found you. So here we are. And there you go." He seemed well-pleased with his logic.

"Who are you, the Riddler?" Charlie stepped back. "Ma'am, I'll be honest. I don't even—"

"As far as you're concerned," the stranger told Charlie, "I'm nothing but trouble. I thought I established that."

"Trouble?" Charlie stepped forward and looked at him closely under the porch light. "Yeah, I see that now. Trouble it is, then." Suspecting he'd been lured into a shakedown—or worse—he added, "This is a bad idea. Let's go." He reached for Trouble's arm, then thought better of it and withdrew his hand.

"Nonsense. This is a great idea." Turning to the woman, Trouble said, "You asked for help, remember?"

Kathleen smiled uncertainly. "Did I?"

"In there." He pointed into the house and wagged his finger.

She turned and looked inside, then gave Trouble a blank look. "How did you know that?"

He said something to her that Charlie couldn't hear. She retreated into the living room, and although she opened her mouth, no sound came out. Trouble stepped inside and beckoned Charlie, who asked, "What did you tell her?"

"I gave her my credentials."

"Which are?"

"Impeccable," Trouble said. Charlie followed him reluctantly, believing he'd walked into some sort of offbeat home invasion that happened to be going very smoothly at the moment.

It was a well-ordered house, though a bit dusty, with a closed-in, old-folk smell. Gas flames danced in the fireplace. "What big eyes you have," Kathleen told Charlie. "Pull up those things so I can see your face." Charlie pushed his goggles up on his forehead. After scrutinizing him for a moment, she said, "You look just like my son." She pointed to a framed photo on the mantel of a young man in cap and gown. "That's Gary. He died in Vietnam."

"That's sad," Charlie mumbled. "I'm sorry to hear that."

"Yes. Yes it is. … Well, where are my manners?"

Kathleen told them to make themselves comfortable while she got tea. Charlie stood by the fire to warm himself and looked at her photos. A family portrait with two kids, a girl and a boy. A framed black-and-white snapshot of a young man in a combat helmet, grinning in front of a palm tree. There were several pictures of the daughter, from gap-toothed girl to middle-aged woman. None showed her with a child or man, though she appeared in pictures with two different women.

"Kathleen needs someone to take care of her," Trouble said.

"Someone like you?" Charlie felt queasy, fearing that when Kathleen returned, the conversation would turn to her bank account and the whereabouts of her jewelry. What if she ended up dead? The halfwit accomplice was always the one that was caught and convicted. If Charlie could just figure out what the bastard was doing, he'd stop this nefarious plot.

"No, someone more down to earth. Like you, to talk to her and wreak vengeance, that sort of thing."

"Wreak vengeance?" Charlie's face contorted in disbelief. He whispered harshly, "You're fuckin' crazy, you know that? This is insane."

"At least she's not shooting at us, eh?" Trouble gave him a rotten-tooth smile.

Kathleen returned with a tea tray, placing it on the coffee table. Charlie watched Trouble from the corner of his eye. The old cadger and Kathleen were talking, but he couldn't make out what they were saying—it was as if they were speaking Greek.

Charlie asked to use the bathroom. Kathleen pointed toward the hall, and Charlie squished his way through the dining room and into the hall.

When Charlie returned to the living room, Trouble was gone. Disconcerted, he checked his companion's cup. Empty. And the box of shortbread cookies Kathleen had offered them had disappeared, as well. "Where'd, uh, Trouble go?"

"He said he had to go see a man about a mule. Or maybe a horse. I don't remember things as well as I used to. I have Alzheimer's, you know."

"Sorry to hear that."

"Comes with the territory," she said with a shrug. "He said his job was to get us together, and his work here was done, for the moment."

"You might want to check your purse." Charlie opened the front door and looked out. No sign of Trouble. He returned and sat in a wing chair by the fireplace, then stirred some sugar in his cup of tea. "You don't know him, do you?"

"I don't suppose I do, but here you are, and you are an editor, aren't you?" She hummed a few notes and picked at some lint on her sweater.

Charlie took a sip. "I'm a writer. I've been a newspaper editor. I don't know that I can do this. Or should."

She gave him a pleading look. "You've come so far. You may as well look at the manuscript. Please."

But he was still perplexed. "Ma'am, aren't you concerned about your safety? I mean, letting strangers in … it's after midnight!" He pointed to the clock and shook his head.

"If you were going to hurt me, you would have already done so. I can tell you're good."

"Aren't you afraid of what you're getting into?"

"Not at all. You've been sent here to help me. It's Providence, you know. He told me we're not supposed to tell anyone about him, by the way."

Even if Charlie wanted to talk about Trouble, what could he say about a thunderstruck stranger who suddenly appeared during his life's lowest moment and offered him salvation in the form of a scam? No, he wouldn't have any problem keeping his mouth shut. And while he didn't understand what was happening, he realized that, no matter how weird it seemed, he was getting a second chance of some sort. So, there it was: stay here, or walk back into the night.

Charlie listened to the rain, which had just started falling harder. "All right. Show me the book."

She led him into the study and pointed to the massive manuscript on the fine old desk—three times the size of any of the novels Charlie had written. "Sit down."

Charlie took a seat. "Ma'am?"

"Yes, dear?"

"Are you sure you're not afraid of me?"

"Oh, quite sure. You're the one. I know that now." She smiled. "And you fit *just right* at the desk."

While Charlie looked through a pile of rejection letters, she talked about her husband. "Thurwood was murdered. They never caught the racist who hit him on the head with that … thing he threw. That's what caused the blood clot that killed him. My dear husband would still be alive today … " She trailed off, tears welling in her pale blue eyes. She jabbed the air with her finger. "It was a beer bottle. I won't forget that."

She pointed at the wall, but Charlie didn't look up, absorbed as he was in the task of figuring out what kind of work the professor had written. Kathleen went to the kitchen to fix coffee. After reading two pages of Talton's dry-as-dust introduction, Charlie glanced up and saw the newspaper clipping Kathleen had pointed at. He positioned the lamp to spotlight the yellowed paper taped to the wall. It was dated Sunday, January 18, 1987. The photo showed a crowd of white rowdies taunting civil rights marchers. It was an ugly-looking bunch: the great-great grandsons of Confederate deserters, their faces grim under baseball caps like the one Trouble had pitched into the flames. One man wore a Confederate soldier's slouch hat. A bareheaded boy in the foreground had a serene, inbred look. Beside him, poised like a baseball pitcher on his follow-through, was a huge, round-faced youth who glared at the camera. His face was encircled by ink, with the hand-lettered caption: "J'ACCUSE!"

Charlie groaned in disgust and disbelief. He knew the guy. Oh, he didn't just know him. The asshole was family—a varmint, Susan's cousin, Rhett "Momo" Hastings, Jr. In the foreground, two steps away from a ducking Redeemer, stood Talton, raising his hand to his head. Charlie cursed Momo (who had once nearly killed him, too). "You bastard, I can't believe you followed me here."

But there they were. Charlie briefly considered telling Kathleen that he knew the guy who threw the thing, then decided against it. After all, what could he say? There was nothing anyone could do now. Besides, cause and effect didn't jibe. An old man keeled over a week after he was conked on the head. That wasn't exactly murder in his book. Anyway, that was twenty years ago. Momo had done time for his misdeeds back in 1987. Just not for this one.

And so, with nothing else to do and nowhere to go, Charlie settled in with the cup of coffee Kathleen had fixed for him and began reading Talton's work. He was vaguely familiar with the events of 1912 and knew that, nearly a century later, locals were still tight-lipped about them. He certainly remembered the two 1987 marches, which had been major media events. During the second one, Charlie and Susan had opened up their home as a refugee camp for Susan's Forsyth County kin, who fled the invading civil rights protesters. With characteristic gall, Charlie had pointed out to his mother-in-law Evangeline that, unlike black sharecroppers in 1912, she could return to Forsyth any time she wanted. He'd stopped short of telling her he'd considered joining the march. That would have incurred her eternal enmity as well as that of her brother, State Rep. Stanley Cutchins, a Reagan

Republican and barely closeted racist who'd flown to Hawaii on a lobbyist-paid junket rather than welcome the civil-rights marchers.

Soon after the event, Oprah herself had traveled south to tape her show in Forsyth County, which by then had become known worldwide as a racist, redneck backwater. Of course, locals believed they'd been vilified unjustly. (Cumming residents told reporters, "We didn't do nuthin' to nobody.") Certainly there had been some progress in the seventy-five years since 1912. For one thing, subdivision signs advertising "Gracious Lake Living" had replaced the infamous county-line postings that said, *Nigger, Don't Let the Sun Set on You Here.*

Charlie knew that since 1987, a few blacks and increasing numbers of Hispanics had moved to Forsyth County. He'd seen photos of an African-American high school track star on the Cumming newspaper's sports page. This showed acceptance, but also suggested that speed was essential for blacks who chose to live there.

Most blacks he knew rolled their eyes in exasperation at the mention of the place. African-Americans certainly couldn't be too comfortable in Atlanta's ultimate suburb. After all, Forsyth's reputation drew the sort of white person who wanted to escape crime, drugs, poor schools, and welfare this and welfare that, but who didn't necessarily use racial pejoratives, preferring to speak in code. Forsyth recently had become the nation's fastest-growing county, a paradise for people of paleness. It also happened to be Georgia's wealthiest and one of the twenty richest in the nation. That was no mere coincidence. There were now polo fields in Forsyth, once the home of *Hee-Haw*'s Junior Samples.

Charlie knew Forsyth's saga was interesting. Talton's manuscript, not so much. "This work is not publishable in its present form," stated one rejection letters he read.

While the old woman thought he could rescue the book, all Charlie wanted was to survive the night. That meant staying as long as he could—until his hostess asked him to leave or the police arrived. But Kathleen didn't tell him to go. Instead, she asked, "How long can you stay?"

"I got nowhere else to go," he confessed. "I have all night."

"You can rest on the couch if you get tired. Use the quilt."

Kathleen retired at 1:30 a.m. Completely at peace with his presence, she was soon snoring gently in the front bedroom. The Seth Thomas wall clock ticked in counterpoint to the rain's wavering beat. Wrapped in a quilt—his clothes remained incredibly damp—Charlie continued reading, mainly to justify his existence.

He reached the hundredth page. There was nothing remarkable written on it; so far, none of what Talton had written was special. Weariness overcame him. He couldn't continue. The scope of this mission was beyond his skills. The past was not within his power to change. The only thing Charlie could do was get some rest and try to save his own life. In frustration, he banged his head on Dr. Talton's desk.

The old sofa was inviting. Perhaps he could sleep off his dampness. He got up and shuffled over to it. The window trembled in its frame. The wind was rising, chasing the storm away. Charlie stood for a moment and considered his plight. He knew a couple of guys who might put him up for few days. Or not. The local Home Depot might hire him. Everyone who worked there knew him already, anyway. Then maybe he could rent a room. But he wouldn't return to the house on Thornbriar Circle, not until things changed. Not until Susan apologized and begged him to come back. But what about Beck (Rebecca) and Ben? What would he tell his children? He didn't know.

Charlie collapsed on the musty old couch. The dust he'd raised made him sneeze. He closed his eyes and dozed off. Soon he was dreaming that he was standing just a few yards away from an unpainted cabin. The world was sparsely furnished and small. He felt like he was on an old, cheaply designed movie set. Trees were bare-limbed silhouettes painted on canvas.

A family of black sharecroppers loaded up a mule-drawn wagon as a mounted gang of masked men watched them from under a spreading oak tree. The nightriders held reins in one hand, rifles and shotguns in the other, all aimed at heaven. Their skittish horses danced to crashing thunder that sounded like sticks hitting tin pans. The scene was illuminated by handheld torches. Charlie suspected that there was a Cutchins in the mob when he saw beady eyes glinting through holes in a makeshift white hood.

The children tearfully protested being dragged from bed in the middle of the night. Their mother, her body wrecked by childbirth and field work, snapped: "Get goin', ain't time to dawdle."

The father, wearing a look of utter defeat, knew his life depended on bowing before the hooded men. He said "Yassuh, yassuh," as he threw his meager belongings into the wagon.

Charlie knew what the sharecropper was thinking: Get to Hall County by nightfall tomorrow, got a cousin there, figure out what to do.

The wagon lurched off with the cotton still in the field. It was a scam: Drive them off at harvest time and take their crops. Affirmative action for white folks. A big, cruel-hearted swindle you couldn't perpetrate on humans and call yourself a moral being. But there was an easy solution: Make the victims less than human. That family became no more important or deserving of reparation than a steer from which you'd carve a steak.

Charlie had to stop this outrage, but how? The book he held in his hand had something to do with it, but when he looked at it, the cover was blank.

Chapter Two

"Darling, you've been working too hard on the book. Come to bed." Charlie opened his eyes and looked up at the ancient woman gazing amorously upon him. Her hair dangled loosely, and the curtain's shadow formed phantom grizzle on her face. For a moment, in the soft glow of reflected streetlight, Kathleen looked like country singer Willie Nelson.

"Mrs. Talton? It's me. Charlie Sherman."

"Oh." She let out a woeful little moan and stood up straight. "I thought you were … I've been diagnosed with Alzheimer's, you know."

"Yes ma'am, you told me. Do you know why I'm here?"

She brightened. "You're the man he brought to finish the book." She went to the desk and turned on the lamp. "How's it going?"

Charlie sat up and rubbed his face with both hands. "I passed out."

"That's all right. I hope it's not boring. I see you read to page one hundred and one." She emphasized those last few words, making it sound like the most fascinating number in the universe.

"Oh, no. It's … interesting. I just … just … had a rough day."

"I understand. I'll make you breakfast and we can talk about how we're going to proceed."

He thought he should proceed out the door. On the other hand: food. "OK."

Kathleen left to putter in the kitchen. Charlie looked at the clock and groaned. It was 4:05. He'd slept less than an hour and had a miserable, hungover feeling without having experienced the joy of drunkenness—a vice he'd sworn off the day Beck was born. (The morning after, actually.)

The dream had seemed so real; the events were etched in his mind. Maybe editing the book was possible, after all. Charlie returned to the manuscript, but he was tired and the words made no sense. They were just scratches on paper. He put his head on the desk.

"Breakfast is ready!" Kathleen called out. Charlie glanced at Momo's picture on the wall, muttered an expletive, and padded into the kitchen in muskrat-scented crew socks.

"What's wrong?" Kathleen set a plate of scrambled eggs and toast on the table. "You look like you've seen a ghost."

"No, no." Charlie shook his head. "Ghost isn't quite the word."

He couldn't get Momo off his mind. He kept seeing his gargantuan cousin-in-law bending over, picking up a Hardee's cup while serving his community-service sentence. In 1987, Momo had pleaded no contest to charges of battery and making terroristic threats after he punched out and threatened to kill a white civil rights marcher during the second Forsyth County protest. And now Charlie was burdened with the suspicion that the racist thug had killed a man in the first march and gotten off scot-free. *Make it go away*!

While thoughts of Momo tended to diminish Charlie's appetite, the smell of fresh coffee revived it. As he ate, he looked at the old lady in a threadbare burgundy robe across from him at the rickety table; she'd pulled her hair up in a bun, so she now looked semi-presentable, which was more than he could say for himself. He studied her kitchen. The finish on the old white curved-top Kelvinator refrigerator had worn to black around the handle. She must have lived here forever, poor woman. He guessed that all she had besides this fixer-upper house was her demented dream to publish her late husband's work. He hoped she wasn't thinking that the book would make her rich, because it wouldn't. He wasn't even sure it *was* a book. After reading a hundred pages, all he could say was that it appeared to be well on its way to becoming a gigantic mess.

"So you'll do it?" she asked.

"I'm sorry. What?" He stopped mid-chew and looked down at his hand, which was resting on a check made out to him—for twenty-five hundred dollars. "What's this?"

"A retainer. Or is it called an advance?"

"For what?"

"Editing Thurwood's book. I'll pay you twenty dollars an hour and we split the royalties fifty-fifty. That's what he said to offer you." She patted her hair. "Don't worry. I'm not in it for the money. We just need to get this done."

He sat there, mouth unhinged, looking like he was about to swallow a rabbit whole. Finally, he managed to say, "You should use this money to fix up the house."

"Oh heavens, I have plenty of money." Kathleen got up and went into her bedroom. After fumbling and clunking around, she padded back into the kitchen holding an armful of papers. She produced statements from brokerage houses, mutual funds, and banks for his inspection.

"You shouldn't be showing me these things," Charlie said. However, he *was* curious, and after a polite pause, started looking through the papers.

Hmm. This certainly changed things.

"And two certificates of deposit in a safety deposit box for fifty thousand each. I was hoping I'd be a millionaire."

"Don't forget to count your house," Charlie said.

She leaned forward like a willing con victim. "I own it, free and clear. How much is it worth?"

"In Virginia Highlands?" He chuckled. "You're a millionaire, easy."

Her face filled with joy. "You're good luck already! You made me rich, just like that!" She snapped her fingers. "As for the house, Angela—that's my daughter, she hates me, you should know—she gets it when I die." Kathleen went on, adopting a grumbling tone. "If I fix it up, she'll have me committed. She already keeps me prisoner here. Made me turn in my driver's license. She claims I'll lose my car, but I think she wants it for herself."

Charlie shook his head and smiled. "Come on. She doesn't hate you."

"You don't know her. She only comes to see me once a week. She's got a girlfriend, a cute young thing. And I do mean *girl*." Kathleen frowned and shook her heard. "She shouldn't date her students. Thurwood wouldn't have put up with that. Don't tell her I told you about the money. Anyway," she said, brightening, "I need a business write-off. A writer, anyway." She laughed, amused by her turn of phrase. "There is one other thing. You have to sign a contract. He's bringing it by—"

"Who is?"

"*Him*. The man you came here with."

"Trouble?"

She gave him an incredulous look. "Is that his name?"

"It's as close as I could get. And it suits him."

"Well, he's bringing it by later today." She looked out into the darkness. "It is today, isn't it?"

"Uh, yeah. I suppose it is, at that."

"Do you have a place to stay? He said you needed one."

"When?"

"Now, I guess."

"No, I mean *when* did he talk to you about all this? He didn't stay five minutes last night, just long enough to introduce us."

"He called me," Kathleen said. "Must have woken me up."

This baffled Charlie, since he hadn't heard the phone ring.

"He said, 'There will be miracles, but you won't like most of them.' Oh, and he said, 'No cops.' I wonder why he said that."

Charlie shrugged. "That's how he rolls."

She wore a puzzled expression. "He rolls? What does that mean?"

"Just an expression. I guess he doesn't like cops."

"Anyway ... you can stay in the basement rent-free while you work on the book. You *are* going to edit it, aren't you?"

Charlie sipped coffee and pondered his situation. He'd been struggling recently to write fiction for an hour at a stretch. Now this opportunity popped up. Funny-strange how a job had come looking for him, brokered by the weirdest dude he'd ever met. And it involved Forsyth County, of all places, land of his accursed in-laws, and Momo, the unnamed assailant. There were also nuts and bolts to consider. A lot of detail work, but the breadcrumbs were there. So what if the book sucked? Many did. Just add it to the pile. And there was that check—with the promise of more to come. The woman had plenty of money, so it wasn't like he'd be bleeding her dry even if he logged some serious time on the project. If he could whip Thurwood's doorstop of a manuscript into shape and get it published, it would look good on his résumé. Royalties would be icing on the cake.

"I can stay rent-free?"

Kathleen nodded and pointed at the door leading to the cellar. "Take a look."

He opened the door and flipped on a light at the top of the stairs. He stumbled down creaking wooden steps into a cold, dark, mildewy little world. He saw a bare bulb dangling from a joist and pulled its chain, illuminating the water heater and furnace. He listened to the whoosh of gas and suspected he'd need a carbon monoxide detector. Old paneling bowed out from cinder block walls. As for furniture, there was a metal-frame foldout cot with an old mattress that appeared to have been home to some hungry rats, a desk, a card table, and two metal chairs. The green shag carpet had to go, but it looked like it would put up a fight.

There was a separate patio entrance; the door's panes, like the overhead windows that ringed the basement, were caked with decades' worth of greasy dust and grime. The basement opened onto a small back yard surrounded by a weather-beaten, gap-toothed wooden fence. The small detached garage behind the house looked like it could topple over or come crashing down at any moment.

He climbed the stairs to the kitchen. At the top, he turned for one last look. *What a dump.* Only a truly desperate man would accept such abysmal quarters. "Can I move in today?"

"Certainly. I don't see why not." She handed him a set of keys along with the check.

"I need to get some things from my house."

"Didn't you walk here?" she asked.

He groaned. "Yeah, I did. I'm kind of stuck."

"Here, take my car." She grabbed a key from a nail on the kitchen wall and handed it to him. "It's old, but it doesn't have many miles on it because I don't drive. It's in the garage out back."

She was handing him so many things: money, house keys, car keys, hopes and dreams. He should give her something, too. A promise, then. "I won't let you down."

"I know you won't. God sent you here. If you cheat me, you'll answer to Him. Or Her." She looked at the wall, then turned back to Charlie. "This is all new to me. Before tonight, I didn't believe. Now I know. It really is amazing."

"Yeah. That's one word for it. I'll be back in a while."

Charlie stepped outside into the cold night and walked along the driveway—two concrete strips separated by patchy grass—to the weathered white garage, which was now illuminated by a spotlight shining from a corner eave of the house. After he struggled with it for a minute, the flip-out door rose with an ominous groan to reveal a silver 1986 Volvo sedan. Charlie squeezed into the narrow space between automobile and wall and fumbled in the dark to unlock the car door. The wind picked up and the garage moaned. He crammed himself into the car, plopping onto the cold black seat.

At first, it wouldn't start, the engine having fallen out of the habit of running. After a couple of tries, the battery started to fade. On the fourth try, the engine went *rur* … *rur* … and started, sputtering badly. He idled the car for a minute, watching the exhaust in the mirror forming a malevolent cloud behind him. A creaking rafter persuaded him to get moving before the garage collapsed on him like an evil tool shed in a Stephen King novel. He inched out and backed down to the street. The car's timing was off. While he waited and hoped for the engine to hit its stride, he picked up a scrap of paper from the seat and turned on the dome light to examine it: a Kroger receipt, two years old.

After a minute, the ancient Volvo's engine fell into a steady rhythm. Charlie drove off, marveling at how the night had turned out. This was madness, of course, but he wouldn't let that stop him. As his beloved Dr. Hunter S. Thompson once famously said, "When the going gets weird, the weird turn pro."

It was time for Charlie Sherman to leave the ranks of the amateurs.

* * *

Charlie couldn't guess what would happen when he returned to Thornbriar, but he knew things couldn't continue the way they'd been going. After all, his marriage had been deteriorating for several years. Susan had grown testy after Beck was born and more so when Ben arrived. The main problem was Charlie's decision—his wife no longer considered it a mutual agreement—to stay home and take care of the kids while he wrote books. This made sense at the time, since she was making more at the bank than he was at the public relations firm. Plus, he hated flacking, whereas she liked money. Years later, his failure to get published made his career path seem like a horribly stupid mistake.

Charlie loved his children, which was more than he could say about his wife these days. Of course, she had plenty to say about him, too. He wouldn't be surprised if, when he returned to the house, the cops were still there, taking notes while she continued her head-shaking, fist-waving rant.

Why had a border-state Yankee (the most ornery kind) from Missouri married this Southern girl from the whitest county in Georgia? Well, first of all, they met in Macon, and the only thing to do there was boink each other. There certainly had been an attraction. She was barely out of high school when they met, not even twenty years old, and he'd impressed her with his intellect and his position as a newspaper editor. He'd fallen for her because she was a saucy blonde and kind of hot. Actually, pretty hot. "Brassy and sassy," she liked to say. That demeanor was a facade to hide her innocence, and as it turned out, she had a hill-country *You Break It, You Buy It* policy. They'd married within a year (most of her relatives were surprised to find out they didn't have to).

Gradually, disappointment had worn off her playful edge, and now she acted like a troll half the time. Charlie thought she was still attractive, though in recent months he'd looked at her more with resentment than desire. Even with all their problems, life together had been bearable until the previous Fourth of July, when their marriage imploded, with the help of two of her most intolerable and intolerant family members—one of whom had apparently killed a college professor for sport.

Charlie rounded the sweeping curve of his block in the old Volvo and saw the porch light burning at 2567 Thornbriar Circle, a ranch much like the other houses on his relatively quiet suburban street. The windows were dark. The cops were gone. As he exited the car, an early morning train rumbled in the distance, sounding its horn at a crossing. He crunched the Volvo's door shut and squished across the driveway on prune-like toes in tattered shoes. He unlocked the front door and stepped into the foyer. Sirius was there to greet him, planting a cold nose on his master's hand.

Charlie walked past the half-bath, switched on the kitchen light, and glanced down the hall. The master bedroom door was closed. He tiptoed down the hall and stepped into his office. He was relieved to see that his computer hadn't been confiscated. He shuddered at the image Susan had seen, and wondered if the dispute over it would end their marriage.

The trouble had begun the previous afternoon while Susan was out shopping for post-Christmas bargains. Charlie was working on a freelance article about Clint Brimmer, a violent racist recently freed from prison. That morning, there had been a newspaper article about Brimmer, once a candidate for governor of Georgia. More recently, he'd been convicted in the cold-case 1965 bombing of an AME Zion church in Montgomery, Alabama that blinded the janitor. After serving ten years, Brimmer had been released from jail on Christmas Eve. Charlie figured he could interview the villain for a magazine article.

During his Internet search, Charlie stumbled across the *Forbidden Speech* website, which contained links to neo-Nazi, skinhead, and Klan sites. And to interracial porn, as well. It was amazing. He'd found a website that featured both racist propaganda and black-on-white sex to taunt the bigots—was the Web great, or what? Out of curiosity, he opened the link for *Jungle Fever*, thinking he'd see something from film director Spike Lee. Nope. Still, it required further investigation.

Charlie slipped a movie in the DVD player for the kids to watch in the family room, then locked his office door, still intending to do more research on Brimmer. But first, *Jungle Fever*. The website was fascinating for about ten minutes, and then, inevitably, it became boring and shameful. Just as he lost interest, he heard the garage door opening, thumping and rattling on its chain drive. Charlie clicked away from the site, signed off the Internet, pulled up his pants, turned off the computer, and went to help his wife bring in packages.

After cooking dinner, eating, and clearing dishes, Charlie went out to the garage. And that's where he was when he'd heard Susan yelling.

Several hours had passed since then, so maybe she had calmed down at least a little. Charlie closed the office door and returned to the kitchen. He opened a can of Alpo for the old golden retriever. Sirius gobbled from his bowl.

Now for a change of clothes. Charlie slipped into the master bedroom, where Susan snored lightly. *Perfect*, he thought. *Sleeping through the breakup of our marriage.* Then again, she could sleep through anything. He grabbed sweat pants and a clean Henley from a chair in the corner, then fumbled around in his dresser for white socks and underwear. He changed in the kids' bathroom.

"Is that you, Daddy?" Rebecca called out from her bedroom at the end of the hall.

"Yes, sweetie."

"Will you sing me a song? I need to go back to sleep."

"My clothes are wet. Let me change." He threw wet garments in the hamper, then checked on Benjamin, destroyer of glasses. The boy breathed softly as his father bent over him and stroked the hair off his forehead before kissing it. In her room, his six-year-old daughter lay under a huge pile of covers, staring up at him with big round eyes.

"You've been asleep, haven't you?" he asked. "You haven't been waiting up, I hope."

"I woke up when Sirius barked. What time is it?"

"It's still nighttime."

"Why'd you go away?"

"So you *were* up."

"For a while."

"I needed time to think."

"Are you mad at me for calling the police?"

"Oh." He slumped down on the bed. "*You* did that?" He stroked Beck's long brown hair. "Why did you think you had to do that?"

"You and Mommy were yelling at each other, so I prayed and God told me to."

"Really." It was just like someone with Cutchins blood in them to bring the Almighty into a domestic dispute.

"Are you still mad at Mommy? I think she's mad at you."

"Mommy and I have problems."

"She says you did something bad, but she won't tell me what. What did you do?"

"Nothing. Really. *Nothing*. Look, you need to sleep."

She propped herself on an elbow and gazed steadily into his eyes. "Are you going to leave us?"

"Sweetie, I will never leave you." He poked her gently in the chest. "Even if I go somewhere, I will always come back."

"I don't want you to go. Christina's daddy left. He has a cellphone but he's never *anywhere*."

"Don't you worry, sweetie. Now get some sleep."

"Sing the Bramble song." Her favorite as well as Ben's, even though it was one of the odder offerings in Mother Goose.

After he finished singing, they kissed and hugged and said good night, even though it was morning.

Charlie pulled a blue-and-gray quilt from the hall closet and bedded down on the family room sofa. He'd tried sleeping in exile back in July, when Susan cut him off, but he'd found that not having sex in a queen-sized bed was preferable to not having sex on the couch. (For the record, Charlie considered it perverse on his wife's part to first deprive him sexually, then complain when he looked at porn.)

Sirius padded in and lay down beside him. As Charlie drifted off to sleep, he thought that maybe, just maybe, Susan would come to him and tug his sleeve, like she used to. Then everything would be all right, and he could laugh with his woman on the way to the bedroom and tell her, "The strangest thing happened last night …"

But this was not to be.

* * *

Susan, picking up where she left off—mercifully, without two cops to shout between this time—stood over Charlie in her frayed pink bathrobe, hair pulled back in a ponytail, face worry-worn. "What the hell's wrong with you?" she said. "You need psychiatric help."

"Good morning to you, too." He looked at her groggily and came up on his elbows. "Is that what you told the police?"

"I didn't call them. Beck did."

"I know. She told me. That wasn't the question."

She put her hands on her hips. "I'm not pressing charges, you'll be happy to know."

He grimaced in distaste. "For what?"

"The officer said there wasn't room in the Georgia Dome to hold everybody who had porn on their computer. They said they'd have to build a hundred new prisons."

"That's because it's normal." He swung his feet to the floor and sat up.

"It's not normal. It's sick. Depraved. Especially that stuff. It should be illegal."

"What, interracial?" He shook his head in disgust, grasping at that rare opportunity to simultaneously appear morally superior and in favor of porn.

"That woman was being abused. That's what I'm talking about."

"I stumbled across it when I was working on an article about a racist, that's all."

She laughed in his face. "Yeah, right. That's your story and you're sticking to it."

"Don't want to argue about it anymore. But I have a right to know what you told the police."

"There *is* an incident number. They made a report."

"Do you think that's a big deal? You act like that makes me some kind of criminal. Wait a minute. What exactly *did* you tell them?"

"I don't know that they wrote down everything." A classic Cutchins response.

Once sassy, now shrewish. "What *might* they have written that would come back and bite me on the ass?" Charlie asked.

She plopped down on the coffee table, took a deep breath, and put her hands on her knees as if to say, *Where do I begin*?

"Do I have to guess?" he asked. "I heard you say I knocked you down."

"Then you already know."

"I was trying to get by you and you shoved me. I didn't knock you down. I brushed past you. I was just trying to get away from your yelling."

"I hit the wall hard. You could have hurt me." She gave a little pout. "You didn't care." The briefest of pauses, then: "I told them you were mentally ill and violent, all right? Holding that hammer that way."

"What way? Come on, cut the shit. You were the one acting crazy. So why are you out here now, other than to continue hostilities?"

"I just can't accept the way things are with you anymore."

"Amen to that. As far as I'm concerned, our marriage is over. Actually, it was over on the Fourth of July."

"*Right*," she snarled. "The Confederate flag ruined our marriage."

Actually, he thought it had. "Well, I—"

"There was a lot of patching up to do, in case you didn't know. Oh, that's right, you were too busy calling everybody names to notice."

"They almost had to patch me up."

"Pappy did not shoot *at* you. Quit claiming he did."

Pappy, also known as Isaac "Ike" Cutchins, was Susan's maternal grandfather and patriarch of her clan. Although well into his nineties, Pappy kept a loaded shotgun in his house, and he was still at least semi-adept at using it, as Charlie had seen firsthand.

Charlie took a deep breath. "You humiliated me in front of your family, and you were on the wrong side of a moral issue. You did everything you could to make me feel like shit about it, even freezing me out in the bedroom. That's worse than porn. It's as bad as an affair, in my book."

"What book?"

"Cheap shot."

"You've been writing for six years with nothing to show for it. And it's not my fault we haven't slept together."

"You want me to leave."

"Like that's going to happen," she said with a sneer. "Where would you go? You don't have any family. You tried to leave last night, and guess what? You're *back*." She sang the last word.

"You win," he declared and stood up, holding up his hands in surrender.

She paced back to the master bedroom. He staggered into the kitchen to make coffee. Sunshine flooded the window above the sink, bathing his face in light. He rubbed the stubble on his chin, feeling weary, but also clever and lucky. Rarely does a guy get a chance to snap off his life so cleanly, with a twist.

Contradicting him, Beck appeared in her white bathrobe, yawning, stumbling, and stretching her arms, her hair tousled and tangled. "You shouldn't fight," she said.

Ben followed in his red pajamas. "'Bout what?" he asked as he sat down.

"They fought last night and Daddy left and then he came back but they're still fighting."

"Over what?"

"I don't know. Daddy did something bad."

Ben was mainly curious. "What bad?"

"It wasn't anything," Charlie said.

"They were being stupid and hateful," Beck explained.

The kids wolfed down Corn Pops and dashed off to play with those Christmas toys not yet damaged or destroyed. Susan returned, still in her robe, and plopped down across from Charlie as he sat at the kitchen table sipping coffee.

"How many orgasms a day you up to? Sheila said men only use that stuff to masturbate."

Charlie didn't want to be reminded of Susan's older sister, whose second husband, Phil, had barely survived the recent raccoon attack. Two months previously, Sheila had arrived at Thornbriar "to calm things down" with a Glock pistol grip sticking out of her purse. After she refused Charlie's request to head back to Forsyth and mind her own business (and Susan backed her right to bear arms in his house), Charlie temporarily vacated the premises. When he returned after midnight, Sheila was still there, waiting up, playing the part of Susan's guard dog. She left at dawn—only after Phil called to demand that she come home and pick him up some breakfast on the way. "Your childless sister, the expert on male sexuality."

"Don't even go there. What happened with Jerry wasn't her fault."

That much was true. Nothing involving Sheila's first husband had ever been anyone else's fault, including his violent death. (He needed killing, as it turned out.)

"In answer to your question, eight," he said brightly.

"Ick."

"On school days. On weekends it's none. As you well know."

"Hard to believe it's humanly possible."

"As we both know, I'm not human."

"At last something we can agree on." She paused. "Just to let you know, I'm not paying for pornography."

He held up his hands. "Fight's over. I'm moving out."

"The hell you say."

"The hell I do," Charlie said. "This morning, in fact. I got a job and a place to stay."

"You got a job in the middle of the night, dressed like a … I don't know what." She sniffed and squinched her face, no doubt catching a whiff of Trouble. "Did you sleep in a Dumpster?'

"The job's been waiting for me. I've already been paid."

"*You've got a job and a place to stay and you've already been paid*?" Susan put her hand to her forehead as if she would faint.

Charlie retrieved the checkbook, along with some bills. Susan watched in disbelief as he paid the mortgage and Visa bill—more than the minimum, less than the balance. He figured that left him enough to live on for a month, if he was frugal. "Don't mail these yet. I haven't made the deposit."

"Could I see the check?" she asked.

He showed it to her. It was drawn on an account at TransNationBank—her employer. "I don't get it. Who's Kathleen Talton, and what is it for?"

"I'm editing a man's book."

"Is that like a men's magazine?"

"No, but thanks for playing. His widow is paying me to fix it up and get it published."

"Where are you going to live?"

He pointed to the address on the check. "There, in a basement apartment, while I'm working on the book. Live cheap or die. That's my new motto."

"There's something majorly screwy about this." Susan bit her lip. "I'm sorry you feel you have to leave. Must be nice to think you can."

Not the apology he was looking for. Too much cheek, not enough knee. "I'll still take care of the kids," he said. "Pick them up, bring them here, fix dinner, leave. How 'bout it?"

She gave him a harsh glare, worthy of her grandfather. "And live in another woman's house?"

He made a face. How could she think such a thing? "She's like eighty years old."

"And you're being paid over two grand for one night's work." She gave him a wicked sneer.

He left the insinuation hanging. *Yeah, I'm that good, but what would you know?*

"If you leave, you're not coming back," she added.

"Let's tell the kids that, then."

She looked down. "OK. Maybe you're right. But I don't see how you'll make this work."

"What I'm doing shouldn't come as a shock, you know."

"I know." She got up and withdrew to the living room.

"Let's call it a trial separation," he called out after her. "I'll come back for the van."

A while later, Charlie broke the news to the kids, telling them he'd see them every day after school. During his tortured explanation of the new arrangement, Beck turned to Ben and said, "Daddy's got a job now. When daddies have jobs, they have to go. Melissa's dad is gone all the time."

That was a better explanation than Charlie could give, so he left it at that. He just wanted a quiet exit—or a last-minute, heartfelt plea from Susan to stay. Contrition was not forthcoming, however, so he kept packing. A couple of duffel bags, three boxes, his bike, and his computer and printer—the basics to begin a new life. As he was leaving, he saw Susan staring into the bedroom mirror, pushing up her hair in a new style. Considering her prospects, no doubt. Perhaps now her prince *would* come. He decided not to disturb her.

Chapter Three

Charlie returned to Bayard Terrace and began hauling in his gear. Kathleen stood in the doorway, her face a mask of incredulity, her voice rising in pitch as she spoke. "You're staying *here*?"

"Yes," he said, brushing past her with his printer. "That's the arrangement, right?"

She spoke to the back of his head. "You don't have anywhere else to live?"

He turned to face her, his expression troubled. "Not *now* I don't. I thought we had a deal." He paused to consider his options. "I suppose I could make a Xerox of the manuscript—"

"Oh, no. That's the only one. It's not leaving this house."

"Not even to make a copy?"

"*Especially* not to make a copy."

Her position, though daft, served Charlie's purposes, so he pressed on, taking the printer into the study. She followed, complaining, "I don't like how this is going. I gave you money and you haven't done anything except drive my car around, without me in it."

"Well, you'd better make up your mind."

She followed him back outside. Charlie took his yellow mountain bike off the car carrier and leaned against it. "Look, Mrs. Talton, I'm going to get some coffee. When I come back, you can tell me what you've decided. I'll return your money if you want. But if you give me a chance, I'll do a good job."

"Can you get it published?" she asked.

"Sure," Charlie said blithely, ignoring his own concerns about the project. "No problem."

When he hopped on his bike he realized he'd left his helmet at Thornbriar. No matter. It seemed like he'd already suffered a major head injury, anyway. The cold air turned his cheeks red as he rolled down Bayard Terrace to its dead end and pedaled to Bay Street Coffeehouse, located in a small set of shops across an alley from the neighborhood post office. He leaned his bike against a brick wall. When he opened the door, a bell tinkled. It was a welcoming place, furnished with old couches and mismatched chairs. Local artists' paintings hung on the walls, and the place was crowded with leisurely Saturday-morning sippers.

At the counter, he ordered a large house blend from a strangely attractive, short-haired, tattooed and pierced woman of indeterminate age. Nearly as big as he was, she wore a black T-shirt with the words AMAZON WOMAN across her ample chest. He gave her two dollars and said, "Keep the change."

"I'd love to," the barista said with an engaging smile, "But it's two-fifty."

"Oh." Even more red-faced, Charlie pulled out another bill. He sat on an old wooden chair at a square table by the door and drank his coffee black, brooding over his unraveling plan. He'd been saved from a terrible fate for some reason, but now his opportunity for a new life was slipping away. If he failed … what was the saying? *An apple never falls far from its bridge. Something like that, anyway.*

When he finished his coffee, Charlie pedaled up the hill and hauled his bike onto the porch. Kathleen opened the door with a smile bright as sunshine. "Good, you're back! Everything's set."

Catching a whiff of Trouble, Charlie eyed her suspiciously.

"He brought the contract," she said. "Just left. Come in and look it over."

Charlie entered, fighting an impulse to gag at the lingering stench. He looked over the contract, which was office-store boilerplate, its blanks filled in with black ink. He would be paid twenty dollars an hour "to do whatever is necessary to complete Thurwood Talton's unfinished historical work." He would live in the basement rent-free while performing his duties and receive "half and only half" of the proceeds from publication. Fair enough, even generous, if there turned out to be any royalties. He raised an eyebrow. "You don't have a problem with this?"

"Of course not. I've already signed it."

"OK." He pulled out his Waterman fountain pen and did likewise. "Deal."

"Deal," she said, shaking his hand. "Make yourself at home."

With the crisis averted, Charlie set up the computer in Talton's study, then turned to the basement. In the dim light that fought its way through the back door's filthy window panes, the place looked only slightly less foreboding than it had at night. He breathed its fetid air, scuffed its crumbling concrete floor with the toe of his hiking boot, and listened to joists creak as Kathleen moved around the kitchen above him. He ducked to avoid overhead pipes. Maybe with a shaved head, he could safely navigate this place.

Over the next few hours, Charlie cleaned up his new living quarters. He threw out a ton of refuse: old bed frames with sharp, rusty edges, sheet metal, fencing, corroded buckets. The decomposing, moldy mattress came out in pieces, along with disintegrating books and an ancient Erector set that once aspired to be a robot. When he nailed up a dark green towel on the door as a curtain, he realized he'd created the perfect hiding place.

He had a bathroom of sorts—a tiny shower stall, a sink with a rusty old faucet, and a toilet that took forever to refill, surrounded by plywood walls. The shower was too gross to bother cleaning—it ran only cold water, anyway. He decided he'd use the Decatur YMCA's facilities to clean up, since he was a member and needed to get back in shape anyway—although he had to admit that cold showers might help him clean up his act. (In fact, he'd been chastened by the porn debacle with Susan and vowed he would be Onan the Barbarian no more.)

That afternoon, he took a shower at the Y, got a crew cut at Fantastic Sams, and bought clothes to create a new image: Dickies work shirts and pants, like the ones he'd worn for his summer job at the warehouse during college. At Optical Shoppe, he bought some offbeat glasses with gray metal frames to complete his trade unionist look, a statement of rebellion against the racist Republican politics of the family he'd married into and the suburbs he'd so recently forsaken.

He also bought a space heater, dehumidifier, carbon monoxide detector, air purifier, and a new laptop computer, so he could get out of the house upon occasion. When he plugged his new gadgets into the basement's lone outlet, he blew a fuse. Nevertheless, he embraced his cold, dank home. In this place of penance he would practice the asceticism his task required. He would be grim, stern, resolute, unrelenting. He would survive and prosper in his dungeon.

* * *

Sunday morning, it took Charlie more than an hour of huffing and puffing to bike over to Thornbriar to retrieve his van. Susan had taken the kids to church and left him a note saying, "I will pray for you."

"Pray for me to *what*?" Charlie said irritably, wadding up the note. Didn't she understand that he wasn't coming back?

He drove back to Bayard Terrace and spent the rest of the day reading Talton's manuscript. That evening, he accepted Kathleen's offer of dinner, free food being a welcome benefit of his new job. As she worked in the kitchen, he sat in the green chair before the blazing fire. The paper's Metro section was open atop the hassock. A small headline on a news brief caught his eye:

Forsyth County Man Shot to Death

> A Cumming man died after being shot in the chest with his own gun outside the Pancake Hut on Hanover Drive late Friday night, according to DeKalb County Police. Robert Logan, 27, of 1287 Dahlonega Highway, was pronounced dead at the scene.
>
> Police seek a suspect, described as a tall, heavyset white man wearing goggles. Witnesses reported the man started a confrontation with Logan, grabbing the victim's hat and throwing it on a stove burner. Police are asking potential witnesses ...

That wasn't what happened! Panic rose like a rocket from Charlie's gut to his brain. He told himself that the guy had been drunk, stumbled on the wet pavement, and shot himself. So why was everyone blaming him? It was as if Trouble didn't exist. There was another reason to worry. If Susan read the story, she'd pick up on the goggles. So would his in-laws, since he'd worn them during the Christmas get-together. The Cutchinses might turn him in, especially if there was a reward. On the other hand, the varmints didn't read—at least not *the lyin' Atlanta newspaper*. So maybe it would blow over.

"No cops," he muttered. Trouble's edict now seemed like excellent advice since Charlie's name was on a domestic incident report, and he was now a suspect in a fatal shooting.

* * *

Charlie awoke Monday to hear women shouting. He laid on his cot and listened to the kitchen floor creak overhead as the combatants shifted positions. Angela Talton was back from Florida, where she'd spent Christmas "with a young redhead that has a tattoo right above her butt," according to Kathleen, who considered her daughter's holiday trip a betrayal. Apparently,

Angela had issues, too. Charlie couldn't make out what they were talking about, but he figured that he was the subject of their dispute.

He fumbled for his watch. It was 7:13 a.m. He didn't want to join a debate that could put him on the street. Besides, he didn't have time to fight; he needed to take care of the kids. He felt an urge to slip out the back door.

But first, he pondered last night's dream, about a black farmer facing a lynch mob in broad daylight. Charlie could recall the scene in photographic detail: The victim, in overalls and a black felt hat, was riding a mule on a dirt road. A half-dozen white men blocked his path. They'd come to tell him to get out of Forsyth County. No, that wasn't right: They wanted to kill him because he *refused* to leave. The farmer didn't flee or beg for his life. He would die like a man. Good for him.

Charlie went into his nasty lavatory. The faucet yielded a sputtering blast of arctic water. He wet a cloth and threw it on his face to shock himself awake, then ran the rag over his buzz cut. Maybe he'd shower at Thornbriar. After all, he was entitled to that after renovating the master bath, even if he had moved out. He stared balefully at the corroded shower stall, then laughed at the prospect of being kicked out of this place, which was just a step above sleeping under a bridge.

Wait a minute. It was *definitely* better than sleeping under a bridge (and infinitely preferable to jumping off one). Furthermore, it was all he had.

His stomach rose to his throat when he realized Angela might have power of attorney, which would render moot Trouble's Office Depot contract. Perhaps she also could have her mother committed to a nursing home, a prospect Kathleen dreaded and one Charlie wasn't fond of, either. It was too late—and would be too humiliating—to tell Susan to hold off paying those bills. He needed this gig, which meant he had to go upstairs and solve this problem. He would be supplicant, diplomat, holy man, professional—whatever it took.

He slipped on jeans, sweater, and boat mocs, then stomped loudly up the rickety wooden steps and tried to open the door at the top, but it was fastened by a hasp on the other side. He rattled the door as he peered through the crack with his left eye.

"See," said Angela. "He could break it down any time he wanted."

"Until you locked it, he could come and go as he pleased," Kathleen countered. "He's going to help me around the house, too, aren't you, Charles?"

"Yes," he said, lips to the crack. "May I come in? Up? Out?"

"By way of leaving," Angela said. "And only because I'm curious about the kind of person who would live down there."

A hand unfastened the hasp. Charlie opened the door and blinked in the light. Kathleen stood by the sink, wearing a pink and white floral-print shift with yesterday's cardigan. Next to him stood Angela, a slightly rotund, middle-aged woman with salt-and-pepper, close-cropped hair, black framed glasses, and an owlish face that made the glare she gave him almost comical. She wore Doc Martens, blue jeans, and a black sweatshirt underneath a denim barn coat. She was holding the contract.

"Hi, I'm Charles Sherman. I guess you heard I'm editing your father's book." He held out his hand. When she regarded it with disdain, he made a point of closely examining it for cooties.

"I understand my mother wrote you a check for twenty-five hundred dollars," she said, enunciating the amount as if she were addressing a jury, "on the recommendation of someone whose name she can't recall. Please return the money and leave."

Angela might be in the right, but she had to be stopped. "Is it your money?" he asked.

"It's my money," Kathleen snapped. "And my house."

"Do you have power of attorney over your mother's affairs?" Charlie asked.

"No, she doesn't," Kathleen said firmly. "I won't give it to her. I can take care of myself."

"I've been trying to since Mom gave five hundred dollars to the Southern Law Foundation."

"I thought it was a civil rights group," Kathleen said.

"It's a homophobic group, Mom! They were behind Georgia's gay marriage ban. Now they've got more money to deny me my rights, thanks to you."

Kathleen stage-whispered, "My daughter's a lesbian." Then to Angela, who was rolling her eyes, she said, "I thought they fought the Klan. I just got confused, that's all."

"Exactly. And this is the latest, most egregious example of your confusion." Angela turned to Charlie. "You're taking advantage of a helpless old woman."

"I'm not helpless," Kathleen said. "How dare you!"

"Look," Charlie said. "I agreed to do a job, and I'm staying in the basement because it puts me closer to the manuscript and Dr. Talton's papers."

"How long have you been working on Dad's book? What stage are you at?"

"I started reading Friday night. I brought a computer and I'm converting files from his old word processing program so I can edit."

"Why are you here, though? Really? You know what I mean."

"I need a place to stay," he confessed with a shrug.

"Are you an alcoholic? Do you have a drug problem?" She glanced at his wedding band. "Don't you have a family?"

"My wife and I are estranged," he said, instantly liking the exotic-sounding term. "Look, the manuscript needs work, but it's publishable." He had to say that, even if he wasn't exactly sure that this was true.

"What are your credentials?"

"I'm a writer. I was an editor with the Macon newspaper."

She sneered. "Macon?"

"It's a good paper," he said defensively. "Since then, I've written freelance articles." He didn't mention his PR work, sensing she might be hostile to the concept. Actually, he was hostile to the concept, which was why he'd quit to raise babies and write novels.

"What makes you an expert on Forsyth County?"

"I'm not. Your father was."

"He comes with the highest recommendation," Kathleen said. "And he fixed my bathroom faucet. The one that's been leaking for ten years."

"Just needed a new washer," Charlie said modestly.

"Great. Look, nothing against you," Angela said, "but I'm a sociology professor, and I—"

"You never looked at the manuscript or showed an interest in your father's work," Kathleen said. "So don't come in and pull that."

Angela sighed. "Mom, I was going up to Forsyth that day, remember?"

"Dr. Talton, I—"

"Ms. Talton," Kathleen corrected. "She teaches at Perimeter College. Unlike Thurwood, she doesn't have a PhD."

Charlie was starting to sympathize with Angela, but expressing any such sentiment wouldn't help his case. "Professor Talton," he said. "It's a great story. And it's tragic that your father died without getting it published. It would be worse if it never got into print. I'm committed to making it happen. If you want someone to review the contract and my credentials, that's fine. I understand. I want everything open and aboveboard. But we'll get it done."

"So don't you come in here messing up the only chance I've got at getting Thurwood's book published!" Kathleen cried out, ignoring Charlie's conciliatory tone. "Not after you refused to do it. I don't have much longer, and I *know* this man can do the job. He was sent here for that purpose."

Angela turned to Charlie. "Ah, yes. That mysterious stranger she talks about. What's his name?"

"Trouble," Kathleen said.

"Trouble," Charlie agreed.

"Double Trouble," Kathleen said, then giggled.

Angela shook her head. "I'm not buying it. I'm going to do some investigating. Meanwhile, Mr. Sherman, I want a curriculum vitae, writing samples, *and* a detailed proposal on your plan to get this book published. But you can't stay here."

"It will take a couple of days to work up a marketing proposal, and I don't have a *curriculum vitae*," he said, pronouncing the term like it was an intestinal disorder. "The résumé and writing samples I can give you. Hang on."

He went to the study. He was reviewing his six-year employment gap when Angela stuck her head in the door. He printed the single sheet and handed it to her. "This project means as much to me as it does to your mother," he said. "I can do it. And I'm not a bad person. I just … fell down."

Her expression softened. She glanced over her shoulder. "Are your parents still alive?"

"No. My father disappeared a long time ago. Eventually, he was declared dead. My mother got cancer. She hung on long enough to see me graduate from college."

"Where'd you go?"

"University of Missouri. Where I'm from."

"Good journalism school."

"I know. I graduated from it."

She raised her eyebrows appreciatively. "Any brothers or sisters?"

"A brother who died before I was born. I was a replacement part," he added, marveling that he would tell her such a thing. He blew air through his lips in a gentle *huff* and gave her a wan smile.

Angela whispered, "Sometimes I think I'm a replacement part, too. It's hard for me to help her when she's like this."

"I heard that!" Kathleen said, sidling past Angela into the room.

"You did not," Angela said. "She always says that. Just trying to keep me quiet."

Charlie grinned. "Look, I gotta go take care of my kids. You two talk. Angela, I assure you that all I want is to get the book published. I'll be gone soon. Your mother's basement is not exactly prime living quarters."

When he left, he grabbed a trash bag from the kitchen and put it in a wheeled garbage can behind the house. It was partially overcast and the sun was playing peek-a-boo. Charlie's breath clouded the air. He inhaled deeply and told himself not to worry. After all, things could be worse. While Angela might dislike him, at least she didn't call the cops or shoot at him. Then again, that's what family was for. When he rolled the waste bin down the driveway to the street, he made a racket, not wanting his good deed to go unnoticed.

* * *

Charlie glanced at his watch as he pulled off Hanover Drive onto Thornbriar. He was running late; Susan would be stressed. She had a meeting scheduled with bank attorneys to discuss a class-action lawsuit filed by black employees. She'd been nervous about the case for weeks. "What can I tell them?" she'd asked Charlie in early December. "I don't discriminate. All I know is that a couple of blacks were passed over for promotions. This started with a woman at the branch too busy polishing the chip on her shoulder to do her job. Now attorneys are coaching branch managers to cover their asses. I hope they're not looking for a scapegoat."

"Don't tell them you're from Forsyth County," Charlie had suggested.

"I'm not. I mean, I won't."

He'd given her the benefit of the doubt back then, having always assumed she was a moderate like her father. Bradley Roy Powell, while a Forsyth County native, was no varmint. In fact, he was Charlie's hero. But now Charlie could no longer ignore the fact that Susan was half-varmint, and therefore capable of poor behavior on issues of race. Not that she'd ever admit it.

When he pulled into the driveway, the garage door was closed. He unlocked the front door. Inside, he was shocked to see his mother-in-law sitting at the kitchen table sipping coffee from his favorite blue cup. *How did she know*? Evangeline Powell, a stocky woman with a dyed brown mini-bouffant, pulled her white cardigan close around her neck, as if he'd brought in a draft. She set to the task of watching Charlie with bright, beady eyes like mall security would a shoplifter. An impish grin lit her round face as she blew her coffee to cool it. The instant Susan's dryer fell silent, Evangeline shouted, "Hon! You need to change them locks!"

"I've been thinking about it," Susan yelled back.

Evangeline smirked. "Hey, Charles."

He sat down across from her. "Hey, Evangeline. What are you doing here?"

"Taking care of my grandbabies."

"Beg pardon?"

"Didn't Susan tell you? Bradley Roy won't pick me up until six. Lord, I don't know what he'll do with himself now that he's sold the auto parts store to Phil and retired. Probably make a nuisance of himself."

"Bradley Roy's a saint," said Charlie, intending to piss her off.

It worked. Evangeline raised her voice to say, "He's a man, that's what he is. But I'll not get into it with you."

Susan walked into the kitchen dressed for work, looking ready to kill someone without caring who.

"What's going on?" Charlie asked.

"Mom dropped in."

Like a bomb, Charlie thought.

"Sheila drove me down," Evangeline said.

Charlie was confused. "I thought Bradley Roy—"

"He's picking me up. People will do anything for me 'cause I do right by 'em. Something you wouldn't know a thing about."

Charlie turned to his wife. "Didn't you tell Sheila that I was taking care—"

"Sheila didn't come in," Susan snapped.

"Everything just falls into place, doesn't it?" Charlie punctuated his remark with a derisive snort.

"Don't you worry none. Everything's under control," Evangeline declared. "We're not going to let what he did hurt the children."

"*He*?" Charlie asked.

"I didn't know this was going to happen," Susan told Charlie semi-apologetically. When he gave her a look of disbelief, she threw up her hands. "I called your cellphone and the number you gave me to tell you not to come over, but you didn't answer, and the woman there said you'd already left."

"*The woman*," Evangeline said.

"Well, here I am," Charlie said. "So there's no need—"

"I was here first," said Evangeline, making it sound like a playground game.

"But I'm taking care of the kids."

"They don't need you to babysit 'em. They got me."

"I've told you a hundred times, I'm not a babysitter. I'm their primary—"

"Look," Susan interjected. "I'm sorry it's working out this way, but I gotta go."

Charlie shook his head. "I'm amazed you let this happen."

Evangeline sat smugly while man and wife fought over her undeniably brilliant three-point plan: She was there, she was staying, and that was that. The battle was won. On behalf of her daughter, grandchildren, and all things good, holy, and Cutchins.

"You've got a job now," Susan wheedled. "This will free up your time."

"Bradley Roy and me gonna take the kids up to Cumming for the rest of the week."

"Mom, we haven't talked about that."

"We just did, right before he came."

"I said I needed to talk to Charlie about it."

Evangeline was a cruel and powerful enemy, and Charlie knew that victory over her was unlikely. Just being around her was giving him a headache. Clearly, compromise was called for. With his temples throbbing, he tried to do a cost-benefit analysis. He didn't want to leave his kids alone with her, for fear they'd wind up sounding like hillbillies and filled with Evangeline's spitefulness, saying "*You got that right*," or "*Lord, look what the cat drug in*."

But their visit to the land of varmints would only last a few days. After that, what could Evangeline do, besides hang around Gresham Elementary School every afternoon? If she did, he could have her arrested for stalking. He had to admit that Evangeline's power grab would give him time to work on the book. He cleared his throat. "So you take them tonight. I'll come and get them Wednesday afternoon."

"No, we keep 'em all week. Susan can pick Becky and Ben up Sunday. We'll take 'em to church."

Alarm bells sounded in his head. *Not the First Church of Varmintville*! Evangeline's Baptist congregation was so primitive the preacher spent more time talking about hell than heaven. Charlie refused to let Ben and Beck set foot in the building. As an adult, Susan had become a Methodist. This tilt toward godlessness still rankled her mother, whose faith placed Catholics in hell, along with *those who did not accept Jesus as their personal savior*—meaning Jews, Muslims, "them" in general, and Charlie in particular.

Susan wore a pained expression. "Mom, I'm going with Charlie on this."

Charlie didn't have a chance to put his hands over his ears before Evangeline started screaming. "He ain't got no rights! Not if he walks out on his family!"

"Excuse us," Charlie said, taking Susan by the elbow. "We need to talk."

Evangeline followed them to the master bedroom. Charlie closed the door in her face.

"We need to solve this in like sixty seconds." Susan glanced at her watch. "I've got to meet the lawyers. I told you I'm being deposed."

"I know who should be deposed." Charlie nodded toward the door.

"OK, what she did is rude and wrong," Susan whispered.

"And you know why she did it."

"Yes. But I don't necessarily feel that way. I don't want to fight. I just want to find something that works. If you could just go along this time, it would really help out."

Necessarily? He felt like he was being asked to take a dive in a boxing match. "It can't happen again."

"You know I can't control her."

"Next time she tries this, she can sit here alone all day. Like a vulture."

Susan scowled. "I gotta go."

"So I'll pick them up in Cumming Wednesday evening. No sense in you driving up after work."

"Or I can," Susan said. "No sense in you and her being in the same zip code."

"Good point. You're it, then."

Then came an awkward moment, since kisses had ended back in July and now their relationship had sunk to an even lower level. Susan grabbed her purse. "Bye." She walked into the hall just as Beck emerged from her room. She called for Ben, then hugged her children so hard they yelped.

After glancing around the room he'd painted last summer, Charlie stepped into the hall and braced for serious man-against-mother-in-law action. The door to the garage slammed shut and Evangeline herded the kids toward the kitchen. She began ransacking the place in an attempt to fix breakfast. Charlie stepped in wordlessly, grabbing bowls and boxes.

"Is that all you got to feed them, cereal?"

"Save it, Evangeline. If we're going to get through this—"

"Where's the milk?"

Ben pulled a jug from the refrigerator. Evangeline grabbed it and scrutinized it like she was a lab technician at the Centers for Disease Control. "I can't believe you give them skim. Children need whole milk to grow. You must buy the groceries. Susan wouldn't do such a thing."

"We have rules about TV," he reminded her.

"Nothing I can do about that in Cumming," Evangeline snapped. "We got cable."

"So do we, but we hold it to an hour a day."

"Movies run more than an hour, everybody knows that."

"Average, Evangeline. Average. They can watch a movie every other day."

Evangeline's stiff body language suggested she was not subject to his pronouncements. "Don't you worry. I know how to make children happy."

"That's wonderful," he deadpanned. He looked around the kitchen. After an awkward silence, he said, "Well, I'd better go. Kids, I'll see you Thursday."

Beck and Ben hugged him. He noticed they didn't seem sad to see him go. Then again, they knew Grandma would let them watch cartoons all day. No doubt she'd seize this opportunity to make up for her Charlie-induced time deficit with them, suck out their brains, and mold them into little Cutchinses. Was that the payoff he got for marrying Susan and helping pay her way through college? This truly was an outrage.

Charlie left Thornbriar with a pounding headache. He hadn't had any coffee yet, so he stopped at Starbucks to fix his caffeine deficiency. Then he called Susan's work number from his cellphone.

"I'm busy, Charlie."

"I'll just take a moment. Have I told you that your mother is a difficult woman?"

"I believe you mentioned it once or twice. So what's your point?"

"You're making this worse than it needs to be," he said.

"I didn't do this."

"Your whole family is already fighting the custody battle."

"Don't be paranoid. Oh, the attorneys are here."

When he laughed, she said, "What's funny? Oh, forget it."

"Fine. Bye." He hung up, vowing that if he came across the Cutchins name in Talton's book, he'd prominently feature the family's role in the outrages. Just then, the sun jumped out from behind a cloud and beamed down on him as if to say, *You got that right.*

Chapter Four

Charlie had left Bayard Terrace hoping Angela would accept the situation. After all, she seemed to be warming to him. A little. However, when he returned with milk and bread, he learned that the feud between mother and daughter was far from settled, and his job was still in jeopardy.

"Angela just left with the contract," Kathleen said, greeting Charlie at the door. "She's getting an attorney to break it. Fat lot of good it will do her." She closed the door behind him and moved to the window, spying on the street from behind a curtain. "I warned her, but she wouldn't listen. That was a big mistake. She has no idea what she's getting into." She shook her head and let go of the curtain. "She said she'd call the police if you don't leave, so you're in this, too."

No cops. "Maybe I should—"

"You're not going anywhere. Get to work." He looked into the woman's sky-blue eyes. She seemed equal parts sweet and creepy right then. "I think my daughter hates men," she added. "She didn't love her father. What do you think?"

"I don't, not about that." His problem with Angela was her opinion of him, not vice versa. Live and let live, that was his motto. "I wish you two could get along. Maybe try a little diplomacy."

Kathleen shook her head. "She didn't hug me when she left. And I'll never have grandchildren. She's fifty years old. I suppose her girlfriend could have some procedure done."

"I suppose."

Kathleen sighed. "She's going to have to change her attitude. Or else," she added in a sinister tone.

OK. More creepy than sweet. "Or else what?"

"I'll put a curse on her, that's what I'll do."

"A curse? Don't go medieval on us," he pleaded, laughing.

She narrowed her eyes to slits. "Thurwood's book is my baby, the most important thing in the world, and she's trying to kill it."

"I can take a hint," he said. "I'll get to work."

"It's best that you do."

"Just don't put a curse on me."

"Don't worry. You're immune."

"That's good to know."

"At least I think you are. Haven't tested it on you yet."

* * *

That afternoon, Charlie took a break and strolled down to Bay Street Coffeehouse. He was encouraged to see Amazon Woman working the counter and delighted when she smiled at him. He sat by the large front window and sipped coffee laced with a double shot of espresso. He gazed out at a thin, beautiful platinum-haired woman in black tights jogging by. No time for that: He was an ascetic with a job to do. The idea that his life had been boiled down to one essential thing brought a peaceful feeling—until he picked up a discarded newspaper from the next table and glanced through the Metro section. A news brief caught his eye:

Diner Gutted by Flames

> DeKalb County investigators are probing a late night fire Saturday that destroyed a Pancake Hut on Hanover Drive. No injuries were reported.
>
> Arson investigators believe an incendiary device may have been involved in the 11 p.m. blaze. Pancake Hut waitress Lila Beth Richards reported a "suspicious-looking man with goggles lurking around" just before the fire. Police believe this may be the possible suspect in the fatal shooting of a Forsyth County man at the same location Friday night.
>
> The Pancake Hut chain is the target of a class-action discrimination lawsuit filed by black customers. Investigators declined to comment on motives in the case.

Charlie gulped down the rest of his coffee, quickly returned to Bayard Terrace, and frantically searched the dungeon for his goggles. He was sure he'd brought them back from Optical Shoppe on Saturday. After reading Sunday's article about the shooting, he'd made a mental note to get rid of them, but now he couldn't find them. He paced around the basement, afraid that Trouble was framing him for crimes the weird old fellow himself had committed. Clearly, something beyond his understanding was at work: the fight with Susan, Beck's 911 call, his eviction, the lightning, the shooting, the bus ride, the manuscript, the deal. Rescues and vengeance at random.

Desperate to figure out what was going on, Charlie hopped into his van, and despite a gnawing fear of getting busted, returned to the scene of the crime. Or crimes. After a twenty-minute drive, he pulled his van into the Pancake Hut's deserted parking lot and looked into an orange-purple twilight. Lines of yellow tape surrounded the place like it was a poorly wrapped gift. The building had been gutted and charred to cinders; only brick walls remained. He exited the van and stared at the burned-out building, then glanced toward the bus stop and saw a dark patch on the pavement. Logan's blood. Charlie's knees buckled and he nearly fell down.

What should he do? What *could* he do? Report Trouble to the police? *No cops*, Trouble had said. *We'll handle this ourselves*. Charlie had to face it: Someone—or something—capable of shaking off a lightning strike, then smiting left (diner) and right (dead guy) was more powerful than cops.

Was he under Trouble's power now? Was he leaving the laws of man behind? Charlie had to concede something was out there, something that could reasonably be called God—and It knew who he was. It also seemed to go out of Its way to keep him alive *and* push him underground. Apparently, God had something to say about the affairs of men, and Charlie was part of Its plan. Quite an epiphany for someone who'd spent his life a millimeter away from atheism.

Charlie ventured past the yellow tape and picked up a shard of blackened glass as a souvenir. There was no point in lingering. He scrambled back to the van and drove off as darkness fell.

* * *

The next afternoon, when Charlie returned from a workout and shower at the Decatur Y, Angela's black Camry was in Kathleen's driveway. He parked on the street and waited for her to leave, but he grew bored after five minutes and decided to confront his nemesis—or at least say howdy.

A freckled young strawberry blonde in overalls and an Indigo Girls T-shirt answered the door. She had boyishly short hair and a nose ring along with three small gemstone studs in her left ear, one in her right, and a tattoo on the back of her neck, some kind of elf-rune design. He wished he could see the lower one Kathleen had mentioned, but it seemed rude to ask.

"You must be the Bogeyman. I'm Hyacinth Vickers. Angela dragged me over for moral support in her fight against the evil witch." She spoke with a straight face and a twinkle in her eye.

"Which old witch?"

"Whichever."

Angela was talking on the phone in the dining room. He heard loud chopping coming from the kitchen and shouted, "Hi Kathleen!"

"Glad you're back, Charles. Lots of work to do," Kathleen said, sounding gruff and purposeful.

Charlie plopped into the green easy chair. Hyacinth returned to the sofa and held up a book: *Killers of the Dream*, by Lillian Smith. "I found it in the study. She was a lesbian and a friend of Dr. King's. I learned about her in a graduate women's studies class at Emory."

Grad school? Kathleen had practically accused Angela of child molestation for dating her! Angela didn't teach at Emory, either. It seemed that she'd done nothing wrong—except to piss off her mother, that is.

"By the way," Hyacinth said, "Angela called a history professor at Georgia State. Turns out he knows you … says you're great and they're lucky to have you. Name's Sherrill."

Charlie burst out laughing. Angela's inquisition had led straight to his old *Macon Telegraph* colleague and drinking buddy, back during his days of imbibing. "Hank Sherrill's a history professor? I'll be damned."

Angela appeared, wearing a scowl and a red-and-black lumberjack shirt.

Kathleen followed, beaming triumphantly. "You didn't say you won a Pulitzer Prize!"

Charlie stood. "I was just the editor on that series. I didn't write it."

"No, you *edited* it. I think that settles it, don't you, Angela? You can take your letter and—"

"He can't stay here," Angela said. "He can work on the book somewhere else."

As Kathleen fumed silently, Hyacinth bounced up from the couch. Playing Tigger to Angela's Eeyore, she said, "We have to go if we're going to meet Mary Alice at five."

Angela gave her a warning glance. "Mr. Sherman, I'm not letting you take advantage of my mother. There will be a new contract. You'll get an agent's fee if the book gets published. I mean, the book's finished already. It either works or it doesn't."

"I'm not an agent. I'm an editor. If I was going to take her money, I'd already be gone." Out of the corner of his eye, Charlie saw a crow perched in a bare-limbed dogwood by the street. It cocked its head and regarded him with a beady eye. "Anyway, it's Kathleen's decision."

"It's good to have him here," Kathleen said. "He weather-stripped the back door."

"She's not in her right mind," Angela snapped, pointing at her mother. "She babbles about angels and prayers."

Kathleen recoiled, her eyes wide with anger. "I babble? I babble? That's it for you, Missy."

Missy? Before Charlie could utter a conciliatory word, a boil erupted on Angela's right cheek. *Whoa*.

Hyacinth grew wide-eyed. "What are you looking at?" Angela snapped.

"Your face," Charlie said. So much for diplomacy. But this was *weird*.

Angela reached up and touched her cheek. "A blemish. So what?"

Yeah, you could call it that. But he'd never seen one erupt so … volcanically. It was *gooshy*.

"If you're not out by tomorrow morning, I'll begin legal proceedings to have you removed. If that happens, you'll lose the right to edit the book."

No cops. Charlie fought panic and told himself not to act like he was wanted for murder. He took a deep breath and said, "I don't think this is about me. You two just don't get along."

"I brought a letter from my attorney. It lays out the family position with great clarity."

"I never told you how to live!" Kathleen shouted. "I'll be damned if I let you do that to me!"

"My God!" Hyacinth cried out, staring at Angela's forehead.

"So I've got a zit. Big deal."

"It's huge!" Hyacinth said. "And there's another one! You're breaking out!"

Angela shook her head in exasperation. When she touched her neck, her eyes widened in alarm. Then she felt her forehead. "This is giving me a lot of stress. Please, Mr. Sherman, don't make this any worse than it has to be." She rushed to the bathroom. Charlie and Hyacinth exchanged bewildered looks. Kathleen turned away and coughed. Or cackled.

A minute later, Angela shrieked. By the time she rushed out of the bathroom, more boils had erupted. "Come on," she snapped to Hyacinth. "I need to see a dermatologist."

"You know where I stand," she told Charlie as she stomped out. Hyacinth trailed behind.

"*Stand*? Looks like she's running." Kathleen chuckled, peeking out the window. "Running sores. But she brought this on herself. Honor thy father and mother. Ha! Instead, she tries to kill my project. She has no idea what she's dealing with. *You* know what I mean."

"No, actually. What *do* you mean?" Charlie asked.

"I put a plague on her."

"A plague?"

She nodded grimly. "Told you I'd do it. She asked for it. Don't look at me that way. She's got to learn. She'll be OK when she realizes she can't interfere."

Charlie shook his head, unable to accept what he'd just seen and heard. He picked up the envelope Angela had left for him on the coffee table. Inside was a letter from an attorney named Bethany Campbell demanding that he immediately vacate the premises and declaring the agreement he'd signed with Kathleen null and void. "Blah, blah, blah," he said as he read.

Kathleen returned to the kitchen, and Charlie went outside to see a crow about a contract, but the bird flew off at his approach.

* * *

The next morning—New Year's Eve—Charlie found it difficult to concentrate on editing due to a draft, so he weather-stripped the study's window. While he was working, Hyacinth showed up and spoke with Kathleen in the living room. Charlie came out of the study just in time to see money change hands. The redhead gave him a choppy wave, then skedaddled out the door and bounced down the steps.

"What's that about?" he asked Kathleen.

"She needed money to go to Florida," she said. "She wants to be with her family."

Charlie took a step back and raised his eyebrows. "You're paying her to get away from your daughter, aren't you? What if Angela finds out?"

"Don't you dare tell her," she snapped. "And I mean business, Buster."

Charlie gave her a look he used on Ben when the boy misbehaved. "You should check on her."

"What does it matter to you? She doesn't care if you live or die."

"She may need medical attention."

"She needs to apologize and stop trying to kill the book. It's my job to make sure it's published, so I'll do what I must do," Kathleen declared, sounding righteous.

"I thought that was my job."

"It's my job to make sure you do your job," Kathleen said, poking him in the chest. He stared at her expectantly, trying to make her feel awkward. She averted her gaze for a moment, then turned back to him. "You're right. I do need to see her. Will you drive me over there?"

"Glad you changed your mind. Let's go." Charlie moved toward the closet to grab his coat.

It was a sunny day, though chill. Charlie drove the Volvo to Angela's house in Decatur, a liberal enclave east of Atlanta and just a few miles from Bayard Terrace. He parked in the driveway and waited. Kathleen knocked on the door and disappeared into a house that looked remarkably like hers. She came out five minutes later and got in the car. "Not a pretty sight," Kathleen said. "I don't think she's ready to get better yet. She needs to—how should I say this—*come to Jesus*."

"You said you were a Unitarian," Charlie pointed out.

"Well, that denomination has limits. I see things differently now. The past few days have been ... spiritually enlightening."

"What about Hyacinth?"

"Angela didn't mention her and neither did I." Her tone was snippy.

"Don't pray for anything bad to happen to me, OK?"

"Don't worry. We're friends." She patted his hand. "On the same side."

On the way home, they stopped at RightPrice Drugs on Vesta Drive to refill Kathleen's prescriptions. While searching for shavers, Charlie heard Kathleen bickering with the blue-jacketed pharmacist. "I was here before her, and she's getting service. You're treating me unfairly, like always," she fumed at the man. She came to Charlie and repeated her complaint. "He's shifty-eyed. Cheats on prices, too."

At her insistence, Charlie went to the back of the store and watched the druggist in action. He did look a *little* sketchy, with slick black hair and narrow slits for eyes. Charlie felt a bump and turned into Kathleen, who was peering intently at the druggist from behind him. "Maybe dealing drugs has affected his world view," Charlie said. "You wanna pull your prescriptions?"

"No. I want him to treat me right. He's never nice. Last week, I had to wait while he filled a prescription for a pretty young thing. Angela noticed too, and made a comment."

"About the young thing?"

"No!" she snapped.

"Well, go ahead and take care of your prescriptions. Uh, are any of them for anger management?"

"Watch it. I'm not in the mood for your smart remarks."

"*Yes ma'am.*"

By the time she returned to the counter, another customer was standing there. Charlie watched as Kathleen tried to excuse herself to the front of the line, claiming she'd been there first.

"I'm sorry," the pharmacist told her. "You'll have to wait your turn."

"It's already been my turn. You'll pay for this!" Kathleen muttered.

Charlie paid for his grooming supplies, then looked for Kathleen. He found her hiding behind a display of paper towels, holding her old prescription bag, eyes closed, moving her head back and forth like Stevie Wonder in a creative trance, chanting an incantation.

"Pestilence, Pustulation, Corpulence, and Stenches, a dose of these for favoring wenches!"

"Kathleen!" Charlie cried out. "What's with the bad rhyming? Are you a witch?"

"No. I just put some thought into it, that's all. And 'witch' doesn't begin to describe—"

A few feet away, the pharmacist stared in horror into an overhead mirror as his face erupted with horrible boils, swelling up instantly. It looked like his face was turning into to a batch of popcorn. Very oily popcorn. Toily, troubling popcorn. This was much worse than Angela's affliction—as far as Charlie had seen, that is. Within seconds, a huge swarm of buzzing flies came from nowhere and surrounded the victim's head. Then came the sound of trombones and tubas from hell as the poor wretch cut a series of the loudest, longest, soul-deflating farts Charlie had ever heard. The druggist went down behind the counter, grasping at it with white knuckles and groaning in agony as he tumbled out of sight.

"That was truly nuclear," Charlie said, marveling at the multiple afflictions. If he hadn't met Trouble, he wouldn't have believed such a curse was possible. Now, as a disciple of weirdness, he could only conclude Kathleen was getting good at it. He grabbed her elbow. "So quit it!"

"Whatever do you mean, dear?" She smiled at him sweetly.

"Giving people the plague. Put him back the way he was."

"He charges too much."

"This isn't going to change things. Reverse the curse, or whatever it is you do."

"No." She paused to admire her work. "He'll think twice before he mistreats customers again."

"He doesn't know what's happening!"

"That lecher had it coming," she snapped. "He'll be over it in a week. Or two. And you're not my boss, so watch your step."

Well. She certainly was being huffy. "I didn't watch my step. That's why I'm here. You need to be a nice lady, not the Wicked Witch of the West."

"Or what?" she snarled.

"Or else I won't work with you." He took her elbow and nudged her toward the door.

"That's not your choice anymore. All I've got to do is pray—"

"I know there's something strange going on. But you're like a kid with a BB gun, running around shooting up the neighborhood. I don't know what Trouble gave you, but it was a mistake. You should use it to make the world better, not settle petty grudges."

"It's not him. It's me. He came when I called, remember? I've got superpowers. So what if I punish evildoers? That's one way to make the world better."

"You afflict your daughter and a guy who works in a store. How's that improve anything?" He shook his head. "I can't believe we're having this conversation."

"You don't understand. Before you get high and mighty, remember we're doing God's work. Anyone who gets in our way will pay the price." She nodded grimly and stared into Charlie's eyes.

He returned the look. "I'm not working with you if you go around starting plagues. Anyway, you know what starts plagues? Rats. Ha! Got you there. And I'm not working for a rat!"

"You do *not* have me there," she insisted.

"Well, you need to get your prescriptions—if he's in any shape to fill them." Charlie peeked around the corner. The popcorn-headed pharmacist was wavering on his legs, shooing away flies. And spitting out a few. Charlie clamped his nostrils shut with thumb and index finger. "Oh, God. I can't stand the smell. That's at least fifty years' worth of evil, right there."

"Come on," Kathleen said. "I'm transferring my prescriptions. If they can't treat me right, to hell with them. Don't look at me that way. I'm only talking figuratively. I haven't figured out how to do that yet. But when I do, watch out!"

"You're turning into the world's worst Baptist," Charlie groused. "Let's get out of here."

The pharmacist cried out in agony and let loose a series of gut-wrenching farts that chased them from the store.

After a stop at a supermarket with a polite (and lucky) pharmacist, they returned to Bayard Terrace just after noon. Charlie brought in two bags of groceries and set them on the kitchen table. "I need to go to the Y," he said. "It closes early on New Year's Eve."

"No," Kathleen declared. "You need to get back to work."

"I don't think so. And don't talk to me that way."

"You work for me. I say when you can take time off from the book."

"Get this straight. I'm not working under these conditions."

"You'd better read the contract."

"I don't care about the contract. I'll pay you back the money and walk out, if I have to."

"I'm afraid you can't do that." Her tone was chilling.

Again with the creepiness. This was *not* the sweet, slightly demented lady he'd made a deal with. No, she'd definitely gone evil on him. He sighed.

"Have you tried it?" she asked, sizing him up for some sort of a wizard's battle. "Don't have the power, do you? Ha! You don't!" She gave him a cruel smile. "That's because you're just a hired hand."

He retreated to the study and pulled his copy of the contract from its manila folder in the wire rack on the bookcase. As he read, his eyes widened. *The terms had changed.* Furthermore, his signature was now dark reddish brown, with two circular splatters underneath. He remembered signing it with his fountain pen in blue ink, but it now looked like dried blood. And what was *this* phrase? "The party of the second part will succeed, or die in the attempt." He hadn't agreed to a suicide pact!

Charlie's fledgling belief in God didn't mean he had to accept this kind of double-dealing. If the Almighty was going to smite people on a crazy old woman's whim, he'd reject the deal. He would not be trapped in her prayer and become a mime in her phone booth. *Wait. If the contract's in blood—*

He charged into the kitchen, where Kathleen was putting away groceries. "Deal's off."

"You can't leave," she said.

"Watch me." He went downstairs and packed quickly, although he had no idea where he'd go. He just wanted out. As he stuffed his duffel bag, he heard a rumble and looked out one of the basement's small, high windows. Clouds were rushing in from the south. To the north, it was clear blue. The rumbling grew louder as the sky darkened. He tossed his new laptop into a half-full duffel and reached for the knob on the patio door.

Zap. He yelped at the shock. His hand flew from the metal as he heard a tremendous *Crack*! The house shook like it had been hit with a wrecking ball. He felt a strong charge of static coming from the doorknob, and then he saw a thin, jagged white bolt of electricity leap out, arcing … *searching*. But not for him. It retreated. A second later, Charlie heard loud, bizarre, guttural sounds coming from upstairs that sounded like an audio tape running backwards—or aliens slaughtering pigs. Absolutely horrific. Then there was silence. Curiosity and dread mixed in his gut. He crept up the stairs. Smoke and ozone filled the kitchen. No flames, though. He looked out the dining room window. Sunshine fell in shafts through rapidly dissipating purple clouds.

In the living room, Kathleen sat stiffly on the couch, staring at the blank TV screen. The wall directly behind the old set was freshly blackened. "Kathleen."

She turned and looked at him blankly. "Are you my son?"

"No. I came here to work on your husband's book."

"Thurwood? Is he here?"

"No ma'am. He died. Do you know what just happened?"

"Did something happen? It's smoky. Was there a fire?"

Charlie looked into her eyes. They were mournful, not cruel. The malice he'd seen moments ago was gone. Some kind of operation had been performed on her.

"I think lightning hit the house. I'll check outside."

He went outside and walked around the house. There were no signs of damage. When he returned, Kathleen looked at him with friendly interest. "Who are you?"

"Charlie Sherman. I'm an editor. I live in the basement."

She nodded, as if this made perfect sense. "I'd like to rest."

"Fine, yes. If you need anything, let me know."

"I wonder if you'd make me some tea. I feel empty-headed."

"Sure." Charlie went into the kitchen and turned on the burner under her brass teakettle. As the water came to a boil, he wondered what all the fire and brimstone was about. *Flight from Forsyth* was just a book, voluminous and not particularly well-written, about events that happened long ago. Why would its completion have such cosmic importance?

Charlie helped Kathleen up and persuaded her to sit at the kitchen table while she drank a cup of Earl Grey. He went to the living room and looked out the window. He prayed for a rainbow. Just as a little test.

A crow flew by, circled low, cawed twice, and shit on his van's windshield.

* * *

Kathleen gently slurped chicken noodle soup and then sat on the sofa listening to public radio. She didn't seem capable of any more mischief. If she wasn't herself tomorrow—her good self, because there were definitely two versions of her—Charlie would call Angela and see about taking her to a doctor. Or maybe the two of them could carpool to the hospital.

At 10:00 p.m. Charlie helped Kathleen to bed. He hoped whatever damage she'd sustained would be repaired by a good night's sleep.

After that, he called Thornbriar, but Susan wasn't picking up.

As he walked down the stairs to the dungeon, his phone trilled. "Hello."

"It's late. Are you sober?" Susan asked.

"For six years, seven months and … eight days," he guessed.

"You at that woman's house?"

"In the basement."

"I'll have to check it out."

"Sure. Any time. Bring the kids. Are they up, by any chance?"

"Probably. But they're not here, They're still—"

"No! No! Don't say it!"

"Stop," she said. "So why'd you call me?"

"To wish you a happy new year. Happy New Year!"

"Happy New Year. And good night."

He'd expected a longer conversation than that. Why, he couldn't say.

Charlie climbed into his sleeping bag and waited for sleep, but it didn't come. He kept thinking about how a higher power had hunted down a loser named Charlie Sherman and given him a place to stay and a job to do. And protected him—or at least spared him. Other than that, he didn't have a clue to this mystery. For some unexplainable reason, it was imperative that *he* bring some old dead book to life.

A few minutes later, Kathleen cried out. Charlie rose and padded upstairs in his mocs, sweat pants, and blue thermal shirt. He knocked on her bedroom door. No answer, just sounds of anguish. He tiptoed into her room and stood beside the bed, watching her toss and turn. A look of distress was etched on her face. "Help me," she moaned.

He was sure she was still asleep. In the distance, a string of firecrackers exploded: *pop-pop-pop-pop*. Then came the whistle and bang of a bottle rocket. She whimpered again. He reached over and held her hand. A smile crossed her face and she fell quiet. He wondered who she thought he was, but since she took comfort from his touch, it really didn't matter.

* * *

On New Year's Day, Charlie kicked his way out of his sleeping bag and slipped on his mocs. A squeak from a dark corner told him he wasn't alone. "Happy New Year," he called out even as he plotted to kill his roommate. When he examined his face in the mirror, he noticed that he looked *younger*. The wrinkles on his forehead had disappeared. He felt better, too. He would credit his increased vigor to workouts at the Y, although he'd only had three so far.

Still dressed in his sweat pants and thermal shirt, Charlie stepped out the dungeon's back door, circled around the house, and retrieved the newspaper, which leaned picture-perfect against the second concrete step at the edge of the yard. The sky was pale blue, with a few cottony wisps directly overhead. The air was chill, the grass dew-sparkled. Feeling strong, he took porch steps two at a time. He unlocked the front door, went into the kitchen, and started a pot of coffee. He pulled the paper from its wrap and laid it on the table. The front page headline declared, "Lawyer Killed by MARTA Bus." Upon seeing the woman's name, he jumped up, knocking the wooden chair back against a cabinet, and rushed to the dark cherry secretary in the living room. He grabbed the letter Angela had delivered Tuesday, raced back into the kitchen, and slammed it on the table next to the newspaper. Same name: Bethany Campbell.

He looked up and saw Kathleen approaching. Her hair stood out in all directions and her eyes were blank. She zombie-walked toward him like an extra in a George Romero movie, her bathrobe open with nothing on underneath. Stifling a yelp, he looked away. She collapsed on a chair and gazed at him with those unfathomable blue eyes. "Coffee," she croaked.

That seemed somewhat human. He breathed a sigh of relief. "It'll be ready in a minute. You're going to catch a chill dressed that way. Go on, pull that robe closed. That's better. Do you know what happened yesterday?"

Kathleen shook her head. "I don't feel good. It's like I drank a bottle of wine. I rarely drink, and I only have a glass of sherry when I have trouble sleeping." She groaned. "My head hurts."

"We should visit your daughter. Make sure she's OK."

"I'm sure she's fine."

"I'm not." He poured her a cup of coffee.

"Milk please, and sugar. Is there something I don't know?"

"Her attorney was killed yesterday."

Kathleen pursed her lips and wrinkled her brows. "Oh. That's too bad." She dumped two teaspoons of sugar in her cup and stirred. "I didn't know the woman."

"Did you pray for that?"

"What on earth are you talking about?"

"Did you put a curse on your daughter's attorney?"

She eyed him like he was crazy. "Why would you say such a horrible thing? I never hurt anyone."

He saw that her hands were trembling. "Sorry," he said. "My bad."

Figuring an ascetic doesn't take holidays, Charlie started working on the manuscript.

A while later, Kathleen walked into the study and said, "Angela called. She's been under the weather. She's feeling better now, but she wants company. A friend of hers died. Could you drive me over?"

"Sure."

"What a run of bad luck she's been having. I can't believe her girlfriend dumped her when she got sick. That's horrible, don't you think?"

Charlie bit his lip. "I suppose."

"I do so much for Angela," Kathleen mumbled as she left.

"To Angela, you mean."

Kathleen came back. "What did you just say?"

"Nothing."

* * *

Kathleen emerged from Angela's house after staying thirty minutes. Charlie jumped out and opened the car door for her, shooting her a questioning look. "Well?"

"Her attorney died," Kathleen said. "She doesn't know if she's going to get another one. She said she'll see how this goes. I think it helped that you brought me to see her. I told her it was your idea. I figured you need her good will more than I do. I'm her mother. Nothing either she or I can do about that now."

"True. But what about Angela's … condition?"

"It's clearing up, whatever it was. Bad acne, I think. Probably brought on by self-induced stress. She gets all worked up over things. Who knows?" Kathleen shook her head at the mysteries of life. "Oh, by the way. I think my TV is on the fritz."

"I checked. It's dead. Lightning hit it."

"Oh, dear. Maybe I should get another one. Could you help me get one and set it up?"

"In time for football? You bet."

* * *

Friday morning, Charlie drove to Thornbriar and made coffee, relieved to see that Evangeline wasn't there and his favorite blue cup was. Susan entered the kitchen dressed in a dark gray suit and found a cup already prepared the way she liked it, with milk and Equal. "I've only got a minute," she said, glancing at her watch, then taking a sip. "So what are your plans for today?"

"I'm taking the kids to Kathleen's."

"Really?"

"We talked about this. You said you'd pick them up."

"Oh. Is that today? So I get to meet the mystery woman. Is she as old as you say?"

"Older."

"I guess I'll see for myself soon enough."

"I guess you will."

She took a long gulp of coffee. "Well, time to go."

Susan hugged the kids and gave Charlie a limp-wristed wave on her way out the door.

"We're having a tea party!" Charlie announced as the garage door rattled closed.

"Like *Alice in Wonderland*?" Beck asked.

"Along the same lines," Charlie said, blinking rapidly. "But better."

On their roundabout way to Bayard Terrace, they dropped by the library and checked out picture books, then stopped at a market to pick up snacks and items on Kathleen's grocery list.

Thrilled to have company, Kathleen gushed over the children when they arrived. She insisted on reimbursing Charlie for the groceries and went to get her checkbook, then returned to the kitchen with a troubled look on her face. "Oh my. I spent three hundred dollars on flowers. In the middle of winter? How is that possible?"

"Let me see." Charlie looked at the entry and laughed. "Hyacinth is a *person.*"

"Is she a friend?"

"You paid her not to be."

"I don't know what you're talking about."

"Never mind, then."

He showed the kids his living quarters after their loud, insistent pleas began to bother their hostess. This worried Charlie, since an unnerved Kathleen could be a smiteful Kathleen.

"You're right. This *is* a dungeon," Ben marveled as they creaked down the steps.

"I see a rat!" Beck shrieked and ran upstairs. Ben, jealous of her discovery, kept exploring.

"Don't go into any dark corners or reach under anything," Charlie commanded.

"All the corners are dark. And the bathroom is icky."

"I know," Charlie said, stretching the word. "I shower at the Y."

After a lunch of grilled cheese sandwiches, Beck sat with Kathleen on the sofa and looked through old photo albums and scrapbooks while Ben played with Legos at the dining room table. Charlie seized the chance to work on the book. When he heard sobbing, he came out of the study and saw Kathleen weeping, with Beck's arms wrapped around her. The scrapbook was open to pictures of Gary as a little boy, and Beck was assuring her that her son was in heaven.

"I don't know about that," Kathleen said, dabbing her eyes with a Kleenex.

"Sure he is," Beck said. "He didn't kill anyone, did he?"

"He was a soldier."

After a thoughtful pause, Beck said, "That's what soldiers do, so it's not so bad."

"He didn't want to be a soldier. He wanted to build things."

"That might help."

Kathleen pulled herself together, and after a while she declared it was time for the party. Beck dressed up in a borrowed red shawl, floppy hat, and loads of beaded necklaces. Kathleen wore her blue dress. Ben and Charlie came as they were. Ben didn't like tea, so he got cocoa. When she heard he was getting cocoa, Beck insisted on tea *and* cocoa. Kathleen fixed both drinks. The kids found her shortbread cookies acceptable, though Ben asked if they could have chocolate chip cookies next time. Kathleen sniffed at the idea, saying, "Those aren't cultured and refined enough."

"Sure they are," Ben said. "They've got chips."

Kathleen squinted at the boy in disapproval. "Don't contradict me, young man."

Charlie steered the conversation away from the dispute, fearing that if she started smiting the children, he'd have to go woodsman on her ass. Some tea party *that* would be. Fortunately, the moment passed without further incident, and the controversy over cookies ended with no fatalities to report.

Later that afternoon, Charlie took the kids to a nearby park, returning just before dusk. When he walked in the door and saw the black marks on the wall behind the new plasma screen TV Kathleen had bought on New Year's Day, he realized he needed to clean up the evidence of divine rebooting before his wife arrived. He scrubbed off the last soot marks just before Susan pulled into the driveway and parked behind the van.

When Kathleen answered the door, Charlie could see that Susan was quite pleased, perhaps even smugly so, to see how old his employer was. Beck interrupted introductions to announce: "Daddy lives with rats. And not the pretty kind either, like in Mrs. Coppins' classroom."

A look of alarm crossed Susan's face.

"There might be a mouse in the house," Charlie admitted.

"It was a rat," Beck insisted. "Big big."

Susan shuddered and said, "I've got to see this place for myself." First, Charlie showed her his new office. (He'd pulled down Momo's picture since he couldn't stand to look at the ugly bastard.) Susan gave a cursory glance at page 758 of the manuscript but said nothing. Then again, he'd told her nothing about the book, not even its title. (She hadn't asked about it, either.) When they went downstairs, she laughed, unwilling or unable to conceal her scorn. "You weren't kidding. It *is* a dungeon. How can you live here?"

"Beats the alternative."

"What does that mean?"

"The street."

Susan rolled her eyes. "You think *that's* the alternative? You're crazy."

"It smells bad, too," Ben said, standing behind Charlie, holding his nose. "I think there are monsters here. They stink with all their might."

"They're rats, stinky rats!" Beck shouted down from the kitchen, not daring to venture closer.

Susan groaned in distaste and tromped back upstairs. "You're going to have to get rid of the rats before the kids come over here again," she called out from the top step. "If ever."

He frowned. "Don't worry. I'll put out traps."

Shortly after that, Susan bundled up the kids and everyone said goodbye. Charlie stood on the porch and watched the Camry disappear.

"You have a beautiful family," Kathleen said when he came back inside. "I hope everything works out. There are too many divorces these days. 'Til death do you part. That's the way to do it."

"We'll see," said Charlie, feeling downhearted. It was difficult and terrible to see his family drive away. After being with them constantly for their entire lives, he realized he might not be emotionally equipped to handle his children's constant departures. But what choice was there? He had to do what he had to do.

He returned to the manuscript and spent several hours banging his head against the wall of the past, which beat the hell out of thinking about the present. That night, he finished copying the entire book to his hard drive. By then, his brain had turned to mush. He stumbled downstairs, kicked off his shoes, turned off the dangling bulb, and slipped into his sleeping bag. He heard a squeak and made a mental note: *Buy traps in the morning.*

Chapter Five

When Charlie finished reading Talton's 1,087-page manuscript, he knew more than anyone else alive about what had happened in Forsyth County nearly a century ago. The nugget of Dr. Talton's *magnum opus* was buried deep inside myriad observations and countless facts, starting with the weathering of the Blue Ridge Mountains, winding along the Trail of Tears, and ending at a hateful, crudely lettered sign at the county line.

The incident that originally sparked Forsyth's madness was an event of questionable authenticity: an alleged "outrage" against a white woman near Deep Creek, five miles north of Cumming, the county seat. On the night of Thursday, September 5, 1912, the unnamed victim (first identified as a farmer's wife, then as a young woman living with her mother) awoke to find a black man in her bed, so the story went. "Imagine her surprise!" Talton wrote. "Like *Casablanca*'s gendarme, she was shocked, SHOCKED, at this occurrence!" More likely, the professor suggested, she was caught in bed with a black man and cried *Rape*! to save her honor, which, to white folks, was infinitely more precious than a black man's life, especially in Georgia, the state responsible for half the nation's lynchings that year.

The man and his rumored accomplice (whose existence was debatable) were frightened by the woman's screams and ran off. Almost immediately, posses formed and combed the area for suspects. While Talton's account was prosaic, Charlie's espresso-fueled reading allowed him to see vigilantes whipping galloping horses through the night, accompanied by silent-movie chase music.

Meanwhile, a man variously identified as the victim's father or husband rode into the sleepy town of Cumming, population 813, and tried to stir up a mob, failing only because there was no suspect. Lynching prospects improved the next day after two black men were arrested. One, a field hand named Ronnie Harris, immediately confessed, according to the nearby Gainesville newspaper. Such "confessions" often came after torture, beatings, and threats of lynching coupled with a lack of legal representation for the accused. Then again, the newspaper could have fabricated the claim. Nothing increased circulation like the terror threat/morality play of black-on-white rape, not to mention the resultant mob activity. "In 1912 Georgia," Talton noted, "black suspects were lucky if they were considered innocent until proven arrested."

While Harris was presumed guilty, he had supporters among Forsyth's 1,159 blacks—ten percent of the county's population. At noon on Saturday, September 7, a stocky, bald black Baptist preacher named Lincoln Roberts stood in the dusty street outside the courthouse where Harris was jailed. Roberts, born shortly after the Civil War, had lived in Forsyth County all his life and claimed to know the parties involved, none of whom were Ronnie Harris. Declaring that the prisoner had been unjustly accused, Roberts called for Harris's release. A crowd of black workers, sharecroppers, and farmers gathered around him. There was no rape or attempted rape, Roberts stated, but simply consensual sex. "The woman's affection for her black paramour was so great she refused to name the man who slipped from her bed and out the window!" Roberts shouted.

The white press would later denounce and condense his speech, stating, "The insolent Negro made remarks about the woman's character." Claiming that a white woman would willingly have anything to do with a black man carried the death penalty by mob back then, of course, so Roberts's "insolence" was cut short when a dozen whites broke through the crowd and roughly seized him. Several drew pistols and pointed them at his head. He was forced to kneel. A man uncoiled a horsewhip and laid into the preacher, lashing through his coat and cutting strips of flesh. Roberts tried to run, but he was clubbed with a pistol butt and knocked down in the dirt. The whipping continued, along with beating and kicking.

Eventually, Sheriff J.A. Wright and deputies emerged from the courthouse to arrest the half-dead Roberts. As they dragged off the preacher, a growing white mob called for his lynching. Wright would later explain that he'd arrested Roberts to save him. It's worth noting that none of Roberts's assailants were charged in the assault. "A white man's right to beat a nigger is the cornerstone of Georgia law," State Sen. Preston Standers proclaimed in 1910, and nothing had changed in the two years since.

The preacher's arrest did not calm things down. In the collective white mind, a black conspiracy to commit outrages against white women grew and festered. Four other blacks were arrested on the rather vague charge of "suspicion," also a lynching offense, though one that was used mainly to fill county chain gangs for road work. (The state's infamous convict-lease system had been abolished in 1908.) Word of Roberts's beating spread, angering local blacks who believed he had been attacked for telling an unpleasant truth. Apparently, *everyone* knew this woman.

By this time, Atlanta papers were covering the story, adding fuel to the fire—as they did in 1906, when false reports of black-on-white crime helped spark the Atlanta Riot. Whites responded by threatening mass lynchings. Rebecca Felton, a populist race-baiter, summed up white feelings succinctly when she said, "If it takes lynching to protect women's dearest possession from drunken, ravening beasts, then I say lynch a thousand a week."

While reports of black insurrection turned out to be false, feverish whites made good on their threat to form mobs. Word of Harris's confession brought armed whites cascading from the hills. By Saturday afternoon, hundreds surrounded the courthouse. As a barrel-chested, red-headed farmer in work clothes waved a hangman's noose in the air, the crowd called for Wright to deliver Roberts and Harris to "justice"—meaning them, of course. The sheriff refused; the mob tested his mettle. A hundred men rushed the building. Wright fired a single warning shot. The crowd fell back after this massive display of firepower but didn't disperse. A chant arose: "Burn 'er down! Burn 'er down!" In a footnote, Talton wrote: "Courthouse arson is a proud Forsyth County tradition."

Following a series of frantic phone calls between the mayor of Cumming, Sheriff Wright, and Gov. Joseph M. Brown in Atlanta, martial law was declared in Forsyth. Brown, the son of Georgia's Civil War governor (and who would later participate in the 1915 lynching of Leo Frank), ordered militia units from Marietta and Gainesville to quell the riots that threatened to tear apart the rural county. Thirty heavily armed troops from Gainesville were quickly dispatched to Cumming, arriving late Saturday afternoon. That night, under tight security, the sheriff moved Roberts and Harris—"the cause of all this trouble," according to the *Atlanta Citizen*—to the Marietta jail in Cobb County, thirty miles away.

Wright hoped his actions would defuse tensions, but outrage among poor whites kept growing, fueled by long-standing antagonisms toward blacks. Not surprisingly, there was a run on rifles and ammunition at Whitsitt's General Store. Heavily armed whites milled about Cumming looking for insolent Negroes and breaking the windows of black-owned houses, since home ownership was the surest sign of uppityness. Sensing trouble settling over the town like an oppressive fog, black families packed their belongings into horse- and mule-drawn wagons. The most prescient of them were halfway to Gainesville or Atlanta by Sunday morning, when newspapers published stories reporting that Negroes were plotting to blow up Cumming with dynamite in retaliation for the attack on Roberts.

In Cumming, as cocks crowed and cattle lowed in pastures, armed whites who'd slept in wagon beds with rifles woke with empty whiskey bottles beside them and faced the ugly truth of a new day: There was no one to lynch and only church to attend. For the moment, all was quiet. But that wouldn't last. "Violence begets violence," Talton wrote, "and the mob's darkest desires and prayers to an angry God would soon be answered."

Around ten o'clock Sunday morning, nineteen-year-old Martha Jean Rankin skipped off the front porch of her father's home in Oscarville in north Forsyth. A pretty girl with long brown hair, she wore a lacy white dress as she hiked past a fenced field of tall, ripening corn on her way to her aunt's house, where her two little sisters had spent the night. She was supposed to take them to church, but before she reached her destination, she ran into Bernie Dent, an employee of a neighboring farm. She knew Dent slightly, though she would not likely have wanted to stop and chat. He was black, scrawny, deformed, and walked with a limp. "There are no photos extant of Dent," Talton wrote, "but newspapers called him 'a barefoot, country Negro,' as well as 'brutish, low-browed, and apelike.'"

By all accounts, he attacked her. She tried to fight him off. He dragged her off the path into the woods, where he grabbed a rock and struck her repeatedly on the head with it. Then he raped her and left her for dead. Later that day, he told some friends what he'd done and asked them to help get rid of the body. After dark, he returned to the crime scene with his half-brother, Thomas Oscar, Thomas's sister Jane, and a friend named Ted Galent. They found Martha Jean still alive, lying in a pool of her own blood. As Jane held a torch aloft, Oscar and Dent took turns raping Martha Jean. When they finished, they left her there, apparently having forgotten the original purpose of their trip.

After a night of frantic searching, Martha Jean's distraught father found her clinging to life Monday morning. He swept her up in his arms and stumbled back to his house. Two local doctors were summoned to her bedside, but it was too late. She was in an irreversible coma, though that evening's Gainesville newspaper reported she had named her attackers and would recover. (This was most likely a calculated piece of misinformation intended to help force a confession.)

When Martha Jean died late Monday afternoon, Dent was already in custody. A hand mirror at the crime scene was traced through a local store after a clerk recalled selling one like it on Saturday to Dent. Threatened with lynching if he did not confess, the slow-witted man quickly admitted to the crime. He was taken to Cumming, then whisked to the larger town of Gainesville before angry whites could re-form a mob to overwhelm the small company of troops ringing the courthouse.

News of Martha Jean's death put whites in a fury and brought a hundred vigilantes roaring into Gainesville Monday night. Mob members with clubs pounded on the locked front doors of the Hall County Courthouse and threatened to break them down. Wright, who had stayed with his prisoner, knew he had to act quickly to save Dent. At this point, many sheriffs would have simply looked the other way or handed the keys to the mob, but Wright slipped out the back door with the prisoner. He commandeered a touring car and took off for Atlanta with Dent and two deputies. The fifty-three mile trip over mountain roads took three hours—record time back then. Meanwhile in Cumming, the mob of angry whites surrounding the courthouse broke up when they learned Dent had been twice removed from their grasp. They would return, however.

Tuesday morning, deputies brought in Dent's three alleged accomplices and two men Wright considered material witnesses with knowledge of the crime, Ike Driscoll and Sam Hardaway. That afternoon, a mob of 300 stormed the courthouse during Wright's absence, smashing doors with crowbars and rushing past outnumbered and outgunned deputies to the jail cells. They were frustrated to find only Galent. Deputies had hidden the two witnesses and Oscar, while Wright had spirited the woman away that morning. Talton believed lawmen deliberately chose to sacrifice one black victim to the mob in hopes of limiting the violence.

As the cowering prisoner kneeled on the floor and begged for mercy, several men with pistols and rifles stepped forward and started blasting away. After they riddled the body with bullets, mob members beat his lifeless corpse with crowbars, then dragged him outside and down the town's main street before stringing him up on a telephone pole near the spot where Roberts had been whipped. Upon his return, Wright found that the white community's bloodlust had been satisfied, so he seized the opportunity to transport the remaining prisoners to Atlanta.

The mob was only temporarily sated, however. After admiring their work, posing for pictures beside Galent's bloody corpse, and collecting some ghastly souvenirs, it was time to get back to lynching. There was unfinished business in Marietta, so they set off to find Ronnie Harris and Preacher Roberts in connection with the earlier "attack" on the unnamed white woman. Wright called the circuit judge in Marietta and advised him a mob was heading his way. The judge ordered the prisoners moved to the Tower, Atlanta's heavily fortified city jail, where they would join Dent.

Once word spread that there would be no fun that night, the crowd dispersed, its members melting back into the hills from whence they came. Wright regretfully advised the judge that there were no warrants for Roberts's arrest, so the black preacher was released from jail that night. He did not return to Forsyth County. Nothing more of his fate is known.

White sentiment continued to run at fever pitch. "Great emotion against these brutes persists," the *Atlanta Sentinel* noted after Galent's death. Closer to home, the *Gainesville Democrat* editorialized, "The good people of Forsyth have behaved themselves with noteworthy self-control," complimenting them for not tracking down more victims to lynch.

In any case, with the suspects gone, prospects for violence seemed to decrease and reporters left town. There wouldn't be much news coming out of Forsyth until trial coverage began in early October. Contrary to the Gainesville newspaper's editorial, however, Forsyth whites showed no signs of calming down. Every store in the county sold out of guns and ammunition; armed men continually roamed the countryside, looking for blacks to harass.

Crime—both real and imagined—became the rallying cry for poor whites, but their primary motive no longer involved punishing rapists. Instead, they saw an opportunity to knock blacks down a peg or two.

For nearly a half-century, lynching and terrorism had been used in the South as a means of racial control, and Forsyth whites were ready to find a new use for such violence. No longer content to make bad examples of individual blacks, the white community quickened with resolve and grand ambition. While most white Southerners could live with blacks as long as they remained powerless and subservient, Forsyth County's poor whites were tired of competing with black labor and especially weary of seeing African-American landowners performing better economically than they did. Such whites were often envious of blacks, the preferred tenants of landowners. Talton stated that the South's ruling class found blacks cheaper, more dependable, and easier to work with than whites, who insisted on higher wages for less work and had an undeniable mean streak. The Southern aristocracy had a history of pitting poor whites against blacks, and in Forsyth County, the conflict turned extreme.

Blacks could not stop this reign of terror without powerful white allies, and therefore, they were out of luck. While not unique, Forsyth County, pinned against mountains to the north, was not a typical plantation county. Farms were small and soil was not rich. Unlike the cotton belt, this region lacked a large, entrenched aristocracy with paternalistic ties to former slaves and their families. In Forsyth, blacks had few white benefactors, and none willing to stand up for their rights. In the end, local leaders bowed down to the mob.

The whites began a process known in later decades as "ethnic cleansing." Then, it was called "whitecapping"—nightriding in the tradition of the once and future Ku Klux Klan, disbanded during Reconstruction and resurrected atop Georgia's Stone Mountain in 1915 in response to *The Birth of a Nation* and America's most famous lynching, that of Leo Frank, a Jew, in Marietta.

As in other Southern states, Georgia blacks were emasculated politically in 1912, especially in rural areas. In 1908, constitutional disenfranchisement capped two decades of legislation designed to keep blacks in a state approximating slavery. Talton called this process "affirmative action for whites."

And so, with the tacit approval of their wealthier neighbors, Forsyth's poor whites pushed forward with their pogrom, inviting comparisons to the treatment of the area's Cherokees in the previous century. "These fierce, warlike Scotch-Irish hill folk reverted to their old ways, fueled by an ancient rage and rekindled by this unspeakable act," wrote a Northern reporter. "All would pay for the sins of the few. The issue was no longer justice. This was war: Defeat the enemy and take the spoils."

Talton called Forsyth County's 1912 troubles "an ultra-violent labor action against blacks by poor whites, egged on by their upper-class neighbors who wanted little to do with either of them."

Shots were fired into sharecroppers' cabins and landowners' homes. Warning signs were posted: *Nigger Git Out of Forsyth*. Fires were set. Barns, houses, schools, and churches burned. As a consequence, more blacks joined the exodus. In the great diaspora of a displaced people, this was a minor eddy in the ocean, but it was remarkable in its completeness. Furthermore, it was the major event in the lives of those forced out. In a 1983 interview conducted by Talton, eighty-year-old Isaiah Smith recalled the day he left town "sometime late September the year of all the trouble":

> "I was nine years old when they ran us out of Forsyth County in 1912. My father let me take one thing I wanted when we left. I chose a baseball he'd bought for me in the spring. I remember gripping it tight in my hand as we pulled away from our house. My mother was expecting my sister then, so she laid down in the back. We had a mule named Sam that Pop sold when we got to Atlanta. White men on horseback watched us with their rifles pointed in the air. Pop was staring forward with the reins in his hands. 'This is what they do, son,' he told me. 'This is what they do.' I heard the sound of glass breaking and turned to see a lighted torch fly through the front window. Pop grabbed my head and twisted it around so hard he hurt my neck. 'Damn it, boy, don't look back,' he said. 'Don't give them the pleasure of seeing your pain.' Most of the day passed before he talked again. He never got over it. That was his land, handed down to him by his father. So the white men stole it, just like they stole the land from the Indians. Took our crops, too. And they've had their way up there ever since. Today's not one bit different in Forsyth County than the day I left."

* * *

On September 30, 1912, the Blue Ridge Circuit grand jury sitting in Cumming returned indictments against Dent and Oscar in the rape and murder of Martha Jean Rankin. One grand juror happened to be the victim's uncle. To the modern observer, this might seem like a conflict of interest, but it was a minor infraction of protocol compared to what happened when the trial began.

Fearing more lynchings and negative publicity, Governor Brown had declared a state of insurrection in Forsyth County and called up four militia companies to escort the prisoners from Atlanta to Cumming. Their orders were to protect the suspects and quell any racial disturbances that might occur, but they were told nothing of the nightriding that was still going on.

There was no train service to Cumming. The closest stop was in the Gwinnett County town of Buford, a dozen miles away. The soldiers, 150 strong, arrived in Buford around noon on Wednesday, October 2, and deboarded with the prisoners—Dent, Oscar and his sister Jane, along with the two hapless witnesses in the case. Harris—the suspect in the earlier "phantom" case—was also brought for trial.

The soldiers marched the prisoners across a rolling stretch of land that would disappear several decades later under Lake Sidney Lanier. Idly curious whites watched as the ring of militiamen surrounding chained prisoners tromped through the mud. As the sun set, the procession arrived at the courthouse in Cumming. The soldiers presented the prisoners to Sheriff Wright, who locked them up in holding cells. The soldiers then formed a circle around the courthouse and set up bivouac.

As the county prepared for trial, farmers stood around the courthouse in sweat-stained work shirts, spat tobacco, cussed the soldiers, and talked about "niggers needing hanging." However, word quickly spread about the overwhelming opposition a mob would face. While Brown was no friend of blacks, whites knew he was willing to give "shoot to kill" orders to protect Georgia's law-and-order image. This same battle-hardened militia unit had recently enforced martial law in Augusta during a violent streetcar workers' strike, killing two passers-by who failed to halt on command.

The separate trials of Dent and Oscar began Thursday morning and ended that night. One company of soldiers stayed inside the courthouse while the others ringed the building, standing in picket with fixed bayonets. This show of force relieved locals of their civic duty to burst into the courtroom and lynch the defendants, so they turned their attention elsewhere. Vendors took advantage of the crowds and set up an impromptu street fair, selling drinks, sandwiches, and cheap jewelry to the gawking hill people. Meanwhile, the town's remaining blacks went into hiding.

With Judge Clement Riley presiding in the courtroom, the victim's father, William Rankin, served as the main prosecutor before an all-white, all-male jury (as required by Georgia law at the time). "This was proof that the trial was a sham and an extension of mob law," Talton wrote. "What juror could resist his pleadings and *testimony* when he cried out in anguish and banged the jury box, railing as he recounted his horror at finding his darling girl lying on the ground, broken beyond repair?" Sitting beside Rankin was Robert Hay, the Blue Ridge Circuit solicitor general. Like Brown, he would, just a few years later, have a hand on the rope around Leo Frank's innocent neck.

While Dent and Oscar had attorneys, whether they actually had a defense was another matter. Their lawyers argued that they were Negroes and knew no better, then called on jurors for mercy. The evidence consisted mainly of the testimony of their accomplices. Driscoll and Hardaway, the two material witnesses who had been held for a month, testified in exchange for their freedom—even though they had never been charged with any crime.

(Talton drily noted that "freedom" meant safe passage out of Forsyth.) The most damaging testimony came from Jane Oscar, who testified for her life as she spoke against her blood kin.

Dent and Oscar were both convicted of rape and murder, the jury returning its verdict shortly after 9:30 p.m. By then, a heavy rain had begun falling and the crowds had dispersed. Inside the courtroom, only court officials, lawmen, the defendants and their attorneys, soldiers, and reporters remained. Word filtered out through town and countryside that night, but any talk of lynching was quelled by inclement weather—and the soldiers' sputtering campfires encircling the courthouse, which served to remind locals of the resistance they would face. The next morning, Judge Riley sentenced Dent and Oscar to death by hanging on October 25. He ordered the troops to return the prisoners to jail in Atlanta so they would survive until their executions.

Riley postponed Harris's case, which was already falling apart. The prosecutor openly stated that the evidence against him was slight, and that his alibi witnesses were afraid to testify because they feared mob violence. The judge stated his hopes for trying Harris in calmer surroundings and assured the public there would be no need for a military presence at the upcoming trial. Talton interpreted this as an apology and invitation to the mob: "Y'all come back now, y'hear?"

The case against Harris was eventually dropped due to lack of evidence—a good thing for him, since his witnesses had left town. Local legend held that he stayed on in Forsyth for another thirty years until he died of natural causes, but Talton found no record of him in the 1920 census and no further mention of him beyond a notation beside his name in a 1913 docket book: *Nol prossed.*

Late Friday morning, the troops decamped and marched all six prisoners back to the rail station in Buford. An eerily quiet crowd watched them pass, content to let the law take its fatal course; the condemned men's lawyers had announced there would be no appeal. It was a strange procession, a four-hour slog through the mud by a ring of soldiers a hundred yards wide at times. They reached the depot in Buford by mid-afternoon Friday and boarded the waiting train.

Meanwhile, the ethnic cleansing continued. A week after Dent and Oscar were convicted, an Atlanta newspaper took note of anti-black outrages in Forsyth, reporting that "a state of terror grips the black community." Signs on every road leading into Forsyth carried the community's new motto: *Nigger, Don't Let the Sun Set on You in Forsyth County*. By then, five black churches and two schools had been burned to the ground. Shots were fired into the houses of blacks who refused to leave, as well as those of their white allies, whose tiny numbers diminished as the horror increased. As an unwelcome consequence, a tremendous labor shortage developed during the crucial harvest time.

Media attention forced local whites to act like they cared about Negroes. Resolutions passed at mass meetings in Cumming calling for federal and state aid to suppress the growing campaign of intimidation, arson, beatings, and nightriding. By then, violence had spread to nearby Cherokee, Dawson, and Hall counties. Black carpenters building a barn were forced off the job at gunpoint in Gainesville, where warrants against their white assailants were issued. However, in Forsyth, no whites were ever arrested for crimes against blacks despite the massive campaign of violence.

After the meetings, Governor Brown again declared Forsyth County in a state of insurrection. This was required so he could mobilize troops to escort Dent and Oscar to the gallows. The governor did nothing to stop the white-capping, which by then had almost completely accomplished its purpose. Brown advised moderate Forsyth whites who wanted to stop the lawlessness that they were on their own and should employ private detectives if they wanted security. None were hired.

Two companies of National Guard troops were detailed to the death march. They quick-stepped the two prisoners from the Tower in Atlanta to Terminal Station, leaving on Southern Train No. 18 at 4:30 p.m. on Thursday, October 24. After a night march from the Buford depot, they arrived at the Cumming courthouse at 1:30 a.m. on the day of the hangings. The press mocked Dent and Oscar, reporting, "They marched along as gaily as if they were in a circus parade."

The gallows were constructed near the courthouse in a pasture belonging to Randolph Carswell, a wealthy doctor and son of Forsyth County's largest antebellum slave owner. A high wooden fence had been constructed around the scaffold to prevent curious onlookers from witnessing the execution, in line with the judge's order that the hangings "shall be in private, witnessed only by the executioner, guards, clergy, family members of the defendants, and two physicians to certify the deaths."

The local citizenry would have none of that, however. As soldiers marched into town late at night, the fence was doused with kerosene and set ablaze. By dawn, the view of the gallows was unobstructed. At daybreak, soldiers cordoned off the area and stood around the scaffold in a circle 200 yards across as the crowd poured in—on foot and by automobile, horseback and carriage. Families came with picnic lunches. According to one report, a boy sitting on his father's shoulders pointed at the gallows with its twin hangman's nooses and said, "That's where bad niggers go to die."

The hills that ringed the gallows formed a natural amphitheater, and by mid-morning, 8,000 people had gathered. They waited eagerly and burst into loud cheers and Rebel yells when Dent and Oscar were marched from the courthouse and led up the steps. Sheriff Wright tied blindfolds on both of them, then asked if they had any last words. Rankin family members were present to hear Dent confess his crime and Oscar protest his innocence. The nooses were slipped around their necks and tightened. Wright stepped back. Two deputies pulled levers simultaneously and the condemned men's necks snapped as they plummeted through the traps at 11:05 a.m. It was the county's first legal execution in fifty years. Forsyth residents went home happy, since a public hanging was the next best thing to a lynching. The cadavers of Dent and Oscar were sold to a medical school.

Many people thought the hangings brought this sordid chapter of local history to a close. But it wasn't over yet. The day after the execution, prosecution witness Jane Oscar was shot in the head in Atlanta's West End, reportedly by a white man. A few days later, a white Forsyth landowner who had spoken out against the anti-black violence was ambushed while driving a wagon back from Gainesville and beaten to death. Neither killing was solved. By the time the 1912 harvest was over, virtually all blacks had fled Forsyth County. Media coverage devolved into a spitting contest between Atlanta and Forsyth County; each community accused the other of being a pack of lawless racists. Carswell pointed out that "no innocent Negro was killed in Forsyth County," whereas in Atlanta's riots of 1906, white mobs had murdered scores of blacks who simply happened to be in the wrong place at the wrong time.

By 1913, the true nature and scope of Forsyth's tragedy had become brutally clear. White women, some of them from the finest families, were forced to do their own cooking and cleaning.

What happened did not go completely unnoticed at the state Capitol. Brown's successor, John Slaton, specifically addressed the horrors of Forsyth and other counties in his 1913 address to the General Assembly. However, there would be no legal recourse for those who fled the violence and intimidation.

Talton argued that what happened in Forsyth County was a microcosm of and precursor to the Great Migration. Many Southern blacks first moved from the country to towns, then later to the North. They were pulled toward cities like New York and Chicago by the lure of better jobs and a better life and pushed away from the South by enforced poverty and rampant persecution. Eventually, Northern blacks would become an important constituency of the urban politicians who voted to pass civil rights legislation. Talton called this "poetic justice, though insufficient."

A handful of blacks stayed on in Forsyth, but their numbers eventually dwindled to zero. By 1920, only thirty African-Americans lived there; by 1940, only two—although Talton had marked through this number with a pen in the manuscript. By 1980, they had officially disappeared from the county.

Meanwhile, Atlanta grew, and 38,000-acre Lake Lanier was impounded on the Chattahoochee River in the 1950s, submerging much of Forsyth County. Over the succeeding decades, local land prices rose as more and more people bought homes along its shores. Civilization's encroachment brought sporadic acts of violence, since succeeding generations of Forsyth County whites remained vigilant. Black truck drivers returned to Atlanta depots reporting they'd been fired upon while trying to make deliveries in Cumming. Unsuspecting black families were chased away from Forsyth County's beaches on Lake Lanier when they came to picnic or swim. In 1980, an urban Boy Scout troop packed up its pup tents and rushed back to Atlanta at midnight after the young campers at Lake Lanier were threatened by men wearing white hoods.

At the time, the brother of one of these scouts was a student of Dr. Talton's at Georgia State. His unsettling tale about that nightmarish camping trip piqued the professor's interest. Having researched the case of Leo Frank, Talton recalled Governor Slaton's remarks and started working on an article about Forsyth County's violent past.

It turned into something more. Talton tracked down children of black victims and interviewed them. Unfortunately, no transcripts of the 1912 trial existed, only the damnably inaccurate and incendiary newspaper coverage. While only one county history had been published, Talton found a few unpublished memoirs and letters written by black farmers who had fled. Most old-time locals were tight-lipped, but Talton located two unapologetic white octogenarians willing to talk.

Talton found something especially intriguing. County records of black land holdings had been destroyed in Forsyth County's 1973 courthouse fire, which had been set by arsonists. However, a radical attorney hoping to file a lawsuit on behalf of a black landowner's daughter had made photostats of these records in 1972. Talton tracked down the man, whose client had died.

The lawyer gave Talton the papers in hopes that the good professor could use them to open the issue of reparations for all those who had been dispossessed.

Talton took six years to cobble together his account—along with the many other things he knew—and write a huge, unwieldy manuscript. In June 1986, he finished it and sent copies to academic publishers, then sat back and collected rejection letters. His manuscript was, according to one editor, "comprehensive to the point of being burdensome." To another, it was "incomprehensible."

Then the tide of history seemed to shift Talton's way. (And this part Charlie was already familiar with, having lived through it.) In December 1986, Dan Greene, a martial arts instructor in Gainesville, learned of Forsyth County's sordid past. He contacted civil rights firebrand Redeemer Wilson, who never backed down from a fight. "Redeemer could scare the sheet off a Klansman," a colleague once boasted. Greene met with Wilson to plan a "Brotherhood Anti-Intimidation March" in honor of Georgia's newly enacted Martin Luther King Jr. Holiday. Soon after that, Talton got a call. "Get you some walking shoes and march up to Forsyth with me," Redeemer told his old colleague from the civil rights movement. Talton went.

And after he suffered that fatal conk on the head, his work became an orphan, only to be adopted nearly two decades later by a man who thought Talton's baby was, well, ugly.

Charlie knew it was necessary to chronicle America's racism at its ugliest and most absolute. And it was impossible to ignore the grim, supernatural force shoving him forward. After all, this was Old Testament stuff, to ignore at his peril. People had died, boils had festered, a building had burned, an innocent television had fried, and a tattooed girlfriend had fled into the night. Even the old lady had been smoked, and this was her idea. Ink had turned to blood on his contract and Charlie's life was forfeit upon failure. At this point, it was impossible not to take it seriously.

Still, he didn't know how to turn Talton's doorstop into a real live book. He felt overwhelmed by the monumental ... *shittiness* of the writing. Editors who rejected *Flight from Forsyth* had been too kind. Charlie lost track of the times he'd fallen asleep reading the damned thing. There was no coffee strong enough to keep him awake through Chapter Eight, "The Agrarian Movement in Forsyth County and Environs." Talton's environs included the England of seventeenth-century agriculturalist Jethro Tull—with a footnote discussing the rock band of the same name.

The book began with the Blue Ridge Mountains breaking away from

Georgia's Piedmont, and this geologic pace continued throughout. Chapter Forty-Eight was titled "Aftermath"; Chapter Forty-Nine, "After the Aftermath"; then came the Epilogue and Afterword. Charlie suspected Talton had been one of those professors who kept right on lecturing past the bell, not caring whether his students missed their next class.

How bad was it? Twenty chapters passed before Martha Jean was assaulted. And there was a chapter on Leo Frank, who, while noteworthy, didn't belong in the book, since he never set foot in Forsyth County and died in 1915. Furthermore, Talton's journal entries indicated he didn't trust his sources. He wrote about "a plethora of inaccuracies and contradictions" in contemporary newspaper accounts and the many lies people swore to be the truth. Talton's narrative had several loose ends, along with stuff that just didn't make sense. *Flight from Forsyth* was overlong, incomplete, boring, sometimes nonsensical, and perhaps wildly inaccurate. In technical terms, a megaturd. No wonder God had threatened to kill Charlie if he gave up, since the unlucky editor would have seriously considered fleeing the project if he only had to give up an eye or an ear.

But there was a good story buried in that manuscript, running like a vein of gold through solid rock, and he had to figure out a way to mine it.

Chapter Six

Charlie rummaged through Talton's file cabinets, hoping to find a grand and unifying piece to the puzzle, something that would help him assign a meaning to the madness—historical and supernatural—he was now mixed up in. Besides notes, drafts, and articles, he found a nasty letter from a Forsyth County man, more rejection slips, Talton's dissertation, several audio cassettes, and a large manila envelope labeled "John Riggins, Forsyth County 1930s" dated January 23, 1987—the day before Talton died. Charlie had noticed Riggins's name handwritten in red on the manuscript's last page. The 1930s? Charlie wasn't going *there*, not when he already had to cut the manuscript by more than half. He set the sealed envelope atop the file cabinet and promptly forgot about it.

Charlie pulled the contract from the wire in-basket and glanced over it again. It smelled funky-bad and—this was truly weird—his signature was wet. He shuddered in horror. *The damned thing was bleeding*! He borrowed an old pot from the kitchen and tossed the contract in it, then clamped on the lid. He made a mental note: Buy resealable container and have contract tested for DNA.

* * *

At dawn, Charlie awoke consumed with the brilliant idea that he should be promoted from editor to coauthor. After all, it would take a mighty struggle on his part to save the book from oblivion. Besides, due to its grotesque and seemingly supernatural flaw, the stinking contract, with its bloody clause, was rapidly approaching illegibility. He figured this might work to his advantage, since the original terms were dissolving, and he who remembers best …

He proposed this change to Kathleen over morning coffee. She was not impressed. "No way," she said. "You're not coming in and taking Thurwood's place." She gave him a look that caused him to back off quickly, just in case she still had some mojo left.

"OK, OK. I was merely—"

"Thurwood put ten thousand hours into the book. All you've done is cash a check."

"Sorry I brought it up."

Chastened, Charlie retreated to the study and got to work. Due to a recent fortuitous development, certain matters were more time-sensitive than others. Hank Sherrill had told a reporter named Bill Crenshaw at the *Atlanta Journal-Constitution* about Talton's book, and Crenshaw had called Charlie to set up an interview. Charlie wanted to contact Forsyth County sources for information before they read about him in *the lyin' Atlanta newspaper*, labeled him a meddlesome outsider, and refused to help, as so many had done with Talton. After all, folks up there were still sensitive about having the county's ultraviolent history dredged up. Charlie had seen this aversion to the past in 1987 with his in-laws, and he suspected that older butt cheeks would tighten all over Forsyth when word got out that a Yankee named Sherman was coming to town to finish the Commie professor's book.

Hoping to make some headway, Charlie called Cecil Montgomery, longtime chairman of the Forsyth County Heritage Foundation. Once, when he was bored to tears up at Varmintville, Charlie had read the man's "View from Mount Montgomery" column in the *Forsyth County Sentinel.* He remembered a picture of a dapper fellow with curly hair and a bow tie. Montgomery was more a genealogist than a historian, but Charlie hoped the man could put him in touch with someone whose ancestors had letters or first-hand accounts of events in 1912. It was worth a try.

Montgomery answered the phone pleasantly, but when Charlie told him what he was doing, the man's tone turned frosty: "I met Talton. Never cared for the man. I rather hoped his book died with him."

"Ah, c'mon, that's harsh," Charlie said, trying to sound jovial. "It doesn't deserve to die. Besides, it could be a good thing for the county."

"I don't see how."

Desperate to salvage the conversation, Charlie blurted out, "I've got Forsyth connections, you know. I married Susan Cutchins. State Representative Cutchins is my uncle."

"Why would someone who's kin to the Cutchinses have *anything* to do with a history book?"

Ignoring this slap at his in-law's lack of intellectual curiosity, Charlie pressed on. When he asked Montgomery about the correspondence of a man named Horton Anderson, the man's tone dropped from frosty to one best measured on the Kelvin scale.

"Those are private records, and no one will open them up to you," Montgomery told him.

Before Charlie could ask if they could have a cup of coffee and talk about county history in general, Montgomery cut him off: "I'm sorry. I won't be able to help you on this. It's just not something I care to do. However, I'd be happy to look over what you've got."

I'll bet you would, you plagiarizing old fool. "Great. Thanks for the offer. I'll be sure to send you a copy of the book when it's published." Charlie hung up and muttered, "If you pay full price, bitch."

Twenty minutes later, his cellphone trilled. Someone calling from a number he didn't recognize. "Hello," he said.

"Charlie. How ya been? That's good, that's good."

Charlie hadn't said how he was doing, but he knew the caller didn't care. It was State Rep. Stanley Cutchins, a.k.a. Uncle Stanley. The old Reagan Republican barely tried to get along with Charlie, and for the record, hated reporters. He'd grunted in disgust when he first met Charlie back in 1986 and learned his niece's bridegroom worked for a newspaper that had won a Pulitzer for exposing pork-barrel spending—$3 million of it in Cutchins's district.

"Hey, Uncle Stanley. That didn't take long. How's the view from Mount Montgomery?"

"I ain't mounted Montgomery, but yer welcome to try."

"Oh, he doesn't like me. Not one little bit."

"That's what I hear. I guess you're wondering why I called."

"Not really."

"Cecil called me, sayin' you're stirrin' up trouble, mixin' the family into it."

Time for a brush-off, since Uncle Stanley's twang hurt his ears. Speaking quickly, Charlie said, "Oops, I left something on the stove. Gotta go. Say hey to Aunt Liz."

"Wait a minute. What you got? What years you coverin' anyway?"

"It's Forsyth County. I think you can figure it out."

"Don't start a war you can't finish." Stanley's tone was ominous, even threatening.

"War's over."

"That's what I'm tryin' to tell ya. What's done is done. Don't go diggin' up what's laid to rest."

"We'll talk. Come see us," Charlie said, though he certainly didn't mean it, just like Uncle Stanley never did when he invited Charlie to his house on the lake.

* * *

Montgomery not only called Uncle Stanley but also apparently warned everyone in the county who might have assisted Charlie. Over the next two days, the increasingly frustrated writer was told, "Sorry, can't help you"; "It's just not something I care to do"; and "Those are private records, and I'd rather not open them up." Others simply hung up. After a dozen calls, Charlie quit his solicitations. No sense being a damn fool about it.

Still, if Uncle Stanley and the other white folks up there didn't like what he was up to, then it must be worth doing. Actually, their opposition made Charlie's mission seem even more intriguing and important, rejuvenating him and giving him heart just when his will was flagging. That's just the way he was—at heart a contrary sort, who thought that finishing a dead professor's book about a county that didn't want the publicity seemed like a right contrary thing to do. Besides, he'd die if he didn't do it. There was always that.

* * *

Beck and Ben fought all the way back to Thornbriar from the supermarket. Charlie, busy herding them into separate time-outs, didn't notice Susan standing in the darkened front hall, hands on hips, glaring at him with eyes afire. He bumped into her. "Oh, excuse me. Bought groceries. Gotta get them out of the van."

She followed him outside. "You didn't tell me the thing was about Forsyth."

"*Thing*? You didn't ask."

"Uncle Stanley called Mom all riled up because you're trying to finish some dead professor's book about what happened way back when. I guess they're talking about 1910."

"1912. See, you're from there and you got the year wrong."

"Anyway, they both called me. They want me to look at it, see what it says." Her expression suggested that she knew it was an unreasonable request but he should grant it, anyway. He'd always liked that look. Feisty as hell. The sex was very energetic when it started with that look, but this time she wasn't being the least bit friendly.

"It's a hefty piece of work, so it says a lot. There's the murder."

"It was a rape and murder." As a native Forsyth Countian, she was duty-bound to point that out.

"Yes, but Dr. Talton focuses on the anti-black terrorism."

"Terrorism?"

"Yeah. White folks do it, too, darlin'," he drawled.

She gave him her *I don't like talking to you* wince. "What about since then? That's what they want to know about, what you're going to write about between then and now. Uncle Stanley has a position in the community to protect, you know."

He shrugged. "I guess I have to write an update. Why do they care? They got something to hide? You got something you need to tell me?"

"No," she said loudly. "I assume they're worried you'll put in Momo's 1987 arrest."

"Hey, that's a good idea. Thanks for reminding me."

"Oh no you don't. Don't pin that on me. I just figured it's what you'd do. You know, re-fight the Civil War, go through the Fourth of July again and show everybody how evil your in-laws are."

"Fortunately for them, I've got to cut the book, not turn it into an encyclopedia of white folks misbehaving."

The kids were sneaking away from their time-out spaces like jungle guerrillas. Charlie caught a fleeting glimpse of Beck as she darted into the dining room to hide behind the china cabinet. She giggled when he spotted her. Ben was crawling on his belly up the hall from the family room. Charlie walked over and planted his foot on his son's back, then yelled like Tarzan and beat his chest.

"You da man," Ben said, laughing as he rolled over and grabbed Charlie's shoe.

"No, you da man," Charlie replied, bracing himself against the wall so Ben wouldn't pull him down and break his glasses again. Ben refused to let go. Charlie dragged him along, peg-leg style, until he made it to the kitchen counter, then dug out a family-sized Stouffer's macaroni and cheese from a grocery bag and hoisted it for Ben to see. "Let go, boy. I've got to fix dinner."

Being hungry, Ben relented. Charlie fell into the routine of fixing dinner, all the while wondering why the Cutchins family cared so much about his Forsyth saga. Pappy had been alive—barely—back in 1912. He'd told Charlie a couple of things. "That was the year of the Titanic," he'd said on Easter Sunday in 1987 after Charlie mentioned the subject. "Year I was born. That's when we ran the niggers out. Some of'em needed extry persuadin'." With a spark in his coal-dark eyes, Pappy had gone on to boast he'd once "chunked rocks at a darkie." That didn't make sense, now that Charlie thought about it, since Pappy would have been an infant at the time. All the more reason to talk to the old man. The way things were going, made-up memories would have to do.

He hoped Uncle Stanley hadn't already warned his father not to talk. But there were two things in Charlie's favor: One, Pappy wouldn't listen to anyone telling him what to do. Also, no one would think Charlie was stupid enough to go back there. But Charlie was way past stupid; he was *chosen*, and the voice inside his head told him to go forth and interview the old coot. He was about to mention this to Susan when he had a better idea: *Don't.*

* * *

Wednesday morning, the wind bit Charlie's face as he gassed up Kathleen's car at E-Z Go on Briarcliff. He was taking the Volvo in hopes he could sneak up on Pappy, since a stranger's vehicle would be less unwelcome than his red Caravan. While talking to Pappy was likely to be an unpleasant waste of time, it wasn't the only reason for the trip. Charlie also wanted to understand the geography of events before his newspaper interview. Then, he could speak with authority as he pitched Talton's tale. Charlie also believed it was necessary to make a pilgrimage to Martha Jean Rankin's grave. Talton had shortchanged her in his narrative. Charlie wanted to reach beyond the cold, hard text and touch her world. Make it *real*—something Talton hadn't done.

Charlie took I-85, then traveled on I-285 to Georgia 400 and headed north. He listened to jazz on WCLK until the signal became a buzzing crackle. He clicked off the radio and grabbed the wheel tightly when a strong wind buffeted the car, slapping the Volvo as if to knock him off course. This made him wonder if there was more than one supernatural force at work. What if he was in a proxy war and it was the other side's turn to move? That would explain why the contract was such a bloody mess—and why he constantly despaired of his task. After all, depression was the devil's favorite tool. Then again, he wasn't exactly sure who he was working for, but he wasn't doing anything wrong, so he'd continue on this path.

* * *

Born on August 28, 1912, Isaac "Ike" Cutchins was a short, rail-thin, unsmiling man with big ears on a small head, a bashed-in nose, and coal-black eyes that held a deep-seated animosity. He looked permanently pissed off, and proud of it.

Charlie first met Pappy on July 4, 1986, a month after his wedding to Susan, which Pappy had boycotted. At the time, Evangeline was still furious at Charlie for marrying her twenty-year-old daughter in Macon rather than Cumming ... and for showing up hungover at the altar.

Independence Day meant a cookout, with Bradley Roy manning the grill. Women brought casseroles filled with cheese, Jell-O molds, and cakes and pies for dessert.

Charlie ate in the living room with Jerry Bancroft, Sheila's first husband. Charlie's mullet-headed brother-in-law was wearing an aptly named wife-beater shirt and watching a NASCAR race on TV. Jerry's days were numbered. Within two months, he would be killed in an act of justifiable homicide outside a Gainesville bar. According to police, he pulled a knife on a man with a concealed-carry permit after attempting to pick up the guy's girlfriend. There would be a fistfight at Jerry's funeral—a fitting tribute to the man.

"Anything else on?" Charlie asked, hoping for a Braves game.

"Rasslin, maybe," Jerry said.

"Oh no," Charlie said quickly, waving his hands emphatically. "Believe me. Racing's fine."

That's when Charlie saw Momo for the first time. Susan's gargantuan cousin came through the front door into the living room, shaking the floor with each step. As tall as Charlie, Momo outweighed him by more than a hundred pounds; a mop of brown hair sat atop his pumpkin-sized head. He scowled at Jerry, ignoring Charlie. "Rasslin's on. Why ain't you watchin'?" Momo switched channels.

"Hey, asshole," Jerry said.

"Fuck you," Momo retorted. "If rasslin's on, rasslin's on. House rules."

Charlie winced and glanced at his watch. How much longer did he have to stay before he could leave? Momo checked all the channels but couldn't find Hulk Hogan or Rowdy Roddy Piper. He grunted in disgust and turned off the TV.

"Turn the race back on, asshole," Jerry said.

Momo turned to stare at him. "Don't make me go out to my truck."

"Hell," Jerry said. "Don't make me go out to mine."

Charlie felt like he was watching a battle between bad and evil. "Guys," he said.

Momo looked at him, apparently noticing him for the first time. "Who the fuck are you?"

"He married Susan," Jerry said. "You missed the wedding because you were in jail for stalkin' that girl." (Momo's mother referred to this as a "failed romance.")

Momo gave Charlie a once-over with close-set eyes and grunted, "You lucky." He stomped off, mumbling about the lack of pro wrestling in the world. Charlie shuddered. The guy reminded him of the villain in *The Texas Chainsaw Massacre*.

Right after he washed down his lemon meringue pie with sweet tea, Charlie saw a performance of what Bradley Roy liked to call "the longest-running soap opera in Forsyth County." Momo had returned to the living room, and Charlie felt himself getting pushed out by the toxic aura of the man, who made Jerry look like a college professor in comparison. Charlie was standing in the wide passage between the kitchen and living room of the modest home when the older folks' conversation seized his attention.

"They can put me in the poorhouse, for all I care," declared Pappy, wearing faded Lee overalls and a blue chambray work shirt. Wizened, with grayish-white hair, the seventy-three-year-old man stood at the head of the table, holding court over bowls of potato salad, bags of chips, ketchup, mustard, napkins, and a platter half-full of grilled burgers and hot dogs. On his left sat his only son, Stanley, dressed in white slacks and a pale blue polo shirt, who was running for a second term in the Georgia House of Representatives, having wrested the seat from a Democrat in 1984. On Pappy's right sat his daughters Evangeline Powell and Marie Hastings, who was nicknamed Tantie Marie. Both wore polyester slacks and sleeveless blouses. Stanley's wife Liz was outside, smoking a cigarette.

"What about the land?" Tantie Marie cried out.

"They can have it," Pappy said, waving his hand. "I ain't got no use for it. I quit farmin', if ya ain't noticed."

His children vehemently shook their heads in unison.

"What about the house?" Tantie Marie's tone grew even more anxious. She shared a mobile home with her son Momo, and Charlie could imagine the trailer rocking from side to side whenever the big guy got up to get a beer (although he wasn't allowed to drink while on probation).

"They can take the house, too," Pappy declared. Meanwhile, Gram, Pappy's hatchet-faced wife, washed dishes, apparently ignoring the discussion over the fate of her home.

"Nobody's taking the house," Stanley said.

"Can't you fix the taxes?" Tantie Marie asked her brother.

"Fix them?"

"Talk to the tax commissioner so we don't have to pay. That's what politicians do, right?"

Bradley Roy, passing through the kitchen to get a piece of apple pie, grunted in disgust.

Stanley shook his head. "That's not the way things work. We'll cover it this year," he declared, then glanced at Evangeline and nodded toward her purse. "Anyway, I already got them to appraise it low. I don't know how long it will be before Bill Arnold notices."

"I'll have to owe you for my share," Tantie Marie said.

Stanley reached over and patted her hand. "I know it's been hard since Big Rhett left."

Charlie turned his head toward Jerry, who was laying on the sofa, and asked, "Who's Big Rhett?"

Jerry answered without taking his eyes off the TV. "Momo's daddy. Momo is Little Rhett."

Momo grunted at the mention of his name, but kept his eyes glued to the TV, apparently mesmerized by the shiny cars racing around the track. "When did he leave?" Charlie asked.

"I don't know. Momo, when did the Forsyth County Courthouse burn down?"

"How the hell should I know?" Momo grumbled.

"Nineteen seventy-three," said Bradley Roy, now standing across from Charlie, still working on dessert. "And they never proved anything," he added, stabbing his fork in the air for emphasis.

"'Cept that Cutchins women are hard to live with," Jerry said, letting out a derisive chuckle.

Charlie was curious, but he didn't want Momo's full attention, so he dropped the subject and turned back to the kitchen-table discussion. Evangeline was shaking her head vehemently as she scolded her father: "I don't know why you have to put us through this every year."

Pappy glared at her. She reached for her purse and pulled out her checkbook. "That don't work on me," she said. "You want the money or not? You don't have anything to say to that, do you? Just as I thought." Evangeline started writing. "What's my share plus half of hers?" Evangeline waved the back of her hand at Tantie Marie like she'd forgotten her sister's name. Stanley gave her a number. Evangeline fluttered the check over the potato salad and placed it in front of her father. "I made it to the tax commissioner, so don't get any ideas. Sure you want it?" Pappy said nothing. Whatever he was thinking was locked away behind those smoldering eyes.

"Go on and tear it up if you don't want it, then," Evangeline said. "Just go on." The check remained undisturbed. "I thought so. I'm tired of this poor-mouth nonsense. You gonna say, '*Thank you, Evangeline, for helping me keep my land*?' I thought not. Come on, Bradley Roy. Let's go." She rose and stormed off in dramatic fashion. Bradley Roy took his time finishing his pie, holding the plate close to his face.

A minute passed before Gram hollered from the kitchen. "Vange is out there yelling for everyone to come out and say 'bye to her."

Bradley Roy sauntered over to the trash can and threw away his paper plate, then took his time saying farewell to everyone. On his way out, he turned, winked at Charlie, and said, "Now you know."

"Know what?" asked Susan, returning from a back room heart-to-heart with her sister, Sheila, during which Jerry's sins would have been freshly cataloged.

Bradley Roy kissed his younger daughter on the cheek. "Everything and nothing. Best come out and say goodbye to your momma. Sheila!" he shouted toward the back of the house. "Vange is in a snit and she needs you to say 'bye to her. You know how she is." He turned to Charlie. "She holds grudges."

"I know. She's still mad about our wedding."

"Hell, boy," Bradley Roy said with a grin, "she's still mad at me about ours! As for you, she ain't ready to admit you exist. Give her a few years … she'll come around."

Charlie noticed that his father-in-law sounded uncertain about that last part.

On the long drive home, Charlie told Susan, "Your grandfather is *right unfriendly*. I'm not sure he even said hello. He just grunted when I came up to shake his hand."

"He and Gram are mad we didn't have the wedding up here."

"Why should they care?"

"They care." She shrugged and looked out the window.

"I heard something about your uncle and a courthouse fire."

"Just a rumor. I've heard it, too."

"Well, what's the rumor?"

She sighed and shook her head. "Supposedly, Uncle Rhett burned down the courthouse and left town. No one's heard from him since."

"Why'd he supposedly do it?"

"Don't know. Love. Money. Take your pick."

"Love? Funny way of showing it."

"Well, it wasn't for Tantie Marie."

Now it was Charlie's turn to shake his head. A few seconds later, he had an epiphany. "They're varmints," he declared. "I married into a family of varmints."

"Don't call them that," Susan said. "And especially don't call *me* that."

But the name stuck, at least with him. Pappy's place became Varmintville.

That afternoon, Susan told Charlie things she'd kept to herself until then—the sort of family secrets no sensible person lets their spouse know until after the marriage has been consummated. Thus Charlie learned Pappy's story—part of it, at least.

In the 1960s, Pappy and Gram moved into a new Jim Walter home that replaced the cracker box and outhouse that the family had endured for decades. When Pappy turned sixty-five, he quit farming, sold his equipment, and told his children to pay his property taxes if they wanted to inherit the farm—those he still talked to, anyway.

Missing from family discussions was Pappy and Gram's eldest child, a daughter who'd run away when she was a teenager. "I saw Aunt Shirley once, at Lenox Square when I was seven years old," Susan told her husband during that ride. "I was with Mom and Sheila. Mom said, 'Lookie, girls, there goes your Aunt Shirley.' When the woman saw us, she turned and walked away. Mom didn't follow. Instead, she dragged us into a dress shop, like she was afraid of her sister. I craned my neck to watch the woman. I only saw her a few seconds before she disappeared. I heard she didn't marry but changed her name anyway. Don't know why."

That night, back in Macon, Susan refused his advances in bed. Eventually, Charlie learned to insist on "sex before varmints." If he had to go to Forsyth County, he would at least start out contented, since these trips never seemed to have a happy ending.

* * *

Charlie, fascinated by Aunt Shirley, had missed his chance to meet her after Gram died in November 1986—two months after Jerry Bancroft's brawl-marred burial (which left Sheila having to play the dual role of bereaved widow and referee). Charlie and Susan, having just recently moved to Atlanta, misjudged the drive time to Cumming, so they were running late that day. When they arrived at Haynes Funeral Home, Shirley had been gone ten minutes, but people were still yelling and crying about what she'd done while there.

According to Bradley Roy, Gram was laid out in her casket looking pretty, and her friends, neighbors, and relatives were waiting for the memorial service to begin when in stormed Shirley wearing a white dress. She went up to the casket, hocked a loogie, and spat on her mother's face. Stanley grabbed Shirley's arm and ordered her to clean off the spit. She snarled, "Get your damn hand off me, or you'll be dead before you hit the floor."

Shirley struggled to open her purse with her free hand, and Bradley Roy saw a pistol butt. "Let her go, Stanley," he said. "She just wants to leave. Don't you, Shirley?"

"I do," she said. "Soon as this bastard gets his damn hands off me."

"You're gonna have to answer to God Almighty for this," Stanley said.

"I will," she snapped. "But He got to answer to me first."

Shirley spun out of Stanley's grip and headed toward Pappy, who had remained seated by the wall throughout the fracas. She gave him a twisted, scary smile, wagged a finger in his face, and snarled, "You better hope you live forever, old man, because when you die, you'll burn in hell." Pappy stared past her like she wasn't there, and she left as quickly as she'd come.

So said Bradley Roy, which made it the absolute truth, so far as Charlie was concerned. Unfortunately, Bradley Roy couldn't tell his son-in-law what Gram's sin had been, and Charlie had wondered about it ever since.

After his wife's death, Pappy's life didn't change much. He watched rasslin and sat on the front porch chewing the tobacco Momo brought by when he wasn't in jail. Every year, Pappy repeated his set piece on taxes. Stanley and Evangeline ponied up their portions and loaned Tantie Marie her share at ten percent interest, the maximum allowed by the Bible, to be repaid when Pappy passed on to his reward and the farm became theirs, all theirs, to sell as quickly and for as much as possible. Pappy listened with characteristic ill humor to the flattery of kinfolk who came to visit, Charlie suspected, not for love, but for land.

The stakes grew higher as Forsyth's population exploded and real estate values shot up. In the 1990s, developers showed up on Pappy's porch, hats in hand, asking how much money he'd take for his land. For a man who claimed he was ready to give up his farm rather than pay property taxes, he was amazingly uncooperative, vowing he'd rather shoot them than desert his birthright. No doubt they'd heard he kept a gun handy. They left and didn't come back.

And so Pappy just kept rockin' and spittin' and gettin' more ornery. The last time Charlie had been in Forsyth County, exactly two decades after his first visit, he and Momo got into an argument over flying the Rebel flag on the Fourth of July. Charlie, who had come to resent even being at Pappy's house, saw the flag as an insult to the United States as well as his liberal Yankee world view. After Momo threatened to kill him with his bare hands, the old man called Charlie a "nigger-loving cocksucker" and ordered him to get off the property. Armed with his double-barreled twenty-gauge shotgun, Pappy followed Charlie outside. Charlie retreated to his van and stood beside it. Pappy fired once—not exactly at Charlie, but not away from him either, killing a crow in a nearby oak tree. As Charlie ducked behind his van, Stanley burst from the house yelling about hunting out of season. Bradley Roy came out behind his brother-in-law and calmly took the gun from Pappy, unloaded the shells, and put the live round in his pocket, saying, "That's enough fireworks for today, don't you think?"

* * *

Now, on a winter's morning several months later, Charlie crossed the Fulton County line into Forsyth. Across the median, southbound cars and sport utilities poured into Atlanta. Along each side of the road stood a thin line of pine trees—a Potemkin forest that failed to hide office parks and residential subdivisions. Forsyth's population was 12,000 in 1910; it had grown twelvefold since then. Charlie passed Cumming and exited Georgia 400, driving beyond Coal Mountain on Highway 9. The other lane was jammed with fuel tankers, dump trucks, flatbeds pulling back hoes, and septic service trucks, as well as BMWs and SUVs, all of them stuck behind an old clunker puttering along at thirty miles per hour. The hills were pocked with chicken houses. Some of their roofs were bright and shiny, while others were dull gray and twisted, rusted reddish-brown in spots. Many were vacant, and some of those were in a state of collapse. A survey crew worked in a pasture near some of those ruins, which would soon be replaced with another subdivision or shopping center. The sales prices for these dirt farms—undeveloped parcels, in developers' terms—had to be astronomical. Millions of dollars, at least.

Just past Coal Mountain Church of Christ, Charlie saw the old graveyard on a hill to the left, near the site of an old church that had burned down in the 1920s. He parked in the cemetery driveway and stepped out of the car. With his hands stuck in his coat pockets, the writer strolled about the burial ground, which was dominated by family plots: Fitzgerald, Mackey, Kirkpatrick, MacGregor. No Cutchinses. The Rankin family plot, with its tidy brick borders, was near the center of the well-kept graveyard. Silk flowers were everywhere, along with withered poinsettias left from Christmas.

When he found Martha Jean's grave, a deep chill colder than the winter air knifed through his bones. He stood still for a while, reflecting somberly about what had happened, hoping to absorb history by osmosis. He listened for a voice from the grave. Why not? After all, his mission was shrouded in weirdness. Wasn't he a ghost writer, of sorts? Or maybe even a ghost's writer. For all he knew, the good professor was behind all this.

When he grew tired of the wind whipping his deaf-to-the-dead ears, Charlie returned to the car and drove east toward Lake Lanier. According to local legend, the stone Bernie Dent had used to beat Martha Jean was embedded in a giant white oak on the banks of Sodder Creek not far from the lake. Charlie parked his car near the creek and made a desultory search for it but found neither root nor rock. The air was cold and time was short. Under the circumstances, who was he to argue with local legend?

After he quit his search, he drove across the bridge into Hall County. A few fishing boats dotted the lake. The green water sparkled blue by some trick of light. He pulled into a lakeside park to collect his thoughts. After years of drought and Atlanta's constant sucking need, the coves had turned to mud flats. The boat ramp was long enough to deserve a county road number.

Back in Forsyth, he stopped at Bud's Quikie, a combination convenience store, bait and tackle shop, and fast-food restaurant. Two old men played video poker in back. Charlie bought a Diet Coke and a Baby Ruth for lunch, then sat in the car working up the nerve to see Pappy.

He focused on how to approach the old man. This time, he'd be non-antagonistic, and he'd let Pappy spew racist venom all he wanted. The more, the better.

When he'd properly steeled himself for his task, Charlie drove past Frogtown and a *Cow Crossing* sign, then turned onto Slide Road near the landfill. To the north stood the Blue Ridge Mountains. He passed the First Church of Varmintville (a.k.a. the First Baptist Church of North Forsyth), which permitted no sin. Just down the road stood the Second First Church of Varmintville, founded by parishioners banished from the first First Church who liked to drink, dance, and divorce, most likely in that order.

Within a minute, Charlie was at Pappy's place. He rolled up the semicircular driveway, tires crunching gravel. In the pull-off next to the house sat Pappy's faded blue 1970 Chevy pickup. It was scary to think the old codger still drove, but the truck was kept in good running order by auto experts Bradley Roy and Phil McRae, Sheila's relatively well-behaved, raccoon-troubled second husband. The Volvo's door squawked open, and as soon as Charlie stepped out into the cold sunshine, the house's red wooden door opened and Pappy came out, dressed in his trademark overalls and blue shirt. He stood on the stoop, forcing Charlie to stay in the yard and look up at him.

"Hey, Pappy. Beautiful day," Charlie offered.

"You come all the way out here to tell me that?"

Charlie laughed. "No, sir. Truth is, I'm working on something. Don't know if you heard—"

"You're Susan's, right?"

"Uh … right."

"I heard you got kicked outta the house fer lookin' at smut." He laughed unkindly. "Got to take care of your own, not go looking through catalogs for somethin' new."

"I'll remember that. Actually, I wanted to talk about something else."

Pappy spit tobacco juice, hitting a boxwood. He stared at Charlie with remarkably clear, dark eyes. "So what'd you come here fer?"

"I'm working on a book about Forsyth County history, back in the day."

A pause. "I ain't sure I know what yer gettin' at."

"You know. The rape, the lynching. Running people off."

Pappy's mouth dropped open. After an instant, he recovered and squinted at Charlie. "Wait jest a minute. You mind tellin' me *zactly* whatcher talkin' about?"

"Come on, Pappy!" Charlie laughed in exasperation. "Nineteen-twelve. Martha Jean Rankin."

Pappy's face returned to its normal configuration. "Don't know nuthin' 'bout it. I was a baby. I can tell you the niggers moved out after they raped and murdered a white woman."

"Well, not all of them did that."

"They's all capable. Can't be safe with 'em around." He looked north, then south, as if scouting the horizon for African-Americans. "Looks like you gettin' your way. They comin' back. I seen a couple last week. They better not come near me, if they know what's good fer 'em." He spat again.

"I wanted to ask—"

"Don't let the door hitchoo on the way out." Pappy retreated into the house. "One other thing," he said through the screen. "If Susan ain't got use for you, neither do I, so there ain't no need for you to come by here. And it ain't a beautiful day. It's cold as hell." He banged the door shut.

That went well, Charlie thought as he drove away. Casting a sullen glance at Varmintville in his rearview mirror, he shuddered, causing his vehicle to cross the center line before he regained control.

Chapter Seven

Charlie ditched his shipping department uniform, choosing khaki slacks and a blue sweater for his interview with reporter Bill Crenshaw. As he walked out the door, Kathleen patted his shoulder, making him feel like a kid going to a job interview. On his walk to Bay Street Coffeehouse, Charlie assured himself that it was all right to have his picture in the newspaper, since the police were looking for an unkempt slob in goggles, not a smart-looking editor with specs. He arrived at his destination a few minutes early. Jean—no longer Amazon Woman, now that he'd properly made her acquaintance—gave him a double-take as he stepped to the counter.

"Newspaper interview," he said apologetically.

She raised a sculpted brow. "So the lone wolf is newsworthy."

The lone wolf. He liked that. He took a seat in the half-full room, sipped dark-roast coffee, and started reading a book Talton had cited frequently. Like the others he'd looked through, it told him little about Forsyth County.

Shortly after one o'clock the thirtyish reporter arrived. Crenshaw was tailed by a balding and bearded photographer whose expression wavered between boredom and amusement. Crenshaw had dark, mischievous eyes and wore a blue tie so loosely it seemed like an afterthought. The two men introduced themselves to Charlie, bought drinks, and then sat at his table. Crenshaw plopped a digital recorder in front of his interview subject and turned it on. "Tell me about the book," he said.

"OK." Charlie started with a short bio of Talton, then gave some background on himself before talking about *Flight from Forsyth*. The reporter jotted notes on a skinny pad. After taking a few pictures of Charlie, the photographer drifted off to make a phone call.

"What do people up in Forsyth County think about this effort to dig up their past?" Crenshaw asked.

"We wouldn't have to dig it up if it hadn't been buried," Charlie said, glancing over at Jean, who winked at him, causing his pulse to quicken.

Crenshaw was intrigued when Charlie told him that not only did *Flight from Forsyth* identify several black landowners who had been forced to abandon their property, but that Talton had obtained copies of records backing up claims of land theft. "Of course, a lot of these records were destroyed in a mysterious 1973 courthouse fire," Charlie said, without mentioning the suspected arsonist's name. "I don't know if you're aware of this, but a lack of documentation derailed claims by blacks for reparations in 1987."

"Little did they know the records were safely in a dead man's care."

"Exactly so," Charlie said. "Following Redeemer's march, local officials paid lip service to the idea of reconciliation by forming a biracial committee. I was up at the library in Cumming the other day and read the committee's report. Whites disliked any mention of reparations, and warned that attempts to seek damages over past events—here I quote—'could produce widespread antagonism throughout the nation, with dangerous consequences.' So Forsyth folks continue the tough talk. But, like I said, there are records to back claims for reparations. Unfortunately, the man who held them was unable to attend those meetings, being deceased. But with *Flight from Forsyth*'s publication—"

"Assuming it gets published."

"—much will be revealed. Assuming, yes. Which I do, of course."

"Who said dead men tell no tales?" Crenshaw paused for a beat. "So, can I see the records?"

Charlie gave him a knowing smile and shook his head. "That's Dr. Talton's story to tell."

"Come on," Crenshaw wheedled. "Give me a break."

"Sorry." No way was Charlie giving him *that* scoop.

At Crenshaw's request, they adjourned to Bayard Terrace to take photos of Kathleen. She protested unconvincingly about having her picture taken, then changed into her blue dress and put up her hair. After she posed with the manuscript, Charlie gave the journalists a friendly push out the door and rushed to pick up the kids, rehearsing apologies to their teachers for his tardiness.

Less than an hour later, Crenshaw called Charlie's cellphone. "My editors are putting pressure on me," the reporter said. "You gotta let me see the records. This is Sunday front-page stuff."

"Sorry," Charlie said, fighting back a grin. "The story will come out in due time."

"Well, forget what I said about the Sunday front page," Crenshaw grumbled. "Monday back page now."

* * *

Late Sunday night, after a weekend of plodding through Taltonic prose, smiling through Angela's hints of lawyering to come, and watching a kiddie movie with Beck and Ben, Charlie finally got around to baiting two rat traps with peanut butter and placing them in a dark corner of the dungeon before crashing out.

An hour later, he was awakened by a loud SNAP! The other trap sprang seconds later. That was one badass rat. Charlie listened closely but heard no anguished squeaks. He went back to sleep.

He woke at dawn Monday with the realization that he'd be in the news that day. He poured a cup of coffee before pulling the newspaper from its wrap. He found the article next to the obituaries. "This was supposed to be a resurrection, not a burial!" he fumed, throwing the section on the kitchen table.

The piece wasn't all bad, but he had mixed feelings about seeing his picture in the paper. On the bright side, he could use the article to convince editors and agents of *Flight*'s importance—if only he had a sample to show them. Not Talton's prose. God no. He needed something to persuade readers to keep going, not to kill themselves.

While Charlie sipped coffee, Kathleen shuffled into the kitchen wearing her robe and slippers. He knew she'd see the story right away, since she checked obits first thing. She squealed in delight and clutched the paper like she was a kid with a new toy. The article included the photo of Thurwood she'd given to Crenshaw. "Isn't he handsome?" she asked.

"Yes ma'am."

"It's really going to happen, isn't it? Thanks to you."

"We've been lucky. It's strange how things are falling into place. Fantastic, really."

"Speaking of fantastic," Kathleen said, "I had the strangest, most vivid dream last night. I was in a courtroom, and Thurwood sat down beside me. You were there, too. You were the court reporter, the stenographer who takes down everything. A good sign, don't you think? Thurwood was happy and thought things were going well. He said, 'That young man is an angel, you know.' I said, 'He's the answer to my prayer,' and he said, 'That's what angels are.'"

"I'm glad he thinks we're going to succeed. But I'm no angel."

"You never know."

"I think I'd have an idea by now."

The phone rang. "Could you get that?" Kathleen asked.

He picked up the kitchen wall phone on the third ring. "Hello?"

"Sherman."

"Yeah, that's me."

"They did right, putting your story on the obit-chew-wary page," said a man in a hard Southern accent. "That book comes out, you're dead. What you got to say to that?"

"I'd say it's time to be rude." Charlie hung up.

"Who was that?" Kathleen asked.

"Someone who doesn't think we should publish the book."

"To hell with them!"

"My thoughts exactly."

* * *

At Thornbriar that afternoon, Charlie read the article to Beck and Ben. They were impressed but mainly hungry, so he baked cookies. When Susan got home, she gave him her *I Don't Believe It* look and said, "What did you do, pull strings to get publicity?"

"Yeah, baby," Charlie said, grinning. "I've got *connections.*"

Later that evening, when he returned to Bayard Terrace, Kathleen said, "The house is cold even though I turned on the gas logs and set the thermostat to seventy-eight degrees."

"Seems hot to me," he said. It was cooler in the dining room, however. He set the laptop on the table. He felt a draft as he moved closer to the study. He reached down and felt cold air blowing in from under the study door. When he opened it, the curtains flew up to greet him and a blast of arctic air hit his face. He flipped on the light. The window had been shattered.

He stood gawking for a moment before realizing the room had been ransacked. Two file drawers lay empty on the floor. The computer was gone. So was the manuscript. "Shit," he groaned. His feet seemed to stick to the floor as he walked to the file cabinet. With each step, the magnitude of what had happened increased. Someone had broken in and stolen his work in progress: not only *Flight from Forsyth* and his PC, but Talton's notes and the documents he'd bragged about, as well—the breadcrumbs he needed to find his way home.

"Fuck me," he declared.

"What's wrong?" Kathleen stood in the study door, staring at the fluttering curtains as Charlie dropped to his knees. "Are you hurt? Oh my goodness."

Charlie gripped an open file drawer and hoisted himself to his feet, nearly toppling the cabinet. It crashed against his shoulder. He angrily knocked it against the wall like it was a tackling dummy, then tried to compose himself. "Burglary. Did you take a nap this afternoon?"

She blinked. "Yes."

"Someone must have come in while you were asleep. Did you hear anything?"

"I don't know. If I did, I thought it was you. You keep the door closed," she said as she looked around. "They took the computer, didn't they? Oh, dear."

"They took everything. The manuscript. His notes. Files." He nodded toward the cabinet to signify the loss, the full consequences of which were still sinking in.

"They stole the book?" Tears welled in her eyes. "This is horrible! Who did it?"

She started toward the sofa, which was covered with shards of glass. Charlie grabbed her arm and steered her toward the desk. She slumped into the office chair.

"Someone who doesn't want the book published." He drummed his fingers on the desktop.

"We're ruined." Kathleen buried her face in her hands.

"No. I've got a manuscript file on my laptop. And I parked one on an e-mail server. It's just—"

"You can still do it?" She looked up hopefully as tears rolled down her cheeks.

"Yeah." He paused. "Yeah," he said again, to convince himself. He knew it wouldn't be easy. The situation was terrible, actually. The trump cards—the property records he'd never bothered to look at, let alone make copies of—were gone. Oops. Big oops. Irreversible, unrecoverable error. Maybe fatal. Blue screen of death. He shook his head and shivered. "Check and see if anything else is missing," he told her.

She got up, screeching the chair on the wooden floor, and padded off. As he picked up slivers of glass, he noticed that the bloody contract was undisturbed. Then, as he clinked the glass fragments carelessly into the trash can, he sliced his left middle finger. He retreated to the hall bathroom and found a Band-aid in the medicine cabinet.

"It's going to be OK," he told the defeated face in the mirror as he held up his bandaged finger. Sure, it would be difficult to check all the footnotes now, and he'd have to remark the text. But he understood the story. And the fact that evildoers wanted to thwart him—that should stoke his determination even more, right?

No. It was no use. He couldn't talk himself out of the despair he was feeling.

Kathleen peered into the bathroom. "I think they took the salt and pepper shakers," she declared. "I'm going to sit down."

He followed her into the living room and noticed she was trembling. "They can't stand for the truth to be told," she said. "That's what brought this on. I think it was the Klan."

"Or maybe someone whose granddaddy stole some land."

Charlie grabbed the phone book and thumbed through the pages until he found it: Thurwood Talton on Bayard Terrace. "You're easy to find."

"I never had the listing changed. Just because … just never did." She thought for a moment, then said, "This is a hate crime. We need to call the police. Maybe the FBI. Even though I never cared much for that J. Edgar Whosis who used to run it. He was in bed with the Mafia."

"He was in bed with a lot of men," Charlie said. "But as for calling the law … no cops."

"We should at least call that reporter."

A plan was hatching in his fevered brain. "Uh … no. Can't do that. If Crenshaw found out the records are gone, it would make *Flight from Forsyth* seem like damaged goods."

"What should we do, then?"

"Fix the window. Get back to work. And don't tell anyone about it." He pressed a finger to his lips. She looked at him like he was crazy. He shrugged. "The damage is done. I'm sure they've already destroyed the stuff they took."

He wished he'd returned the desktop computer to Thornbriar as soon as he'd bought the laptop. Now he'd have to buy another PC for Susan and kids.

Kathleen picked up the phone.

"Uh," Charlie said. "Who are you calling?"

"Angela, to see if she has a copy of the manuscript."

"No. We don't need it, and she doesn't need to know."

"Phone's dead," she said, staring blankly at the receiver.

Charlie groaned. He grabbed a flashlight from the pantry and went outside to find that the phone line had been cut at the box. He looked around the other side of the house and found two sets of shoe prints in the mud by the study window. One pair was sunk deep in the mud beside the screen, which had been taken off and cast aside. Charlie shuddered to think what could have happened to Kathleen, especially now that she was back to being powerless. *Would have been nice if she'd woken up and put a smite on their evildoing asses.*

Working in the dark on a rickety stepladder, Charlie patched the window with an old sheet of plywood from the basement. By the time he finished, he could see his breath even as he wiped sweat off his forehead.

He returned to the study feeling a frenzied urge to get back to work, but the room was so ugly and cold he couldn't stay there. He also felt violated. His space had been invaded—his work and thoughts had been stolen. Pissed on, crunched by jackboots. Raped. He walked into the kitchen and slumped at the table.

When he'd composed himself, he used his cellphone to report the service outage.

Kathleen sat down across from him and said, "This is a horrible thing." A moment passed. "You're sure we can keep going?" Another moment slid by. "I need to hear something positive, Charles."

He lifted his head to meet her gaze. He felt like he was a boxer, bloodied, rising off the canvas, not sure what had hit him, what round it was, or how long the bout was supposed to last. And all he had now was a puncher's chance, if he could keep going. "Yes."

She gave him a nervous little laugh. "We've got people frightened, don't we? We'll get it done just to spite them. Anyway, I'm too old to be afraid." She leaned forward and swatted his leg. "Back to work."

She retreated to her bedroom. The study was still cold, so he stayed in the living room, lying on his belly as he worked on his laptop by the fire. But he was too frazzled to do anything. The good professor's words had blurred together in a meaningless clump on the computer screen. Wanting to do something, Charlie retyped the title page, adding his name as editor. Then he replaced Talton's artless epigraph with a Biblical passage that had been uttered by a black preacher after his church just north of Cumming had been burned to the ground: "*I the LORD thy God am a jealous God, visiting the iniquity of the fathers upon the children unto the third and fourth generation of them that hate me …*"

Charlie hoped this was true. He could use some Old Testament justice on his side.

He gave up on the day and went downstairs. He looked around the dungeon and, feeling his dark little world closing in on him, buried his face in his hands.

Then he remembered the rat traps. Soon, the stench of death would be his only companion. He grabbed a plastic bag and his flashlight and went into the shadows to search, but found neither vermin nor traps. He staggered back to the cot and collapsed on it, overcome with a sudden fear that he had killed not a rat, but Trouble, and thereby put a curse on himself. That would explain so much.

* * *

Charlie lay on his cot until noon. When he brought the laptop out of hibernation, he saw the ghastly title of Talton's first chapter: *Geologic/Economic Imperatives and Propensities*. No question: *Flight from Forsyth* sucked, he was lost, and villains grew fat on stolen breadcrumbs.

"Are you all right?" Kathleen asked him when he trudged upstairs. "Have you been drinking?"

"No, it's just hard to get moving today." He stood and stared at the wall as he drank cold black coffee.

"Could you call someone to fix the window?"

"Yeah."

"Oh. I have a friend that could use your help. She bought some ceiling fans."

The idea of doing something other than working on Talton's manuscript appealed to Charlie, so he called the woman, who knew someone else who wanted some painting done. Before he knew it, he had several days' work lined up. The idea of making a living as a handyman appealed to him, and he considered giving up on Talton's turd and returning Kathleen's advance. The contract was a joke, anyway. A bad one.

After calling a glass installer, Charlie went to the Y, where the scales said he'd lost ten pounds since Christmas. At least *something* was going right.

On the way to pick up the kids at Gresham Elementary, he stopped by Office Depot and ordered business cards to advertise the services of "Charlie the Handyman." After Beck and Ben were settled in at Thornbriar, he loaded his van with tools.

Late that afternoon, he noticed the answering machine's blinking light. He played the message and was shocked to hear that someone named Joshua Furst, an editor with Fortress Publishing in New York, had found his home phone number and wanted to talk to him about his "Forsyth saga."

Just as Charlie pulled his cellphone out of his pocket to return the call, the kids exchanged blows. "Stop it!" Charlie shouted, clicking shut the phone. "Time-outs for everyone!"

Returning the call would have to wait until he was safe from sabotage.

When Susan got home she was friendly, even flirtatious, which made Charlie trust her even less. Then he realized he'd misread her. She simply wanted to talk about her job, or more specifically, complain. Just like old times. At least she wasn't griping about *him* this time.

During dinner, Susan and the kids demanded that he return the computer he'd taken back in December—which wasn't possible now that it had been stolen. He wasn't going to admit that, however. After ten minutes, they wore down his resistance. "All right, all right. I'll get you another one," he said.

"I want the old one back," Beck said.

"Uh—"

"You pawned it, didn't you?" Susan said. "I knew it!"

"No, I didn't. Don't worry. I'll get you a better one."

"When?" Susan said, calling his bluff.

"Now!" He jumped up and stomped toward the door.

"And you're paying for it!" Susan shouted after him.

* * *

Wednesday, Charlie earned $150 installing three ceiling fans. He called Joshua Furst's number but got voicemail, so he left a message. That night, Kathleen told Charlie it would cost $150 to repair the study window and suggested that the repair was his responsibility. Since she looked ready to smite someone, Charlie ducked out and went to the coffeehouse. For the record, he didn't care who God or Bad Kathleen thought should pay for the window, he was keeping his handyman money.

Late that evening, he went through the motions of working on the manuscript, but he could only look at the damned thing a few minutes before it repulsed him.

Thursday, Charlie painted bedroom ceilings in a house three blocks away from Bayard Terrace. As a consequence, he was late picking up the kids. For the second day in a row, Beck and Ben were the only children left in their respective classrooms. His apologies were abject; the teachers' smiles were strained. Charlie knew he was pushing it, but what could he say? He had a job.

Friday, Charlie was painting walls. Mrs. Wetherbee's TV was blaring in the living room, so he didn't hear his cellphone at first. When he realized it was ringing, he nearly kicked over a can of yellow paint in his haste to take the call. "Charlie Sherman here."

"Mr. Sherman, Joshua Furst. You're a hard man to get hold of."

"Uh ... sorry. I've been busy." Charlie was perplexed, since he'd been anxiously awaiting this call.

"I wanted to talk to you about the Forsyth book."

"How did you hear about it?"

"One of our authors lives in Atlanta. Arden Davis. She marched in Forsyth in the eighties. Anyway, she e-mailed me an article about you along with your phone number. Were there really twenty thousand people there that day?"

"Not counting the Klansmen."

Joshua laughed. "It's a great idea for a book. Can you tell me more about it? You're finishing a professor's work, right?"

Charlie explained what he was doing, or rather, what he *should* have been doing.

"How soon can you send me three chapters, along with an outline?" the editor asked. "Let me have an exclusive look at it, and I'll get back to you in four weeks. I'm looking forward to seeing it."

"OK. I'll get it in the mail to you." Even as he said this, Charlie wondered how long it would take to make Talton's prose presentable.

* * *

Saturday morning, Kathleen expressed shock and outrage that Charlie was charging her friends to paint rooms and install ceiling fans. "You don't need the money," she told him as he drank coffee and ate toast she'd paid for. "Your job is to edit Thurwood's book, which you're not doing. You should be sending something to that editor you told me about."

"I assure you I do need the money. I've got a family and bills to pay. It's always tight this time of year, and I have to help with the mortgage. Don't worry. I can do both jobs."

"I'm paying too much. I don't plan to give you all my money." She shook a finger at him. "Virginia Wetherbee said you're charging four hundred dollars for painting two small rooms."

"That's a bargain."

"She could have hired a painter."

"She *did* hire a painter!" Charlie said in exasperation. "Hey. Did you take your meds?"

"I don't see what that has to do with it."

"Take your meds."

"It's not your business."

"Angela said it was."

Mentioning her daughter put Kathleen in a foul mood but also forced her to act. After pouting for a while, she got some bottles from the kitchen counter. Charlie watched her take her medication to make sure she didn't palm the pills—a favorite trick of hers, according to Angela. As soon as he turned his head, he heard the garbage can's lid go up.

"Kathleen!" he yelled. "Did you just throw away your meds?"

"Of course not. And I'm not taking them twice!" she yelled back. "Do you want to kill me?"

* * *

Charlie finished his painting job Saturday shortly after dusk. With his paycheck safely tucked in his wallet, he slipped in the dungeon's back door. After cleaning up using gritty mechanic's soap, he put on clean clothes and went upstairs, where he found Kathleen kneeling in the living room by the fireplace. The lights were off and a dozen candles burned brightly on the mantel, their light reflected in the mirror above it. Photos of Thurwood were all over the room: standing on the floor, lying on the couch, sitting on the coffee table—dozens in all. Kathleen wore a baggy old black cardigan sweater. Her faraway eyes danced in the firelight. Was she holding a séance? "Kathleen."

She snapped out of her reverie. "Where have you been all day?"

"Painting Mrs. Wetherbee's bedroom. I finished."

She looked around and laughed. "You must think I'm silly."

"No." *Silly* wasn't the word he was thinking of.

"I wanted to spend some time with Thurwood. He died twenty years ago this month. We were married forty years." She sighed. "Sixty, now. I miss him every day."

"I understand."

"Sit down," she said. "Talk to me for a while."

Charlie glanced at his watch, then looked around. "Where can I sit?"

"I'll make a spot." She picked up photos from the couch and placed them on the coffee table. When they sat down, she held both his hands. "Thurwood wants you to get back to work on the book. He knows you're having trouble, but it's going to be OK."

Charlie grinned. "You talked to him, did you?"

"No, of course not. I can't speak to the dead ... he spoke to me. In my dream."

"Oh." *That's different.*

"He said there aren't any major problems with his book."

Charlie shook his head. "I don't want to talk about it right now. Look, I need some time to myself."

"You have more time to yourself than is good for a person. If that's what you are. I think sometimes that you come from a far place, from—"

"You're getting me confused with the guy I came in with." *The one I killed with the rat trap.*

"What do you mean?"

"Nothing. Look, I'll work on it in the morning. I gotta go."

He left to eat dinner and hang out at the coffeehouse. When he returned at midnight, the house was dark. He slipped in the dungeon door and climbed into his sleeping bag. After a few minutes of tossing, turning, and fretting, he fell asleep.

* * *

The sun was shining and sweat beaded his forehead when he saw her in the distance, walking along the cornfield fence. She wore a white dress and a red ribbon in her curly shoulder-length auburn hair. As he stumbled clumsily along the fence row, he realized she was the rich girl. Her daddy owned several hundred acres of bottomland. "Martha Jean!" The name came easily to his lips. She turned toward him. Even at a distance, he could see her eyes twinkling. She was pretty. "Wait up!"

She kept moving. He persisted, even though something was wrong with his foot. He huffed like an old man as he shambled up to her.

"Daddy kill you if he see you runnin' after me." Her hard tone belied her soft features.

"I gots to tell you. Doan go down to the crick today."

"What do you mean?" She wrinkled her nose. "You stink."

"It ain't safe down there," he panted.

"It ain't been rainin'. The snakes won't be out."

"Not snakes. It's ..." He couldn't remember what to warn her about.

"It's what?" she asked.

His thoughts, already dim, grew darker. "Nuthin'."

"Say 'ma'am,' you stupid nigger. Leave me before you get in trouble."

He looked around fearfully, then relaxed. There wouldn't be no trouble except what she caused. "Doan—" He could feel the anger rising, and there was no use in talking. Words never did him much good, anyhow. He stood and watched as she turned and sauntered down the path, swaying her hips. He felt confused. A terrible urge rumbled through him and stuck down there, chasing away all fear. It wasn't right she should put him in trouble just because she was a white girl. There was that other thing, too. He could tell she needed it.

And then something turned inside him. He pulled the new mirror from his pocket. He looked into it and saw a misshapen black face, dull-eyed and thick-lipped. He dropped the glass and reached down to grab a chunk of granite twice as big as his fist, then chased after her as fast as he could, his determination growing.

* * *

When Charlie woke, he realized he'd had a wet dream—a consequence of living as an ascetic. And now he knew things that had never been written, having seen the outrage, seen it whole. More than that. He'd lived it. He'd committed it. He'd given that little bitch what she deserved. *Whoa. Steady, Charlie.* He shook his head to clear it of that nasty thought and groaned at the repulsiveness of what he'd experienced.

It had been more than a dream. It was all too real. He sat up and considered taking a cold shower. Too late for *that.* He pulled the chain on the bare bulb, then stood up to stretch. It was 4:00 a.m. He stripped off his soiled sweat pants and stumbled to the can. He gave himself a cold-water wash, toweled himself off, and threw his clothes atop the sleeping bag on the cot. He would have to wash the whole mess.

Usually he didn't give a second thought to his dreams, but this time he recalled everything and couldn't go back to sleep. Something burned inside him. He slipped on jeans and tiptoed up the creaking stairs to the kitchen. He groped for and found the red bag of coffee beans on the counter. He started to fill the grinder, then realized he'd wake Kathleen. He took the coffee downstairs and poured beans into his palm, tossed them in his mouth, and chewed them like peanuts. He fired up his computer, then took a swig of water from the bottle he kept in the cooler beside his plastic milk crate. He sloshed the liquid around to wash down the grounds.

Although he'd never been an artist, he grabbed a piece of paper and, using his Waterman with black ink, sketched Martha Jean's face. It turned out better than he had any right to expect, given his lack of skill. If he could find a photo of her, he'd know whether he was on the right track. Going on what he remembered seeing in the mirror, he drew a picture of Bernie Dent, that ugly little bastard. Then he drew the rock, for good measure.

After that, Charlie took a deep breath and started typing. Rather than fading, the dream became more vivid with every keystroke. It was exceeding strange, what was happening, but he seized on the idea that the dream was divine compensation for his recent loss—and just the break he needed. He didn't like channeling a mentally handicapped rapist, but who was he to question such a gift? What else could he do?

He'd need further corroboration before he could fully weave its details into the text, of course. And he'd keep Talton's footnotes in the manuscript, to lend authority to his account. But the story's telling was shifting now, and it was going to be good. No, make that *fantastic.*

Chapter Eight

Dawn peeked into the dungeon as Charlie finished transcribing his terrible dream's rich detail of grit, smoke, dust, lust, and pain. He collapsed on his cot, but after a few minutes he rose and took his laptop upstairs. He made coffee and migrated to the study, where he edited Talton's manuscript for another four hours, until bolts of pain shot from his fingertips to his neck, commanding him to stop.

He wasn't done for the day, however. Sunday evening, after returning from the Y and refueling with coffee, Charlie plunged back into the manuscript, his slate-gray shirt sleeves rolled to his elbows, eyes gleaming with manic energy. For another six hours, he attacked Talton's lumps of coal, compressing them into sparkling diamonds on the page. He could now see the book clearly and whole, running like a river through his mind—from the background of the attack on Martha Jean to Redeemer Wilson's second protest march in 1987, the one Talton didn't make. At the rate he was working, he'd have a package for Fortress in no time.

* * *

He breathed the dust of a commandeered 1910 Oldsmobile as it raced out of Gainesville with Bernie Dent trembling in the back seat. He chased after the accused murderer-rapist along with thirty-eight other mob members, whose names he knew. The would-be lynchers yelled and screamed and kicked rocks in a frustration bordering upon sexual. It took them a few minutes to fully comprehend that their prey was gone. Then they scattered, shouting curses and threats: "Damn nigger!"; "Next one won't be so lucky!"; "We'd be better off if they was all dead."

Suddenly, he was someone else, trudging through the September night into Cumming, the earth falling away behind each footstep, hurrying him along, until he reached his destination. He stopped and waited; the sun rose and burned his face. He smelled rotting meat and swatted at a horde of flies buzzing around his head. On a dusty street, he stepped over the tobacco-spit that had spattered on the courthouse steps like raindrops in hell, passing through a lingering crowd that longed to do the devil's work. Soldiers ringed the building, standing at parade rest with fixed bayonets. He smelled horse turds and heard stray dogs barking at a bitch in heat. He wiped his brow; his sweat was muddy. He took notes for the piece he'd be filing on "The Georgia Troubles" for *The New York Times*. God, he hated this little cow town.

At 4:00 a.m., the courthouse door melted into darkness. Charlie kicked out of his sleeping bag and started writing. The power cord dangling from the overhead socket swayed back and forth as he tapped keys, going at them like a jazz piano player on meth.

Before he knew it, four hours had passed.

Upstairs over coffee, he told Kathleen to take her meds. She angrily refused. "Those pills are part of the control system Angela has," she declared. "You shouldn't be a part of that."

There was a special place in hell for the controllers, he knew. "OK," he said, having no time to argue. He left her sputtering vague incantations, apparently trying to get her smite back on.

That morning, Charlie drove the van up to Forsyth County. The place grew uglier every time he saw its malignant, incurable growth. Houses appeared like mushrooms after rain. In Cumming, he felt a pang of doubt as he pulled into the parking lot of the county's modern, one-story library. He'd traveled fifty miles like a heat-seeking stalker to find something that in all likelihood didn't exist. But his hunches had a supernatural twist now, which made following them an adventure, no matter the outcome.

The library, which had just opened, was empty except for a mother and daughter in the children's section and an old woman returning her serial alphabet mysteries. A plump, pretty librarian with dark hair and gold-framed glasses stood at the checkout counter. "May I help you?"

"Yes ma'am. I'm doing historical research on Forsyth County and I was wondering if the library had any photographs from 1912." He sensed a pair of eyes fix on him.

At the end of the counter, an older, heavy-jowled librarian wearing glasses on a beaded chain regarded him suspiciously. "Your uncle," she told the younger woman.

"Cousin, actually," the young librarian said. "We just call him uncle." Turning to Charlie, she said, "'Cause he's old. He runs the local historical society."

"What's his name?"

"Cecil Montgomery."

The older woman looked away. Charlie whispered, "He's no help."

The younger woman, looking to be in her mid-thirties, wore a white V-neck sweater. She smiled sheepishly and glanced over at the other librarian before returning her gaze to Charlie. "What do you need?" she whispered back.

"Have you ever heard of Martha Jean Rankin?" When she nodded, he said, "I need a picture of her. She died in 1912."

She looked at him critically. "I thought I recognized you. You were in the paper." She wrinkled her face in perplexity. "Do you drive a truck?"

"No. I just wear cheap clothes."

She giggled, drawing a warning glance from her colleague—apparently the alpha librarian.

"You married Susan Cutchins," she whispered.

"I knew that. But how did you?"

"This used to be a small town. My name's Lillian Scott." She looked around. "There aren't any 1912 pictures here." Leaning forward, she whispered, "But I have one. I'll bring it tomorrow. Will you be here?"

"I'll make a point of it." He turned on his heel and walked out before he further irritated the older librarian. "Troll," he muttered under his breath as he passed by her desk.

* * *

That night, Charlie edited the chapter covering the lynching of Ted Galent. Following a ten-page discourse on capital punishment, Talton had written that Galent, had he been properly charged, would have faced the relatively minor offense of concealing a crime. Instead, "Galent was shot to death in his jail cell, beaten to a pulp, and strung up on a telephone pole in the center of town and set afire, disrupting communications throughout the town and causing unnecessary inconvenience to Cumming's wealthier citizens."

Charlie inserted a subhead: *Lynching Disrupts Phone Service*. After that, he took the laptop downstairs along with marked-up manuscript pages and turned on the bare bulb overhead. He fell asleep while rereading the chapter, still wearing his work clothes and glasses; the papers slid off the sleeping bag into a pile on the floor.

* * *

He sat on a rickety chair taking dictation from a dying man in a bed. The stench of shit filled the room, which was crowded with mismatched old furniture. He gagged, momentarily breaking the pen's contact with paper. The dim-eyed man lying in his own filth saw this and stopped talking, then licked his lips with a gray tongue and croaked, "You need to get all this down. 'Cause it the damn truth."

"Sorry." The scribe turned to open the window, but as he placed his hands on the frame, he felt the bitter cold. He turned back to his clipboard. The dying man stared at the ceiling and began talking slowly: "I, Joshua Logan, being on my deathbed, do solemnly swear that I am a sinner and I beg the good Lord to forgive me for the things I done wrong. I took part in the killing of a man named Galent in the year of our Lord 1912 and the taking of another man's farm that same year. I have farmed the land as my own ever since, but because it is not my land by any lawful act, it is not mine to give to my heirs. Though they may not see it that way, the land belongs to a nigger named Buck Smith, who was run out of town. We burned his cabin and drew lots to see who would get his land. I won. And then there was Riggins. Ike Cutchins is the one to answer for that, more than me. You make sure you write that down."

While Logan was talking, a woman with a weathered face came in with a pitcher of water, placed it on the bedside table, waved her hand in front of her nose, and left without pouring any into the empty glass beside it.

Logan motioned for the scribe to put down his pen. "We was all of us caught up in that thing with the Rankin girl," Logan wheezed. "But it wasn't just that. Niggers was doin' better than we was. I was a sharecropper and it didn't seem right. Some of us just hated 'em. Lots of rich folks liked them better than us. Then old man Carswell said how if we got rid of niggers we'd be rid of crime. He was mad 'cause his family couldn't own 'em anymore. I didn't even know I was gonna take the land when we did it. Had to hire a lawyer—Samuel Jenkins—to make the title look good."

Logan paused and licked his parched lips, needing water. Some meanness inside the young fellow kept him from giving it to the old man, however. Logan dictated a few more sentences, then said, "Lemme see what you wrote."

He took the clipboard and read silently before saying, "Gimme the pen." He scrawled his name. "I don't need to say no more. I'm prayin' to the Lord—"

His speech was interrupted by violent spasms. Logan flopped around on the bed, and his eyes popped wide open. His face turned purple. It looked like he'd offended God so badly that the Lord was strangling the son of a bitch. Then Logan was still. "Aunt Lilly! Aunt Lilly!"

The woman came in and regarded Logan carefully, then took his pulse. "He's dead," she declared, dropping the hand. She then slapped the corpse's face hard with the back of her hand. "Been wantin' to do that for the longest time. Cee, you need to get rid of that letter."

"Yes ma'am." They both retreated to the kitchen, where the fireplace burned brightly. The scribe threw the sheet into the flames and asked the woman, "Anything more you need me to do?"

"Don't tell a soul. Nobody needs to know what he said. Not ever. This land's all I got—"

"I know."

She gave him a sullen gaze. "Don't have much choice, do I?"

"Not for me to say, Aunt Lilly."

"You run along and tell your parents. After they take the body away, I need you to come back and help me get rid of the mattress. Guess we burn it." She wrinkled her nose. "Now I got to wash him off before they come. Seems like I pay good money for the funeral home to do it." She considered the issue, then shook her head. "People will talk. Best I do it."

"You want us to say a prayer for him?"

"Ain't no point, where he's goin'."

He shuddered when he saw the cold hatred in her eyes. "I understand."

When he stepped outside into the blustery cold, he recalled that he was due at choir practice in an hour. He realized that his name was Cecil, but his friends called him Monty. He also felt a pang of longing for the high school football team's quarterback, but he would have to keep that to himself. "Oh my goodness," he said as he trotted off, "I'm gay." But that word didn't sound right to his ears, not in 1953.

* * *

Charlie typed Logan's confessional scene, including the letter, into his laptop. Although Logan's name didn't appear in *Flight from Forsyth*, Talton had interviewed Buck Smith's son Isaiah. It was the work's most gripping passage.

And now Cecil was helping, despite his antipathy to the project. Charlie chuckled with glee.

He went upstairs to look for blank stationery. He could hear Kathleen moaning through her own dreams, sounding both intriguing and unladylike. Thurwood must be visiting. He found a sheet of paper that appeared to be the right size, then returned downstairs and rewrote the note using his closed laptop as a backboard. Due to overwork, Charlie was troubled by a knot at the base knuckle of his right ring finger. His grip on his fountain pen was cramped, the penmanship scrabbly—not his own. It was a tricky proposition, using a first-hand account from a lyncher and land-stealer, especially since the letter had been burned, but he'd think of a way to use it. Everything came to him so easily now. Such is life in the realm of the professionally weird.

* * *

Charlie drove past Cumming, continuing northwest, figuring Joshua Logan lay in the graveyard of the First Church of Varmintville, since the Second Church hadn't been built until the 1980s. Less than two miles from Pappy's farm, he pulled into the gravel parking lot of the fading clapboard church. He zipped up his parka and ambled toward the unfenced cemetery. Weeds had overgrown the plastic flowers that adorned the graves; his work boots crunched dried stalks as he conducted his search.

The throaty roar of dual glasspack mufflers shattered the quiet. Charlie recognized the sound. His chest tightened as he ducked behind a tombstone. An instant later, Momo's red monster Chevy pickup truck—*General Nathan Bedford Forrest*—rolled by less than fifty feet away. Charlie knew that Momo, who had threatened to kill him the last time they'd seen each other, kept a gun handy.

The truck's big V-8 engine chugged lethargically at the stop sign before it roared off in the direction of Pappy's house. Charlie stood and dusted off his knees, trying to convince himself that his Caravan was invisible. He glanced at the tombstone he'd been hiding behind.

JOSHUA LOGAN
BORN JULY 12, 1888
DIED FEB. 3, 1953
GONE TO HIS REWARD

Nice delphic touch. And a single headstone. He searched for the wife's grave but found no marker for her. Charlie remembered the vicious slap from his dream. The lonely grave was further confirmation that his vision of Logan's death was true, so true. Clearly, the miracle shouted down the fraud.

* * *

Lillian Scott, sitting at the reference desk, looked up and smiled at Charlie as he approached. Wordlessly, the Forsyth librarian opened a drawer and produced a manila envelope. "You wanted to see this, I believe," she said, pulling out a heavy sheet of paper and turning it to face him. Shocked, he held up his drawing, which he'd smuggled in under his parka. She stared at it wide-eyed. "It's the exact same picture!" she said, drawing the unwelcome attention of the library troll. "My great-grandma drew that picture. How'd you get it?"

"I … uh—"

"Looks like the original, except that the paper's new."

"And cheap, unfortunately. I drew it from a copy. I inherited some stuff," he whispered.

Leaning forward, she confided, "I inherited some things, too."

"Really? What?"

"Some old journals and letters from back in the day. I haven't really read them, but there might be something there."

"I'd like to see them."

She looked at the other drawing he'd placed on the desk. "That's the killer, isn't it?"

"You tell me."

Before he could stop her, Lillian summoned the library troll, who stiffly walked over and hoisted her chained glasses upon her nose as she regarded the picture. "Bernie Dent," she declared.

"Indeed it is," he said.

"Where'd you get this?" the older librarian demanded.

"He inherited it," Lillian said.

The older woman eyed Charlie suspiciously. "You're working on a book about the old days, aren't you?"

"I am," Charlie said. "And I've got some more work to do."

On that note, he departed—without getting the younger woman's phone number (or giving out any information, either). By then he was thinking he already had everything he needed—especially since his dreams were proving to be real and true.

When he returned to Bayard Terrace, Charlie skipped lunch and placed Joshua's death statement on a cookie sheet, then brushed the paper with tea and baked it at low temperature. Of course it wouldn't pass the test of authenticity. Therefore, he would make a copy and destroy the original—if what he was cooking could be called an original. He still wasn't sure exactly what he'd do with it, but he'd keep it handy nonetheless. Only one person alive had ever seen its message. One other person, that is.

Kathleen came into the kitchen looking for her reading glasses. "What are you doing?'

"Experimenting," he said. "Trying to see how somebody might get away with something."

"I see," she said, pursing her lips. "Will they?"

"That's always the issue, isn't it?"

* * *

Another night, another excessively vivid dream, another writing marathon. When he took a break, Charlie glanced at the clock and gasped. The school bell would ring in five minutes! And teachers were already extremely tired of his tardiness. He dashed out the door and sped off in his van. When he was ten minutes away from his destination, his cellphone rang. He winced as he answered.

"The principal called and asked if you're all right," Susan said, her tone flat as a manhole cover.

"Hey, Suse," he said, trying to sound breezy. "Just running a little late."

"That's been happening a lot, and it's not acceptable. They're not babysitters."

"What are they going to do, call Family and Children Services?"

"Actually, they just might."

Ouch. Charlie knew this could be an issue in custody hearings, if it came to that. "I'll do better. 'Bye." He pounded the steering wheel in frustration. It wasn't fair. Couldn't people understand that he had to write? And write and write?

Charlie arrived at Gresham and coached himself to remain calm. He apologized profusely to Beck's and Ben's teachers and meekly accepted separate but equal scoldings. Bottom line: The next time he was late, he would receive a warning letter, and a copy would go "in the file."

Charlie left school ranting about a conspiracy against him, only realizing he'd gone over the top when he saw his kids staring at him in alarm. "I'm writing a story about monsters," he explained. "Sometimes I practice it out loud."

Monsters interested the kids, especially Ben. On the way back to Thornbriar, Charlie told them the story of *Frankenstein*. It had been two days since he'd showered, and midway through his tale, he scratched a sticky armpit.

"You stink worse than a monkey," Beck said.

"Don't be rude," Charlie said.

"Then don't stink," she suggested.

At Thornbriar, Charlie fixed peanut butter and jelly sandwiches. He was pretty sure that the one he made for himself was his first food of the day. On second thought, he had no idea when he'd last eaten.

* * *

The next day, Charlie proudly arrived at Gresham Elementary on time only to find Evangeline waiting in the office. He did a double-take, nearly spraining his neck as karmic tires squealed on psychic pavement. "What are you doing here?" he asked, not bothering to be polite. The school secretary watched the two antagonists impassively, as if she might one day be called on to testify.

"I came to pick up the kids," Evangeline said. "Susan can't trust you to do that anymore."

He grimaced. "Not true. And here I am. You wasted your time. Anyway, you're not on the list."

"Susan put me on it."

"Did she," he deadpanned, making sure it didn't sound like a question.

"She did," Evangeline replied, making sure he got an answer.

"I'm gonna get the kids."

"I'll be at the house, waiting for them," she declared.

Charlie escaped with Beck and Ben out a side door. He took them to Dairy Queen, then the library. They were at Duck Lake Park when his cellphone rang.

"Mom's at the house. She says the kids are missing. She wants to call 911."

Charlie pushed Beck's swing. "No, they're with me, Susan. Too bad she drove all the way to school for nothing. Hey, wanna eat out tonight? My treat."

"Yay!" Beck cheered, waving her arms and almost toppling from her seat. "Pizza!"

"Pizza!" said Ben, twisting the chains as Charlie gave him a push.

Susan continued: "The school counselor called today and asked if anything was wrong with you. She said you showed up at school yesterday mumbling to yourself."

"Why would Ms. Morris claim that? I didn't even see her."

"The teachers told her. They say you've been disheveled and disoriented."

Obviously, someone had gotten to them. *Satan*. And he had evidence! "I'm under a lot of pressure to get the book finished. You have no idea."

"Don't be late again. I can't be pulled away from here. I'm up for a promotion. I need you to focus on the kids. They need you to focus on them, too."

"Fine," he grumbled. She kept talking, but he quit listening.

He dropped the kids by Thornbriar after Susan got home. He didn't bother to go inside, since Evangeline's Crown Victoria sat fat and stupid in the driveway like an ugly old toad.

* * *

Increasingly, *Flight* was becoming Charlie's book. The dreams persisted, and like a side effect from the drugs that were advertised on Kathleen's nightly news programs, they were excessively vivid. Charlie awoke each day at his weirding time of 4:00 a.m. with images and scenes etched into his brain, hearing echoes of rifle shots in the hollow, seeing the fear in a sharecropper's face illuminated by a nightrider's torch, smelling armpits and tobacco spit on the crowded courthouse steps. Charlie had come to believe that *Flight from Forsyth* was a book of lost souls, who now came unto him for deliverance from guilt, shame, and/or injustice—although some of them just wanted to share recipes.

The only way to rid himself of the pressure on his brain was to download these graphic scenes. Charlie's compulsion to write was so strong it often overwhelmed his urge to piss. He scribbled frantically on a legal pad while waiting for the computer to boot, certain that his dreams were true. He was extremely grateful to be gaining more in his sleep than he'd lost in the burglary, though it didn't seem worth it the morning he woke with a severe headache after dreaming the county's 1910 annual budget meeting.

The next night, he found himself in a coffin as clods of dirt thudded on its closed lid. Panic rose in his chest and he clawed at the pine box. Splinters stabbed the quick beneath his fingernails. He awoke clutching his chest. He couldn't describe the horror of being buried, nor could he see its place in *Flight*. He didn't even know who he'd been. Then again, maybe all dead people felt alike.

He went to the bathroom and returned to his cot at 4:02 wishing he didn't have to write this horror, but there was no escaping death. He turned on his laptop and flexed his fingers. Pain shot through them. He typed slowly, then sped up, surprising himself by writing not a dirge, but a letter to a sister-in-law in nearby Dahlonega.

October 16, 1912

Dear Addy,

The last of the coloreds left Oscarville yesterday. Luther burned down their shacks this morning and plans to plant cotton there next year. He says he got the best claim to the land, but it doesn't seem right, what folks been doing. Luther says keep my mouth shut, but everbody knows what's going on. No use to talk about it. I fear there will be a price to pay. That's what the Bible says …

The letter went on to mention an obnoxious mother-in-law and how many jars of applesauce had been canned for the winter, along with the recipe. It would go well with the pork chops from the pig Luther had bought from Lester McCready, the colored man who moved away.

It made no sense, this mix of death and food, but Charlie kept typing. He yelped in torment as he wrote about sewing a new dress, describing its frilly lace in agonizing detail. He wrung his hands to ease the pain. They felt like nails had been hammered through them. Another knot appeared, this one on the palm side of the base knuckle of his left middle finger.

The next night he channeled property records, again waking with a terrible headache. Charlie spent six hours inputting data before collapsing in a heap on his cot. When he was done, he checked Talton's text and realized he'd dreamed the documents that had been stolen from the study. But now Charlie could see black faces and cotton fields, not just names and numbers.

* * *

Day and night bled together. Except for his children, all was darkness, and the stress of dream and dungeon took a toll. Charlie now talked to himself nonstop on his daily shamble down to the coffeehouse. He had learned to mask the odd behavior by pulling out his cellphone and holding it to his ear as he walked, so he looked like a man on the go, not one going insane. These trips, his only breaks from the grind, were also a luxury he could ill afford, since he was nearly broke and hadn't done any handyman jobs in two weeks, having gotten no offers despite leaving his business cards tacked on bulletin boards all over that part of town. He regretted giving Susan his painting money to help pay the mortgage. Meanwhile, Kathleen owed him for more than a hundred hours of work on the manuscript, but she was so crotchety he hesitated to ask for payment. To top off his humiliation, when he ordered a double espresso, Jean told him, "You look like a deliveryman who lost his truck."

By this time, Charlie believed he was more electrical conductor than writer—a wire with its insulation chewed off, stretched to breaking between two unseen points (neither one in the living world), and heated to the melting point. Charlie Sherman was a candidate for spontaneous combustion, if ever there was one.

* * *

He was an attorney in the old courthouse looking through property records. A young secretary flirted with him, showing him a picture she was drawing of the recently deceased Martha Jean Rankin. When he went into a back room, she followed. Hot damn! A few minutes later, he was running out of the courthouse, tucking his white starched shirt into his trousers with a deputy and another man on his heels.

Charlie woke up breathing heavily. No wet dream, just running for his life. He cupped his hands over his face. Now he knew that Randall Pryor, the original attorney for accused murderer Bernie Dent, had been caught diddling a secretary in the file room and had to be replaced by an inexperienced young attorney named Jackson Ponder just days before the trial. He also knew that Lillian Scott's great-grandmother was a hussy. How could Charlie put such scandalous details in the book? There had to be a way—although he'd probably let Lillian Scott's slutty ancestor have a pass, since she was an artist.

By now the dreams were connected like pieces in a puzzle. He knew that the deputy who chased Pryor out of town had stood by when the mob descended on Ted Galent's cell. The other man who'd pursued the horny attorney was named Jim Biddle, a member of Galent's lynch mob. Biddle would later sit on Bernie Dent's jury, brag to his colleagues about the lynching, and fall asleep when Jackson Ponder presented Dent's case, which was not so much a defense as a second-hand confession and plea for clemency. (Ponder had believed Dent was a dead man the moment he'd been arrested, so the outcome was inevitable.)

Charlie started writing, describing the buildings Pryor had passed by on his sprint out of town. Details, details.

* * *

He sat at a table underneath a tree. Everyone in the county, white and black, formed a line that extended all the way to the Chattahoochee River. Each person waited to shove a note card containing personal statistics in his face. He stared at each one for a moment to burn it into his memory, then nodded his head. The person stepped away and was quickly replaced by another.

This census went on for several nights. Orderly and alphabetical, like dead Talmadge voters in Telfair County, circa 1946. Each morning, he typed the data in courier font at speeds in excess of 100 words per minute. The miracle of photocopying would blur and confuse the source, making it seem authentic, he hoped. He now knew everyone in the county back then, and better still, had backup for the stolen documents on landownership.

The high-speed stenographic channeling continued to take its toll. He had two more knots in the palms of his hands: *Carpal Stigmata Syndrome*, he called it. He developed a migraine during his census count. He feared he was growing a brain tumor, and it was doing all the work. But he had to admire such an industrious malignancy, since it certainly was getting the job done.

The next night, he was in a mob chasing after someone. Couldn't see who.

The night after that, he was being chased by a mob. He took down names, then got his ass kicked.

Then he was a she, complaining about having to do her own wash after the maid left town.

He spent one night as a feisty cur sniffing hitching posts. Someone who smelled like a Cutchins threw rocks at him. He chased the boy and bit him on his barefoot heel. Barking vociferously, he called the Cutchins a bitch. That was a good dream.

In the next, he stood in the middle of a stinking, late-summer crowd and felt dull-eyed primitive religion pulsing through the people, sensed an insane hatred of blacks, listened to the brainwashing by Randolph Carswell as the county's so-called Great Man told whites it was time for blacks to leave Forsyth forever. Then he went out and repeated the lies, and by constant repetition, helped to forge a new reality. Making lies the truth—wasn't that how people got things done in the world?

* * *

The file drawer was full again. Charlie had played God's own hack and gone far beyond replacing Talton's purloined documents. He'd lived the story and heard the frightened whispers about a mischievous devil and an angry God.

Flight from Forsyth played in his head constantly, swirling around in endless variations on the same theme.

However, even a feverishly obsessive-compulsive fellow in his manic phase can stare at a computer screen only so long. One Saturday night in early February, he ran out of steam just past eight o'clock. The day was done, shot. Kaput. He turned off his laptop and went to the living room, where Kathleen sat on the couch watching *Casablanca* for the third time that week. Her eyes glowed in rapt attention as Rick told Ilsa what colors she and the Germans had worn in Paris.

Charlie sat down in the green chair, wishing he had enough cash to go somewhere. Friday, he'd asked Kathleen for $500—a fraction of what she now owed him for the hours he'd racked up on the project. She responded by claiming she'd already paid him. No point in asking again. Angela, plague-free and re-lawyered, had come over that morning and seized Kathleen's financial papers, claiming her mother's failure to take her medications was proof that she couldn't be trusted with her own affairs. Kathleen explained that she'd gone off her meds to prevent Angela and the pharmacist from controlling her brain. Before she left, Angela told her mother to quit paying Charlie—which happened to be what Kathleen wanted to hear, anyway. So now the Talton Gang was plotting to starve him. *How had they learned his secret, that he would gladly finish the book for free*?

When his cellphone rang, he answered in the study.

"How's Mom?"

"She's been in a terrible mood all day. I wonder why that is." His tone was dry.

"She thinks you're going to keep asking her for more money."

"I *am* going to keep asking her for more money."

"She's paid you enough," Angela spoke gently, as if she was a nurse telling a terminal patient that he'd be getting no more painkillers.

"That's not the deal. I never would have signed on for that amount."

"It can't be open-ended. I'm looking at the contract right now. My God! What is this?"

"Red ink," Charlie guessed, though he had no idea what Kathleen's copy looked like. His contract, as gruesome and sopping wet as a pound of raw liver, was now packed away in a plastic tub in the dungeon. The vat, he called it. And now he felt the weight of it on his shoulders every waking moment—and even when he slept, for that matter. He assumed the document was saturated with the blood of those lost souls who gave him his dreams. He still needed to get the stuff tested. But not until they'd fed him all their stories.

"It says, 'The party of the second part will succeed, or die in the attempt.'"

"Hey, don't blame me for *that*."

"Die trying?" she said, her voice dripping with disbelief. "No way this holds up in court."

"Who's going to challenge it? I thought you agreed—"

"I never agreed to anything. I just had a setback when my attorney was killed. I've got a new attorney. Sandra Hughes is redoing the contract."

So she was back to boxing with God. "Knock yourself out."

"By the way, Mom thinks she has superpowers."

"Not *that* again. She also thinks she has a cat," Charlie said. "Bounce. I keep kicking the food dish."

"We had to put her to sleep just before Christmas."

The euthanasia had been Angela's gift to her mother just before she left to spend the holiday with her tattooed (now ex-) girlfriend. *Such a sentimentalist.* "It's the gift that keeps on giving," Charlie said. "She puts out food for it once a week. Which is odd in and of itself."

"She's in denial. Tell her she doesn't have a cat anymore."

Being a dog person, Charlie considered an imaginary cat preferable to a real one, so he didn't plan to mention the tragedy, fearing he'd have to drive her to the Humane Society to get a replacement. "I gotta go. Rick's about to shoot Major Strasser."

"What? Oh. *Casablanca*. Yeah," she said wearily. "One thing: If you want to stay there, you've got to take on more of a caretaker role. That's the only way this is going to work."

"I'll do what I can. But there is the matter of payment."

"We'll discuss terms later. Make sure she takes her meds."

"What terms?" he asked, but it was too late. She'd already hung up. When Charlie returned to the living room, Rick and Captain Renault were strolling off into the foggy night. Kathleen was misty-eyed. "That was our favorite movie," she said. "Thurwood and I must have watched it a dozen times together." She hit a button on the remote and turned off the TV. "I heard you talking about my kitty." She went into the kitchen and stuck her head out the back door. "Here, kitty, kitty!"

She returned to the living room. "Have you seen Bounce?"

"Never," Charlie said.

"I think my daughter killed her. That's just the sort of thing she'd do."

"Well, Bounce must have been very old or very sick."

"Yes, she *was* old and sick. I asked Angela to take her to the vet for surgery. But she won't spend money on a cat. Not my cat, certainly."

"If you know this, why have you been putting out food?"

"Well, *something* has been eating it. I thought she might have tossed Bounce out on the side of the road and she made her way home. You know how they have radar. But the food hasn't been touched lately. Maybe she is dead. Maybe it's rats."

"Hmm." *Had Trouble … Nah. Ick. Probably.* He shuddered, imagining the old trickster walking the streets with a rat trap stuck on his face. Which would serve him right, sort of. "Well, don't feed the rats."

"I miss Bounce. Now I've only got you," Kathleen said. "And you should be working on the book right now. That's what I'm paying you for, isn't it?"

Chapter Nine

Shortly after dawn, Charlie finished transcribing his dream of Lincoln Roberts, the black preacher who'd been beaten nearly to death for speaking truth to power in 1912. Unfortunately, he'd *been* Roberts, so he'd woken up at 4:00 a.m. screaming in pain and terror.

He shut his laptop and, with trepidation, climbed the dungeon steps. Kathleen had been through several mood shifts lately, so he wondered whether he'd see good Kathleen (cheerful and hospitable) or bad Kathleen (cranky, suspicious, even a little smiteful). She was in the kitchen, eating oatmeal. Charlie regarded her carefully, then glanced at the stove. None for him. Not good. Also, she happened to be glaring at him.

"Just remember, it's his book, not yours," she said by way of greeting.

"Yes ma'am."

"Don't you 'yes ma'am' me."

"First time I ever heard *that*."

"I know you're a smart aleck and want to change everything."

"No I don't." He planned to keep the title and Talton was still the book's sole author, although that seemed increasingly unfair. Also, the footnotes were staying—some of them, anyway. But there was no point in arguing. He retreated to the dungeon and packed his duffel for a workout.

After a trip to the Y, he worked on his laptop in a Decatur coffeehouse. Shortly after noon, while sipping coffee and ignoring his gnawing hunger, he finished Chapter Three. He stared at the computer screen dumbly for a moment, then … Eureka! He now had the sample he needed to send to Fortress Publishing. Unfortunately, Joshua Furst was an old-fashioned hard-copy kind of guy, so he couldn't simply send the chapters via e-mail.

He hurried back to Bayard Terrace and told Kathleen the good news.

She was unimpressed. "It's about time," she declared.

He went to the study and wrote a cover letter while printing the chapters and table of contents. Afterward, he handed a set of chapters to Kathleen and slid the other one into a brown envelope, then addressed it and taped it closed. He slipped on his jacket, bounced out the door and down the steps, then stopped as suddenly as if he'd hit a brick wall. He wanted to put his imprint on the book. Mark his territory, so to speak. He came back inside.

"What's up?" Kathleen asked suspiciously.

"The title doesn't work."

"Don't change it."

"I'm not changing it. Just adding something to it."

"That's changing it."

"I'll show you."

Minutes later, he handed her a new title page. She looked over her glasses and read aloud: "*Flight from Forsyth: Ethnic Cleansing in America.*" After a moment of mulling it over, she said, "I guess that's OK."

He walked the package down to the post office. After mailing it, Charlie cut across the alley to the coffeehouse, where Jean greeted him with a big smile. "How's the writing going?"

"I sent the first three chapters to my publisher."

"Cool. So you've got a publisher already."

"Kind of. If they like it."

"Well, good luck."

Charlie thought about asking her out. Then he remembered he didn't have a place to take her—or money, for that matter. He drifted to a seat by the window with his double espresso. Once there, he permitted himself to daydream. Really, could success be so far away? Where would he live when he hit the big time? A loft, of course. In a trendy, fashio-industrial section of town, preferably near—or in—an abandoned textile mill. And he'd wall in cozy little bedrooms for the kids to sleep in when they came to visit, which would be often, since he would fight for and win joint custody. But Saturday nights would be reserved for Jean. Or someone like her. Actually, since he'd learned she was bisexual, maybe Jean *and* someone like her. If the marriage thing didn't work out, that is. Hey, an ascetic can dream, can't he?

He finished his drink and returned to Bayard Terrace. It was a school day, and he needed to pick up the kids, but first he had to settle accounts. Susan was demanding money for the mortgage payment, and he didn't want to be browbeaten by his wife on such a triumphant day. He showed his work log sheet to Kathleen, explaining what she owed him.

Her eyes widened in anger. "We've been through this," she said. "I already paid you."

"Yes, for a hundred and twenty-five hours, but I've worked another—"

"No. I paid you that money to edit the book, and you should be through by now. Not just a couple of chapters. I'm certainly not giving you any more money. Do you think I'm a fool?"

"No. I think you need to take your medicine."

"Don't you insult me! I'm not the one making up things!"

How did she know? She was just guessing, right?

He wanted to point out the contract's terms, but his copy was a bloody mess and Angela now held Kathleen's. Another problem: If his employer was too far gone mentally, it could invalidate the agreement, and he would lose all his rights. Charlie alone understood what the real deal was, but he had no time to explain or argue, not when the kids' teachers considered him insane and Susan was ready to sic Family and Children Services on him—or even worse, Evangeline. So all he could do was bluff. "I'm not working on it, then," he declared. "We'll talk when I get back."

"You should earn your keep, instead of asking for money. Start paying rent. I don't have money anymore. My daughter took it. Where are you going? Come back here!"

* * *

It was too nice to stay inside that afternoon, so Charlie took the kids to Duck Lake Park. They walked around the lake, tailed by a mallard and his mate expecting more than the few crumbs they'd been tossed. Beck was playing Cupid. "Mommy asks about you all the time," she told Charlie. "What you're saying. And what you're thinking."

Ben followed after them in his haphazard fashion, hunting down pine cones and tossing them in the water. "About what?" Charlie asked.

"About our family."

"I think about you and Ben. I think about writing. I think about doing my job as a father. That's mainly what I think about."

She squinted into the sun. "What about Mommy?"

He shrugged. "That changed. What does Mommy think?"

"Mommy thinks you're crazy. But I'm not supposed to tell you that."

"It's not really much of a secret, now is it?"

"No, everybody thinks you're crazy." She giggled and grabbed his hand. "That's all right."

"I'm glad you think so." Charlie watched Ben run up to the dock with an armful of pine cones and heave them all into the lake. "What else does Mommy think?"

"I can't tell you. But if you want to come back, that would be OK. You didn't have to leave."

Another mixed signal from Susan. No surprise there. "Well, actually, I did. But I don't expect you to understand."

"I understand," she said firmly. "You're being stupid and hateful."

"No. It's hard to explain, but this is something I have to do."

"Do you think you'll ever come back?"

It was his turn to squint into the sun. "There's always a chance."

She frowned as she pondered this. Ben ran by with another load of cones to throw in the water. "You dropped one!" Beck shouted, and went running after him.

* * *

After dinner that night, Charlie gave Susan $150—all he had left except for a few ones and a twenty tucked behind his driver's license. "Cash?" she asked, raising an eyebrow at him like he'd gotten the money from the old woman's jewelry box. "You're living like a street person. And I need more than this."

He dug out the twenty and slammed it on the table. "All I got."

Susan rolled her eyes and picked up the money, which only served to harden Charlie's attitude. He left, mumbling to himself about "never coming back, not for a long time."

His stance was quite unfortunate, considering what happened to him when he returned to Bayard Terrace. Kathleen greeted Charlie by accusing him of stealing her salt and pepper shakers and pawning them.

"If you can't give them back," she shouted, "at least give me the money you got for them!"

Clearly, Kathleen was losing her battle with dementia. He went into the study and used his cellphone to leave a message for Angela: "Kathleen is off her meds and out of control."

"I heard that!" Kathleen shouted from the living room.

A little while later, Charlie was brewing coffee. Kathleen came up behind him and hissed, "Get out of my house."

He turned to face her, jumping back when he saw the butcher knife in her hand. "Kathleen! What's gotten into you?"

"Don't try to trick me. That's what you all do. Try to sell me a new roof and take my house! You can tell your boss and the other Irish Gypsies that I'll not put up with it. I'm calling the police!"

"I'm not a thief. We have a deal. Thurwood's book, remember? I just sent—"

"Get out!" She stepped toward him, pointing the knife at his crotch.

It was one thing to be an ascetic, quite another to be a eunuch. He raised his hands, but only belt high. "No problem. I'll just get my computer."

Facing her as he backed away, Charlie went to the study and grabbed his laptop. As he retreated through the living room, holding the computer like a shield, he wondered if his extended warranty covered knife fights.

Once he was out, Kathleen locked the door behind him. Charlie stood on the sidewalk and looked at his van, now his home as well, and wondered if he could make enough as a handyman to survive. He called Angela again. No answer; he left another message, this one sounding forlorn. He circled behind the house and slipped into the dungeon to get his stuff. No telling when he'd be back, especially since he could hear Kathleen on the phone upstairs, and it sounded like a 911 call. So much for the printer.

He had just pulled out of the driveway when a police cruiser turned onto Bayard Terrace. "No cops!" Charlie hissed. After the squad car passed by, he watched in the mirror to see if it would turn and follow him. It pulled into Kathleen's driveway instead.

He went to the coffeehouse. Jean wasn't there. He sat in a corner nursing his brew and waited for Angela to return his call. His spirits sank further as he considered his plight. What was he supposed to do? He thought about Beck's invitation to return to Thornbriar. He sensed a trap. Was he being tempted to renege on the contract?

All these attempts to sidetrack him were the devil's work, of course, and Charlie wasn't about to let Satan have his way. There was no turning back. Even if he'd been fired by his earthly boss, he had to finish the book. Now he understood why the contract had been worded so harshly. Because God couldn't trust people to do something unless their lives depended on it, and maybe not even then. Charlie vowed to be someone his grungy, vengeful God could believe in. Having done that, he went back to work.

He left the coffeehouse when it closed at midnight and retreated to his van, parked at the back of the lot behind the building. He took out the middle seat and set it upside down on the back one, then crawled into his sleeping bag, all the while hoping the cops wouldn't find him. Using his parka as a pillow, he curled up, pulled the sleeping bag tight around his neck, and dozed off.

He woke from a terrible, useless dream: black farmers calling each other racial epithets to a hip-hop beat, then shooting at each other from mule-drawn wagons. He looked at his watch: 3:13 a.m. The timing was off. Everything was off. His nocturnal transmission had been hijacked. Had losing his place in the world destroyed his channel into the past?

On the other hand, maybe he could get back to leading a semi-normal life.

Then he reminded himself that he was living in a van.

But at least it was *his* van. With difficulty, he managed to empty his mind and fall asleep.

A while later, a rap on the window awakened him. He looked up and saw a figure standing at the van's side window, crowned by a halo provided by a parking lot light. At first, he was afraid. Then he realized it was Jean. She spoke, her voice muffled by the glass: "Are you homeless?"

What a disheartening question. And rude, somehow. What could he say? He was what he was: a middle-aged man sleeping in a van. Trespassing. And now ashamed. He rubbed his head, leaned over, and opened the sliding door. She plopped on the van floor and looked him in the eye. "How long?"

His mind was as blurry as his vision, but the crisp air forced his world into sharp focus. He was too forlorn to be cute or clever. "My boss pulled a knife on me last night. And I'm broke."

Jean, who knew about Charlie's living and working arrangements, seemed unsurprised. "Why? The violence, I mean. I figured you're broke."

"She was off her meds."

She nodded sagely. "I know how that is."

"I gave all my money … for child support."

She gently touched his chest. He felt an impulse to kiss her, but that would ruin the only adult relationship he had left. She saved him from a bad decision by climbing out of the van. "I've got to open up," she said. "Come inside. I'll give you some coffee and a muffin."

The tall woman tromped off in her hiking boots. Charlie pulled on his own boots and clambered from the van. It was 6:00 a.m. Traffic was sparse. He pissed from the back end of the parking lot onto a wooden fence in a luxurious, arching stream. When done, he admired his accomplishment. That was the shame of modern life: People no longer took pride in their work.

Charlie brought his laptop into the coffeehouse and set it on a corner table under a track spotlight. Jean was scurrying to get the place up and running. A couple of regulars stood at the counter, stamping their feet, gently razzing her. When she was caught up, Charlie ordered coffee.

"On the house," Jean said, her voice just above a whisper.

"It's OK. I've got a credit card."

She laughed. "Less trouble for me to give it to you, then. Here, take a muffin. Cranberry-walnut. I have to throw it out, otherwise."

"Thanks. I'll make it up to you." He returned to his table, opened his laptop, and plugged in, realizing that he'd been reduced to scrounging for power *and* food. The beggar bit into his muffin and stole a glance at Jean. She was heartbreakingly beautiful, inside more than out. Why must the woman he desired see him scraping bottom? They could never be together now. He felt that he was no longer a man to her, just a stray she'd befriended.

He was typing away when he felt a firm, gentle hand on his shoulder. "You're so tense," Jean said. "You never stop working, do you?"

"Got a job to do," Charlie mumbled. "Everything depends on it."

She leaned down, kissed the back of his neck, and walked away. It hadn't felt like a come-on—more like an act of grace. She was an angel, and this was a holy place. He sensed that no harm would come to him in her abode. A minute later, she slipped a CD in the player. The music was organic, Eastern: a wooden flute and a bird that chirped on cue. Charlie wasn't paying complete attention. It sounded like a man was climbing a mountain and crying about the love of a woman. Either that, or his feet hurt.

Dawn brought a storm. Fat raindrops smashing sideways pushed people into the coffeehouse and kept them there. Charlie kept working, looking out the window just as a lightning bolt struck nearby and rattled the building. It reminded him of that night at the Pancake Hut, when all this madness started.

It rained heavily for an hour. When the place filled up, Charlie shared his table with a young man named Ron, who had pierced eyebrows and tattoos on his forearms. "I just got fired from my day job, which I'm better off without," Ron said. "The world sucks. But why does it have to suck so loud?"

"Really," Charlie said. "Why doesn't it have any manners?"

"Life should get people a room when it fucks them," Ron declared.

Charlie laughed. "Unfortunately, that's exactly *not* how it works."

The clouds started to break; the rain stopped. Charlie stood and stretched. He looked out the window. "Rainbow," he announced. The customers cheered and drifted over to see it. A MARTA bus rumbled by. The bell on the door tinkled. Charlie bid adieu to Ron and packed up to leave. Jean thumped her chest with her fist to salute him and wish him well.

* * *

During the next two days, Charlie showered at the Y, took care of the kids, and slept in the van. Fortunately, he landed a couple of handyman jobs and earned two hundred bucks. On the third day, he was eating lunch in a Decatur diner, idly watching a crow on a parking meter. It was, in turn, looking at him. His cellphone trilled.

"*Where are you*?" Angela demanded. "We need you back here with Kathleen. She's been off her meds for weeks. She accused me of going up on the roof and trying to tear off the shingles."

"She kicked me out and called the cops. I left messages. Don't you check them?"

Not one to dwell on her mistakes—that was Kathleen's job—Angela ignored Charlie's question and pressed on. "She doesn't remember kicking you out. Why'd she do that?"

"I'm an Irish gypsy. Apparently, you are, too."

"A what?"

"A fly-by-night roofing contractor. She saw a story about them on the news and now she's convinced they're out to steal her money."

"She needs someone to take care of her full-time. And I can't do it. We'll pay you."

"I'm supposed to be getting paid to—"

"Three hundred a week, plus room and board."

"Is that even minimum wage? For a left-winger, you sure are anti-labor."

"I'll pretend you didn't say that."

"I'll pretend you didn't offer me three hundred and give you another chance. My job is to edit the book. That's what the deal was. Is, I mean."

"We need to talk about that. When can you be here?"

"I think we'd better talk about it now, while we're at a safe distance."

"All right. I finally got power of attorney. This *deal* you've got? We've stopped it."

"Wait a minute—"

"Who do you think you're kidding? Dad was getting senile when he wrote the book."

"Not true." Charlie was sure that the good professor had simply been obtuse, not demented. "It's not that bad. I just sent chapters to an editor who's interested in it." He shook his head. "I can't believe I'm defending a man against his own daughter."

"I know it isn't publishable. I've got expertise, you know. There's so much wrong with it structurally. Plus, it doesn't adequately address feminist issues. Women are treated as victims."

"They were victims!" Charlie said. "Murder, rape. Lack of servants. *Hello*?"

"*Merely* as victims. It's a male-dominated narrative."

"Well, that fits in with the racio-sexio-fascio-ism of that period, doesn't it?" He didn't know what that meant, but at least it *sounded* academic.

"I can't let Mom waste her money. I've voided the contract due to diminished capacity."

"Look, just because you're not thinking clearly—"

"*Her* diminished capacity, Charlie. Don't be a smartass."

He looked out the window. The crow seemed to be enjoying itself. A lone thunderhead hovered ominously to the west—over Bayard Terrace, no doubt. Angela had better choose her words carefully, because she was prime smite bait. "Keep talking," he said.

"If you believe in the book so much, you can finish it on your own."

"She owes me … at least two thousand dollars for the work I've already done." As he spoke, he realized that he was severely lowballing the amount he was due and cursed himself for not keeping better track of the time he'd spent on the book.

"No, she doesn't. Tell you what, you can have all the royalties. Every penny. But academic presses don't pay much. You might get a thousand dollars if you're lucky."

All the money? Not too shabby, especially since he was sure he could do better than a measly grand. And in the meantime, this live-in caretaker deal would keep him alive, at least. It sounded like a briar patch to him. *OK, throw me in.* "Well, then, that's a beating I'll have to take. So are you going to redo the contract with those terms?"

"Yes."

"Five hundred a week."

"Four-fifty."

"OK," he sighed. "You gotta pay me the two grand I earned under the old contract, though."

"I don't know about that."

"Let me know when you do. Have a nice day."

"Wait. All right. But everything from now on is on your own. And you take care of Mom."

"I get coauthor's credit."

"Sure. Fine. Whatever."

"All right. I'll do it," he said with what he hoped sounded like reluctance. "But I have to take care of my kids from two until six."

Angela paused before saying, "All right. We'll see how this works."

After Charlie hung up, he added up hours in his head, realized he should have asked for four thousand dollars, and then smacked his forehead with his phone. He watched the crow fly off. When Charlie cocked his head this way and that, he could see he'd not only survived the ordeal, but stood to prosper, if his reclamation job on the book was as good as he thought it was. He may have sprained his ankles, but he'd landed on his feet. His universe was held together with baling twine and duct tape, but it was still in one piece. And most importantly, treasure far greater than gold had just been handed to him.

That night, Charlie returned to Bayard Terrace and stood on the porch, refusing to enter until Angela handed him a check. Kathleen was delighted to see him and claimed her daughter was holding her hostage.

"I left a list of things for you to do on the kitchen table," Angela said, wrapping a muffler around her neck. "I'll be back by tomorrow with the new contracts."

"Smite bait," Charlie muttered after the door closed behind her. He looked at the list: *Wash dishes, clean out refrigerator, get groceries, pick up prescriptions. Sweep and mop kitchen floor.*

"She irritates me," Kathleen told Charlie as she watched Angela's departure from behind the curtains. "She does it on purpose."

* * *

The next day, there were two contracts for Charlie to sign: one stating that Angela didn't have to pay Social Security taxes, the other declaring that Kathleen didn't have to pay him any more money to edit the book, which was now his baby. He would shoulder all risk and reward from then on. He signed them both, not really caring what the foolish papers said, since he knew that the real deal boiled and bubbled in the dungeon below.

Chapter Ten

Charlie celebrated the first day of spring by digging in the dirt at Thornbriar with his children. After school, he took them to Pike's Nursery, where they picked out yellow snapdragons, orange marigolds, and purple petunias for planting. He also bought fertilizer and grass seed in hopes of bringing the dead lawn to life. A while later at Thornbriar, the kids worked diligently in the flowerbed—until Ben used his trowel as a dirt catapult and ended up with Beck's teeth marks imbedded in his arm. Charlie ordered them inside. After he sowed the grass seed and covered it with straw, he did the same.

Dirty and sweaty, Charlie stood in the kitchen, wishing he'd brought a change of clothes. Surely he still had some jeans and a shirt somewhere. He found what he was looking for in a black trash bag in the corner of the master bedroom closet. He checked the dresser for socks and underwear. Nothing for him, but—*Hello*—he found a Victoria's Secret nightie. His eyes narrowed suspiciously. *So this is what she's buying with the money I'm giving her*. Although he knew he shouldn't rummage around in his wife's drawers, he lingered. *Whoa*. Purple thong panties. Definitely new. Jealousy mingled with arousal as he slipped them back in the drawer.

He figured he had enough time to take a shower before Susan got home. Not quite. She walked into the bedroom as he was toweling off. "This isn't your place anymore," she said, her expression grim. "Don't take liberties."

Without saying a word, he dressed, hugged the kids, and left.

Charlie's heart was cracking anew, now that he suspected Susan of cheating on him. Perhaps it had been going on for a while, and that's why she'd kicked him out. And now she aimed to do better, as her mother would say.

* * *

For several days afterward, Charlie and Susan said little to each other. A week later, while he was fixing meatloaf, she announced her plans to travel to Charlotte for a weekend banking conference: "I'll be gone from Thursday until Sunday, and I really have to do this to have a chance at a promotion and a raise." She sighed. "So can you take care of the kids—here, not at your rathole—while I'm gone?"

This from the woman who hadn't even thanked him for planting flowers. He stared at her, chopping onions rhythmically, trying to think of a way to deliver an insult while maintaining moral superiority.

"If you can't," she added, "I can leave them with Mom."

Damn, she was good! "I'll do it," he said, with tears in his eyes.

When Thursday came, Charlie stayed overnight at Thornbriar, crashing on the family room sofa, since the master bedroom door was locked. He broke in anyway, just to see what she was hiding. Thirty seconds' worth of snooping confirmed his darkest fears. Her sexy lingerie was traveling with her. "You skank!" he cursed, slamming the bedroom door shut.

Charlie was morose for the rest of the long weekend. He didn't want to be in the house, so he took the kids out and stayed on the move, going to Bayard Terrace and then to the cemetery with Kathleen to visit Thurwood's grave. Of all the places he went during that melancholy time, he liked the graveyard best. Not a good sign.

* * *

One day in mid-April, Charlie finished editing a chapter shortly before noon and decided to do yard work at Thornbriar before picking up the kids. When he stepped inside the house, he could tell something was amiss. Sirius was outside, and the kitchen light was on. He hadn't expected to find Susan home, but he heard the shower running. He checked the garage and saw her car. Was she ill? Susan *never* took sick days unless she went to a doctor or hospital.

What was the etiquette for walking in on an estranged spouse?

As Sirius pleaded for entrance at the patio door, Charlie moved toward the bedroom, having decided to tell Susan his intentions. He stood in the bedroom door and prepared to give her a shout, but he was struck speechless by the sight of an unmade bed and clothes strewn everywhere, not all of them Susan's. A pair of men's dress shoes lay on the floor. They seemed *tiny* compared to Charlie's size thirteens.

Part of him recoiled in horror. Not the part that controlled his feet, however. He tiptoed to the open bathroom door and peered in. He saw two figures through the shower stall's translucent glass. Susan was on her knees, though his view was blocked by a hairy-backed man who groaned and hit the glass with his fists as she did something she hadn't done for Charlie since she'd been his girlfriend, back when she was still trying to impress him. He recoiled from the sight, and feeling like a morally outraged burglar, slunk to the garage. He waited a few minutes for his pulse to slow and the throbbing in his head to subside. He knew the man had to be Bryan Speeler, Susan's boss. He'd seen Speeler a few times at social functions; Susan often touted his many virtues. But Speeler was *married*. Wait a minute. So was she!

Flustered, Charlie started to leave, then stopped. He had a job to do. He wasn't going to let her abominable actions rule his life. His hands shook as he opened the garage door. He rolled out the lawn mower and pulled out trash cans to hold straw and grass clippings. And then he had a bright idea. He placed the cans in the driveway beside the van to block Susan's exit, then closed the garage.

He started mowing, humming in accompaniment to the machine's roar. He'd cut half the yard when Susan appeared in the front door, dressed for work and scowling. He killed the engine and gave her a big smile.

"What are you doing here so early?" she asked, trying unsuccessfully to sound friendly.

He pointed to the yard, and shouted, "Had to get the straw off."

She shook her head. "Call next time. We could have lunch," she said, sounding completely insincere—just like Uncle Stanley.

When he thought about what she'd had for lunch, he struggled to keep from gagging. "Next time, maybe."

"Well, thanks for working on the yard. I have to get back to the bank." She glanced at the driveway. "Can you move the trash cans?"

Susan went back inside; he kept mowing. A few minutes later, the garage door rolled up. Charlie killed the mower, then sauntered over and stood beside the cans. With the van in the driveway beside him, Susan's exit was now blocked. As she backed out her Honda Accord, Charlie looked for Bryan in the passenger seat, but no one was riding shotgun. Charlie made a show of picking up the barrels, but instead of moving them out of the way, he dropped them on their sides. Susan hit them with a double *thump*. The sound of crumpling plastic stopped her.

Time for a vehicle inspection.

"Hey!" Charlie shouted. Leaving one of the cans stuck under her rear bumper, he walked around to the passenger side, peering in like a cop looking for a bag of dope. He was perplexed, but only for a moment. *Ah.*

"What?" she snapped. "Move the cans."

He went behind the car. Instead of picking up the barrels, he reached into his pants pocket, pulled out the key fob that Susan had neglected to confiscate, and popped the trunk. "Whoops," he said loudly as he looked in on the curled-up banker, complete with suit and tie. "It appears that we have a hostage situation."

Bryan shielded his face with his hands, as if expecting a beating.

Charlie grinned. "Dude. We were married three years before she made me get in the trunk. Come on. Get out. Make her let you ride in the front seat. You couldn't have been that bad in bed." He offered Bryan his hand. Bryan refused it. Charlie glanced around and shrugged. "Then again, maybe you were."

Bryan tumbled clumsily out of the trunk. "It's not what you think."

"Sure it is," Charlie said. "Anything else would be worse."

Susan gripped the steering wheel, staring straight ahead.

"That's all right, honey!" Charlie shouted as he pulled the trash can out from underneath the bumper. "I understand. Always carry a spare!"

He resumed his work, pulling off the mower bag to empty it. Bryan adjusted his coat and tie, then dusted off his pants and climbed into the front passenger seat. Susan, crimson-faced, backed out and squealed off, laying tire tracks on the street.

Charlie finished his yard work and, a couple of hours later, picked up the kids from school. He was grateful to be with the two people who could help him fend off the psychosis that was spreading out its tendrils within and around his soul. He avoided the defiled house and bounced around the neighborhood, stopping anyplace that could provide a diversion: Dairy Queen, the library, Duck Lake Park. At dusk, he took Beck and Ben back to Thornbriar, a place he now found intolerable. He couldn't stop pacing, and when he was on the verge of pulling out his hair, Susan called him on the home phone. "Are you there?" she asked.

Clearly, her nerves were jangled, too. "Of course not."

"Just like you to be contrary," she said. "It's been a rough day. Could you go so I can come home?"

"Just leave the kids alone?"

"I'm right outside." He walked with the cordless phone to the living room window. Sure enough, she was sitting in her car on the street, her turn signal blinking.

"Don't we need to talk?"

"No. There's nothing to talk about."

"I was in the house, Susan. I know the trunk thing wasn't mob-related."

Click. He turned to the kids, who were coloring pictures at the kitchen table. "'Bye, kids. I gotta go."

"Mommy's not here," Beck said.

"She's right outside. You won't even have time to misbehave before she gets here."

"Thanks for the warning," Ben said, mimicking one of his father's favorite expressions.

He hugged them, then dashed out the door, giving Susan a jaunty wave before driving away.

* * *

Morning came. Charlie couldn't keep his mind off the vulgar spectacle of his wife's infidelity, plagued as he was by the vision of Bryan's hairy back against the translucent glass wall. It was a sunny day, and hammering in the distance sounded like music to him; he didn't want to sit brooding at the desk in Talton's study. When his cellphone trilled, he hoped someone wanted Charlie the Handyman to tear up something and rebuild it, so that he could convince himself that such a thing was possible.

"Charles." It was Susan, sounding stiff.

He heard the whine of a drill in the background. "Where are you?"

"At home. I took a personal day." She spoke in staccato. "I'm changing the locks. I should have done this long ago."

Anger shot through him like a geyser. "I pay part of the mortgage—"

"Not enough, and nothing I can count on. God, Charlie. You come in and hand me grimy twenty-dollar bills like you've been panhandling."

He stood up. "And you take them. I've got rights."

"I don't want to argue with you."

"I need to take care of the kids." He paced around in a tiny circle, almost stepping on himself.

"I've made arrangements with a parent in the neighborhood to keep the kids after school. I've been considering it—"

"Ever since *Bry*—"

"Don't go there," she snapped. "We're separated. And he's going to leave his wife."

"That is *so* daytime TV."

"Don't."

"I have a right to see the kids. We have joint custody, if you hadn't noticed."

"You gave up that right when you walked out. Look, Charlie. You can see the kids on weekends. Take them to a movie or the park. The weather's getting nicer. No way are they staying in that dungeon of yours, though. And you can't come here, snooping around."

"Fine!" he yelled. "Don't take them up to Varmintville, either, then! That's poison they feed them up there. 'Nigger' this and 'Nigger' that."

"It doesn't even come up when you're not around."

"Oh, so I make everything worse."

"*Finally* you get it."

"You're not going to get custody," he said.

"You know how it works."

He did. She had motherhood, income, and house. Three strikes and he was out. And yet ...

"There's the matter of adultery," he pointed out.

"It doesn't matter what you say. You got kicked out for domestic violence and exposing the kids to porn. You're on record with the police as mentally unstable. You really want to take me on?"

"None of that's true, and once upon a time, the story was that I walked out."

"Well, you said you got kicked out. I'm just going by what you've been saying."

"Sounds better for you, doesn't it? So you decided you'd do what you had to do, and that's that."

"Pretty much. I've got to think of the kids. I may move to North Carolina if I get a promotion."

"You must really hate me."

"You must really hate *me*, running off in the night and coming back to constantly mock me."

"First I left, then you kicked me out, now I'm back to leaving. Would you please make up your mind?"

"I don't have time for this. Face it, Charlie, it's over. Give it up. Writing's not working for you. Get a real job. Get a life."

There was so much to say. He hung up on her.

So there it was. The marriage was over and he was locked out. Getting her to beg him to return hadn't worked out so well, after all. She got to have sex and he didn't. She got to keep the kids and he didn't. She got child support and he didn't. No fair.

His nerves were too jangled to work on the book, so Charlie spent the rest of the day doing odd jobs for regular customers. (Despite his agreement to be Kathleen's full-time caretaker, he still snuck in a considerable amount of moonlighting.) He couldn't keep his mind off the kids, however. At 2:00 p.m., he had to resist the urge to drive to Gresham Elementary. Instead, he went to Home Depot and bought mulch and fertilizer for Mrs. Williford's flowerbed.

That night, Beck called. Ben spoke to him, too. They told him about their new playmates and said they missed him. "Mommy said you could see us on weekends," Beck said. "Are you in jail?"

"No," Charlie said, though he wasn't so sure this was true. After he hung up, he wept quietly, then quit when he remembered one of his mother's favorite sayings: "Tears are weakness leaving the body." The sort of thing one says after a spouse jumps off a bridge.

* * *

The next morning, Charlie was in his office when his cellphone rang. He eagerly answered, hoping he'd land a job that would let him use his hands and keep his mind from wandering. "Hello, Charlie here."

"Joshua Furst at Fortress. We want to publish *Ethnic Cleansing*. Is it still available?"

"Do what?" Charlie was blown away. "*Flight from Forsyth*? Great. What'd you just say? Yes!" He took a step forward and jumped for joy, coming down so hard the house shook. "Oh. By the way, I now have full rights to the manuscript as coauthor. I can send you the contract I signed with Dr. Talton's daughter, who has power of attorney. Uh, so what are you offering?"

"We're still developing the offer." There was an awkward pause before the editor continued. "It's a worthwhile book. But we don't see it as a blockbuster."

"There were twenty thousand marchers in Forsyth County that day."

"Yes, we want the book out for the anniversary of the march next year, to give it a publicity boost. We need a clean manuscript by the end of September at the latest, and that's pushing it. Can you give us that?"

"Sure. Fifty grand would be a good offer," Charlie suggested.

"We'll see."

After the call, Charlie stared at the phone, wondering if he should get an agent or send the book to another publisher. After so many years of failure, this was a nice dilemma to have. But he needed quick money, so Furst things first. He drummed the desk with his fingers. A narrow shaft of sunlight cut through the window and behind the blind to warm his hand. This almost—

Wait. It did! Of course! This was all part of the plan. He felt the burden on his heart lighten. Life seemed bearable. Caring for the kids every day was a barrier to success, and it had been lifted. Now he could meet the deadline. Yes, he was better off locked out of Thornbriar, forbidden from that house of pain. He went into the kitchen and told Kathleen what had just happened.

"That's wonderful, Gary!" she exclaimed.

He didn't correct her or mention that Angela had given away her rights to the book. Why spoil a celebration?

They celebrated with tea. After a couple of heavily sugared cups, Kathleen was puttering happily around the house, doing tasks Angela had assigned to Charlie. Meanwhile, he was busy daydreaming about shooting to the top of the bestseller list.

* * *

Shortly after noon on May 15, a mailman in Bermuda shorts and long dark socks folded a manila envelope from Fortress Publishing into the black mailbox by the door at 432 Bayard Terrace. In it were two copies of a contract that would pay Charles T. Sherman a $20,000 advance—roughly a dollar for each 1987 marcher. (Charlie wished he'd told Furst there had been 25,000.) His deadline for completing the book was September 30, and Fortress planned to put it in bookstores on MLK Day.

Charlie signed the contracts with a flourish. After he mailed the documents at the post office, he crossed the alley to the coffeehouse and told Jean about his accomplishment. She seemed almost as happy as he was. They shared a toast, he with a double espresso, she with a bottle of spring water. Now that he was successful, Charlie thought that maybe she was attainable after all. But he was afraid of losing his only friend. Who would he celebrate with, then? After downing his drink, Charlie bid adieu.

He walked out into the sunshine, thinking about his kids, wondering how much he'd spend on attorney's fees to win them back. When he returned to Bayard Terrace, he told Kathleen, "I signed the contracts on Thurwood's book and mailed them."

"That's wonderful! Do I owe you any money?"

"No. It's between the publisher and me now."

She patted his arm and he saw adoration in her eyes. "Thank you, Charles."

"You're welcome, Kathleen."

* * *

Summer brought a thaw and more mixed signals from Susan. When the school term ended, Susan agreed to let Beck and Ben attend YMCA day camp, if Charlie paid for it. Every weekday morning, Susan dropped off the kids and every afternoon, Charlie picked them up. He brought them to Thornbriar after Susan got home, but rarely stayed more than a few minutes.

On June 26, the Shermans celebrated Ben's birthday together with a trip to White Water amusement park. Charlie had another reason to rejoice. He'd just received $10,000—the first portion of his author's advance. He'd given half that amount to Susan for child support, and she grew increasingly friendly throughout the day—laughing, joking, and even wiggling a little in her black tank suit. She complimented him on his appearance. Months of steady workouts and eating light had produced a salutary effect. He'd lost thirty pounds. While they were sitting on lounge chairs by the wave pool, she reached over and rubbed sun block on his heavily muscled, hairless chest. "After we get back to Thornbriar, we're having cake," she said. "Maybe you could stay and lick the icing."

She blushed and looked away, then fumbled in her canvas beach bag, seeking something she couldn't find. Even though Susan had told him she was no longer seeing Bryan Speeler, Charlie suspected some kind of feminine trickery. If he tried to kick the football, she might pull it away at the last instant. Besides, he'd been doing so well, succeeding as a writer despite her, not because of her, that he had another reason to be wary. Like a boxer who believes sex will make him soft, he reasoned that going back to her would make him weak just when he needed to be strong. And when he was successful, he would have … *options.*

Besides, she hadn't apologized. Or begged him to return.

That evening, they had cake at Thornbriar. Her coy invitation was not repeated, and Charlie left before the children went to bed, pausing in the driveway to shuffle his feet and shadow-box. A *contenduh.* That's what he was.

* * *

Charlie began work on the epilogue to *Flight from Forsyth* and scheduled an interview with Redeemer Wilson, which ended up costing $300 in the form of a contribution to Wilson's Holy Way House and Hunger Palace Foundation. Charlie met Redeemer at Thelma's Soul Food Kitchen near the Inman Park MARTA station for lunch on a hot July day. The writer wore his shipping uniform; the civil rights movement's working-class hero showed up in trademark overalls and blue work shirt, his salt-and-pepper hair in a mini-Afro. When the ancient warhorse walked into the restaurant, people rose to greet him, hugging, and kissing Redeemer as he playfully struggled to make his way to a back booth.

They ordered lunch, which was on the house for Redeemer. For two hours—and through constant interruptions from old friends, well-wishers, and admirers—the barrel-chested World War II veteran talked in a hoarse voice about fighting Germans, coming home and getting beaten for drinking out of the wrong water fountain ("It was a beating I had to take," he said), leading marches in his hometown, and later joining forces with the Reverend Martin Luther King Jr.

"I was the shock trooper. I'd go into these racist towns and wear 'em down. After a week of me, the town fathers were ready to negotiate," he said with a throaty laugh. "I got shot at four times, hit with clubs, bats, and bottles, beaten with fists fairly regularly, and arrested one-hundred-and-eighty-nine times," he boasted. "They needed someone to do that, and I was their man. Then they killed the dream in Memphis." Sadness etched Redeemer's weary face as he talked about "the wilderness," those years after King's death, but his eyes lit up when Charlie talked about Thurwood's book.

"Oh, yes, I knew Doc Talton well. I was lookin' for him for that second march in 1987. Had a place for him right up front. He was walking the walk back in the sixties, you know. There were some days we'd have an event, and he was the only white man there. The only one." Redeemer let that sink in. "Didn't find out he'd passed until somebody called me the next day about his obituary. So sad."

The old lion shook his head. "He told me about the book, but I figured it died with him. Now here comes you, and got him a publisher. So, I guess you want to know about the marches up in Forsyth. First time, it was just a local thing with Dan Greene from Gainesville. The Klan and their friends ran us out of town. Nearly killed us. Well, I didn't go through what I went through to take that as an answer. So we came back twenty-five thousand strong. It was a sight to behold, a line miles long on a nasty winter's day. We told the world that you can't just hide yourself away and say you got your own laws to keep people out, no sir. Nothing like it since. Think of it, man! This was 1987, a generation after Selma. All those white folks in Forsyth told reporters, 'I didn't do nothing wrong to nobody, so I don't understand what they protesting about.' Well, if they didn't do nothing, what exactly did they do?"

"I've heard that, too," Charlie said. "They never did much for anybody, either, as far as I can tell."

"Exactly!" Redeemer said, thumping the table. "Twenty years passed since then, and it's no different now, is it?"

After the interview, Charlie took a photo of the grizzled old civil rights hero and they parted with a hug, new best friends. Charlie promised to come down and work at the Hunger Palace, Redeemer's soup kitchen on Memorial Drive in Atlanta. "On any day *but* Christmas or Thanksgiving," Redeemer admonished. "That's when all the fakers come down. We need for you to be real, Brother. Especially these days. You gotta be the man who's down there at six on a Monday mornin', knowin' what to do and doin' it. Just remember this," he said, peering intently into Charlie's eyes. "It's not just what *they did* that matters. What *you* do matters more. And like I always tell my marchers: 'Look up when you walk.'"

* * *

The final stretch: In mid-September, Charlie was polishing *Flight*'s next-to-last chapter. Fueled by coffee and Gatorade, he worked fourteen hours a day while watching over Kathleen haphazardly, ensuring her cooperation by telling her he'd quit editing her beloved Thurwood's book if she failed to take even one of her meds. She was fine most of the time, and they conspired to keep Angela in the dark about the true nature of their relationship, which boiled down to Kathleen helping Charlie help Thurwood get published. She was quite proud of the fact that they'd found a way to flip that nasty old "publish or perish" rule on its head. Charlie, being a contrary sort, was rather pleased about it, too.

He took his breaks and slipped out for coffee during Kathleen's naps. On one of these afternoons, he was sitting by the window at Bay Street Coffeehouse when an extraordinary woman walked in. He smelled her before he saw her. Her cologne—sharp and musky, almost industrial, a chemical compound designed to break the laws of nature, yet still entice—distracted him from the Georgia governor's 1913 message to the legislature. The woman's dark, glossy hair was a sophisticated pageboy, and she wore a sleeveless white-trimmed beige dress. She took off her round-rimmed sunglasses at the counter, grabbed Jean's shoulders, and kissed her lightly on the lips. Charlie felt a pang of jealousy for whatever they had going.

The woman slipped four paper cups of coffee into a caddy and turned to look at Charlie, who happened to be staring at her. She winked and slipped on her sunglasses, then eased out the door with the subtlest of sashays. Charlie was smitten. And not in a bad way.

Entranced, he ventured to the window and watched her walk down the street and climb into the passenger seat of a silver Porsche Carrera. He turned toward Jean, who leered at him and said, "I know what Writer-Boy wants for Christmas."

"I have no idea what you're talking about," he said as he approached the counter. "So, uh ... who is she?"

"As far as you're concerned, that's Danger Girl," Jean said in a hushed tone as she toweled off a white cup. "I told her about you, and she thinks you're *interesting*. Her name is Dana Colescu. She owns a Midtown art gallery. Knows all the right people."

"Too bad for me. I have *never* been one of the right people."

"That may change, if your book's a bestseller." She poked him in the chest. "So get to work, you."

* * *

Charlie completed the manuscript on Wednesday, September 26, a few days before it was due. (If he hadn't already believed in miracles, getting the book done on time certainly would have changed his mind.) As the bibliography printed out, he leaned back in the swivel chair and smiled at Talton's photo on the wall. Thurwood smiled back. The younger man had done well, and the dead guy knew it. Charlie wrote a cover letter, then signed it and put it in a box with the manuscript and a CD containing the book's text.

When he came out of the study, Kathleen was napping. He decided not to disturb her, even though she'd be overjoyed to hear the news. Anyway, this was *his* moment.

After paying for priority delivery, he emerged triumphantly from the post office and stared into the bright sunshine like a man exiting a cave. Yes, it was over. *Finally*. Night had been conquered; the long storm was over. Perhaps now the contract would stop oozing blood. Or did the manuscript have to make it to New York? Be published? Arrive in stores? Win the Pulitzer? When exactly is a writer finished? He'd never come close enough to know.

And what next? Work as a handyman, to take his mind off his mind? Maybe he'd get a regular job and look for a loft. With Susan's help securing a loan—was it too much to ask?—and the second $10,000 check, he might be able to buy a fixer-upper. Would Susan resent his attempt to solidify their separation? She'd been acting like a woman scorned since that day at White Water. Well, she hadn't asked him back, and he had to go somewhere, because his days in the dungeon had come to an end now that his mission was accomplished.

In any case, he should celebrate. A sudden chill wind whipped through his shirt as he crossed the alley to the coffeehouse. Jean, alone in the shop, looked up from the magazine she was reading when he walked in. Pat Metheny was playing jazz guitar over the sound system. The triumphant coauthor gave her a weary smile. She glanced outside. "Getting cloudy. Sometimes I think you bring the rain."

He looked over his shoulder. Where had *those* clouds come from? "I finished."

"You what?"

"The book. I just mailed the manuscript to my publisher. It's done!"

"Yay!" She ran around from behind the counter and hugged him. Her scent was surprisingly feminine. She pushed him back and smirked at him, arching her eyebrow, the one adorned with a tiny gold ring. "Whatever will you do now? Besides fix up people's houses and take care of kids and write another book, that is. This calls for a cup on the house."

A lightning bolt flashed close by, followed by a loud crack of thunder. "That was random," she said.

"Not exactly," Charlie said. "Gotta go."

He left the coffeehouse at a dead run. It was dark as twilight when he bounded up onto Kathleen's porch. He burst into the living room, fearing something terrible had happened. The old woman stood befuddled, pinching her black cardigan tight around her bosom. "Freaky weather," she said.

He leaned over and put his hands on his knees, panting to catch his breath. "You all right?"

"Kinda cold," she said, sounding nervous. "Cold and creepy. I don't know why."

Charlie brushed past her and went into the study. A chill wind blew in through the window. He slammed it shut, sensing that something was coming. Trouble, perhaps? Maybe the old guy wasn't so dead after all and was coming to say "Job well done" or "Congratulations, earthling, you're free to go."

Charlie tiptoed down to the basement, trying to sneak up on the dreadful, loathsome contract vat that he'd tucked away in the dungeon's darkest corner. The vat was dark to the top. Charlie lifted the lid and saw roiling blood. He staggered back in horror. This was damnation, not celebration!

Outside, lightning flashed, followed quickly by a clap of thunder that shook the house and rattled its windows. Then came several strikes in quick succession.

Kathleen shrieked. Charlie heard a heavy thump on the porch, then another. There came an ominously soft knock. Telling himself he had no reason to be afraid, Charlie clomped up the stairs, pulling himself along the rail.

"Don't answer it," Kathleen whimpered.

"Not an option," Charlie said. He felt an electric shock as he grabbed the doorknob. He twisted it and gave it a jerk, swinging it open, kicking it sideways to finish its motion.

Lo and behold, there stood Trouble, fully charged, the lines in his face deep and sharp. His eyes were dark and haunted. Something was terribly wrong. "Dude," he said. "Where's my book?"

"I finished it," Charlie said. "Mailed it. Fire in the hole." He punctuated the statement with a jaunty gesture, swinging his fist playfully.

"Did you?" Trouble was covered with a patina of filth. Charlie fell back as the weird one entered the living room, filling it with his choking aura of physical decay, body and engine oils, sweat-matted grime, farts, and ozone. Trouble stank fiercely, as Ben would say, with all his might.

"Yeah. Just got back from the post office," Charlie wheezed, trying not to inhale.

Kathleen continued to whimper. She'd covered her eyes like a child trying to hide. Trouble breathed heavily, rumbling like a bison with a chest cold. "Show it to me."

"Gladly," Charlie said with the confidence of Mark Twain's Christian with four aces. Trouble followed him into the study, where Charlie pointed to the spare copy of *Flight from Forsyth*.

Trouble picked up the manuscript and held it under the overhead light. He seemed to stare into it, then set it down, leaving grimy thumb prints on the title page. He inhaled and roared at the top of his lungs, "THAT'S NOT THE WORK YOU AGREED TO FINISH, YOU STUPID ASSHOLE!"

Charlie flinched from the hurricane of bad breath. "What do you mean? A deal's a deal."

"And this ain't the deal."

Charlie laughed uncertainly. "You're joking. Look, I did my job. Anyway, why did I have all those dreams?"

"Dreams? I don't do dreams. I do small animal impressions. And by the way, thanks so much for trapping me. *Twice*. Nearly broke my neck and shoulder." Only then did Charlie notice that Trouble's head tilted to the right.

"That's what you get for stalking. But the dreams—I saw everything, clear and whole."

Trouble snorted in disgust. "This book was already finished. It was your ego that told you there was something left to do on it. That and sloth. The deal is to complete Talton's *unfinished* work."

Charlie couldn't believe what he was hearing. "Sloth?"

"Laziness. Look it up."

"But he hasn't been lazy," Kathleen said, appearing behind them, holding her nose.

Trouble ignored her. "You still have to fulfill the contract. And you haven't even started."

He stomped away, brushing past Kathleen, who looked like she was going to throw up.

"What are you talking about?" Charlie said. "I don't have any idea—"

"You have everything you need," Trouble declared over his shoulder.

Charlie rushed to the window and opened it for some fresh air. He turned and saw that Kathleen was starting to keel over, so he parked her on the study's sofa and rushed after Trouble, who was at the front door. "Wait, wait," Charlie pleaded. "I don't know what you're talking about. If you mean Talton had something else, they stole everything in a break-in right after I started."

Trouble didn't stop. He walked out the front door and didn't bother closing it. Charlie grabbed the knob but left it open, since the house needed airing out. He watched Trouble stomping away with incredibly high steps, as if he was a life-size marionette.

Charlie turned around and saw Kathleen standing in the dining room. "He stinks so bad," she said, then lurched to the bathroom and started vomiting.

Charlie returned to the office and looked around the room where he'd spent countless hours. This was supposed to be a moment of triumph. Instead, he'd been told he'd performed a fool's errand. Nothing made sense. "Damn it!" he yelled. He grabbed the manuscript and threw it at the wall, sending pages flying all over the room.

That was a start. He grabbed a file cabinet drawer and yanked it out. He threw it at the sofa, spilling out the fake documents he'd drawn up to replace the stolen ones. The second drawer did not come out so easily. This irritated Charlie even more, and he tugged harder. The cabinet toppled and crashed to the floor. A corner clipped his knee, cutting through his jeans and slicing open his skin. Charlie cursed and kicked wildly at it. His hiking boot dented the metal side.

He bent down, put his hands on his knees, and grimaced, looking around for something to destroy. A dusty manila envelope that had been wedged between the file cabinet and the wall stood edgewise on the floor. He picked it up, intending to rip it apart, but there was something small and hard inside that piqued his interest. He flipped the envelope over and read aloud, "John Riggins, Forsyth County 1930s." There was also a 1987 date in magic marker, a burlesque of Talton's elegant scrawl—perhaps this was the last thing the good professor ever wrote. Charlie recalled putting this atop the file cabinet months ago. The thieves must have knocked it behind the cabinet during the burglary.

What the hell was he supposed to do, now that he was a few thousand hours off course? He calmed down, took a seat in the chair, and fanned himself with the envelope. "Fuck me," he said.

Kathleen appeared in the doorway. "What's that?" she asked.

"Something about a man named Riggins," Charlie said. "You ever heard of him?"

She shook her head as he emptied the envelope on the desk. There was a cassette tape and some typewritten notes. The back of a photo was dated Oct. 12, 1937 and the name John Riggins was scrawled on it. He flipped it over. "Oh my God," he said. It was a picture of a human body charred beyond recognition, hanging from the limb of a dead tree. Wisps of smoke were visible, giving the eerie impression that the soul was departing the tortured body.

Outside, a crow cawed loudly. Charlie looked up and saw the bird flying toward the window, only to veer off at the last instant. He heard a bus rumble in the distance. Kathleen stood transfixed, paler than he had ever seen her before. Charlie held the cassette in his hand and glanced at the old black-and-white photo. There were several men in the background. Beside the still-smoldering corpse, pointing up at it like it was a prize marlin, knelt a bantamweight man with a straw hat pushed back on his forehead. Charlie couldn't bear to look at the picture and averted his gaze as he gingerly slid the photograph back into its envelope. "That's horrible," he said.

He needed a break, but Trouble's visit had convinced him there was no such thing—not for him. How could finishing *Flight from Forsyth* have been such a mistake? How could the death of one man outweigh the horrors that occurred in Forsyth County in 1912, with more than a thousand victims? He shook his head; it made no sense. But maybe this was what Trouble had been talking about. Charlie looked around. He couldn't think of anything else.

Since there was nothing else left of the professor's papers and documents, the only thing he could do was to find out more about this last iota of Talton's work. He went to the dungeon to retrieve his boombox so he could play the tape. He snuck a glance at the vat. The blood was receding. The weight was still on his shoulders, though, pushing him down—and forcing him to stumble forward.

Charlie took the boombox out to the front porch and plopped down, stretching out his legs and resting his feet on the second step. His knee had stopped bleeding. Overhead, the clouds were breaking up. He slipped the cassette into the player and turned it on. He leaned into the gentle breeze that stirred the bushes around him and listened to the otherworldly hiss of the tape. After a few seconds, Talton's high, clear voice piped up. "Interview with Jasper Riggins, January 23, 1987, at 237 Agate Drive, Atlanta, Georgia." A pause, then: "Please tell me about your cousin's death, Mr. Riggins."

Chapter Eleven

Charlie knew that a black man named John Riggins died at the hands of persons unknown on October 12, 1937 in Forsyth County, and that the man's widow, Lettie, drowned in the Chattahoochee River less than a year later in an apparent suicide, leaving her infant daughter Minnie an orphan. Riggins had been an only child; his wife had two sisters, one of whom had raised the girl. Both of Minerva's aunts died in the 1970s. As for the gruesome photograph, Talton had written a note saying that it arrived in the mail at his house on January 20, 1987 with no return address and a Cumming, Georgia, postmark.

Charlie listened to Talton's tape again the next morning, struggling to understand Jasper Riggins's Deep South black dialect, mixed in with the interplanetary hiss that Charlie suspected contained the real message he was supposed to hear.

The old man's sad, defeated mumble still echoed in his ears as Charlie drove to Summerhill, a poor neighborhood south of downtown Atlanta, virtually sitting in the shadow of the gold-domed Capitol. The address he sought was within walking distance of Turner Field, home of the Atlanta Braves. He turned onto Agate Drive and looked for 237, but the old houses on that side of the street had been razed and replaced with townhomes. Charlie parked the van in front of 240, a dilapidated wood frame house turned gray. He glanced around for signs of urban danger, saw none, and exited the van. He strode up the cracked sidewalk, stepped past a rotten railing onto the porch, and banged on the torn screen door.

There was shuffling inside. A moment later, an elderly, overweight black woman with a kind face and bulging eyes opened the door. She wore a blue house dress and slippers. "May I help you?"

"Yes ma'am. I was trying to find out about someone who used to live on this street." He pointed over his shoulder to the townhomes. "Before those were built, most likely."

"You a bill collector?"

"No ma'am. I'm a writer." The woman bent toward him and leaned on the doorframe. He said, "I'm looking for a man named Jasper Riggins."

"He dead."

"I'm sorry. When did he die?"

She turned and shouted, "Will! When Jasper Riggins die?" She nodded at the homes across the street. "They built those right before the Olympics. He gone by then. Musta died in ninety-four, mebbe. What you need?"

"I'm writing a book. About something that happened to his cousin." The woman raised an eyebrow and gave him a *Go On* look. "He was killed. Lynched. In Forsyth County."

Her eyes lit with a glimmer of recognition. "Where Redeemer had that march."

"Yes ma'am. Exactly so."

The woman's face filled with wide-eyed curiosity. "When this man killed?"

"A long time ago. 1937."

"Before the Olympics," Will said, shuffling up behind the woman. He was dark-skinned, with a wrinkled face. "I had a great-uncle got lynched down by Valdosta," he said. "Happened 'fore I was born. He was young. Got in a fight with a white man over nuthin'. Whupped the man, and they couldn't have that. Shot him and hung him and sold picture postcards of it in the drugstore. Heard they even cut up pieces for souvenirs." He shook his head. "Everbody knew who did it and that was fine by them. You could lynch a black man and run for mayor. Didn't make no nevermind."

"What was his name?" Charlie pulled out his legal pad.

"Henry Etheridge. On my mother's side."

"Back then, everbody knew someone it happen to, or their family," the woman said.

Charlie took notes. Since he had so little to start with, he wasn't going to ignore any information. He might need a couple hundred pages of context (à la Thurwood Talton, ironically) to flesh out the story. They were the Thompsons, he learned, married forty-two years. "So you knew Jasper? Do you know if he had any relatives?"

"He kept to himself, mostly. I don't remember meetin' any of his kinfolk."

"A woman named Minnie Doe? He talked about her in an interview."

Mrs. Thompson shook her head slowly. "Don't recall the name. He didn't have a woman I know of, and he live there a long time. Someone came to look after him sometime. That might be who you mean." The couple conferred for a moment, mumbling names, tossing them out one by one until all possibilities were gone. "Don't think he had kids. Maybe his niece."

Charlie chatted for a few more minutes before he left. He gave them his phone number in case they thought of anything or ran into anyone who'd known Jasper. Discouraged, he drove off.

* * *

After breakfast the next morning, Charlie listened to the tape a third time and tried to transcribe Jasper Riggins's gummed-up dialect. He found himself guessing much of the time. There was another problem: The old man's fifty-year-old memories weren't even firsthand. His was the collective knowledge of the family. Thurwood had made a note to contact the daughter, Minnie, but Charlie could find no sign that he'd succeeded. The day after the Riggins interview, Talton died. Thanks a lot, Thurwood.

So now it was Charlie's turn. The phone book listed one M. Doe with an east Atlanta address on Arcadia Avenue, only a few miles south of Bayard Terrace. He sat for a moment at Talton's desk considering the consequences of failure before grasping at this straw. Taking a deep breath, he dialed. An automated voice told him the number had been disconnected. He cursed and hung up, worried that she'd died while he was working on *Flight*. It would be just like God to trip him up like that.

Early that afternoon, he left to check the address after making sure Kathleen took her medication. "And no faking," he scolded, wagging a finger as she gulped her water.

"Stop that," she said. Showing remarkable quickness, she reached out and grabbed his finger with her free hand. She gave him a one-eyed squint. "How long have you been staying here?"

"Since the beginning of the year."

"Really? When do you have to leave?"

"I'm not exactly sure." He extricated his finger from her grip and grabbed his computer satchel.

"Well, stay as long as you like."

"OK." He gave her a big smile on his way out the door.

* * *

Arcadia, a side street filled with close-set bungalows in an older neighborhood near Memorial Drive, was undergoing a dose of gentrification, giving it a combination of rundown and renovated housing. As Charlie drove down Arcadia, birds chattered, a car alarm blared, and a child squalled on a screened-in porch. He found M. Doe's address and pulled to the curb across the street. A Georgia Power Company truck was parked in front of the house; a uniformed worker knelt before an electric meter on the side. The small yard was manicured, and empty flowerbeds beneath the windows had been neatly mulched. Two rosebushes were in bloom.

The front door opened and an oval-faced black woman with wavy silver-gray hair peered out at the truck. She seemed about the right age, but Charlie couldn't tell for sure. She wasn't terribly overweight, but her body appeared to have settled comfortably in on itself. She stepped off the porch and onto the sidewalk, building up speed as she passed the rose bushes. She confronted the utility worker, waving her arms and shouting, "What are you doing, cutting off my power? I pay my bills!"

Charlie slumped behind the steering wheel and watched the woman harangue the man. Without ever opening his mouth, the utility worker returned to his white pickup truck, her eyes burning into his back. He drove off, shaking his head as he glanced at Charlie.

Exiting the van in his industrial clothes and carrying his satchel, Charlie looked like he might spray for termites or survey her lot. He cleared his throat. "Good afternoon."

"What do you want?" she yelled. "I'm not giving up my house! Get off my property!"

Charlie stopped in the middle of the street and held up his hand to signal peace. While this was clearly a bad time to wrangle an interview, there might not be a better one, especially if she faced eviction. "I'm not here to cause trouble, ma'am."

She glared at him in disbelief. He saw anger mixed with dignity. Mainly anger, though. Charlie shielded his eyes from the afternoon sun. "Are you Minnie Doe?" he asked, resuming his approach. "I want to talk about Forsyth County."

She regarded him suspiciously. "Minerva. Nobody calls me Minnie anymore. And why would I want to talk about Forsyth County?"

He stopped. "I'm writing a book about a man named John Riggins. Died in 1937."

"Riggins is my maiden name." Her eyes narrowed further. "How'd you find me?"

He took a step forward. "I looked you up in the phone book after I listened to an interview with Jasper Riggins."

She put a hand on her sagging bosom. "Lord, he passed on more than a decade ago."

"So did the man who interviewed him. I was finishing a book on what happened in Forsyth County back in 1912, and I stumbled across the tape." Now Charlie was on the sidewalk, just a few feet away from the woman, who stood with her arms on her hips, appearing at least temporarily interested in what he had to say.

She fanned herself as beads of perspiration appeared on her forehead. "John Riggins was my father. Died before I was born. Murdered." The last word hung in the air, ugly and alone.

"Yes ma'am, that's what I understand. He must have been very brave to stay in Forsyth."

"You're writing a story about it seventy years later?"

"Yes ma'am. It's important." At ease with the weirdness of his task, Charlie felt no further explanation was necessary. Certainly not if he could get his foot in the door without one.

"And you want me to talk to you about it."

"If that's all right."

"It's not." She turned and walked away. Over her shoulder, she said, "Got other things on my mind."

He followed slowly up the sidewalk. She stepped onto the small porch and eased into a weathered wooden rocker, which took up nearly half the available space, with the welcome mat and potted plants taking up most of the rest. Looking down on him seemed to calm her. She rocked for a moment before she spoke again. "What did you say your name was?"

He smiled hopefully. "Charles Sherman. Charlie."

"You're a reporter."

"Yes." He reached up to hand her a clipping of Crenshaw's eight-month-old article. "I finished that book. Now I'm writing about your father."

She looked at the story, then glanced at his face like she was checking an ID. "Well, as you may have noticed, I can't help you right now. Can't even invite you in. Power company cut me off even though I paid the bill. I always pay my bills."

She leaned forward to hand the clipping back to him. She had a gardener's hands, clean but weathered and short-nailed. Lined and familiar with work. A pair of dirty cloth gloves lay beside the chair.

"Did you pay it this morning? Maybe they haven't credited—"

She waved off his assertion. "I gave the money to Demetrious the day before yesterday to get the money order, just like I did last month. Can't find my checkbook. Didn't know I was late until they hung a cutoff notice on the door."

"Who is Demetrious?"

"My grandson. I haven't seen him since I gave him the money to pay the bills."

"Uh … maybe that's part of the problem," Charlie suggested.

"Humph. Might be. He's never done me this way before, that I know of. But now I'm stuck. I don't have a car anymore."

Charlie seized the opportunity. "I can give you a ride to the bank or the power company."

"I had to sell it to help pay my house note. I took out a loan to get my roof fixed. Some men from Augusta. I got a raw deal. Interest is high. Whoo-wee. They call them Irish gypsies."

"Oh. Them."

"You heard about them?"

"They're everywhere."

"They need to be in jail."

Charlie shifted his feet awkwardly, figuring he'd stay until he was asked to leave. She gave him an irritated look, then wagged a finger at the clipping. "Is that book getting published?"

"Yes ma'am." He pulled out a letter from Joshua Furst he'd brought to prove his legitimacy and stepped forward to offer it to her.

She glanced at the letterhead without taking it. "So you're writing about my father. Hmm. It's important because it happened up in Forsyth County … after they said we all got run out, is that it?"

Who could say these things? "I started working on it yesterday. I have no idea where it will take me."

She rocked. After what seemed to Charlie like an eternity, she spoke. "Call me crazy, but I believe you. I had a dream that someone would come to me about my father."

"When?"

She shut one eye and looked at the tiny porch's ceiling with the other. "I don't know. But it's fresh in my mind." She looked back at him. "You don't seem surprised."

"I'm not. I can't explain why, but I was meant to do this."

She mulled the statement for a moment. "All right. I'll take that ride. Need to pay the phone bill, too. Wait here." She went inside. Charlie rushed to the van and cleared off the passenger seat, then the floor, moving papers and tools so that she could sit beside him.

Minerva came out clutching her purse and climbed into the van. She stared at the monkey wrench on the floor between them. "I thought you were a writer. Looks more like you're a plumber."

"I'm a handyman on the side," Charlie said. "Mouths to feed."

"I heard that."

The engine grumbled to a start and Charlie drove off. He took her to Citizens Savings to get cash. On the way to the power company office, she told Charlie that her father's cousin Jasper, a lifelong bachelor, had left her some money when he died, but she'd spent it keeping her daughter out of jail and trying to raise Demetrious. "Although that is proving difficult," she added, "since the boy doesn't want to grow up. And now he's messed up the simple task of paying the utilities before they got cut off. All I have is my pension and Social Security. I retired early, never dreaming I'd be spending so much money raising other people's children."

"What did you do before you retired?"

"I was a teacher. Atlanta schools. I'll bet you didn't know that."

"I didn't, but I'm not surprised."

"Why's that?"

He laughed. "I'm just not. I don't know why. Maybe because you talk better than I do."

"I take pride in my diction," she declared. "Now if I could only keep Demetrious from dropping out of school. I'm afraid he's beyond my help. When I get hold of him …" She trailed off and looked out the window. Charlie saw defeat in her eyes. The money she'd given the boy was likely long gone, spent on nothing she'd want to know about.

"Well, what do you want me to tell you?" she asked, turning her attention back to Charlie. "I'm not sure I have much to share. Like I said, I never knew my father. He died before I was born. Nine months before. Aunt Lizbeth told me I was the last thing he did. I don't remember my mother. Her name was Lettie. I was the last thing she did, too. Died right after I was born. She drowned."

"I don't know much about your mother other than that. Your father died a terrible death, I'm afraid."

"Hard to imagine." She shook her head sadly. "It always seemed odd that he was up there after everybody else got chased out, though."

"There were reports of a few others. But we—Professor Talton and I—couldn't prove they existed. I'd always wondered if their names appeared on the census even though they were gone, you know, maybe so the county revenue commissioner's kinfolk could farm their land without paying taxes, or something like that." He paused for a moment as he recalled that Talton's manuscript had originally listed two black residents in Forsyth County in 1940, but the good professor had struck through that number.

Minerva looked out the window. "People need to know their past. Too many lies have been spread. Everybody talks about 1954 and 'I have a dream.' Well, I'd been teaching ten years before I saw white children in my classroom. Some poor kids from Cabbagetown in 1970. That's history. So … what do you want to know?"

"Everything. You married?"

"My husband's gone. Never found another man." She paused, as she did frequently. "I met James Doe after I started teaching." She chuckled lightly. "My car broke down one day and he rescued me. He was a mechanic by trade, and he pulled his car over and helped me. Went to a store and came back with a fan belt. Replaced it right there on the side of the road. Within a year, we were married even though he was a few years younger than me. He was drafted and went to Vietnam. Didn't come back. We had a baby girl, but he never saw her."

"What year did he die?"

"I don't know that he's dead. Haven't heard from him in forty years."

"Oh." *Awkward.* Charlie drove into downtown Decatur. He pulled into a parking space in front of the Georgia Power office and asked, "Do you want me to go with you?"

"No, I'm fine."

While she was inside, Charlie furiously scribbled notes on his legal pad.

She returned, clutching a receipt. "They say the lights will be back on by the end of the day."

"Good. Glad that's taken care of."

After a side trip to pay the phone bill, he drove her home. Meanwhile, Minerva continued her story. "I was expecting Shaundra—my daughter—when James went off to basic training. I raised her the best I could, but she was always finding trouble." She watched a cop making a traffic stop, then turned back to Charlie. "Shaundra got pregnant with Demetrious and claimed she didn't know who the father was." Minerva shook her head. "She was an adult by then, but she couldn't take care of herself, let alone a child, so it's been up to me to raise him, old as I am. He was doing all right until high school. Held back his freshman year. Now he cuts class so much he's not going to graduate. Running with bad people, too. My house is supposed to be his address, but I don't know. He stays with his mother sometimes, but she keeps moving."

She flipped her hands up. "Honestly, I don't know where else he ends up some nights. Comes and goes as he pleases. I didn't think he'd do that with the power company money, though. I'm afraid he's gotten mixed up with gangs. So, Mr. Sherman, that's my life. I spend a lot of time worrying about where my daughter and grandson are and what they're doing, and ... well, I can't say that has much to do with your story, but I do have some things that might help you out. Letters, pictures, and such."

"I'd like to see them. Anything that would help me get to know your parents."

When they returned to her house, she invited him inside. The place was neat, its furnishings modest. A throw rug covered the living room's worn wooden floor. An old TV equipped with rabbit ears sat on a cart in the corner. Jesus pictures and needlepoint adorned the walls. Minerva pointed to a framed picture among the bric-a-brac on an end table. The photo showed a smiling youth in a black suit and tie. "That's Demetrious in his go-to-meeting clothes. He doesn't dress that way now, oh no. He dresses like a *gangsta*." It took her awhile to say the last word, one she obviously despised.

Minerva directed Charlie to retrieve a footlocker from her bedroom closet and carry it into the living room. "Don't slide my treasure chest on the floor," she warned him. She opened the shades and blinds so they could see and started digging through it as he booted up his computer on battery power. The strong scent of mothballs reminded him of his grandmother's dark closet back in Missouri.

"Can we open the windows?" he asked. "I think I may be part moth."

"Go ahead."

After Charlie caught a breath of fresh air, Minerva showed him her family memorabilia: a Bible with the family tree filled in back to 1840; a diploma from Savannah State College, where John Riggins had graduated in 1934 with a degree in agriculture; photos of John and his bride Lettie and their correspondence. Best of all, a journal Riggins had kept. Charlie was ecstatic. "I'd like to make copies," he said.

Minerva glanced over the papers. "You can do that, but they're not leaving my eyesight."

Charlie nodded, recalling Kathleen's possessive attitude toward Thurwood's manuscript. He read through the journal and took notes on his pad, which was bathed in the western light that cut through the living room window and fell on the coffee table.

When the power came on just after five o'clock, Minerva offered him dinner. "Nothing much, just what I'm having," she said.

"That's fine."

Soon after that, he was staring at a small plate containing kid-sized portions of Chef Boyardee ravioli and canned peaches—exactly what he fed Ben and Beck when he was in a hurry. Karmic payback, he reckoned.

"Thanks," he said. After eating quickly, he returned to the task of getting to know John Riggins, a lanky, dark-skinned man, and Lettie, short, plump and slightly fairer. Charlie surreptitiously held the photo up while watching Minerva rock her way through the evening news. *Hmm.* Perhaps the old photos had darkened over the decades.

"It's getting late," Charlie said when he realized the sun was setting. "I don't want to bother you anymore today, but I'd like to come back. This stuff is fascinating." He shut down the computer.

"That would be all right."

As he slipped his laptop into its case, he heard a car squeal to a stop. Then arguing and yelping, the sounds of a scuffle, a thump on metal, a car pulling away, and a long wail of anguish.

"Oh Lord, please don't let it be what I think it is," Minerva said, choking back a sob. "I'm afraid they just dumped him out there. You look. I can't bear it."

Charlie inched toward the living room window, fearing a shotgun blast or automatic weapons fire. When he peered out, he saw a girl standing on the sidewalk in front of the house. A middle-school student, he guessed, maybe five feet tall, thin and knock-kneed, her short hair pulled in tight pigtails with ragged ends. Her face may have been pretty, but it was puffy from crying—and maybe a beating. She wore blue jeans, a T-shirt, and windbreaker, with a backpack slung across her shoulder. She looked lost. "It's a girl."

"What?" Minerva got up and brushed away a lace curtain to look out. "Oh dear Lord."

"Do you know her?"

Wearing a worried look, she shook her head. "No. Don't think so."

When Minerva opened the door, the girl called out, "Are you D's grandma?"

The old woman made a face. "Who is *D*?"

'Demetrious."

"Yes. Who are you?"

"Takira. I heard he stay here. I need to talk to him."

"Haven't seen him." Minerva started to close the door, then paused. "Baby girl, what's wrong?"

"D won't talk to me. And I need some money."

"What you need money for, child?"

"I missed my period. I need a pregnancy test and I don't got a place to stay. They'll beat me if I go back home." This all poured out in a plaintive, rapid-fire delivery. It was the most eloquent and succinct description of a living hell Charlie had ever heard.

Minerva looked wide-eyed at Charlie, whose mouth was hanging open.

"Come in, girl. Mr. Sherman, looks like we're through for the day."

"So, I'll come back, and—"

"You can bring a copier or something if you want."

"How about tomorrow?"

"Monday," she said firmly.

The girl trudged in and slumped on the sofa. Charlie left, giving her a sympathetic smile. She averted her gaze and stared at the floor. As Charlie drove off, he saw two teenage boys walking in the street. He couldn't make out their faces in the darkness, but fear crept into his gut. All kids in this part of town looked sketchy, if not downright dangerous. And these two had predators' eyes. He shuddered, glad he had a metal frame and 170 horsepower between his hide and them.

He turned the corner and sped off, his mood improving immediately. After all, this was a major accomplishment. John Riggins was no longer unknowable (which would have made him the deal-breaker in the contract), but a real-live dead human being, someone Charlie could write about with authority and confidence, since his subject had possessed the good grace to tell so much about himself in his journal.

Yes, a good day overall.

* * *

Later that evening, Charlie called Susan to tell her he'd completed *Flight from Forsyth*. She congratulated him, and then quickly changed the subject, saying he could either cough up $150 a week for after-school care or go back to picking up the kids. He chose the latter, since he missed Beck and Ben—and had more time than money. Also, she was willing to give him a key to Thornbriar, indicating a further thawing—but without mention of icing or licking.

Meanwhile, there was other work to do. On Saturday, Charlie started building a deck near Little Five Points, so his return to Minerva's house was delayed by several days. He knocked on her door Thursday morning, balancing his computer atop a new scanner still in its box. Minerva answered, her expression grim. "Something wrong?" he asked as he stepped inside.

"We did the test, and now we know. The girl is pregnant," she said, closing the door. "Claims D is the father. Lord, now *I'm* calling him that."

"The father?"

"No," she said, irritated. "D."

"What does he say?"

"He came by after you left the other night. He called her all sorts of names and stormed out. I haven't seen him since."

He fidgeted. This was all very terrible, and furthermore, he needed to get to work.

"Eighth grade," Minerva said. "Fourteen. She's staying with me now, since her mama kicked her out. I want to turn that hateful woman in for child abuse and neglect, but I'm afraid she could get Demetrious arrested for statutory rape. I don't believe in abortion, or in babies having babies, either." She sighed. "This is like Shaundra all over again. Worse by ten years. And if Demetrious is ..."

She waved her hands helplessly in the air. Charlie waited for her to finish her thought, but she didn't, so he busied himself pulling the scanner out of its box.

After a minute, Minerva spoke again. "He brought back the money Friday. Most of it, anyway. Said he didn't get a chance to get to the power company. I hate to think what all he did ... I'm lucky I got any of it back. Lucky he's alive. I'm afraid *of* him and *for* him. The people he associates with." She growled in disgust. "That friend of his he brought by the other night is nothing but bad news. You can see it in his eyes. He got beat up in a fight and talks about getting a gun and killing the other boy. D said he'd help him. They both spend all their time playing the fool."

"Oh really," said Charlie, scrutinizing the scanner's instructions.

"My grandson's no bigger than me and talks about killing people. Too much anger and hatred inside. It's all messed up. I don't want to trouble you with that." She waved her hand as if she was shooing away her problems, but they hung in the air like thick smoke over a fire in a valley.

Charlie looked up. "Where's Takira now?"

"I got her back in school. She'll be doing well if she makes it through this semester. She'll be showing pretty soon, skinny as she is. But you go ahead and work on your book."

He set up his scanner in the living room while she cleaned up in the kitchen. He felt guilty about using her precious electricity. When she came out to check on him, he said, "If there's some way I could, uh, reimburse you—"

She tut-tutted him. "Just give me some copies of your book when it's published. I don't want people claiming I made up a story and sold it to you. What's that called? Checkbook journalism?"

"Yes. No. We don't want that. I don't have much of a checkbook, anyway."

"You do the work. You get paid. That's the way it should be."

Minerva went into the kitchen and worked noisily for an hour. Then she came into the living room and started energetically dusting around him, wondering aloud how long he would take, asking why anyone would care about something that happened so long ago. He looked up from a letter he was copying. "You having second thoughts? Don't you want to know what happened?"

She picked a piece of lint from the sofa arm. "Maybe not. I was just thinking there's a reason the past should stay buried."

Unsure how long Minerva would let him stay, Charlie picked up his pace.

Her mood improved after Charlie offered to buy her lunch. They ate in a diner called Café Max near Little Five Points. After they returned, Minerva got a phone call, which she took in her bedroom. She came back into the living room and rolled her eyes. "That was the high school attendance office. Demetrious has gone missing from school again. He was out most of last week. I quit signing excuses for him two years ago. Now he doesn't even bother. He's out roaming the streets."

To Charlie, the boy seemed not so much a troubled teenager as a storm building to critical mass. He glanced at the photo of the truant, gangsta wannabe, and statutory rapist. He didn't want to deal with Hurricane Demetrious, but he could sense the manchild bulging out of the picture frame, pushing against the fabric of Charlie's universe.

* * *

Charlie showed up at Minerva's house the next morning, hoping to finish copying Riggins's papers. She was in a better mood, cheerfully serving him coffee and cinnamon rolls. He found papers in the bottom of the chest that quickened his pulse—a title deed to a farm in Forsyth County, along with tax records. The Holy Grail, if what Jasper had said was true: John Riggins had been lynched for his land. Charlie recalled the 1987 biracial commission's report and its white-led disparagement of claims for reparations. *Suck on this, biracial commission bitches*!

He showed Minerva what he'd found and asked if she'd ever made a claim on the land.

"There was an AME preacher named McDougal who tried to do something back in the 1970s. I gave him my information, and he talked to a lawyer, but nothing ever came of it."

"Was that in 1972?"

"Yes. I think so. How'd you know?"

"There was a courthouse fire about that time. Some records were conveniently destroyed."

"Hmm."

"Hmm, indeed. I think I need to take a trip to Forsyth County."

She bugged her eyes and grunted. "You can go without me. Anyway, they're not going to give it up. That's how they are. No offense." She shrugged. "If you prove the land should belong to me, you know what they'll do, don't you? Make me pay seventy years' taxes, that's what."

Charlie couldn't say they wouldn't. But still, it was worth fighting for. "The land is worth millions in the current market."

As he was making a copy of the title, he realized that this may have been what the burglars were looking for back in January at Bayard Terrace. "Do you have a safety deposit box?" he asked.

"Yes."

"You should stash this away for safekeeping."

"You really think the land's worth some money?"

"Yes. Definitely."

Charlie finished copying and gave Minerva a ride to the bank, where she tucked away the records. After that, he returned to her house and dropped her off, then sped away to pick up the kids, thinking about how to proceed with his investigation. Obviously, the land grab was the central part of the story—and most likely the murder motive. He knew Riggins's farm had been located in northern Forsyth but wasn't sure exactly where. He needed to find out who owned the land now. He snapped his fingers. Pappy must have known John Riggins! Hell, everyone in Forsyth would have known the only black man who lived within twenty miles. Whenever Riggins went to town, a hundred eyes would have followed him, just waiting for him to lunge at a white woman. Charlie wondered what pretext they'd used to kill the man. Then again, when violent racism was Forsyth County's official policy, how clever did they need to be?

Chapter Twelve

Two weeks after finishing *Flight from Forsyth*—and two days shy of the seventieth anniversary of John Riggins's lynching—Charlie was compelled to return to Cumming. On a sunny day that seemed more summer than fall, he parked his van downtown in a large lot near a poultry plant (where Hispanics now flocked for jobs). Huge cooling units droned as he crossed Main Street to the square and glanced at the modern red-brick City Hall before turning his gaze back to the courthouse.

The brick courthouse had white-trimmed windows that Charlie found irritatingly small, front and back porticos with tall, spindly white columns, third-story dormer windows, and a white phallic clock tower topped by a spike. It replaced the old courthouse, which had burned down in November 1973—at the hands of a varmint, or the spouse of one, according to family rumors. But he knew from working on *Flight from Forsyth* that there had been several other suspects, and this had always been a county of arsonists. (In the early 1970s, the state fire marshal for North Georgia had declared that eighty percent of his work was in Forsyth.)

Inside the courthouse, Charlie passed through security and took the stairs down to the records room. Once there, he watched as several white folks searched land records. They moved quickly, plopping big red log books on counters and taking notes. Charlie found the books covering 1917 to 1950. He suspected the records he was looking for may have been destroyed for the same reason Talton's documents had been stolen from Bayard Terrace. Therefore, he was both shocked and relieved to find two entries under the Riggins name. One index item listed Thomas Riggins as grantor on February

18, 1935 and (illegible) Riggins as grantee. This was the transfer from father to son that Charlie already knew about. He needed to find a later transfer. Then he'd trace the title to the current landowner. His pulse quickened when he saw that the information he sought was in Deed Book 12, on page 123.

Charlie pulled out the big book and flopped its frayed cover open on the slanted tabletop. He took a deep breath and leafed through pages, marveling at the permanence of fountain pen ink. There it was, the description of the property in Land District Three, in the northwest portion of the county. Sold to—

"Fuck me," Charlie said softly. *Bam*. It was right there.

A man standing nearby chuckled. "Not what you were looking for?"

"This ... has been looking for me," Charlie mumbled, feeling dizzy.

—Isaac Cutchins for $500.

Right out there in public. *Damn, Momo's daddy missed a spot.* Then again, everything had been duly noted and endorsed by the county clerk on October 17, 1937. All neat, tidy ... and bogus. John Riggins's signature didn't match the signature on a letter Charlie had brought for comparison. The date of death was October 12, 1937, according to the marking on the photo and Riggins family recollections, but there was no official record. Riggins had simply ceased to exist on that day. Charlie lugged the book over to the Xerox machine and made a copy of the transaction. Then he got the hell out of there.

Feeling that doom was his destiny, Charlie trudged back to the van. The photo, which he had never examined closely, waited for him there. On the verge of tears, he slid into the driver's seat and groped around behind him until his hand found the manila envelope. His head hung as he pulled out the picture. It had been there all along, of course. Something had simply prevented Charlie from seeing the truth until now. But there was twenty-five-year-old Isaac Cutchins, pointing to a lump of human charcoal and claiming credit for the catch. The glint in his eyes said, *Lookie here*! *Look what I caught*!

So this is why I've been chosen, Charlie thought. He threw his head back against the seat and stared at the photo with melancholy eyes. It was all so clear: God wanted him to destroy his world.

Then again, why did he think he'd been working for God? God wouldn't trick him into signing a deal like the one that kept mutating on him, would It? No. Charlie feared he was a pawn working the back end of an infernal contract—nothing more than some kind of debt collector, with his own signature the bloodiest of all. Whether he was working for God to punish the wicked, the devil to close a deal, the ghost of John Riggins to seek justice, or a stinky old trickster to settle a score, the boiling blood gave him little choice.

But of course there was a choice. There is always a choice.

Should he go to the Forsyth County sheriff with this information? No. The idea was ludicrous even without throwing Trouble's admonition about cops into the equation. And maybe this is why he'd said *No Cops*.

With grim resolve, he recommitted himself to the task assigned, even if it meant doing the devil's work. He would make the same decision another Missouri boy once made on his way down the river: "*I was a-trembling because I'd got to decide forever betwixt two things, and I knowed it. I studied for a minute, sort of holding my breath, and then says to myself, 'All right, then, I'll go to hell.'*"

* * *

Now that he knew who he was up against, Charlie rented a safe deposit box. No way would he allow a second set of documents to be stolen. Then, after a few days spinning his wheels and brooding, he returned to Cumming the next Monday.

"There you are," said Lillian as he stood at the library's reference desk. "I haven't seen you in *months*." She wrinkled her eyebrows. "Did you finish the book?"

"I did," he said with a short nod.

"Congratulations!"

"Thanks. Now it's on to something else."

"So … you didn't need to look at my great-grandfather's journal, after all." She smiled sheepishly. "I'm glad you didn't depend on it. I was looking through it after we talked about it, and there are pages missing—on 1912. I think Mom cut them out with a razor. Probably in 1987. People were really uptight back then, you know. Other than that, it looks complete up to his death. He died in 1950."

"Really?" Charlie said, trying not to sound too interested. "I'd like to see it. I'm thinking about writing more about Forsyth. It's … an interesting place."

"That would be good. We shouldn't have our reputation based on just one bad thing."

"I agree," Charlie said, wide-eyed. "People should see there's more to Forsyth County. Have you read through it, by any chance?"

"No, I just looked to see if it was readable. It's at my house. I'm off Thursday. You should come by." She gave him a promising smile.

"Really?" he gushed. "That would be great."

She wrote her address and phone number on a slip of paper and slid it across the desk. "It's near here. Call me first."

Charlie pocketed the paper and glanced around. He wanted to look at some 1937 newspapers, but a recent edition of the *Forsyth Sentinel* lying on a table caught his eye, and a front-page headline jumped out at him:

Investors Take Option on Cutchins Land

> Southland Associates, a Memphis-based shopping mall developer, paid a $1 million option on the purchase of the 200-acre farm in Forsyth County belonging to Isaac Cutchins, father of State Rep. Stanley Cutchins.
>
> Richard Davis, a partner in Southland, declined to discuss plans for the site, though he noted that its proximity to the proposed Outer Perimeter "will make it increasingly valuable in the years to come."
>
> Negotiations began late last fall, Davis said. The option is good for a year …

Late last fall. The varmints had huddled around Pappy after Christmas dinner at Thornbriar, and a hush had fallen over the room when Charlie entered. They must have been talking about the money coming their way. Susan had been sitting there, soaking it all in. Whaddya know, the next night, he was out on his ass. And he'd been bouncing on the pavement ever since.

There are no coincidences.

"A year, eh?" Charlie muttered to himself. "Let's see what comes up between now and then."

* * *

Lillian Scott lived near downtown Cumming, on a side street just off Main, not far from the library. Her small white frame house was freshly painted, with black shutters, neatly trimmed shrubs, and a concrete driveway that looked like it had been recently poured. In deference to its pristine condition, Charlie parked on the street. Holding the scanner under his left arm and his computer satchel in his right hand, he hit the doorbell button with his left pinkie. Lillian answered the door in jeans and a baggy sweatshirt, her brown hair cascading to her shoulders. She looked cute. He smelled potpourri and sensed a trap. He warned himself to be careful. Lillian's great-grandmother had attempted a liaison in the courthouse with that hapless attorney back in 1912, so there was a possibility that horniness ran in the family.

"Come on in," she said, grabbing his arm and pulling him into the living room, which had landscape paintings on the wall and a blue sofa with white lace arm covers. She pointed to the dining room. "You can work in here." Two cats—one black, one black and white—entwined themselves around her legs. "You want coffee?"

"Sure. Thanks."

"I've got some old letters, too, but I haven't read through them. If you see anything you can use, you're welcome to make copies."

"Okie-doke."

She poured Charlie a cup of coffee, and he sat down with it at an antique table, where family papers had been carefully laid out. He debated telling Lillian what he was looking for, then decided against it. After all, he didn't know if he could trust her. Anyway, she didn't seem that interested, since she hadn't read either journal or letters.

While Charlie worked, Lillian curled up with a book in a living room chair. He pored over old correspondence and soon hit pay dirt, becoming entranced by the story that unfolded. This was the stuff of dreams (his kind of dreams, at that).

The dispute between Ike Cutchins and John Riggins had been going on since 1935, when Riggins returned to farm the family land, which had lain fallow since 1912. The feud was a constant source of entertainment to the men who ran the county. The letters from local justice of the peace Lucious Fervil to wealthy landowner Horton Anderson, Lillian's great-grandfather, born in 1886, would fill a chapter. (Talton had heard of this mother lode of information and written about it in his notes, although without any mention of Riggins.) Needless to say, Charlie was overjoyed to stumble across it. The stuff was rich and gossipy, rife with strife, as the feud escalated:

June 12, 1936

Dear Horton,

Here is the latest news on Ike Cutchins. He wanted to swear out a warrant against John Riggins for cussing him. He said Riggins called him a damn Cracker and told him to get off his land. I asked him why would John-Boy do that? He's a sensible nigger. Ike must have given him cause.

He said it wasn't my business. Ike always has been a hothead and can't stand that John runs a better farm than him. "It ain't right," he says, "for a nigger to own land when I don't."

Envy is the root of Ike's troubles.

I refused to draw up a warrant. I looked him in the eye and told him he'd have to handle this himself. That is all for now. Keep your eyes wide open.

Yours truly,

Lucious

Charlie stared at the meticulous handwriting and thought: *Everyone knew the little bastard was up to something*. He put the letter in the flatbed scanner and made a copy on his hard drive.

There was much more. He felt a spike of nervous energy when he found some letters from local historian Cecil Montgomery to Lillian's mother, his "dearest cousin." Montgomery would not be pleased to know that Charlie Sherman was looking at his letters. Indeed, Charlie was tremendously surprised to find them. Apparently, Cecil hadn't covered this base and collected them from Lillian back in January when he'd warned the townsfolk to beware the strange invader. Maybe Cecil was getting old and forgetful—or didn't think these papers mattered.

Well, they did now. Charlie's gaze froze on a brown envelope he uncovered near the center of the table. *Hello*. "Joshua Logan" was written on it in thick black ink. The lyncher and land stealer of 1912. He of the deathbed confession, dictated to a young Cecil Montgomery and promptly burned. Unless—

No. Nothing like that in the envelope. But he could now see handwriting samples and signatures from both men. *Get while the getting's good*, Charlie told himself. As he scanned a letter from each man, he stifled a laugh, worried that an outbreak of glee would alert Lillian to the true nature of his mission and the pending danger to her family's good name.

After that, he sought more documentation for his main story, but no worries. It was all around. He was practically whistling when he found this letter:

June 6, 1937

Dear Horton,

Just to keep you posted on the Cutchins-Riggins problem. Here is the latest. On the night of June 3 Ike Cutchins showed up at John Riggins house with a homemade gasoline bomb and threw it on the porch. Riggins stepped outside, picked up the bomb, a canning jar stuffed with a burning rag, which had failed to explode. He threw it after Ike, who was running away down the road as fast as his stubbly little legs could carry him.

Unfortunately, there was a casualty. Ike's fyce, who apparently possessed a fair deal more courage than his master, stayed behind to bark at John. When the jar hit the road, it blew up, and a piece of flying glass so mangled the dog's back leg that it had to be amputated.

Sheriff Ware told me this after both parties reported their own versions of the incident and demanded that an arrest be made. Riggins must understand that a white man has more rights than a nigger will ever have.

Yours truly,

Lucious

Lillian fixed ham sandwiches for lunch. By then, Charlie had scanned thirty pages into his laptop. "What exactly are you looking for?" she asked as they ate in the newly remodeled kitchen, complete with granite counters, maple cabinets, and black appliances. "Like I said, I haven't read that stuff."

"Local color," he said in his best deadpan. "The sort of things that make a story come alive."

That seemed to satisfy her, but as it turned out, she was interested in something else. As they chatted amiably, she told Charlie with a shy smile, "There isn't a man in my life, at present." She also said that she considered his separation "the same thing as a divorce." He took these statements as a warning, along with her tendency to reach over and touch his hand when she laughed at his jokes.

After lunch, Charlie kept reading, but didn't find anything of particular interest until his eyes fell on a partially blacked-out journal entry by Anderson on October 13, 1937, the day after the date on the back of the lynching photo: "Yesterday marked the death of (name redacted) at the hands of (several names redacted), and especially (name redacted), who started all this. I am not happy about it, but the nigger had to argue, so he died."

While Charlie was staring at this entry, the phone rang. Lillian took the call in the kitchen. A few seconds later, he heard her mention his name, which was precisely when things went wrong.

"Oh," Lillian said. "I didn't know. Nobody ever told me that." She became more apologetic and agitated. Finally, she said, "Yes, Cecil."

Shit. Montgomery.

When Lillian returned to the dining room, Charlie glanced up and flinched when he saw the look on her face. "You have to leave," she said between gritted teeth.

"What's going on?" he asked.

"Logan's coming. He's won't be happy," Lillian said. "It's best for you if you're gone."

"Who's Logan?"

"My brother. I'm not telling you anything more. You're a snake." She hissed the last word.

"Sorry," Charlie said, doing his best to look confused. "I don't understand."

"Yes, you do," she said. "Why else would you be sitting at my table, taking notes?"

He glanced around at the papers. All those sources, all that history … fading before his eyes. But at least he now had more damning information on the old man. Charlie cleared his throat and gulped. "Tell … Logan that I'm not working on 1912 anymore. This is a Cutchins thing I'm doing now."

She glared at him, arms folded across her chest.

He closed his computer, unplugged the scanner, and quickly packed up his stuff. With his gear in his hands, Charlie turned to her and said, "I've got a job to do. That's all it is."

"Like I said, it's best that you go. I'm only giving you this warning because I don't want blood on my carpet. And delete whatever you put on your computer. You don't have rights to use it."

"Goodbye." Charlie marched out of the house and quickened his step. He opened the van door and tossed his equipment on the floor in front of the passenger seat. As he drove off, he cast a glance back at Lillian's house and shook his head mournfully at the history he'd left behind. When he was a half-block away, a blue Ram pickup sped by going the opposite direction, running a stop sign. Racing the engine, its driver turned toward Lillian's house.

"It's good to be gone," Charlie muttered as he drove off. As for deleting the copies he'd made on his computer, she'd have to take that up with his boss.

Of course he felt badly, but his mood brightened when he realized how much treasure he'd rescued from behind enemy lines. What occupied his mind on the drive back to Atlanta were those blacked-out names. How could he learn the lynchers' identities? *Maybe Lucious Fervil also had a horny great-granddaughter.*

He crossed the line into Fulton County and breathed a sigh of relief. Soon afterward, his cellphone trilled. He was glad it was Joshua Furst at Fortress, but his relief was short-lived. "What the *hell* is going on down there?" his editor asked. "I haven't even finished reading the manuscript—it's absolutely fantastic, by the way—and people are already calling me. You're really stirring up trouble, and I say that with the greatest admiration. Some guy named Cecil called demanding to see everything you've written. Then some woman called to say your life is in danger and gave me her number. Your first groupie. Ha, ha."

"Uh, thanks. Don't let Cecil Montgomery see the manuscript. And it's not about him, anyway. I'm working on something else. What's the woman's name?"

"Wouldn't give it. Just a number." Joshua rattled it off.

"Hang on," Charlie said, tossing the phone on the passenger seat, pulling out his pen, and writing the number on the back of his left hand. He picked up the phone and checked with Joshua to make sure he'd got it right. "OK, thanks." Charlie hung up.

He dialed as he drove past the first sign of civilization, the North Springs MARTA station. No answer.

A minute later, a call came in. "Hello," he said, trying not to sound agitated.

"You called me," a woman's voice declared.

"I did? Oh. Did you leave a message with my editor?"

"Is that you, Mr. Sherman?"

"Yes. And you are—"

"You don't need my name," she said in an accent torn between drawl and twang. "I got some information for you. I wanted to warn you, but your editor wouldn't give me your number."

"Warn me about what?"

"Logan Scott is looking for you."

"Yeah, I heard," Charlie said. "What's his problem?"

"He was nervous about something 'that damned writer' is working on and said his uncle's gonna kill his sister. I said, 'What writer?' And he said, 'The one working on the dead man's book about 1912.' He 'bout had a conniption on his way out."

"The dead man's book." Charlie liked it as a title. Maybe for his memoir, if he wasn't careful. "Now … who's his uncle?"

"Cecil Montgomery."

"You mean his cousin."

"He said uncle."

"Whatever. And they were talking about me?"

"Not by name, but I knew it was you. I been followin' you. Saw an article earlier this year. I Googled you about a book deal, then I called Fortress. I didn't think the guy was going to help me out. Glad he got in touch with you."

"You told him my life was in danger?"

"Logan carries a gun. Probably end up shooting himself, though, like his cousin did down in Atlanta last Christmas."

Charlie's sphincter clamped shut. He was stunned into silence for a moment, then attempted a recovery: "Wouldn't know about that."

"Got into it with a guy at a Pancake Hut. I figure he had it comin'. Anyway, Logan works for the county. He's an auxiliary deputy, thinks he can arrest people."

"Does he work for the sheriff?"

"No, the planning—you don't need to involve me in this."

The planning commission. That would make Scott one of the county bigwigs. And Joshua Logan's farm was out there near the proposed superhighway, too. Lillian's family probably had as much at stake as Pappy's clan did. "No, of course not. Uh, thanks for the warning, I'll certainly—"

"You married a Cutchins."

"That's true." He stared over traffic into the blue sky. A smile crossed his lips. "We don't get along so well anymore."

"I figured as much, if you're working on what I think you are. So Evangeline Powell's your mother-in-law." She cackled. "What do you think of her?"

"A little goes a long way," he drawled.

"I hear you. Her act got old with me a long time ago."

"So what is it that you think I'm working on?"

"I figure you're writing a book about the Cutchinses and by now you know they're all evil and crooked as snakes. Stanley Cutchins cheated me on my insurance. Told me the policy he sold me covered my boat, even charged me for it, and then I found out the hard way it didn't. He knew what he was doing, and it cost me dearly. Now one of their own is going to do it to them. If that's not poetry, I don't know what is. But you need to be careful. There's people up here who have worked for generations to keep this quiet. But some of us think the Cutchins' time of ridin' high needs to come to an end, what with the news about the farm."

"I saw that there's an option of a million dollars on the land."

"Purchase price be twenty times that. If you know how they got it, you know it's not right."

"OK. You called me, and I got a feeling you want to help. Is there something else you'd like to share?" He still wasn't sure exactly what she knew, and he didn't intend to tip his hand.

"Yeah. Get in touch with Danny Patterson. Lives on Crooked Hollow Road. Know where that is?"

"I've been by it a few times."

"My daughter's best friend—his niece—takes care of him. If you talk to him, he might have something to tell you. But be quick. He ain't gonna be around much longer. Got cancer real bad."

"What will he tell me?"

"I don't know what he'll tell you, but he seen it."

Bam. Charlie felt like he'd been shoveling in the dirt and just hit something hard. "It?"

"The thing itself. He's your eyewitness, Mr. Sherman. I gotta go. People can listen in on these cellphones. Good luck," she whispered. "I hope you nail their butts to the wall."

* * *

The next morning, Charlie drove on Crooked Hollow Road for several miles before he found a gray mailbox with "Patterson" painted on it in crude red letters. Atop a hill, an old two-story house stood at the end of a long, two-track grass and gravel driveway that cut through an overgrown pasture. No cars or pickups. It was a scenic view, if you didn't look too closely, but Charlie could see signs of decay even from a distance: peeling paint, torn screens, plywood on a window, and a sagging roof adorned with a dish antenna.

It was a sunny October day and the air was still; leaves from oaks and poplars dropped straight to the ground. Across the road, behind him, stood a new subdivision. A half-mile away, work had begun on yet another one. The clanking union of a front-end loader and a dump truck broke the morning stillness. The van's tires crunched and popped along the driveway. Charlie parked beside the house, climbed out with his satchel, slammed the door, and shouted, "Hello!"

He didn't trust the broken stair railing or front porch to hold his weight (or the porch roof not to collapse on him), so he walked around the house and knocked on the kitchen door. He heard a chair squeak, then slow thumping. The door opened and a grizzled, wild-haired, and rheumy-eyed old man in a ratty pale blue bathrobe stood before him, giving Charlie the blankest stare he'd ever seen. Underneath the robe, the man wore a frayed T-shirt and graying briefs. A tube from his nose connected to an air tank on a two-wheeled cart he pulled behind him. The man's free hand hung trembling uncontrollably.

"Mr. Patterson?"

"I doan wanna … buy anything," the old man wheezed. "Ain't got … money."

Charlie spoke quickly. "I don't want to sell you anything. I'm working on a book about Forsyth County. I understand you know what happened to a man named John Riggins, and I wondered if you might be willing to talk about it."

The old man gasped, either in surprise or for breath. "Ain't heard that name … in a long time. Someone finally caught … up to it. So that's … what it's all about."

"Beg pardon?"

"Been a car … parked down the road … past day or so." He pointed feebly toward the side of the house. "Ain't there today. Not so far as I see, anyway. You know anything … 'bout that?"

"No. But people have expressed an interest in what I've been doing lately. I can say that."

"What you mean?"

"They broke in and stole a bunch of papers. They didn't find what they were looking for."

"What they looking fer?"

"A land title and this." Charlie pulled out the lynching photograph from his satchel. "You ever seen it?"

Patterson stared, his mouth open slightly, his wheezing almost a whistle. "No."

Charlie's spirits sank as he put back the photo.

"But I remember … 'em takin' it."

Charlie's spirits bounced back. "Go on."

"Don't suppose … you got smokes." Patterson pulled a bloody handkerchief from his robe pocket. He weakly coughed up a red patch of phlegm and spit it into the cloth, then tucked it away.

"Afraid I don't."

"Come inside anyway." Patterson let him in, apparently as starved for company as he was for nicotine. Charlie followed him as he slowly shuffled to the kitchen table and sat down in an old metal-legged chair with a torn vinyl cushion, the oxygen cart pressed against his leg. Charlie remained standing.

A TV blared away in the living room, which it shared with a hospital bed. A pile of dirty dishes sat in the sink and more were scattered across the table. There were competing stenches: a backed-up toilet or septic tank, rotting food, and/or a dead animal under the house. Charlie doubted that Patterson could smell any of it.

"I heard that land's gettin' sold. That picture … worth a million dollars," said Patterson.

"More than that," Charlie said, raising his voice to be heard above the TV's din.

"All right. This is somethin' … needs to be told. Nuthin' nobody can do to me now. I'm dyin'. Cancer. That's what the tube's for." He pointed to his nose.

"I'm sorry to hear that. Uh, mind if I turn off the TV?"

The old man nodded. "Go ahead."

Charlie went into the living room. *The Matthew Steele Show* was on. Trash TV of the worst sort. Two mothers were pregnant by their sons-in-law, and their daughters sat beside them. The graphic at the bottom of the screen said, "*She's my half-sister, she's my step-daughter*!"

Charlie shook his head in disgust.

"You got to turn off the VCR, too. That's an old show I was watching"

"Oh. OK." Charlie turned off the machines, then stepped to the front window and looked out. "Where was the car parked?"

"Down the hill … under some trees."

Charlie saw a wide, flat shoulder on the road about a quarter-mile east. No sign of a stakeout. Returning to the kitchen, he sat down across from Patterson, pulled a small digital voice recorder from his shirt pocket, and cleared a spot for it on the table.

"Excuse the mess. My niece … supposed to come by … and help me. Hasn't been here … for a week. I'm runnin' outta food. She probably … shacked up with somebody … met in a bar … and forgot about me."

"I can get you something after we talk." Charlie realized how cold that sounded, especially since he meant to say it that way.

"Something from … Pancake Hut. I'll trade you … interview for eggs 'n grits."

Charlie grimaced at the mention of his least favorite restaurant. Nevertheless he said, "Sounds like a deal."

"I just turned eighty-two … Longer than most … nonsmokers. Outlasted … everybody. Wife … kids. Now all I got … is that niece … lucky she comes by … once a week."

"I'm going to turn on the recorder now." Charlie pushed the *Rec* button.

"I reckon … I got to do this," Patterson said.

Charlie reckoned he did.

Patterson began in his wheezing rasp. "OK. It was 1937 … my birthday, October 12 … just a few days ago."

"Happy birthday."

"Nobody pays any attention … anymore. But you don't need to hear … 'bout that. I was playin' hooky to celebrate. Bad year. Weevils was everywhere. We lost half our crop."

Charlie pointed to the window and swept his hand around. "On this land?"

"No. My daddy owned land. I rent this house now … with my Social Security. Anyway, Bobby Jeter and me cut school to go fishin' … near the ford at Long Creek not far from here. Didn't have a bridge back then … built one the next year. Back then you had to go a mile to a bridge, but it was so shallow at the ford you could drive across.

"We heard a car coming … and ran to hide. It pulled up on one bank. A minute later, three or four men rode up on horses on the opposite side. They didn't cross the creek. Waited on the top side. We hunkered down. Heard 'em talkin' but couldn't … make out what they said. Before long, we hear some whistling … clopping along the road. John Riggins. His mule started acting up … 'cause of the crowd waiting, I reckon. I 'member Riggins calmin' it down … just 'fore they came into the open. Riggins stopped when he saw the men. He bent down and talked in the mule's ear. We were so close I heard him say, 'We gonna let these men pass.' He backed his mule … and pulled it to the side. He was close to us … where we was hidin'."

Charlie gazed into the man's clouded eyes. Patterson broke contact and looked out the dirty kitchen window. "There was four men in the car. The men on horses … splashed across and the others got out of the car … the little fella with a face like the devil was one of 'em. He got out and waded across … splashing water. Ike Cutchins, wavin' his arms. Riggins looked at him and said, 'What you want, Ike?' I never talked to the man … but everybody knew him, he was the only colored man … left in the county. Deep booming voice. I could tell he didn't respect Cutchins. … I bet Cutchins' veins was bulging … to be talked to … that way by a … well, you know how it was back then." Patterson shook his head. "It's the lowlifes … always wanna be called sir. Don't get me started … on Ike Cutchins. I ain't got the breath for it."

He asked for a drink. Charlie couldn't find a clean glass so he washed one. He filled it from a leaky kitchen faucet that spurted airy water and waited for the man to collect himself. The interview was taking a tremendous toll on him. Patterson took a few sips, then continued.

"'You know why I'm here,' Ike says. Riggins says he don't. 'Tell 'em what you did to my woman!' Ike shouts." Patterson coughed. "Riggins says … he didn't do nothing. Ike goes into a rage, like a little demon. Stomping up and down, shoutin', 'You a liar. You was, you was!'

"As soon as he says that, he pulls a pistol … out of his waistband. Shoots the mule in the head. It flops over … thrashin' around. The other men yell at him … for not getting a clean shot. He always was a lousy shot. My dad said when he'd go out hunting … he'd as likely shoot out … the neighbor's window … as bag a rabbit. Riggins is stuck under the mule. Ike laughs. 'Who's the big man now?' Riggins doesn't say anything. Cutchins kicks him." Patterson paused for another drink of water and wiped away some moisture from his eye. He started coughing again and pulled out his bloody wet handkerchief. "I need a Kleenex."

After a minute's search, Charlie found a box of tissues in the living room. Patterson hacked weakly and this time wadded up the tissue without looking to see what landed in it. A few moments passed before he continued. "Riggins wiggles his way out … from under the mule while Cutchins jaws at him. Somebody with a shotgun … Tom Dempsey … puts the mule out of its misery. Tom turns to Cutchins … says, 'Get it over with.' But Cutchins ain't through. Says 'Beg for your life, nigger!' Riggins says … 'Go on.' Cutchins screams, 'I wanna hear you beg for your life, nigger!' And Riggins, say what you will, he was a man."

Patterson choked up and tears welled in his eyes. "He say, 'I'm not gonna beg for something I got a right to. You can't give me life. You can just take it away.' 'Then I'll take it away,' Cutchins says. Riggins knew he was a dead man. No point in being a pussy about it. He wasn't givin' Cutchins no satisfaction. He tries to stand up … Cutchins pistol whips him. Riggins a big man. Strong. He just keeps gettin' up … towers over Cutchins, who's pointing the gun at him. He grabs the gun. They fight over it. Cutchins is cussing. Riggins says, 'You ain't … gonna be the one to kill me.' That's the last … thing he said. Tom Dempsey runs up … clubs him from behind with the shotgun butt. Riggins staggers backward … lets go of the gun. Cutchins shoots him in the gut."

Patterson stopped talking and gasped for breath. Charlie pushed the glass of water toward him, but Patterson shook his head and held up his hand to signal for time.

Charlie listened to him wheeze, accompanied by the ticking of a clock and birds singing outside. After a couple of minutes, the old man continued:

"Riggins don't go down at first. He wobbles on his legs for a minute … then drops to his knees. Cutchins laughs and says, 'Looks like I am the one to kill you!' Then Cutchins shoots him in the face … two or three times. Riggins falls over. My buddy pisses himself … and runs away, making a racket in the underbrush. The men hear him. They run after him and catch him … but they don't see me. He don't tell 'em about me. They drag him … over to Riggins … and Cutchins orders him to shoot the body. He didn't want to … but they tell him, 'You're one of us now.' Bobby's cryin'."

Patterson's voice broke again and he sobbed. "Cutchins is a sick bastard. You put that down."

Charlie nodded grimly as he jotted on his pad.

"Bobby told me years later … he had a thousand nightmares about it. I told him … the man was dead already. What they did was bad wrong. Murder. But it was even worse, makin' … a child be part of it. I know … now … we was all a part of it. It wasn't just a thing that happened. We all had to own it. It wasn't just a thing."

Another pause. Patterson drummed the table. "What Cutchins does next … he pulls down his pants and pisses on Riggins. Laughin'. He says, 'I ain't even started yet.' Then he runs to the car and gets some gasoline … kerosene … coal oil or something. Douses the body and somebody else … Joshua Logan—"

"Really."

"—he gets some rope and throws it over a tree and makes a loop. 'Cause I guess you got to have a hangin', even though it makes no sense. One of the men rides off on horseback … takes Bobby with him. And they haul the corpse across the creek. Logan puts the rope around Riggins' neck. A bunch of them pull him up and Cutchins lights him … and Riggins hangs there burning."

Charlie broke in: "Were you still hiding? What were you thinking?"

"I was still in the brush … I thought they were going to kill Bobby. Afraid they'd kill me."

"Why?"

"Because I thought they were … in league with the devil. They mighta been. They didn't … care about nobody. But the devil … don't take you … where you don't want to go."

Charlie didn't want to dwell on that statement right then.

"Did you ever talk to anyone about this?"

"Other than Bobby and my niece, not till today. I figgered it wouldn't do no good. But now … I got nothin to lose." Patterson took a sip of water. "They left Riggins hangin' … took a picture."

Charlie pulled out the photograph. "Can you identify these people?"

"Yeah," the old man said with disgust. "That's Ike Cutchins, lookin' like ... he caught hisself a fish." Patterson sneered as he pointed. "He's the only one ... still alive."

Patterson named the other men in Cutchins's mob: Joshua Logan, then fifteen years younger than the dying man Charlie had dreamed about; Tom Dempsey; Bob Parkhurst; Hank Suches; Tom Montgomery. Eight men in all, six in the picture, most of them clad in overalls and dungarees. Charlie struggled to contain his excitement as he wrote down the names, especially Montgomery—Cecil's father and Joshua Logan's brother-in-law. (Charlie had figured out that both Logan and Montgomery were Lillian Scott's great-uncles.)

The seventh man, who owned the car and had enough sense not to pose at a crime scene, was named Carswell; he'd been the photographer. Patterson's mention of that name caused Charlie's eyes to light up and his heart to beat even faster. The Carswells had practically run Forsyth County back in 1912 and for many years before and since. Plus Bernie Dent and Thomas Oscar had been executed on Carswell land. "I forget his first name," Patterson said. "But it won't be hard to find. He was mayor of Cumming ... during World War II."

"What about the man who rode off with Bobby Jeter?"

"That was Bill Roark. He was Bobby's next-door neighbor."

Charlie listened to the birds outside for a moment, hoping in vain that Patterson could use the time to catch his breath. "Murder by lynching," Charlie muttered. It had been a cold-blooded killing in broad daylight on a pretext so flimsy it was only worth mentioning due to its perverse irony. "What was it that Ike Cutchins claimed Riggins did to his wife? Was he trying to claim there was a rape?"

Patterson snorted in disgust. "There was a rape all right. Not the way he claimed."

Charlie's heart skipped a beat. "What do you mean?"

"Well ... I didn't see this myself. Bobby told me a few years later. I asked him how come Ike Cutchins ... ended up with John Riggins' farm. He said Parkhurst told him ... Ike Cutchins went to Riggins' house ... later that day and told Riggins' woman to leave ... Forsyth County or he'd kill her, too. And then he ... made her sign somethin'. But he wasn't through. Then he ... had his way with her. That's what Bobby told me."

"Oh my God." Charlie's head throbbed. This was too much.

"Then that posse of his ... run her outta town next day ... burned her house down. I was just a kid," Patterson said. "Nuthin' I could do."

"Nobody did anything back then."

"Everybody wondered why … they even bothered livin' here when they was the only ones for years in either direction." Patterson paused to catch his breath, then continued. "More recent … in the 1960s. The civil rights movement. I remember hearin' Cutchins brag … about the good ol' days and killin' niggers. But he kept his mouth shut … about the specifics. What he did was cold-blooded murder. And what he did after was worse … you ask me. I hear he's gonna sell the land for a ton of money. Special place in hell waitin' for him. Maybe … he made a deal with the devil already. That's all I know." He took a long pause, then said, "I'm tired a talkin'."

Charlie let out a deep breath and slumped in his chair. Both men were quiet for a moment. Charlie thought, *Damn, I got it.* "Thank you." he told the old man. "This was important, what you told me. People need to know."

"Well … we made a deal. And I ain't eaten in a day. So go get me … them eggs and grits. Cup a coffee. Sugar. Cream. Pack of Camel straights."

This was the best deal Charlie had ever made. "I'm on it," he said, then stood up and wiped sweaty palms on his pants. Before Patterson could protest, Charlie pulled out a small camera and took a snapshot of Patterson's age-lined face, then grabbed his things and hustled out the door.

It took awhile to find a Pancake Hut, and almost as long to get service. He just had incredibly bad karma when it came to that restaurant chain. He was gone for more than an hour, and when he came back with the food, he saw an ambulance and a car beside the house. He passed by the driveway and turned around a minute later. He returned in time to see a black car pull off the road onto the shoulder right where Patterson said one had been parked the day before. Charlie would have liked to check in on the old man, but he knew it was best to keep moving. He'd forgotten the Camels, anyway. He also had the feeling that Danny Patterson was about to leave the house for the last time, poor guy. At least he'd gotten that terrible secret off his chest. Charlie owed him a moment of silent remembrance—when he had a spare moment, that is.

Charlie stopped at a park in Cumming and ate the food he'd bought for the dying man. The egg yolk and grits ran together on the Styrofoam plate. He stirred the mess around, sopped it up with buttered toast, and sipped lukewarm coffee. While he ate, Charlie listened to the recording of Patterson's faltering voice telling the tale in both past and present, an acknowledgment that, to those who remember, what *was, is.* And then Charlie realized he had not told Patterson his name. All in all, he felt luckier than he did sad, like he'd cheated death somehow—or at the very least, eaten its lunch.

Chapter Thirteen

By the time he read Danny Patterson's funeral notice in the next morning's paper and finally observed that promised moment of silence, Charlie had already typed a transcript of the conversation, made copies of the audio file, and stashed spares in his safe deposit box. The death notice stated that Patterson died of a lengthy illness, but Charlie's mourning turned to concern for his own safety when he considered the possibility that his eyewitness had fallen prey to Black Car Syndrome. The more he thought about it, the more he believed the man had been a victim of foul play, not nasty habit.

After all, Forsyth folk had a history of violence, and so did the Cutchinses: death threats on July Fourth, Momo's general behavior, courthouse arson, John Riggins, a thousand blacks fleeing Forsyth for their lives (surely Pappy's father had scared a few out of town). Plus, there had already been a burglary, and Charlie figured that when the evildoers found out that they'd missed the thing they sought, they would return.

So he set up a firewall by hiding his files and papers. If anyone searched Bayard Terrace in his absence, they'd find only the manuscript for *Thoracic Park*, his unpublishable novel about evil heart surgeons—but nothing concerning his current project, unless they walked in on him or ambushed him in his van. And then … well, publish or perish, that *was* the deal, wasn't it?

Minerva called Charlie that afternoon and said she'd found another of her father's journals while cleaning a bookcase. Then she started talking about Takira. "That girl is going to be the death of me. She's keeping the baby. I tell her having it is good but keeping it isn't, not at her age. Her family doesn't have insurance, so I'll be paying a lot of the bills and the delivery will be at Grady Hospital. Demetrious came by and told her to get rid of it. He said if she doesn't, he will. He got her all upset, so I told him to leave. He gets this *attitude*, but I encourage him to stay around—when he behaves, that is. I don't want to give him an excuse to leave Takira and abandon the baby."

Too much information. Charlie shifted uncomfortably in his office chair. When she paused to take a breath, he asked, "When can I come by and look at the journal?"

"Tomorrow, if you want. How's the book coming?"

"Fine."

"Do you know who killed my father?"

"Can't say just yet."

A moment's silence. "Can't say, or won't?"

"I still have some people to talk to."

"I see. You'll tell me as soon as you can."

"When I've got it nailed down, I promise."

Truth was, Charlie was troubled by his newfound knowledge and didn't know what to say to Minerva. She'd said she was born nine months after her father died, and now he had information that Pappy had raped her mother. He was afraid of where this was taking him and dreaded the prospect of telling her it was *her father* who had done the killing and stealing. He also might need her help to prove this terrible fact. It was all twisted and ironic, the stuff that migraines are made of.

But there were other things to talk about. "Your father's body was never recovered, is that correct?"

"Jasper said there was a memorial service, but there's no grave. They had a white man go up there to find out what happened, but no one would say anything. My mother was run out of the county, and the house was burned. But we never got him back."

"OK. Well, I've got work to do. I'll see you tomorrow."

"Tell me what you can, when you can."

Charlie hung up. For the next few hours, he sat at Talton's desk, writing the death scene. John Riggins had been murdered by a mob that made it look like a lynching—as if that somehow justified the killing. He ended the chapter with the body hanging from the tree. He hated the thought of Riggins rotting in the sun, but he feared the brave man's body had been left for crows to eat. A thought burned in his mind: *Perhaps it's my job to find him.*

* * *

Charlie arrived at Minerva's house shortly after 9:00 a.m. They briefly danced around the issue of the identity of John Riggins's killers, but Charlie wasn't ready to tell her everything—only that more than one person had been involved.

Minerva looked him in the eye sand said, "It was a mob, wasn't it?"

"Yes. I can tell you that much."

"Do you have names?"

"Yes. Nothing I can share yet."

"Nothing you can share," she said with a note of disdain.

Minerva made coffee and gave him a cup, muttering about how she wasn't sure he deserved it, but she wasn't going to be inhospitable. Then she left him to work while she read a magazine. Riggins's journal—which he'd been filling in at the time of his death—was great stuff. Although no poet, the murder victim had been bright and eloquent, in a way. His college grades showed Riggins had been more interested in math than literature, but he also had a sense of history. A practical man, he kept close track of his money and was determined to succeed. "Silence is best," he wrote after enduring catcalls in Cumming on Saturday, April 26, 1936. "Although they want me to grin at their foolish jokes and laugh at myself, I hold my peace and move on, careful not to step on any toes or gaze too long at any white women."

Riggins clearly had not suffered Isaac Cutchins gladly. He mentioned his nemesis several times, always in relation to a conflict: "Cutchins is abrasive and confrontational, though cowardly when push comes to shove. He is a fool, but a dangerous fool. Usually, when he does anything, he makes sure he has backing." This entry had come three months before Cutchins assembled the lynch mob.

The day before he died, Riggins made his last entry, writing late at night during the harvest season: "Lettie works hard in the corn field. Jasper, fearful of white men, refuses to come up from Atlanta to help. I told my wife this evening that I love her, something I sometimes forget to do." Charlie hoped Minerva had been conceived that night, but Riggins, a gentleman, kept such details to himself. Charlie was copying this passage when a key turned and the door swung open.

In swaggered Demetrious Jackson, five-foot-six and rail-thin.

"Hey, Gee-ma!" he called out cheerfully, then did a double-take when Charlie rose to greet him. The grin returned. "You the writah!"

"Yes," Charlie said as he offered his hand.

Demetrious regarded it with amusement. "Old school," he said, and shook it. "I'm a writah, too. I write rap songs. Little bit a' dis, little bit a' dat, know what I mean?"

"Why aren't you in school?" Minerva asked.

"Out early today," Demetrious mumbled. "Bomb threat or somethin'. I'm hungry."

"You eat some lunch and get back there, you hear me?"

Demetrious went into the kitchen. Minerva shook her head and told Charlie, "I hope he's not in trouble again. Last grade report had all F's. I gave him a desk to study at, but it doesn't do him any good if he's not here."

"She thinks I should work at Mickey D's!" Demetrious shouted from the kitchen.

"I never said that. I want you to finish school so you can get a good job. But working at McDonald's would be better than what you're doing now."

"You mean eating your food," the teenager responded.

"Eating my food's fine. I mean cutting school and staying out all night, hanging out with hoods like that one with the handkerchief on his head, that—"

"P-Dog," Demetrious said, returning with a turkey sandwich and orange juice. "And it's called a doo-rag."

"They arrested one of the boys he runs with for robbing a convenience store," Minerva said.

Demetrious shrugged. "He stupid. I don't hang with him no more."

"That's good, since he's in jail."

The teenager ate his sandwich in quick bites, washing the food down with juice.

"Have you talked to Takira lately?" After she didn't get a response, Minerva said, "You need to look after her. She's carrying your baby."

"I don't know that. We been through this. If it was mine, I say get rid of it."

"Don't talk that way." She flipped on the TV and turned her attention to the noon news.

"Where do you go to school?" Charlie asked.

Demetrious ignored the question. "What about you, Book Man? I heard what you doin'. How much you payin' us for our story? You make a movie 'bout somebody, you gotta pay 'em." He nodded solemnly. "I know that's right."

"I'm not making a movie. I'm writing a book."

"Well, my name in it, I need to get some green, ya know what I'm sayin'?"

"I hear ya," said Charlie.

"You be thinkin' about it." Demetrious emptied his glass and sauntered out the door, slamming it behind him, leaving his dishes for someone else to clean. Minerva opened her mouth to say something, then closed it and shook her head.

An hour later, Charlie left. As he unlocked the van, Demetrious popped out from between two cars down the street. "Yo, Book Man. Wait up."

Charlie placed his laptop and scanner on the floor behind the passenger seat and slammed the door shut. "What?"

"It's about my baby momma." Demetrious was standing close now. He rubbed his chin thoughtfully. "I need some money."

"Don't we all."

"I'm Gee-Ma's business agent," he declared.

Charlie laughed. "After the episode with the power bill, I doubt she wants you to represent her."

"I invested it, man. To make a rap CD." He shrugged. "Didn't work out. But that's done. I want to talk about what's goin' on now. How much you get for writing the book?"

"Nothing so far. And there's no guarantee it will get published or that I'll get anything."

The teen looked at Charlie like he was stupid. "I hear you sold a book. What you get for it?"

"The one that's finished? About minimum wage so far, and it's all gone."

"This book make you a lotta money."

Charlie chuckled and shook his head. "Not necessarily. Most books aren't bestsellers."

"Well, this be a good movie. Make a lotta coin."

"I wish."

"I need money, man," Demetrious said, adopting a wheedling tone. "Two large to take care of my woman."

Charlie decided to take him literally. "You're never too big to take care of your woman."

Demetrious laughed. "I see what you sayin'. I mean two gees."

"I'd advise you to stay in school and get a part-time job."

"Everybody wants to put me in a McJob, man. I ain't gonna be a sucka. I need to pay for an abortion, so I need money quick. I figure if you give it to me, at least that's honest. Takira too young to have a baby. Best for Gee-Ma, too. You know that."

"I can't be part of this."

"Can't, or doan wanna be?"

"Take your pick."

"Doan tell me you never."

"You put yourself in an adult situation. Time to act the part." Charlie got in the van and started the engine.

What happened next startled Charlie. Demetrious pounded the window and shouted, "You steal my family story to make money! If you want my hep, it's gonna cost! Hell, just don't come 'round no mo! This my house!"

Charlie drove off, leaving the boy standing in the street—small, alone, and angry.

* * *

Isaac Cutchins's parents had come to Forsyth County from Pulaski, Tennessee. This Charlie knew because Susan's Bible told him so, and being a border-state Yankee, Charlie never forgot it, since Pulaski was the birthplace of the original Ku Klux Klan—the terrorist arm of the Southern Democratic Party during Reconstruction. When Charlie thought of Momo's monster truck, *Nathan Bedford Forrest*, he realized that it was only fitting that Pappy's trail would lead back to that town.

In an attempt to find out more about the family's roots, Charlie searched the Internet for genealogical background data, hoping to find dirt on the cheap. No dice: The Net would have nothing to do with the varmints. Therefore, duty called for a pilgrimage to the Tennessee town—Pulaskipalooza, Charlie dubbed the trip. Angela would cover for one night with Kathleen, and Susan agreed to pick up the kids from school that day, even though he wouldn't tell her what he was up to.

Well before dawn on that crisp October day, Charlie departed Bayard Terrace for the four-hour drive with two peanut butter sandwiches and a Thermos full of coffee. The moon was a waning crescent when he passed through Chattanooga, switching from I-75 to I-24 for the trek across southern Tennessee.

Charlie pulled into Pulaski with the morning sun at his back. He parked near the Giles County Courthouse. The Beaux Arts structure, built in 1909 to replace its burned-out predecessor, was garishly beautiful, with large columns on the front portico and smaller ones supporting an oversized dome. Bleary-eyed and road-weary, Charlie saw it as a hungry Chinese dragon preparing to eat the town. When he stepped out of the van, the smell of sulfur hung heavy in the air.

He walked past the statue of Count Casimir Pulaski and went inside to the records room. He found some old deed books containing relevant information and took notes on land ownership by Cutchinses in Giles County after the Civil War. The trail disappeared after 1907, when the antebellum courthouse was destroyed by fire. *Hmm.* He tapped the tabletop with his fingers. There had to be more. He trudged out of the courthouse into the bright sunlight, squinting and shielding his eyes with his hand, then waving off the stinkpit odor that permeated the town. It smelled ... like hell. Or maybe he was crazy.

His next stop was Pulaski's one-story gray stone library, which looked like a sawed-off federal office building. When he entered its special collections room, an older woman wearing a blue floral print dress looked up from her book and frowned at him over her trifocals. Charlie stood before the local histories and found an authoritative-looking work, *The Big Book of Giles County History* by William Conger, published in 1939. Thurwood would have envied the 1,000-page tome. Charlie turned to the index and found four marvelously dreadful entries under the Cutchins name:

> *Cutchins, Lemuel, Shot by commanding officer for cowardice, 234;*
> *Cutchins, Render, Received letters of dismissal from First Baptist Church 301—303;*
> *Cutchins, Samuel, Talbot, et al., Ordered to leave Giles County, 323—324*; and
> *Cutchins, Talbot, Tried in absentia for Giles County Courthouse fire, 324.*

Charlie hooted at this mother lode of varmintry. The woman gave him the evil eye. "Sorry," he muttered. He turned to page 234 and read as he stumbled to the table next to her spread-out genealogy books:

> Lemuel Cutchins, born in 1839, joined the Tennessee Militia, a fighting unit of the Confederate States of America. A chronic deserter, Cutchins received a bullet in his backside from his commanding officer, Capt. Wilson Johns, an excellent shot and first-rate horseman, on August 14, 1864, while running away from a skirmish with Union foragers near Sandy Creek. This was the third time Cutchins had shown cowardice, and he was listed as deserting under fire.
>
> Lemuel disappeared and later returned to Giles County amid widespread and well-deserved enmity from neighbors, since, in addition to being a known coward, he was rumored to have been a highwayman in Kentucky. Reportedly, he used his ill-gotten gains as a robber to purchase a homestead in Giles.

Charlie turned to page 301 and learned, to his shock, horror (and delight), that Render, son of Lemuel, had been

> … found guilty of gross immorality by the First Baptist Church's board of deacons in 1895 for having engaged in a practice too loathsome to mention. Following his expulsion from the church, Render Cutchins was believed to have tried to make a fresh start with his three wives, a male cousin, and several beleaguered and degraded sheep in Utah, where such perversion might be deemed permissible. Render Cutchins and his ilk will have to answer to a higher power than the Mormon Church when their wretched days on earth are done.

These entries were all the more scandalous coming as they did in an otherwise dry, pedestrian book that consisted mainly of lists of names and histories of gristmills. Indeed, Conger failed to mention Pulaski's glorious role in the birth of the Klan—an exclusion that in and of itself spoke volumes about Southern history. Charlie wondered if any Cutchinses had belonged to the original Klan. (However, he suspected that the varmints didn't meet that organization's standards. Bradley Roy had told him that Momo tried to join the Klan in 1987, but his dues check bounced.) In any case, the Cutchinses' outrageous behavior awoke the prose stylist in Conger, who railed against those miscreants in righteous indignation.

Charlie became engrossed in the transcription of the minutes of the meeting at which Render Cutchins was cast out of the local church. There were smudges all over the page, while most others in the book remained pristine. One subsequent summary passage was especially well-read:

> The banishment of Cutchinses from the county was tied to Render's expulsion from First Baptist Church, although they did not leave all at once. While Render took his leave of Giles, family members who remained took offense at his "ill treatment," and there was a war between them and their neighbors involving arson and livestock killings lasting several years. The conflict culminated in the jailing of Lemuel's brothers, Samuel and Talbot, and two of their sons for burning down the First Baptist Church. The men would escape confinement before trial, however. After that, their families

> were driven from Giles at gunpoint. For several months, the valiant men of Giles remained on alert to prevent any of the Cutchins clan from sneaking back into Giles to cause more destruction and mischief. Their vigilance proved insufficient, however. According to the trial record, Talbot Cutchins evaded the patrols and set fire to the Giles County Courthouse, then disappeared. He was tried in absentia and found guilty of arson in the first degree. His whereabouts remain unknown to this day.

Charlie rejoiced as he fired up his laptop and typed in these Tennessee tales of varmintry.

After finishing *The Big Book*, Charlie looked through *Geography and Geology of Giles County* so he could place the horrible melodrama in its proper setting—the Land of Milk and Honey, as Giles was nicknamed. After a couple of hours of work, Charlie took a break.

On a librarian's recommendation, Charlie drove to Goodspeed's Diner for lunch. He took a seat at the counter and ordered meatloaf, mashed potatoes, green beans, fresh baked rolls, and sweet tea. The waitress assured him that Pulaski had nothing to do with the Klan anymore and that blacks and whites there got along "right nicely." She didn't know what Charlie was talking about when he mentioned the sulfur-smell he noticed everywhere he went in town. After Charlie paid his check and stepped outside, the smell seemed even stronger than before—almost overpowering, in fact.

He returned to the library and scoured bookshelves for more dirt. From *Giles County Marriages and Births: 1866—1910*, he learned that the Cutchins family's sexual habits included not just polygamy (and something unspeakable with that male cousin and the sheep), but also incest.

Silas Cutchins—brother of Lemuel, the Confederate deserter—had escaped mention in Conger's book but appeared twice in *Marriages*.

First, he married Elizabeth Dranger in 1875.

They begat Jeremiah Cutchins in 1880.

In 1878, Silas married Tess Smith.

In 1880, Silas and Elizabeth Dranger begat Lucretia.

"*Awk-ward,*" Charlie sang as he wrote down this last morsel of information.

But there were more complicated arrangements than simple bigamy. Local genealogists had added helpful handwritten notes in the margins to keep track of the comings of Cutchinses: "Silas and Tess had a daughter named

Annie Smith Cutchins in 1881—Jeremiah's half-sister"; and "In 1905, Jeremiah married an Annie Smith—but her married name should have been Annie Smith Cutchins Cutchins. They begat Carl Cutchins four months after the wedding."

From Susan's Bible, Charlie knew Jeremiah Cutchins had moved to Forsyth County, Georgia in 1906. He also knew that Gram's maiden name was Henshaw. According to *Marriages*, the Henshaws were the unbanished branch of the Cutchins family. Charlie felt nauseous when he recalled Evangeline's boast that Pappy "went back to Tennessee to marry a hometown girl."

Clearly, the story had turned ugly—not that it was pretty to begin with. Charlie knew he was treading on dangerous ground. Best if he just stopped there. Actually, he wished he'd stopped sooner, before finding out that the apples on this family tree had hideous worms writhing in them. It was all so obvious: Recessive genes had risen to the top of this bubbling, maggoty stew. "Cutchins blood is thicker than thick and likes of itself way too much," Charlie wrote in his notes.

He shuddered when he realized this family curse had poisoned his own children. Thankfully, he'd been there to chlorinate the gene pool—but had it been enough? And why did the Cutchinses resent other people swimming in it? From his own experience, he knew that the varmints regarded in-laws as outsiders, barely tolerated and often resented. He was beginning to think that these people would support gay marriage, but only between cousins.

Confounded by the burden of Cutchins history, Charlie stumbled out of the library just before closing time. Declaring his work in Pulaski done, he drove out of town both horrified and enlightened, glad he wasn't going to spend the night smelling Satan's spew, for he was now convinced the town had been built over the mouth of hell.

He worried that this was some kind of Abrahamic setup: a test of how far he was willing to go or what he would be willing to do. It came back to that essential question: Who or what did he work for, really? He'd once believed he was working the back end of an Old Testament deal—either as a scourge of God or as a debt collector for a fallen angel. Either way, it was a relatively simple, straightforward arrangement. But now the blood-soaked contract was forcing him to turn on his own family and defame his wife and kids. Unfortunately, Charlie couldn't march into war with the deity he wanted; he was forced to go into war with the deity he had.

That night, Charlie stayed in a Chattanooga motel room and, with great and grim resolve, wrote the Pulaski chapter without pulling any genetic punches, even making a fleeting (if not bleating) reference to those unfortunate sheep. He thought of his mother-in-law's poor impulse control, close-set beady eyes that crossed when she got angry, and her addiction-to-bling magpie personality. Militant inbreeding explained so much. Even Beck's 911 call made sense now. *The hellish varmint gene is transmitted by the women. Pass it on.*

* * *

This nightmare of a book had to end soon, one way or another. Paranoia had set in and constant fear was fraying Charlie's nerves. Shadows caused him to jump. When he went outside, he looked over his shoulder for black cars and monster trucks. The sooner he went public, the better, but he wasn't ready to do so just yet. Puzzle pieces were missing. He was able to fill in some gaps by conducting research at the Cumming library on Lillian Scott's off days. When he put all the pieces together, he would confront Pappy with his findings.

On Halloween, Charlie got a phone call from the mystery woman—that is, the secretary of the Forsyth County Planning Commission's executive director, although he would continue to pretend he didn't know who she was. "Trick or Treat," she said. "I hope you talked to Danny Patterson before he passed."

Trust no one. "Oh," he said. "I meant to do that. Are you saying it's too late?"

Her voice turned shrill. "I said you didn't have time, and he died the day after I talked to you."

Charlie groaned. "I *knew* I should have gone out to see him. Shoot."

"He's the only one I know of that could tell you about it. That would, anyway." He could see her slumping in her chair, her hopes of vengeance thwarted. "Hope you can find out somehow."

He sighed. "Not sure I can go ahead with the project now. Maybe I should hang it up."

"No. Don't do that. There is somebody you could talk to, but I'm not sure she knows about the killing."

"Who's that?"

"The missing Cutchins."

That was a bolt from the blue. "Are you talking about Shirley? I don't know how to reach her."

"Now her name is Cartier. Arlene Cartier." She pronounced it "Cart-ee-er."

"Arlene?" That didn't make sense. "Is she married?"

"Doubt it. Changed it legally. Didn't want to be a Cutchins. Can you blame her?"

"No. How do you know this?"

"I worked with her in a restaurant in Kennesaw back in the 1980s. She got drunk one night and told me a lot more about her family than anyone would ever want to know."

"You seen her lately?"

"A year ago. She was living in a trailer park near Kennesaw named Shady something. She keeps moving. Maybe she's still there. Go see for yourself."

"I will. Keep in touch."

"I got your number."

"You're not the only one."

* * *

On November 2, Charlie drove to Kennesaw with some burning questions to ask Arlene Cartier about her days as Shirley Cutchins. He hadn't found an address or phone number for either person, so he followed his only lead. Regretting his failure to capture Danny Patterson's account on video, this time he took a tripod and camcorder borrowed from Thornbriar while Susan wasn't looking.

North of Marietta but still part of Atlanta's suburban sprawl, Kennesaw had achieved notoriety in the 1980s for legally requiring residents to own guns. Charlie wondered if that's why the missing Cutchins had moved there—to become part of an armed camp. He exited I-75 and took Old Highway 41 north toward Lake Allatoona until he reached Shady Haven Trailer Park. Just before noon, he stopped by the office, also a mobile home. The frowsy middle-aged blonde who answered the door told him to look for an old trailer near the Dumpsters. She closed the door before Charlie could ask her where those were. He sniffed, but the cool breeze gave no clues.

Charlie drove along the perimeter gravel drive until he saw the trash bins, and beside them, a ramshackle little trailer on the smallest lot in the park. It shared the tiny triangular space (which seemed to be an afterthought) with a battered old white Toyota, some spindly young pines, and utility feeds. He skidded to a stop on the gravel and opened the door. He slammed it as gray dust and the sour smell of garbage drifted toward the van.

The trailer was nothing more than a camper, easily towed by a pickup truck—not that anyone would want to take it anywhere. It looked like it had come there to die. Ancient and round, with a porthole window near the rear, it was painted primer gray and sported copious amounts of rust around rivets and along seams. Two bent poles held up a faded and tattered green awning.

A flower bed was filled with the dried husks of weeds, candy wrappers, and plastic grocery bags.

He carried his camcorder and tripod to the door, banging on it twice with his elbow before a gruff, raspy voice cried out, "Hold on, I'm acomin'."

The door opened. The first thing Charlie noticed was the gun, a big, Dirty Harry-looking automatic. "And I know how to use it," the woman said by way of introduction. Cigarette smoke seeped out of the door from behind her. He set down the camcorder case, rubbed his eyes and blinked. The woman looked so much like Pappy he thought for a second he'd walked into a trap. Courtesy and a sense of self-preservation would keep him from mentioning the resemblance, however. Although she wasn't aiming at him, she seemed a bit twitchy. Her arms were folded across her chest, and the gun was pointing haphazardly toward the crows in a pine tree by the fence. With a moment to adjust, he saw differences: She was shorter than Pappy and had ear-length, imperfectly chopped, greasy black-gray hair. Like her father, she wore blue jeans and a work shirt.

"I'm Charles Sherman. Are you Arlene Cartier?" He pronounced her last name like the jeweler's.

"You here for the lawsuit?" He gave her a blank look. "The blow-dryer that caught on fire. I called that eight hundred number on the TV and left a message. I figured Chad Armstrong would take my case. You don't work for him?"

"No, I'm a writer."

"So this ain't about the dryer." Her weary tone suggested disappointment came often. "What's it about, then?"

"I'm working on a history book."

"A history book." This seemed to make as much sense to her as the blow-dryer lawsuit did to him.

"About Forsyth County. I heard you were from there." She conceded nothing, so he continued. "I'm doing a story about a man named Cutchins."

Silence followed, but Charlie was determined to wait for an answer. Eventually, the woman spoke: "I used to have that name, but I got rid of it and do not care to hear it anymore, thank you." Her formal twang was unmistakably familiar.

"I thought you could give me some background on your father."

"Don't call him that." She looked like she regretted not shooting him to begin with.

"The son of a bitch, then."

"That's better."

"May I come in?" He started up the rickety wooden step to the door and stopped, watching her gun hand. The rank smell of countless cigarette butts assaulted him; this was like stepping into an ashtray. "Or we could sit outside."

"Too cold for that."

She stepped back from the door but didn't close it, so he walked in, bracing himself for a secondhand headache. She slipped the gun into a cabinet drawer in the trailer's micro-kitchen and sat down at a table, across from a thirteen-inch TV tuned to *Judge Maybelline Mayhew.*

She was a bit on the thin side, though slightly disproportioned, as if the load of her body had settled awkwardly on her frame. She sat with her legs bowed, knees wide apart. When she yawned, he saw that she was missing a few teeth—though not many, and not in front. She either had a palsy of some sort or was nervous; her left hand trembled slightly. Her cigarette hand was much steadier. "Charles Sherman," she said. "The name rings a bell."

She didn't object as he set up the camera in the cramped quarters, though if she was anything like her father she'd let him go through the trouble of doing the work before declaring, "I never said you could."

"We've never met, but for purposes of disclosure, I should tell you I married—"

"My youngest niece."

Younger, actually. That entire generation consisted of only three people (that he knew of): Sheila, Susan, and Momo. "Yes! How'd you know?"

"Wedding picture in the paper. You were a reporter or some such. You plucked her when she was young. Nowadays young, anyway."

"That was a long time ago. Were you at the wedding?"

"No, just saw the announcement." She nodded toward a discolored white album on a nearby shelf.

Charlie didn't know what to say. Apparently, she watched her family from a distance and only threatened relatives on special occasions, like funerals. He turned on the camera. "My wife said the only time she saw you was at the mall, but she didn't get to meet you."

"That's because I saw them first. I ain't got no use for her mother."

"Me neither." He gave her a sympathetic grimace. "I've got to admit I don't know much about you. No one likes to talk."

"I doubt they would. They ain't got nuthin' to be proud of."

"I've been learning a lot about Ike Cutchins, though."

"That he's the devil?" She snorted in contempt. "That's the only thing you need to know."

He looked one way, then the other, then right into her eyes. "I've seen evidence to that effect. And now I want to talk to you about it."

"What did you find out that made you wanna talk to me?"

"I was working on a book about what happened in Forsyth County in 1912, but then I stumbled across something else. I thought you might be able to help me with it." Her face went pallid. She lit a Salem, took a drag, and looked out the window toward the trailer park's fence and the shedding trees. Charlie continued. "It happened in 1937. Your father—"

"I told you, don't call him that. I don't have one."

"—killed a black man and stole his land."

"Go on."

Now Charlie had her full attention. He told her a few details of the crime and said Danny Patterson had lived just long enough to tell the tale.

"I remember Danny. He was several years older. He always avoided me. Now I reckon I know why."

When Charlie mentioned his suspicions about Minerva's lineage, she slapped both palms on the table. Staring into Charlie's eyes, she said, "Well, I give you credit. You told me something I didn't know. Not that I wanted to. I wasn't much more than a baby then, but I don't doubt for a second he did that. He hated black people worse than anybody else I ever knew. And there weren't any black people around, because of him and people like him. I'll bet that man Riggins worked harder and did better for himself and that devil couldn't tolerate it, because he can't stand to see other people do well. And especially not no black man. He was always filled with spite. Piss and vinegar." She returned her gaze to the window. After a moment, her eyes took on a bright, malevolent cast. "I stole it off a dead nigger," she crowed softly.

"Beg pardon?"

"That's what he told me once, when I asked him how he got the farm. I thought it was a joke. Thought he was just bein' ugly. Shows what I know." She stared into his eyes. "So nobody knows about this? But that's fixin' to change. Ha." She finished with more of a snort than a laugh.

Charlie nodded. "A lot of people knew, but nobody's talked about it. Seems like they're afraid."

"He's a monster. He ain't gonna die, not of natural causes. I thought about going up there and killing him myself. Still do, from time to time, when I'm bored and lookin' for somethin' to do."

Charlie laughed.

"Think I wouldn't? Well, I would."

He decided not to tell her about the pending land sale, lest he become an accomplice to murder. He glanced around at her pathetic little home, not knowing what to say. As if reading his mind, she said, "I never had a chance."

"I'm sorry. What do you mean?"

"You're writing a book about the bad he did. But you don't know everything."

"No ma'am, I don't. That's why I'm here. I heard you could shed some light—"

"You know about ! *this*?" She rolled up her sleeve to expose an ugly scar on her arm.

"No. *Ouch*." He squinched his face sympathetically. "What happened?"

"Punishment for tryin' to kill him," she said. She looked around and took a deep breath. "It was after the first time he raped me, when I was thirteen. I was the oldest, by two years. He waited till I … till … I came of age. I wanted to kill myself 'cause of what he done, but something in me had enough sense to say I wasn't the problem. So I snuck into his room that night with a butcher knife. Only she cried out. I froze. Then he woke up and grabbed my arm and hit me in the face. He dragged me out of the room and threatened to do it again right there. Only I knew he wouldn't because the others were around. I spit in his face and he slapped me, then pushed me back in the room with the others—there was just two rooms, so all the kids slept together. I remember lying on my mattress on the floor, thinkin' it ain't over, it ain't over. Sure enough, it wasn't. Next day, I was doing the ironing, alone—"

"Did your mother know that he'd molested you?"

"She was fine with what happened so long as it didn't happen to her. She just had her youngest and didn't want to be bothered. Now let me tell you. He grabbed the iron—it was one of those old ones you had to put on the stove to heat up—and pressed it on my arm. Says, 'You're mine now, you little bitch.' He branded me." Tears brimmed in her eyes. "And he said if I ever told anyone what was going on, he'd kill me. So I didn't."

"That's awful." Charlie reached toward her. She gave him a warning look, and he pulled back his hand.

"That was just the beginning. I wish I'd run, just run away back then. But I stayed. It went on for three years. Every week. He bought this car. Saturday afternoons he gave her some money to take the other three out for ice cream. I had to stay home. *To keep him company*." Her lip curled in disgust. "So I didn't get any ice cream. No, I got raped by that hillbilly. And they'd come back and she would always honk her horn as she drove up, give him time to pull up his britches."

Charlie's head reeled as he tried to figure out how the family dynamic had functioned. Or dysfunctioned. Gram, Pappy's wife/cousin/sister/whatever, was worn down from his hatred and abuse, as well as haggard from producing four babies. Tired of her, he'd turned to a younger, fresher version. What had kept him from treating his younger daughters the same way? Or had he? They both idolized Stanley. Perhaps their brother had protected his younger sisters, after allowing Shirley to be sacrificed to the devil. With this messed-up family, who knew?

"So you never told anyone? You never went to the law?"

"He was the law. People were afraid of him. And now you tell me he got away with murder." She shook her head. "Make a long story short, I got pregnant and ran off when I was sixteen. They didn't none of 'em come after me. Weren't no rescue, just good riddance."

"Was he—"

"Yes."

"The father? My God."

"God didn't have anything to do with it. And I wanted to get rid of it. I went to a black woman in Atlanta. I hadn't never seen a black person but in pictures up till then. Everything they taught me about 'em was wrong. She saved my life. Don't know what I would have done, having to carry a baby around. Probably starved myself to death, just to kill it, knowing whose it was. Whole family's that way. Can't keep their things in their pants around family. I bet you know that much."

It was true. He remembered how Momo and Stanley kissed Susan and Sheila on the lips when they hugged at family gatherings. *Cutchins blood loves itself.* The woman gave him a wicked smile. She sure knew how to look ugly when she wanted to. A family thing, Charlie supposed.

He silently cursed Pappy for getting away with all these terrible crimes as he thought about Lettie Riggins, rest her soul, as well as Shirley/Arlene, ruined, waiting to die in a little white ghetto while those proud of their Cutchins blood—fattened on ice cream—now stood to become rich.

She gave him a crooked smile. "Some family you married into, eh?"

"Yeah. But my marriage isn't working out."

"So now you know the deep dark secrets. Though with that crowd, there may be more." She chuckled drily. "You gone too far to stop now."

"I'm not sure I follow you."

"On your book. You better be careful. They don't take criticism too kindly. They went and put one of their own in the government to protect themselves."

"You talk like it's a conspiracy."

Again, the wicked smile. "It *is* a conspiracy. But you aim to bring it all down, right?"

"I aim to tell the truth, and if that brings him down, so be it."

She folded her arms across her chest. "You get the bastard. Get him good. That's what you need to do," she wheezed. "It's bigger than you know. I prayed for something like this to happen, that his own would do him in. I reckon you're close enough."

Charlie sat back in his chair and thought: *No. I can't be the answer to her prayers, too.* Surely they would be too dark, too damaged in transit, to make it through. Otherwise, Pappy would already be in hell.

"Don't tell him where I am." She stubbed out the third cigarette she'd smoked since his arrival. "He'll send somebody if he knows where I live."

"I won't."

"Promise. Blood oath."

"No problem on that," Charlie said.

In return for the promise, Charlie got as much dirt as an investigative reporter could hope for from one source—a cold, hard, gritty, and hateful firsthand account of life with Isaac Cutchins. He learned that after she'd run away, the high school dropout had worked in factories and restaurants, bouncing from job to job, never finding anyone to love, having grown tired of men before she ever had a chance to know a decent one, if he knew what she meant. And now she lived on Social Security.

As he loaded his equipment into the van, he remembered Evangeline talking about going out for ice cream every Saturday. It was her fondest childhood memory. Could he put it in the book? Hell, yes. Maybe he'd follow up and ask her if she'd known what was going on while she went out for happy time. He'd ask her: What flavor did Shirley always get? But first he'd talk to Pappy. That monster.

And there it was, his title: *American Monster.*

Chapter Fourteen

Charlie stepped out from the dungeon into the back yard and paused to bask in the afternoon sunshine, but his mood on this mid-November day was grim. A most unpleasant task lay ahead. He had finished the rest of his research, and it was time to ask Pappy a question: "Did you kill John Riggins, rape his wife, and steal their land?" Face to face, man to monster. Charlie had cleared his schedule for the confrontation. Beck and Ben were staying at friends' houses, and Susan would retrieve them. Kathleen would nap.

"Let's do this thing," Charlie muttered to himself as he marched to the van, slamming his right fist into his left palm. "The motherfucker isn't going to get away with it. Let's bring the pain." Not exactly a calming mantra, but it served his purpose, to get him moving in the direction he needed to go.

As he drove up Georgia 400, Charlie considered the other missing piece to the puzzle: how to prove that Minerva Riggins, lighter-skinned than either of her parents, was Pappy's daughter. He had enough to convince a neighborhood gossip, but not an all-white jury in Forsyth County—or a reputable publisher. Of course, neither Minerva nor Pappy would cooperate with him on DNA testing, which was what Charlie needed to build an airtight case and help Minerva reclaim her family's wealth. Reparations. That's what this was all about, wasn't it? That and to wreak vengeance upon the evildoers. Go Old Testament on their asses.

Joan Osborne's *One of Us* came on the radio, reminding Charlie of Trouble, riding on a bus that ferried the righteous away from danger and smote the wicked. Had Trouble been on that bus that ran down Angela's lawyer? And had Bethany Campbell deserved smiting? Maybe the Almighty's wrath was random, but whatever. *God is not mocked.* The idea that there was *any* kind of divine justice heartened him as he launched himself into this time of trial.

North of Cumming, Charlie exited the highway and drove by Coal Mountain. The surveyors were gone, but flags marked the right-of-way for the big road they planned. A half-mile away stood Stableford Farms, Phase II, Now Open! A forest of two-by-fours jutted from the ground. Eventually all the farms in the area would be gone, replaced by subdivisions and a megamall.

The pace seemed to be quickening, as if the devil and developers knew that time was running out. Well-connected builders were snatching up parcels of land every day, aided by state and local officials who insisted on literally paving the way for them by financing road improvements. Charlie was sure Stanley Cutchins had his dirty little hands in all of this. He'd devoted several pages of *American Monster* to the legislator's misdeeds. *So much to cover, so little time.*

He drove past Pappy's place without slowing, scouting it out. The only vehicle at the house was the old man's battered pale blue Chevy pickup. He made a U-turn and pulled into Pappy's semi-circular drive, his tires popping rocks and making it nearly impossible to take Ike Cutchins by surprise. With palms sweating, Charlie got out with his clipboard, which held the incriminating evidence. "Pappy!" he cried out heartily, attempting familiarity. He twisted his neck and adjusted the collar on his work shirt. Crows cawed in the distance. *Ours or theirs?*

His work boots crunched gravel as he walked toward the house. He checked his watch as he thunked onto the porch. The red wooden door was open and the sun shone through the screen, bleaching a patch of living-room carpet. Inside, an old table radio broadcast a low-watt AM fire-and-brimstone preacher from Ellijay, who was hollering eternal damnation at the top of his lungs.

As Charlie lifted his hand to knock, Pappy's voice came from a back room: "Come on in."

Although shocked by the invitation, Charlie opened the screen door and stepped inside.

"I left it on the coffee table!" the old man yelled. "Stanley said you need to get rid of it before that cocksucker finds out about it."

Charlie looked around the living room and saw a pint Mason jar filled with amber liquid on the spindle-legged coffee table. Something in it half floated, touching the bottom. At first he thought it was moonshine Mezcal. He stepped closer and saw it wasn't a worm.

"Shit," he said, stepping back when he realized what it was. A memento, just like they used to keep in the bad old days, a souvenir of a successful lynching. He considered grabbing the jar and running away with this great prize, his personal Rosetta Stone. Before he could act on this impulse, Pappy walked into the living room, rubbing his face with a towel.

"That asshole—"

He lowered the towel and looked straight at the aforementioned asshole. Pappy's mouth dropped open as he staggered backward two steps and clutched his chest with his right hand. Charlie thought the old man was going to drop dead, but Pappy's look of horror was quickly replaced by his natural expression of dyspepsia. "Get the hell outta my house," he said in an ominously quiet, clipped tone.

"Ah, but you just invited me in," Charlie said, forcing a smile.

"I sure as hell didn't know it was you."

Charlie gave a sidelong glance at the Mason jar. The black finger was crooked like a question mark. "Do you know why I'm here?"

"Ain't no reason for you to be. I told you to get off the property last time you was here."

That finger kept beckoning him. Charlie had to force himself to look away from it. "I'm glad your memory is so good," he said, "because I need to talk to you about something."

"I don't wanna talk to you. Ain't got nuthin' to say."

"Is that part of him?" Charlie pointed toward the jar.

"What the hell?" Pappy gave Charlie a one-eyed squint.

"That finger. Is that what's left of John Riggins?"

"Don't know who you talkin' about. And you're trespassin'. Get out."

"I know what happened."

"You don't know a damn thing."

"I have the photo of you with—"

"Photo don't prove nuthin'. Get the hell out or I'll shoot you."

Charlie looked around. The shotgun wasn't in sight, though he knew Pappy kept it handy, standing in a corner of the kitchen. Loaded.

He shoved the clipboard toward Pappy. On it was the lynching photo inside a transparent plastic report cover. Pappy glanced at it, then looked away. "That ain't me. You need to head on. After what you did to my granddaughter, I'm not worried about what you got to say, anyway. Nobody gonna believe you."

"What did I do?"

"You know what you did. A man like that shouldn't even walk this earth. You want money, is that it? You tryin' to blackmail me?" He grew more animated as he spoke, shifting his weight, casting a furtive glance toward the kitchen. Calculating time and distance, no doubt.

"No. No amount of money could keep me from telling the world about John Riggins."

"Ain't no one left to tell no tales. And you're a liar on top of bein' a wife-beater."

"That reminds me: Did you rape your oldest daughter?"

"Shut up, you bastard. I'll not have you talkin' that way in my—"

"I got a statement from Danny Patterson. And from Shirley."

"Get out."

"Did you know Riggins had a daughter?"

"You're a damn liar. He didn't have no kids."

"I thought you said you didn't know him."

Pappy snarled, "I told you, get outta my house!"

"She was born nine months after he died. She's still alive."

"I've worked for everything I got. You can lie about me all you want—"

"I'm not going to lie. I don't have to." Charlie pulled his printed list of questions from behind the plastic-covered photo. "I'm giving you a chance—"

"I'm givin' *you* a chance to get outta here before I kill ya."

Charlie would have laughed off the old man's threat except there was one thing he didn't know: Where *was* that gun? Charlie wanted to break toward the kitchen and go for it himself, but it would be hard to explain to the Forsyth County sheriff how he'd killed Pappy. Plus, it would ruin the book's ending. Anyway, a reporter should avoid inserting himself into the story, if possible. "Why'd you do it? Did you rape John Riggins' wife?"

That hit a raw nerve. "You accusin' me of sleepin' with a *nigger*?"

The old man licked his lips and proceeded to make one of the biggest blunders of his execrable life. He hocked up a loogie and spat at Charlie's face—but the wad of saliva fell short and splattered the plastic report cover on the clipboard, instead. Charlie glanced down. At first he was grossed out. Then he realized Pappy had voluntarily and vehemently given him exactly what he needed: a DNA sample. He glanced at his watch. "This interview is over," Charlie declared. "I'm out of here."

When Pappy broke toward the kitchen, Charlie grabbed the Mason jar and dashed out with it, still clutching his clipboard, wondering how fast the old man could move. He struggled to open the van door, then placed the clipboard on the seat beside him and the jar in a box with his papers on the passenger-side floor. He started the van and rolled down the driveway. "Hot damn!" he yelled, panting in relief.

A second later, the rear window shattered and he felt a bright, hot patch of pain in his neck. "What the hell!" he shouted. A splotch of red spattered the inside of the windshield in front of his face. He grabbed his neck. It was wet. He looked at the red on his fingers. Shit! He glanced in the rear-view mirror and saw Pappy standing with his shotgun on the porch. Charlie grabbed his chest with his right hand and steered with his left as he hit the gas pedal, throwing up rocks and dust, then swerving onto the county blacktop without checking for oncoming traffic. There was a second blast, and a rain of pellets sprayed the roof.

He felt his neck again and put his hand in front of his face. He'd either been hit with birdshot or a piece of glass. It wasn't bleeding much, but it stung. Only a scratch, Charlie told himself. Only a scratch. He checked the mirror. No sign anyone was following him. He'd gotten away. He would live to tell the tale. He'd have to swear out a warrant on the old bastard for aggravated assault. This would bolster the book's credibility, and more importantly, get the asshole arrested. Charlie wouldn't mind if the old bastard died in jail.

"That is one serious motherfucking footnote!" he yelled, holding his neck and checking his mirror one last time, just to make sure that old pickup wasn't barreling after him.

Charlie hit the highway and sped out of Forsyth, bleeding *and* laughing. Beside him, the spittle glistened with promise in the late afternoon sun.

* * *

DNA Testing Lab, located in a small strip center near Northlake Mall, looked like a cross between a copy shop and a medical clinic. A few minutes before closing, Charlie walked in wearing duct tape on his neck and placed his clipboard with the bespittled cover on the counter. He perused the pricing sheet, wishing he could simply opt for the Personal Satisfaction package, but knowing he had to spring for the more expensive Court Admissible deal. *Do it up right. Gift wrap the package.*

When the young black technician wearing a white lab coat turned around to serve him, she did a double take. "You're hurt. We're not a clinic. You should—"

"I know," Charlie said. "It's just a scratch. I'll patch it up better in a minute. First things first."

He pointed to the clipboard. She grimaced in distaste.

"It's saliva," he said. "Manspit." Then, because he couldn't resist, he added, "Spitacular."

"How long ago did this happen?"

"A little less than an hour."

"No. That." She jabbed her finger at the photo.

"Oh. Seventy years."

"Did somebody spit on the picture?"

"He was aiming at me," Charlie said.

"Uh-uh." The technician's castor-oil grimace was so severe it was almost comical. "I don't want to know. Do you have a match for this sample?"

"I'll have to bring it in later."

"Any other testing you want done today?"

Charlie looked over his shoulder at the van and wondered if he could get the finger tested, then decided against it. A historian's artifact could be a lab technician's 911 call. Besides, if his theory was correct, John Riggins was related to no one he knew, since Minerva was an only child. And he didn't want to pay to find out that Riggins's closest relative was a pickle.

The technician took the sample. "I guess there's enough," she said.

After learning that the results would be available five days after he brought in a comparison sample, Charlie paid the technician and returned to the van. The vehicle looked like it had been involved in a drive-by, with pellet marks peppering the tailgate. He counted eight new holes in the back of the driver's seat. He was lucky he'd only been hit by a single pellet. If Pappy had been a few seconds quicker, used buckshot, or Charlie had been just a bit slower, he and his van would be spending the night at the bottom of Lake Lanier. "Helluva contract," he muttered.

Now all he had to do was convince Minerva to help prove her father was a white rapist. He debated driving over to her house, but that would have to wait. There was too much else to do. Even though Trouble had that *No Cops* rule, Charlie needed to drive back to Cumming and swear out warrants, for the record and the story. First, he needed to patch the rear window to decrease the chance of getting pulled over by police.

As the sun was setting, he drove to a nearby office complex and circled around behind the buildings. Next to a Dumpster, he found a large corrugated box. Working in the glow of a yellow security light, he pulled a utility knife and duct tape from his tool box and cut a patch of cardboard. Then he fastened it over the shattered rear window. In the process, he cut himself on crumbled safety glass. He used several bandages from his first-aid kit to dress his newest oopsies, then repatched his gunshot injury, a flesh wound that had already stopped bleeding.

Then he remembered Kathleen. *Oh, yeah. That.* He should have been back at Bayard Terrace an hour ago. He pulled out his cellphone and tried to call her, but her phone was out of service.

That was creepy. *Just like before.*

It took Charlie a half hour to drive to Bayard Terrace, where he found, to his horror, that both Atlanta police and Angela were on the scene. One patrol car sat in the street and another in Kathleen's driveway. Neighbors stood on the sidewalk, talking amongst themselves. Charlie parked on the street and rushed up to the young couple who lived next door.

"What happened?" he asked.

"Somebody broke in again," the wife said, shaking her head.

Charlie silently cursed himself. This was his fault for not returning straight to Bayard Terrace.

"I heard Kathleen yell," the woman said. "And I saw somebody in that room." She pointed toward Talton's study. "I knew it wasn't you, because it was a short person. Wearing a ski mask. So I called 911 and then I yelled out the window. I think I scared him."

"Young or old, fat or thin?"

"Normal. I couldn't tell the age."

Not Momo, then. Maybe they hired someone.

"He was gone when the police arrived," she added.

"When did they get here?"

Husband and wife exchanged glances. "Ten minutes ago, maybe," she said.

"Have you seen her?"

"No. We didn't go in. We weren't sure they were gone."

"I'm going to check on her."

Charlie rushed up the sidewalk. A black cop pushed against his chest when he tried to enter the house. "You family?"

"I live here. I'm her caretaker."

"Not anymore," said a voice from the bedroom. Angela came out glaring. "They bound her up with duct tape and strapped her to a chair. She nearly had a heart attack! If that wasn't enough, she said this has happened before. And you didn't report it! Is that true?"

"Uh ..."

"She hasn't been taking her meds, either."

"Is she all right?"

"No thanks to you, she is."

"I know who's behind this," he offered. "It's about the book."

"It's definitely about you," Angela said. She turned her back on him and returned to her mother's side. Charlie found himself talking to Officer Tanner. He breathlessly told the officer what he knew—some of it anyway. Enough to point a finger at the Cutchinses—without mentioning the finger, of course. That was his, all his. But he did happen to mention the shooting. Tanner said a detective would talk with him.

Charlie tried again to see Kathleen, but Angela wouldn't let him near her. After a short and heated argument, she told him to pack his things and get out. "You're fired!" she said.

"I couldn't smite him!" Kathleen cried out from her bedroom. "It wouldn't work."

He saw no point in arguing. Angela didn't know about *American Monster*, and Kathleen didn't understand its heavy familial implications, since he'd never told her about them. So much the better. Charlie handed Angela his key and went into the study. The manuscript of *Thoracic Park*—his decoy novel—seemed to be the only thing missing, since all his papers were in his van or the safety box. He didn't tell police about the theft of 350 sheets of paper. He just wanted to get out of there and swear out warrants in Forsyth.

Charlie bagged the few possessions he kept in the study and grabbed the printer, then went downstairs and began hauling stuff out of the basement. There was one tricky moment, when he snuck out the dungeon's back door with the contract vat, something that would be extremely difficult to explain to police. It had filled to the top, so it was very heavy. He carried it gingerly to the van and put it behind the back seat, managing to do so without spilling any blood.

By then, the neighbors had drifted away. The officers stayed inside the house. Feeling more like a perpetrator than a victim, Charlie left without talking to an investigator. As he drove away, he noticed a black car following him. The detective? Not likely. Charlie zoomed through a red light, barely avoiding a T-bone crash, rounded a corner, took a left, a right, and then pulled into an empty driveway. After waiting ten minutes, he left the neighborhood via a back way. While he was driving along Briarcliff, his cellphone rang. The call was coming from the place he had once called home.

"Hello," he said uncertainly, having deep misgivings about talking to anyone right then, especially a varmint.

"I heard you went up to Pappy's." Susan's tone was hard as rock.

"That's true."

"Mom said you broke into his house and threatened him, and you're going to spread lies about him if he doesn't give you a bunch of money. She says you heard about the deal on his farm, and you're trying to get a cut."

"That's what she'd say."

"Are you?" she demanded.

"I find your question offensive. Did she tell you the nature of these so-called lies?"

"She says you stole something, too."

"*Something*? Ask her what I stole, Susan. Ask her what I stole."

"So you did take something."

"Nothing that belonged to your grandfather." He liked his answer, nice and legalistic.

"You've been going downhill for over a year, ever since that thing with the Rebel flag on the Fourth of July. This grudge you've got is *insane*. This is the second time you've been up there, even though you're not welcome. That's *stalking*, Charlie. You're mentally ill! The phone's been ringing off the hook! The Atlanta police are looking for you. Hang on. There's another call."

Charlie hummed the *Jeopardy* theme as he drove, checking the mirror for black cars. Susan came back on again: "That was the Georgia Bureau of Investigation. An agent wants to talk to you."

"I'm sure you gave them my number."

"I had to. Hang on. Another call." Click.

Please remain on hold while your life is destroyed.

"That was the Forsyth County Sheriff's office. They've got warrants, plural, out for you."

"That was quick. Pays to have connections." So much for going back to Cumming to swear out one of his own. *Unless* ... "I suppose it would be too much to ask if you'd post bond."

"I'll say it is. You've turned against my family. I can't have that. If you come here, I'll have to call the police. I'll tell you this, too. Stay away from the kids, or I'll file charges."

He didn't bother to ask "what charges?" He knew she'd think of something. "How much money are they giving you? Or do you have to wait for the land sale?"

"I don't know what you're talking about."

"All right. Détente is done. Just one thing: Don't let Beck and Ben near your grandfather ever again. He may be old, but he's dangerous."

"You are so full of shit, Charlie. You're going to jail. I hope you rot there."

Susan hung up. Charlie slammed his phone on the dashboard. After that, he drove around aimlessly, checking his mirror to see if he was being followed. He figured Uncle Stanley had called in the GBI, and they'd triangulate his ass or catch him using some other nefarious method that involved both technology and varmintry. When the cellphone rang again, he shut it off.

He traveled on the Perimeter for a few miles, then exited at Hanover Drive. He didn't know why he was being drawn toward Thornbriar, but he turned left at the George Bailey Bridge, as he now called it, and passed the gutted shell of the Pancake Hut, where this madness had started. A few blocks away, he stopped at the Nights Inn. After stomping his cellphone to death in the seedy motel's parking lot, he checked into a second-floor room that smelled of booze and disinfectant. It took him ten trips to haul up his stuff from the van, which was, due to its cardboard window, no longer secure. Again, he didn't spill a drop of blood. Apparently, it would not abandon him.

He sat down on the bed, rubbed his face, and reflected on his sorry state. He was on the run, homeless, nearly broke, and completely screwed, with what was left of John Riggins as a roommate. He picked up the jar and examined it carefully. Had to be the man's middle finger. Charlie bet that raising it in Ike Cutchins's face had been the last thing Riggins did on this earth. He put the jar on the bedside table. It didn't distress, haunt, or scare him. Indeed, what was left of Riggins was Charlie's new best friend.

He grabbed a towel from the bathroom and covered up Riggins, to keep him snug. "I'm gonna take care of you now. Good night, John," he said, then patted the jar reassuringly.

Chapter Fifteen

When Charlie left the auto body shop, workers were admiring the shotgun pellet marks on the van's rear door. "Check out the roof!" he shouted through cupped hands from the parking lot.

A few seconds after he reached the curb, a MARTA bus stopped to pick him up. It dropped him off right at the motel, too. He wondered: Did he, like Trouble, now have special bus powers?

Back in his room, Charlie checked first for his computer under the bed, then for the Mason jar, which he'd stashed in a duffel. To his great relief, both were still there—as was the blood vat, hidden in the closet underneath a jacket. He brewed courtesy coffee, put the laptop on the table, jammed his knees under it—and then listened to an argument between the Hispanic prostitute next door and her client, a middle-aged man in a business suit Charlie had seen slinking up the stairs. After some bilingual yelling, a door slammed.

In the silence that followed, Charlie realized that a momentous change had occurred. By snatching that Mason jar, he'd inserted himself into the story. Ergo, *American Monster* was now a memoir. And so he started rewriting, from page one: "*On the night after Christmas I met Kathleen Talton. I was newly destitute, trudging through the rain with a man whose name I still don't know. She had prayed for a miracle. What she got was me.*" He would keep out the story's supernatural elements, however. (He knew that some people would argue that if he was the answer to someone's prayers, then there was no God.)

After a few minutes of tapping away, his thoughts drifted to the jar. He pulled it from the duffel and placed it on the table. In the lamplight, the formaldehyde seemed to take on a radioactive glow. When he picked up the jar, the finger touched bottom and moved as if tracing an answer on a Ouija board. Charlie watched it, entranced. In a less-than-lucid moment, he said, "What is it, John? Is the story trapped in a well?"

He shuddered, realizing that his mental hygiene (as Susan called it) was slipping.

Never mind that. There were decisions to make. Being dispossessed, exiled, and hunted, Charlie figured that pulling a disappearing act was the best thing to do. He couldn't go to jail. He'd lose his stuff—and what was left of John Riggins. To avoid that, he would stay underground until the book was finished. Unfortunately, he had no cash, and if he didn't get the second half of the publisher's advance soon, his house of credit cards would collapse. When he got the money from Fortress, he'd rent an apartment. And where the hell was that check, anyway? He reached into a pocket for his cellphone, then remembered he'd killed it to elude capture.

So be it. If the world conspired to keep him holed up in a motel with John Riggins's finger and his computer, then he had nothing better—and little else—to do than work on the book. He returned to his task, writing *American Monster* at a furious pace, without regard to time or creature comforts, of which he had much and few, respectively.

At 4:00 a.m., the prostitute next door and her client broke the bed with a mighty crash. Charlie paused to listen to their laughter, then resumed his writing.

* * *

For three days, Charlie stayed in his room and pounded the laptop's keyboard, recasting *American Monster* as his own story, sticking his head out the door only for Papa John's pizza and Mongolian beef from the Hungry Wok. By the time he called the body shop and learned that his van was ready, he'd completely rewritten the first ten chapters.

Charlie stashed away his valuables and stepped outside, blinking in the sunshine. He crossed the street to wait for the bus. It appeared immediately. He accepted his good fortune with a nod to the sky as he boarded the vehicle. The female bus driver, who nodded at him, looked just like the one that had picked him up with Trouble that night outside the Pancake. Then again, the motel was on the same route. Still, his life was weird. No doubt about it.

He picked up the van—now unblemished, repainted royal blue, and boasting a new rear window—and charged the repair, whistling at the cost. He drove back to the motel and checked out. At Southern Trust Bank, he smuggled the Mason jar under his jacket into the vault and placed it inside his safety deposit box, which was, fortunately, the largest available. Still, there was barely room for the purloined digit.

Not a proper burial, but at least John was secure for now.

He'd spent a couple of nights out on the street after Kathleen had pulled a knife on him, but that now seemed like some kind of urban camping trip. This time, Charlie fully embraced his homelessness. He rented a post office box at Mailbox Decatur, then went to Cellular USA and bought a prepaid phone with a new number. He immediately used it to call his editor at Fortress.

"Where have you *been*?" Joshua Furst asked, his voice hitting a high note on the last word. "I've been trying to reach you all week. People are *threatening* me."

"I'm hiding out. I've been shot, burglarized, shadowed, threatened, and, to top it all off, maligned—by my wife, of all people." *The unkindest cut of all.*

"I called your cellphone and there was no answer."

"It died a violent death in a motel parking lot. As so many of them do."

"Then I tried *another* number. They said you were evicted. What gives? Where are you now?"

Charlie gave him his cellphone number and his new address.

"You live in a post office box?"

"Yeah, that pretty much sums it up."

"Anyway, some attorney calls and tells us he's going to get a cease and desist order and prevent us from publishing your book. His name is, hang on a minute … Stanley Cutchins."

Charlie broke out laughing. "He's an insurance agent! He's a legislator, but I assure you that he is *not* burdened by a knowledge of the law."

"What is his problem? This stuff happened a hundred years ago. It's like somebody getting pissed off at a book about the *Titanic*. I searched through the manuscript and the only thing about a Cutchins I found was a quote from some guy born in 1912."

"They've got the book confused with something I'm working on now. Uncle Stanley will have plenty to yelp about later."

"*Uncle* Stanley?"

"By marriage. Long story … and I'm not proud of it, OK? Let me just point out that if they're trying to block publication, well, you simply cannot *buy* publicity like that."

"I agree. Sadly, Legal says we must have threats in writing before we can advertise them."

"By the way, I've got another manuscript to show you."

"Oh. Hmm. Another book, eh? I should warn you: Things are in flux."

"What do you mean?"

"We have a new publisher. Now isn't the time to approach him with another book."

"Who's the new publisher?"

"Evans Barclay, of the Las Vegas casino Barclays. I think he may have won us in a poker game. He says we paid too much for *Flight.* Called it a bad bet. He's looking to cut losses. Know when to fold 'em—"

"Wait a minute!" Charlie struggled to control his anger.

"Don't worry. We're going to publish *Flight.* I got the galleys in, and I need to send them to you for proofing. And you need to compile an index."

"If you've got the galleys, I should have been paid already!"

"I'll send them. You get them proofed. Gotta go. There's a call on the other line."

"When am I gonna get paid?" Charlie demanded. "*Am* I gonna get paid?"

But Joshua had already hung up.

At least Charlie now knew he needed to find a different publisher for *American Monster.* But there was a bright side. Hopefully, Uncle Stanley would keep harassing Fortress, barking up the wrong tree. The critter that Cutchins wanted to kill would come crashing down on him from a completely different direction.

Charlie then drove to Store-All, where he rented a closet-sized unit and stowed away his stuff: tools, bicycle, spare clothes, cot, boombox, papers, even the van's two bench seats, and the vat (nearly full of blood), keeping only a few days' worth of clothes and what he needed to write, including his printer. That night he went to a multiplex cinema and after watching a movie, camped out in the van at the periphery of its parking lot.

He slept fitfully until daybreak, waking with a stiff back. He washed up in a nearby supermarket's restroom, then bought a cup of coffee, bagels, cold cuts, fruit, bottled water and a bag of ice for the cooler. He still wasn't ready to write because his van was not yet home—or office. He drove to the Store-All and got his tools, then to Home Depot for lumber, hinges, and a lock, putting all the purchases on his credit card. There would be hell to pay when the bill came, but he pushed that thought out of his mind. He built a locker and shelves for the van, along with a frame to secure the cooler. After eating turkey on a bagel for lunch, he bought an air mattress at Target. He inflated it in the back of the van and laid his sleeping bag atop it, then admired his work. *Van sweet van.*

To throw his enemies off his trail, Charlie did something sketchy. When he saw a red Caravan that looked like his in a shopping center parking lot, he switched license plates with it while repeatedly murmuring his mantra: *No cops*. The next day, he came across a similar vehicle and repeated the process. If they wanted to swear out warrants and try to tail him in a black car, then he'd play Three-Van Monte with them. His new motto: *Drive safely, damn it.*

Then he shifted his operations to the north side of town. The next morning, he exercised and showered at the Dunwoody Y. He worked in the local library branch until closing, then set up shop in a coffeehouse, enduring the raucous conversations of rival high school cliques. After the shop closed, he drove away and found a secluded place to park in a strip mall. He sat in the rear of the van, resting his back against the passenger seat, and typed away on his laptop until the battery died.

The next day he bought a car charger for his laptop battery. Now he could write until he maxed out his MasterCard and ran out of gas.

* * *

Charlie arrived at Minerva's house while she was cooking supper—fish, mashed potatoes, and green beans—and she invited him to eat. Takira was there; Charlie noticed the girl wasn't showing yet. He shuddered to think that the poor child was carrying Pappy's great-great-grandchild in her womb—if she was still pregnant, that is. Charlie didn't mention Pappy or her pregnancy while they ate. Instead, he listened to Takira talk about school. Apparently, her middle school was a hellpit, but he'd heard from other parents that most of them were.

After dinner, Takira left to see a new friend in the neighborhood. Minerva and Charlie stepped out on the front stoop. It was a clear, cool evening. Minerva sat in the rocker bundled in a sweater, and Charlie, wearing a tan jacket, leaned against a wrought iron support as they watched the girl walk down the street. Recalling Demetrious's habit of lurking, Charlie scouted the shadows. "You seen your grandson lately?"

"Not for a couple of days. Sometimes he comes by to eat. That's why there was extra tonight."

"It was good," Charlie said. "Thanks again."

"You're welcome."

A minute passed before she sighed and said, "Well, I know you didn't show up just to eat my food. I tried calling you, but your number didn't work."

"I got a new phone." He wrote down his new number and gave it to her.

"Some woman said you didn't live there anymore."

He laughed. "Which woman?"

She rolled her eyes and shook her head. "Men. They're all the same. What's your new address?"

"Actually, I'm looking for a place."

"Where are you staying now?"

"Here and there."

"Hmm, as Arsenio used to say. So, are you going to give me the news about my father?" She clucked her tongue. "Seventy years ago, and it's the news."

Charlie cleared his throat. "There were eight men involved in the murder of John Riggins, and it was over the land."

"I'd always heard that he was lynched by a mob."

"I'd say that's true. One of them is still alive. He owns the land your family held."

She leaned forward, her good ear cocked toward him. "Go on."

"The sale's on record, with John Riggins' signature, but it's bogus, since it was dated after his death."

"My father's death," she said. "So the man stole it."

"I know the man who did it, the main one." He stepped off the porch, then stepped back up, since the small stoop offered little room for pacing. "His name is Isaac Cutchins. He's the one who's still alive."

"What do you mean, you know him?"

"I married his granddaughter."

She looked like she'd been slapped in the face. "Ain't that a revelation," she said, putting her palms to her temples. "He and you are mixed in your children."

"Yes," he said, feeling a pang of longing for the little varmints.

"My Lord, he must be nearly a hundred years old."

"He is nearly that. And spry." Charlie looked across the street, recalling how close he'd come to being shot by the old man. Twice.

She raised an eyebrow. "You're still going ahead with it, though?"

"Yes." He gave her a crooked smile. "I never liked him, anyway. The whole family is going to try to stop the book." Charlie sighed. "It's gotten quite ugly."

"But it's your family. The blood is all mixed up."

"No." He shook his head. "I'm estranged from all of them. I'm an exile now, and I have a job to do. One of those 'die trying' things."

She narrowed her eyes, but then a look of pity crossed her face. "What about your own people? Your parents still around? Brothers and sisters?"

"All gone. I'm an only child of only children. Well, I had a brother, but he died before I was born. He fell off a cliff when he was with Dad, out in the woods. My mother died of cancer right after I graduated from college."

"Dear God."

"When I was young, my father got this great notion to jump in the river and drown. Gravity has not been our friend."

"Hmm. Like my momma." She rubbed her chin and regarded him carefully. "Perhaps your father couldn't live with his regret over what happened."

Charlie shrugged. "He lived with it for nine years. That's all I know."

"You're a very lonely man, aren't you?"

Charlie didn't see what that had to do with anything. "I have a job to do."

"And you're going to do it no matter what your wife's people think."

"I have no choice."

"There's always a choice."

"Well, then, it's my choice to believe I have to do it."

"How close are you to finishing the book?"

"I've collected almost everything I need," he said, stretching out his arms to indicate the size of his task—or the fish he planned to catch. "I've got to get comments from some people. I've identified members of the lynching party and I want to talk to their children. There is something you can do to help."

"What's that?"

He drew a deep breath and said, "I need a DNA sample from you. Probably just hair."

She regarded him suspiciously. "Why do you need that?"

"There's no gentle way to say this, so I'm just going to put it out there. There's evidence to suggest that Isaac Cutchins—"

She gave him a look that told him to shut up. But he was God's Own Fool and therefore had to say what he had to say.

"—is your father."

"No. You *did not* just say that."

"When I went to see Pap—Cutchins, he denied killing Riggins, but I caught him in a lie about whether or not he even knew the man. More importantly, I got a DNA sample from him–"

Minerva gave him a look of disbelief. "And he went along with this?"

"Not exactly. He spit it at me."

"*He spit it at you*?" She looked like she'd just swallowed poison. Her eyes were wide. Her nostrils flared. Then she exploded, yelling, "Where do you get off coming here trying to tell me I'm not *me* based on an old white man's *spit*?" She appeared ready to do what Pappy had done.

"No, I—"

She popped out of her rocking chair and wagged a finger at Charlie. "John Riggins is my father. I am the daughter of the man I believe in. I would be less of a person if it was any other way. There's science, and then there's foolishness. I'm not a fool, I can look at the photographs and see what I see. But what that man did—if that's what he did—doesn't make him my father." She took a breath and continued. "No. John Riggins is my father. That's the way I grew up. That's what I've believed all my life. I made something of myself just like my father did and his father before him. I'm not going to let you come in and change that. I am who I am, a combination of what God made me, what I do with my life, and who I choose to be. You can tell me that I've got ... those genes in me, but that's not my soul. I know who I am. No sir, you are not coming here and convincing me at my age that I'm somebody else."

Charlie didn't want to argue. He threw up his hands.

"Don't look at me that way," she snapped. "God gives us our souls, Mr. Sherman. I have the soul of the daughter of John Riggins. If you write anything about me, make sure you get that down. My father was a brave man and he died for it. That's what I always knew. This other, there's none of him in me. John Riggins is my father. Says so on my birth certificate." She fretted with the front of her dress. "No. I won't help you on this. Write what you will. I'm done with you." She scowled and gave him a dismissive wave of her hand.

Charlie stared at her, resentment smoldering in his eyes. He wasn't so much hurt by the rejection as he was pissed. Damn right he'd tell it his way. Why did she think she could deny the truth? The truth—that's what this was about. She needed him more than he needed her. Actually, he didn't need her at all. Would be nice to be on good terms with her, but it wasn't necessary, not now. He had a job to do. The idea that she owned the story and could make the truth a lie—that was just ridiculous.

Sensing his antagonism, she took a step away, then turned back toward him. "I want that land back. Maybe not even for myself, but that's not your business. I'm not helping prove John Riggins is not my father. Do you understand?"

He stared down at the steps. "I understand how you see things and I understand the big picture."

"I'll thank you to go now. And don't come back."

He swallowed his shock at the banishment and said, "I'm sorry if you're offended, but maybe you shouldn't be so upset."

"Apologize for what you've done wrong, not how people take it. Now get gone!"

Charlie held up his hands. He was done with her, too. However, he did want to giver her a piece of advice. "Fine, I'll go. But you should get an attorney and put a lien on that property."

She stood with her arms on her hips, waiting for him to leave.

He stepped down onto the sidewalk. She stormed inside, slamming the door behind her. On his way to the van, he saw Takira approaching, talking with her friend. He waited for her, and when she was a few feet away, said, "Takira, can you do me a favor, please?"

"OK."

He wrote a note on his legal pad: *Demetrious, I have a lucrative proposition for you.* He signed it and included his cell number. He tore off the sheet and handed it to the girl. "Have D call me. There's some money in it for him, but don't tell Minerva. She'll kill the deal."

* * *

Charlie figured the varmints wouldn't look for him in Scarlett O'Hara country, so he shifted operations south to Clayton County. As the wind blew the last reluctant leaves off the oak tree above him, Charlie sat on a picnic bench in Jesters Creek Park with his much-abused clipboard next to the laptop. It was chilly; he wore fingerless cotton gloves as he keyed in the changes he'd made on a hard copy of Chapter Fourteen. His cellphone buzzed—an exceedingly rare occurrence. He glanced at it skeptically before answering. "Hello?"

"Yo. Sher-Man."

It was the call he'd been waiting for. "Demetrious, where you been?"

"In 'n out. Heah 'n theah. Heard you wanted to deal."

"Yeah, I do. I want somethin' you got."

"I ain't believin' this," he said. "Man want to *part-ee*."

"No, no. Not that. I want to do a DNA test on you."

"I already told the bitch."

"This isn't about Takira. It's about the book I'm writing. I need a sample. Your blood is required." While saliva would do, he thought Demetrious should bleed for the cause. *A prick for a prick.*

"My blood." Demetrious made it sound like the stupidest thing he'd ever heard. "You a vampire?"

"I need to prove something."

"What?"

"I need to see if you're related by blood to someone."

"Who? Gee-Ma's daddy? I heard 'bout that. Whew."

This was too easy, Charlie thought. *It doesn't even require lying.* "In a word, yes. It could be worth a lot of money down the road. *Way* down the road. As for right now, I can give you … a hundred dollars." Charlie winced, doubly embarrassed at practicing checkbook journalism *and* hoping he could do so on the cheap.

"Humph."

"You can't tell your grandma. She'll cut you off if she knows you're doing this."

"Like she did you."

"Yeah, something like that."

"Bet it worth a lot more'n a hundred dollars to you."

"Well, that's the offer."

A beat passed. "A thousand."

Charlie laughed in disbelief. "I don't have a thousand!"

"Well, I ain't got no extra blood then. We through."

"Wait. Wait. I'll give you three hundred. Final offer." Demetrious didn't say no, so Charlie added, "Meet me tomorrow. Noon. Edgewood-Candler Park station. If you're not there, deal's off."

"I might be there."

"Show up on time, playah," Charlie said, but he was talking to himself. Demetrious had already hung up.

* * *

Demetrious sauntered out of the Edgewood-Candler Park MARTA station a half-hour late. His smaller companion gazed intently at the old, beat-up van parked in a Kiss-Ride spot. Charlie reached over and opened the passenger door. "Hop in, Demetrious."

"P-Dog needs to go, too."

Charlie gazed impassively past D's companion, who gave him a malevolent glare. This was not part of the deal. Furthermore, P-Dog was bad news. "No, he doesn't. I don't have room for him. Don't have a place for him to sit."

"He can ride in back."

"No he can't."

Demetrious peered inside the van, then looked to his friend and shrugged. He gave Charlie a sour look. "You got the money?"

Charlie noticed what looked like the hammer of a black automatic pistol sticking out of the friend's back pocket. "I'll get the money after you've done your part. Get in, Demetrious. Just you."

Demetrious weighed his options. "I ain't goin' without homey."

His friend stood behind him, glowering and acting twitchy. A bus stopped fifty feet away. The driver, a round black woman, opened the doors and stared at them. A flock of crows descended from the west, landing tumultuously in a bare-limbed oak nearby.

"Fine," Charlie said. "Sorry for the inconvenience." He started to pull away.

Demetrious banged the side of the van. Charlie stopped and the teenager opened the door. "P-Dog say he cool. He wait here for me."

"What's the 'P' stand for?"

"Punkass," Demetrious said, laughing. P-Dog gave them the finger.

"Hop in." Demetrious climbed in and tuned the radio to a rap station; Charlie tolerated it as long as he could—ten seconds. "That stuff's offensive," he said, hitting WCLK's preset. Jazz. Better.

"What, you don't like niggas?" Demetrious laughed at him.

"I don't think Gee-Ma wants to hear you talk that way. And buckle up. I want the blood sample in the lab, not all over the windshield."

"Gee-Ma been tryin' all her life not to be a nigga." Demetrious looked around. "This is embarrassin', driving around in this piece a shit van. Smells bad, too. He pivoted his head and looked in back, furrowing his brows, giving Charlie a piercing gaze. "You *sleep* in here? You homeless motherfucker." He broke out laughing long and loud.

"I got some things going on," Charlie said. "Money's coming in. Don't you worry about me."

"I ain't worried about you. 'Cept the part about payin' me."

A half hour later, the sixteen-year-old manchild was sitting in a plastic chair with a needle in his arm. Fortunately for Charlie (and he hadn't thought about this), the kid had a fake ID saying he was eighteen. The same lab technician who had served Charlie previously said results should be in by the following Monday, but Charlie already knew Demetrious and Pappy had to be kin, because they were both such assholes.

Afterward, Charlie drove to a bank and got a cash advance on his credit card. When he handed Demetrious an envelope with $300 in it, the teenager took it without a word of acknowledgment.

As Charlie drove to the MARTA station, Demetrious asked, "You think we can get the land back?"

Charlie was thrown off guard by the attempt at civil conversation. He took a moment before saying, "I don't know. Your grandmother has an excellent claim."

"That means we need a lawyer and go through the courts and shit, right?"

"Yes. But don't tell her about what we did today. If you do, I'll tell her I gave you enough money to pay her back for the Georgia Power bill."

"Our little secret," Demetrious said, patting his pocket. "This mean I'm gonna be in the book."

"Oh yeah, you'll be famous."

"Famous," he snorted. "Hell, I'll be notorious."

"Notorious DNA," Charlie said.

"I like that, man." He held out his knuckles, and Charlie punched them.

Chapter Sixteen

Charlie stuck to his simple plan: charge all purchases, even coffee, and keep moving. As dusk came earlier and nights grew colder, he divided his time between three libraries, two YMCAs, and four coffeehouses that provided free refills and electricity. Shut off from his family and having no comforts of home, he had nothing to do but write. He had to finish quickly, since he was running out of money and the time that it bought. To make matters worse, his mental state was deteriorating due to lack of sleep and malnutrition, along with fears of lightning strikes, Trouble's static cling, and assassination. He dreamed of shotgun blasts and woke to their echoes.

Having burrowed to the lowest level of a Sandy Springs parking garage, Charlie woke in darkness on the day before Thanksgiving. He fumbled for his watch, cursed when he saw the time, slipped on work boots, and catapulted himself into the driver's seat. He raced out an open exit gate, passing the glaring attendant who trudged up the sidewalk to start the day shift. Scratch off another place from the list of places he could stay.

After downing three sample cups of coffee at the nearest Kroger, Charlie went to the Dunwoody YMCA. He changed into grungy workout clothes and pedaled thirty minutes on a stationary bike, then lifted weights. He showered, brushed his teeth, shaved, and put on his last set of clean clothes.

He was the first patron of the day at the Dunwoody library. The matronly blonde who unlocked the door smiled approvingly as he walked in. He picked a table in the rear corner of the main reading room and plugged in his laptop, writing for two hours about Aunt Shirley/Arlene—"Shirlene" as he now called her—before quitting for lunch. He ate a bagel with peanut butter, then drove to Decatur. Desperately hoping for a check from Fortress, he opened his box to find junk mail—*how did these people find him*?—and a note to ask at the counter for a package. He handed it to the slacker clerk, who disappeared into the back and returned with an oversized brown envelope: galleys for *Flight*. A handwritten note from Tracy, whoever she was, told him: "Correct and return within 10 days WITH INDEX, otherwise cost of indexing will be charged to you. HAVE FUN!"

He lugged the galleys and his laptop across the street to Java Joe's. He checked his e-mail, with typically disappointing results. No one he knew wished to communicate with him, just "Herb Tarkania" offering to increase his penis size. Depression loomed. He shook it off. He had work to do. He spent two hours reading and correcting page proofs for *Flight*. The first thing he did was remove all mention of Joshua Logan. He didn't want to tip his hand to Cecil Montgomery until the time was right. Logan, as one of Pappy's fellow lynchers and land thieves, would get special treatment in *American Monster*.

The nomad moved on to another of his favorite spots, the Decatur Library's special collections room. He worked on *Monster* until it was time for supper: a bagel and cream cheese with juice. How long before he was sick of bagels? After this modest repast, he migrated to a nearby Starbucks and used the bathroom to brush his teeth, since he didn't want them falling out on his book tour. Charlie marked galleys until the coffeehouse closed, then drove through an open gate into a bank garage, parking beside an SUV. He climbed into the rear and leaned against the back of the passenger seat to begin the tedious work of compiling the index, working until his mind faded out.

Around midnight he left the garage to take a leak. A Decatur cop noticed him just before he committed a crime upon some bushes, so he kept walking, changing direction and going to a nightclub he hadn't been to in years. He walked past the folk singer onstage on his way to the men's room. When Charlie exited the restroom, the bartender told him he'd missed last call. Charlie shrugged apologetically and left, then circled back to the garage, making sure the cop wasn't staking out the place. He darted to his van and slid fully clothed into his sleeping bag.

When he woke up Thursday morning, Charlie tuned to the news and heard a familiar voice. "Every year, it's a struggle," Redeemer Wilson rasped through the van's radio speakers. "But somehow we make it. People open their hearts and we have enough to go 'round on this, one of our humblest and holiest of days. So, if you're cold and alone and need a good meal and some fellowship, come see me at the Hunger Palace today. And if you got money, don't forget to donate to the Holy Way House and Hunger Palace Foundation Christmas Feast Fund!"

On this day, Redeemer would be the media's designated hero, of course. Reporters weren't always so kind. They often went "looking for my human flaws," as the civil rights icon so aptly put it. Charlie recalled a few, though nothing could outweigh Redeemer's courage and service to the cause of justice—and for the last thirty-some years, his noble attempt to keep street people from starving. To hell with his critics. That's how Charlie felt.

In late 1987, Redeemer purchased a Pentecostal church on Memorial Drive along with an adjacent lot, using money from his Feed the Neediest charity, which had prospered in the aftermath of the Forsyth County marches. He then built the Hunger Palace as a community center next door. According to one investigative report, the equipment used to set up its kitchen in 1988 should have been delivered to an Atlanta public elementary school, although the school's needs were eventually taken care of and no charges were ever filed. Redeemer also bought a red Cadillac around the same time. This fact had been covered ad nauseam by the media, because everyone knows that black preacher + red Cadillac = scandal.

With defiant good humor, Redeemer endured bad press over his interlocking charitable funds. "I'm bloody but unbowed," he'd told Charlie during their July interview. "Unbossed and unbought. And on the holidays, these TV stations that been tryin' to rip me a new one all year send their anchors to work in my kitchen for an hour and get their pictures taken with me. Go figure."

Charlie loved the guy, and he remembered his promise to volunteer at the Hunger Palace. Until he heard Redeemer on the radio that morning, he hadn't given the idea a second thought. Ironically, now he was as much a potential beneficiary of Redeemer's charity as he was a donor/volunteer. Nevertheless, the idea of doing good works while cadging a meal held great appeal for a liberal with an empty belly.

After putting in a couple of hours proofing *Flight*'s galleys in the back of his van, Charlie drove to Memorial Drive in East Atlanta. The day was cloudy and cool. As Charlie approached his destination, he saw a crowd standing in front of the Hunger Palace, the larger of Redeemer's two buildings, next to the Holy Way House of the Social Gospel, which paid a salary to Redeemer and listed him as its minister—another source of controversy. Once, when he'd been accused of lacking proper ordination as a preacher, Redeemer retorted: "Neither did Jesus. You gonna doubt the Bible just 'cause the Lord didn't get a license?"

Charlie passed the Holy Way House, a dilapidated white frame church set close to the street. The gravel lot was jammed with cars, including Redeemer's ancient, banged-up Cadillac. Charlie parked on a side street. He left his coat in the van and approached the church from the west, Atlanta's skyline behind him. Shopping carts piled high with possessions and black garbage bags surrounded the building's concrete stoop. The door was open, and he peeked inside. Several men and a few women were scattered throughout the pews; perhaps half were awake. At the pulpit, an enormous, dark-faced man with a booming voice demanded repentance. With a beefy paw, the preacher beckoned Charlie to enter, but the writer moved on, threading his way through the anarchy of parked cars in the gravel lot toward the Hunger Palace.

Charlie stopped to watch the bearded civil rights lion holding court in front of the building's double doors, greeting his shabbily dressed flock. At least twenty people surrounded Redeemer while a perky blonde from Channel Six interviewed him. Flanked by her cameraman, she was asking him about his latest run-in with the law: Redeemer had been found passed out in his car in the middle of an intersection, and DUI charges were pending. (Charges were always pending, but Redeemer hadn't spent a night in jail since the 1960s.)

"Why we talkin' about this? That's not what this day is about. We have a desperate and continual need for donations large and small, but especially large," Redeemer declared, pausing to shake hands with an insistent admirer, a bearded black man in an army jacket and watch cap. When he turned back to the camera, he said, "And don't forget to send your donations to Reverend Redeemer Wilson's *Feed the Needy Food Fund* in time for Christmas. Give until it hurts!" He flashed a grin.

"Are you saying you're innocent?" the reporter asked, returning to her line of questioning.

Redeemer's eyes bugged out. "Well, scandalize my name! After all these years, I gotta put up with that?" he yelled. "I *never* claim I'm innocent. Been through too much to say that. But I paid my dues. Now you're tryin' to make me look bad on Thanksgiving. Can you believe that?" He held out his arms to implore the crowd to action; its members took the cue, booing and jeering the reporter. She cringed under the weight of public disapproval. Redeemer lowered his hands like a quarterback calling signals in his home stadium. His supporters hushed.

"Come back Monday morning, you wanna make me look bad," Redeemer continued. "We came up short this year, and we may not even be around next year. I'm eighty-two years old, so you can't do nuthin' to hurt me. It's these people that come here you'll be hurtin'." He swept his arm to include the crowd. Its members, unsure what sound effect to produce, let out a collective grumble.

"Just doing my job," the reporter said.

"And I'm just doin' mine. Tellin' you to BACK OFF!" He then returned his attention to his flock. The reporter did as she was told and went inside. Charlie wanted to say hello, but Redeemer was too busy being adored to notice him at first. Volunteers and vagrants pressed in on their hero. Charlie stood on the edge of the crowd debating how to proceed. A minute later, Redeemer looked at him and shouted, "Hey, I know you!"

"Yes, I—"

"The writer. I'm gonna put you to work for a change." Redeemer glanced around until he found the person he was looking for, right behind him. He gently pushed a young blonde woman holding a small black girl in her arms toward Charlie. "Take her and the kids in and get them fed."

The woman wore heavy makeup, a black miniskirt, high-heeled boots and a denim jacket. She was striking, with an aura of seedy glamour—and an overdose of mascara. A down-on-her-luck stripper, Charlie guessed, though she wasn't large-breasted. For some reason, she looked vaguely familiar, but he couldn't place her. She drew leers from men in the crowd. One shouted, "I'll take care of her, all right!"

Redeemer gave the offender a sharp look and said, "You ain't trustworthy. You can look at this man," he said, pointing at Charlie, "and know he loves children. Ain't that right?"

Surprised by the question, Charlie quickly bobbed his head.

A boy about Ben's age with an Afro stepped forward wearing a dirty jacket. Like the girl, he was black, or rather mixed-race. The girl's frizzy hair was bound in a ponytail. No more than three years old, she wore a sweater over a gown that looked like a Halloween princess costume.

The woman handed Charlie the girl, who smelled like she could use a bath. He held her easily in his right arm. She put her hands around his neck and gazed at him with impossibly green eyes.

"What's your name?" Charlie asked.

"Romy."

"Romy? I like that. I'm Charlie."

"I'm Tawny," the woman said. She hugged the boy's shoulder. "This is Wyatt."

"Hey," Charlie said.

"You work in a factory?" Tawny asked, taking in Charlie's rumpled clothes.

"No, no. Just poor." He stepped to the door and pulled it open. Tawny and Wyatt walked in; Charlie followed. Inside, they paused, momentarily stunned by the size of the crowd. It seemed like a thousand people were jammed into the Hunger Palace's main hall. Tables were crowded with people; the queue was so long it had quit being a line and turned into a blob.

"What the fuck," the woman said. "We'll never get any goddamn food."

"I'm hungry," said Romy.

Charlie looked down. Wyatt had a fierce grip on his right leg. "Come on," he told the boy. "We'll get you something to eat." Still holding Romy, he bulled his way toward the head of the line, repeatedly muttering, "'Scuse us, hungry kids coming through."

The little girl pointed at people and said, "*Pop, pop, pop.*" Charlie was amazed when they turned and not only smiled at the girl, but stepped aside. In just a few seconds, the four of them stood at the head of the serving line. "It's a miracle," Charlie said, staring into the face of Charlene Guy, Channel Six morning anchor, who stood behind the steam table wearing a white apron and a Braves baseball cap.

"I suppose it is," said Charlene. "But children always move to the head of the line here." The news personality turned and smiled for her station's camera as she dished out dressing.

A stout black woman appeared behind Charlene and stared out at the crowd, then turned toward the kitchen and shouted, "We ain't got enough food!"

Charlie skipped dinner for the time being, not out of altruism, but because he didn't have an extra arm to carry two meals and Romy. They moved through the line and got turkey, dressing, sweet potato soufflé, green beans, cranberry sauce, rolls, cans of Coke, and pumpkin pie slapped on foam plates. They were served by a team of three news anchors, a rich white woman with her silver hair done just so, and a couple of everyday people—the ones who knew what they were doing. Romy grabbed her roll and stuffed it into her mouth as Charlie, already despairing of finding a place to sit, led Wyatt and Tawny to the dining area. Lo and behold, two shabbily dressed black men rose as the four approached the first row of tables, sweeping their arms gallantly to offer the family their places. When Charlie set Romy down, she kneeled on her chair to eat.

Charlie looked around and realized he and Tawny were sprinkles of salt in a sea of pepper. "Get us some paper towels or a rag or something," she commanded him. "This table's filthy."

He moved toward the kitchen to look for rags. His path was cut off by the large woman he'd seen before. "Tell me you just drove up a truck with five hundred meals on it," she said, not looking like she would take No for an answer. Reluctantly, Charlie shook his head.

"We gonna run out of food before we run out of people. Gets worse every year."

"Sorry," Charlie said. "I'm just lookin' for some rags to wipe tables."

"You here to volunteer? Cause if you are, then volunteer to wash pots and pans. That's where we need help. Gettin' nuthin' but lip from the back of the kitchen. My name's Lucinda. Lucinda Persons. If you need anything, just keep working." She chuckled, then widened her eyes and snapped, "I mean it."

"Yes ma'am," Charlie said, backing away to avoid her wrath.

Lucinda stormed off to find another volunteer/victim. Charlie looked back wistfully at Tawny, who was already drawing the attention of several men. And then he caught a whiff of a familiar and most unwelcome odor. He surveyed the dining hall but didn't see Trouble.

Charlie walked through double doors into the kitchen, past the cooks working at stoves and a six-year-old inspection notice on the wall with a "71" score, which was barely passing—and probably a charitable grade, at that. Beyond an old, broken-down Hobart dishwasher, an emaciated figure in a ratty T-shirt and tan corduroy pants with his back to Charlie was scrubbing a large pot in the middle trough of a deep triple sink. As Charlie approached, the drudge reached over with his free hand, scooped out a handful of dressing from a smaller pot on a shelf, and stuffed it in his mouth.

"Heard you need some help," Charlie said to the back of the dishwasher's head. He felt a crackle of static when he grabbed a green scrubbing pad from the metal shelf overhanging the sink. When the fellow turned to face him, Charlie rocked back on his heels, took a deep breath, choked on the smell, and yelled, "You son of a bitch, you nearly got me killed! I was thrown out of the house and there are warrants for my arrest. You're—"

"Trouble?" The dishwasher grinned and stripped off his plastic apron, offering it to Charlie. "Told you so. Here. Your turn. About time my replacement got here. I'm not cut out for this kind of work." He wiped food from his face and gestured to the pots and pans stacked up on the counter and the floor beside the sink. "Here," he said, flipping a wet rag, hitting Charlie in the face. "If you'll excuse me, I gotta keep Redeemer away from that *whore.*" Trouble snarled the last word.

"I'm not through with you!" Charlie shouted, but Trouble was already halfway across the kitchen's red-tiled floor. Charlie followed, talking to the back of his head. "Why is this shit happening to me? I want to know." In frustration, he cried out, "You made me homeless!"

Trouble turned and laughed contemptuously. "No, I didn't. And welcome to the club. Rest assured, you belong here. You're just too stupid to know it. Get to work and quit messing up my plans."

"I had a home," Charlie said, his face forlorn.

"No, you were out in the rain. If I had to do it over again, I wouldn't rescue your ass!"

"Rescue *my* ass! Some rescue." Charlie looked around. "Is this where you stay? How long have you been working for Redeemer? If you call what you do working, that is."

"You got it wrong about who works for who."

"Are you saying he works for *you*?"

"Not that, either. He's just contrary. Not good at following orders."

"Just like me, right?"

"Hardly. You work for yourself, asshole. That's why we had to have a contract. And even that doesn't seem to be working. Fair warning: You're in violation, home boy." Trouble pointed an accusing finger at him. "You're lucky I don't smoke your ass right now."

Charlie sneered at him. "Do it."

"Won't."

"You mean *can't* … *bitch*," Charlie added, being in a somewhat self-destructive mood.

"I'll ignore that. Usually, no one talks to me that way and lives. I guess you know something the other assholes don't, is that it?" He snorted. "Consider yourself fortunate."

"That would be a stretch right now. Anyway, I'm not afraid of you."

"Figured that much." Trouble started to saunter away, almost making it to the dining hall door before stopping. He turned and regarded Charlie critically. "You're not even close to fulfilling the contract. So just do your job and stay away from the whore. She's filthy, nothing but bad news."

"Wait! I need to talk to you about the book, about—"

Trouble walked out. Charlie tried to follow, but when he touched the swinging metal door, a jolt of electricity knocked him back two steps. He tried again. A bigger shock this time. *But not fatal.* Charlie narrowed his eyes. *Trouble wasn't fully charged.* He might have a chance to beat the shit out of the old asshole, consequences be damned. The third time, Charlie touched the door with his elbow. *Zap.* He cried out in pain. He tried a fourth time.

A pan fell off a rack and hit him on the head. "OK," he grumbled, his hair standing on end. "I'll wash dishes."

Mumbling obscenities, Charlie returned to the sink and slipped on the dirty apron. He drained filthy water from the tubs and refilled them, squirting soap into the middle tank. Then he started scrubbing. There was a mountain of dirty pots and pans—several hours' worth of work. He struggled to find places for clean cookware, hanging some up on an overhead rack, stacking others on vacant counters and stove tops.

No one came to help, and everyone else in the kitchen ignored him. When the food was all gone, cooks and servers brought more pans, trays, and utensils for Charlie to wash, making a pile on the floor larger than the one he'd started on.

Afternoon faded into evening. The dull roar of the crowd on the other side of the double doors died down. By the time Charlie dried off the last pot and hung it on a rack above a butcher block table, he was alone in the kitchen. While he was draining and wiping down the sinks, the lights went off. "Hey!" he hollered, groping around in the darkness. "I'm not through back here!"

Trouble's voice rang out. "Hey back atcha. I think the circuit breaker tripped. Give me a hand getting it back on. I'll hold the flashlight."

"You do it," Charlie said, ripping off his apron and putting it on the sink. "I'm outta here."

"There's people trippin' over themselves. Sure, we've got our differences, but we all gotta do what we gotta do to keep this place workin'. Come on," Trouble wheedled. "Do the right thing."

Charlie hesitated, unable to see well enough to make an exit. "Where is it?"

"Back this way, I think."

Trouble shone a beam on the floor as he walked into a pantry. Charlie followed him and heard the click of a metal door latch. "I'll hold the light," Trouble said. "Looks like the main breaker tripped. Flip it. Be careful." The flashlight beam danced over the switches. As Charlie pushed it back into place, a hand clamped down on his. "Take that, sucker!" Trouble screamed in his ear.

Charlie's body spasmed as electricity surged through it. When Trouble released his hand, Charlie went flying against a wire rack on the opposite wall. The lights came back on, but he was blinded by the universe of dancing red spots that dominated his vision. He felt like he was having a heart attack. Through ringing ears he heard Trouble say, "That's what you get for consorting with the whore and her bastard child."

Charlie had no idea what that meant, but he still wanted to kick Trouble's ass. He tried to rise to his feet with a vague idea of striking back, but he seemed to be paralyzed.

"That whore is the source of all your problems, and you're too stupid to know it!" Trouble screamed. "Not that it matters what I say. You aren't capable of learning."

"Gah," said Charlie, drooling.

"You're the stupidest prick I've ever worked with. You're lucky you're still alive." Trouble looked to the ceiling and muttered. "You picked one blind bastard. Absolutely useless. Can't I just enforce the contract? I'm tired of looking at him. Why, I oughta just enforce the contract right now. Really. Let me do him." He held his ear as if listening to a distant voice. "Might have to, anyway. Ah, c'mon. You'll be *sor-ry*," Trouble sang. "*Truly you will.*"

The next thing Charlie knew, Trouble was huffing and panting, dragging him by the feet from the pantry across the kitchen floor. He wanted to resist, but his limbs were useless. He tried to call out, but his voice made no sound. A trickle of electricity continued to course through his body. Trouble grunted as he pulled Charlie out the rear door of the kitchen onto the loading dock. After stealing Charlie's boots, Trouble left him lying on the concrete facedown, drooling.

At that point, Charlie passed out.

When he came to, it was dark outside. A yellow light burned overhead. He tried to remember where he was. "Redeemer's," he muttered. He struggled to get up. The cold concrete was trying to tell him something. He looked down at his shoeless feet. "We was robbed," he moaned, falling sideways against the wall. He patted his pants pockets. He still had his keys and his wallet. A cold wind hit him, and he realized he'd pissed himself or gotten dishwater on his pants.

He stumbled around in a circle and then tried to get inside, but the steel door was locked against him. This seemed to present an insurmountable problem. Then he turned around and faced the night. *Walk around the building, dumbshit.* He shuffled down the dock steps onto the empty rear lot and staggered around the building, leaning on it for guidance and support, since he was still dizzy and blurry-eyed. He rounded the front corner and faced the gravel lot, which he dreaded crossing without shoes.

Nearly all the cars were gone, but two children sat in the open side door of a cargo van. He blinked and tried to focus his eyes. Those were the kids he'd helped. The tiny girl saw him and called out, "Hi, Charlie. Are you hurt?"

"Hey," he mumbled, unable to remember her name. He was about to say he had been injured when he realized he was beginning to feel better. He took a step toward the van, then saw it wasn't the seedy enchantress who'd been with them before. This woman was black. Older and rounder. Ah, of course. "Are you their mother?"

"No, their momma went out with Redeemer," she said. "There they are, coming back." She pointed toward Memorial Drive just as the red Cadillac came barreling into the lot.

Charlie stood dumbly as Tawny exited the car with a bag of groceries and sang out to the kids, "We got food for tomorrow." She stood in a halo underneath a streetlight by the building's corner.

Redeemer climbed out of the driver's side and said, "You can't keep doing it the way you been. Here, take this." He handed Tawny something small. "What I promised."

Tawny glanced Charlie's way but didn't seem to notice him. She turned and walked over to her kids.

"She's a whore," said a grimy whitish-gray man through a faceful of hair. He was sitting down, his back against the building. "Not judgin', just sayin'. She works the stoplight down the street. Bunch of 'em do."

Charlie turned to stare at the guy. "Have you seen … Trouble?"

"Nuthin' but," the man responded. Charlie turned back to watch the family for a moment. Weird: That little girl was the only person who cared what had happened to him. He couldn't remember her name, but he knew that she deserved saving from this terrible world she lived in. Not that he could do anything about it, since he was no better off. He left, gingerly stepping and ouching his way across the gravel, taking the shortest route to the sidewalk.

Once he had escaped the torturous parking lot, Charlie cast a backward glance at the woman named Tawny, the one Trouble had been screaming about. *The whore.* He felt like his mind had been poisoned against her, but he was also filled with desire for the woman underneath the mascara. Anyway, if Trouble hated her, she couldn't be all bad.

The side street was empty when Charlie climbed into the Caravan. His crotch was wet and cold, and he could smell the taint of homelessness upon himself. Since the Y was closed and he couldn't afford a motel room, there was no shower in his immediate future, so he did what he would be forced to do more and more frequently in the days to come—change into dirty but dry clothes, put on secondhand sneakers, and wipe down his body with moist towelettes. Pantless, he crouched low as a cop car passed by.

Charlie drove off and stopped at a service station to use the restroom. He recoiled in horror when he saw his face in the mirror. Tracks of dried blood ran down each cheek. His eyes were beyond bloodshot. They were pools of red. The bastard had nearly blinded him. Correction: *had* blinded him, but he'd recovered, somehow. He wanted to kill Trouble, if such a thing were possible.

He ran water and splashed his face with both hands, then looked around and realized there were no paper towels, only a hand dryer. He left the restroom shaking his head like a wet dog.

Having missed two meals already, Charlie looked for a place to eat. The supermarkets he drove by were closed; so were the restaurants he passed. Finally he saw a Pancake Hut and despite his misgivings, pulled into the lot. He sat at the counter of the otherwise empty diner and waited. Fifteen minutes later, he realized the waitress, like Lil Bit, was intent on ignoring him. He left without getting so much as a glass of water. As he departed, the cook hollered, "Thanks for taking the hint, you homeless fuck."

Chapter Seventeen

November 30: DNA Day. According to lab results, there was a 99.989 percent certainty that Demetrious Jackson was related to Isaac Cutchins. Charlie attributed the .011 percent (one ten-thousandth) ambiguity to incest-related mutation. He put the results in his safe deposit box alongside the Mason jar containing Riggins's finger, which spent its days circling endlessly in its dark prison. It was a sad, awkward moment. Before locking the door on his box, Charlie apologized to the lonely digit for breaking the news that way. "Sorry, John. Sooner or later, you had to know."

That afternoon, Charlie checked his mail in Decatur. The only piece was his dreaded credit card bill. He hadn't kept track of expenses, and his fingers trembled as he opened the envelope. When he saw the total, he despaired, slumping against the wall of the store and sliding to the floor. Nearly thirty-two hundred dollars! Shocking! There it was, his life on paper: Fast food, gas, coffee, the first DNA test, camping gear, a duster coat and wide-brim hat to keep off the rain—all of it piled onto the previous balance. Being homeless was more expensive than he'd realized. He'd have to get a cash advance on his card and buy a money order to make a payment, putting off the day of reckoning for another month. Unfortunately, he was close to his credit limit; he wouldn't make it to the end of the year unless he signed up for another card—or two. But one blood-soaked contract was enough. He'd left Bayard Terrace without getting paid for his past month of caretaking for Kathleen, but in truth he'd done little to earn it, so he didn't press the issue.

Now he only had fifty bucks left in his checking account. He desperately needed money. Across the street at Java Joe's, he called Fortress.

"Mr. Furst no longer works here," said the woman who answered Joshua's extension.

"Who is my editor, then?" Charlie asked, stomping the floor in frustration and rattling the table, sloshing coffee on his legal pad.

"That depends. Who are you?"

"Charles Sherman. I wrote *Flight from Forsyth.*" Silence. "You are publishing it, aren't you?"

"Could I put you on hold?"

"No! Absolutely not! I demand—"

Click. Charlie listened to *The Impossible Dream* for three minutes before hanging up. He feared he'd entered into a contract with the very worst sort of devil, one who refused to keep its end of the bargain. In other words, a publisher.

* * *

Facing grim financial prospects, Charlie had to sell *American Monster*. Fortress was out of the question, due to lack of interest (or editor) and its abominable payment policies, which vacillated between slow pay, no pay, and what, me pay? He needed an agent to protect him from such deadbeats. Following a marathon espresso-driven indexing session for *Flight* at Java Joe's, he wrote a query letter that, due to his increasingly paranoid state, read somewhat like a Nigerian confidence e-mail:

> Dear ___________:
>
> I have been shot and my house has been ransacked twice. I need to send what I've written someplace where the people who are looking for me can't find it. Perhaps I could pay you a storage fee. But I have heard you are a bright and resourceful agent and recognize an excellent opportunity when you see it. I will finish my book by the time you read this letter and I am quite sure it will sell a million copies, maybe more. It is all true and documented. There are things I can't say yet, but when the time comes I will turn my evidence over to the authorities. First I must tell the story and force them to do their jobs. Their ancestors are involved, so good luck with that—this is what I tell myself.
>
> This is the true crime I have documented in *American Monster*: My wife's grandfather, Isaac Cutchins, 95, lynched a black farmer in 1937. Then he raped the dead man's wife

and stole his victims' land, which is now worth $20 million. The woman who was raped gave birth to a light-skinned daughter, whose life is plagued by her seventeen-year-old gangsta wannabe grandson.

By the way, Cutchins raped his oldest daughter 150 times while he sent his wife and other children out for ice cream during the early 1950s. That's six hundred cones! The victim showed up at her mother's funeral to spit on the dead woman's face and curse her father to hell. My wife and I stopped by the dry cleaners and missed it, but I tracked down the woman and heard her terrible nightmare story.

This is the family I married into, and *American Monster* is the story I was chosen to tell the night I agreed to edit a dead man's book—*Flight from Forsyth*, soon to be published by Fortress, I think. I have built a strong case and the killer knows it. When I confronted the man on these issues, he tried to kill me. His family—my family—has turned against me. I've been banned from seeing my children. I am on the run. I write this letter from a coffeehouse with a liberal electric outlet policy and it closes in ten minutes, so I must be brief. I know this all sounds insane, but it is the story of murder and greed and it's all true. I'm an excellent writer. Read the sample I've enclosed. You will see for yourself. Thank you.

Sincerely,

Charles Sherman

* * *

The next day Charlie rewrote the query, making it more coherent, though it still wasn't completely sane. On the way to Java Joe's that gray, cloudy morning, he stopped to consider his image in a plate glass window. He was turning into a ghost—or, upon further reflection, a zombie. He had dark circles under his eyes and looked gaunt; he'd lost more than fifty pounds in less than a year—although that, in an of itself, was a healthy thing. It was his psyche that was suffering most. Living on the street had exacted its toll in sleeplessness and constant hunger; his drifter's loneliness grew heavier on his heart each day.

But there was work to do. He printed *American Monster*'s first three chapters at a copy shop and mailed them with his semi-sane letter to Barbara Asher, the only literary agent who had not rejected *Thoracic Park*. (Actually, she'd never responded, but Charlie took his omens where he could find them.)

He received a letter that day from Fortress demanding the galleys and index. Angry, he called the company; the receptionist refused to put him through to the publisher. Charlie hung up, convinced he'd seen the last dime from that hellbound outfit. Still, he'd finish *Flight from Forsyth* because it would have his name on it and prove he existed, matters of no small importance to a man in danger of falling off the face of the earth.

* * *

Having worked double-time to put the final touches on *Flight*, Charlie grunted in triumph as he shoved the galleys and index into a big envelope. After he mailed them to his publishing company, that worthless pack of bastards, he turned his full attention to *American Monster*, where his head and heart already were. He wrote quickly and well, even obsessively. His fingers flew over the keyboard like he was Chico Marx playing piano.

He was protective of his *Monster*, of course. He wasn't just the book's author, he was also its bodyguard, Secret Service, and Army of One. He locked away notes, hid copies of disks and flash drives, and e-mailed chapters to himself, leaving them safely on Hotmail, he hoped. He shadow-boxed in preparation for throw-down time, and when he came across a dinged-up aluminum baseball bat at the Goodwill Store, he bought that, because if he had to go down, he'd go down swinging.

His attempts to contact the living relatives of John Riggins's other lynchers yielded three denials, including a terse, awkward one from Cecil Montgomery, who wanted to know where Charlie was calling from, two "no comments," and an anonymous death threat, all of which he wrote into the story. Forsyth County officials weren't very helpful, either. Tempting fate, Charlie had tried to contact District Attorney Eric Stockwell to talk about the case, but the prosecutor didn't return his calls. (Charlie thought that was weird. After all, he was jailbait. Didn't Stockwell know or care that the sheriff's office was holding warrants for his arrest?) He'd mailed questions about John Riggins's death to Pappy, with a copy to Uncle Stanley, requesting a written e-mail response to his Hotmail address. If he got none, then Pappy's denial, lie, and spit would be the family's final word on the matter.

Unless, of course, they killed him. Then Trouble would have to dig around in a Dumpster for another writer, wouldn't he?

* * *

After a parking attendant called the cops on him, Charlie fled Atlanta again, traveling even farther south than Clayton, hiding in Butts County, of all places, camping out in a state park, cooking hot dogs on a black-grated grill, and rubbing his hands together over it like it was his very own barrel fire. He refused on principle to roast marshmallows until his children returned to him.

As winter approached, Charlie had the park mostly to himself. Sometimes he slept in the van, other nights in the tent he'd pitched for appearances' sake. Fueled by instant coffee, Gatorade, peanut butter sandwiches, fresh fruit, and yogurt smoothies, Charlie wrote and edited almost constantly. For a break, he'd go for a walk with his computer, talking to bare trees and fearless squirrels. Sometimes he'd rent a boat and, ignoring the danger involved, row the laptop back and forth across the park's lake like he was on a cheap date. The ascetic writer had become closer to his computer than the most fervent porn junkie. After the sun set, he kept writing and editing until words became blurs on the screen.

One day, while he was out for a walk, a state trooper came by and checked out his vehicle at the campsite. Charlie hid behind a pine tree and watched. After a few minutes, the trooper drove on. It was good to know the license plate hadn't been reported stolen.

Nevertheless, he packed up his tent and vacated the park, shifting even further south, down to Indian Springs State Park in Middle Georgia. Along the way, he saw a likely looking Caravan, so he switched plates again.

Sitting by a campfire, he finished the first draft of *American Monster*, concluding with this epilogue:

> As I write these final pages, I am homeless. I have been banned from seeing my children. I cannot afford an attorney. Whether this account ever sees the light of day is out of my hands now. I made a solemn vow, a covenant, to do this, as distasteful as it has become. It is important, because people—living and as yet unborn—need to know the truth about their past. The problem isn't so much that, as Shake-

> speare put it, "The evil that men do lives after them, the good is oft interr'd with their bones," but that the evil becomes the unchallenged norm, and is eventually mistaken for good. The lie becomes the truth.
>
> We ignore the past and think that those who suffer do so because of some inferiority on their part, and we take strange comfort in that. And when we prosper we are certain we are blessed due to our innate goodness and superiority. Our ignorance of history and refusal to take responsibility for the past—as well as our acceptance of unfair benefits we derive from it—allow these evils to thrive.

Five minutes later, he began his rewrite. *Time enough for rest in the grave.*

* * *

On the verge of completing his third and final draft, Charlie drove up to Decatur to check his mail and found a letter from Barbara Asher. "Is this for real?" the agent wrote. "You seem very strange, but the samples are great! Mail me the manuscript and I'll look at it over the holidays, if you give me an exclusive."

"Yessss!" Charlie shouted, pumping his fist in the air, jolting the slacker clerk from his customary elbows-on-counter torpor.

He didn't go back to Indian Springs. Instead, he spent the night in a Decatur parking lot. On the cold, overcast morning of December 24, he finished work on the 275-page manuscript in the special collections room of the Decatur library, completing it a week ahead of his self-imposed deadline.

He went to the bank and rented another large safety deposit box so that he could stash his most crucial papers for *Flight from Forsyth* and all of those for *American Monster*. Desperate to see a friendly face, he drove over to Virginia Highlands and lugged a duffel bag containing his writing gear into Bay Street Coffeehouse. The place was decked out with wreaths. Charlie breathed in the doubly invigorating mix of pine and coffee. Jean rushed around the counter to hug him. "Where have you been?" she cried out. She wrinkled her nose at him, but she was too polite to mention why.

"Finishing another book," he proclaimed. "I'm done."

"So soon? How prolific of you!" She stepped back and frowned. "You're skinny now."

"Yeah. I've got authorexia."

"You." She smiled, showing a dimple in her chin he'd never noticed before.

"I need to borrow a cup of electricity to print it up."

She laughed. "Sure. By the way, people have been asking about you. I don't remember who, though a couple of them acted like detectives." She gave him her most potent gaze, her head cocked to the side. "I told them I know nothing. Nothing!"

"Good." Charlie hoped he didn't look as scared as he felt right then. "I've been hiding out. But that part of my life is just about over. I'm looking for a place," he said, trying to sound properly ambitious.

"Where have you been staying?"

"Here and there."

She pursed her lips, appearing deep in thought. "I know a guy who wants to sublet his loft. I'll talk to him."

"That might work," he said, although he had no idea how it would, since he was flat broke and thousands of dollars in debt. He gave her his phone number, anyway.

Coffee was on the house in celebration of his grand achievement—and in recognition of his poverty, which, he assured Jean, was about to end. "Somebody owes me money," he explained.

Charlie finished printing the manuscript shortly after noon and slipped the manuscript into a box and hand-printed the address. He asked Jean to watch over his stuff while he went to the post office, where he stood in line behind procrastinating holiday shippers.

Roxanne, the postal worker Charlie knew best and trusted most, took his package. He turned away from the counter. When he looked at all the holiday-numb people behind him, he realized he'd completed his mission. It had nearly killed him, but he'd done it. His knees shook and he almost fell to the floor as a wave of joy and relief swept over him. Feeling holy and humble, he returned to the coffeehouse and packed his gear into the duffel. When he went to the counter to thank Jean and wish her a happy holiday, she pointed overhead at mistletoe hanging from a pipe, then pecked him on the lips.

Grinning broadly, he hauled his gear out to the van in the back lot. And now to rid himself of the horrible burden of the blood-soaked contract—and Trouble the Terrible, hopefully. Although he'd stashed the vat in the storage unit, it always seemed to rest on his shoulders, pushing him down and forward all at once. How heavy it had been, how it made him stagger! He could already feel it lifting away into the sky as he drove off to the Store-All.

* * *

The Dumpster saved Charlie's life. He was alone at the Store-All, holding the contract vat over his head, pouring its odious contents into the green bin when a deafening blast threw debris, shrapnel, and chunks of asphalt in all directions. He was shielded from the explosion by the trash bin's considerable bulk. Metal screeched on asphalt as it shifted on the parking lot pavement and crashed into him, sending him sprawling.

The plastic tub landed upside down on his head, dousing him with blood. It stayed there for a moment while he flailed his arms wildly. Frightened out of his wits, he first thought the blood had exploded to punish him for trying to get rid of it. Still on his butt, Charlie flung the tub to the side. His world was an inferno: heat and fire everywhere, dust and smoke in his eyes and lungs. His ears were filled with intense ringing.

"What the fuck!" Charlie screamed, but he could barely hear himself. Wide-eyed, he scrambled to his feet. Chaos surrounded him. On the other side of the Dumpster, flames shot twenty feet into the air, and a thick cloud of black smoke roiled upward. Fires burned all over the lot. Store-All's office window was shattered and flames licked the inside walls. The top of the Dumpster was burning, too. Smoke from burning plastic pierced his nose and stabbed his lungs.

Dazed, with his heart racing, Charlie spit out coppery, foul-tasting blood and took a few unsteady steps around the Dumpster, crunching glass with every step. To his shock and horror, his van was now a blackened, burning hulk. Make that *three* burning hulks, along with a hundred minor parts—the pieces of his life—scattered all over. He looked up at the mini-warehouse's roof in disbelief. Was that the driver's seat on top of the building?

It was difficult to think with that thing up there. He shook his head to clear it and realized that it wasn't the blood, but the van that had exploded. And it was no accident. The engine was off, which meant that someone had tried to kill him with a car bomb. "Holy shit!" he cried. "I'm in Iraq!"

His sticky-lidded eyes stung from smoke, ash, and dust. He put his forearm over the bottom half of his face and staggered around in a circle, dripping blood like Carrie at the prom. He looked at the front gate on Wynburn Avenue. Traffic had stopped. People stood beside their cars. Some moved toward him slowly but couldn't get through the security gate. *Stupid zombies.*

Yelling and honking filled the air, cutting through the ringing in his ears. "They're trying to kill me!" he shouted, then fell to his knees and wailed, "They destroyed everything!"

But they hadn't—not yet, anyway. He patted the flash memory drive in his pocket. The final draft of *American Monster* was with him, and his Waterman pen was in his pocket, so he was still in business as a writer. He patted again and felt his wedding ring. Which was strange, because he couldn't remember putting it there—or even carrying it with him. Had the explosion—*Nah*. Maybe he'd planned to hock it and just couldn't remember now that the blast filled his head.

In any case, everything else was in danger. The door to his unit, which he'd left open, was hanging precariously by its top hinge, and a fire burned inside. In a few minutes, his possessions would be destroyed. He needed to save what he could and get out before the zombies got to him.

In desperation, he sprinted across the lot, leaping over wreckage, shielding his face from the flames consuming the van. With a loud grunt, he yanked the broken door off his storage unit. He blinked against the smoke, grabbed his mountain bike, its chain lock draped around the handlebars, and wheeled it out. He'd taken off his duster inside the unit earlier to wrestle with the vat. He dove back inside and grabbed it along with an old backpack. Choking on fumes, he dug into a garbage bag filled with old clothes and pulled out an armful, then stumbled out the door and stuffed them in the backpack.

The uninsured vehicle's burning frame now stood between him and the street. Fifty yards away, a half-dozen people were at the front gate, shouting at him to open it. "Help is on the way," an older man yelled. But Charlie Sherman didn't operate under man's laws and therefore expected to derive no benefit from them.

"No cops," he muttered, turning away from the growing crowd. He saw the license plate on the ground. He crammed it in his pack, too. *For me to know and you to find out.* While he figured the police would eventually identify him, finding him was another matter. He was safer as a moving target than a sitting duck. He checked the bike's tires. Soft, but rideable.

To escape through the back fence, he needed his bolt cutters. Holding his breath, he stumbled back inside his unit. The heat was nearly unbearable, and smoke burned his eyes. He fumbled with the hasps on his big metal toolbox, then felt around inside and grasped a rubber-gripped handle. He rushed outside with the cutters, exhaled, inhaled, slipped on the duster and backpack, then hopped on the bike. Holding the cutters across the handlebars, he started to pedal, stopping when he saw what was left of his computer on the pavement twenty yards away from the van—the bottom half containing the hard drive. He ripped out the drive and jammed it into his pack, then pumped the bike to the back of the lot. He was now screened from Wynburn by several warehouse buildings. As he neared the fence, he heard an emergency vehicle's *whoop-whoop*.

He jumped off the bike and started snapping through fence links. Pop, pop, pop, pop, pop, pop. He stuffed the cutters in his crowded pack. The wire scratched him as he rammed the bike through the slit he'd made. A steep embankment covered with thick tufts of brown grass led to some railroad tracks. He half slid, half walked down, using the bike for support, then pedaled away to a rising chorus of sirens. He bumped along on the gravel beside the tracks. When he hit a hard, smooth patch of dirt, he put the bike in high gear and pedaled fiercely, glancing over his shoulder at the towering black cloud—his life up in smoke. He wondered if this was Trouble's work—a double-cross by the Party of the First Part. If so, he was doomed and all he was doing was stretching out the inevitable, ugly ending. Which would leave him crushed like a bug, most likely.

Several minutes later, he stopped beneath an overpass. A jumble of shopping carts lay at the foot of a concrete embankment rising diagonally to the bottom of the bridge. Above the two pillars that supported that side of the Arbor Drive bridge, a cardboard hut was wedged between concrete and iron—a refrigerator box some poor wretch called home. The flaps were open and it appeared vacant, though its inside was lined with blankets and old coats.

Charlie hollered out a greeting and got no answer. He leaned the bike against a concrete pillar and scrambled up the incline. As he drew near the shelter, an acrid stench assailed his nostrils. He entered and held his breath as he stripped off his bloody clothes. He flung his foul duds into the brambles beside the bridge and put on clothes pulled from the backpack. He had no pockets, so he put his phone, wallet, and keys into his pack and pedaled off in paint-covered sweat pants and a bulky sweater, the cold wind whipping his face.

First things first. He got off the railroad right of way, took a side street, then zigged and zagged while trying to think of somewhere he could stay, someplace warm and safe.

Unfortunately, he could think of no such place. On top of that, his credit card was nearly maxed out and there was a price on his head, set by man or God—or maybe both. And while they hadn't killed him, he hadn't survived yet, either.

His heart raced from exertion and fear. The shock of the bombing and the winter bike ride sapped Charlie's strength and played tricks on his mind. He kept looking over his shoulder, expecting to see motorcycle cops—or a black car—racing up behind him. He felt like the world was made of quicksand, and if he stopped he'd sink into it and disappear. Every so often, he laughed at the ugly joke his life had become, with its mixed-up punch lines. Once he cried because his daddy killed himself, and now—for the hundredth time—he understood why.

Charlie was pretty sure that the varmints had tried to kill him, since no one else cared whether he lived or died. Then again, there was Trouble, but explosives weren't his style. Still, Charlie wasn't letting him off the hook, not after the old trickster had suckered him into this mess in the first place.

After an hour of riding around, feeling like a hunted animal, he needed shelter from the cold. He went to the only place he felt he could reasonably claim a right of access. Charlie locked the bike to the rack in front of the Decatur YMCA and went inside. The people there were strangers to him. A black staffer stood by the registration desk and held up a hand. "Stop."

"Stop?" Charlie said. "I need to—"

"You can't come in here like that."

Charlie held his membership card like a badge. "But I got to. I got to." He turned and looked over his shoulder, half expecting to see cops rushing up on him from behind. "I just need to clean up." His hands trembled. His eyes filled with tears. His voice cracked. "Please, sir. Please. I don't have a place to stay. I don't have anything anymore. I just need to clean up and go away. That's all."

The man folded his arms across his chest. Charlie turned to another black staffer, the clerk sitting behind the front desk. "I pay my dues. Every month. I got a right. You can't discriminate just because—"

The clerk grabbed the card and gave her colleague a nasty look. "What part about the reason for the season do you not understand?" Then to Charlie: "We close in fifteen minutes, due to the holiday. You'd best hurry."

"Thank you, thank you," Charlie said. "I won't forget this. Ever." He shuffled straight toward the locker room, leaving the employees to argue about his worth. Fortunately for him, the place was nearly deserted. Charlie threw away his sweat pants and sweater, which were sticky with blood. He groaned when he glanced in the mirror and saw that his bloodstained face was covered with stuck-on ash and soot. After his shower, he put on brown corduroy pants and a white shirt, then wiped off his blood-crusted boots with a Y towel. When he looked in the mirror he was amazed to see the only marks on him were a couple of scratches where he'd pushed through Store-All's fence.

On the way out, he rifled through the lost-and-found bin, searching for a coat. He had to settle for a red quilted vest. He put it on under the duster and slipped out. It didn't matter how ridiculous he looked; he felt worse.

Now what? Crash at a cheap motel and figure out what to do next, that's what. He pedaled into downtown Decatur and stopped at Mailbox. Even though he'd locked his bike to a lamp post, Charlie walked into the store backwards, ever watchful of his most prized possession.

Taking time out from explaining to a customer that he couldn't give next-day delivery on a package shipped Christmas Eve, the slacker clerk smirked at the writer's new outfit. Ignoring him, Charlie went to his postal box and struggled to unlock it, then stopped to rub his hands together and blow on them. After a minute's work on his hands, he was dexterous enough to turn the key. There was one piece of mail, a thin envelope from Fortress. He pulled it out and tried to open it, but his raw, red fingers were useless for such detail work. He saw a pen attached to a beaded chain on the counter. He slipped it under the flap and ripped the envelope open. Inside was a sheet of paper with numbers on it—and a check for $10,000.

Charlie stood with his mouth open, blinking and shuddering as a great, grumbling evil lifted off his back, pinching a nerve just to be mean on its way out. He stared at the check. He could feel himself getting taller. He cried out in joy, "I made it! I made it! I made it!" and bounced out the door, dashing back an instant later to retrieve his keys from the mailbox.

"Happy Festivus!" the slacker yelled after Charlie. "And to all a whatever!"

Soon afterward, Charlie sauntered into Southern Trust Bank and proudly deposited $9,500 in his checking account. He kept the rest in cold, glorious cash. He stepped out of the bank a new man, bursting with joy at the realization he wasn't going to starve or freeze to death, at least not for a while. He could start over: cheap car, cheap apartment, new shipping department clothes, even a steak and baked potato, with sweet tea to wash it all down.

As he unlocked his bike, the wind stiffened. It would be a tougher ride now, and he had many miles to go. He hopped on and pedaled along the sidewalk, then jumped the curb into the street, his duster streaming behind him. A bus passed by. The warmth of its diesel exhaust comforted him.

Weary and fatigued from his murderously busy day, the raw-lunged, adrenaline-spent bombing victim pedaled into the lot of his favorite Nights Inn just before dusk. He hid the bike from view and registered, sneaking a peek at the license tag in his pack, since he couldn't remember its number. "Can I have a room on the first floor?" he asked.

G. Patel shook her head. "You're lucky we have anything," she said in a lilting accent. She took his credit card and handed it back a moment later. "I'm sorry. It is not going through."

He'd hit his limit. His credit had crashed on Christmas Eve.

"I can pay cash," Charlie said with a catch in his voice, almost sobbing when he realized how close he'd come to sleeping on the street. She gave him a doubtful look. "You do take cash, don't you?" he asked. The look on her dark, pretty face remained. "I'll pay two nights in advance."

This appeased her. Charlie signed the forms and walked outside, then wheeled the bike to the stairs and carried it up to the second-floor room. Inside it was frigid. He turned the heat up, leaned the bike against the register, and collapsed on the queen-sized bed. He couldn't remember the last time he'd laid down on a mattress. Within minutes, he was asleep.

He woke in near-total darkness. Only a thin strip of light cut between the panels of the window curtains. He jumped out of bed, threw on his boots, then sprinted out the door and down the stairs. The desk clerk looked at him impassively. "Yes?"

"I need to get a cab. Do you have the number—"

She put up her hand to stop his question and made a phone call. Within three minutes, a Yellow Cab pulled up. Charlie was impressed with this transportation system's near-buslike efficiency.

"Where to?" asked the driver, who looked like he might be related to the desk clerk.

"Toys R Us." They drove in silence through the thinning Christmas Eve traffic. Charlie glanced at his watch and silently fretted that he was too late.

"Wait for me," he told the cabbie when they reached the toy store, which was, miraculously, still open. Barely. He walked in and a manager locked the doors behind him.

He looked around in amazement and dismay. The place had been ransacked. The popular toys were gone, but some board games, dolls, trucks, building sets, and stocking stuffers remained. He ran around grabbing things and throwing them in his cart. He stood in the checkout line behind two black men, one in a business suit, the other in a DeKalb Sanitation uniform. He supposed they were absentee fathers trying to buy their way back into their children's hearts—just like him. Self-consciously, he slipped on his wedding ring, hoping that somehow this would make him invisible in the world of bad parents.

He made a generous donation to the junior cheerleaders staffing the gift-wrap table and pushed a cartful of brightly wrapped packages out the door to the waiting cab.

And then Charlie returned to the motel. For dinner, he ate two Nip-

Chees and drank a Diet Coke from breezeway vending machines. In his room he watched *It's a Wonderful Life* long enough to see George Bailey jump from the bridge. He gave a raucous cheer, then turned it off.

He dozed again and woke when the room's stultifying heat got to him. It was nearly 11:30 p.m. In the bathroom, he splashed cold water on his face. He called the desk and asked for another cab. He waited with his gifts at the bottom of the steps. The same driver showed up.

"2567 Thornbriar Circle. It's not too far."

Only a few minutes away, in fact. Inside his old house, lights were on. No doubt Susan was up late wrapping gifts, something they'd done together for so many years. While the driver waited on the street, Charlie tiptoed up the driveway and put the first batch of gifts in front of the door, then repeated the process. As he returned to the taxi, the porch light came on. Charlie dove into the rear seat. "Go!" he shouted as he slammed the door.

"Back to the motel?"

"Head that way."

The cab driver gave him a questioning look but complied, following the route Charlie had taken when he left home that rainy night nearly a year before—and what now seemed like a lifetime ago.

As they approached the George Bailey Bridge over I-285, Charlie said, "Let me out here." The bemused cabbie pulled over. Charlie paid him and got out. He watched his breath as the car drove away on the near-deserted street, then looked up the hill at the burned-out husk of the Pancake Hut, a monument to God's wrath. Two blocks further on was his cheap motel. As he started moving toward it, the wind picked up, and his duster billowed behind him.

The bridge trembled beneath his feet. On its narrow walkway, Charlie stood and gazed out on the night traffic rushing at him like a river full of stars. In the opposite lanes, demon eyes receded. A driver passing by honked at him. Perhaps an old neighbor, or simply someone angry at him for taking up space.

In the distance, a church bell tolled twelve times.

Charlie started walking again. He'd fulfilled the contract, but he knew that his battle was just beginning. Something evil wanted him dead. Which was reason enough to keep going, since he was, after all, a contrary sort.

Chapter Eighteen

On Christmas Day, Charlie wished he could have been a fly on the wall at Varmintville when Susan gave her people the bad news: *He's alive*! Or better yet, when Beck and Ben did—that is, if their mother hadn't destroyed his gifts. But he wasn't an insect, no matter what Evangeline claimed, so instead, Charlie sat in his motel room and watched TV. Any thought he had of going to the police—(and he didn't think much of the idea to begin with)—was quashed when news updates linked the Caravan to a meth lab discovered in the fire-damaged warehouse unit next to his. They'd have to figure out who he was on their own.

He received some good news the next day, on the anniversary of his flight from Thornbriar. Jean called him that morning and said, "The guy with the loft to rent wants to meet you. He's a history professor. Lots of books. You should like that."

"Sounds nice," Charlie said, envisioning a stuffy, cramped old place filled with cat hair. Which would be infinitely better than the nothing he had. Maybe he could get the place without a credit check, which he was sure he wouldn't pass. "Uh, you ever been there?"

"I went with a friend who lives in the building. Très chic."

"Really?"

"Yeah. I told him great things about you. By the way, when you meet him, don't act so … oh, how do I put it? Homeless. Can you be here at noon?"

"Yeah, if I get my ass in gear."

"Do so, then."

When Charlie arrived at Bay Street Coffeehouse in his newly laundered Christmas Eve outfit, Jean introduced him to Dr. Edward Satalin, an Emory University professor, who planned to leave on New Year's Eve for six months in France. He wanted to sublet his apartment as much as Charlie wanted to get out of the motel, and a good word from Jean was all Satalin required as a reference. The two men hit it off immediately. Charlie tossed his bike in the back of Satalin's Pathfinder.

They drove downtown, then turned south. "You don't even need a car," the bearded professor said, pointing at the Garnett MARTA Station as they passed it. "You can bimodal on MARTA all over town."

"Cool."

"I really admire your ... *greenitude*, Charles. It takes commitment to ride a bike in weather like this."

"Oh, it's nothing really," Charlie said, waving his hand nonchalantly. "I'm used to it."

The loft was located on the third floor of a converted Farm and Home Furniture warehouse on Castlegate, a street crowded with three- to five-story buildings that ranged in style from old brick to aqua-tinted glass and steel. The building's north brick wall sported a mural—repainted with loving care—of the defunct company's billboard, featuring a black-and-white Holstein cow.

The professor's lodgings were amazing. Charlie loved Satalin's spacious, open-room apartment, with its high ceilings, heavy steel entrance door, polished cement floor and exposed black ductwork. Best of all, it was furnished in an understated, masculine style and had all the electronic amenities, including cable and high-speed Internet. It was filled with stuff Charlie would have chosen, if he'd had money. Eight-foot tall dark cherry bookcases, equipped with a sliding ladder, took up an entire brick wall. Satalin had thousands of books and CDs, most of which were jazz and classical. Beyond the balcony/fire escape stood a fence topped with razor wire to thwart hobo invasions from the railroad tracks behind the lofts. It was the best of both worlds—luxury, with a hint of dungeon.

Charlie gladly agreed to hand over half of his advance check up front to stay there until the end of June, utilities included. He knew he was getting a great bargain. And so with a handshake, the beleaguered writer went from squalor to splendor. He hoped that he'd turned the corner and put the ugliness of the past year behind him. Then he could concentrate on enjoying his accomplishments and become the success he'd always daydreamed he'd be.

* * *

On New Year's Day, Charlie sprawled out on Satalin's weathered brown leather sofa clad in only a towel and watched a bowl game on the big-screen plasma TV. His new work clothes were in the dryer, and he had no plans to leave the loft, since there was a bounty on his head and he was suspected of running a meth lab. In the kitchen, a sirloin patty sizzled on the Thermador gas range's grill. Satalin had left a week's worth of food in the matching stainless steel side-by-side refrigerator-freezer.

He'd figured out why he'd gotten such a great deal on rent. While surfing the Net on Satalin's desktop computer, Charlie learned that his landlord was heir to an investment-banking fortune. The professor didn't need the money; he just wanted someone to babysit the place.

Charlie got up and sliced a red onion with a hundred-dollar knife. After eating and clanking dishes in the sink, he settled back with the game. After a while, he grew bored with the lopsided contest and turned off the TV. A freight train rumbled by. Across the hall, a door slammed with a resounding *thump*. He listened to the sounds of the building: Indian music next door, pots and pans clanging upstairs. He wondered what his new neighbors were like. Good-looking? Cool? Female? Alone, as he was?

Charlie pulled his clothes from the dryer and dressed, then played a jazz CD, pianist Kenny Barron's *Things Unseen*. He searched Satalin's shelves for a book to read and picked one on ancient Greece, figuring that since he had this history gig going, he'd start at the beginning, more or less.

After reading a chapter, Charlie again grew restless. He needed to work. Yes, writing. That which had driven him crazy would now keep him sane. The lumps and bumps in his hands had disappeared, and with access to a computer again, he could crank out some magazine articles. Or put together a new final chapter for *Monster*, one with a furtive, bombed-out fugitive feel.

Charlie sat down at Satalin's glass-topped computer table and turned on the desktop PC. An instant later, a knock on the door caused his heart to skip a beat. How had the varmints found him so quickly? He tiptoed in his white crew socks to the door and peered out the peephole. It wasn't a hillbilly with a shotgun. It was *her*—the unforgettably upscale woman he'd seen at Bay Street Coffeehouse back in September. *Danger Girl.* He swung the door open, a look of wide-eyed amazement on his face.

The woman's expression matched his. "I came by to see if you vur here," she said. "You're here, but you're not you." She strung out the last word, puckering her lips and almost purring it in an intriguing accent Charlie couldn't place. Russian? Transylvanian?

She was in her early thirties, he guessed, with silky raven hair, and dressed entirely in black—jeans, thermal Henley, and high-heeled boots adorned with silver chains. *Damn, she was fine.*

"I'm not myself today," he said in an attempt to recover.

"I've seen you." She wrinkled her nose in puzzlement, then snapped her fingers. "Bay Street Coffeehouse. Jean's place. I'm Dana. Dana Colescu," she said, extending a hand, which he gladly took. "You're the writer."

The writer? Cool. She retrieved her hand and peered around his shoulder. "Is Eddie—"

He stepped aside, hoping she'd come in. No such luck. She gazed at him with questioning eyes. "Gone to France," Charlie said. "Without seeing England, as far as I know."

"So soon? I vas going to give him a bon voyage—Oh, vell."

He was sure that whatever she was going to give him would have been worth sticking around for, the overeducated fool. Charlie hoped that perhaps he could get the "velcome" version.

"How did you end up here?" she asked.

"I'm subletting. Thanks to Jean, who introduced me to … Eddie."

"*Ah* … I'll have to call her and find out all about my new neighbor." She flashed a seductive smile and put a finely manicured hand on Charlie's elbow for a moment before withdrawing it. He decided she sounded like a vampire. *Vlad the Impaler's hot girlfriend.*

"She'll tell you I'm a starving writer," he volunteered. "Quite crazy. Even daft."

She stepped back to appraise him. "Too well-built to be starving." In truth, his bout of homelessness had left him leaner, and riding his bike for the past week had toned his muscles. "But, daft, *yesss*. Like a daft horse, big and strong? I call you Budviser." She laughed. "How tall are you?"

"Six-four."

"Nice." She nodded appreciatively. "Only your clothes hint at hunger." She pinched the fabric of his new warehouseman's shirt. He gazed at her hand in amazement.

"Things are looking up. My book is coming out this month."

"Vonderful! Vot's it about?"

"History. Ethnic cleansing."

Her eyes narrowed and her expression clouded. Had he said something wrong? What if her family had been murdered? How horrible! If he only knew more, he could console her properly. Repeatedly. "Right here in Georgia," he added. "Believe it or not."

Her face brightened as she pointed at the floor. "This Georgia? Ah. I love to read it."

"So how do you know Jean?"

"She's one of my new artists. I'm putting together an exhibition of her vork."

Charlie did a double-take. He'd seen some of Jean's paintings on the coffeehouse wall but had no idea she'd advanced to the gallery stage. "Wow. That's great. … So, you live here, too?"

She pointed up, toward the building's corner. "Overlooking Castlegate." She sighed. "Vell, I'm off to a party. *Futbol*, you bet." She rolled her eyes. "I was going to see if Eddie vanted to come along, but he's gone to Burgundy for his Burgundy. Vot are *you* doing—" she raised her eyebrows "—for this holiday?"

"Hiding out."

She laughed. "Ve all do that. Vot besides?"

"Writing."

"Vell, I von't disturb you any longer."

"It's quite all right. I'm disturbed by nature."

She gave him a wonderful laugh, rich and throaty.

"Come back any time," he added, hoping she wouldn't go.

She left, closing the door behind her. He banged his head against it in frustration. Who was he kidding? He had no money, no car, and no chance. And when she talked to Jean, well … that would be the end of whatever dream he had of getting something started with her.

"Shit," he said as he threw the deadbolt. "You homeless motherfucker."

Enough of that. He put on another jazz CD, Miles Davis's *Kind of Blue*, and went back to work, bending over the keyboard as the light in the eastern windows faded. By the time he'd finished his session, he'd written a 2,000-word update to *Monster*. A good day's work on the best day he'd had in a long time. On the psychological and social front, he hadn't ranted to himself—well, maybe once—and he'd chatted with a real woman who had not run screaming from the encounter. Who knew? Maybe he did have a chance with Dana, after all. They *had* hit it off well, hadn't they? Now, if he could just get on the bestseller list … and get some decent threads. Just erase everything and start over. That would be cool.

Seeking a diversion, he clicked on the DVD player. Something was already in the machine, so he played it, figuring Satalin's taste in movies would be as erudite as it was in books and music. Not quite. Before Charlie knew it, he was watching *Anus and Andy—No Holes Barred* from *The Bros and Hos Collection*. He was about to stop the porn video, but his hand became … *con-*

fused. He found it difficult to tear his eyes away from the TV as the strangely attractive woman entertained a basketball team in a locker room. Ah, the agony of ecstasy, the method of acting, the pain of unnatural acts. Her face did its own stunts, that was for sure.

Hold it. Charlie knew that face. He shuddered and every hair on his body stood up. Meanwhile, something else of his collapsed. A chill ran up his spine. The picture that had been on his computer, the one that got him kicked out of Thornbriar—was a still from this movie. Not only that. This was the woman with the kids he'd helped on Thanksgiving Day at Redeemer's soup kitchen. The one Trouble ranted about. Shaved, thrusting, and threatening to become 3-D and pop out from the plasma screen.

In the interest of research he played on, but the movie grew more foul. Amid shouts of "Eat it, bitch," the guy who would have been the team's center grabbed … what was her name? Tammy? Terry? … by the hair and roughly forced her to go down on him. It was abusive. They weren't using protection. He wondered if she'd gotten pregnant from this shoot.

Enough. He felt weak, overwhelmed. Exhaling loudly, he ejected the disc and picked it up like he was handling a used condom. Even though it wasn't his to destroy, he couldn't let it sit on the shelf, a reminder of his failure, mocking him. He couldn't allow it to sap his soul and rot his brain. He took the DVD out on the balcony. Grasping the disc between thumb and forefinger, he whirled it away and watched it sail over the razor wire, flashing in a patch of fading sunlight as it flew toward a southbound MARTA train in the distance. He went back inside and switched the TV to football.

That night, he dreamed of the soup-kitchen whore, waking at 4:00 a.m. in ecstasy and relief.

In the morning, he stepped out on the balcony with a cup of coffee. As he scanned the train tracks, the DVD flashed in the sunlight, winking as if to say *I know what you want*—just as it would for the next six months, whenever he dared to look its way.

* * *

Another great thing about Satalin's place was its proximity to Le Patisserie, a cinnamon-scented bakery on the loft building's ground floor. It quickly became Charlie's favorite hangout, and he developed a bit of a crush on its owner, Amy Weller, who wore her brown ponytail sticking out the back of an Atlanta Braves cap. That's where he was one morning less than a week after moving into his apartment, sitting at a small table near the door, drinking Mocha Java, eating a pastry, and comparing Dana Colescu to the bright-eyed woman behind the counter. A hard rain during the night had left the street slick, and a MARTA bus sloshed by as a customer entered, leaving a whiff of diesel to mingle with the spices. Charlie's cellphone buzzed. He pulled it out of his duster pocket and regarded the New York area code suspiciously. "Hello."

"Charles Sherman?"

"That's me."

"Barbara Asher. I got your manuscript, and I've got to tell you I *love American Monster*!" she gushed. "Mother of God, it's Bob Woodward, Hunter Thompson, and Erskine Caldwell rolled into one. And, as you put it, 'a healthy measure of *I am a Fugitive from the Georgia Chain Gang*!' But is it true?"

The agent! He launched into his spiel: "All that and more! Backed up by photographs, recorded eyewitness accounts, primary sources, genealogical research, and the kicker: DNA test results. I've got documents and recordings to back the footnotes." *On this book, anyway*. He left out the part about nearly being killed—but he was still working on that section, anyway.

"Excellent. Fortress is publishing your other book, right?"

"Yes ma'am. It should be out soon."

"This is great! And you don't have an agent?"

"No, I don't."

"Does Fortress have rights on this book?"

"They passed. New publisher."

"I heard. Did you have trouble getting paid?"

"I got the money eventually. Right when I absolutely had to have it." Thinking about that day made him shudder. His knee rocked the table, almost spilling his coffee.

"I've dealt with them," she said. "They're problematic. Best to move on to another publisher with your next work. This … has potential. I'd love to represent it. I've got a good feeling. I think it's going to be a great success. So, are you still interested in having me as an agent?"

"Definitely. And there'll be an update. Things keep happening. Arrests, hopefully."

"Arrests would be good publicity. A happy ending. Closure, anyway. Uh … you're talking about them, not you, right?"

"Actually, it's a donnybrook. We may all be in jail before this is over."

"Even better! *Devil Went Down to Georgia* and all that."

"You're getting warmer, actually."

"Are you doing a publicity tour for the Forsyth book?"

"They haven't set up anything."

"They won't. Bear in mind, you'll have to do all the marketing yourself. Call the media. Get something started. It will help sell the next book, too."

"I'm working on a couple of articles right now."

"Excellent! Charles, your book is going to be great. I just know it. But we've both got work to do. I'll send you a contract. We'll send everything by e-mail now and be modern about it."

He gave her his e-mail address and said goodbye. In wide-eyed disbelief, he stared out the bakery window at traffic on Castlegate. He'd just done a deal! With an agent! For the next few minutes, he imagined his coming prosperity: new loft, new clothes, new car, and Dana, the new woman for his new life. Or maybe Amy. Who could say these things?

While he was daydreaming, his coffee grew cold.

* * *

Since the police linked him to a meth lab, Charlie would remain most unhelpful to authorities, who reported little progress in the Store-All bombing investigation. However, there were news leaks—or, as Charlie called them, tidings of comfort and joy. The mini-warehouse's office had burned to the ground, company records had not been properly backed up, and the bombing victim's identity remained unknown.

Charlie was sure police had found *something* to identify him—either a vehicle ID number or his name on at least one of the unburned papers that littered the lot after the bombing. If not, something else was at work, something strange—although weirdness had become normal, from his point of view. Perhaps the *No Cops* rule was not only divinely inspired, but also had a corollary, since the police didn't have him, either.

Then came another leak that wasn't so comforting. According to an article Charlie read while sitting by the front window in La Patisserie one Tuesday morning, someone had left the scene of the bombing on a yellow mountain bike and changed out of bloody clothes under a bridge a mile from the crime scene. While reading this, Charlie experienced a cold, hard feeling surging from his groin to his throat. When he finished the article, he rose slowly from his chair and backed out the rear door into the building's garage, whistling drily as he went.

* * *

This seemed like an ugly thing to do, but Charlie did it: He bought a can of black enamel, took his bike out on the balcony/fire escape, and spray painted it against a plastic dropcloth. Even before it dried, he knew he'd have to do more. People in the neighborhood had seen him riding a yellow bike, and a scratch would reveal its true color. Also, police would have tread prints. He needed to get rid of it.

Thursday afternoon was bright and chilly. Charlie rode his bike to Garnett Station and wheeled it onto a northbound train. He got off at Tenth Street and left the bike outside, unlocked, after wiping off his prints. Then he slipped on his backpack and jogged over to a bike shop on Monroe Drive. He bought a new blue hybrid with slightly knobby tires and twenty-four speeds. It was *so* not yellow.

Charlie surprised himself by pedaling toward his old haunts in Virginia Highlands rather than back downtown. Despite an urge to see Jean, he pedaled onward, waving as he passed Bay Street Coffeehouse just in case his favorite barista was looking out the window. He pumped up Bayard Terrace and stopped at Kathleen's house. He carried the bike up the porch steps and leaned it gingerly against the wobbly railing. (He'd always meant to fix that.) Floorboards creaked as he stepped to the door and knocked. A pudgy, middle-aged white woman peered out suspiciously from the window. "I'm Charlie Sherman," he announced.

She shook her head.

"Yes, I am!" he insisted. "A friend of Kathleen's. I used to live here. I edited a book for her. Is she home?" He tried to speak with gentle confidence, but he was afraid he came across as desperate, loud, and strange.

The woman disappeared, leaving him to think that Angela had placed her mother in a rest home and rented out the house. As he turned to go, the door swung open and Kathleen stood with open arms, her blue eyes sparkling. "They came this morning!" she said, advancing on him and hugging him fiercely.

"Who came?" he asked, his arms pinned to his sides.

"The books!"

"The books?" His eyes grew wide and his face lit up. "So soon?"

"Seemed like forever to me."

The woman appeared behind her. "Now Mrs. Talton, you can't just—"

"Shush, Betty." Kathleen pulled Charlie in the door. "Where have you been? Betty, make some tea, please. This is my writer! The one I told you about! My, what a wonderful day!"

Instead of making tea, Betty made a phone call. Meanwhile, Kathleen bent over a box on the living room floor and pulled out a hardcover of *Flight from Forsyth: Ethnic Cleansing in America*. Beaming, she handed it to Charlie, her eyes filling with tears of joy. He admired the glossy black-and-white jacket's stark line art: silhouetted nightriders outside a cabin. The title's bold letters had ghostly trails of ink, suggesting motion. Charlie's name was on the cover, below Talton's, as coauthor. A beautiful book, albeit one covering an ugly subject. Charlie read the dedication aloud: "To Kathleen, who made everything possible."

He flipped through the book and glanced at the index, checking an entry on Governor Brown to see that it matched the page. It did. He sighed in relief. He had worried about the index, since he couldn't remember anything about the damned thing except that he'd compiled it in anger.

"We did a great thing, didn't we?" Kathleen said.

"We did indeed." He flipped the book over and glanced inside the back flap at his picture below Thurwood's. Ouch. He wished he had that one back. He rather liked being incognito these days. Would his newfound fame be his downfall? He suspected that he'd be navigating some treacherous waters soon.

In the kitchen, Betty talked to Angela on the phone. Meanwhile, Kathleen stared lovingly at Thurwood's photo. "Did they say anything about how handsome he was?"

Charlie was touched by her love for the man. "I'm sure they were jealous."

"I'll bet they were," she said, nodding emphatically.

Charlie gazed at the white back cover, which contained several blurbs in red ink from eminent historians, who praised the work effusively. Charlie felt a pang of conscience for compromising their academic integrity with his divinely inspired literary derring-do. But everything happened according to a plan. (That was his story, and he was sticking to it.)

Kathleen narrowed her eyes. "You got all the money, didn't you?" He nodded. After a moment's pause, she said, "Well, there was no guarantee there would be any. Everyone got what they wanted. I'm just glad it's done." She grabbed the book and kissed Thurwood's picture, then closed it and hugged it to her chest. "We did it, sweetheart!" She turned to Charlie. "So how do *you* feel?"

"This is one of my better days." He gave her a smile both weary and triumphant. "It's all good."

"I want to see Thurwood. Can you take me?"

Before Charlie could answer, Betty handed him the cordless phone.

"What are you up to?" Angela spoke in her most demanding voice.

"I came by to see your mother. Is that permitted?"

A pause. "I suppose, since you're there already. Took me by surprise. There are warrants, plural, for your arrest. Family feud, I gather."

"They're BS. 'Git offen my property,' mainly."

"I bet you get that a lot," she said. "So you've taken care of them?"

Silence.

"I'll take that as a 'No.' You're a train wreck, you know. I don't suppose I should blame you for everything, though," Angela said, her tone softening. "Tell me. Did they find what they were looking for that night?"

"No, they most certainly did not."

"Mom doesn't remember. What were they looking for?"

"The first time, someone took your father's notes. Uh, tried to, that is. The next time, they were looking for something else I was working on." He paused. "I'm sorry. I never meant to put your mother in danger. Things happened fast that day."

"A lot of excitement, I'll say that. She still talks about her 'great adventure.' Funny. When you were there, she was happier than she'd been since Dad died. She spent twenty years moping around, then you come along and she thinks she's on a holy quest. Now, she just babbles a lot."

"She's not babbling now."

"No? She's been going downhill fast, but maybe she'll be on her best behavior around you. She thinks you're some kind of angel. She's been asking for you. In a way, I'm glad you came by. But you can't have your job back."

Charlie chuckled. "You'll be happy to know my replacement is very protective."

"Good. So, congratulations on the book. How does it look?"

"Great. Thanks."

Kathleen tugged on his jacket sleeve. "You need to take me to see Thurwood."

"Kathleen wants to see Thurwood," Charlie told Angela. "I don't have my van. I biked over."

"Use her car. I've got a class to teach right now. Stick around. I'll come by later. I've been staying there lately."

"So all is forgiven?" Charlie asked.

"Most of it."

After Charlie hung up, he announced, "Angela's not so bad."

Kathleen cleared her throat and looked away. Betty rolled her eyes.

"Ah. So it's not just me," Charlie said.

This time, Betty cleared her throat and looked away, while Kathleen rolled her eyes.

"All right! All right! Let's go see Thurwood," Charlie said.

He locked his bike to the porch. When Kathleen came out in a black coat, Betty announced she was leaving for the day. Kathleen told Charlie, "Angela sleeps here now so that I won't run away."

"Good. Cause you're hard to catch when you build up a head of steam."

She laughed at his tease and playfully swatted his arm. Charlie helped her down the steps. In the sunlight, she looked terribly pale. She paused on the way to the car to catch her breath. In the cemetery, Charlie parked on the grass underneath the spreading, bare-limbed oak that served as Kathleen's navigational marker. Thirty paces to the east lay Thurwood's headstone. Kathleen leaned on Charlie as they walked to the grave. Once there, she stared at her name carved in granite beside Thurwood's. She leaned over and spoke as if she were waking her husband from a nap. "Sweetheart, it's me. I brought the young man. Didn't I tell you we'd get it done? Didn't I do well? Look at this!" She held the book over the grave so the headstone could see. "I know it took awhile. Please forgive me. But it's all right now. It's all right, sweetie. All the people who've read it think it's wonderful. This is how you live on. I am so proud of you. I hope you're proud of me." She laid the book atop his grave. "You can feel it better this way."

She turned to Charlie. "Do you have anything to say?"

He stepped forward. "It's been an honor to work on your book, sir. I believe it will do very well." He thought for a moment. "If you see John Riggins, give him my best."

Kathleen touched Charlie's arm and confided, "Sometimes I think you're my son. But I know that you're not." She took a moment before she spoke again. "I never got over Gary's death. Thurwood's, I could accept. His days were cut short, but he lived a full life. But Gary. Oh, Gary."

She walked over to her son's grave. Charlie gave her some space.

When she returned, she said, "Should we leave the book with Thurwood? He might like that."

"It would get wet," Charlie said. "I bet he'd like it if we gave it to Georgia State's library."

"Wonderful idea!" She picked up the book and took his arm. As they walked back to the car, a crow circled overhead. "My life is complete now," she said. "There's nothing left for me to do."

"I'm impressed. Not many people can say that."

"Although I wish they'd caught the man who hit Thurwood on the head. That caused his death, you know. But that was long ago. Vengeance is mine, sayeth the Lord," she murmured.

Charlie was glad to see she'd finally accepted what had happened to Thurwood. It made him feel a little less guilty about keeping Momo's identity a secret from her (although he did devote a chapter in *American Monster* to that debacle up at Varmintville on the Fourth of July).

When they returned to Bayard Terrace, Angela was there, and she was in a surprisingly good mood. They ate dinner at Gamille's on North Highland, Charlie's treat. The women drank wine, and by the end of the evening, Charlie had purchased Kathleen's ancient Volvo for $1,000. He left with five copies of *Flight from Forsyth* and his bike in the trunk. A very good day, all in all. On the way home, he drove by the Tenth Street Station and saw, with a nod of approval, that his old bike was gone.

* * *

Two days later, Charlie was working at the computer when he got a phone call from Angela. "Mom died in her sleep last night," she said.

Charlie was stunned. "Oh God. I … that's terrible." Even as he spoke, he knew that her time had come. After all, she was eighty-three, and her life was, by her own admission, complete. "What happened?"

"She died in her sleep. It was peaceful, I think. She was so happy after the books came. I think she wanted to be with Dad. Does that sound weird?" She sniffled and started to sob.

"No, not at all." Charlie thought of her dreams of Thurwood and suspected she wasn't alone when she died. "I wish she had lived to see the book succeed, though."

"At least she saw the book completed."

"Yes. She finished the drill."

"It would be nice if you said a few words at the funeral."

"I'd be honored."

* * *

The service was held at the Unitarian Church in Northeast Atlanta. A small crowd attended: a sister, nieces, neighbors, colleagues of Thurwood. Angela sat with her current partner, Sandra Hughes, the African-American attorney who had drafted the current contract on *Flight from Forsyth*.

Afterward, a small procession traveled to the cemetery. Feeling both empty and full, Charlie stood at the edge of the crowd as the casket was lowered into the ground. When the graveside service was over, he drifted away and sat in the Volvo. He'd passed on the chance to eat one last meal at Bayard Terrace because he had something else in mind.

After the other mourners had driven off, two black men with shovels filled in the grave and tamped down the dirt. When they left, there was just Charlie, the sunset, the rising wind, dead folks all around, and an almost imperceptible shadow behind the caretaker's shed. He'd expected Trouble to show up, but when a bus passed by on the highway without stopping, Charlie figured the trickster wasn't coming. That was for the best. After all, fistfights at funerals were a varmint thing. And while Charlie liked to think he was above that sort of behavior, he wasn't sure what he'd do when he saw Trouble face to face.

He exited the Volvo and tiptoed across the grass, carrying a copy of *Flight*. He stood before their graves: Thurwood's carpeted with fescue, Kathleen's covered with the dirt of the newly dead. A patch of sod and a few chisel blows to date her tombstone, and she'd be set for eternity. Ignoring his own recent advice, he kneeled and placed the open book face-down between them, so they could share again. "Goodbye, friends," he said. "Don't know that I'll be back. But you live on, both of you." He struck his chest with his fist as he backed away.

Charlie returned to the car weighed down by the knowledge of how fleeting and few his friendships had been. He decided to reestablish contact with Minerva. It was wrong to be on the outs with her. Eventually, she'd understand that what he'd done was necessary—though he hoped she hadn't yet found out what exactly that had entailed.

It turned out to be an awkward meeting. When he came to her house that evening, Minerva stood at the door and didn't invite him in. She shook her head when he asked about Takira and Demetrious. Either she was unwilling to talk about them or reluctant to speak to him. Maybe both. But Charlie figured Demetrious hadn't told her about the blood test. Otherwise, she would have slammed the door in his face. He handed her an autographed copy of *Flight*, then told her he had finished *American Monster*. "*Flight from Forsyth* is going on sale on MLK Day," Charlie said.

"There's something wrong with trying to make money that way," Minerva declared.

He turned and left without saying another word.

Chapter Nineteen

Charlie woke early on MLK Day and checked Amazon.com. *Still no sales. None*! What was wrong with people? Or maybe it was him. Bad karma. Or bad marketing? He needed to get busy and generate some buzz—line up signings, schedule interviews, get media coverage. At least he'd managed to sell an article about Forsyth County's inglorious history to *Atlanta Week*. Now to plot his next move. Maybe he'd finally write that Brimmer article, the one that had been so rudely interrupted by his eviction from Thornbriar. But how could he be both a celebrity *and* elusive, even invisible?

He slipped on his duster and walked to the end of the hall, clomped down two flights of stairs, and stepped out onto the sidewalk. He lingered for a moment to savor the winter air, gazing northward at downtown Atlanta's looming skyline. Even though it was slate gray overhead, Charlie slipped on his shades, being a wanted man with no book sales to his credit. He turned and walked toward the bakery with his hands in his pockets. A loud noise drew his attention. He turned to see a southbound MARTA bus speeding down Castlegate toward him, engine roaring, going airborne for an instant when it hit a bump. "Whoa dude, slow down," he muttered.

Meanwhile, a white Chevy pickup pulled from a parking space on the south side of the bakery and rolled slowly toward him from the other direction. Charlie passed the garage entrance and heard someone shout, "Hey, nigger lover!" He looked up as a blue Toyota pulled from a parking space in front of the bakery, moving directly into the truck's path. As the pickup swerved into the opposing lane to avoid the car, Charlie faced a man in a ski mask pointing a shotgun out the truck window at him.

Then, mayhem and carnage: In an instant, the gun fired, the speeding bus plowed into the truck, and the shooter hurtled through the windshield. All this was accompanied by an ear-splitting cacophony of gunshot, shattering glass, and crashing metal. Wounded, Charlie stumbled backward into the void that had once been the bakery's front window. Flailing his arms, he crashed into a display case, landing atop a German chocolate cake and smashing it flat. He thrashed wildly in the mixture of broken glass and baked goods. Meanwhile, terror-stricken customers screamed and dove under tables.

Bolts of pain shot through Charlie's jaw, giving him a terrible, ear-splitting headache. Dazed, bewildered, and bleeding—his face seemed afire—he struggled to comprehend what had happened. An automobile door slammed, and he thought: *They're coming to finish me off.*

Struggling to his feet, he pulled himself through the broken window onto the sidewalk, slashing his right hand in the process. "FUCK!" he screamed as he whirled around, looking for an attacker who wasn't there. His mouth tasted—and felt—like hell. There was a bloody hole in his left cheek near his jaw, the exit wound from the buckshot pellet that had shattered a molar just above the gum line. He'd been hit by two other pellets. One had glanced off his left cheekbone and ripped off a chunk from the bottom of his earlobe; the other had grazed him above the left shoulder blade. The gashes on his right palm, right thigh, and right forearm he'd received from the window glass were bleeding more heavily than the gunshot wounds.

Charlie's boots crunched glass as he surveyed the scene. The shooter was lying on the truck's crumpled hood, his head a foot away from the bus grille. Flames from an engine fire licked the man's clothes. The driver was slumped over the steering wheel.

The bus driver tried to back away from the burning truck, but the vehicles were locked together. Its engine straining, the bus dragged the smaller vehicle twenty feet before the truck's bumper tore off with a screech and clang. A horn blared as a taxi peeled away in reverse. The driver—who somehow escaped injury—stopped the bus. After her passengers had exited the vehicle, she stepped off and yelled, "People, get away from the fire!"

As the flames rose higher, passengers poured out the bus's back door. Braving the inferno and spitting blood, Charlie dragged his assailant off the truck hood. "Who are you?" he demanded.

The man didn't respond. His bloody head flopped like a fish when Charlie put his arms under the man's armpits and dragged him away. The victim laid his shooter down on the pavement by the bus's rear tires. A moment later, the truck's gas tank exploded with a roar, spewing burning gas all over the street and vehicles parked on the curb. Charlie, protected from the blast by the bus, watched the pickup become its driver's funeral pyre.

Charlie turned back to the shooter, and with his left hand, pulled off his would-be assassin's ski mask. A white guy. A stranger. He felt for a pulse. Nothing. Meanwhile, bus riders and bystanders scurried north toward downtown. Charlie spit out more blood and bits of broken tooth. As he backed away from the body, a black BMW buzzed by and nearly clipped him, its horn blaring as it raced away. "Athhole!" Charlie shouted.

The bus driver, a matronly black woman wearing sunglasses, approached him. "I'm so sorry," she mumbled, shaking her head. "So sorry." Charlie stared at her in dull amazement. He thought he recognized her. Then again, maybe all female bus drivers looked alike. "Police be here soon," she added.

Taking that as a warning, he backed toward the garage, leaving a bloody trail. He paused when he reached the sidewalk and peered through the bakery's broken window at the pandemonium inside. An employee was using a fire extinguisher on a burning bundt in the broken display case. Fortunately, the shotgun blast had angled upward, over people's heads, only to destroy the wall clock and knock holes in ceiling tiles.

"What the hell is going on?" someone shouted at Charlie.

Amy Weller, stooping to coax a customer out from underneath a table, looked up at him in alarm. "Were they shooting at you?"

"I think tho," Charlie lisped. "Ith anyone hurt?"

"Besides you? I don't think so. You need an ambulance. Just hang on. We called 911."

The pain in his jaw was screaming. No cops was one thing. No paramedics was another. Charlie retreated to the garage like a wounded beast into its cave, unsure whether he should run, hide, or seek treatment—which would mean turning himself in, most likely. He slumped against a concrete wall near the elevator and slid to the oil-spotted floor. "Thith day ith completely fucked," he observed, lolling his head around and closing his eyes.

"Hell-o?"

Charlie looked up to see Dana Colescu standing over him, wearing a red leather jacket and black jeans. She stared at him in horror "Ohmygawd! Writer Guy! Vot happened?"

Blood dribbled down his chin. "I got thot."

She took a step back. "Who did this? Vere are they?" She whipped out a formidable black automatic pistol from her purse. *Damn.* He pointed a bloody, trembling finger toward the garage door as smoke wafted in. "Is it safe?" she hissed.

He shook his head. "They're dead."

She clomped up to the garage entrance with the pistol behind her back and looked around, then returned to Charlie's side. "I'm impressed," she said, tucking the gun away. "You do good vork. And you kept your shades on."

"The buth hit the truck. I gotta get out of here before the polith come."

"Vy? Are you in trouble with the law?"

"Not ovuh thith." He struggled to get up. "But they have ithues."

"Issues?" She put a hand on his shoulder and tried to push him down. "Maybe you should vait—"

"No copth," he said, fighting to stand.

She watched with a worried expression as he staggered toward his car.

"OK, I'll help you. Just calm down. You're bleeding all over the place."

He looked down. It was true. He was dripping on the floor.

"I'll take you somewhere. In your car."

He dug keys out of his coat pocket with his left thumb and forefinger and gave them to her. "Old Volvo."

"Vait. Don't get in yet."

Weak from pain, he watched her get a brown blanket from the trunk of her powder-blue Mercedes. She unlocked the Volvo, then used it to cover the back seat. She looked at him and said, "You'll live. I've seen vorse. But you are a bloody mess."

He crawled in and laid down on his right side as the rest of his teeth hummed in sympathy with their fallen comrade. He lifted his head to peek out the window. Dana drove out of the garage and slipped through a narrow gap between gawkers and a silver car. "Move, bitches!" she shouted as she wove through the growing crowd, barely avoiding a fire truck as it angled to block off the street. Seconds later, an Atlanta police car sped by, its siren screaming. "Vo," said Dana, her face a mask of concentration. "That vas close."

It hurt too much to talk; Charlie rested his head against the door. He closed his mouth and swallowed a bit of himself. He gagged but held it down. Dana checked the mirror, then hit the gas and dodged a pothole. She pulled a cellphone from her purse as they approached Marietta Street. Overhead, Newschopper Six thumped by on its way toward the burning wreckage.

"Vot hurts vurst?"

"My toof."

"I know vere to go, then."

Charlie expected to go to Grady Memorial, where gunshot wounds were part of the ER's daily routine—but Dana embraced his *No Cops* rule. And so, as Atlanta police searched local emergency rooms for a big white dude with half his face shot off, Charlie sat in a chair in a Midtown dentist's examination room. Dana stood in the door, arguing in a foreign language with a silver-haired man she called Victor, who wore a blue tunic. Victor ended the debate by touching his finger to his lips and stroking Dana's cheek. Then he left the room.

"I used to vork with Victor years ago," she said. "He is a teddy bear."

"You were a nurth?" Charlie asked.

She shook her head. "No. Something else, back then."

Victor returned with a medical bag. "I am Dr. Blaga," he told Charlie. "Only Dana knows I vas army surgeon in previous life. Now I'm oral surgeon. I fix you all up. One price for all." He thought this was tremendously funny and laughed until he coughed.

Blaga produced a syringe and injected Charlie with a painkiller. Charlie wouldn't remember much about the office visit after that—a mercy, since he got more shots in his jaw, root canal surgery, and a temporary cap to replace his shot-out tooth, in addition to a total of thirty-two stitches on his hand, cheek, and thigh. Plus a bandage on his ear, a gauze patch on his shoulder, and a sympathetic *tsk*. "Nothing more to do for those," Blaga said. "But they vill heal."

Before Charlie knew it, Dana and Blaga were hauling him back to the underground garage. When they reached the Volvo, Blaga handed Charlie two bottles. "Take every four hours. One for pain, one for infection." The doctor pushed him into the front passenger seat of the car and kissed Dana on the cheek.

"Thankth," Charlie mumbled, now slurring *and* lisping.

"You vill come back for permanent crown in three veeks," Blaga said as he backed toward the elevator.

Dana snapped Charlie's seat belt with ruthless efficiency.

"I'm thorry I took your day away," Charlie said.

"That's all right," she said, checking the mirror. "The gallery's closed today, anyvay."

Talking was difficult, so Charlie shut up. He just wanted to lie down in Satalin's wonderful bed and not be shot at for a while. He dug out the last of his cash to pay the parking fee.

Dana listened to electronic dance music as she drove. After a few blocks, she said, "The police vill be vaiting for you at Castlegate, you know. And whoever sent those people, too, maybe. Tell me: How vorried should I be for you? And me, for that matter. And vy did this happen?"

He owed her at least some of the truth. "I think ith about a book I wrote that ithn't out yet. About a lynthing theventy yearth ago."

"A what?"

"Lynthing. When a mob killth a man."

"Seventy years ago?"

"The victimth land wath tholen, and now ith worth a lot. A *lot*." He held his arms wide.

"Enough to send people after you?"

He nodded. "Thith ithn't the futh time. Theeth people will kill you for fifty dollah."

She blanched. "You veren't kidding ven you told me you ver hiding out. Vot vent wrong?"

"With the hiding out? Got me." He knew he'd made a mistake that gave away his position; he just didn't know what it was.

"Vot about the other time they tried to kill you? Vot happened then? Vas it just vunce?"

He shuddered. "No comment."

"They came close this time. You're lucky that bus came along."

"I have great faith in public tranthpotathan."

"You should go to the police."

"No copth. They have a warrant out on me."

"Vot is the vorrant for?"

"Nothing." He waved his wounded hand. "Minor."

"I don't see—"

"Look," Charlie said, becoming agitated. "I can't ethplain. There are other fotheth at work. Powerful fotheth."

"Vot-ever. I don't understand, but I accept. I have deals like that, too. So how do ve sneak you back into your place vithout the cops seeing you? I guarantee it vill be crawling vith them. And people saw your car. It vas the last one out before the police came."

He thought. She thought. Then Charlie came up with the Man-in-the-Trunk Plan, even though it hadn't worked the last time he'd seen it attempted. But at least it was something. Dana parked a couple of blocks away and walked to the lofts to retrieve her Mercedes. When she returned, he climbed into the trunk, making her, like Susan, a man-stasher. Charlie felt like he was trapped in a coffin—like he had been in one of his 4:00 a.m. dreams—and could barely tolerate being inside during the time it took for Dana to drive to the lofts, flirt with the cop who stopped her at the garage entrance, and park the car.

When she popped the trunk open, she hissed, "Hurry! The officer is on the radio."

Charlie saw a black patrolman standing in the garage entrance with his back to them. As he and Dana scurried toward the elevator, Charlie saw that the bus and truck were gone. Two satellite news trucks were parked across from the bakery, and another cop sat in a squad car. Looking from the garage through the bakery's rear glass door, Charlie saw workmen placing plywood sheets over the broken window. He crouched behind Dana as they entered the elevator vestibule door.

They reached his loft undetected. "How's that for a first date?" she joked as he stepped inside.

He smiled wearily. "Thank you for thaving me."

"You owe me one." She handed him a business card with her cellphone number on it and received his number in turn, then kissed him on his undamaged cheek before leaving. He lingered in the door before closing it, watching her walk to the elevator.

Charlie knew that discovery was inevitable, but he hoped for a few hours' rest before the world found him. A glimpse in the full-length mirror revealed one messed-up individual with torn, bloody clothes, a bandaged right hand, and a spot of blood coming through the gauze pad on his cheek. He rummaged around in the bathroom cabinet and found a jumbo Band-aid. There. Now he looked like the victim of a cat fight, not a shootout. His right hand hurt more than anything else. Could he write? Not that he had any desire to—he just wanted to crawl deeper into his cave. He took two of the pills Blaga had given him, laid down on the couch, shifted his keys in his pocket, and let the world quiet down.

* * *

The cellphone's buzz woke Charlie. He answered it before thinking maybe he shouldn't. Fortunately, it was Dana: "I bring you soup, if you can eat."

"I can eat. Thanks. You are so good to me," he said, his lisp receding.

"You have no idea how good I can be."

He was groggy and wounded, but he wasn't dead. "I'd like to find out."

He hung up and slipped on a clean set of work clothes. Day had turned to night. A MARTA train clacked by. Moments later, there was a knock on the door. He jumped up and opened it, smiling expectantly—

Whoops.

—at four uniformed Forsyth County deputies in the hall, two with guns drawn. Of various shapes, sizes, and ages, but of one color, they seemed whiter than most people and reminded Charlie of toughass Pillsbury Doughboys. "Charles Sherman?"

They pushed in and before he knew it, Charlie's hands were cuffed behind his back. Pappy's warrants were being served. After his rights were read, one of the deputies asked Charlie how he'd been injured.

"Right to remain silent, and all that," he replied, sure that they already knew, since the world conspired against him.

Two deputies perp-walked him down the hall toward the elevator. Its doors opened. Dana, holding a brown paper bag, took one look at Charlie and his escorts, froze in mid-step, then lunged sideways inside the elevator and disappeared. Seconds later the doors closed in the lead deputy's face. "We'll take the stairs," he said.

Charlie and the lawmen stepped outside into the cold night air. Two deputies stuffed the suspect into the back of the second of two patrol cars double-parked on Castlegate. Then came a high-speed blue-light trip north on Georgia 400. Apparently he was a high-value target, given the manpower devoted to his arrest. Even so, Charlie hoped he could post bond that night and go home, though the taxi fare would be huge. Oops. His wallet was still on the kitchen counter. As were his meds and cellphone. At least he had his keys. They would come in useful if he ever made it back.

Who to call? The one person he should be able to count on was most likely part of the conspiracy. Even if she wasn't, it had been months since he'd spoken to Susan. And he recalled that she'd already stated she wouldn't bail him out of jail.

Although the Novocain had worn off and he could speak normally, Charlie continued to take advantage of his right to remain silent. He assumed someone had given the sheriff his address after the hit job failed, but the lawmen seemed to know nothing about him, except that he'd pissed off Ike Cutchins, which apparently put him in good company. He learned that the two deputies he rode with had, over the years, served three criminal trespass warrants on the old man's behalf—two on hunters who had merely stepped over the wrong fence.

The squad cars pulled into the parking lot of the Forsyth County Jail, a low-slung building across the street from the courthouse in Cumming. A metal garage door rattled up and the car pulled in. The door rattled down on chains behind him, and Charlie realized this was the real deal, dungeon-wise. At the booking desk, Sheriff's Captain Morgan told Charlie, "We have you as a flight risk. You'll need a bond hearing."

"What does that mean?" Charlie asked.

"Means you're staying here tonight."

"How long can you hold me?"

"Seventy-two hours. You'll be out in the morning, most likely."

Charlie was taken to a cluttered room, fingerprinted, and photographed. When Morgan asked what had happened to him, Charlie stood mute. "Note his existing injuries," Morgan told the booking deputy. "We don't want to get blamed for someone else's doing."

Afterward, the young deputy gently pushed Charlie into a room with a phone, closed the door, and stood outside. Forsyth's newest inmate picked up the receiver and felt a burst of butterflies in his empty stomach. Who does a hermit call at a time like this? He didn't know anyone he could impose upon, even to save his ass. He couldn't ask Dana for help after all he'd put her through that day. Besides, her number was in his wallet.

He had to call someone. "Don't be a pussy," he said as tears of self-pity welled up. "So you don't have friends. You must have at least one ally. Think, think, think."

Charlie snapped his fingers, even though it hurt. Angela. *Ironic, eh*? He hoped he remembered her number, though he was by no means sure she'd help him. He guessed correctly and got her answering machine. He made an impassioned, rapid-fire plea: "Angela, I'm in the Forsyth County Jail. They're holding me without bond on bullshit charges that are part of a vendetta against me because there are *certain people* who don't want the truth to get out. I need to hire Sandra. If you could get a message to her, I'd appreciate it. This is my one phone call, so if Sandra can't represent me, could you get in touch with an attorney? Please help. Of all the jails in the world, this is the one I do *not* want to be in. I repeat: I do *not* want to be here, so please—"

Beep. "Thank you for your message."

After that, Charlie exchanged street clothes for an orange jumpsuit. He hated that color. It reminded him of Tennessee's football team. He was placed in a large gray and white holding cell, joining two DUIs and a wife beater, all Caucasian. Charlie lay awake on his green mat, staring at the bars. Over the next few hours, a dozen more prisoners shuffled in. As his medication wore off, the pain sharpened. To keep his mind off his misery, Charlie tried writing a prison novel in his head, tentatively titled *Nobody's Bitch*. After a couple of hours, his brain grew tired of the literary effort. Shortly after he dozed off, four noisy drunks were thrown into the cell, now full to the max. So much for moving to Forsyth County to escape crime.

He slept fitfully, waking when the pain from his injuries intruded on his oblivion. In a semi-conscious state, he saw visions: signs of a coming Apocalypse, when the wicked would pay for their sins in the fiery pit, the righteous would smite their own sons and daughters, and then take their parking spaces. There would be bats aplenty in his Apocalypse, and for some reason, a groundhog. He realized he wasn't taking Armageddon seriously, but the pain that lingered in his thigh and jaw made it hard to properly concentrate on the End Time, and even more difficult to sleep. *How much brimstone could a woodchuck chuck if a woodchuck could chuck brimstone?*

* * *

Charlie looked up and saw a jailer holding a folded-up *Atlanta Journal-Constitution* outside the cell. "Sherman, looks like you got your name in the paper."

Bleary-eyed, Charlie rolled off the mat and shuffled toward the deputy. "Can I see?"

The jailer laughed and walked away, leaving Charlie to wonder: Why would a misdemeanor arrest merit a newspaper story? The answer: Uncle Stanley, of course. If the varmints couldn't kill him, they'd discredit him by throwing him in jail. Then they'd kill him—but only after showing him that no one would miss him. *Nice touch.*

And to think he'd been on the verge of success. Now this, his ruin. All his money would go to fight these charges. The varmints would win. He'd end up with nothing. After a few hours in jail, he understood perfectly why inmates, lonely and abandoned, hanged themselves. He didn't understand why every time he worked through his life equation, he ended up dead, one way or another. But there he was. *Mental note: Get rich, buy friends.*

While other prisoners made bail, Charlie stewed. Apparently he was pariah to local bondsmen. Again, he blamed Uncle Stanley. The cell's TV was broken, and other than asking twice for a newspaper (to no avail), Charlie kept his mouth shut. Still no word from Sandra. Then again, why would an African-American woman want to set foot in Forsyth County? Obviously, he'd wasted his phone call. After all, his relationship with Angela was nothing more than a series of battles, truces, and one-sided deals. She probably wanted him to rot in jail. But surely not in Forsyth, where her father, too, had suffered. She would resent the irony enough to do something about it. Wouldn't she?

Shifts changed. Day turned to night in Charlie's windowless world. More prisoners came: meth dealer, probation violator, burglar, girlfriend beater. None talked much. Instead, they slept. When fatigue overcame his pain, Charlie joined them in slumber.

Wednesday morning came, and still no word on his release. Ridiculous! Surely someone was trying to get him out. If not, why go on living? Damn. Zeroed out *again*. The jailers fed Charlie and barely noticed him otherwise. That night, he ran a fever. His wounded leg had swollen, straining the sutures and oozing pus. He shivered, shook, and sweated through the night. When the lights came on, he was haggard and pale. He'd barely spoken a dozen words since he'd been brought in. Now he felt too weak to talk.

Several other prisoners were released to a bail bondsman. Meanwhile, Charlie lay in a heap on his mat. After pondering his situation for a while, he decided (yet again) that he couldn't go on. The problem wasn't just being in jail. What made it worse was the knowledge that everyone outside was content to leave him there. He had a blanket, and though tall, he was clever. But there were still a half dozen inmates lounging around in the cell. First he'd rest. Then, as soon as he was alone …

* * *

As it turned out, Charlie was no more successful at ending his life than his enemies had been. Actually, he never got around to trying. Thursday morning, a young, fresh-faced deputy ripped his baton along the cell door's bars. "Get up! Time for your bond hearing, Mr. Famous."

Bleary-eyed, Charlie squinted at the deputy and staggered to his feet—disheveled, weak-kneed, and burning with fever. "I'm sick," he groaned.

"You'll be out soon, and you'll be someone else's problem."

Charlie declined to eat breakfast, and a little while after a trusty took his tray away, Deputy Strayer cuffed Charlie's hands in front of him and led him to a white van outside. Charlie winced and put his shackled wrists over his eyes to shield them from the sun, which seemed overpowering, even as a wintry wind cut through his jail uniform. He tripped over a parking curbstone and fell to his knees, yelping in pain. The deputy grabbed Charlie's arm and pulled him up, then helped him into the van. The door slammed shut. Charlie, alone in back, marveled at the growing spot of blood on his pants leg where his sutures had popped.

The van crossed the street, circled the courthouse, and backed up to a door. "Looks like you're going to be even more famous," the deputy said over his shoulder, through the mesh. "Bunch of reporters from Atlanta to cover you. So be cool." Charlie dropped his head in shame.

Strayer came around and opened the rear door. "What the hell did you do?" he yelled.

"I'm hurt," Charlie mumbled, his jumpsuit leg now covered with blood.

Strayer was joined by a young deputy, who stared open-mouthed at Charlie as a stream of journalists rounded the building's corner, pushing, shoving, and jockeying for position between the van and the courthouse entrance. Charlie was befuddled by the cameras. How did he merit this kind of coverage? When deputies pulled him out, Charlie hit another curbstone—God, he hated those things!—and fell on the pavement again. He broke the fall with his hands, popping more sutures.

"We gotta take him to the hospital," said the younger deputy.

A middle-aged sergeant forced his way through the crowd. "After the hearing," he said. "We gotta get through the media circus first."

Two lawmen grabbed the prisoner around the waist and half-carried him into the building while reporters barked questions Charlie didn't comprehend. After taking the elevator, the three men burst unceremoniously into a second-story hearing room. It was packed with people, mostly young women, several of them black. Journalists poured in after them. Charlie saw Angela standing along the back wall. And there was Sandra Hughes, sitting at a table in front. A bolt of energy ran through him. The sisterhood had come to his rescue!

Crenshaw, the newspaper reporter who'd interviewed Charlie at the coffeehouse a year before, sat on the front row along with some TV reporters. Video cameras on tripods lined the far wall. The deputies led the prisoner to his stout, short-haired African-American attorney, who was conferring with three earnest-looking white women in dark business suits leaning in over her table. Looking gruff and purposeful, they whispered and shuffled papers. All four lawyers looked at Charlie in amazement and horror, then turned in unison to stare at the deputies, who sat Charlie in a chair and backed away like he was a suspect package—instead of a packaged suspect.

"You made it!" Charlie cried in amazement. "I was afraid—actually, I just

… wow." He looked around. "How does an arrest for theft by taking draw this kind of attention?"

Sandra looked at him like he'd come from another planet. "God, have they been beating you?"

"I got shot. But you wouldn't know that."

"Are you kidding? *Everyone* knows. Somebody took a picture of you coming out of a window. You looked like *The Terminator*. It's actually pretty cool. You kept your shades on." She pulled a copy of Tuesday morning's paper from her briefcase to show him the front-page photo. Above it, the headline: "Writer Missing after Shooting." "You made *The New York Times* and the *CBS Evening News*. We thought you'd died until Angela found your message on her machine. We alerted the media, forcing them to set this hearing. She also brought her Intro to Sociology class for moral support. You'll be happy to know you are now extra credit."

"Wow. I've never been extra credit before."

He turned to wave at Angela, who gave him a clenched-fist salute. His spirits were rising. He had some fight left in him, after all. There were things people needed to know, and he was the one to tell them. "Why has it taken so long?" he asked. "Where have you been?"

"I'm sorry." She gave him a hangdog look. "I didn't hear from Angela till late Wednesday."

"She doesn't check her messages very often," he said glumly.

"I know. But I worked all last night, and I brought reinforcements. Charles, this is Debra Biello of the ACLU, Karen Janus of the Georgia Criminal Defense Project, and Callie Wollcroft with Prisoners of Conscience." *Sotto voce*, she said, "They're considering declaring you a political prisoner. I'm sure they will after what we've seen here."

Charlie nodded to the women and held up his shackled hands. They all complimented him on his first-class suffering, then Ms. Biello handed him a Kleenex for his oozing hand. "That's some book you wrote," she said, pointing to a copy of *Flight* on the table. Seeing people leaning forward, taking notes, he grabbed the book with his bloody hand and posed with it, in case anyone wanted to take a picture. Several flashes went off.

"Mr. Sherman," said Ms. Janus, "I was reluctant to review a misdemeanor charge, but we're definitely opening a case file now."

"You need medical treatment," said Ms. Biello.

"And a press conference," said Ms. Wollcroft.

"You're a *cause célèbre*," Sandra said. "Savor the moment."

Charlie gave her a look of disbelief. "*Savor the moment*? Press conference? I want the hell out of here!"

The ACLU attorney said, "Didn't you know everyone wants to hear from you?"

Charlie stared at her, dumbfounded. "Hell, I had trouble coming up with a number for my free phone call. I thought I was going to disappear in there."

"You didn't know everybody knew you got shot?" Her tone was incredulous.

Charlie shook his head sadly. "I didn't know what I didn't know."

Sandra held up the latest front page: "Wounded Writer Held Without Bond." She patted his arm. "You shouldn't even be in jail on these trumped-up charges. Isaac Cutchins is crazy. He threatened to kill two reporters if they didn't get off his property."

"*Offen* his property," Charlie corrected. "And he's not crazy. He's got something to hide."

A side door opened. Charlie's mouth shut. A slight, balding man with a shaggy fringe of hair and wearing a threadbare blue suit entered the room. A few people stood. The man motioned for them to sit down. "I'm just a magistrate," he said in a nasal twang, then did a comical double-take at the civil rights lawyers as they scrambled to find chairs. "It's just a bond hearing, ladies," he said. "An informal proceeding. I don't even need a plea today, let alone a full-blown defense."

He took a seat behind the desk by the window and put on a pair of spectacles. The sergeant stepped forward to hand him a file. He looked over it briefly and grimaced. "So you're Charles Sherman." The man glanced at the defense table, lowered his gaze, and squinted. "Is that *blood*? Stand up, Mr. Sherman."

Charlie stood. The magistrate's face wrinkled in distaste. "What's going on?" he asked.

"Your honor, Sandra Hughes, lead counsel for the defendant."

"And I'm Hugh Toomer, Ms. Hughes. Sit down, Mr. Sherman. I must say, the defendant has brought an awful lot of legal talent for a bond hearing on—"

He looked over his glasses at the files.

"—criminal trespass and theft by taking. Why was this postponed so long? This note says 'Hold until four p.m. Thursday.' What does that mean?" He gave the sergeant a piercing look.

Sandra, still standing, spoke: "Your honor, that statement may be a key to the problem. My client's treatment has been an outrage. He has been held incognito nearly to the law's limit and denied medical treatment. These offenses follow an assassination attempt on him by two Forsyth County men and his arrest on flimsy charges contained in questionable warrants. This doesn't seem like America to me. More like Guantanamo or Abu Ghraib."

Two Forsyth men. Charlie wore a blank expression as he mulled over this fact.

"Save the histrionics for the trial," Toomer said.

A flash of anger crossed Sandra's face as the magistrate glanced down at paperwork. "You go, woman!" Charlie whispered. "I love pre-trial histrionics!"

"I'd say what we have is a misdemeanor defendant who's bleeding," Toomer observed. "Is the sheriff already out of money for treating prisoners? We're not even through January."

The sergeant and Strayer offered conflicting explanations—"Your honor, they were self-inflicted" and "He fell on the way over"—delivered simultaneously. Audience members hooted derisively.

Wearing a sour expression, Toomer shook his head. A second later, a man in a suit burst through the same door Toomer had entered and blurted, "My apologies." He turned and looked in horror at the crowd, then at Charlie.

"Our late solicitor general, Paul Armitage," Toomer said, drawing titters from the crowd. "All right, we need to set bond. And frankly, I don't understand why you're here."

"The sheriff considers him a flight risk," Armitage said. "He was hiding out. If we could just hold him until four—"

Sandra was up like a shot. "This is outrageous! Obviously, Mr. Sherman was hiding out because people wanted to kill him. Your honor, we seek immediate removal of the defendant from Forsyth County for his personal safety. We ask that he be released on his own recognizance, though I must admit I'm curious about the state's interest in holding Mr. Sherman."

"Perhaps at a more pertinent time, Ms. Hughes." Toomer glanced at the warrants on his desk. "All right, I signed these two months ago for a couple of misdemeanors. Not felonies." He squinted at Armitage. "These charges don't even make it to trial most of the time. Why is he being held for nearly the full seventy-two hours?"

"It wasn't my doing, but I would point out the victim is a prominent—"

"Ixnay on the ominentpray," Toomer said. "Let's send Mr. Sherman home. Mr. Sherman, I'm releasing you without requiring you to post bond, providing that you give us a proper address. And we should have a doctor look at you right now. Any objections?"

Charlie stood. "Your honor," he said, feeling a steel grip on his left arm. "Why is there no property listed on the theft warrant?"

"Shhh," Sandra hissed.

The magistrate looked down and said, "The warrant says 'certain personal items.'"

"I suggest you ask them what I stole," Charlie said. Sandra wrapped both hands around his forearm and pulled with all her might, forcing him down.

"Discovery is not the purpose of this proceeding, Mr. Sherman. The defendant is released on his own recognizance." Toomer looked around. "All right. Mr. Sherman, please obey any court summons or subpoenas you receive. Everybody knows who you are now, that's for sure. Deputy, would you please uncuff Mr. Sherman? Next case."

"That's all we got," the sergeant said.

"What a waste of time," the magistrate muttered.

Armitage, looking like he wanted to be elsewhere, was immediately surrounded by reporters, who interrupted his attempt to make a cellphone call. "No comment! I'm not trying this case in the media," he said, waving his hands in the air as he retreated, punching buttons.

The reporters then pressed in on the defense table, but before Charlie could speak, deputies laid hands on him. "We'll take you back to the detention center and get you looked at by a doctor and processed out," the sergeant told him, then turned to a fellow deputy. "Call the EMTs."

As journalists shouted questions, Charlie told Sandra, "You handle the media. I'm too tired to talk."

The sergeant said, "Ma'am, if you're going to hold a press conference, please do it outside."

"I suggest you do your job, not try to keep me from doing mine, deputy," Sandra snapped.

The prisoner stood and presented himself for uncuffing, but the deputies hurried him away in shackles. "I need a ride back to Atlanta," he said over his shoulder, then shouted for all to hear, "Ask them what I stole!"

As the door closed behind him, a young woman yelled, "Speak truth to power, Charles!"

Unfortunately for Charlie, it was still power's turn to talk. Waiting at the jail were two navy blue-suited, middle-aged white guys with dark hair: Finch and Drew. They claimed to be GBI agents armed with a material witness warrant that allowed them to detain Charlie for questioning. Although his jailers had called paramedics to treat Charlie, Finch and Drew pulled rank, claiming Charlie was involved in a terrorist drug-smuggling conspiracy. The locals ceded authority, washing their hands of Forsyth's most famous jailbird. They called off the paramedics. By this time, Charlie was merely oozing blood, anyway.

As soon as one set of cuffs was removed, another was slapped on. This time, Charlie's hands were placed behind his back. Agents Finch and Drew were in such a hurry to move their prisoner that he had to literally dig in his heels before they would allow the desk sergeant to retrieve his keys from the property lockup. They pushed him out the side door into the transfer bay. Charlie saw their car and stopped cold. The Crown Victoria looked like the vehicle that had followed him briefly when he left Kathleen's house back in November. And the one that staked out Danny Patterson's place. The damned car was everywhere—maybe it had even blended into Kathleen's funeral procession. So that's how—

"Oh, hell no!" Charlie yelled. "I'm not letting you take me into the woods and shoot me! Help!"

The agents pulled harder. Charlie shook them off and staggered backward, then started kicking at them, which was, in retrospect, a mistake. The agents called for help. Two deputies came running and tackled Charlie, pinning him to the concrete floor. While Charlie was down, Finch kicked him in the ribs. *Oof.* The four men brought him to his feet and shoved him into the back of the car. "They're going to kill me!" he shouted. "Third time's a charm." He thought for a second. "Fourth time, overall. But who's counting?"

As deputies retreated into the building, one cast an uncertain backward glance at Charlie. "You know what it is!" Charlie shouted. "They're not real GBI agents!"

"Shut up," said Finch, slamming the door. Drew took the wheel and started the car.

Charlie's right side was killing him. He was sure the bastard had cracked a rib. Well, maybe not, but he'd claim so, anyway. He coughed up phlegm and spit on the back of the front seat to check it for blood. None yet, but the day was young. "Where are you taking me?" he demanded.

"Where your lawyer can't find you." Finch turned to give him an oddly pleasant smile. It was evil, that face, bought and paid for by Uncle Stanley and the Cutchins's ill-gotten gains, no doubt. Who else had the clout to keep this *habeas corpus* nightmare going? As if to taunt his prisoner, Drew drove by the courthouse. Charlie saw Sandra surrounded by reporters, too busy discussing his plight to notice him. Here he was, drowning, slipping under the water's calm surface while lifeguards held a training session on the beach just a few yards away. This was *not* a fitting end to his contract, to be shot while in custody, especially not after he'd regained his will to live.

He recalled Redeemer Wilson's chilling account of such times: "*If there were reporters in the town where they arrested you, they moved you to a place where no one knew you. A small town, back in the woods. That's where they did their dirty work, things that couldn't be proven. They'd say they gonna beat the nigger outta you, but what they meant was they gonna beat the man out of you or kill you, one."*

Charlie thought his ordeal wasn't going to end well, either.

The agents took him into Cherokee County and on to Canton, passing over I-575, a spur off I-75 that ran north to merge with the Appalachian Highway near Nelson. Drew took a right turn into an industrial park. At the bottom of a hill, he pulled off the street and stopped before an electric gate. The agent produced a plastic card. The gate opened, and he stopped beside a nondescript building hidden from the street at the back of a heavily wooded lot. A few cars were parked near the front door. This was heartening to Charlie, since he had feared he would get the abandoned warehouse treatment.

So maybe they wouldn't kill him. Surely their prisoner-grab had been too public for that. That was a theory, anyway. And they probably were GBI agents—rogues or moonlighters, based in Forsyth County and beholden to Uncle Stanley or someone even higher up. And they were playing a game, keeping him out of public view.

"So you want to tell me what this is about?" Charlie asked.

"You're being detained as a material witness to a crime—the drug-related bombing at the North Atlanta Store-All on Christmas Eve," Finch said, pausing like he expected a confession.

"Whatever do you mean?" Charlie's tone was a mixture of innocence and insolence. After an awkward silence, he said, "If you really wanted to question me, you shouldn't have taken me away from my attorney. Now you're screwed as far as information is concerned. And furthermore, I don't know what you're talking about."

The agents pulled him from the car and led him into the building's side entrance. As they tugged him down the hall, Charlie looked around for other people but saw none. Finch and Drew pushed him inside a small, windowless room near the back of the building and closed the door. When Charlie refused Drew's command to sit on a cushioned metal chair beside a folding table, the lawman kneed him in the groin and pushed him down onto the seat. They uncuffed him, then recuffed his hands behind him so that he was fastened to the chair.

"We need a statement," Finch said, pressing a button on a digital recorder and placing it on the table. Charlie stared at it balefully. He knew that anything he said could be edited and then held against him. It was simply outrageous that anyone would do such a thing. He was shocked, *shocked*, at the very thought of doctoring information to achieve an end.

When he was ready and able to speak, Charlie said, "Hey, don't you need a good cop to make this dynamic work?" Finch scowled. Charlie leaned forward and spoke into the microphone: "Fuck yourselves. Thank you, I'll be here all week. Wait! I already have been."

"We know you're involved. That was your van that blew up. We can hold you till you talk."

Technically, the van was Susan's, but he saw no need to point that out. Now he realized she had another reason to be pissed at him, as if she needed one.

"Could have done this in Forsyth and saved yourself some gas. I want my attorney. I also need medical attention—" Charlie raised his voice "—more now that the man who identified himself as Finch cracked a rib and the man who identified himself as Drew kicked me in the balls! I also want to eat. I want to speak to a representative of Prisoners of Conscience and the ACLU, too. And clean clothes and a ride home. Other than that, deponent sayeth not."

Finch restarted the recorder, then both agents left the room. Charlie recited the only clean limerick he knew, sang a couple of lines from a Sinatra tune, and hummed for a while.

The door opened. "Then, when I was four years old—Oh, hey."

Finch grabbed the device and walked out.

A few minutes later, Drew came in and asked, "Anyone ever tell you you're an asshole?"

"Anyone ever tell you this interview is over?" Charlie stared straight ahead until the agent left.

* * *

Finch and Drew stayed away for a while, leaving Charlie to strain against his cuffs and count the holes in ceiling tiles. They didn't feed him, but they did pipe in rap music over a speaker mounted on the wall. This made Charlie think of Demetrious. Then Demetrious dancing. That kid had all the moves.

When Drew returned, he said, "You're free to go."

"Wow. Giving up so easily? Well, this was pointless. OK by me. I need a ride back to Atlanta."

"We're not taking you anywhere. Just go."

"I'm entitled to a free call. Where's a phone I can use?"

"You don't get a phone call. You weren't arrested."

"I'm a taxpayer. Let me use the phone."

"Just get out," Drew growled. "That's the deal."

"You're just going to dump me out on the street in prison clothes fifty miles from home?"

"You should have thought about that before you showed your ass."

"That's one thing I haven't done. Yet."

"Well, thanks for sparing."

Drew uncuffed Charlie. He stood up and stretched. His orange pant leg had stuck to his oozing wound, and when it pulled loose, he winced in pain. Charlie's arms felt like logs hanging from his shoulders. He shook his hands to restore circulation. "Well, it's been surreal," he said, looking into the agent's eyes and seeing emptiness there.

At the front door, Drew gave Charlie a push to send him on his way. Despite misgivings about the agents' motives, the newly freed man stumbled forward, squinting at the cold sun in the afternoon sky. He needed to get home, but how? The loft was nearly an hour's drive away, and not having a car complicated things immensely. Sick, wounded, bloody, and tired, with a sticky red right hand, he coughed as he stumbled down the drive. He rubbed his goose-pimpled arms. When the gate swung open, he walked through, then up the hill toward the Canton-Forsyth highway.

Problem: A man in a jail uniform who looked like he'd been in a knife fight would attract serious attention. How long could such a person go unnoticed?

Not long, it turned out. A minute after Charlie reached the highway and pivoted toward the Interstate, a Canton motorcycle officer roared up and squealed to a stop beside him. The cop jumped off his Harley and pulled his gun, yelling, "Put your hands over your head!"

Charlie complied, standing open-mouthed as two squad cars appeared and cops came out of their vehicles like they'd captured an escaped convict who'd been in a knife fight. "All right, all right," Charlie said. "I'll—"

The motorcycle cop kicked Charlie in the back of the knee, forcing him to the ground.

"Please don't—"

A blow between his shoulder blades put Charlie's face on the pavement, scraping his cheek raw. While sprawled out on the road shoulder, he was handcuffed for the third time that day. He coughed and said, "I'm not going to cause any—"

He was kicked in the side. Then again. He looked to the west and wondered if the beating was ever going to stop. The sun grew dimmer and smaller, as if fleeing his plight. The cops shouted, sounding like dogs barking at a wild animal they'd cornered. One of them placed a gun to his head. He looked down on the asphalt and closed his eyes. *This is a setup. This is how it ends.*

A car horn sounded. Charlie opened his eyes and turned his head to see a black man in a car at the stop sign. He was leaning toward the open passenger window, holding a cellphone like a camera.

"Keep moving!" the motorcycle cop shouted. Only when he advanced on the driver did the man roll up his window and turn toward the Interstate. The cop radioed in some numbers.

"Got a witness now," Charlie muttered, his face stuck in roadside gravel.

"All right, that's enough," said another cop. He grabbed Charlie under the shoulders and lifted him. Charlie blew grit off his lips and tried to spit the taste of oil and tar out of his mouth. The cops placed him in the back of a squad car.

Their prisoner learned during the ride to the police station that—as he suspected—he'd been picked up following a report of an escaped prisoner. At least now he could make that phone call. *Simple pleasures are the best.* Charlie could hear anxiety through the static on the police radio. The cop shouted back through the partition, "Is your name Sherman?"

Charlie smirked. "I have the right to remain silent."

Soon they were in front of the police station. An older man in uniform stood on the sidewalk, waving the patrol car away, as if he wanted no part of its cargo. The officer stopped anyway, got out, and opened the rear door. Charlie slid out and looked around.

"Let him go," the older man said.

"Chief, he resisted—"

"He's free to go."

The officer hemmed and hawed. "Somebody with a camera—"

"Nothing happened, right?"

Charlie gave the older man a crooked smile and said, "Right."

Once uncuffed, he turned away, then glanced back at the police chief and the cop, who gestured madly and yelled at each other in the secret language of the damned. That's right: No jail could hold him. *No cops? Ha! Cops say, "No Charlie!"*

Trembling, weak with fever, hungry, nauseous, and bleeding through the sand, glass, and gravel that peppered his wounded left cheek, Charlie started the long march home. He knew he had to hide his leg wound. A quarter-mile up the street, he found a tattered black trash bag and picked it up in hopes it would keep people from paying too much attention to him. He tore off a piece and wrapped it around his pant leg to cover his wound.

After a mile or so, he stopped at a convenience store in hopes of calling Angela or Sandra for help. But the payphone was broken, and when he asked to borrow a customer's cellphone, the man dialed 911 while the clerk shouted, "Get out!" In hopes he'd at least get a ride to the county line, Charlie waited outside for the cops to show up, but none came. No one wanted anything to do with him. He was radioactive.

He tried hitchhiking, but after two drivers swerved off the road and tried to hit him—or at the very least, scare the shit out of him—he gave up on that method of transportation. From then on, he kept moving, lurching up a hill and shambling back down the next, passing under the Interstate bridge and shuffling out of town on his way to Fulton County and civilization. With the sun to his back, Charlie trudged onward, wheezing his way up a long, winding incline. As he walked along the narrow shoulder of the two-lane road, Charlie tried not to think of the miles that lay before him. *Just cross this desert*, he told himself. *Be a Kung Fu prophet.*

Near dusk, he got the Talton treatment. A flying beer bottle hit him—only this one came considerably faster than the one that Momo threw at the good professor back in 1987. Fortunately, he'd seen it coming from a red Ford pickup. Turning away and putting up his right fist kept it from hitting him full in the face. Instead, it struck a hard, glancing blow on his right temple, like a beanball. He staggered away from the road and went down as his assailant's Rebel yell faded into the distance. He stayed down in the brown grass until the cold got to him, then stood and wobbled on his feet. He took a few shaky steps before he recovered his equilibrium and continued his march. It was colder now, and his head hurt like hell. Tears welled in his eyes. *Cry all you want, but keep moving forward*, he told himself.

For several hours, he stumbled on, semi-delirious from fatigue, fever and chills, and hunger. Eventually, he reached Alpharetta in Fulton County. Traffic was sparse, it was late, and the temperature was near freezing. Suffering from hypothermia, he came to a bus stop and declared he would go no further, even though he didn't know what time it was, or if buses were still running. His arms were numb. He leaned against the MARTA signpost and collapsed, sliding to the ground. He wrapped his arms around himself, then blew on his hands to warm them. Within seconds, lights appeared over the hill. Hissing and squealing, something stopped beside him and opened up to swallow him.

Charlie thought he was looking into the mouth of a dragon. He stood up to address the beast as a supplicant, then realized it was a MARTA bus. Recovering his sanity, he said, "I don't have any money. I just walked from Canton, and I need a ride the rest of the way home."

"I seen your picture on TV." The driver, a stocky black woman wearing a wig, regarded him critically. "You the man wrote the book about Forsyth County." She shuddered. "Won't catch me goin' up there. Everybody's looking for you, you know."

"I don't want to be found," he said wearily. "I just want to go home."

"Nobody give you a ride? Well, doesn't that say something about the way they treat us."

Us? She must have just made him an honorary black person.

"Come on in," she said.

He faltered on his way up the steps. She reached out to steady him. "I thought you'd be cold as ice in that jail outfit, but you're hot as fire!"

The bus's interior was lighted and warm. It smelled of humanity, but Charlie was the only passenger. He slumped on the seat behind the driver. "What time is it?" he asked.

"Past midnight. I'm not supposed to be here." She slammed the door shut. The bus rumbled forward.

He looked out the window and soon fell asleep. The driver woke him when she pulled into the North Springs Station—the northern end of the line.

"Train take you the rest of the way," she said. "Pay double next time."

"OK." He took a step down to the curb and turned. "Thank you."

"That bus driver got suspended."

Charlie gave her a puzzled look. "Sorry. What?"

"The driver took out those men tryin' to kill you. Limits to what a bus driver can do in this world, I reckon."

"I suppose." Charlie paused to think about this, then saw a train's headlight approaching from the south. He limped away as fast as he could, grateful that bus riders didn't have to pay for transfers or pass through turnstiles at the rail station. He hustled up to the platform just as the train pulled in. A few travelers from the airport disembarked with wheeled luggage. Charlie boarded and slumped in a seat. It left on its southbound journey immediately. He had the car to himself until the train stopped at the Dunwoody station. There, a young white man in a waiter's outfit—black slacks and vest, white shirt, and thin black tie—stepped into the car, followed by a couple of African-American teenagers. He heard cursing, but it was aimless, with no anger in it—something he could ignore.

Charlie dozed off and woke at Five Points, one stop short of his destination. A black transit cop was staring at him. When Charlie got off at Garnett, the cop followed him to the exit, talking into his radio. "I'm out on bond," Charlie hollered over his shoulder as he walked into the night.

Now only a short walk from home, Charlie felt a surge of energy as he hit the sidewalk. The homeless man who lived in the vacant lot on State Street had extinguished his barrel fire and retired to his cardboard shack for the evening. A car honked and Charlie quickened his pace, hoping to get home before another policeman spotted him. As he entered the garage on Castlegate, he saw that the bakery window had been replaced but not yet relettered. He looked for the Volvo. It took him a minute to remember that Dana had parked it somewhere else. How many days ago had that been? He couldn't recall. He wasn't going to look for it now, that was for sure.

He rode the elevator up to his floor and trudged along the hall carpet, marveling at how luxurious it felt compared to the road he'd just traveled. He fumbled with his keys at the apartment door and pushed it open with his uninjured shoulder, half-expecting to see the place torn apart by evildoers, but it was just the ordinary mess. Several notes had been slipped under the door.

After draining a half-liter bottle of water, he headed to the bathroom. After washing his hands and splashing water on his face, he went to the kitchen, but there was little to eat. He gobbled an apple and a handful of crackers. Then he took a double dose of antibiotics and painkillers, the latter more for his distressed feet and ankles than his gunshot and glass wounds.

Charlie took a long shower to wash off the dust and caked-on blood. After he dried off, he ripped up a towel and tied strips around his wounded thigh and hand. When he'd done all he cared to do for himself, he turned out the lights and climbed into bed.

"No cops," Charlie murmured sleepily as a freight train rumbled by. "I get it now."

Chapter Twenty

His hair damp and sheets sweaty, Charlie woke from a dream of drowning. The loft's vague shadows seemed unfamiliar, but the sound of a MARTA train clacking by comforted him. His back and leg muscles were red-hot clothes hangers beneath his skin, and his knees were busted hinges, but his fever had broken, and the pain from his wounds had subsided. A remarkable recovery.

The radioactive orange jumpsuit lay rumpled on the floor, looking like the man inside had vaporized. Would the sheriff charge him with stealing it? Charlie didn't care; he would keep his trophy, stenciled with that dark, magical lettering: **FORSYTH COUNTY JAIL**. When *American Monster* was published, he'd pose for his author's photo in it and have the last Georgia chain gang laugh. Anyway, it was a fair trade for the shipping department clothes still in Cumming. He threw the blood-stained uniform in the washing machine along with his battle-tested duster.

The kitchen was trashed: dirty dishes in the sink, old food and bloody bandages on the counter. He cleaned up and brewed coffee, reveling in quotidian tasks that marked his return to normalcy. While eating eggs and a bagel—practically the only food left in the place—he looked at notes and reporters' business cards that had been slipped under his door. One said, "Fight the Power! Peace, Kim #416."

He fired up the computer and checked the Atlanta newspaper's website for news. "Writer Missing: Law Agencies Under Fire" was the top story, accompanied by that fortuitous, perhaps lifesaving cellphone photo of Charlie with a cop's boot on his head. *Thank you, Alphonsus Hester, wherever you are.*

The picture's poor resolution didn't hide the defeated look of a whipped dog in Charlie's eyes. He'd been shamed, humiliated, and dominated, and now the world knew it. This pissed him off and pushed his blood pressure back to a proper boil. He wanted to fight back.

Fortunately, there was plenty of ammunition out there—and shots were being fired. His story had gone national, even international, and Redeemer Wilson had proposed a prayer vigil for him. Crenshaw's article was replete with quotes from Sandra, law professors, and civil rights attorneys expressing their outrage at his treatment. Rep. Stanley Cutchins claimed no knowledge of the dispute between his father and his niece's estranged husband. A photo of Pappy's house showed a "no trespassing" sign by the driveway. And there was this lovely sentence: "When asked what Sherman had stolen, Isaac Cutchins threatened to kill a reporter." There was a sidebar story ("Forsyth Book No. 1 on Books.com") and an editorial blasting the GBI, Forsyth County sheriff, and Canton police for their mistreatment of a man "most likely hiding from assassins, not warrants ... although one has to wonder if there isn't a connection." *Cool.* Charlie hit the print button.

The story in Tuesday's paper had identified his feckless assailants as Forsyth County meth dealers. The shooter's name: Robert Suches. Someone with that last name had been in the mob that killed John Riggins. "Suches it is," Charlie muttered.

And the brilliant part: Through it all, Charlie Sherman remained a man of mystery, whereabouts unknown, his survival in doubt. He'd be the hottest interview in America. Once upon a time, he would have done anything for this kind of attention, but now he didn't want the scrutiny—mainly because he was too burned out for a news conference, and furthermore, he wasn't sure what to say.

He was still Googling himself when his cellphone rang. Seeing it was a New York number, he took a chance and answered it.

Fortress's young publicist was on the line. "Charles Sherman! My God, you got shot *and* arrested. You're like our most famous author right now," Heather Schwartz gushed. "We're *inundated* with interview requests, in case you didn't see my e-mail. Oh, and we sold an excerpt to the Atlanta paper. It was weird. Your editor said it was a boring chapter, mainly a list of land documents and stuff."

"Oh." Those would be the records Crenshaw had long coveted. "Wait. Who's my editor?"

"Joshua."

"I thought Joshua got fired."

"We've got three Joshuas. Well, two now. By the way, the book's selling out everywhere. People want to know what got you shot and arrested and tortured or whatever. We're going to a second printing. Oh, and the *Times* is reviewing it. You've already been on the front page twice. This is so exciting!"

"Yay," Charlie deadpanned.

"I'm e-mailing you like sixty interview requests. You take care of them, OK? And send me stuff I can use for a press release about you being shot. And arrested."

"I got assaulted, too."

"Were you raped in jail?" she asked, sounding hopeful.

"No, just run-of-the-mill police brutality."

"Somebody said there's a picture with a cop's boot on your head. Was that posed?"

"Uh, no. Not that one. The mug shots were, though."

"Send us something, anyway. We'll issue a statement. And congratulations! This is so awesome!"

"Thanks." He hung up and broke out laughing so hard he fell out of his chair, causing himself more pain.

Next, Charlie listened to the saga play out over his cellphone's voicemail. First Angela, from Wednesday night, apologizing for not playing his message. Then Sandra, excitedly saying she was calling in her human-rights allies "because the Forsyth sheriff won't return my calls and that place is an American gulag." Then, late Thursday morning, after he'd been taken by Finch and Drew, a WTF call from Sandra. She'd called again Thursday night: "God, Charles, where are you? What have they done? I've demanded that the governor call out the National Guard to search for you!"

There were more calls: Jean, his oldest friend from his new life, worried and crying. Dana, on her way out of town Thursday night, saying, "You've manufactured enough publicity to get on the bestseller list." Laughing! A wonderful laugh, too. Nothing from Susan. But she didn't have his number. With good reason. Yet they found him, anyway.

And a recent one from Barbara Asher: "Charlie? Charlie?" she cried out in anguished hope. "Are you alive? There's an article about you in the *Times*. This is absolutely insane! Your sales must be through the roof! I'm putting *Monster* up for auction. Call me when you're out of intensive care or solitary confinement. There's so much more to do. Editing and a new ending. Without you around, who would do it? Publishers don't have real editors anymore. Please, please, don't die on me, darling."

His e-mails included the usual junk along with a "semi-desperate" plea from Crenshaw for an interview. And one from *Atlanta Week* editor James Hadford: "Charlie—We'll pay you $2,000 for your first-person account of whatever the hell's going on. By the way, we mailed a check for your last article."

Charlie was out the door in a flash. He found an envelope from Hadford in his vestibule mailbox. Five hundred bucks. Cool. He snuck a peek through La Patisserie's back door. A painter was lettering the bakery's new front window. There was a rack inside, by the door, with free copies of *Atlanta Week*. He was reluctant to show his injured face in the shop after causing so much chaos there, but he snuck in anyway and snatched a copy, retreating undetected. He stood in the garage admiring the front-page promo: "Georgia Diaspora: Forsyth's Blacks are (Finally) History."

A bus rumbled by, reminding him of his brush with death. He shuddered, realizing that this wasn't over. *American Monster* was far from being published, and he was still in danger. Then he realized that Minerva might be in danger too. He needed to see if she was OK. Should he call her? No. She'd hang up on him. He needed to pay her a visit, even if she slammed the door in his face. He returned to the loft, got his coat from the dryer, and rushed out. He slipped on his shades and raised the duster's collar to cover his damaged ear as he walked past two news trucks parked on the sidewalk. After spending twenty minutes searching for the Volvo, he found it on a side street with two parking tickets stuck under a wiper and a tow-away notice plastered on the driver's window.

On the way to Minerva's, he called Sandra. Her assistant shrieked, "Mr. Sherman's alive!"

Sandra came on the line. "Charles! Are you all right?"

"I am now."

"They wouldn't tell me where you were, then I got a call from a reporter. They had pictures of you getting stomped. I called the Canton police and they claimed they had no record of you."

"They let me go. It was just a courtesy stomp."

"How'd you get home?"

"I walked to Alpharetta and caught MARTA. Or maybe MARTA caught me."

"You should have called me. We were worried sick. Now the Justice Department is involved. I talked to the governor for twenty minutes yesterday afternoon. He promised a full-scale search."

"He lied," Charlie said. "I walked along the main road for thirty miles. I was out there for eight hours. I wasn't hard to find."

"He was probably hoping you'd get hit. Do you realize how much media this has gotten?"

"Yeah. The paper's running an excerpt from the book Sunday. *The New York Times* is reviewing it. I've got sixty-five requests for interviews, last I checked."

"Hell, Charlie, *I've* got forty. We need to go on the attack."

"I don't want to do anything today. Maybe Monday. I don't know what to say, anyway."

She hesitated. "All right. You must be exhausted. Should I tell people you're all right?"

"That seems like a bit of an overstatement, but go ahead."

"OK. Call me. Oh, by the way … maybe this isn't the right time, but I promised Angela I'd mention it. She wants to renegotiate the contract on the book." Charlie flinched. The car swerved to the left. "And your wife called."

The car swerved back to the right. "Really. What does she want?"

"She's worried about you," Sandra said, sounding surprised. "You should call her."

Actually, Charlie had been talking about Angela, but there was no point in getting into that now. "Thanks for the warning. And thanks for bringing the legal army."

"I'll bill you. Thank goodness you're a bestselling author now, so you can afford it, right?"

Charlie laughed, but stopped when he hung up, since the prospect of forking over a bunch of money to Angela didn't amuse him all that much.

Minutes later, he parked in front of Minerva's house and rang the bell.

She opened the door, gasped, and stepped back. "First I hear you were shot, then the next thing I hear is that you got yourself arrested, then you disappear. You all right?"

"More or less."

She examined his face, tut-tutting at his injuries. "So what brings you back to my doorstep, Mister Bad Penny?" she asked, distrust in her voice.

"Came to see how you were doing. I figured if I was having troubles, you might be, too."

She sighed, stepped inside and gestured to the sofa. "Come on in. I'll make tea."

When she returned from the kitchen, she sat in her chair and regarded him this way and that. "Looks like you didn't get shot up too bad."

"I'll be all right." He nodded toward *Flight from Forsyth*, which sat on the table by her chair with a bookmarker stuck in the middle. "You've been reading it."

"I'm halfway through. Terrible stuff. What happened, not the writing. Writing's good."

"Thanks. How's Takira doing?"

"She's at school."

"Heard from Demetrious lately?"

She looked out the western window. Before Charlie could break the awkward silence, the tea kettle whistled. Minerva went to the kitchen, returning with cups on a tray. "Tell you the truth," she said, seemingly apropos of nothing, "I gave up on you." She sat and took a sip. "There have been things happening. About that farm."

Charlie took a sip of bitter, unsweetened brew, then put down the cup. "Did you get an attorney and file a lien on the property, like I suggested?"

"You were shot," she said, casting her gaze on the floor. "What time of day did that happen?"

"Monday morning. About ten, I think."

"At noon that day, some men—lawyers—came by with papers."

"Really." Charlie sat up straight.

"Of course I didn't know what had happened to you at the time."

"What were their names?"

"Jackson and Stout. That's the law firm. The men had a quitclaim on land in Forsyth County. They wouldn't say it was my father's, but obviously it was, because they were willing to give me twenty thousand dollars to sign it."

"How'd they know to find you?"

"They didn't say."

"Hmm." Charlie had already come to suspect that the evildoers had found Minerva after finding *him*, perhaps picking up his trail at Kathleen's funeral. That pissed him off. He couldn't even mourn folks properly anymore. "Damn. You didn't sign it, did you? Because that land is worth millions—"

She held up her hand to silence him. "I told them I'd think about it. Unfortunately, Demetrious and his friend came in while they were here. I didn't want to tell the boy what was going on, especially not with that P-Dog—" she sneered at the name "—standing there. Demetrious got upset and started yelling how this was about the book you're writing. One of the men told Demetrious this was grown-up business and for him to run along and mind his own."

She sighed. "Now you know Demetrious can't stand to be *dissed*, he calls it, and really, the man had no business saying that since this isn't his house. The boys have a problem with white folks anyway, but these two men ... well,

P-Dog acts the fool and pulls a gun!" She threw up her hands. "This isn't even an ounce of his business, and he's yelling that they're trying to cheat us—like it's his money, can you believe it?"

Minerva fanned herself with her hand before continuing. "Anyway, Demetrious and he start carrying on, saying they're stealing what is rightfully ours. The boys are shouting to get out before they kill them. Let me tell you, those men left in a hurry." She paused and looked down. "I told the boys they had no business doing what they did. I should have told them to get themselves gone."

Her eyes widened. "Not ten minutes later," she said, her voice high and indignant, "The law comes and takes Demetrious and P-Dog away. Now his friend is nothing but bad news, and this isn't the first time Demetrious has been in trouble, and with a gun, well—that's not good at all." She shook her head. "I expected to get a phone call from him, but not a word. The next day, I saw your bloody face in the paper and found out that you'd disappeared. That's when I knew."

"Knew what?"

"That it was over. Things weren't going to work out the way I'd hoped. And it wasn't safe to fight about it. While I'm trying to get Demetrious out of jail, calling lawyers—and I can't even find his mama, but Shaundra is a whole 'nother story—the men come back, real confident now. They say they can make the boys' problems go away, drop charges, clear the record, if I just sign the quitclaim." She laughed ruefully. "They'd pay me ten thousand. Half what they'd offered before."

"That's extortion!" Charlie cried.

"Well, I've got to look out for mine. I took the money. I had to. There's going to be some big bills coming with the baby. And now Demetrious is out of jail. Not that he'll stay out."

"*Oh, Minerva*," he said, unable to hide his disappointment in her.

Anger flashed across her face. "Don't you 'Oh, Minerva' me. Looked like they got rid of you. Those men said there wasn't going to be a book, and even if there was, it wouldn't matter, because they'd fix it so nobody would believe anything you said. Next thing I know, you're in jail, then you're all bloody on the news yesterday, then you disappear again. I figured they put you on a chain gang, or did you like they did my father." She shook her head.

"I wish you hadn't signed the quitclaim."

She stood up. "Well, that happens to be *my* business. And what would you have done besides give me free advice that would keep my baby in jail? Don't know why I'm explaining myself to you," she huffed. "Anyway, you got your story. That's what's important to you, and that's all I've got to say." She held up her hand to fend off his arguments.

Obviously, it was time to go. Charlie stood up. "Did you get the name of the cops?"

"No," she snapped, then added, "They were dressed in suits, like detectives. They said they were GBI."

"Really." He took a sip of bitter brew for the road and left, mumbling apologies for their awkward reunion.

Minutes later, Charlie pulled into the parking lot of a Memorial Drive convenience store next to a check-cashing service crowded with workers on payday. He was thirsty, but when he saw the news rack—and the photo of his head under a boot—he opted for the grisly souvenir instead. As he fed change into the machine, a derelict rushed up with his hand out. Charlie turned away and retreated to the car, ignoring the panhandler's pleading eyes.

He laid the paper on the seat beside him. Only then did he see the front-page story by Crenshaw he'd missed on the Internet due to his obsession with himself: "Forsyth Farm Sells for $22 Million."

"Shortly after 3 p.m. Thursday," the article stated, "retired farmer Isaac Cutchins of Coaltown took time off from feuding with Charles Sherman to become a multimillionaire." Crenshaw reported that Department of Transportation Commissioner Robert Mann had been "actively involved" in pursuing a portion of the parcel for development of the Outer Perimeter highway. The rest of the land would be used in a major retail development. "While Cutchins, who has repeatedly threatened reporters with bodily harm, refused comment on the sale, his son, Rep. Stanley Cutchins (R-Cumming) called it 'a blessing.' However, a spokesman for GrassRoots Georgia called the sale 'a blatant conflict of interest.'"

A blessing. Charlie laughed bitterly. *Shortly after 3 p.m.* Finch and Drew had held him until the deal closed, released him, and then, he was certain, sicced the local cops on him. Good times. Obviously, the varmints thought he was a lot smarter and more dangerous than he actually was. In fact, he felt like a dumbass, knowing that he could have shouted the truth from the rooftops early on and perhaps stopped the sale, or made sure Minerva received what was rightfully hers. *But no. That wasn't his style.* Instead, he had sandbagged and played coy, planning to release *American Monster* according to his own agenda—thereby making his grand entrance in the fourth act of a three-act play. So the wicked prospered, thanks to God's incompetent avenger. And the joke was on Minerva.

Then again, she should have gotten a lawyer, like he'd told her to.

To hell with it.

Charlie drove toward the afternoon sun with no idea where to go next or what to do. He just knew he didn't want to return to the loft and risk an interview or another assassination attempt. He wanted neither to talk nor die, and he especially didn't want to think about the sale, for that would be dwelling on the land of his enemies. He couldn't concentrate and grew angrier with each passing second. Was God mocking him, or had God Itself been mocked? "Fuck it!" he shouted, banging the steering wheel.

As he approached Redeemer's church on Memorial Drive, Charlie wondered if Trouble might be lurking about. Whether the supernatural creep was fully charged or operating on a dead battery, Charlie wanted answers. He pulled into the empty gravel lot of the Holy Way House and scouted for danger. Two middle-aged black men in hard hats walked along the other side of the street. Charlie exited the van and stepped toward the church. Dusk brought a chill, and a gust of wind swirled a plastic bag around the lot. Down at the stoplight, a young black woman in a mini skirt stepped into the street and leaned into the open passenger window of a red Lexus.

One of the church's broken-out windows had been boarded up. Another hadn't, and a taped-up towel covered the broken pane. Charlie stepped up to the church door. It had been kicked in and the lock was busted, so it didn't close perfectly and swung loosely on its hinges. As he entered, his boots crunched glass. He smelled smoke and stared into a dark corner of the sanctuary at a woman and a small boy partially illuminated by late-afternoon sunlight cutting through a side window. Coals glowed in a stubby-legged charcoal grill. Smoke danced through sunbeams on its way out an open rear window.

"This is our place, asshole," the woman said.

"I'm just looking for someone."

"Nobody here but us." She stood and appeared ready for a confrontation. He suspected there might be a weapon in the paper bag she held by her side.

"He works for Redeemer," Charlie said, taking a step closer. As his eyes adjusted, he realized that he was gazing at the porn star from Satalin's DVD. The home wrecker. Trouble's whore. Why did this woman keep showing up, like a thumb in his eye, to remind him how shabby his life was? She was most likely diseased, living here in an abandoned church, mocking God. Not that Charlie was particularly fond of the Almighty right then, himself. And she *was* good-looking. Still. She had a lot of nerve.

"What's his name?"

"I call him … he's the dishwasher. At least he was on Thanksgiving."

She shook her head. "The kitchen was open again on Christmas. Just that day, though. Anybody worked over there," she said, nodding in the direction of the Hunger Palace, "is out of a job."

A second child emerged from the shadows. The girl. Charlie plopped down on a pew and rubbed his face with his hands. There was no reason for him to be in this place. He should go. Yet here he was, troubled by feelings of both revulsion and desire.

The porn star was close now, blocking the light flooding the western window. She wore jeans and a gray sweatshirt. No makeup. This gave her a winsome, vulnerable look—just someone who did what she had to do to survive. "I know you," she said.

"We met on Thanksgiving," Charlie said. "I helped you and the kids in the serving line."

"Oh. OK." Her tone was warmer, softer. Her accent wasn't Southern, just nondescript American. She drew nearer. "That's right. Redeemer knows you. You been in a fight?"

"Somebody tried to shoot me."

"No," she corrected. "Somebody *shot* you. They just didn't do a good job."

He smiled. She reached down to touch his face. He pulled away, embarrassed, ashamed—and afraid of her, too. He jerked his thumb over his shoulder toward the door. "It's not safe here."

"I can take care of my own." The boy approached and stood at his mother's right hip.

The girl tiptoed up behind them. "You're always hurt," she said.

"I'm sorry. I don't remember your names. I'm Charlie. Charlie Sherman."

"I'm Tawny Carson. This is Wyatt. And Romy. Short for Rosemarie."

"Hi," the children said in unison.

"Hi." Charlie gazed at frizzy-ponytailed Romy, who wore a ratty pink sweatsuit. Such a beautiful little girl. The boy reminded him of Ben, for some reason. These poor kids deserved better than this. "Anybody can come in, just like I did. It's not safe."

"It's not safe anywhere, Charlie. You should know that."

He nodded toward the grill. "Is that what you're using for heat?"

"For now."

"I could fix the door," Charlie said, surprising himself. "In the morning. The front window, too. But you could … you've got to watch out for carbon monoxide."

"I'll be OK. Unless you got a better idea where we could stay." She raised an eyebrow.

"It . . . you could freeze to death here," he said. "Do Romy and Wyatt have sleeping bags?"

"We got blankets."

"Look . . . I have kids their age. I'd like to get them some sleeping bags."

"I'm not stoppin' ya. That wouldn't be right for me to stop you, if that's what you want to do. Just don't tell anyone we're here. They'll take my kids away. No telling where they'd end up."

"OK." He paused to think. "You want one, too?"

"A sleeping bag? Sure, if you're handing 'em out."

"I'll get some food, too."

He stood and inched slowly out of the pew.

She touched his arm and whispered, "You can fuck me when you come back. Any way you want."

"Sorry," he said. "I'm ascetic."

She nodded knowingly. "I know how that is. I don't feel so good myself sometimes."

He drove off and considered not coming back, but he couldn't break his promise to the kids. Maybe she didn't belong in Redeemer's house. On the other hand, if Trouble hated her so much, maybe she wasn't all bad. Somehow he was caught between the two of them without understanding why. But a deal is a deal, and that little girl was worth saving. No doubt.

* * *

It was bright and chilly Saturday morning when Charlie showed up at the Holy Way House with a new framed steel door and a window-sized plywood sheet tied atop his Volvo. Inside, he saw the sleeping bags he'd brought by the night before, but no people. He slipped on gloves and, despite having no legal right to do so, started tearing out the old door. His hand injury slowed him down. So did tearing the wrapping off the new tools he'd bought. He fixed the broken window first—or at least nailed the plywood over it.

It was noon before Charlie wrestled the new door into place, and he had nearly finished shimming it level when a black sedan pulled into the lot, causing him to flinch. Out stepped a man in a suit, wearing a fedora and trench coat, looking like a darker version of Lieutenant Kinderman from *The Exorcist*. He stood with his feet apart, arms akimbo. Charlie set down his carpenter's level and gave him a questioning look.

A broad grin spread across the man's face. "The elusive Mr. Sherman. Nice of you to fix Redeemer's door. I wonder if he broke in himself one night when he forgot his keys. Don't get me wrong," he said, holding out his hands, palms down, as if to calm the waters. "We love him. But he is what he is." He stepped up onto the porch. "I'm Detective Sanders, Atlanta Police. And in case you haven't noticed—and judging by your face, I'm guessing you have—somebody would prefer it if you weren't breathing. I'd like to talk to you about that."

"Hang on. There. That should hold." Charlie dropped his screwdriver and shook hands gingerly, wincing at the detective's viselike grip.

"You're the most interesting person in the world right now, you know."

Charlie shrugged. "I had an interesting week. How'd you find me?"

"I didn't. He did," Sanders said, pointing across the street to a patrol car sitting in a warehouse parking lot. "We have an APB out on you. Nothing to worry about," Sanders said, holding up a palm. "I just have some questions to ask."

"I'll talk, so long as I can keep working. I'm not going anywhere."

Sanders looked around. "Fair enough. I imagine you've had your fill of cops."

"I was handcuffed by three different law enforcement agencies Thursday," Charlie said, beaming proudly.

"On one day?" Sanders chuckled. "Those are Redeemer-type stats. You should be proud." He pulled out a white notepad. "No need for that today."

The interview proceeded, punctuated by Charlie's grunts and groans as he leaned in to drive screws by hand, regretting his refusal to buy a cordless driver.

"You may know by now that your would-be killer was a Forsyth County meth dealer," Sanders said. "We found $10,000 cash in the truck toolbox. I also know Isaac Cutchins had you arrested."

"There you go." Charlie grunted as he worked on installing a lock.

"Which is interesting, since I learned from a beat cop's incident report of a break-in at … hang on … Bayard Terrace … that Cutchins allegedly shot out your van window in November. You were going to speak to a detective, but you disappeared. So, there *you* go. Went. And the next thing we hear from you is … *kablooey*!"

Charlie balanced his screwdriver on two fingers and blinked at him. "Whatever do you mean?"

Sanders laughed. "I mean that you're standing there with a screwdriver because all your power tools got burned up on Christmas Eve! Look, I know why you don't want to admit being at the Store-All. They shouldn't have linked you to the meth lab in the unit next door. I don't believe you're connected to it, even though the GBI is still investigating that angle."

Charlie gave him the blankest look he had available.

"And when you pop your head up again, all hell breaks loose on Castlegate. Again with the meth dealers. Speed kills." He shook his head in bemusement. "So who wants to do you harm? Besides Mister 'Get off my lawn' and the dead guys, that is. Did you know them?"

"Nope." Charlie grabbed the level and peered at its bubble. "Start with Cutchins' son, Stanley."

"Ah, the man finally says something useful. That name sounds familiar."

"He's a state legislator."

Sanders groaned, then jabbed his pen at Charlie. "What did you take from the old man to cause this trouble?"

"Right to remain silent and all that. I suggest you ask the *alleged* victim."

"The warrant doesn't state what it was."

"All the more reason to ask."

"I've seen your book. I understand why folks up in Forsyth County don't like it, but the reaction seems ... harsh for something that happened nearly a hundred years ago."

Charlie shrugged. "Ask *them*."

Sanders gave him a peeved look. He shook his head and glanced over his notes. "Something's missing."

"Besides one of my teeth and part of my ear?"

"Yeah," Sanders said. "Like honest answers."

"Well, that's all I've got to say, for now." Charlie reached for a tube of caulk.

"Gee, thanks for all your help," Sanders said, his voice dripping with sarcasm. He took down Charlie's cellphone number and handed him a business card. "I'll be in touch," he said as he walked to his car.

A moment later, Charlie's phone buzzed. "Hello."

"Just checking." The detective waved at him, then hung up and drove off.

Charlie finished installing the door. While cleaning up the job site, he heard a squealing engine belt behind him. He turned to see a banged-up red Cadillac sedan veer across two lanes of oncoming traffic and jump the curb, throwing a hubcap. Charlie leaped over the porch railing, landing behind a scraggly bush. The car skidded to a stop ten feet away, raising a cloud of dust that floated toward him. Only when the dust settled and he recognized the driver did Charlie come out into the open. A puffy face wearing oversized sunglasses poked out the open car window. "Did I hire you to do that?" the man rasped.

"No sir," Charlie admitted.

Redeemer Wilson slid across the seat and exited the passenger side. Wearing a suit without a tie, the old man wobbled toward Charlie and flashed a grin. His breath reeked of whiskey. Charlie grabbed his elbow to steady him and wondered if the old icon/reprobate had been out carousing all night.

"I been meanin' to get that fixed," Redeemer said. "But if I didn't hire you, I don't gotta pay you."

"That's true. It's on the house," Charlie said.

"On the house of the Lord." Redeemer frowned pensively and wagged his finger. "I know you."

"I interviewed you for a book about Forsyth County."

Redeemer snapped his fingers. "You the one been in the middle of that mess all week. I was gonna pray for you. I coulda told ya that those white folks up there don't like people criticizin' 'em. Glad to see you survived. Bloody but unbowed. My kind of guy." He gave Charlie a hearty whack on the back.

"Here," Charlie said, dangling the keys at eye level. "I made spares. Three sets in all."

Redeemer watched them swing. "It's your door," he pointed out.

"No, I just fixed it."

"You went and made it your door. You're it." He laughed and tagged Charlie on the shoulder.

"It's your church."

"I haven't been able to keep it open. Or closed." He gestured to the boarded-up window. "So you can come here any time you want. 'Specially if you're going to fix it. It needs a lotta work inside. Buncha derelicts trashed it. I ran out of money. People won't give anymore. Don't know what's wrong with 'em." He paused. "Actually, I do. Buncha cheap-hearted bastards is what they are. Glad to see somebody cares. Keep up the good work. I'm goin' home now."

Charlie again tried to give him all the keys. Redeemer consented to take one set. "You keep the others," he told the younger man. "Since you're the only one who cares. You gotta give her one of them, too, since she lives here now. I assume you're doing this to keep her safe."

"Who?" Charlie asked, trying to look innocent.

Redeemer gave Charlie a look that made him blush, then guffawed. "The young woman with the kids. Does tricks. She's around here somewhere. Her little girl is special. You know what I mean."

Charlie didn't. He tried to hand Redeemer the rest of the keys. The old man refused. "Go on. Keep a set and give one to the gal," he wheezed. "I got cancer. No tellin' how long I'll be around. How long? Not long. It's a joke, son. You had to be there. Take care of yourself. If you want to do more, here's how to get in touch." Redeemer fished out an old, grimy business card from his wallet and squinted at some writing on the back. He laughed. "Don't call that number," he told Charlie, handing him the card. "Call the one on the front."

Redeemer turned and walked unsteadily to his car. Charlie watched and worried about letting the man drive. Then he recalled that, despite all the negative publicity, Redeemer had never been convicted of a traffic offense or had a wreck. He decided that the old man had some sort of protection, too, better than anything some shot-up, just-out-of-jail white guy could give him, especially in this part of town. Charlie trotted over to the light pole and retrieved the hubcap. As soon as he had reattached it to the wheel, Redeemer drove off, blasting the horn three times.

Charlie unlocked the new door and immediately felt better, like he'd just kicked Trouble in the teeth. He packed up his tools and drove to a shopping center to get some gifts for Romy and Ben, because he missed getting things for kids.

When he returned, Tawny and her children were back from a shelter where they'd gone to wash up. Tawny looked nice in the daylight—even beautiful. He gave her a set of keys, keeping the last one for himself, only because there was no one else to give them to and Tawny insisted he keep them. She thanked him again for the sleeping bags, food, and the kerosene space heater he'd brought by the night before. When he gave a stuffed bear to Romy and building blocks to Wyatt, each child grabbed one of his legs and hugged him fiercely, nearly toppling the big man. He handed Tawny a fifty-dollar bill, surprising himself more than her, especially since he was running low on cash.

When he said he had to go, Tawny walked him to the door and played with it, opening and closing, stepping in and out of shadow and light. "Thank you for all you're doing for us. Come back any time," she whispered in his right ear, adding a nibble and a lick.

He ducked away from her, smiling and gently swatting his ear. The woman was dangerous, and if he let his guard down—well, he wouldn't let his guard down. He couldn't afford ... he just couldn't, not when she'd caused him so much pain, getting him thrown out of his house and all.

Once in his car, he cleaned out his ear with a moist towelette. Then another, for good measure.

Chapter Twenty-One

One thing was certain: Since the ordeal of his shooting and arrest, Charlie Sherman was no longer anonymous. He had to come out of hiding and make a statement, so he set up an interview with Bill Crenshaw, the reporter who'd been with him at the beginning. After lunch Saturday, he parked the Volvo in Decatur near the library and fed the meter. A young couple on a bench across Sycamore Street snuck glances at him as he shoved his hands into the pockets of his battle-worn duster and shuffled up the sidewalk. He crossed at the light, passing a bearded young bohemian in a blue peacoat who gave him a raised-fist salute.

A bell tinkled as Charlie stepped inside Java Joe's. Crenshaw sat at a table facing the door, working on his laptop. "Congrats on surviving an assassination attempt and jail," the reporter said, giving him a once-over. "Looks like something chewed on your face. You sure this is safe?"

Charlie glanced around at the half-full room. He'd given the subject some thought, but he didn't believe there would be another attack. After all, the varmints had their money and the book was already published. Now they could hire someone to read *Flight from Forsyth* and tell them Pappy's murderous land grab was not mentioned. (He could see the Cutchinses all tucked in snugly, listening to *Flight* being read like a bedtime story, complete with a happily-ever-after ending.) They'd be fools to attack again. Unfortunately, they *were* fools. He only hoped God's imperfect protection would hold out, at least until he could afford bodyguards. "Hell if I know. I may die tonight."

"Hey, your wife called. Said she's been trying to find out how you're doing, but you didn't give her your phone number."

"How do you think I lasted this long? Uh, that was off the record."

"That's OK. It's common knowledge that most married people want to kill their spouses. By the way," Crenshaw said with a smirk, "we're publishing that stuff you wouldn't let me see last year."

"Heard y'all had to pay top dollah," Charlie drawled. "I'm getting coffee to celebrate. I'd offer to buy you a cup, but that would be corrupt."

Crenshaw gave him a sick grin.

Charlie ordered a double espresso and returned to the table, taking a seat across from the reporter. Crenshaw was on his cellphone. "Hey, Jack, I got him! All shot up, dust on his boots and holy shit … is that a bullet hole in your coat?" He reached out and fingered the shoulder of the duster. "I'll check."

Crenshaw asked Charlie, "You talk to any other reporters?" Charlie shook his head. "That's a negative. Yeah, hold it for me. And you're welcome." Crenshaw hung up and slapped his laptop. "They just cleared the top of Sunday's front page for you. So tell me all about it."

Charlie laughed. "Not so sure about that, but I'll give you twenty minutes. Which is twenty more than anyone else is getting. I owe you that for old times' sake."

Glancing at his watch as he talked, Charlie coyly answered Crenshaw's rapid-fire questions. He admitted the arrest had been the result of "a family feud" only after Crenshaw told him he knew Isaac Cutchins was his wife's grandfather. Charlie wouldn't speculate on the motives and identities of the people behind the shooting, since it was under investigation. He did mention the lack of cooperation he'd received from the locals and suggested that many of Forsyth County's most prominent citizens would be unhappy when the newspaper published the excerpt showing how blacks' land had been stolen. He made no mention of John Riggins or Minerva Doe. Of course, Crenshaw wanted to hear all about the shooting, his jail time, his "false imprisonment" by Finch and Drew, and his "charming little encounter" with the Canton police. (For the record, the GBI would deny that any of its agents had held him in a warehouse.) With less than a minute left of his allotted time, Crenshaw asked, "What about Isaac Cutchins's land sale last week?"

"I'm not sure it's his to sell," Charlie said.

"What do you mean? I didn't see anything in the book about his land."

Charlie stood. "*Buzzzz.* Time's up. Good day."

"Damn it, Sherman, this isn't a game!" Crenshaw said, but Charlie was already up and moving toward the door.

* * *

After a good night's sleep, Charlie tiptoed into La Patisserie Sunday morning, worried that Amy Weller would be pissed at him for nearly getting her customers killed. It would be terrible if she was, since he still had a crush on her. Instead of being angry, she rushed around the counter to hug him, clucking like a mother hen over his injuries.

"Thank God you survived!" she said. "I was worried about you."

"I nearly got the place destroyed," Charlie said, savoring the cinnamon and nutmeg aroma of her clench.

"It was scary," she said, pulling back, her brown eyes popping wide open. "Why'd they do it?"

"Money."

"But who paid them?"

"Somebody from Forsyth County."

She nodded knowingly. "Those people should be ashamed, all of them." She brightened. "Hey, breakfast is on me. You wouldn't believe what it's done for business. You getting shot, that is. It sounds ghoulish, I know. But before, hardly anyone knew we existed. Then all the reporters started hanging out here waiting for you, like you were Godot or something. '*This is Casanthia Clayton, reporting live from La Patisserie on Castlegate*,'" Amy mimicked, holding a mixing spoon like a microphone. "Since then, it's been packed in here."

While the place was crowded, it didn't take many people to fill a bakery with four tables inside. Charlie took his cup of Mocha Java and a raspberry croissant outside and sat at a black wrought-iron table in the shade, reading Crenshaw's article. By this time, he'd lost track of the media coverage he'd received. Had he really been on the front page six days in a row? Inside the paper's first section was the book excerpt from *Flight*, which filled Page A-6. Thc paper also ran a laudatory review. Plenty of blurb material there.

Despite his time constraint on the interview, Charlie had been a relative chatterbox compared to lawmen, all of whom had refused to comment. While Charlie's willingness to talk put him at an advantage in the main article, the locals fought back in a sidebar story: "Forsyth County's resident historian Cecil Montgomery said, 'No one wants him dead, of course, but we would like him to cover some other poor, unsuspecting county if he's going to do things that way.'"

"You wish," Charlie muttered. "And somebody does want me dead, asshole."

He finished reading and folded up the paper. He had something else to think about: Angela's request to renegotiate the deal on *Flight from Forsyth*.

Charlie was willing to go back to the original contract. Sure, he'd lose half the royalties, but the old deal had called for an editing fee, so she'd have to cough up some cash, which Charlie desperately needed following his purchase of a bike, a car, and all that stuff for Tawny and her kids. It would be a long time before he saw another check from Fortress—six months at least, even if it was a bestseller.

He also had something up his sleeve. He'd decided that, as part of the deal, Angela would be barred from making a claim against any and all other works. That way, he would keep everything from *American Monster*, the existence of which would remain … *understated* during negotiations, of course.

He called Angela. This time, she surprised him by answering. Charlie thanked her for getting Sandra to represent him (though he was still pissed she'd taken so long) and gave her a brief account of his adventure. Then he proposed the deal, reading talking points from his napkin. "You want half the royalties, I'll give you half the royalties, but only if we go back to the original deal. And that pays me twenty bucks an hour."

"Twenty bucks an hour?" She sounded stressed.

"I'm willing to cut you some major slack. Let's round it off to twenty grand."

"I'm supposed to pay you twenty grand up front?" Angela asked, her voice rising even higher.

"Hell, I worked two thousand hours on it." He was guessing, but that number sounded about right. "That's worth forty thousand, less the money I got paid already, and deducting half of the advance, which Kathleen would have been entitled to, that was ten thousand, so that's fairly close to thirty, but I'll settle for twenty. For you, a bargain. You'll get a five hundred percent return, easy."

"Hmm. I don't know. I'll have to think about it."

"You've got a bestseller on your hands. One you claimed was unpublishable before I started working on it. In your professional opinion." He couldn't resist the dig.

"You'll never let me forget that, will you?"

"Never and a day. It's sold out all over town and already in a second printing. Plus rights sales …"

"Wait a minute. Why are you so eager to offer the deal?"

"Full disclosure: Because it avoids a lawsuit, you being so litigious. Plus I need money right now."

"Hmm. That sounds pretty straightforward."

"One other thing."

"What's that?"

"You can't make any other claims on any other works."

"Why would that matter?"

"It shouldn't. I was just thinking about magazine articles and such. Never know where the road leads. Anyway, think about it. But don't delay," he said, sounding like a late-night infomercial announcer. On that note, he hung up.

Before he'd finished his coffee, Angela called back to say she'd accept his offer and agreed to write him a check. He assured her it would be the best deal she'd ever make.

* * *

Monday, Charlie called Susan at work. "Charlie. My God, is that you? I've been so worried."

"What, you don't recognize me? Guess it's been awhile."

"You never gave me your number," Susan said, adopting an injured tone.

"You threatened to have me arrested, remember? Now maybe you understand why I was reluctant to let that happen."

"And now you're getting even."

He ignored her comment. "How are the kids? I want to see them."

She ignored what he'd just said, too. "An Atlanta police detective called and asked about the bombing and shooting," she said. "I couldn't believe it was your van that got blown up by drug dealers."

"Drug dealers? Did he say that?"

"Well, no."

"Where'd you hear that, then? Never mind. I know where. The evildoers."

"You told him my family is involved. Uncle Stanley is really upset. That detective made it sound like I was a suspect! Charlie, I'd never do anything to harm you. I mean, I … I—"

"Yeah, right. Are you telling me you don't have any idea what's going on?"

"I know you've been running around with meth dealers, that's all."

Charlie was incredulous. "Cut it out. You don't actually believe that."

After an awkward silence, she said, "I saw where your book is the number-one bestseller."

"Pretty good for an abject failure, eh?"

"Now you can pay me the eight thousand dollars child support you owe me."

"D'oh." He hung up.

* * *

Under a gray sky that threatened rain, reporters crowded the sidewalk and spilled into the street in front of La Patisserie, waiting for the start of Charlie's Tuesday afternoon news conference. Some leaned against TV trucks; a few lounged on parked cars, holding digital recorders above their heads. Charlie saw Detective Sanders (who had been staying in touch, to no effect) in middle of the crowd. To the far right stood some suspicious-looking straight-laced characters who probably had Finch's and Drew's numbers on speed dial. In the rear, Crenshaw lurked, wearing a rumpled trench coat.

Charlie stood in front of the bakery's newly painted display window to address the assembled media. In exchange for the exposure, Amy Weller donated coffee and muffins for the event and furnished a wooden podium she'd borrowed from a cousin who belonged to Toastmasters. Having doffed her Braves cap and slipped on a blue blazer to go with her jeans, Amy handed out her favorite writer's news releases and background sheets.

"This is better than facing a gunman," Charlie joked as he began. "But I'm not sure by how much."

He spoke for ten minutes, first talking about Thurwood Talton, then mentioning his own role in publishing the book. He gave a chronology of events in Forsyth County and referred journalists to the background sheet he'd worked up. However, reporters weren't there for a history lesson, so he talked about the shooting. Then, to the delight of TV crews, he reenacted it. He was properly remorseful over the fact that two men had died, but grateful no one else had perished.

Characterizing his arrest and subsequent ordeal as "something out of Kafka," Charlie confidently declared, "I will be cleared of these ridiculous charges." He dismissed the warrants with a wave of his hand, like they were gnats. "The *people* behind my arrest refuse to say what I allegedly stole. You should ask them what I took."

"What did you take?" several reporters shouted.

"Ask *them*!" Charlie reiterated loudly.

When he finished his remarks, hands shot up and reporters yelled for his attention. After fending off some easy questions, he called on Channel Six political reporter Arch Bano.

"You think there's a conspiracy in all this?" Bano asked.

Charlie's abused face was grim, his tone somber. "There are powerful people in this state who do not want what I write to be published."

"Isn't it too late to worry about?"

"They didn't know the book was out. Or what was in it, for that matter.

Again, ask them what they're worrying about."

"A follow-up," Bano said. "Do you support House Resolution Three-Ninety?"

"Sorry," Charlie said, shaking his head in puzzlement. "I'm not familiar with that legislation."

"It was introduced by Representative Bannister today. He said it was *not* in response to your book. Just a coincidence, one he intends to take full advantage of. Have you talked with him?"

"No," Charlie said. He only knew State Rep. Tyrus Bannister by reputation. An old ally of Redeemer's, Bannister was a civil rights veteran with a reputation (among whites, at least) as a shakedown artist, with a history of organizing protests against corporate and government misbehavior and proclaiming the miscreants cured after money changed hands. Charlie knew that Bannister was currently leading a boycott of Pancake Hut.

"It's a resolution calling for the state to pay reparations to African-Americans for slavery."

A black radio reporter corrected him: "To *explore the concept* of reparations for slavery and discrimination in the years since emancipation."

Interesting. Although Charlie doubted it would pass, this might help him sell books. He decided to endorse the idea of exploring the concept. It seemed like the least he could do. "Certainly," he said. "So much wrong has been done, especially in places like Forsyth County. I believe we need to look into these issues. When I edited Dr. Talton's book, I found many things that needed repairing." *Not to mention the book itself.*

Suddenly, he had a queasy feeling. *No*, he told himself. *It won't go that far.*

"So, would you be willing to testify in favor of the resolution?"

Shit. It *was* going that far. Charlie blanched, but he recovered quickly. "Uh, yeah. Of course. If I'm not being shot at or arrested at the time." The crowd's laughter gave him a good note to end on, so Charlie closed the news conference, amazed that the Christmas Eve bombing hadn't been mentioned. But if the cops weren't leaking his identity as the victim, he sure as hell wasn't going to, either.

Afterward, Crenshaw and a few other reporters hung around with follow-ups. Charlie let his guard down, connecting the Cutchins farm sale to the Outer Perimeter Highway project, Department of Transportation, and governor's office, then drawing a line back to State Rep. Cutchins, of course. He hinted at a nefarious conspiracy without going into detail or mentioning the murder/lynching of John Riggins. Let them sniff it out on their own and report the facts, thereby paving the way for *American Monster* to become his next blockbuster.

* * *

Charlie thought he'd made it clear that his after-event musings were off the record. Instead, his attacks on high-ranking officials received prominent play on the evening news. Before he even had time to worry about their reactions, he received a phone call.

"Charles Sherman, Tyrus Bannister here," boomed a hearty voice.

"Representative Bannister. How are you tonight?"

"Wonderful! This is great, what you've done, resurrecting Professor Talton's work! I met him back in eighty-seven, you know, during the first march. Fine man. A pity his work was lost in the wilderness for so long. I commend you for seeing it through."

Charlie knew Bannister hadn't been at the first march, but he'd been right in the middle of the front row in the second one, posing for the cameras. "Thank you."

"Anyway," Bannister continued, "I saw the article about land records. Names, dates—the stuff we needed back in 1987, after Redeemer's march. But it's never too late—"

"For reparations." *Ka-ching*!

"Heh-heh. Straight to the point. I like that. You've heard of HR Three-Ninety, my resolution on this issue. We tried before. No luck. Now, thanks to you, we have records to back up our claims."

The fake records. Charlie recalled those 4:00 a.m. sessions and the artificially aged papers in his safety deposit box. But if the burglars knew genuine copies existed, how would they know he hadn't made spares? All part of a grand and cosmic plan, right? Then again, maybe not. He gulped. This was treacherous territory.

"You and I have a synergy, a symbiosis," Bannister continued. "When this resolution comes up for a hearing, the victims of injustice need you to speak, since you're the documenter of the misdeeds we seek to rectify." Not hearing an objection, Bannister forged ahead. "This goes beyond Forsyth County, of course. But Forsyth is the epicenter, the epitome, the … *worst-case scenario*, if you will, of so many of the evils that have befallen us on our road to equality. So, may I count on your testimony at the hearings? It would give you an excellent opportunity to promote your book, of course."

What choice did Charlie have? "Of course."

"Excellent. I have a good feeling about this. I think your work, and your presence—after all the trials and tribulations you've gone through, will be

… nothing short of providential. Very well, Mr. Sherman—Charles. Do you have any questions?"

The questions Charlie had were ones he couldn't ask: *Will I have to testify under oath? And what is the penalty for perjury*? "No."

"So you'll be there with those records."

"If the good Lord's willing and the creek don't rise."

Charlie hung up, hoping that God had other plans for him and already knowing that a hundred-year flood was on the way.

* * *

Wednesday, Charlie taped a radio interview at the local NPR affiliate to be aired on *All Things Considered.* As he left the radio station, a GBI agent with a search warrant accosted him. "Why do you all have to be such stalkers?" Charlie asked.

The lawman didn't answer his question. Instead, he took the writer to the State Crime Lab to get his fingerprints and a blood sample. Though no explanations were given, Charlie figured it had something to do with the large amount of blood recovered from the Store-All. (Well, that and mouthing off to reporters about the governor.)

This time, at least, Charlie got a ride back to his car. When he returned to Castlegate, he found a cream-colored envelope in his mailbox from Cantrell, Bachman, and Gaithers, the silkiest of silk-stocking law firms (John Cantrell was a former governor). In the letter, attorney Ken Mason demanded that Charlie "cease and desist making false statements about the recent land sale by Isaac Cutchins, or legal action will be taken against you on behalf of our client, Southland Associates."

"Blah, blah, blah," Charlie said as he read. Fair enough. He was in a cease-and-desist mood, having said too much already.

* * *

For a writer who had tried for six years to get an agent, it was strange to be hounded by one. But it was all good. "Great news!" Barbara Asher exclaimed over the phone Thursday afternoon. "I have a preempt offer. Spence Greene, the head man at Brubaker Publishing, heard you on NPR yesterday and called me with a deal just as I was setting up the auction. They'd already been talking about it, but he is *terribly* impressed with you—did you quote Orwell?"

"Yes. I said, 'Being shot is interesting.' From *Homage to Catalonia*."

"Smart move. Plus he saw the *Times* review of your other book. Perfect storm!" she belted out the last two words like Ethel Merman.

Charlie shifted his phone to his left ear, since she'd just scorched his right one. "What's the deal?"

"Two million! Your wildest dream has just come true!"

Not quite. His wildest dream would be this, plus Jean and Dana, along with a sprinkle of cinnamon. Nevertheless, it was a struggle to recover from the shock of suddenly becoming a millionaire-to-be.

"Not too shabby, eh, Charles? ... Charles ... Charles!"

"Two million?"

"With all that money on the line, they want to publish quickly. You should go with this."

"Let's sign the papers before they change their mind."

"Charles, you're my kind of guy. I'm on it. I've put everything else aside to work for you. Britney Spears' makeup artist wants to do a tell-all. We need a ghost writer. You interested?"

"I'm close enough to being a ghost already. Her makeup artist?"

"They know everything. Absolutely everything. It's scary."

Charlie hung up and danced around the loft to AC/DC's *Thunderstruck*. He jumped up and pumped his fist in the air, shouting, "I'm rich! I'm rich! I'm rich!"

It was hard to believe that a month ago, he'd been living in a van.

* * *

Friday morning, Charlie checked the *Forsyth Sentinel* website and found an interesting item: State Rep. Stanley Cutchins announced he was tithing a million dollars, to be divided among "all the Christian churches" of Forsyth County. Either the varmints wanted to buy their way to heaven, or Uncle Stanley had just launched the most expensive General Assembly campaign in state history.

On the same page, he saw an article headlined "Local Historians Denounce Forsyth Work." In it, Cecil Montgomery ridiculed *Flight from Forsyth*'s "many inaccuracies, factual errors, and glaring omissions. For example, everyone knows Sodder Creek runs west-east." Charlie would have laughed off the criticism if Montgomery hadn't also challenged the footnotes: "I'd like to see some of those land documents allegedly in the author's possession."

"I'll bet you would," Charlie muttered at the computer screen. "And so would I."

However, now Charlie wondered if Montgomery hadn't already seen them. When he'd first found out about John Riggins, Charlie thought Uncle Stanley was behind the burglary at Kathleen's house a year before. Later, he realized Montgomerys and Logans would have had just as much motivation, since their ancestor had stolen a farm, too. *Hmm.* Cutchins and Montgomery had so much in common. Both were descended from lynchers. Both had profited from land thefts. Both had secrets to keep.

Charlie decided he should make the Logan and Montgomery clans' lives more *interesting*, as well. He owed them that.

* * *

Groundhog Day: Wearing a new coat and tie, Charlie arrived at Buckhead Booksellers five minutes before the hastily arranged Saturday night signing was set to begin—the first of what he hoped would be many. Inside, a line of people holding copies of *Flight from Forsyth* stretched from a square black table to the coffee shop, then disappeared into the travel section. Charlie took a deep breath and sauntered over to the author's chair.

A young Goth bookseller named Esmerelda briefed him. "We sold out of your book, but we received a rush shipment this morning. There's a stack of books behind the register for people who can't be here, so if you read the slips and sign them, that would be cool."

"Fine." Charlie gave the crowd—a roughly equal mix of black and white—a quick once-over. "Do you have security here?"

"No. Should we?"

"My publicist was supposed to request it." He shook his head. "Too late to worry now. All right. Let's do this. I'll sign as many as I can before they get me."

"Interesting tattoo." She reached to touch his face. He pulled away.

"It's not a tattoo." The scab from the gunshot wound had fallen off to reveal a bright pink rose-shaped scar on his cheek.

"I'm sorry," she said. "You probably have space issues after all you've been through."

Space issues. What a concept.

Charlie pulled out his trusty Waterman pen, laid it down, and rubbed his hands together. He threw out his fingers and stretched them like he was preparing to play piano, then popped his knuckles.

He signed books carefully and quickly. People congratulated him. Consoled him. Thanked him. Told him he was brave. Esmerelda stood beside him, holding books open and cutting conversations short, semi-politely encouraging people to move along once they had Charlie's autograph. A woman pushed her book toward Charlie on the table, said her name, then added in a whisper, "I'm from Forsyth County. I knew those men who tried to kill you. They got what was coming to them." Charlie kept his mouth shut as he wrote. She gave him an embarrassed smile and left. After he'd signed a book to Beverly Tucker, Charlie felt a tug on his sleeve.

"Hey, Daddy."

Charlie jumped up and cried out, "Benny boy!" He picked up his son and hugged him fiercely. "I miss you, guy. Incredibly much. It's been forever since I've seen you. What are you doing here?"

"Mommy brought us. I heard your voice."

"Did she tell you I was here?"

Ben shook his head and stared at him intently. "I heard you got *shot*," the boy said, overemphasizing the last word.

"Did Mommy tell you that?"

"No, Tyler told me at school. Mom said you were OK."

"I am. It's not a big deal." He waved his hand to brush off the injury and sat down, then realized this was a teachable moment of sorts. "I was lucky. Usually, guns kill. So stay away from them."

"You've got a scar." Ben looked at the line. "Are all these people here to see you?"

"Yes. They're buying my book." Charlie showed a copy to his son.

Ben countered with his own book. "Can I get this? Will you read it to me?" He held up Lemony Snicket's *The Bad Beginning*. A bit of a reach for a kindergartner, but Charlie had to admire the boy's ambition.

"Sure, I'd love to, but—"

Ben was already climbing up onto his lap. Charlie grinned at an older black woman. "What can I do?" To Ben, he said, "Stay with me, but I'll have to read it later."

Beck appeared, holding a copy of *Stellaluna* and rushed to hug him. "You got shot," she said.

"No big deal."

"Is too. You're famous now," she said, looking over the line of autograph-seekers. "We're kind of famous, too. You can sign my book."

Charlie wrote "To My Special Princess—Love, Daddy."

Ben got similar treatment: "To My Favorite Guy."

While Ben sat on his lap, Beck stood by her father's left shoulder and read aloud softly. Susan stepped into view around the corner of a bookcase with her copy of *Flight*. Charlie squinted at her, a bemused smile on his lips. She gave him her semi-pissed look, as if he had, for the thousandth time, made her late. In a dark blue dress and a trench coat, her long blonde hair falling in curls to her shoulders, she looked better than ever. The sharp features of the bank teller he'd met in Macon had softened with age. He beckoned her; she ignored him. *God, what a contrary woman.*

Beck and Ben returned to the children's section. Charlie grew chattier and more charming with customers as Susan drew nearer. When she stood before him, holding her book and looking grim, Charlie gave her an easy smile and drawled, "Hey, stranger."

"How many books have you sold today?" Susan asked, sounding like she expected a cut of the take.

Charlie glanced at Esmerelda, who said, "More than a hundred. I'm counting the stack behind the registers."

"That's some stack," Charlie replied.

Susan shoved her book at him. "Sign this please, Mr. Sherman."

Her tone was not especially friendly, and Charlie could tell she was nervous. Clearly, she did not like playing the role of supplicant. "Why of course, Mrs. Sherman."

"Oh, are you two married?"

"Kind of," Charlie said.

"I'm working on it," Susan countered.

"Whatever *that* means," Charlie said. "Look, you didn't have to do this. I would have given you one, if only you'd asked."

"You've been so busy," she said with more than a trace of sarcasm.

"Yes, getting shot by people who were paid by those who shall remain nameless."

"What the hell does that mean?" she snapped. "Never mind. Just sign the damn book."

Esmeralda backed away from the bad vibe disturbing the air around the signing table. Charlie stared at the title page. With a dozen people still in line, there wasn't time to talk to her much longer, nor did it promise to be a pleasant conversation if he did. He had to write something. The Waterman flew over the page, and he signed his name with a flourish.

Susan read, "Thanks for making this possible. Love, Charlie." She stared at the page. "*Love*?"

"Somewhere," he said sadly. "Maybe not with me right now."

"No. I suppose you left it somewhere else." After receiving no response, she continued. "Why do you have to take this psycho feud of yours public? That news conference was over the top, claiming Uncle Stanley is in some kind of conspiracy with the governor."

"*My* feud? I'm the one getting shot."

"That's what comes with—" she bent down and whispered "—messing with drug dealers."

"I keep hearing this. Is that what you think?"

"It's what the GBI thinks."

"How would you know?"

"Because they showed up with a warrant and searched the house for drugs," she said, finishing by mouthing the word *asshole*. "I don't know why I bother."

She turned on her heel and marched toward the children's section. Esmerelda flowed back into the vacuum.

"And she *does* bother," Charlie noted.

He kept signing. A few minutes later, Ben ran up and hugged him. "I miss you, Daddy. I hope we can be together again."

"We will be." Even as Charlie said it, his spirits sank. Not only did he no longer believe what he'd just said, but there seemed to be no way to make that lie the truth.

"When you get out of your dungeon," Ben said.

"Yes."

Susan called for Ben. He ran off. Beck walked past, waving happily to him.

"Mr. Sherman. Mr. Sherman." A gray-haired black man bent over the table.

"Huh? Sorry."

"If you could make it to Clyde Simmons. My grandfather was run out of Forsyth in 1912."

Charlie looked up. "Rufus Simmons?"

"Why, yes." The man stepped back, looking shocked. "My Lord. Is he in the book?'

"Yes. A footnote, too, I think." I'll sign it to Rufus Simmons' grandson, Clyde."

"Thank you so much for doing this."

Charlie looked out the window and saw Ben's head bouncing up and down as the boy skipped along the sidewalk. "Huh? Oh, yeah. You're welcome."

After the signing was over and his audience had drifted away, Charlie learned that Susan had left the marked-up and unpaid-for children's books at the counter. He was irritated at first, but then realized this gave him a legitimate, non-stalking reason to return to Thornbriar. Where he'd left his love in the first place. He'd see if any of it was still there.

* * *

Charlie showed up unannounced at Thornbriar the following Saturday afternoon. "I come bearing tribute," he said when Susan opened the door. She wasn't wearing her wedding ring. Neither was he, but he wished he was, just to trump her. Prosperous from Angela's $20,000 buy-in, he waved a $6,000 check with a flourish, then handed it to his stunned wife, figuring it would bring him almost up to date on child support and get him inside the house to see the kids. He pushed inside and patted Sirius on the head. At least the dog was glad to see him.

"Is this money from the book, or from selling drugs?" Susan whispered harshly.

"Hey kids! It's me!" he shouted.

They came running. "You're back!" Beck squealed. Ben stumbled into the foyer, his arms full of toys, dropping them at Charlie's feet. Susan stood blocking Charlie from the family room, so he stepped into the living room, kids tugging his hands. Charlie put the books on the coffee table and plopped into the easy chair.

They ran off to get more stuff. Susan said, "I'll need two thousand more."

Charlie shook his head in exasperation. "You know, you're such a … skip it."

"Consider it skipped."

The kids returned with artwork from school and squeezed in to sit beside him. They'd grown since he'd last sat with them in that chair, and Charlie felt like a big sardine, but he was too grateful to be near them to complain. As he marveled at their drawings, Beck scrutinized the scar on his cheek and poked it. "A flower is growing there."

Ben pulled his injured ear and asked if it would come off. "It will if you keep pulling on it," Charlie said. "OK, I'll read the books now."

"Mine first," Beck said, grabbing *Stellaluna* from the coffee table and handing it to her father.

Susan took a seat on the sofa across from Charlie and folded her hands in her lap. "How long do you plan on staying?" she asked, her tone crisp.

"He just got here," Beck said, scowling.

Susan stiffened. Charlie snuggled in deeper with the kids in the chair. As Sirius lay contentedly at his feet, he read *Stellaluna*, then moved on to *A Series of Unfortunate Events*. Susan waited impatiently. He grew hoarse but kept reading, fearing that if he stopped and asked for a glass of water (which she wasn't about to offer), Susan would declare the visit over.

After an hour, Ben said, "All for now. You can read to us tomorrow."

"No, we'll be going to church," Susan said. "Charlie, you need to go."

Charlie stood up. "All right. Bye, kids. I love you."

Beck hugged him, then Ben followed suit. Sirius, moving slowly, came up and brushed his master's knee. Charlie bent down and rubbed the old dog's neck, wondering how much longer the pooch would be around.

"Beck, Ben, put your things up, please," Susan said, then followed Charlie to the door. When he stepped outside, she said, "Wait up a minute."

Charlie saw a look on her face that he'd seen a thousand times before, that of hesitant confession. "Did you have something else to say?"

Susan cleared her throat. "I guess you know that Pappy sold the farm."

"Yeah. The article about it was right under the picture of me getting stomped by the police. I also saw that Uncle Stanley's spreading money around to all the churches. I figure they already divvied up the profits." Susan looked like she'd eaten a green apple. "I guess your mother and Uncle Stanley figure they're due a cut since they've been paying taxes on it."

Susan looked away. So there it was. Pappy had already given up his wealth to his offspring. Charlie smelled Shakespeare at play. Hadn't that been King Lear's tragic mistake? "Have they evicted Pappy?"

"The developers are letting him stay in the house until they have to level it."

"Mighty white of them," Charlie said. "So everybody's rich now. You get your cut yet?"

"That's not your business," she said angrily, waving her finger in his face. "And I know you. You're just trying to avoid child support. No matter what, you still have to pay."

"What's Bradley Roy say about all this?"

She bit her lip. "Daddy won't have anything to do with the money. Mom's threatening to leave him."

"I don't understand. How is that a threat?"

"Stop it. I know you hate her. But they've been together fifty years."

"Well, no one can say he didn't try. He's a saint," Charlie said.

"Well, I'm not." Susan laughed drily.

"Just curious. Why won't he have anything to do with the money?"

"You," she snarled. "He says something's fishy. Thinks you know something about Pappy, but he doesn't know what it is. I told him you were just making up stuff." She sighed. "He's worked hard all his life. He should enjoy a little luxury now that he's retired. I don't see the problem. Uncle Stanley said whatever you were trying to accuse Pappy of got edited out because you couldn't prove it. Because it was a lie."

Far from being insulted, Charlie was overjoyed to hear that the varmints thought the storm had passed, which meant they had no idea what was coming. He couldn't help grinning, but Susan wasted no time wiping the smirk off his face. She said, "Before you get any ideas about spending the money from *Flight from Forsyth*, I'm entitled to half of everything you make, especially considering all you put me through the past twenty years."

"When it's over, you'll be rich one way or another, won't you, dear?"

"Like I said, I'm entitled."

"I'll set up college funds for the kids," Charlie said.

She glanced back into the house, as if to gauge the children's IQs and scholarship potential. "I'll be the custodian."

"Now you're starting to get on my nerves."

"C'mon, we've been on each other's nerves since I opened the door."

"Well, you look good angry." Charlie grinned. "Then again, that's the only way I see you."

"I wonder why that is?"

"Look, I want to get back to spending time with Beck and Ben."

He watched her jaw muscles bulge. Time for him to *git*, as Evangeline would say.

"Mommy," Ben hollered from inside. "Are you going out with Harold tonight?"

"Harold?" Charlie asked.

Susan turned to give Ben a withering look. Without changing her expression, she turned back to face Charlie. "Just be careful what you say about my family. I'll bet all those reporters who think you're a hero would like to know why you left that night." She shut the door in his face.

"I'll be back next week," he told the peephole.

* * *

Charlie's return to Thornbriar was blocked, however. On Valentine's Day, he received another cream-colored envelope from Cantrell, Bachman, and Gaithers. Same law firm that had threatened him before, different lawyer. In her letter, Leslie Volcker, Esq., advised him that Susan had filed for a restraining order to keep him away from Beck and Ben "due to your heavy involvement in drug trafficking." Ms. Volcker advised him to keep his distance while the matter was pending.

Charlie was infuriated. He resisted the impulse to tear up the letter and tore up the envelope instead. Obviously, Susan had used the money he gave her to hire an attorney. That sucked. It also meant he'd be spending his *American Monster* loot on lawyers, both his and hers.

Volcker's letter didn't mention divorce, and that seemed odd. Charlie puzzled over this for a moment, then realized Susan didn't want a divorce. After all, divorcing a man who was about to become rich wouldn't make sense to a varmint, would it? No, better to wait until he actually *was* rich from the royalties on *Flight*. Clever girl. But clearly, this was war. And he was determined to win, since Susan was going to fight that way. She might not beg him to come back, but in the end, she *would* be on her knees, by God.

Charlie called around and came up with the name of a suitably cutthroat divorce attorney named Richard Muncie. A few days later, Charlie met Muncie and told him the deal with Susan. The bald lawyer was both impressed and appalled when Charlie said, "In conclusion, there's no point trying to keep this civilized."

"Not even for the children's sake?" Muncie asked with a wry smile.

"Souls, sir. We are fighting for their souls. The choice is bruised and battered on one hand, or stolen on the other. So let's gear up for a monumental battle between good and evil. And we'll see who's left standing when all this is over."

"It'll cost you," Muncie said, "in ways you can't even imagine."

"Whatever it takes," Charlie replied. "Bring it on."

Before the ink was dry on the check he wrote to Muncie, the restraining order against Charlie had been issued and the media alerted. This time, Charlie didn't answer reporters' calls. Just as well. Nothing he had to say was fit to print.

Chapter Twenty-Two

Charlie woke at 4:00 a.m. from a dream about Romy. The girl was moaning and kicking off her sleeping bag in a filthy room, terribly sick and feverish, babbling about a dark angel trying to kill her. Since Charlie trusted his night visions, at least those that came at four o'clock sharp, he jumped out of bed and paced around in the dark on the loft's cold concrete floor, worrying about the girl and fighting the urge to hop into his car and drive over to Redeemer's church to check on her.

He hadn't seen her in three weeks. Why was the well-being of a street urchin—the daughter of a prostitute God apparently despised—so important to him? Maybe he was just a sucker for an underdog—or had issues with the Almighty, himself. Whenever he saw her, he'd been wounded or injured, and the little girl always seemed to take away some of the hurt. There were dangers in crashing in on a whore in the middle of the night, however, so Charlie waited.

But not for long. At dawn he burst out the door, ran down the stairs, hopped in the Volvo, and drove to Redeemer's Holy Way House. Tawny answered the door, opening it just a crack, then swinging it wide when she saw it was him. Her face was plain and pale, her eyes bleary.

"Thank God you're here," she said, hugging his neck as he stepped inside. "You're the only person in the world I'm glad to see right now." He pressed his forearms against her sides in an awkward embrace. He could feel her ribs. How long had it been since she'd eaten? "Romy's bad sick. I was going to call 911, even if the cops come and kick us out."

"If Redeemer says you can stay, you can stay," he said, watching his breath in the early morning sunlight. He turned and made his way between the pews to the corner where the kids lay in their sleeping bags. That part of the sanctuary was warmed by the kerosene space heater he'd given them.

Romy moaned pitifully. "What's wrong, little girl?"

She opened her eyes and pointed to her throat.

"She can't swallow," Tawny said, coming up behind. "Hasn't eaten since yesterday morning."

Charlie touched the girl's forehead and drew his hand back. White-hot fever raged through her. A hundred and four, he guessed, having been there and done that. "Let's get her to a doctor."

"I don't have any insurance. I don't have any money, either."

He held up his hand. "It's all right. I'll take care of it."

Wyatt, sleepy-eyed and apparently untouched by his sister's malady, slipped on clothes and old, torn sneakers. Charlie turned off the heater, picked up Romy in her sleeping bag, and carried her out to the car. Tawny and Wyatt followed.

Charlie drove to Childmed Group in North Atlanta, being especially careful since he didn't have child safety seats in the car. After Tawny filled out paperwork and the cashier verified Charlie's credit card, Tawny took the kids back to an examination room while Charlie waited out front.

An hour later, Tawny returned with Romy in her arms; the woman staggered under the weight. "Strep throat," she said. "I'll need help with the medicine." She gave Charlie a pleading look.

"In for a penny, in for a pound," he said, and went to the counter.

"That will be three hundred thirty-five dollars today," the cashier said, pointing to filled-in lines on two yellow forms. "One child's sick visit, one's physical. And vaccinations for both."

Once he got over his sticker shock, Charlie signed for the expense, then carried Romy, limp as a rag doll, out to the car. Tawny put a hand on his elbow. "We need groceries, too. If we could stop on the way back to the church, I could—"

"I can't take you back there. You don't even have hot water. And even with the space heater, it's freezing there. That's no place to get well. I'll put you up in a motel for a few days, and I'll see about getting the utilities turned back on."

Charlie slipped Romy into the back seat. Wyatt slid in beside her. Tawny turned to Charlie and looked at him plaintively. "I know it's a lot to ask, but what about your place?"

Interesting question. But the answer had to be No. He didn't want to compromise his position in the war with his wife and lose his own kids.

There would come an accounting someday, hopefully soon, so he'd let Susan be the one to engage in extracurricular activities.

He struggled to come up with a simple answer. "I don't even have a place. It's a sublet." He winced, knowing his excuse sounded lame.

Disappointment spread over her face. "Oh."

Charlie took Tawny to Redeemer's church so they could get their things. He saw that both hot water and heat were electric, which meant he'd only have one bill to pay. Another window had been broken, and Tawny had covered it with a blanket. He worried about squatters, burglars, and worse. He needed to secure the windows, at least.

After stopping at Target to buy groceries, car seats, a prepaid cellphone, and Romy's medicine—and spending nearly $300 this time—Charlie checked Tawny into a motel with weekly rates and a kitchen. When she unlocked the door to their first-floor room, Wyatt ran to the bathroom and Charlie laid Romy on a double bed. "You're going to get well," he told her.

When Charlie brought in the car seats, he said, "These are yours now. For a cab, or—"

"When you come back," Tawny said. "I'll keep them for you."

"I paid for a week," Charlie told her. "In the meantime, I'm going to board up the broken windows at the church and get the power turned back on. Here's some money for cab fare and whatever." He handed her a hundred-dollar bill.

Tawny clutched it. "This means a lot."

"It's nothing, really."

"No, it's a big deal. I've been with a lot … never mind who I've been with. I've just never …" She took a deep breath. "You don't make this easy, you know. I don't want to sound cheap, but I would like to, you know … I don't just mean *that*. But I do mean *that*," she said with a laugh, "Any time, any place." She looked at him earnestly. "I can make you happy. I want to make you happy. Don't you want me to?"

"I have other plans," he said.

* * *

Having decided that *Flight from Forsyth* was worth promoting after all, Fortress scheduled its bestselling author for a publicity tour. Finally, after all these years, Charlie had hit the big time. On February 21, he would fly to New York to meet his agent, sign the contract for *American Monster*, interview a writer with *The New Yorker*, appear on TV, sign books, and give a lecture at The New School. Then on to Boston and a speech at Northeastern University. The tour would end in Los Angeles in early March. Charlie's booking agent had lined up eight lecture dates for him. When the tour was over, Charlie could pay cash for a new BMW, if that's what he wanted. (It was.)

With fame in his pocket and fortune on its way, Charlie couldn't wait to leave Atlanta. He also wanted to escape Tyrus Bannister, who had been pestering him about HR 390. The legislator expected him to testify before the House Special Judiciary Committee and explain why reparations "for slavery and historical discrimination" were necessary. Despite his promise, Charlie had no intention of doing so. No way would he sit at a table in the state Capitol and let Rep. Stanley Cutchins (D-Cumming) grill him about his "documents" and ... *other stuff*. Anyway, the concept of reparations was a dead end. A nonstarter. Nothing he could do about it.

Even though he believed that it was to his advantage if the varmints thought they were home free, paradoxically, the idea that they thought they were in the clear bothered him. Still hoping to make Stanley's and Cecil Montgomery's lives more *interesting*, Charlie gave Bannister something he could use in his battle for reparations. Two days before his flight to New York, Charlie retrieved his forgery of Joshua Logan's deathbed confession—the original having been burned in a 1953 fireplace incident—from his safety box, pausing to say hello to Riggins's finger and again apologize for its confinement.

He had already compared the handwriting on his work to that contained in letters he'd scanned at Lillian Scott's house in October. Both text and signature matched Montgomery's and Logan's handwriting, respectively—close enough for Charlie's purposes and government work, at least. In any case, the miracle shouted down the fraud, the way he saw it.

When Charlie mailed Joshua Logan's "document" to Bannister (hoping it would serve to placate the politician, too), he wondered how Montgomery would respond. Then again, what could the old third-rate historian do? Cecil's name hadn't been linked to the letter, so how could he claim it didn't exist when *there it was*? At least it didn't seem like he could. Anyway, Charlie didn't care what Cecil thought—or what happened to him, for that matter. Although he wouldn't mind causing Montgomery some embarrassment, his real purpose was to fire a shot across the varmints' bow by connecting John Riggins and Isaac Cutchins, which the letter did nicely. And the Montgomerys and Logans would go down along with the Cutchinses when Charlie's next book came out. In the meantime, with luck, the General Assembly would adjourn and the dust would settle before Charlie returned from Los Angeles. Consequently, there would be no need for him to testify before a bunch of politicians. That, he thought, would be an excellent way for things to work out.

* * *

In New York, Charlie was the toast of the town. The signing at Village Books was well-attended, the *New Yorker* writer was snarky yet sympathetic, and the co-hosts on *Good Day America* called him "our Southern Salman Rushdie," though Charlie joked, "I might be more of a Boo Radley."

After the show, Charlie huddled with Barbara Asher in a Manhattan Starbucks. Outside, it was gray and sloshy. His petite agent, a sixtyish ball of energy and enthusiasm, brought him some bad news. "They've changed the terms," she told him between sips of coffee minutes before their 10:00 a.m. meeting with Spence Greene, Brubaker's publisher, and the company's top editors. "They don't like the secrecy we're imposing, not with the amount of money involved. But they'll live with it. You have to be cleared of those criminal charges before they'll pay the advance. Spence said they'll publish books about stalkers, but not by stalkers." She laughed lightly.

"No big deal," Charlie said, his fists clenched beneath the table as he fought to conceal his irritation.

Barbara patted the table instead of his missing hand. "Don't worry. You'll get your money, just as soon as—" she paused to give him the slightest of frowns "—you *will* be cleared of the charges, won't you?"

Charlie opened his mouth to respond, but Barbara bolted from her chair. She made it to the door before she stopped and returned to the table. "A three-time Pulitzer finalist just walked by outside," she explained. "And he doesn't have representation at present. Whew. Too fast for me. I guess a younger agent will catch him." She glanced over her shoulder. "He won't last long on *this* street."

She took a moment to study Charlie's face. "You really should do something about that." She pointed to his scar, which was not only rose-shaped, but looked like it had a stem. "It doesn't inspire confidence. It's … like you killed a gardener in prison or something. Maybe we could cover it up with concealer." She reached into her purse.

"No way!" Charlie protested, pushing back from the table. "If my scar is good enough for a national television audience, it's good enough for you."

She drew out an empty hand. "I just want you to take this seriously. Did you really have to send mug shots of yourself in a prison uniform for the jacket photo?"

Charlie shrugged. "Why not?"

"I hope that's the last time you have to wear it. That reminds me. We'll need a wrap-up for the criminal case." She sighed, and seeing that Charlie's hands had reappeared on the tabletop, patted them both. "Don't worry. Someone will publish it even if you do end up in jail." She took a sip of coffee. "Let's get this done, Charles. I'm repping Britney's makeup artist's tell-all, and I have an auction to prepare for. I'm hoping high six figures. Nothing like yours, of course. Not unless she gets shot."

"I know some people."

"Don't tempt me. Hmm. I may call you after I get the manuscript." She brightened. "We should have some champagne after we sign the contract."

"I'm an ascetic."

"An ascetic?" Barbara said. "Well, you'll soon be living in style."

"That's nice," Charlie said. "I don't have a style right now."

"You do too. Militant trade unionist." Barbara's green eyes twinkled. "I've seen pictures. Oh! I know what. I'll buy you monogrammed uniforms. In case—so everyone knows who you are."

"To knowing who you are," Charlie said, raising his cup in toast.

* * *

Contracts were signed, interviews given, speeches made. In Chicago, Charlie had time to kill before his lecture at the University of Chicago that evening. He was walking along Lake Shore Drive on his way to the Field Museum. He'd wanted to go there ever since his father had promised to take him for his eighth birthday, before that nasty old bridge got in their way. He was upbeat, even serene, about fulfilling this lifelong dream. When his cellphone rang, he saw it was Crenshaw. "Hello, stalker."

"Why didn't you answer my voicemails?" Crenshaw sounded pissed.

"My battery went dead. Had to buy a new charger. Very busy. Dog ate—"

"How many more excuses do you have?" Crenshaw asked.

"How many do you need?"

"I figure by your caginess that you've heard."

"I'm figuring by my relatively good spirits I haven't. What's up?"

"My God, you *haven't* heard."

"Heard what?"

"About your competition."

"I wasn't even aware that I had any competition," Charlie said, adopting a mock-elitist tone, hoping it came across as a joke.

"You know Cecil Montgomery, right? Forsyth County's local historian?"

Charlie's sphincter tightened. *Careful.* "I've talked with him. Never met him. Saw where he was in a snit about my book. Figured him for jealous. Wouldn't call him competition, though."

"You being a famous author and all, yeah, yeah," Crenshaw said in a bored tone. "Did you know he was related to Joshua Logan, the subject of Tyrus Bannister's most recent news conference?"

"I *did* know that," Charlie said, holding the cellphone away from his mouth, whistling through his teeth to relieve the sudden rush of tension that hit him. "Why? Is he denouncing me again?"

"Probably would if he could, but he can't 'cause he's dead."

"That's … that's terrible. What happened? I mean, not a big surprise, I guess. The guy's in his seventies, right?" For some reason, Charlie was already thinking of alibis.

"He was murdered during a burglary."

Wait a minute. Charlie wanted to ask: Was Montgomery the victim, or the perpetrator? However, he had the good sense to bite his tongue instead. *Be calm.* "What did the burglar get?"

"Shot. Montgomery walked in on him and they killed each other. Burglar's name was Suches. Ring a bell?"

"One of the guys who came after me was named Suches," Charlie said.

"Yeah. Interesting. Deputies say the thief was holding some documents."

"Documents?"

"You know. Paper thingies with writing on them."

"What kind of documents?"

"Kind the sheriff won't talk about. Bannister wants 'em, but it ain't gonna happen, him being black, talkin' about reparations and all," Crenshaw said, using his best *In the Heat of the Night* voice.

"Strange," Charlie said. "When did this happen?"

"Last night, the day after Bannister's news conference. Go figure."

Charlie's eyes widened. Had the varmints hired another Suches for this job? What a bunch of fuck-ups. "You think there's a connection?"

"Why, do you?" Crenshaw asked.

"You're the one who mentioned it."

"You're the one who gave the Logan letter to Bannister."

"So?"

"That's what I'm saying. *So* ..." Crenshaw trailed off.

"Sorry, man. Can't help you. I gotta go."

"You think of anything, let me know. And answer your damned calls, man. You used to be in the business, so be a good source. And don't leave town."

"Too late for that, I'm afraid."

Charlie hung up. Well, *that* certainly was an unintended consequence. He shuddered as a chill swept through him. Or maybe it was just the wintry Chicago wind. In any case, after what he'd been through the past year, he took the weather personally.

Montgomery's death brought him no joy, even if the guy was a pissant. But Charlie didn't see how he was to blame if the old bastard fell into the line of fire. Unto the third and fourth generation and all that. Clearly, the day of judgment was at hand. And there was a bright side. Montgomery couldn't denounce the letter or challenge him on his footnotes anymore. All part of a divine plan, obviously. Montgomery had been hit by a bus, so to speak, and the wheels must keep rolling. Time to check out the dinosaur bones and fulfill his father's broken promise.

He took the steps to the museum two at a time.

* * *

Charlie drove to Redeemer's church the morning after he returned to Atlanta from the West Coast. The visit was a surprise to all parties involved. He didn't know exactly what he was doing or why, but he was feeling more attracted to the young hooker than repulsed. Absence, he supposed. He brought toys and books for Romy and Wyatt. When he pulled up in front of the church, the lights were on, and after a moment of shock, Tawny let him in. Charlie was relieved that she didn't have male company.

The children seemed happy and healthy. While Wyatt unwrapped a Nerf football, Romy hugged Charlie's leg and sang, "I'm better now."

Just then, Tawny lashed out at him. "What is wrong with you? It's been weeks and you didn't even call to see how we were doing."

Her anger surprised Charlie. "There wasn't anything I could do a thousand miles away," he protested.

"I thought that's why you got me the cellphone, to stay in touch."

"I got the cellphone for you, not me," Charlie said. The football hit him in the shoulder. "Hey!"

"Thanks," Wyatt said. "It was my birthday this week."

"Happy birthday! How old are you now? Five?" Wyatt nodded.

"You're my son's age." Charlie turned to Tawny, frowning. "He needs to be in school."

"I know," she said, looking away. "But there's no requirement until first grade, next year."

"You read to them?"

"Yeah, but I don't need you acting like you're from Family Services," she said, her voice rising. "I mean, if you're going to take care of us, then take care of us. *Do not* just string us along and show up whenever you want." She folded her hands across her chest and glared at him.

Tawny reminded him of Susan back when she was young and feisty, before his wife turned malevolent. He wanted Tawny right then. But that didn't matter, not with the kids around, even though he suspected they hadn't been spared the sight of their mother at work.

"If I get my act together," she said, "I could have any man."

More like every man, he thought.

"I know what you're thinking," she said, wagging a finger at him and nearly poking him in the chest. "But you're no better than me, Buster. Not when you've got that asshat problem."

Charlie puzzled over that for a moment. "Oh. Ascetic."

"That's what I'm sayin'."

"I didn't come here to fight," Charlie said. "I should go. Take this." He handed her a wad of hundred dollar bills—ten minutes' worth of talk to a bunch of college kids.

Tawny clutched the bills and waved them at him, looking for a moment like she was going to throw them in his face. Instead, she bit her lip. "Fine. Go. Don't expect me to beg. Anyway, you're worse off than I am. At least I got my kids." Then she laughed at him.

Nothing he could say to that. Charlie left, his face burning with both shame and anger. He wanted to scream in frustration, knowing that he couldn't stay with this disreputable, irresponsible woman nearly twenty years his junior, and he couldn't desert her, either, because she and those kids needed him when no one else did.

* * *

If the varmints had any doubt that another book was in the works, the call from Brubaker attorney Ray Washburn to Uncle Stanley dispelled them.

Charlie got one of those calls, too, and after conferring with Washburn, he started revising *American Monster*.

He was in the process of removing some of the more colorful adjectives describing Pappy when he heard from his divorce lawyer.

"Your wife and her attorney are playing hardball," Richard Muncie said. "They obtained an extension on the restraining order until mid-June. The fact that you face criminal charges helpeth you not. You working on that?"

"Yeah. I hired Cornelius Searles."

"Are you facing a death penalty I don't know about?"

"I figure I'd get the best."

Cornelius Searles was a well-known African-American defense attorney, a protégé of Johnnie Cochran, who often appeared on CNN as a legal analyst. He loved high-profile cases, and while this was just a misdemeanor, Charlie's notoriety and ability to pay his fee proved irresistible to Searles, who looked forward to the prospect of doing battle in Forsyth County in front of a dozen TV cameras.

"*Whew.* That'll cost you. Not to be racist, but you couldn't go with a white attorney for Forsyth?"

"Where's the sport in that?"

"You're gonna need to hang onto some of that money you're making. Your wife wants ten grand a month child support."

"What? I'm not rich yet!"

"She wants the kids in Northside Christian Academy next year."

Charlie grunted in distaste. "Does she know about the book contract?"

"She will. By the way, assume you're under surveillance. There's a chance your cellphone calls may be intercepted, too. Her lawyer's got game." Muncie's voice was filled with admiration.

Charlie thought of his latest visit to Tawny. He'd wanted to go back and patch things up with her, but now he realized he couldn't afford to be seen with her. The varmints and their allies would use her against him. "Damn."

"Yeah, I get that a lot," said Muncie. "Rough business, breaking up. I will say this: Your wife's a real piece of work. From a purely professional standpoint, I gotta just step back and admire her. You don't get clients like her every day."

"She's not your client," Charlie said. "I am."

"Don't remind me," said Muncie, sounding glum.

* * *

After a whirlwind speaking tour across the South, Charlie returned to Atlanta late on the night of April 1. The next morning, he was in La Patisserie, sitting by the window enjoying a muffin, fruit cup, and coffee. Two men in business suits entered and approached him. Fearing for his life, Charlie stood and looked around wildly for a weapon. "Are you Charles Sherman?"

"Yes," Charlie said warily, casting his gaze upon a plastic spork. His would not be a heroic death.

The first man handed him some papers. "You've been served," said the other.

They left. Charlie opened the envelope. It contained a petition for divorce—on grounds of desertion and mental cruelty. His hands shook as he held the paper. Lies, all lies! He hadn't deserted Susan. She'd kicked him out. What about all the money he'd given her? As for mental cruelty—what about Bryan? And now *Harold*. God, the woman had gall.

The petition removed any iota of doubt left in his mind that Susan was involved in the varmints' plot. What else could the divorce petition be but part of a conspiracy to ruin his reputation and destroy his credibility?

After he sent an e-mail to Muncie vowing to "fight this thing to the bitter end and beyond," Charlie glanced through the morning paper. A brief on the legislative news page caught his eye: *Reparations Bill Dies in House*. Ah. So that's why Bannister quit calling him. But really, what could he have done? In this case, given his own weakness as an ally, wasn't it better to let the dead past bury the dead, and let the living move along? He certainly thought so.

* * *

Charlie spent much of April holed up in his apartment. Besides polishing *American Monster*, he worked on a book-length, profanity-laced defense of himself as a husband and father for a yet-to-be-defined audience. Muncie's warning about the possibility of surveillance had become an obsession. Obviously, life was unfair. Just when people stopped trying to kill him, they started spying on him.

Consequently, when he should have been enjoying his newfound freedom and wealth, he was more alone than ever. Tawny was untouchable—grungy, ungrateful, and off-limits due to his fear of Susan's spies; Jean, his oldest friend in his new life, now seemed distant—and knew too much about his time in the gutter to see him the way he wanted to be seen. Plus, she'd probably shared this information with Dana, who remained illusive. He hadn't seen Danger Girl since she'd dropped by his loft briefly one afternoon in

March with a box full of copies of *Flight from Forsyth* for him to sign, saying, "Just in case, vell, you know." In case he got killed and drove up the value of signed copies, she meant. But that was understandable; she was an art dealer. Didn't they wish for bad luck as a matter of course? And then there was Amy—or rather, there wasn't. A trace of cinnamon was all he'd had of her.

Perhaps he should just start over and find a new life in a new loft. He'd read about an absolutely fantastic development on Industrial Avenue. It, too, had train tracks and razor wire, requisites for urban living. He could soon afford nearly anything the city had to offer, but he couldn't motivate himself to go out and look. Instead, he sat at his computer, worked on his rant, and waited for whatever it was that was hurtling toward him.

* * *

Charlie decided he had to get out more, but he didn't want to go out alone. So he hired a pretend bodyguard to escort him on his outings—Armand Parsons, a beefy, underemployed African-American actor. He'd met Parsons at the bakery one day after a drugged-out panhandler followed a young couple into the shop, demanding money. When Amy Weller told him to leave, the man said, "Suck my dick, bitch." Parsons, standing at the counter, grabbed the guy by the collar. Charlie, sitting outside, had gotten up for a coffee refill and opened the door just in time for the panhandler to sail through it. Impressed with Parsons's physical presence, Charlie bought him a cup of coffee and struck up a conversation.

The former high school football player lived across the street from Charlie and hoped to get a part in the next Tyler Perry movie. In the meantime, he needed money.

"If you're looking for work, I could use a bodyguard on an ad hoc basis," Charlie told him.

"*Ad hoc*? I need a job so I can get my stuff *out* of hock," Parsons said. "Just one problem. I'm not a bodyguard. I don't even have a weapon. Matter of fact, it's at the pawn shop."

"Oh, I don't want you to carry a gun. I just need you to act like a bodyguard."

"Acting." Parsons rubbed his chin and took a sip of coffee. "How much?"

"Twenty an hour."

"Twenty-five."

"All right."

"When do I work?" Armand asked.

"Whenever. Give me your cell number."

They reached an agreement: If there was any shooting—whether on location for a movie or during an assassination attempt—it would be every man for himself. That afternoon, on the way to Lenox Square, Parsons said, "I'm like that merchant in *The Godfather*. You know, the neighborhood guy who came to see Don Corleone in the hospital and Michael posted him as a guard when the hit men drove by."

"Exactly so," Charlie said. "I wouldn't have it any other way."

"And when they make a movie from that book you wrote, you can get me a part."

"Victim or criminal?"

"Either one," said Parsons. "Just needs to be a speaking role."

They rode for a while before Parsons spoke again. "Man, I hope you sell movie rights soon. Get you a Navigator or an Escalade. This old Volvo ain't doin' nuthin' for your style points. Mine either."

"Next check comes in, I'm gonna buy a BMW."

"That's cool, but an Escalade be better."

* * *

In mid-April, *GQ* interviewed Charlie for an article: "Big Shot Writer." Charlie found the idea silly, but it was the kind of foolishness that sold books, so there he was, posing for the photographer in front of La Patisserie, wearing a new black duster coat, black custom-tailored, form-fitting Dickies, tight lace-up black boots, and new industrial-grade sunglasses that the shabby-chic young reporter and grungy German photographer found cool. Charlie thought the outfit made him look like a worker in a chic morgue—or somebody waiting for Neo to show up so they could access the Matrix.

Dana, having just returned from Munich, happened to be in the bakery. She came out to watch and soon took over, strutting around like a runway model in high-heeled, knee-high boots over jeans and a bright red sleeveless T-shirt emblazoned with the words *Mangez Moi!* Soon she'd talked the photographer and Charlie into visiting her art gallery to finish the shoot. There, in her native element, Dana continued to work her magic, breezily greeting customers, terrorizing her assistant, and setting up a backdrop for the photographer. She found time to convince Charlie to spend $12,000 for an abstract painting. "A bargain at any price," she said. "You vill be thanking me for this. Many times. In many vays."

When Charlie left for another appointment, the photographer stayed to negotiate a fee for taking photos for a gallery catalogue. That evening, before Charlie could get a return on his investment, Dana called and asked him for a ride to Hartsfield-Jackson Airport. This time, she was going to China. She kissed him lightly on the lips as she got out of his car at the Delta terminal. He pined for her on the drive back to Castlegate and all that evening. He went to bed alone for what seemed the 665th night in a row.

Hoping to learn more about Dana, and feeling nostalgic (as well as horny), Charlie strayed over to Bay Street Coffeehouse to see Jean the next day. He learned from her that Dana's negotiating tactics with the photographer had included sex. It was a dagger through his heart. How could she do such a thing, when he'd been waiting for months?

Seeing the stricken look on his face, Jean said, "I'm telling you this for your own good." Without delving into specifics, she said that Dana, originally from Bucharest, had a shady past. "And present, I found out recently," she added with a frown. "You're better off without her."

Charlie despaired. He'd suffered so much to be rich and famous, and here was Dana, screwing the help. Jean was right, of course. Dana was no good for him. Unfortunately, that only made him want her more. He returned to Castlegate and stumbled into La Patisserie to cry on Amy Weller's shoulder, hoping his favorite baker would take pity on him and relieve his torment. As soon as he walked in, the cinnamon girl shouted out, "Guess what? I'm engaged!"

Charlie went to bed alone again that night, convinced that a curse hung over his head.

* * *

While Charlie bided his time and kept quiet about *American Monster*, the varmints were being attacked on another front. Clearly, *someone* smelled blood in the water, and during the last week of April, Forsyth County Commissioner Randolph Dempsey—son of Tom Dempsey, a member of the 1937 mob—qualified to run against Stanley Cutchins in the Republican primary. On April 30, a third GOP candidate plunked down his fee in the House race. (Democrats didn't bother to qualify a candidate; the district was too white and conservative for them to stand a chance.)

Crenshaw called Charlie and said, "Your uncle has drawn opposition."

"Like shit draws flies," said Charlie.

"Come on," Crenshaw said. "Give me something more diplomatic I can quote."

"Fuck him if he can't take a joke."

"Gotta be civil."

"Sorry. Can't think of anything else. The guy's evil."

Charlie got off the phone and wrote a check for $2,000 to Jimmy Townsell, the third and least-known candidate. The only thing Charlie knew about Townsell was that, unlike the other two, he didn't have a lyncher's last name.

* * *

After refusing a plea deal that included a suspended sentence, Charlie received a summons to appear for trial on May 26 in Forsyth County State Court. He had believed that the varmints would flinch in this game of chicken and the charges would be dropped. They didn't and they weren't, however. Consequently, Charlie grew more anxious as the trial date approached, since a book deal worth two million dollars was on the line.

On May 25, Armand Parsons escorted Charlie to the bank to retrieve John Riggins's finger from the vault. Charlie drove back to the loft with the Mason jar in a velvet cognac bag he'd borrowed from his bodyguard. The writer hemmed and hawed before saying, "Armand, I need you to go up to Forsyth with me for the trial."

"No way," said Parsons, even though he wasn't privy to the bag's contents.

Charlie wheedled. "You'll be on TV."

"I ain't goin' up there without an AK-47 and fifty brothers," Parsons declared, his hands folded across his chest. "Besides, I got a part in Tyler Perry's new movie, so I can't do this gig anymore. You'll have to get a new entourage."

"Well, it's been real."

"Not really," drawled Parsons, shaking his head as he checked out a young woman on the sidewalk.

When Charlie got back to the loft, he called Cornelius Searles. "I'm bringing the pain. I need bodyguards. Lots of muscle. And not to be racist, but I want my posse black."

* * *

On the morning of May 26, Searles and his assistant, an attractive young black woman, drove up to Cumming in the attorney's Lexus. Charlie rode in a Chevy Suburban with four off-duty DeKalb County police officers in ersatz SWAT uniforms, although their client would have rather seen them in suits, bow ties, and white gloves, armed with copies of *Final Call.*

People stared at the white man in the gray suit and his black storm troopers as they crossed the street from the parking lot to the courthouse. The media was there in force to record their grand entrance, which was carried out with crisp precision. Charlie, his face grim, looked like he'd shown up for a grudge match with Satan.

Oddly enough, Charlie's satchel containing the metal-lidded jar passed through the courthouse's X-ray machine unnoticed, but the group was detained at the security checkpoint, anyway. After a brief but loud dispute between Searles and a sheriff's lieutenant, calls were made and Charlie's bodyguards were allowed to proceeded to the second floor.

While the defense team was waiting in the hall, Solicitor Paul Armitage showed up waving affidavits and depositions. He seemed mighty pleased with himself and ready to present the case of The People against Charles T. Sherman. Searles warily eyed Armitage. When the two lawyers huddled in the hall, Charlie heard Searles whisper harshly to the prosecutor, "What the hell are you trying to pull?"

After that, there was more waiting, since the court session started late that day. Finally, a deputy told Charlie and his attorney to go into the court room. They took seats at the defense table. His bodyguards cooled their heels in the hall.

For the defendant, reality was sinking in. This was actually happening, and since Pappy didn't respect truth or law, he could claim Charlie stole a TV and the family silverware. What if the jurors believed the varmints and not him? Charlie could be convicted and sentenced to serve a year in the Forsyth County Jail. An eternity in hell, in other words.

No, don't even think that, he told himself. *You shall prevail.* Charlie cast a sidelong glance at his dapper black attorney, who no longer seemed like the ideal defender of his freedom in such a place. "We're going to win, aren't we?"

"Those affidavits don't say anything, really," Searles assured him. "Just that you and Isaac Cutchins don't get along and you're not a nice person and therefore capable of anything. It's bullshit, and I know how to deal with that. Look, here's what you need to do: When the jurors come in, watch their faces. Half of them will give away their vote before they even sit down."

None of what Searles had just said was particularly reassuring to Charlie.

A few minutes later, in came the jury pool, thirty people of all shapes and sizes but only one color. Charlie looked over the men and women and decided that none of them liked him.

At twelve-thirty, the jury of seven women and five men had been picked and seated. Charlie's throat was dry as he stood and Judge Robert Bascom read the charges. Searles entered a plea of not guilty on his behalf. Bascom, an older, heavyset man, declared a lunch recess. Charlie, now genuinely nervous, threw himself back in his chair and ran his hands along his temples.

"Don't do that," Searles whispered harshly behind his yellow legal pad. "It doesn't look good."

"This is un-fucking believable," Charlie whispered back, shaking his head.

"You wanted a trial, you got it. Be careful what you wish for." And then Searles gave him a wicked smile. "Although I can't wait to see their faces when you whip out the jar."

Bring the pain. The thought cheered Charlie. "I can't believe they're pushing their luck this way. Murder will out, but this is really poetic. If I don't go to the slammer, that is. I wish there was a plea for Not Guilty by reason of Check It Out!"

Searles chuckled. "Just remember, it's not a felony. No more than a year in jail. Probably get you a suspended sentence, although they might want to teach Smartass White Boy a lesson for not taking the deal." Searles adjusted his tie. "You know a good place to eat?" He surveyed the courtroom. Several men on the back bench were staring at him. "Correction: a safe place?"

"McDonald's had a black assistant manager last time I was there. It's just a few blocks away."

Searles sighed. "All right. If all else fails, lower your standards."

The defense team ate Big Macs, Charlie's treat. People stared at the black SWAT team members, who joked and laughed. While some people may have resented their presence, the locals kept their comments to themselves. After all, it wasn't as if they didn't know what black people looked like. Most of them had seen too many; that's why they'd moved to Forsyth County.

Charlie and his team returned to the courthouse, where Searles gave an impromptu news conference for a dozen reporters covering the trial. Crenshaw caught Charlie's attention and mock-hanged himself by his tie. *What did he know*?

Shortly after two o'clock in a packed courtroom, the bailiff called out, "All rise."

The judge entered. "Be seated," Bascom said. He called counsel to approach the bench, and a moment later, both lawyers returned to their tables.

"Call your first witness, please."

"The prosecution calls Isaac Cutchins to the stand." A deputy left the courtroom. Charlie pivoted in his seat and braced himself for his first face-to-face confrontation with the ancient villain since Pappy shot out his rear window.

The deputy returned and whispered to a superior officer sitting on a back bench. The deputy again left and returned. Charlie turned in his chair and raised his eyebrows, giving the reporters a quizzical smile.

A growing buzz filled the room. Jurors exchanged puzzled looks. The ranking deputy rose and went to the railing. Armitage leaned back in his chair to listen; a look of unhappy surprise spread across his face.

"Your honor," the solicitor said a few seconds later, "Mr. Cutchins was here this morning, but apparently, he's suffering a bout of ill health. We ask for a postponement until tomorrow morning—"

"Who's your next witness?" the judge asked, glancing at a sheet.

"We plan to call Representative Stanley Cutchins—"

"Objection, your honor," Searles said, rising. "Without the alleged victim's testimony, this proceeding is nothing more than a character assassination the prosecution has planned and laid out—"

"Objection!" Armitage shouted out.

Searles did a double-take at the objection to his objection, then continued. "—that serves no purpose other than to damage my client's reputation. It would cloud, rather than clear, the issues surrounding the case."

"Is Mr. Cutchins in the hospital?" Bascom asked.

Armitage looked around helplessly.

"Ten-minute recess," the judge continued. "Please ascertain your witness's whereabouts."

Armitage scurried off. He was back in five minutes, ashen-faced. The bailiff retrieved the judge. Armitage and Searles approached the bench. Bascom grew angrier as the solicitor talked. He threw down the papers he was holding and grabbed his gavel.

"Case dismissed!" the judge roared. "My apologies to the ladies and gentlemen of the jury. Mr. Sherman, you are free to go." He bowed his head to the defendant.

Searles returned to the table, suppressing a grin.

"What just happened?" Charlie asked.

"Seems the victim told the solicitor, the judge, and everybody in Forsyth County to go fuck themselves." Searles took in a deep breath. "Kind of anticlimactic, but what the hey. I just won a trial in Forsyth County, Georgia before an all-white jury. You can damn well bet I'm putting that on my résumé!" He punctuated his statement with hearty laughter.

And so Charles T. Sherman walked out of the courtroom a free man. His guards joined him in the hall and with rare precision, the group quick-stepped down the stairs and outside. They waited for Searles, who followed with his assistant a few minutes later, then they all crossed the courthouse square rapidly on the way to their vehicles. There would be no post-trial interviews, not until they were out of town. The media could cover the aborted trial any way they pleased. Charlie just wanted out of Forsyth alive.

Most amazingly, the secret of *American Monster* had been preserved.

Charlie made a phone call before his Suburban even cleared the Cumming city limits.

"Barbara Asher here."

"Tell Spence Greene to cut me a check," Charlie said, savoring each word. "And I'm writing a new ending."

Seconds after he finished that call, Charlie's phone buzzed. It was Crenshaw. "I just heard something strange," the reporter said.

"What's that?"

"That Isaac Cutchins is missing a finger."

"Do what?"

"How many fingers does Isaac Cutchins have?"

"Don't recall," Charlie drawled. "I usually see just the one."

"There's another book coming, isn't there? That's what all the trouble is about! I've talked to three people saying you're working on a lynching. A man named Riggins. Why didn't you tell me?"

"Not time yet. Thought it might happen today, but no dice. Have to wait."

"Screw you. You got some bad karma, dude."

"Have a nice day," Charlie said.

Crenshaw got even. The headline in the next day's paper said, "Victim a No-Show, Sherman Case Dismissed." In the article, Crenshaw quoted Evangeline: "It's terrible when the guilty walk free."

To which Charlie said *Amen.*

Chapter Twenty-Three

The sunny June morning promised a hot afternoon. Charlie left Muncie's office grumbling about Susan's hostility. He had just finished—endured, rather—a conference call between both parties, their attorneys, and the judge in his divorce proceeding. Tempers had flared, especially Susan's. In the end, Judge Belinda Jackson lifted the restraining order after lecturing Susan and her lawyer about their winner-take-all tactics. Charlie would have Beck and Ben for a full day that weekend—his first time alone with them in seven months.

Charlie wore his wedding ring that morning to fortify his position. Muncie had chided him: "I don't know who you're trying to impress. Nobody else can see it."

"Nobody else needs to see it," Charlie countered. "I know what the deal is. I'm still married."

Muncie shook his gleaming head and chuckled. "Hate to break it to you, but it's the terms we're haggling over, not what's going to happen."

"Well, I don't want a divorce," Charlie declared. "Not when she's acting this way."

"I've noticed that there's just one thing you two won't give each other," Muncie said.

"What's that?"

"Whatever the other one wants."

"Well, can you blame me? Look at what she wants. She's dead set on cutting me off from the kids."

"Look on the bright side. You're going to be a millionaire. And chicks dig millionaires." Muncie gave him a wicked grin.

"Alas, I fear I'm cursed in that regard."

"See a doctor, then."

That wasn't what Charlie meant, of course. His fear was that his sexual mojo was being controlled from beyond, to no good end. Or more precisely, no end at all.

Afterward, Charlie stood in the parking lot beside his new space-gray metallic BMW 328i and tugged until his knuckle ached, but the ring remained stuck firmly on his finger.

At the loft, Charlie squirted Ivory Liquid on his hand to ease off his symbol of lost love and unrelenting torment. He was tugging away at the band when he heard a *whump* in the hall followed by a knock on the door. He wiped off the soap and sauntered to the peephole. A black man in a brown uniform stood in the hall. Charlie opened the door and saw a box with a Brubaker Publishing Company label. The deliveryman was already gone.

He threw out his arms and laughed maniacally before dragging the box inside. With a knife from the kitchen, he sliced the tape, feeling like he was exhuming a corpse and on the verge of bringing it back to life. Inside were twenty-four jacketed author's copies of *American Monster*. Though he'd seen a mock-up and knew it was coming, the cover was a shock: grim and humorless, with stark black type on the gray background, drawing the eye to the old, grainy photo of John Riggins hanging from that limb.

"That ought to get their attention," Charlie growled appreciatively.

On the back jacket flap: front and side profile photos of the author's scarred face. His staged mug shots made a powerful statement, although the orange jumpsuit's effect was lost in the black-and-white format. And now he worried that readers might be confused and think he was the monster.

No. That would be terrible. They couldn't. He shook his head to rid himself of the thought.

An instant later, his wedding band hit the floor with a *ping*. Charlie pocketed it and read the back-cover blurbs from prominent authors who loved his *Monster*. They really, really loved it. In exchange for their adoration, their books were listed on the cover of a book that was sure to be a bestseller, because it had been written by Charles Sherman. If anyone could appreciate the irony inherent in that concept, Charlie could, although perhaps not at the moment.

* * *

A grim and awkward task lay ahead. Charlie knew Minerva wouldn't like *American Monster*, but he'd promised her a copy and figured she should have it before the book hit the stores.

She was outside when Charlie, wearing old shipping department clothes and driving the Volvo instead of his new BMW, parked at the curb by her house for the first time in five months. Wearing a faded old blue dress and a floppy straw hat, she was pulling weeds from around the red, white, and purple petunias in her flowerbed.

"I like your flowers." he said as he approached. "They're rowdy."

She turned and regarded him warily. "I'm trying to make them a little less so." She stepped onto the sidewalk. "Haven't seen you in a while. They quit tryin' to kill you?"

"So far. Though they might step up their efforts now."

Takira appeared at the screen door. Hugely pregnant, her body shape resembled a basketball taped to a broom. "Hey," she said, smiling at Charlie.

"Hey."

Minerva glanced at the girl, then at Charlie. "Any day now," she said. She wiped her brow with a gloved hand, then eyed the spine of the book clasped against his thigh. "So what brings you to our neck of the woods?"

He held up *American Monster*. She took a step back. "Oh. My. God. Is that … that my father?"

"I'm sor-sorry," Charlie stammered, horrified at what he'd just done to the poor woman. "I thought … thought you'd seen this."

"No. You never showed it to me." Her tone was hard.

"I'm sorry. I thought—I guess I saw too much of it myself, and … sorry. Well, I want you to have the book." He handed it to her—or tried to. She took a step back and regarded it like a hiker would a coiled snake beside a path in the woods.

She heaved the longest sigh he'd ever heard. After a moment, she slowly raised her hand. "I guess I should have a copy. You autograph this one?"

"I did. To Minerva, whose dignity is unmatched."

"Take off the cover. I don't want to look at it."

Charlie complied and tucked the jacket in his back pocket.

"Well, thank you. Mr. Childress—that's my lawyer—wants a copy. He's been waiting for it. Did he get in touch with you? I think he had to go through your publisher. The number you gave me didn't work. Again."

"Yeah, I talked to him. I thought I'd give his book to you. I've got a couple more in the car. I wanted Demetrious to have one. I'll give you his copy, too."

"He won't read it. Doesn't read anything. He's still angry about what happened."

"I want one," Takira said.

"Have you seen him lately?" Charlie asked the girl.

"He come and go," Takira volunteered.

Minerva frowned at the girl. "He do," Takira insisted.

"He's fallen on a rough patch," Minerva said. "He and his mother, both. She hooked up with some bad people. Owes them money. But that's not your problem." She sniffed and pointed her trowel at the flowers. "Sometimes I just plant whites. They look like a choir in robes, singing."

Charlie allowed himself a smile. "Not to change the subject, but the book hits stores tomorrow. I'm holding a news conference. I was thinking maybe you could come and—"

She shook her head. "I don't want to talk to people about this. That's your thing." She waved and called out a greeting to a neighbor walking by, then fixed her gaze on Charlie. "I bet you made a ton of money off this book. It's a nasty story, and people love nasty stories."

Charlie shrugged. He figured she was too proud to ask for money and wouldn't want it, since the book said exactly what she feared it would, and accepting the money would mean accepting the fact. Then again, maybe God's plan was to give Minerva something. "If you need help, I'd be glad to … share what I've got." *Before my wife gets it.*

"Mr. Childress said I shouldn't take your money. I don't want it, anyway. What's mine by rights is mine by rights, that's the way I see it."

Charlie realized that this was essentially what John Riggins had said the day he died.

"You were going to give me another book, I believe," she said.

"Sure." Charlie went to the Volvo. He took off the jackets from two copies and returned. Takira had retreated into the house. He handed Minerva the books.

"I don't even know if I want to read it," she said. "I'm afraid what it will say. Let me have a cover so I can give it to my lawyer."

"It's the truth. I swear." Charlie pulled a book jacket from his pocket and folded it inside out to conceal the photo before handing it to her.

"Sometimes there's more than one truth, and they contradict. If you don't believe it, try reading the Bible sometime." She looked at him, waited for a response, then shrugged. "Whew. Must be ninety degrees." She wiped her brow with her forearm. "Did you put the part in about the quitclaim?"

"Yes I did, along with the GBI's denial that they sent anyone over here. They tried to deny that two agents held me in a warehouse, but the Forsyth

Sheriff's Department wouldn't back them up. So then they had to deny that they denied anything."

Minerva gave him a rueful chuckle. "Well, I better call Mr. Childress. He needs to know the book's out."

"Good luck. I told him I'd testify for you."

She was already on the steps. "Goodbye." She waved, giving him the back of her hand.

That went well, Charlie thought as he went back to the car. *Better than the last couple of times, anyway.*

He drove off. At the stop sign a block away, Demetrious flagged him down, coming out into the street and putting his fist on the car hood. Charlie looked around for P-Dog, D's little gunman.

"Yo, yo, yo." Demetrious came around and banged on the driver's side door.

"Hey." Charlie rolled down the window and tried to sound breezy. "You stalkin' me?"

"Got my eyes out. Heard you was in the neighborhood. Just wanted to stay in touch."

Charlie looked ahead and saw the silhouette of a head just barely above the driver's seat of an old Buick. He was glad he didn't bring his BMW.

"Look," Demetrious said. "I need hep to get someone outta a jam."

"A little late for an abortion, isn't it?"

Demetrious waved his hands like he was signaling an incomplete pass. "I'm not worryin' 'bout that no more. I need to help out my momma. She owes some money. And you rich now, what I hear. Bestseller, on TV and all."

"Can't help you."

"You mean you *won't* hep me. Get this straight. This where Ima comin' from. Man rips us off for twenty million and then you come in and clean up and make yo own. Where's ours? That's what I'm talkin' about." Looking anguished, Demetrious crisscrossed his chest with his hands. "You owe us half what you make, man. It's our story! It's my blood!" Demetrious pounded his chest with his fists. "A dealer threatenin' to kill my mama," he said. "I need twenty large, man."

"I don't have that kind of money to hand out."

"At least enough fo me to get a gun," Demetrious pleaded.

"A gun will get you into more trouble than it will get you out of."

"She die, it gonna be on yo head."

"No, it won't. And don't even talk that way."

"You say you tryin' to hep my family. That's a laugh."

"I said I was seeking justice. That might not help you personally. You made your bed, now–"

Demetrious reached in to grab his collar. Charlie hit the gas, causing his head to hit the door. The kid let go, yelling, "Fuck you, motherfucker!"

Charlie glanced in the side mirror just before he turned right. "Don't worry," he mumbled, rubbing his stinging left temple. "You'll get what's coming to you."

A minute later, when Charlie turned onto Memorial Drive, his phone buzzed. "Hello."

"We're going to rip you a new asshole, asshole," Uncle Stanley said. "We've hired a lawyer and we're going to tear apart every assertion in that book. Did you think you could get away with this?"

Charlie's tone was cool and proper. "You had every chance to respond."

"I can't wait to see you get what's coming to you. We're going to beat on your head until your ears bleed."

Charlie gave Redeemer's church a sidelong glance as he passed by. Before hanging up, he said, "I reckon that's a beating I'll have to take."

* * *

Charlie's news conference was scheduled for 2:00 p.m. on June 23, the nationwide release date for *American Monster*. This was his day, his time to shine, his party. At his own expense, Charlie had hired the local public relations firm of Jacoby and Ruthers to stage the event.

That morning, Charlie visited bookstores and found, to his great relief and joy, that *American Monster* was ubiquitous. He gave an impromptu signing in Buckhead, smiling and posing for a photo with a rich white woman who bought three copies for her "African-American friends." When Charlie suggested that it might be instructive for her to read the book, too, she laughed. What a funny thing to say!

He stopped by Bay Street Coffeehouse, walking in the door in his new blue-and-white seersucker suit from Jos. A. Bank Clothiers—a perfectly respectable summer outfit for a Southern writer. He also wore a white button-down oxford shirt, a yellow-and-blue striped tie, and cordovan Cole-Haan tasseled loafers, accented by a sharp, clean-smelling fragrance he'd bought on a whim at Nordstrom's. *GQ* was on the newsstands, and while Charlie's Industrial Chic was in, now that he had money, he wanted to set new trends. Anyway, he was tired of the working-class look. He was going uptown from here on out.

"This is my Tom Wolfe look," he proudly told Jean, who gave him a disapproving frown.

"I liked it better when you were a truck driver. Now you look like a man who's full of it."

"That's cold."

Jean mumbled something about "putting on airs" and turned her back on him as soon as she took his order for a double espresso on ice.

As he sat at his old table by the window and watched a car drive up Bayard Terrace, he thought of all the time he'd spent in the dungeon, helping Kathleen complete her life. That world was gone. Angela had sold her mother's house recently for a huge amount of money. She'd get another large chunk of change when royalties and movie rights money from *Flight* came in, but he reminded himself of the happy fact that she'd cut herself out of any share of *American Monster*. He'd buy a pricey gift for her August commitment ceremony with Sandra. It was the least he could do. Chuckling, he raised his glass toward the dungeon, and said, "Here's to happily ever after."

* * *

The news conference went reasonably well, although there was a rough part when Charlie had to explain why he hadn't gone to the police after the bombing, which had suddenly become common knowledge (and pushed him to the top of the front page again after news of his trial died down). He told reporters that, as far as he knew, there were no new leads in the case. He referred questions to Detective Sanders, who had talked to him three times since their original meeting. Reporters were reluctant to forgive his recalcitrance (along with his disappearing act after his Forsyth County trial), so Charlie tried to thaw the mood with some candor about what it's like to be shell-shocked and homeless on Christmas Eve, although he no longer looked the part.

Reporters might not like him, but so far the news coverage had been generally positive. TV stations repeated his accusations, along with a confusing mixture of no-comments and denials from the Cutchinses. He'd heard from a reporter that they'd called him a pervert, but that accusation didn't make the evening news. Charlie was more interested in what Crenshaw would write, since the newspaper reporter had been on the story since the beginning and knew more about it than all the other journalists combined.

The next morning, he was awakened by a freight train's rumble halfway between four o'clock and dawn. Charlie watched shadows dance on the ceiling. Abandoning sleep and fortifying himself with coffee, he checked e-mails. The haters, who'd been slow to respond to *Flight*, reacted more quickly to *Monster*. He'd gotten twenty messages, half of them hostile, and half of *those* threatening, like the one from Aryan@earthbank.com: "Nigger Lover, you betray your family for silver. Go to hell with my knife up your ass." Charlie winced and shifted uncomfortably in his chair. Maybe it was time he hired real bodyguards.

After checking news coverage on the Internet, Charlie shuffled downstairs to buy a paper, first peeking around the corner of the garage entrance. The coast was clear—at least there were no pickup trucks. He ran to the box, quickly slipped in coins and snatched a copy, then trotted back to the vestibule, humming through his teeth, and tapping his foot nervously while awaiting the elevator.

Safely back in his loft, he read Crenshaw's front-page coverage of his news conference: "Wealthy Forsyth Farmer Accused of 1937 Lynching." The photo of Charlie highlighted his scar. Another picture showed Momo's monster truck in front of Pappy's house along with three *No Trespassing* signs and a crudely lettered notice stating *Violaters will be shot*! Forsyth District Attorney Eric Stockwell was dismissive of Charlie's claims, saying, "A finger in a jar doesn't make a case." But Charlie didn't expect much sympathy from that quarter, since Stockwell had refused to return Charlie's phone calls about *American Monster* in December. There was also a promo blurb: "Coming Sunday: A Look Behind the Book—The Cutchins-Sherman Feud."

"Reruns," Charlie muttered.

* * *

Charlie spent the rest of the morning looking for a new loft. Everything he saw was too big or too small; nothing was just right. He missed having Armand, his faux bodyguard, to talk to. When he checked his voicemails after lunch, there were thirteen messages, mostly from reporters—and one from Matthew Steele, inviting Charlie to appear on his TV show: "Of course, we'll have some Cutchinses on, too. Think of it, Mr. Sherman! An episode dedicated to families who lynch, and the courageous in-laws who expose them!"

The trashiest of trash TV. Charlie groaned in distaste and shouted, "Oh, hell no!" at his new cellphone.

That evening, he cruised bookstores and held impromptu signings, accepting business cards with private numbers written on them from a couple of fine-looking young women. He thought that perhaps his curse was about to be broken.

Late that night, Charlie returned to Castlegate and parked his BMW in the garage. Rather than face his lonely loft, he walked out to the street. Traffic was sparse and the night was balmy; some of the day's stifling heat had dissipated. Charlie gazed at the few stars he could see over downtown. La Patisserie had been closed for several hours. A few far-off voices called, and when he stopped to listen, he heard the reassuring rumble of a midnight bus and the throaty gospel of the barrel-fire guy who lived near the MARTA station. A freight train rolling slowly through downtown blew its horn.

Feeling restless, Charlie started walking. A block south, on the right side of the street, the flickering neon sign for Max's Place beckoned him. He'd never been inside before and decided to check it out. He listened to soles of his Cole-Haans slap the sidewalk, proud of their echo in the still night air. When he reached Max's, he hesitated before pulling the door's long wooden handle. It was weird to walk into a bar after so many years of sobriety. But things were different now. He'd proved he could handle just about anything, hadn't he? A drink wouldn't be that big a deal. Besides, Max's was the only place open to him right then, so there he was.

Charlie stepped inside to a blast of cold air and funky old R&B, the Bar-Kays' *Holy Ghost*. Max's was nearly empty and a soft reddish glow permeated the place. The carpet smelled of old beer and stale cognac. He glanced at a couple in a corner booth and stepped to the bar. "What'll ya have, buddy?" asked the bartender, a stocky black man with a knife scar on his face. He gazed appreciatively at Charlie's rose while awaiting his order.

"Budweiser." The word just came out. Sounded right. "Yeah."

The bartender placed the bottle on the counter. Charlie slipped him a ten and stared at the beer. A woman in a sleeveless green dress was slouched over a drink a few stools over. She took an interest in Charlie when his change came back. "Hey, baby," she cooed.

When he glanced her way, she gave him a bleary-eyed smile. She had chocolate-brown skin. Her hair was teased out and unruly, and her make-up seemed misapplied, as though her mirror didn't function correctly. She was swaying to the music in a burlesque of seduction. Charlie thought she might have been attractive if she'd kept herself up—but she'd still have that tattoo. He squinted at her. Had she been beaten? Was she crying? Most likely she was a junkie or alcoholic. Maybe she was crashing off crack. He drummed his fingers on the bar, letting them inch toward the bottle.

"Shaundra, leave the gentleman alone," said the bartender, scrutinizing the mug he was drying. "He don't need your nonsense."

She ignored him and bumped down the bar toward Charlie, stool by stool. When she was close, she reached out and touched his cheek, brushing his blue polo shirt. "What happen to you face?"

"Got shot," Charlie said, pulling away from her and picking up the beer.

"My kinda man." She laughed, flashing a gold-tooth smile.

When he looked into her eyes, there was something familiar and terribly wrong about them. They were small and beady, following him everywhere, looking for a chance to bore a hole through him. Creepy. Evil.

"You dress good. You smell good," she said, leaning in close. "Wanna party with me? You look like you need a date. No doubt."

The whiff of beer in his nostrils, the woman coming in on him like a crow on roadkill—all this was wrong. Without taking a sip, Charlie set down the bottle and pushed away from the bar, leaving his change laying there.

"Shaundra workin' her magic again," muttered the man in the booth, who then broke out laughing.

Moving quickly, Charlie stepped outside. Feeling like he'd dodged a bullet, he shuddered in relief in the warm night air. The woman staggered out behind him, her heels clicking on concrete. "This ain't over," she declared. "You and me need to have some fun. Do some business. You a businessman, right?"

He crossed the street, walking faster with each step. She shouted out after him. "I 'member now! I know you! I know you! You owe me! Come back, honey! We can work it out."

Everyone knew Charlie. That was his problem. He quickened his pace and ran back to his loft. Once inside, he looked in the mirror and pounded his fist on the wall beside it. Through gritted teeth he said, "You're an alcoholic, motherfucker. What part of that don't you understand?"

* * *

Charlie dreamed of waking at 4:00 a.m. He heard a revolver's cylinder spin, and the next thing he knew, he was holding a gun to his temple. Beck and Ben were watching him, waiting to take their turns with the gun. A pile of cash lay on the table in front of him. Three men also sat at the table, strangers all, their faces lit by a dangling bulb in a dank, dark-cornered room. "Your turn," the bald man said, then nodded to the children. "Or theirs."

When the alarm rang at 5:00 a.m., Charlie awoke terribly confused.

Where had he been the last hour? He hit the clock's button and looked around. The doors were closed. He touched his chest. He existed. He stuck out his foot. The floor was there. The shadow of a tree limb danced on the ceiling. The shadow was real.

Maybe it was a witching-hour dream, maybe it wasn't. In any case, Charlie wanted to call Thornbriar and check on Beck and Ben, but he worried that Susan would use any ill-timed communication as evidence of stalking and get the restraining order reinstated. But he had to know the kids were all right. He was due at Channel Six's studios at seven o'clock for a live interview with *Atlanta Dawn* host Charlene Guy. That gave him enough time to shower, don his new khaki suit, grab a cup of coffee at the bakery, and drive to Thornbriar—not to stalk, of course, but just to check and see that everything was OK.

And so he found himself slowly driving past the house at 6:10 a.m. A BMW larger than his sat in the driveway. Had to be a 528i. Jet black. Paid for with his child support, no doubt. Wait a minute. Why wouldn't she park it in the garage? He drove on to the stop sign down the street and circled around in the intersection, then backtracked. As he passed by the house again, a gray-haired man in a suit was stepping out the door. Susan, in a bathrobe, kissed him. *Harold? God, he was old.*

Charlie felt his face burn and fought the urge to slam on the brakes. However, he'd taken his foot off the gas, so he was just coasting away. What should he do? What could he do? The little skank was out there cheating on him publicly, with impunity! At the Hanover stoplight, he dialed Muncie's cell.

"What the hey," said the groggy lawyer.

"I want a detective to trail my wife."

"Why?"

"I'm countersuing on grounds of adultery. I need documentation, I tell you!"

"What time is it?" Muncie groaned. "Oh, no. Stalking is bad, Charlie. You're not outside your wife's house right now, are you?"

"Of course I'm outside her house. Otherwise, I'd be inside it and that would be even worse."

Muncie spoke slowly, as if to a child. "Charlie, how far away are you from your wife right now?"

"Infinitely far," Charlie replied.

* * *

Charlie arrived at the Channel Six studio expecting a friendly interview, since he'd never heard of a guest segment on that show turning ugly. *Atlanta Dawn* host Charlene Guy smiled warmly at Charlie when she introduced him to the city's largest morning audience, but the interview quickly became adversarial. Charlene started by asking if Charlie was involved in drug trafficking. He laughed off the question and mentioned the racist death threats he'd been receiving recently. She parried by asking about his "conflict of interest" in writing about his family. The interview went downhill from there: Charlene told him twice to lower his voice, and on one occasion, he suggested that she didn't know what she was talking about.

He staggered out of the studio greatly displeased with TV news, his cheating wife, and life in general. "Six minutes of hell," he called the interview on his way out the door and into the sunshine. Another performance like that and he'd have to get out of town—maybe even move to Canada. In a voice hoarse from all the talking he'd done during the past few days, he'd said some ugly things about the varmints, but he meant every word, especially when he declared that Representative Stanley Cutchins "is a bad joke Forsyth County voters have been playing on the state of Georgia for the past two decades"; "Isaac Cutchins is a thieving murderer"; "My wife's divorce petition is filled with lies"; and "The governor? Don't get me started on *him*."

Charlie consoled himself with a leisurely breakfast at Midtown Diner. He'd just paid the check when he felt his cellphone vibrate. It was Crenshaw. He considered ignoring the call, but their relationship had reached a tipping point, and Crenshaw now gave *him* useful information half the time. Charlie took a deep breath and stepped outside. "What do you want?" he growled, hoping he sounded friendlier than he felt, but not caring much.

"What do you have to say now that your monster's dead?"

"Say what?"

"Isaac. Cutchins. Is. Dead." Silence. "You don't know? My deepest condolences," Crenshaw added with mock sincerity.

"Shit." Charlie grimaced at his tasteless response. *Think, think, think. Say something appropriate. Hmm. Difficult.* "What was it? Heart attack, stroke? Both?"

"Lead poisoning."

"Lead poisoning," Charlie repeated dully.

"Bullet in the brain. Through it, actually. Last night. Messy, from what I hear."

Charlie resisted the urge to shout, *I didn't do it*! "He was *murdered*? Wow."

"No. The family says it's a suicide. You're to blame, you'll be happy to know."

"No. Absolutely not. Pap—Ike Cutchins would never kill himself. That's not in his nature."

"Your mother-in-law—Evangeline Powell ... she still is your mother-in-law, right?"

"Never heard of her."

"Cut the shit. I'm just checking to make sure you haven't snuck off and gotten your divorce yet."

"Oh, you'll know when that happens," he assured the reporter.

"Fair enough. Back to the dead guy. Your mother-in-law says, and I quote here, 'Daddy heard about that pack of lies coming out about him, and he couldn't live with being slandered. That man'—and here I'll insert your name, since she refused to say it—'may as well have stuck the gun to my daddy's head and pulled the trigger himself.' Now, *that*'s a money quote. What say you?"

"I say it's a homicide."

"Really, you think somebody read the book, got pissed off and came up here—"

Charlie thought about Aunt Shirley. *Say it ain't so, Shirlene*! "No, I'm not saying—wait. Are you up there now?"

"Yeah. Your in-laws just finished putting on a show for the cameras. Representative Cutchins was there, and then Tant or Taint—

"—Tantie Marie. It's actually Marie Hastings. His sister."

"Whew. Thanks. I had her down as Stanley Cutchins' wife."

Charlie broke out laughing.

"What's so funny?" Crenshaw demanded. "Oh, the Pulaski stuff. *She's my sister, she's my daughter, she's my wife*." He made a sucking noise through his teeth. "I'm not going there. Hey, there's this huge, hulking guy with a monster truck. Everybody calls him Momo. That's Rhett, right?"

"Rhett Butler Hastings Jr."

"Ostentatious name for a mouth-breather. Well, he says he wants to kill you. Off the record."

"He'll have to wait in line."

"Anyway, much crying, wailing, gnashing of teeth, and blaming you. You'd think they'd just go off and count their money. Look, I'm going to cut you some slack and give you a chance to act properly. So, what's your on-the-record reaction?"

Charlie needed a minute. He wasn't a good mourner to begin with, and especially not in this case. While the world would be a better place without Pappy in it, Charlie figured that if it seemed he was in some way responsible, book sales *could* suffer, and he certainly would be sad about that. He heaved a sigh. "It's unfortunate. My condolences go out to his family. This was a man who caused much pain to others. I hope that, before his life ended, he was able to find repentance."

"Rising above it all to slip the knife in," Crenshaw said. "Nice."

"And bye."

Charlie hummed on the way back to Castlegate. Sunny sky, God's in heaven, all's right with the world. It seemed like a providential plan was playing out. As he approached the lofts, he saw a spectacle: Two news trucks had collided in front of La Patisserie. Amy the baker, all in white, with her baseball cap on backwards, stood on the sidewalk, snapping photos as two TV cameramen yelled at each other and reporters—one white male, one black female—wandered around in circles, wearing dazed expressions and holding disconnected microphones. The feeding frenzy had begun. Or perhaps the End Times were near. In either case, the oblivious reporters didn't notice Charlie, and he escaped undetected.

A few minutes after he'd parked in the garage, he watched Charlene Guy's face fill the screen during a *Channel Six Action News Breaking News Alert*. "Go ahead, Dave," she said.

"Charlene, Forsyth deputies are asking why a man nearly one hundred years old would kill himself, but relatives say they know the answer. This," Decker said, holding up *American Monster*. "The latest effort by Charles Sherman, whose previous book on Forsyth County made waves earlier this year."

"It's still making waves, jerkwad," Charlie told the TV.

The shot cut to Evangeline, wearing dark sunglasses. "It's that pack of lies what did it," she declared.

Charlie stared in fascinated horror as Susan's kinfolk took turns in front of the camera to trash him. He plopped on the sofa. When his cell rang, he shouted "No comment" without picking it up.

Tantie Marie yelled off-camera: "He didn't want to go to the nursing—"

"Hush up," said a voice off-camera that Charlie recognized as Stanley's.

Evangeline continued: "That, that—I don't know what to call him—"

"Estranged son-in-law," Charlie suggested.

"—has libeled and slandered a good man. Daddy couldn't live with it."

The cellphone rang again. Charlie waited for it to quit, then checked his voicemail. "You have thirty unheard messages. *Mailbox full.*" Someone was giving out his number like candy on Halloween.

When Channel Six cut to a replay of Charlie's disastrous interview, he turned off the TV and listened to messages, deleting them as he went. One from Susan, simple and cold: "It would be best if you didn't attend the funeral." That was a severe understatement, considering the history of violence at varmint burials. He wondered if Shirley/Arlene—if she wasn't in jail for murder at the time—would pay her disrespects as her father lay in his coffin. *There will be spit.*

Charlie checked Amazon.com. *American Monster* was No. 5. People were buying *Flight*, too. Sales had risen into the top 100 for the first time since Charlie's last book tour. But he really was sad that the old man had met his end this way. He would have preferred to see Pappy die in jail.

* * *

At least a dozen people knocked in vain on Charlie's door that day. When he left the apartment that afternoon, he had the good sense to peer around the elevator door before stepping out into the glass-walled vestibule. He could see into the bakery and through the garage entrance to the street. The coast was *not* clear. While the wrecked news trucks had been towed away, a pack of reporters now camped out in La Patisserie. No way was he doing interviews when he was considered an accomplice to suicide.

He returned to his apartment and exited the patio door, rattling down the fire escape's iron steps. He sprinted away, running beside the razor wire-topped fence at the property's back boundary without looking at that telltale DVD of Tawny gleaming in the sunlight. After three blocks, he slowed down. It was too hot to be on the lam. At Barista's, he got a bottle of water and an iced café Americano. He sat on the patio under an umbrella and plotted his next move. Avoiding the media was the only tactic he could think of.

Charlie thought he saw a reporter walking toward him and ducked behind the low patio wall, knocking his cellphone out of his pocket. When he reached down to pick it up, it spoke to him: "Charles Sherman? Are you there? Answer me!"

He peered over the wall like a soldier engaged in trench warfare. False alarm on the reporter. Just a normal person. "Hello?"

"Charles! Where have you been? We've been trying to reach you all day!" It was Randall Blaine, Brubaker's head publicist. "I've got Spence Greene on the line."

"I hate three-way calls," Charlie said.

"Too bad. We've got the opportunity to go on national TV, but we have to act quickly."

"I don't know if you've heard, but Ike Cutchins is dead."

"Yes!" Greene hissed, making his presence known. "Opportunity of a lifetime!"

"People think I killed him. I'm laying low."

"Why? Do people think you put a bullet in his head?"

"They think I might as well have," Charlie said with a hillbilly twang. "Anyway, I was on *Atlanta Dawn* today. The book is getting plenty of publicity without any need of putting my scarred face on TV again, especially under hostile circumstances."

"Not enough publicity," the publisher grunted. "You're not number one yet. You've got to get your mind right on this, brother."

"What show do you want me to do?"

"Matthew Steele!"

"No. Not *Steele*." Charlie sneered. "No way."

"Yes. Way," Greene said. "I heard you didn't return the man's phone call when he reached out to you *himself*. What the *ef* is wrong with you?"

"That must be one of my eight hundred and ninety-five unheard messages."

"Five are from me," the publicist pointed out.

"I've seen that show. Not that I'm proud to admit it. I'm not going on Steele with the varmints. They'd have home field advantage!"

"We insist," said Greene. "Your contract specifically states that you will actively participate with the media to promote the book."

"Does the contract say I have to be a media whore?"

"In no uncertain terms," Greene said. "Look, millions of people watch the show."

"But none of them *read*," Charlie protested. "It's not my audience!"

"Do it," Greene growled. "Don't be hard to work with."

"I held a news conference *at my own expense*. Today, I was on TV and also talked to a reporter. One I'm not particularly fond of anymore."

"Charles, most authors—hell, ninety-nine percent of them—would *kill* for this chance."

"Don't you see? People think that's precisely what *I* did! Let's just—"

"You're going to reach an entirely new audience," Blaine said. "People who need to know lynching is wrong, damn it! It's like, just say 'no' to mob violence."

"So go there," Greene said. "Lend dignity to the program."

"That's a virgin in a whorehouse argument," Charlie said.

"You, sir, are no virgin."

"Yeah, but I'm an ascetic." Charlie gripped his phone tightly while he considered throwing it across the street, then relented. "Shit. All right."

"That's my bestselling author! Talk to you later."

Greene hung up; the publicist stayed on. "You'll fly to Chicago Sunday for a Monday taping. Steele's people will call you with arrangements. Let me know if you need anything else."

"I want Oprah!" Charlie wailed. "She understands this Forsyth County shit!"

After the phone call, Charlie snuck back to the loft and watched Matthew Steele's tried-and-true formula of bright lights, dim crowd. Steele, a short man with wavy blonde hair, wore a sharply tailored black suit. On this show, a mother and daughter—both immense, with teased-out hair—were pregnant by the same man. It was the standard fare: bleeped expletives, hair pulling, and security guards dragging contestants back to their chairs, where they'd rest during the commercial breaks and come out swinging for the next round. At the end of the show, Steele turned to the audience and gave a what-can-I-do? shrug. "Well, I guess the lesson for today is, 'Don't foul your own nest.'" Brightening, he said, "If you thought this was something, wait until you hear what we've got lined up for next week, when a controversial bestselling author takes on folks from Forsyth County, Georgia, lynching capital of America! Join us Tuesday for 'Racist Murderers and the In-laws Who Rat Them Out!'"

Charlie shook his head in disbelief. The show had been taped the day before, when Charlie had no intention of appearing on it. So how could Steele make such an assumption? What a presumptuous, arrogant, sleazy bastard! The fact that he was prescient made it even worse.

Following the show, Charlie went downstairs to check his mail. He was standing in the vestibule reading a letter from Satalin politely reminding him to vacate the premises by the end of the month when someone grabbed him from behind. On the verge of delivering a sharp elbow, he realized his attacker smelled too good to be a varmint assassin. He turned to face Dana, her dark eyes merry with mischief. Despite his lingering hurt over her liaison with the photographer, he was happy to see her. Still, he had to say something. "You've been ignoring me."

"I'm sorry." She looked down and pouted. "I've been busy. Don't be mad at me. I *vill* make it up to you."

He regarded her suspiciously. "When?"

She pursed her lips. "Soon. Vot's that?" she asked, pointing at a lavender envelope.

"Don't know. Forwarded by Fortress's publicity department. From Aimee Duprelier."

"*The* Aimee Duprelier?"

He wrinkled his face. "How many could there be?" He opened it up. "I am invited to ... a fundraiser for Redeemer Wilson."

"A party! Take me!" she cried out, bubbling like a schoolgirl.

Charlie gave her a bemused laugh. "Do you know her?"

"Who doesn't? She's very rich. This is a great opportunity ... to get out and have some fun ... vith you, you stick-in-the-mudge."

"Mud. Just when I'm going back into hiding," he said, punching the elevator button.

"Vot for, this time?"

He squinted at her, and gave her a John Wayne drawl: "They say I killed a man, Missy."

Dana giggled. "You are constantly entertaining. And the most dangerous writer I know." She glanced over her shoulder while stepping into the elevator, then put a hand on his chest. He pressed a floor button. She didn't. Was she going to—

Her cellphone broke out in balalaika music. Suddenly she was talking in her native tongue. He raised a brow as the doors opened on his floor. Dana closed her phone and frowned. "Business crisis."

"Temperamental artist?"

"Temperamental customer," she muttered darkly. "I vas hoping to spend time vith you."

Charlie sulked. The doors banged shut on him, then bounced open. "Don't be disappointed," she said, patting his scarred cheek. "The party's only two days avay. You take me?"

"You bet." She kissed him lightly on the lips and pressed her floor button. He backed out of the elevator and the doors closed. He vowed to himself that if she said "take me" one more time, he would.

Crenshaw appeared beside him.

"Whoa," Charlie said, recoiling and falling against the wall, then righting himself. "What do you want?"

"The GBI released the results of lab tests from the Christmas Eve bombing. They say they found a *huge amount* of goat blood at the scene, along with your fingerprints. They figure some kind of animal sacrifice was involved." Crenshaw paused.

"Go on."

"Do you understand that sources in a major law enforcement agency claim that you worship the devil?"

Those assholes Finch and Drew, no doubt. Charlie laughed. "Sorry, I'm not that religious." He slipped his key in the lock. When he opened the door and stepped inside, Crenshaw tried to follow. Charlie pushed him back.

"Nice place," Crenshaw said as the door closed in his face. "So!" he shouted through the door. "Do you have any comment?"

"Yeah!" Charlie shouted back. "The part about the goats ain't true!"

Charlie was furious that his tax dollars helped fund an agency that would say such things about him. Spence Greene and Blaine would love it, of course, since any publicity was good publicity, so far as they were concerned. As for the blood, he was glad it wasn't human and fortunate it hadn't been his. As far as the devil was concerned, well, the deal was done, whatever it was. He had the better part of a million dollars in the bank and a hot date lined up for Saturday night. No use worrying whether there was hell to pay, he told himself, but he was fighting a nagging fear that those assholes might be right.

Chapter Twenty-Four

Friday morning, Charlie temporarily put thoughts of the devil aside and read the e-mail from his attorney confirming his right to pick up his kids that evening and keep them for twenty-four hours. "Be cool. Be very cool," Muncie cautioned. "Susan is hostile, holding you responsible for her grandfather's death, and wants to revoke your visitation rights immediately, but I worked with her lawyer and got her to back off."

While Charlie was debating whether to celebrate his victory or buy an athletic cup for his next trip to Thornbriar, he received another e-mail, this one from his publisher:

> Charles,
>
> Cutchins politician threatens to sue for libel if we don't pull the book. Since our lawyers vetted the ms and the main bad guy is dead, I'll stand firm. But if you lose, we don't pay for the defense. If there's anything we need to step back from, better let me know. Now. Just got off the phone with Cutchins attorney, Georgia ex-governor—charming fellow, btw.
>
> Spence
>
> PS They claim you faked footnotes in the other book. I said we have nothing to do with that. I hope for your sake that's another of their lies. They are lies, aren't they?
>
> PPS Be a man. Answer your phone.

When the phone buzzed, Charlie answered it manfully. It was Crenshaw. Charlie refused to talk until he read the morning paper—the real one, not the Internet version, so he could see his relative importance—and the reporter didn't want to hang up, so Charlie slipped on sandals and stayed on the line while he padded downstairs to get a copy of the *Atlanta Journal-Constitution*. The article was atop the front: "Target of Lynching Book Kills Self."

Target? *What the hell does that mean*? Charlie perused the article, then said, "Hey, where's the devil-worship stuff?"

"It was not for attribution."

"As opposed to off the record," Charlie said. "Cowards."

"Yeah. Managing editor wouldn't let me print it. No cheap shots without a name. Journalistic ethics, or some such shit. Just when it's getting interesting, too. I think it's a blatant conflict of interest. I mean, most editors worship the devil, too. You were an editor once, right?"

"Yeah."

"See what I'm sayin'? You should thank them at your next black mass."

"I'll be sure to do that. Moving right along …"

"So, if it wasn't a suicide, as you maintain, who do you think did it?"

"No comment."

"That's worthless. By the way, the Forsyth DA calls you 'Miss Marple.' He doesn't appreciate your speculation on the manner of death. But that's not what I'm working on. I got a whole new thing. Yesterday I talked to some history professors. They had questions about the documentation for *Flight from Forsyth*."

"Not *that* again. Why is it coming up now?" Charlie asked, though he knew that his work represented the mule's toe in the tent on reparations, so to speak. Now he feared he'd screwed the mule.

"Oh, to attack your credibility, definitely," Crenshaw said. "And I get to watch. Oh boy."

"Old news. I'm concentrating on *American Monster* now, so—"

"Charlie. Charlie. You promised me documentation a year and a half ago."

"Nuh-uh."

"Dude, I am so tired of you and the history you rode in on."

"Whatever," Charlie said. "Gotta go."

* * *

After spending the afternoon cruising bookstores, signing *Monsters*, and buying a small library for Beck and Ben, Charlie arrived at Thornbriar just before six o'clock. It was hot and sunny, with a few hours of daylight left. When she answered the door, Susan was wearing a white summer dress. She looked good, except for her glower.

"Hey," he said.

"I told them Pappy died. They're sad, of course. I'm not taking them up there for the service."

"When's the funeral?"

"You are *not* coming." Her voice could have carved an ice sculpture.

"No, of course not." He thought he heard something inside. Harold? He'd been repeatedly warned to be cool during his visit, but he pushed his head inside the door, anyway. "Sirius?"

Susan pushed back. He looked into her eyes. They were smoldering like a poorly doused campfire. *What the hell did you do to my dog*? "Do you want to talk?" he asked.

"Not to you."

"Give your mother my condolences."

"Fuck you, Charlie."

"No. Really. It's a terrible way to die, to have somebody kill you."

She looked at him in disbelief. "What do you mean? *You* killed him with that book, even if—"

"I didn't pull the trigger myself," Charlie twanged.

She clamped her jaw shut. He could tell she was in a slapping mood; he took a step backward.

"It's not just about him." Shining tears of anger filled her eyes. "You called me a *mutant*. You're an asshole."

Ah, so that was it. He had debated whether to put that in the book. "That just means I think more highly of you than the varmints. Anyway, you called me a pervert."

"The difference is, you put it in a book."

Now it was his turn to show outrage. "You put it in court documents!"

"OK," she said, carelessly brushing back her hair. "We're getting nowhere."

The powder keg was defused when Beck and Ben marched up, freshly scrubbed and dressed in bright, clean clothes, wearing backpacks like they were going to their first day of school.

"Where's Sirius?" Charlie asked Ben.

"In the back yard."

Charlie gave Susan the evil eye. "Lawyers didn't say anything about not seeing my dog."

Susan gave it back. "Didn't say anything about seeing him, either, did they?" She broke off the staredown to stoop for goodbye kisses. "Bring them back tomorrow by six." To the kids, she said, "I'll miss you."

"Miss you too," Beck said, embracing her. Ben got dragged into the group hug, looking up at his father for something Charlie couldn't give.

Susan pushed them out and closed the door. Charlie stared at it and shook his head before turning to tend his children. He buckled the kids into their booster seats, then climbed behind the wheel. When he started to back out, a horn honked behind him. That obnoxiously big BMW had snuck up behind him and was waiting to take his place—or bugger his car. So she was going out, probably to celebrate being one step closer to all that money. Despite his joy at being with his kids, he resented the fact that Susan was using him as a babysitter so that she could step out on him. Charlie couldn't wait to see what Muncie's detective dug up.

"Always carry a spare." Charlie scratched his nose with his middle finger as he drove by Harold. "Let's go eat."

Charlie took the kids to Chik-fil-A for dinner. To his disappointment, they didn't talk much. Everything was basic with Ben ("Do you still have rats?"); Beck wasn't in a talkative mood. They didn't ask him when he was coming back, something they'd always done before. Maybe they'd accepted his disappearance, or perhaps he'd already been replaced. Once he thought he heard Ben say "Harold," but Beck quickly shushed her little brother. Charlie was afraid to ask them about the man, fearing that he wouldn't like their answers.

At the loft, Beck and Ben ran around and bounced on the bed. They agreed that this place was much nicer than the dungeon, and they especially liked the big TV. No rats, he assured them. Charlie laid out mats and placed sleeping bags on them, then read aloud from a new Lemony Snicket book. After that, they camped out on the floor and watched a movie. Charlie fell asleep with them, waking to find Ben cuddled next to him, breathing warm and soft in his ear. *My boy*. Tears welled in Charlie's eyes. Being close to his kids made sleeping on the cold concrete floor worth the discomfort, so he stayed there all night.

And woke up with a stiff back.

For breakfast, he took them to the bakery. Amy marveled at the kids as they ate muffins and drank juice. Charlie sipped coffee and read the paper, amazed that it didn't mention his name. He was glad, for even he had grown tired of seeing his name in the news. Then he thought of that scumbag Matthew Steele and shuddered. He glanced at his watch and realized that Pappy's funeral had started. The burial had been pushed up a day, since several family members would travel to Chicago Sunday for Monday's taping of the Steele show. Charlie shuddered at the thought of sharing a flight with them.

After flying kites in Piedmont Park and visiting Fernbank Museum, Charlie returned to Thornbriar promptly at six. The garage was open. Sitting inside was a new silver Mercedes C300 sedan with dealer tags. So that was her ride now. He wondered how much of his child-support money had gone to the down payment.

Susan, dressed in black, opened the door. After the kids went inside, she told Charlie, "From now on, don't get out of the car."

He looked at her like she was crazy. "I'm going to walk them to the door."

"I can't even stand to have you on the property."

"Y'all get right testy about real estate, don't you?"

"I can't condone what you've done."

"What, tell the truth? If Pappy and his supporters, including you, can't handle it, that's your problem. You should come to the light."

"*You're* the light?" she scoffed. "Listen. I love my family. And I'll always protect them." She took a deep breath. "Don't ever set foot in this house again. Consider it fair warning. You know what I'm saying."

"I assume you're telling me you'll kill me in my own house."

"Get over the notion that it's your house."

"And you know the rule we've always had. There better not be any guns in there."

"You don't make the rules anymore."

"Those are my kids, too."

"I don't want to talk to you. Not after what I went through today. You should go. So go."

"You're really hateful."

She laughed bitterly. "I'm a varmint. Can't help it."

Charlie expected her to slam the door in his face, but instead she stood there looking slender and really quite beautiful in an ugly way, watching him get in his car and back into the street.

Charlie returned to the loft and dressed for Aimee Duprelier's Buckhead soirée. He thought he looked rakish in his seersucker suit and blue polo shirt with suede bucks, along with new rimless glasses—part of his spending spree for the upcoming "Monster Book Tour."

Just after eight, Dana knocked on his door. She was wearing a little black dress; her raven hair was lustrous. She twirled. "You like?"

"Always. Come in."

She gave him a promising smile. "Do you have anything to drink?"

"We must go out for that. My drinking days are over." It helped to remind himself of that.

She pursed her lips thoughtfully. "Ve'll have to go to my place for a nightcap then, von't ve?" she asked, her voice an exotic purr.

Yes. This would be the night. *Finally.* He fought back a whimper of desire. As they left, Charlie caught their reflection in the wall mirror and thought they looked like models in an upscale vodka ad. He was glad to see that she wasn't a vampire. (With all the supernatural crap he'd been through, he was beginning to wonder.)

In the hall, she took his arm. "I like your new look. Prosperous. Less of a bloody mess than I'm used to seeing." She laughed and squeezed his bicep.

In the garage, Dana ran her fingers along his new BMW's trunk. "I like." And then she ran her fingers along his face. "I like this, too. It's … rugged."

Charlie cast a glance back toward the elevator, then reluctantly opened the car door for her. On their way to Buckhead, Dana told Charlie about their hostess in a clipped, Eastern European news-anchor delivery: "Aimee got half the company in the divorce. It vas privately held back then … and not vorth nearly so much as it is now. They did an IPO and raised three hundred and fifty million. Baldvin sold off his stock and she ended up vith the controlling share. Now he's an employee in his own company, and she votes on all his raises. He's probably the only chief executive officer in Atlanta vithout a stock option."

"How do you know so much about her?"

She gave him a knowing smile. "An art dealer has to know these things. I am so looking forward to meeting her … and her money."

"Dana the Dangerous."

She gave him an impish grin. "You don't mind, do you?"

"No. Should be fun."

* * *

Aimee Duprelier's Buckhead "cottage" seemed like a cross between a mansion and a grand hotel. It boasted Italian marble in a foyer with a twenty-five-foot ceiling and wide, sweeping staircases left and right. As Charlie and Dana entered, Aimee broke away from a conversation to greet the new arrivals underneath a chandelier that looked like it cost more than Charlie's BMW. "Why,

Charles Sherman!" she cried out, her penciled eyebrows etched in flight. Aimee—a woman of indeterminate age, heavily bejeweled yet somewhat plain-looking, with the skin on her face unnaturally tight—wore an emerald green dress with a gigantic bow in the back. "Someone just told me you live in a *dungeon*," she whispered conspiratorially as she touched his arm.

Charlie found her air of familiarity amusing. "I used to. Now I live in a castle, but it's under siege."

Aimee gave him a high, throaty giggle. "You're as funny as you are notorious. I've been reading about you every day. You've caused quite a stir with that new book of yours."

"Oh, that." He introduced his date to the hostess. A couple entered and Aimee turned to greet them. Dana's dark eyes darted about. Was she casing the joint? Recalling the outcome of the GQ photo shoot, he kept a grip on her arm. When he regained Aimee's attention, Charlie asked, "Is Redeemer here?"

"No, unfortunately. The cancer."

"Oh, no. That's terrible. Last time I saw him—I was fixing the door on his church—he wasn't doing well." He didn't mention that Redeemer seemed to be on a bender at the time.

Her face grew long. "Do you know him well?" She took a confidential tone, as if asking Charlie to admit he was a liberal.

"Oh, sure," Charlie said breezily. "I interviewed him for *Flight from Forsyth*, and spent Thanksgiving washing pots and pans at the Hunger Palace."

"Ah, a man of many talents." She laughed. "Feel free to help out in the kitchen."

He gave her a wry smile.

"He really is in a bad way," she said. "I don't think he'll march again. Of course, that's not what I'm fundraising for." She gave him a little laugh that he found disturbing. He wondered if Redeemer had any intention of setting foot in this place, regardless of his health. These were not his people.

"Wouldn't bother me if it was."

"This is for the *homeless*," she chided. "Not that reparations thing." She waved her hand to dismiss the thought. "Thank God that bill in the legislature died, right?"

Charlie frowned. Something sounded wrong about the way she'd said that, even though he was even more thankful for that outcome. Before he could respond, Dana chimed in. "Charles is making a contribution, aren't you, sweetie?"

Aimee pointed to a basket sitting on the table beside the book. "Put it there."

Charlie pulled out his checkbook and wrote a check for $1,000. Easy come, easy go. This was the sort of thing wealthy people did, he supposed.

Still, this strengthened the feeling he had that Dana Colescu was one very expensive person to hang with.

Aimee stood at his shoulder. "To Redeemer Wilson's—"

"Holy Way House and Hunger Palace Foundation," Charlie said. He really did almost know the man.

Aimee slid away once the money was in the basket.

"Let's vork the room," Dana whispered in Charlie's left ear. "By the vay, her gown's a Kabertigan. As a writer, you should know."

"She's wearing enough diamonds to keep an African civil war going," Charlie observed.

They drifted into a large, crowded parlor buzzing with conversation. Expensive colognes and perfumes vied for Charlie's attention. Near the front window, a tuxedoed black man played a Cole Porter tune on a grand piano. Charlie recognized several African-American partygoers as members of the city's political elite. The look was semi-formal: Many men wore suits, a young Indian woman wore a sari, and an older Japanese man also wore a tuxedo.

The event was half charity ball, half trade mission. Welcome to Atlanta.

"I'm famished," Dana said, moving toward the food table. "Vould you get me gin and tonic?"

Charlie ordered Dana's drink, along with a Diet Coke for himself. The green-eyed black bartender gave Charlie's scar an appreciative glance. While Dana ate finger sandwiches from a plate, Charlie served as her drink caddy and watched men steal glances at his date when their wives weren't looking, even though plenty of women were also checking out Dana.

When she finished eating, Dana grabbed her drink and said, "I'm going to mingle and try to sell some paintings. Vy don't you find your next true crime story?" She laughed lightly as she glanced around the room. "Looks like here there are plenty of evildoers," she said, savoring the last word.

Left on his own, Charlie stepped out onto the patio, returning seconds later, coughing, his eyes stinging from cigar smoke. After that, he gave himself a tour of the house—those parts that weren't cordoned off. He paused at the top of the wide, curving marble stairs to gaze down on Atlanta's elite. He suspected they'd all done something similar to Pappy's misdeeds—or at the very least, inherited their grandfathers' ill-gotten gains. In any case, he was looking at the result of nearly 300 years of affirmative action for white folks.

Aimee looked up from the foyer and beckoned him to join her. Then she called out to a distinguished-looking man in a gray suit: "Pitts, come here, you rascal you." She introduced the two men, though Charlie recognized W.

Pitts Scudder from countless photos in the newspaper. He was the CEO of Susan's bank. In fact, Scudder had interviewed Susan for her first job in Atlanta many years ago, when he was a lowly VP. Charlie saw no point in mentioning their connection, however.

"Ah, Sherman!" Scudder said, rolling his eyes as he shook Charlie's hand. "You've certainly got things stirred up in Forsyth. What's the latest on the development of the Cutchins land?"

"Minerva Doe's attorney filed a lawsuit Friday."

Scudder shook his head. "That's going nowhere."

"I don't know about that. She has a strong claim. There was extortion."

Scudder gave him a stern look, then broke it off with a scoff. "Don't be ridiculous. Be a shame if that got any traction. I know the developer. Good man. Played a round with him just last week. I'm sure he'll survive any so-called *exposé*. Or should I say, airing of a family's dirty laundry?"

Charlie grinned. "There's always that chance, isn't there? Next time you two go golfing, tell him to settle." He patted the banker on the shoulder for good measure.

The banker gritted his teeth at the patronizing gesture. Aimee said, "Let's change the subject."

"Good idea," Scudder said. "Aimee, did you know this muckraker's wife—or is it ex-wife?—is one of my employees? She's testifying for the bank in an upcoming class-action case. Charming woman. Always liked her. I don't think she shares Mr. Sherman's views on affirmative action."

"What case is that, Pitts?" she asked.

"It seems one of our African-American employees didn't get a promotion and decided to involve all her friends. They'll lose, of course. Perhaps Mr. Sherman could share his royalties with them. That's the way you liberals work, isn't it? Now, if you'll excuse me." He bowed to Aimee and turned his back on Charlie as he walked off.

Charlie opened his mouth to say something witty and scathing, but Aimee was already drifting away. Just as well, since he could only come up with profanities. Scudder joined some friends across the room. Charlie saw the glint of contempt in Scudder's eyes as the banker glanced back at him and gestured over his shoulder with a thumb. He said something Charlie couldn't make out, but if he'd lip-read correctly, Scudder had just bragged about fucking "that asshole's wife." His buddies guffawed.

No. It couldn't be.

Charlie knew he had to get out of there. "Excuse me," he said, squeezing past two gossiping doyennes in a hall on his way to the kitchen. He found Dana chatting up the caterer. He felt a pang of jealousy and a sense of dread, suspecting that screwing the help was just her way of doing business. He whispered, "This party's gone south. We need to go before I kick somebody's ass."

Dana took the caterer's business card and walked with Charlie to the foyer. There they saw Charlene Guy laughing merrily, her arm interlocked with that of her escort, a handsome blue-eyed man in a tux with a rim-collared shirt. Charlene gave Charlie a purposefully nasty glare. She looked like she was going to pull a microphone out of her black clutch purse and continue the disastrous early-morning interview they'd conducted earlier that week. Charlie pivoted away, dragging Dana behind.

When he found Aimee, Charlie said, "Wonderful time. Gotta go."

"But it's so early!" Aimee protested.

"Sorry," Charlie said. "I have pumpkin issues." He left her laughing.

Once out the door, Charlie breathed a sigh of relief. At least Dana was still with him.

"I have come to the conclusion," Dana said as Charlie pulled her along, "that those vere not your people."

"No, they're not. Then again, I'm not even sure I have people."

"They're not mine, either," she confessed as they got to the car. "I only came to try and separate them from their money. Vot is your excuse?"

"I guess I just wanted to see how the other half lived. I'd rather wash dishes at Redeemer Wilson's soup kitchen than party with these folks."

"Vell then, you should."

"I should."

The drive to Castlegate seemed to take forever, due to Charlie's anticipation of a happy ending to the night. As soon as he parked in the garage, Dana popped out of the car, laughing gaily. "Come on! I've been vaiting for such a long time. When I saw you looking like burly truck driver at Jean's coffeehouse, I said to her, 'I *vant* to taste that.'"

And he *vanted* her, too. Once they were inside the vestibule, she pressed the elevator button insistently. The doors opened to reveal a stranger in a suit. "Which floor?" he asked.

Before Charlie could step inside, Dana dug her fingers into his arm and pulled back.

"Aren't you getting off?" she asked.

The man smiled and said, "Of course."

After he exited, Charlie and Dana stepped inside and the elevator door closed. "Let's go to your place," she said.

"I thought you wanted—OK." Charlie pressed the button for his floor.

As the elevator rose, Dana gave Charlie a tight-lipped smile.

The doors clanked open and Charlie looked down the corridor. He stepped out, and Dana followed a half-step behind. Suddenly Charlie was staring down the barrel of a pistol. From the corner of his eye, he saw another armed man grab Dana's right hand as she reached into her purse. He pulled her thumb back, hard. She shrieked in pain, and a black Glock automatic flew from her hand and hit the floor. The man cinched her waist from behind and lifted her off the floor.

Charlie was about to go for the gun pointed at him—multiple attempts on his life had made him fatalistic—when a badge holder flopped open in front of his face. "FBI," the man said. A rumble of footsteps came from the stairwell. Seconds later, a SWAT team burst through the exit door into the hall. With a dazed expression, Charlie looked around, his hands in the air. A half-dozen helmeted men in body armor pointed assault weapons at him.

Dana would not go gently; still held from behind, she reared up and kicked a SWAT member in the helmet with both feet, knocking him to his knees. Two other men grabbed her legs. She was hogtied in mid-air, hair disheveled, spitting and spewing foreign curses, her right breast exposed and flopping.

"Rodika Arcos, we have warrants for your arrest," said a stocky white man with bristly gray hair—FBI Agent Brisco, who looked like he'd neglected to shave his head for a week.

"Rodika Arcos? There must be some mistake," Charlie said.

Four men carried the writhing, screaming woman to the open elevator. Charlie, stunned and shocked, remained passive as an agent pressed his face to the wall and cuffed his hands behind him. A door opened and a neighbor peeked out, then disappeared.

"Am I under arrest?" Charlie asked.

"Not yet," said Brisco. "Come downstairs with us." Not that there was a choice with a SWAT member holding each arm. Charlie walked down the stairs under his own power, thereby avoiding Dana/Rodika's rough treatment. Once outside, Brisco called Charlie over to a spot on the sidewalk in front of the bakery while three SWAT members stood nearby, their assault weapons pointed in the air.

Dana got special treatment. A black SUV roared up the street and squealed to a stop in front of the garage. As she was stuffed into the back seat, she shouted, "Cancel my dentist appointment!"

"What's that about?" Brisco asked Charlie.

"I have no idea," Charlie said as he watched the SUV speed off, even though he did.

As it turned out, Brisco knew who Charlie was and treated him with a modicum of respect. He uncuffed the writer for a sidewalk interview that convinced both men Charlie didn't know much about Dana/Rodika, except that she was incredibly hot. Brisco then released Charlie without telling him why she'd been arrested, though Charlie was sure the charges would be exotic, since that's how she rolled.

Back in his apartment, Charlie fretted. Why couldn't they have busted her in the morning, after he'd spent the night with her? And should he, as a gentleman, post bond? Nah. She was a flight risk. Based on her travel habits, a frequent flight risk. Still, he owed her some consideration in exchange for what she'd done for him when he'd been shot. He dug up the bill for his root canal and cap and called the dentist's office. He realized that his phone might be tapped, but at this point, what did it matter? The voicemail message gave him an emergency phone contact. When he called the second number, a woman answered. "Buna Zeewa."

"Doctor Blaga, please. It's an emergency."

A moment later a man said, "Hallo. Who iz thiss?"

"A friend of Dana Colescu. Or Rodika Arcos. The FBI arrested her about an hour ago and took her … I don't know where, actually. She asked me to call you and cancel her appointment … whatever that means."

Apparently, Charlie had said too much. Foreign curses filled his ear, and the man hung up.

After a few minutes of moping, Charlie remembered he needed to check on something. He went downstairs and bought an early edition of Sunday's paper from the rack in front of the bakery. Atop the front page: "Sherman's March Through Forsyth." The subhead: "Do Author's Character Defects Mar Books?"

Another story inside bothered him more: "Sherman's Sources Disputed." Crenshaw had interviewed historians from Emory University and the University of Georgia, who didn't say anything conclusive. Their professorial hemming and hawing served mainly as ballast. The real accusations came from David Clark, Cecil Montgomery's self-appointed replacement as local historian. "Bullshit!" Charlie cried out and stomped around in a circle in front of the bakery. *There is a special place in hell for historians who bear false witness … against those that do God's will, that is.*

Charlie was so restless from the night's tumult and drama that he couldn't sit still, let alone lie down and sleep before the trip to Chicago, where he and his character defects would match wits with varmints on that abominable TV show. Having no idea where he would end up, he hopped into his BMW and drove into the night. He headed north on the Downtown Connector, then northeast on I-85. Before he knew it, the car was idling on Thornbriar Circle and Charlie was staring at his old house, wishing he was inside it. He even missed Susan, if only because she held a broken-off piece of him and wouldn't give it back. That nasty BMW now occupied his old spot in the driveway, and another man slept in his former bed beside Susan, who was breaking vows and commandments left and right. But mainly she'd been lying. First with Bryan. Now with Harold.

Had Susan slept with Scudder, too? Charlie's face burned hot with anger and jealousy. He couldn't drive the horrific possibility out of his mind that Scudder was Ben's father. But when Charlie thought about it, Ben did resemble Susan's CEO. *No! Don't go there!* He couldn't help himself, however. He kept matching the bank president's face to his son's until one became the other. He told himself that no matter who the father was, Ben was his son. This was the same concept Minerva had tried to preach to him about John Riggins. At the time, Charlie had been too involved with his own version of the truth to listen to hers.

He is my son, Charlie told himself. *And I know better than anyone on earth that he can be taken from me.*

And what about Beck?

Was this the payoff for his heroic efforts on the Almighty's behalf? Had he fulfilled his contract only to be mocked and have his children stolen from him? This was an outrage on a cosmic scale: Not only were they being stolen from him, but now he was being stolen from them, his genes sucked out of them like he'd never existed. Why was his reward this crushing loneliness? No, this couldn't be Satan he was dealing with. Even the devil would have cut a dude a better deal than this. The devil was logical and cunning. This was random and cruel, to give him a test that had all wrong answers.

Charlie knew he should leave before something else weird happened. He drove off and circled the city on I-285 until he came to the Memorial Drive exit. He took it, turning away from the giant Confederate monument at Stone Mountain and heading west toward Atlanta, listening to a late-night DJ pretend the world was a party. When he reached Redeemer's church, Charlie pulled into the parking lot. Aimee had hinted that Redeemer was dying. The man's dream—his shelter for the homeless—was withering away, too. Charlie wondered where the money would go. Probably to pay Redeemer's medical bills, but no one would admit that, because it would sound *corrupt*, and some twenty-four-year-old TV reporter might get hold of the story.

Charlie wasn't there looking for God or answers this time. He was looking for Tawny. It had been months since he'd seen her, and now maybe it was time …

A car barreled past on Memorial, weaving in and out of its lane, horn blaring. This part of town was surreal in the middle of the night. Certainly not a safe place for his BMW. As he sat with the engine idling, contemplating how to proceed, a woman's unearthly screams tore the air.

They seemed to be coming from down the street.

What was he thinking, coming to this place? There was nothing he could do but save himself. He drove off, testing the car's acceleration. On the way back to Castlegate, he managed to convince himself that the cries of torment hadn't come from the church.

* * *

Fueled by bad news and lack of sleep, Charlie's depression was in full force Sunday morning. When the alarm rang, he rolled over and looked at the clock. If he hurried, he could eat breakfast and catch his flight to Chicago. On the other hand, if he went back to sleep, he'd miss it. An easy choice: He would let the varmints have their undisputed say. They could steal hotel towels, too, for all he cared. Charlie turned off his phone and avoided the computer. When he finally got up, he watched a baseball game on television, then an old movie. After that, he listened to jazz. He figured that if the food held out, he wouldn't have to leave the loft until Friday, when he was due in court to battle Susan for the kids.

Sunday bled into Monday. Just before dawn, Charlie woke up. Curious about Dana's fate, he ambled downstairs to get a newspaper. Her late-night arrest hadn't made Sunday's paper, but now it was front-page news. Only then did Charlie learn what had kept Rodika Arcos flying all over the world: international art fraud, drug smuggling, gunrunning, and—according to Romanian authorities—espionage and conspiracy to commit murder. There were also "crimes against humanity" on her rap sheet, stemming from the time she spent with a Serbian man. Then, her name had been Arca. And what was *this*? What kind of woman would participate in an armed attack on an *orphanage*? Wow. Could he pick 'em, or what?

Although Charlie escaped mention in the arrest story, he'd been linked to the international fugitive in a society brief about Saturday night's soirée. "I'm toast," he muttered when he saw his name in bold print next to Dana Colescu's.

He stared at the painting he'd purchased from her. Why did he have to go and buy art from a forger? Hell, he didn't even know if it was hanging right side up—or if it was backwards, for that matter. Did the artist really live in Paris and have AIDS, or did a twelve-year-old Filipino girl paint it using photographs and mirrors?

The first knock on the door came at 7:03 a.m., and he was officially under siege. That morning, at least a dozen people pounded on the door. Each time, Charlie stood still and waited for the knocking to cease.

He considered packing a suitcase and getting out of town, but he didn't. Instead, he laid on the sofa and stared at the sunlight on the ceiling as it faded through the morning hours. Then he listened to his bedside clock ticking the seconds away. When a few thousand had passed, he realized that at that very moment, varmints were taping the Steele show in Chicago. Spence Greene and Barbara Asher would rip Charlie a new one for being a no-show, but only if he talked to them. Another problem easily solved. Other than avoiding all human contact, he didn't know what to do. So he did nothing and quietly waited for the world to go away.

The knocking came intermittently throughout the rest of the day.

Morbid curiosity about Dana drove Charlie to click on the evening news. He stared in disbelief as Susan appeared on the plasma screen, standing beside her Mercedes beneath the TransNationBank sign in front of Hanover Mall's landmark clock tower. Channel Six reporter Trent Bozier asked, "How do you feel about your husband's relationship with an alleged war criminal?"

Susan took a deep breath. "Obviously, he continues to engage in disgusting behavior and associate with dangerous criminals, on top of harassing my family, and I will do everything I can to protect the people that I love from him."

"Does that include a restraining order?"

"Definitely. We're getting the restraining order reinstated. It never should have been removed."

Tears of frustration and rage welled in Charlie's eyes. "You'll pay for that!" he screamed. "You'll pay and pay and pay! On your knees begging is too good for you!"

* * *

Charlie didn't eat or sleep much for the rest of the day, and he continued to ignore phone calls, e-mails, and knocks on the door the next day. Tuesday afternoon, he worked up the nerve to watch *The Matthew Steele Show*, hoping the scheduled episode had been cancelled because he hadn't shown up for the Monday taping. No such luck. The host, wearing his trademark black suit, opened the show with a seething denunciation of "Charles Sherman, the man in the empty chair." Steele pointed to said chair and declared, "He didn't have the courage to show up after his Eastern European lover's arrest on espionage charges." The crowd jeered. "Mr. Sherman, this is what people think of you." Steele held his microphone overhead and urged the crowd to boo even louder.

"Why the fuck should I care?" Charlie muttered at the screen. "You idiots don't read."

Steele prowled the stage like a greedy preacher. "Theft and trespassing, domestic violence, child pornography, meth dealing, and adultery. With a spy, no less! Libel, war crimes, art forgery." Steele, who didn't care whose offenses he was talking about or if they'd actually been committed, sucked in a deep breath. "The list is endless, but the bottom line is that Charles Sherman is one reprehensible individual!" Steele stopped pacing and bowed his head, appearing to be deep in thought. When he looked up into the camera, he said, "Charles Sherman … is a vermin!"

He repeated the line. On the third try, the crowd took the cue and started chanting it. They kept this up until Steele silenced them by proclaiming, "And now, it's time to meet Charles Sherman's victims!"

"Victims?" Charlie jumped up from his seat on the sofa, yelling, "Them there is perpetrators!"

Uncle Stanley, Momo, and Evangeline walked out on the stage. To applause! As Steele introduced them, the clapping and cheers grew louder. All of them were dressed in black, like they'd flown straight to Chicago from Pappy's funeral without changing clothes. What a pack of fakes! The hulking Momo, wearing a hateful scowl and dwarfing Steele's security guards, wore a suit instead of his usual Confederate T-shirt. Stanley was wearing his legislative ID badge on his lapel, and Evangeline wore a black suit with her trademark mini-bouffant. Puffy-eyed, she broke into tears when Steele asked her how she was doing.

"My daddy died," she said. "That's how I'm doing."

Steele knelt and patted her hand

Next to her sat Momo, forehead wide, brow low. "Pappy was the best man I ever knew," he said. "He taught me how to hunt. Pap was always there to help. Until … until." He hung his head.

Stanley spoke up. "Sherman was always trying to destroy the family, but things turned really bad when he got caught with child pornography on the computer in the house. He didn't have a job, by the way. Except for writing porn."

"My daughter wasn't standing for any of that," Evangeline said.

"It got violent," Stanley said. "He beat Susan up pretty bad. She was able to call 911. He was so out of control the police had to draw guns— "

Evangeline interrupted. "It would have been better if they'd a—" Suddenly she was staring cross-eyed at a microphone a foot away from her face. "Lord, I can't say such a thing."

"Shot him to death," Momo said helpfully.

Stanley continued the narrative: "Sherman got kicked out of the house and soon after that, he began stalking us and plotting his revenge."

"How so?" Steele asked.

"Well first, he tried to build up his credibility by putting his name as the author of that first book even though somebody else wrote it, and it wasn't factual to begin with."

"You're talking about *Flight from Forsyth,*" Steele said. "So that never happened?"

"Not the way he told it, that's for sure. Anyway, once he does that, he starts making up this cock-and-bull story about how this black man lived in Forsyth and how my father supposedly killed him and stole the land." Stanley put air quotes around killed and stole. "Even worse things, nonsense and lies I won't repeat."

Without missing a beat, Steele asked, "When did he start worshiping the devil?"

Enough. Charlie turned off the TV. He paced around the room until he couldn't stand the silence anymore. He turned the TV back on just as Steele was cutting to a commercial: "When we come back, we'll hear from someone who has a different perspective on these matters."

Different perspective? Who could it be? Charlie wracked his brain for the answer while advertisers tried to sell him toilet cleaner and hemorrhoid ointment.

Steele returned. "Ladies and gentlemen, our special guest, Arlene Cartier!"

Aunt Shirlene!

The varmints' mouths dropped open in unison at the announcement. Apparently, they had no idea this was coming. *Nice touch, Steele.* Charlie pumped his fist in the air and cheered raucously as Arlene, wearing a red dress, walked onstage. As she passed Stanley, he rose from his chair. She raised her hand to slap him. When he recoiled from the anticipated blow, she laughed in his face. The crowd broke out in guffaws and jeers. She turned and glared at this newest source of dissatisfaction, apparently scouting for more targets. Her eyes were lit with fire as she sat down in a chair set well apart from the others.

"Now, is Cartier your married name?" Steele asked, holding his microphone in front of her face.

"No. I never married. I changed my name as soon as I legally could. Wanted nothing to do with 'em." She gave a backhanded wave toward her relatives.

"Now, sister," Stanley cautioned. "I know you're upset by Pap's death, but—"

"Don't you even talk to me!" Arlene screamed. Turning to Steele and calming slightly, she said, "First, I want to tell everyone that I believe every word in Mr. Sherman's book. That … my father—" she patted down her red dress, which didn't fit like it belonged on her "—was capable of what was described in the book, and I know 'cause I lived through it. You have no idea how many times I've prayed to be able to tell my story to the world."

Charlie crouched by the sofa and bit his thumbs in anticipation. "Yes, I do. You go, girl!"

"That man was a monster. He raped me every week for three years, and the woman he married just looked the other way." Arlene's rapid-fire delivery let everyone know she would not be outtalked.

"Your mother," Steele added helpfully.

"And as far as I'm concerned, the whole family can burn in hell."

Stanley, now two shades paler than at the start of the program, cried out, "You can't believe her! Sherman planted that story in her head!"

Arlene continued: "I left home when I was sixteen years old and pregnant by my own father." Audience members cried out in disgust. "I was so ignorant I had no idea what to do. I heard about a place to have an abortion up in Ringgold and I went up there, but then they wanted me to have the baby so they could sell it. They took care of me all right, but when my baby was born, no one would take it. He was retarded. My boy's nearly sixty years old and he's in a state home, and that's where he'll stay until the day he dies."

"No, no!" Charlie shouted at the screen. "That's not what you told me! That's not what's in the book! Stick to the script, goddamnit! Stick to the script!" He reached up and grabbed his hair with both hands. "You were supposed to have an abortion!"

"I blamed myself," Arlene said, "but it was due to the inbreeding. I know that now because of this book. That *Monster* married his half-sister. I gave birth to my brother! There's crimes against God going on in that family! Dig the (bleep) up! Do those tests on him and my son! He stole that land, and worse!"

This was too much even for Steele, whose face went pale. Charlie felt nauseous, too. His source was refuting him. What had he been thinking? Never trust a varmint! *Never, never, never*!

Arlene leveled her gaze at Stanley. "I heard you already took his money from selling the stolen land and been spreadin' it around, like good works will get you into heaven. You livin' a lie."

"You should have come to us," Stanley said, his face a mask of pain and suffering. "We would have helped you!"

"Come to you?" She scoffed. "Hell. You knew what was going on."

"I protected my sisters."

Charlie's eyes widened at this admission.

"You protected your other sisters. Not me. You could have stopped him. Instead you decided that monster was your role model."

"Oh my goodness!" Steele said in alarm. "Are you saying—"

"He tried to do it to me himself. Once. I fought him off with a butcher knife."

"That's a damn lie!" Stanley shouted.

"He has a scar on the inside of his left thigh. Pull down your pants and show your rape scar, you (*bleep*)! You're lucky I didn't cut it off. Maybe somebody did. He ain't got no kids, you know."

The crowd started chanting, "Pull 'em off! Pull 'em off!" Charlie, having recovered somewhat, joined in.

"And as for how that man died, I don't believe he shot himself. Too damned mean for that."

"Do you think somebody killed Isaac Cutchins?" Steele asked. "Police say it was a suicide."

"Wouldn't put it past his own people, not with money on the line." She pointed at Momo. "His daddy burned down the courthouse, and he's no better. Maybe he did it. You kill your granddad, boy?"

That was too much for Momo. "I can't stand this no more!" he bellowed, and rose from his chair. He took a step toward Arlene, who stood to face him. As the security staff closed in, she pulled a small canister of mace from her bra and sprayed her nephew in the eyes, then gave two guards the same treatment. Audience members screamed. Steele jumped off the stage, and with security guards semi-disabled, the melee began in earnest as people in the crowd rushed to join the fight.

Arlene had also smuggled a knife into the studio, and she was determined to cut someone, bless her heart.

Chapter Twenty-Five

The brawl on the Steele Show reminded Charlie of his brother-in-law Jerry Bancroft's funeral, so he switched channels and happened upon a car chase in progress. At first he thought he was watching *COPS* and started singing the theme song. Then he realized it was live and local. Newschopper Six was hot on the trail of a silver sedan weaving through traffic on I-85 in Gwinnett County. He put down the remote. After seeing the horrific performance of Aunt Arlene ... or Shirley (who was that woman, anyway?) Charlie was glad to watch bad news that didn't involve him. Best of all, he knew that Channel Six (*If it bleeds, it leads*) would stick with the chase, preempting other local coverage—including the daily beat-down of Charlie Sherman. He settled in to watch.

The vehicle proceeded north, running on the shoulder at highway speed. Traffic reporter Trey Denison gave a breathless report: "The suspect car is taking the exit at Pleasant Hill. It's on the grass now ... almost slid down the embankment."

Early evening anchor Gayle Huggins cut in. "Trey, we have some information on the suspects. Two black males in their late teens or early twenties, both about five-foot-six. Wearing baggy shirts and basketball shorts—"

Trey: "Did you see that? He just clipped a car when he ran the red light, then sideswiped another. Traffic's too heavy to get through. This is Gwinnett Place Mall at rush hour we're talking about! He's going the other way now, taking a right, heading east."

"Trey, where are the police cars?"

"The ones on I-85 are about a quarter-mile back, working up the ramp. I see some other police cars now." The camera panned to show two units in pursuit.

"One going westbound on Pleasant Hill just did a U-Turn at a traffic light to join the chase. The suspect is accelerating, but this can't last long. He's cutting through a parking lot, just hit a car. *Look out.* He almost hit a pedestrian."

The anchor broke in: "For those of you just joining us, we are covering an apparent carjacking in progress. Police spotted the suspect vehicle northbound on I-85 after the alleged carjackers shot the victim about an hour ago. We've got a reporter at the shooting scene, and we'll bring you a report when we're able."

The chase continued for a few minutes without commentary before Denison said, "Police have a roadblock at Highway Twenty-Nine. Unless he … yep, there he goes on Ronald Reagan Parkway. Police are setting a blockade there, too. It's going to be over soon."

The camera zoomed in on the car as the driver slowed to negotiate the snarled traffic. Two patrol cars rolled onto the parkway's grassy median just as the stolen car—now identified as a Mercedes sedan—left the eastbound lane and barreled across the median toward oncoming traffic.

Denison shouted, "He's going the wrong way!"

The Mercedes shot up onto the westbound lane, going against traffic. It immediately collided head-on with a pickup truck. The car spun into the median and came to a rest. The camera closed in on one suspect as he jumped out the passenger door and sprinted toward the mass of cars in the roadblocked eastbound lane. He charged up on a car sitting in traffic. "He's wearing a red cap or something on his head, and it looks like he's armed," Denison said, his voice on edge. "I think he's trying to steal another—"

The carjacker's body jerked once, then collapsed on the ground.

"He's down." The camera panned to armed officers advancing on the suspect, guns drawn. The video shot was too distant for Charlie to make out anyone's features clearly, but he had a bad feeling about what was happening.

The helicopter's camera pivoted to show the Mercedes driver running along the median grass back the way he'd come. A county police car raced up behind him. The carjacker scrambled up the incline to the westbound lanes and tried to sprint across, but got clipped by a car and fell down. He staggered to his feet and tried to hobble away, but an officer jumped out of the pursuit vehicle and tackled him from behind. The camera stayed on the suspect for a minute, then switched to his fallen accomplice, who remained motionless.

"It looks like the police have the situation under control now," Denison said. "But at least one of the suspects appears to have been shot. It doesn't look like he's moving, either."

Gayle Huggins cut in: "We're going live to DeKalb County and Monica Crowley at TransNationBank on Hanover Drive. Go ahead, Monica."

"No!" Charlie shouted as he stared at the face of a woman he'd known for several years. "No!"

The camera cut to the reporter on location. "Gayle, right now I'm where the scene of this alleged crime in north DeKalb County. I'm with an eyewitness, TransNationBank assistant manager, Allison Fugate." The blonde reporter put a hand on the weeping woman's shoulder. "Take a breath and compose yourself."

The bottom dropped out of Charlie's stomach.

"It was terrible," Allison said, clearly distraught. "I was looking out the window and saw it happen. When Susan went to her car—"

"And that's branch manager Susan Sherman?"

"Yes," Allison said. "They shot her and took her car. They just shot her. They didn't have to do that. They already had the keys." The woman sobbed deeply and gasped for breath.

"Could you describe the suspects?"

"Two young black males. They were short. The one who shot her was wearing a red handkerchief on his head."

"This isn't happening," Charlie told himself as Allison sobbed and sniffed her way through the interview. But it was happening, and he needed to do something. *Get moving*, he told himself. *You've got to help.* Through the fog of confusion that was clouding his brain, he heard the reporter say, "The shooting victim has been taken to Northeast Atlanta Regional Medical Center with life-threatening injuries."

Get Beck and Ben. Where were they? With the woman who babysat for them after school? He didn't have her phone number, so he'd have to drive there. He burst out the door, sprinted down the hall with long strides, and hurtled down the stairs, grabbing the handrails and taking a half-flight at a time. He slid to a stop in the garage and thought for a moment before deciding that luxury cars were bad luck and taking the Volvo.

It seemed to take forever to reach his old neighborhood. Along the way, Charlie listened to the news, fretted, and kept switching radio stations. No updates, just traffic reports telling him that the world was slowing down on its way home. His gut churning, Charlie drove past the school and Thornbriar, feeling like he'd entered hostile territory. And what if the worst happened—if, at that very instant, that incessant beeping in the hospital changed to a solid, flat tone?

The kids needed a parent, especially now. He wasn't going to apologize for doing his job. Thank God the restraining order had been lifted. Or was a new one in place? Susan was so vindictive, he couldn't keep track. Damn! The letter with his visitation rights was in the other car. He hit the steering wheel in frustration. He'd had problems with this babysitter back in October. Well, she'd just have to understand. He turned onto her street. At least he thought it was her street.

But which house? They all looked the same to him. He parked in the driveway of a likely looking tan brick ranch. When he rang the bell, the woman opened the door a centimeter and said, "Her sister came and got them just a few minutes ago."

How did Susan get in touch with Sheila? "Why didn't she call me?" Charlie asked.

The woman closed the door in his face. Charlie stood on the porch feeling dumb and empty. From inside, a man said, "If you don't leave, we'll call the police."

"Ridiculous!" Charlie shouted over his shoulder as he stormed off. "I'm just trying to help!"

* * *

Northeast Regional Medical Center's main building was white, modern, and square, with two large wings spreading east and west. Its windows shone golden against the evening sun. When Charlie rushed into the emergency entrance, a funky chemical smell filled his nostrils. He spotted a sign-in desk and quick-stepped toward it. "I need to know about Susan Sherman," he said, slamming his palms on the counter. "She came in with a gunshot—"

"She's in surgery," said an older white nurse standing behind the young black desk attendant.

"Do you know—"

The woman shook her head, wagging her double chin. "You can take a seat over there." She pointed toward the waiting area.

Charlie turned and saw Evangeline sitting on an orange plastic chair, clutching a black purse with both hands. His mother-in-law glared at him with dark eyes, her jaw clenched tight, face ready to explode: The very picture of hatred and rage, though it appeared that she'd survived the Steele show without any noticeable wounds.

As Charlie approached her, she rose from her seat and walked stiffly away. He looked around for his father-in-law for a moment before recalling that Evangeline had left Saint Bradley.

Evangeline returned, a white cop with a butch haircut in tow. He took one look at Charlie and a storm of worry crossed his face. "Holy smoke! You're the guy who wrote the book about the in-laws!" He turned to Evangeline. "And you're the in-law!" He spoke into the radio unit on his shoulder. "I'm at the ER waiting room and I need backup."

The officer's radio crackled: "Gwinnett County advises suspect has implicated white male subject Charles Sherman in the carjacking."

"What?" Charlie asked, his face contorting in disbelief, even though he already had more than an inkling of what was going down. "That's absurd!"

"He's in on this. I knew it," Evangeline declared, her face a mask of grim satisfaction.

"Ma'am, could you please take a seat over there?" The cop pointed to a chair by the wall. Evangeline stood ramrod straight for a moment before complying.

"I'm taking you into custody," the cop said, clamping his hand on Charlie's wrist.

"I don't understand. What do they mean, the suspect has implicated me?"

"Place your hands behind your back." The officer pushed Charlie's right hand into position as eh cuffed him. Charlie had been through this enough times to know it was counterproductive to struggle.

"What's going on? Just because she told you—"

"Doesn't have anything to do with her, all right?"

Charlie found that impossible to believe. As he was perp-walked out of the hospital, he noticed that seeing him in handcuffs brought a smile to Evangeline's troubled face.

* * *

Two detectives transported Charlie to the northeast precinct station and led him to a drab little interrogation room with pale green walls. It contained a gunmetal gray table, two chairs, and a mirror on the cinder block wall. They took off his cuffs and confiscated his cellphone.

The first interview was short. Sergeant Foley, who was white, stood in the corner with his arms folded and watched while Detective Nance did the talking. Nance, a light-skinned black man with freckles, asked Charlie about his marriage. "Am I under arrest?" Charlie asked.

"Not yet," Nance said.

"I want to talk to my attorney."

Nance left the room and returned with Charlie's cellphone. Charlie called Muncie's cell number and left a message. Nance took the phone and left. Foley followed him out.

Charlie spent the next hour drumming the table and walking around the room, which was so small he kept brushing against the wall.

The detectives returned. "Sit down," said Nance. "No word back from your lawyer. Sure you want to wait, or would you rather talk? We found out a few things we can share."

As far as Charlie was concerned, the cops didn't need his help. They had their suspects in custody. Only stupid people in situations like this talked to police without a lawyer present. But this was beyond stupid. He needed to know about Susan. "Is my wife alive?"

"As far as we know," Nance said. "But we want to talk about you. What am I sayin'? Everyone wants to talk about you. You're famous. Your name's been in the news every day this past week."

"None of it good," Foley added.

"I've had better weeks," Charlie admitted.

"How'd you know about the carjacking?" Foley asked.

"I saw it on TV. I knew it was Susan because Channel Six interviewed a coworker who said they shot her. Plus, she has a silver Mercedes."

"Nice car. How can she afford it?"

"She's a banker, duh. Plus I give her a couple grand a month child support."

"Only a couple grand a month?" Foley scoffed. "Rich as you are?"

"It's going up soon. She wants ten grand a month."

"Does she?" Nance interjected, making a note. "Interesting."

Damn. Where was that lawyer?

"When you heard, did you try to call her, just to see, you know …"

"She blocked my number," Charlie said.

"Ouch," said Foley. "Not on good terms, eh?"

"A pending divorce," Nance told his partner. "Rather nasty, I hear."

"And they said they were taking her to the hospital," Charlie said.

"So you rushed right to the hospital," Foley said.

"First I went to check on the kids, but her sister had picked them up. I don't know what happened there. She must have gotten in touch with Sheila, or had somebody call her. That's a good sign, that she was able to do that," Charlie said, trying to sound hopeful.

"So you didn't know this would be happening?" Foley asked.

Charlie looked at him with a mixture of contempt and disbelief, calculated for maximum effect. "If I had, I would have done something to stop it."

"Un-huh," said Foley.

"Un-huh," said Nance.

"You know the guys who did it," Foley said.

Foley and Nance both gave him piercing stares.

No way would Charlie admit he knew the carjackers unless he had to. "I heard in the hospital that somebody knows my name. Obviously, they're trying to blame me. Look, I've been the victim of hit jobs more than once. I don't know who did it, OK?" Charlie threw up his hands in exasperation.

"Got any ideas?"

"You tell me."

"OK. You know Kwame Taylor?"

"Never heard of him." Charlie felt relieved. Perhaps he was wrong. Maybe—

"How about P-Dog?"

Charlie gulped. "Yeah. I've heard of him. Didn't know his real name."

"He's the shooter, by the way. How do you know him?"

"I'd like to try calling my lawyer again."

"Sure. Detective Foley."

Foley pulled Charlie's cell out of his shirt pocket and handed it over. Charlie dialed but got no answer. He left another message, his voice tinged with desperation. The cops found this amusing. When he was finished, he put the phone on the table.

"How about Demetrious Warner?" Nance asked. "Nickname *D*."

Charlie knew it was leading to this, but it was still a jolt to hear the name. "Yeah. I wrote about him in a book. P-Dog is the one who got shot, right?"

"The book," Nance said, looking at Foley. "We gotta get a copy." Nance sat down across the table from Charlie and looked him in the eye. "So how you know Demetrious Warner?"

"Through his grandmother. The book's about … something that happened to his family."

"Did you know today's his birthday?" Nance said.

"Must have wanted a present," Foley cracked.

"His eighteenth, to be precise," Nance said. "He's looking at the death penalty."

Charlie rose out of his chair, his heart in his throat. "You told me Susan was alive!"

Foley put a hand on Charlie's shoulder and forced him down. "She is, as far as we know. But see, the way the law works, he can be charged with a capital crime for his partner's death."

"Is that the deal that's going down?"

"Yeah," Nance said. "Looks like it."

"That's cold," Charlie said.

"You should be feeling a little chilly yourself, right now."

"Yeah, wait'll ya get a load of this." Foley glanced at his notepad. "Party to a crime. Everybody who did the crime is responsible. His partner, anyone who participated. You know, like, say, paying them to do it."

"Who paid them to do it?'

"This guy and his questions," Nance told his partner. "He cracks me up."

Nance said, "We have info says you gave money to D. That's who."

This was ridiculously dangerous, and Charlie realized that he was the guy the cops would not want to cut a deal with: The Great White Defendant. Especially if the GBI and governor's office got involved. "Bullshit," he said.

Nance pulled a fax sheet out of his pocket. "What's this, then, that we just got in from Gwinnett County? 'Demetrious, I have a lucrative proposition for you.' That your signature?"

Charlie stared at the note he'd written months ago about the DNA test. "Ha ... Jeez ... hmm ... yeah, like I said, I'm gonna need my attorney."

"I figured you'd say that."

The cops got up with looks of disgust on their faces. "Make your friggin' call," Foley said.

He handed Charlie's cellphone to him, then both detectives left the room. Charlie autodialed Muncie and again left a message. As soon as he was done, Nance came back into the room and retrieved the phone, then exited, leaving Charlie alone with his thoughts.

Nearly two hours later, Foley burst into the interrogation room holding Charlie's cellphone like it was a dead rat. "Call."

"Hello, Sherman here," Charlie said, feeling a sudden and strange hope that Susan was calling to tell him it was all a mistake, and she was doing just fine.

"Charlie," Muncie said. "What kind of trouble are you in?"

"Susan was shot in a carjacking, and I'm being held as a suspect. Northeast DeKalb precinct."

"Shit. Have you been talking?"

"Somewhat."

"Double shit. What the—don't say another word. I'm on my way. ... Charlie. Charlie." A long pause. "OK. Good. Just keep doing that until I get there."

* * *

Muncie arrived at 11:05 p.m. and huddled with his client. Whispering, with a legal pad blocking the view from the mirror, Charlie told Muncie what he knew of the carjacking, including the incriminating information about paying Demetrious for his blood sample—a piece of information he'd neglected to include in *American Monster*. Another instance of sandbagging he now regretted. He also mentioned Demetrious's demand for $20,000.

"Do you know if that's why he targeted her?" Muncie asked.

Charlie shrugged. "I don't know much. I just know him."

"Did you tell him where she worked?"

"No. I never talked to him about my family, but she wouldn't have been hard to find. She was on TV last night denouncing me, standing in front of the Hanover clock tower."

"Well, due to the divorce, they've got a motive for you," Muncie said. "They'll say chickens have come home to roost."

"It's bullshit, though. What do we do?"

"We don't talk to them. Nothing to gain. Make them prove everything."

"They could arrest me."

"Then we'll get you out on bond."

"I was hoping for something less ... stressful than that."

"What can I say? You lead an interesting life. Looks like you'll have a sequel to your book."

"I don't want it to be a jailhouse memoir."

"I hear ya." Muncie looked into the mirror and smiled broadly. "We're ready."

A few minutes later, Nance entered the room alone, hitched up his pants, and stared at Charlie for a moment, then switched his gaze to Muncie. "He's free to go."

"Why?" Charlie asked, which was, he had to admit, a very stupid question. Muncie was already pulling him out of his chair.

Nance sneered at him. "Because you're rich and famous. But don't leave town."

"Come on," Muncie said. "Let's go."

Once outside, Charlie said, "What just happened?"

"Well, they don't have much on you, despite what they said. And for all I know, they bugged the room and heard everything we said."

"That's illegal! They can't do that!"

Muncie shrugged. "Whatever. I'm sure they'd say they didn't. Good thing you didn't confess. By the way, when the cops tell you you're free to go, don't ask why. Just go. Come on. I'll give you a ride. I guess I'll have to include taxi fare as part of my fee. Where to?"

"Northeast Regional. Susan's there." Muncie gave him a questioning look. "So's my car."

"Just don't do anything we'll regret while you're there."

They climbed into Muncie's black Porsche and roared away. Charlie checked his cellphone's voicemail: "You have twenty-eight unheard messages." He played through the voicemails, skipping as soon as he heard who they were from: reporters, mainly. He erased them all.

"I still don't know how she's doing. The divorce—"

"Don't worry about that. Just do what you can to help her. Wouldn't hurt to pray."

"I kinda think that's dangerous, right now."

Muncie gave him a peeved look. "You're one weird dude, you know." After a minute, he said, "Look, even if they don't have enough to hold you on right now, they're probably going to try to get an indictment. I'll put my investigator on this case. If we have a package to give the DA, we may be able to avoid an indictment. We have two jurisdictions to worry about."

"I didn't have anything to do with this. I just want you to understand that."

"Good. That will help."

Muncie turned into the hospital entrance. "We'll beat this rap," he said. "Not bad for a divorce lawyer, eh?"

"You were bound to turn into a criminal lawyer dealing with the family I'm tangled up with," Charlie said. "And speaking of your PI, what did he find out about ... uh, Harold?"

"Some other time." Muncie's tone was curt.

He pulled to a stop at the parking lot gate and let out his passenger. As the lawyer drove away, a siren wailed in the distance. It was past midnight and most of the hospital windows were dark. Charlie looked at the streetlamp, then at the waxing moon, partially hidden behind a cloud. He walked slowly toward the main entrance. He passed through the sliding doors and approached a woman in a suit sitting behind the information desk.

"Visiting hours are over, sir," she said.

"I just need to know—"

A uniformed guard appeared at Charlie's side.

"She's in the ICU. There's nothing you can do now. Get some rest, Mr. Sherman."

Charlie looked perplexed. "Do you know me?"

"Everyone knows you."

Regretting this unfortunate fact, Charlie turned and walked out.

Chapter Twenty-Six

As Charlie drove to the hospital early Wednesday morning, the thoughts that had kept him up all night continued to hammer his burned-out brain. First: this was Susan's fault. By going on TV, she had willingly participated in the Cutchins family's evil scheme to defame him and defraud Minerva Doe, thus exposing herself to the wrath of God. It was so obvious. Second: Of course, Charlie would do everything he could for his stricken wife. Third: If the unthinkable occurred, he would take Beck and Ben and flee this accursed place.

These audacious thoughts did not comfort him. Instead, they made him increasingly nervous. When he arrived at Northeast Regional, his throat was so dry he could barely swallow. His sneakers squeaked on the ICU's polished floor as nurses popped in and out of rooms. The piped-in music sounded inappropriately perky. When he came to 332, he opened the door and spied Bradley Roy in the corner of the private room, his head lolled back on the cushion of an aqua-colored armchair. Charlie's father-in-law looked like he'd aged a decade in the year and a half since they had last seen each other. The old man's dark hair had turned steel gray; his face was careworn and wrinkled. This was alarming, since it contradicted Charlie's belief that leaving Evangeline would have had the opposite effect on a man.

Sunshine came in spots through loose-weave drapes, dappling Susan, who lay in the bed breathing in rhythm with the respirator's slow, steady *pock*. On a monitor, a line blipped relentlessly; her heartbeat was now mathematical. Charlie tiptoed to her side, grimacing at the tubes and wires sticking out of her. Her left elbow was bandaged. There was an abrasion on her forehead. Her hair was matted and disheveled. She wore the slightest of frowns.

Charlie gently took his wife's hand and held it, cruelly aware he couldn't have done this if she was awake. Looking at her now, he knew she didn't deserve this. If things had worked out differently on that winter's night so long ago, the children would be sleeping in their beds right now, Susan would be stepping out of the shower, and Charlie would be leering at her. *If.*

Bradley Roy stirred, half-opened an eye, then came fully awake. He sat up straight, blinked, and stood. The old man hitched up his pants and gave Charlie the evil eye. "You."

"Me."

"I don't want to believe the things I'm hearing. But if they're true," he said, sighting down a pointed finger at his son-in-law, "I will for certain kill you myself."

"Fair enough. But you'll have to get in line."

"I heard that." Bradley Roy nodded. "Suppose you tell me what happened with the police."

"I'll tell you, but first I want to know about Susan." Charlie brushed a strand of hair from her forehead. The frown straightened out. She never could stand for her hair to be mussed.

Bradley Roy scratched day-old stubble and shook his head. "She's not out of the woods yet."

"The one who shot her is dead."

"Can't say I'm sorry about that." Bradley Roy cleared his throat. "She was in surgery for three hours. They didn't take out the slug. It was small, at least, a twenty-two, but it's lodged in her spine and she's got a cracked vertebra. They don't know . . . if she's paralyzed. But it doesn't look good." He choked a sob, then composed himself. "They're keeping her in a coma so she don't try to move."

"Have you seen Beck and Ben? How are they doing?"

"Sheila's got them. She's puttin' 'em in Bible Camp."

"Not at First Baptist, I hope."

Bradley Roy shrugged. "Best place for 'em right now. I wouldn't worry about it if I was you."

"They should be with me."

"Leave 'em be. They're in good hands. Away from this." He gestured weakly toward the bed, then checked the silver watch he'd worn as long as Charlie had known him.

"Do they know what happened?"

"Lord, I hope not. They know she's hurt. Or maybe that she's sick. I don't know exactly what Sheila told them." The old man gave him a penetrating stare. "All right, I gave you what you wanted. Now you tell me. Why did this happen?"

Bradley Roy was no varmint—in fact, he was the only in-law Charlie felt he could speak to honestly. "I can't say why it happened, but I can make a guess, since I know the people who did it."

Bradley Roy turned and reached down to pluck a newspaper section from the floor beside his chair. He leaned over the bed and shoved the headline in Charlie's face: *Author Implicated in Wife's Shooting*. "So what's this about?"

Charlie shook his head vigorously and held up his hands. "I had nothing to do with it."

"How'd they find her, then?"

"Hell, Bradley Roy, you can use my name to look her up. And then she was on the news Monday night standing right where the carjacking took place. Even showed her car. Shouldn't have gone on TV."

"She was mad at you."

"She's always mad at me."

"Well, this time for cheating on her with that foreign woman that got arrested." Bradley Roy paused. "She was a looker, I'll give you that."

"Don't see why *Susan* was jealous," Charlie muttered.

"What's that supposed to mean?"

"Nothing."

"You're a fool. She loved you."

"Come on. You expect me to believe that?"

"Well, she's a Cutchins," Bradley Roy said. "She's just got a contrary way of showing it. So tell me what else you know about what happened yesterday."

"The one that died, I only met once or twice. The one that's still alive, Demetrious, is Minerva Doe's grandson."

"Shit. *That* wasn't in the paper."

"I don't know how much you know about this, but that makes him Pappy's great-grandson."

"I'm followin' you. Go on."

"He told police I gave him money to do it. Which is exactly opposite what happened. A week ago, I took a copy of the book to Minerva and while I was driving away, he ran up to my car and told me he needed money to help out his mother."

"How much?"

"How much?" Charlie wrinkled his face. "Twenty grand."

"You ever give him money before?"

Charlie hesitated. "I paid him for a blood sample. I needed it for the book."

"The book. Damn thing's been a tornado rippin' through the family. Made everyone crazy, includin' you. You got like a million dollars, didn't you? So why didn't you give him the money?"

Charlie wore a look of disbelief. "Why didn't I give him the money?"

"Yes. Why. Didn't. You. Give. Him. The. Money. You took advantage of those people's story—I mean, it is their story, and hell, everybody else is profiting off what happened. If it was a movie about their lives, you'd have to pay them, right?"

"Hold on. It's *not* a movie, and Minerva doesn't want my money. Doesn't want anything to do with the book. She's suing over the farm sale, though, so I don't want to taint the case."

"Phooey." Bradley Roy gestured toward Susan. "You tellin' me there was a way to avoid this and all it took was money? I am sick and tired of being surrounded by greed. That's what broke up my marriage. You aren't in the clear. There's blood on your hands."

"I told you, I didn't have anything to do with this."

"Just because you wash your hands of it, doesn't mean you're clean. You're in this nastiness along with everybody else, and it ain't over, not by a long shot. Well, all right. You been here. You found out what you needed to find out. And now I'll kindly ask you to leave. So go."

When Charlie hesitated, Bradley glanced at his watch and said, "They'll be here soon, anyway, and I'll not have the lot of you screaming at each other like it's some damned TV show while my daughter lies here ..."

He choked up, unable to continue. Charlie reached over to touch his shoulder. Bradley Roy swatted the hand away. "You're a prick."

"I'm sorry you feel that way."

"My feelings are the least thing you need to feel sorry about."

Charlie turned to leave, his face burning with shame.

"Wait. There's something I was going to tell you," Bradley Roy said, his features softening. "I owe you that much, I suppose. They took half of Pap's money after the sale and split it up. Vange moved out with her money and got a fancy house by the lake. I ain't had much to do with her or any of'em lately. I bought a copy of your book. I'm reading it now, and I gotta admit, it makes sense."

Bradley Roy paused to reflect, then continued. "Way back before your time, I said something Pap didn't like, because, well you know how I feel about the N-word. He looked at me across the table—this was in his old house—and he said, 'I don't need you telling me about *niggers*.'" Bradley Roy whispered the last word. “He said, ‘We ran ’em all out and there was one too stupid to leave, so we took care of it, and I’ll damn well not put up with any shit from you about it.’ I’d come back from Korea owing a black man my life.”

Charlie nodded. “I know. So he as much as said he got rid of John Riggins.”

“Seems like it now, don’t it?”

“Maybe you should tell that to the family.”

“I think they know. I think they knew all along and kept it a secret. That’s the real shame of it. All right. You go on, then.”

Charlie cast one last glance at Susan before he left. As he approached the elevator, the doors opened and Evangeline stepped out, gazing at her shoes. When she looked up and saw Charlie, she yelped and lurched backward, throwing up her hands. Charlie walked past her as she inched along the wall, glaring at him with fear and hatred. “Don’t you touch me!” she warned, then pulled her cellphone from her purse.

Charlie took the stairs, exiting before she could have him arrested again. He crossed the drive to the parking lot and saw Stanley giving a television interview. The Channel Six crew broke away from the politician in mid-sentence and chased after the elusive author. Charlie had too much of a head start on the overweight cameraman and the blonde in high heels, however, and thereby made his escape.

* * *

Back at the loft, Charlie called his sister-in-law to check on the kids but got no answer. Then he called Muncie, who said the private investigator had been reassigned from “Harold Watch” to find out what the police had on him. After that, Charlie sat on the sofa, occasionally glancing at the wall mirror to see if he was still there, and tried to convince himself that Susan’s paralysis wasn’t his fault. He skipped breakfast and ate a piece of dried bread for lunch. He ignored knocks on the door and refused to turn on the TV or computer. The news could rage; he would stay in his safe place. Every hour on the hour, he turned on his cellphone and called the hospital for a condition report. Susan remained critical.

Time’s passage was glacial. That afternoon, he sat on the bare concrete floor with his legs sprawled out, contemplating the nature of his suffering. His work was a failure. His reputation as a human being was destroyed. Everything he should have accomplished, all the things that should have been his, had slipped away like sand through his fingers. He was alone in the world. His children would be taken from him and turned into Cutchinses, becoming as distant as stars in the sky—the dim ones, at that.

He didn't belong in this place or any other. Well, maybe on a bridge.

The sun set. The otherworldly fire in his mirrored doppelganger's eyes faded. He cast yesterday's newspaper on the floor beside him and put his face in his hands. He wanted to cry but couldn't, because he was a dry and hollow man.

When it was time to make his hourly call to the hospital, he turned on the phone. Before he could press the "send" button, it buzzed. He pinched his chin fiercely, enough to hurt. The number looked familiar. "Be a man," he told himself. "Answer the phone." He took a deep breath. "Hello."

"Charles." It was a deep schoolteacher's voice. Minerva.

"Hey."

After a minute, she said, "Are you still there?"

"Yes."

"I heard about your wife. And Demetrious. It's terrible in so many ways. How is she doing?"

"She may never walk again. But she's got to survive before we even worry about that."

"It's that little gangsta Demetrious hung around with. I realize this is no consolation, but he's the one who did the shooting."

"I know. And you're right. It isn't."

"That boy was a shark. But Demetrious went along with it. He believed everybody owed him something, and he was going to take it. Now they're charging him with the other boy's death, that's what I hear. He's being held without bond. I'm afraid he'll never see the light of day again."

Minerva continued in a halting voice. "I took no joy in that man Cutchins' death. If I could change things, I'd drop the suit in a minute. Tell me. Would you do what you did if you had it to do over again?"

"It's beyond that now," Charlie said, his voice etched with weariness.

"Takira's baby won't have a father."

"Do you need somebody to talk to? I'm not the best person for conversation right now."

She laughed derisively. "If I need somebody to talk to now, I talk to Jesus. No, that's not why I called. I need you to give me a ride. Please."

"Well, I—"

"I know you've got other things on your mind, but you need to see this."

He was tired of the other things on his mind. "All right. When?"

"Sooner rather than later. Now would be good."

"Is it an emergency?"

"It's beyond that now," she said, either mimicking him or simply matching his world-weariness.

"You're not talking about going to see Demetrious, because—"

"It's too late for him. Too late for a lot of things."

"OK. So where are we going?"

"I want you to see something. I want you to understand."

"I already know."

"You know nothing." Her tone was flat and cold as ice. "I'm at my house."

* * *

Minerva was rocking on her stoop when Charlie arrived in the Volvo. She stood up and strolled slowly down the sidewalk in heels. Charlie had never seen her dressed up and figured she wanted to go to church, although it seemed awfully late for Wednesday evening services. He got out and opened the passenger door for her. She was wearing makeup and a floral print dress.

"You look nice," he said. She waved off the compliment like a bug in the summer night. He hopped in, eyeing her anxiously. "Where to?"

"The morgue. It's on Pryor Street, off Memorial downtown. They want me to identify a body," she said, sounding empty and defeated.

"Oh. Oh. I'm sorry." Charlie concentrated on starting the car. A minute later, he pulled up to the stop sign where he'd last seen Demetrious.

"They think it's my daughter."

"D's mother?" The news hit him like a brick. He gulped nervously and said, "I'm so sorry. What happened?"

"She was killed. Probably over drugs or money." She waved her hands hopelessly in the air.

"It may not be her," Charlie said.

"It's her," Minnie Doe said, and stared out the window at the gutter, absently picking at a loose thread on her dress. "Lord, I'm gonna have to pay for the funeral. I should have gone to Atlanta Life and got a policy on her. We used to get these policies. Small ones. The agents would come by and collect premiums. We called it life insurance, but it was just burial insurance. Nicest thing some folks ever had was a coffin. Seems a shame, but there was dignity to it."

He pulled onto Memorial. "I'm sorry. I don't recall her name."

"That's right. You don't. She didn't merit a mention in your book. Her name is Shaundra. Shaundra Warner. And now she's gone. I read a brief in the paper this morning about some no-name murder and didn't even know it was her. Police found the body yesterday. Beaten to death and thrown in a Dumpster. That one, I think," she said, pointing at the trash bin behind Redeemer's church as they drove by. "Somebody killed her and just threw her away. Oh my Lord," she wailed. Violent sobs wracked her body as she wept.

Charlie reached over to touch her arm, but she drew away and squeezed herself against the door. She produced a white handkerchief to wipe her face. Charlie stared straight ahead as he drove.

"I promised myself I wouldn't cry. But what good are promises?" She honked her nose and sniffled. "Oh, what would you know? You keep a tight control on your emotions. Sometimes I wonder if you're even human."

After that, they rode in silence. Charlie turned left onto Pryor Street, driving by the pillars supporting the western edge of the huge interchange of the Downtown Connector and I-20, at the core of Atlanta. The Braves were out of town, and traffic was light.

The Fulton County Medical Examiner's Center was a new building, its parking lot bordered by a wrought-iron fence. Charlie parked under the yellow glow of a streetlight. They entered the front door. Minerva was stone-faced and silent as they approached the desk. A dark-skinned man closed a copy of *Sports Illustrated* and placed a call. Moments later, an even darker man in a white polo shirt came out. A surgical mask dangled from his neck. "Ms. Doe. Thanks for coming."

Minerva pushed Charlie away with her hand like she was a swimmer and he was the pool wall. She and the man spoke quietly as Charlie stood off to the side. The two of them walked toward the back. Minerva turned, looking peeved, and beckoned Charlie to follow. They entered a large room and walked through a corridor into an adjoining building. Here was a room like ones Charlie had seen in movies, with autopsy tables in the middle. Along the wall stood a bank of metal lockers. The place gave no sign of recent activity except for the strong scent of industrial disinfectant.

The man went straight to the middle section of lockers, opened a door, and slid out a corpse on a tray. Minerva staggered and grabbed Charlie's arm, bracing herself for a shock. The stench was subtle, due to the low temperature, but Charlie could smell garbage mixed with death's decay.

"She came in about this time last night." The attendant spoke gently, with an accent. Nigerian, perhaps. "We believe she died during the weekend. There will be an autopsy to tell us such things."

He pulled a sheet back to reveal the head. Charlie and Minerva studied the brutalized face, which showed neither horror nor peace. The woman's visage was puffed up and purplish, her eyes swollen shut, as if she had been holding her breath. There were puncture wounds and welts all over her head. Her skull, shattered and misshapen, rested flat like a deflated basketball. Its back had been crushed.

Charlie stepped backward, his stomach churning. He swallowed hard, trying to keep from puking. The attendant glanced at him and nodded toward a white bucket. "Do it in that."

"That's Shaundra Warner," Minerva said. "My daughter. That's her tattoo." She pointed at a red serpent on the corpse's left arm. Charlie felt dizzy, having also recognized the marking. This was the woman he'd seen in Max's Place, the one who chased after him, shouting that he owed her something.

"I am sorry for your loss," the man said. "Unless you want to stay for a time, we will leave this place."

"I'd like to leave, please." Minerva turned away, putting her hand over her mouth. The attendant covered the face and slid the body back into its slot, then closed the locker door with a *click*.

They returned to the front desk, where Minerva filled out a form. When she finished, she sighed and looked at Charlie, then handed the clipboard to the man in the polo shirt. He gestured to the *Sports Illustrated* guy, who held out his free hand for it. "Is that all?" asked Minerva.

"We'll call you if we need anything," the front desk attendant said. "Otherwise, after the autopsy, we'll contact the funeral home." He checked to see that he could read what Minerva had written, then nodded sympathetically. "I know how difficult this is. May God be with you."

"Thank you," Minerva said.

Charlie was already backing toward the door. Minerva followed. Out in the parking lot, he said, "I'm sorry. That's so terrible."

She breathed deeply and muttered, "I hope I don't end up in there."

"Me neither."

"You're likely to," Minerva grumbled. "You keep messing with people."

She marched quickly to the Volvo, rubbing her arms as if warding off a chill, even though it was a hot summer's night. In the car, she said, "I prayed that they catch those people who did this, but I don't think anyone even cares. If something happens to you or yours, Mr. Sherman, it's a big deal because you're ... you know. At least you, of all people, should know. Dirt gets done to a poor black woman, it's the same as it was a hundred years ago. Well, I needed for you to see her. I didn't want her to go without a trace, without you noticing or understanding. So now you know."

"Now I know."

She looked out the window, then turned back to him. "It's wrong, the way they make you pay to tell the world your loved one's gone. That doesn't seem right. I'll pay for an obituary notice in the paper. I want people to know she's gone. They can't just stuff her in a Dumpster and throw her away. That's not right. I'm not living in a world like that, no sir. But I may have to let the county bury her. I need to save my money to pay for Takira's baby. I have to put the living before the dead. Demetrious doesn't know yet. I guess I'll have to find somebody else to take me to see him."

"That would be best."

"In his own twisted, stupid way, he was trying to help his momma, but he doesn't know how to do things right. You may not understand it, after the hurt he's caused, but that makes him worth saving." In a voice full of heartbreak and hopelessness, she said, "I just don't know how to do it. Don't know that I have the strength. They want to kill him with the death penalty, that's what I'm hearing. That's not right. It's not like they ever gave … a damn about the boy that died. Now they claim they do. That's the biggest lie of all."

Charlie stared straight ahead as he drove away from the morgue, passing a black car as it entered the lot. His face was expressionless.

"The other night when your wife came on the TV," Minerva said, her eyes downcast, "He was at my house and saw her standing by that Mercedes, and—I shouldn't say anything else."

"I figured it was something like that." He turned onto Memorial and drove past state offices and the old Archives building.

"I look in your eyes and you seem lost," Minerva said. "I used to think you did the Lord's work. Don't know why. You get showered with money and you just get lonelier. You can't buy back what you lost. Listen to me." She shook her head. "I'm sitting here talking and I don't even know what all you lost." She looked out the window at men in the projects, drinking from brown paper bags. "Don't know you at all."

Perfunctory, pragmatic, and polite. That's how Charlie wanted to play this—without mentioning that he'd met her daughter, because that certainly wouldn't help. "Do you need anything from the store before I take you home?"

"No. Thank you."

They rode quietly the rest of the way to Minerva's house. When Charlie pulled onto her street, Minerva gave him a wide-eyed look like he'd frightened her.

"What?" he asked. He pulled to the curb and cut the engine.

"There is something strange about you. Once I thought you might be an angel, and then I realized I was being a fool, you were just a man, a selfish man at that, with a small version of the truth. Oh, it was truth. And it was a hammer. All metal and cold. But now I think there's something behind you, backing you up, a huge dark shadow I can't see through. I'm not afraid of the devil. And I know you're not him. You don't have the power, especially not over me, and you don't have the tongue for it, either. But tell me, is that who you're working for? Because the kind of things that have happened don't just happen. And they *are* evil. This is … this is some kind of Bible curse. On everybody. You're not talking." She paused a beat. "You're not saying I'm crazy. You do know what I'm talking about, don't you? In the name of God," she cried out, her voice taking on a keening quality, "tell me I'm not crazy!"

A moment of silence passed. "You're not crazy."

"I can't tell if you're good or bad. I can't figure out your nature. Are you trapped? Did you make some sort of deal?"

He hung his head. "Turns out it was a trick."

"I'm entitled to more than that."

"I thought I was, too." He sighed. "I met a stranger. He doesn't have a name, and he … I've seen him come with a storm."

"With a storm?"

"Out of nowhere, on a sunny day."

"Go on."

"I was given a job. I was going to tell the truth about wrongs that had been done." He laughed sardonically. "It seemed so *right* … but no good deed goes unpunished. There's wreckage everywhere. Boils and pestilence. People killed. Shootings and bombings and lightning strikes. The contract that I signed started out normal, just something from an office-supply store. But then it changed."

"How?"

"A penalty for failure was written in blood. And then my signature turned to blood. And then the whole thing turned to blood." Charlie took a deep breath.

"Oh, Lord. I suspected something … but it's hard to believe."

"I'm so sorry all of this happened. I was going to kill myself the night this started … and this thing came along."

"You were going to kill yourself. And then you made a deal when you didn't have anything left to lose—"

"That's never the way it is, no matter how we see it. I know that now."

"All along, you were a dead man walking," she muttered. "It all makes sense now. Doesn't make it any easier, though."

They got out of the car. On the sidewalk to her house, Charlie reached to touch her arm. She pulled away from him and said, "You're cursed." She shook her head and surveyed the neighborhood. "It is hard for me to be strong. There's nothing left but that girl and the child she carries. I'm burying my baby, and her boy's life is over before it begins. All I have to look forward to is to see my great grandchild being born into a world like this."

The porch light flashed on and the door opened. Takira came out, her belly as swollen as the full moon overhead. She looked forlornly at Minerva as the old woman trudged up onto the porch.

"Take care of her," Charlie told the girl.

Minerva embraced Takira. "You and the baby are all I've got."

"Yes ma'am." Takira returned the hug. "We need each other now."

"You go inside now," she told the girl, then spoke to Charlie in her sternest tone. "I don't care if you *are* cursed. You need to take back what you wrote about me. I am *not* that man's daughter. My father is John Riggins, and he died before I was born."

"I can't change what happened." He thought of Ben and wished he could.

"You changed *everything*. You laid out a path of destruction like poison breadcrumbs. You changed the past and that changes the present and that changes the future."

"I'm sorry."

"Don't say you're sorry when you're not. But now that you've said it once, and used my boy for your precious, scientific DNA tests, don't ever say it again. That man is *not* my father. He didn't have anything to do with me. Just leave him out of my life. I don't want any part of anything he touched. I'm dropping the suit. Let the greedy bastards have it." She waved her hands in disgust.

"But Minerva—"

"And you're a greedy bastard, too. That's why you signed some contract in the first place, one you stuck with. You have no idea what the truth is. And now there's no way to heal the wounds. There's no balm that will get rid of the hurt. Not just me. All around." She held out her arms wide. "I don't know what I was thinking, talking to you in the first place. You just caught me at a weak moment. It's best if you stay away from me. Like it does me any good to tell you that."

"I just want you to know—"

"I am sincerely tired of you wanting me to know things. Goodbye, Mr. Sherman."

"I want to pay for your daughter's funeral."

"No thank you. Your money's cursed."

"Just promise me you'll consider it, and I'll go."

"All right, fine. I'll think about it!" she snapped. "Now, good night, Mr. Sherman! Good night!" She stepped inside the house and slammed the door.

Charlie walked to the car, thinking that God's bitter curse, which he knew by heart, was coming true: ... *upon the children unto the third and fourth generation of them that hate me.*

How much longer would it go on? Charlie counted out on his fingers. Minerva, Shaundra, and D. And the one to come. Closer to home, Evangeline, Susan, Beck and Ben ... and their children, too.

It was true: The deal he'd made had been a trick. The house he'd been hired to tear down was his own. And it was falling in on him, sure enough. He tried to shut that thought out of his mind, but it kept knocking. And maybe the reality was even more terrible, given the way he felt about God. Perhaps he'd started his own curse, and the only hope for Ben was to be Scudder's son, after all.

He had no doubt to hide behind anymore. The devil, once just a convenient straw man, was now his only hope. After all, if he was indeed working for God, he could do no worse by switching sides. If he wasn't in hell at this moment—cut off from the wife he'd once loved and stripped of his children, completely alone and publicly reviled, repellent to women, his vision turned to blindness, his only gift the Reaper's touch—he had but to take one tiny step in any direction, and to hell he'd surely go. And it was a step he'd have to take, for there was no other place left for him.

As he pulled away from Minerva's house, the moon vanished behind a thick patch of swift-moving clouds, and a moment later, rain splattered the windshield. With the old car's wipers squeaking and thumping, Charlie turned onto Memorial Drive. He tried to think of something pleasant and calming, but all such thoughts had fled. Instead, he saw Shaundra's puffy face in the morgue's pale light and smelled her death, just as he'd heard her die. For he knew now that the terrible screams he'd heard Saturday night could have been nothing else.

He hated Trouble, the deadbeat deceiver, and his boss, that vengeful, unlovable God that tricked desperate fools for fun and prophecy. If he could just do something to end this bloodbath he'd initiated before Beck and Ben were ground up into a pulp along with everyone and everything else he'd touched ... but how? He had no answers. He was helpless. Hopeless. Worthless, clueless, useless.

As he drove past Redeemer's church, a lightning bolt cracked the eastern sky, illuminating a skulking figure bending over a trash barrel near the soup kitchen. Just who Charlie needed to see. Of course. He'd first found Trouble lying by a Dumpster where he'd been scavenging like a carrion feeder. Which should have been the tip-off.

Charlie slammed on the brakes and jerked the steering wheel to the right, skidding into the church's far entrance, then drove across the gravel lot toward the Hunger Palace, figuring he was back to square one, with nothing left to lose. Time to get a new deal. Or die trying.

Chapter Twenty-Seven

The place seemed abandoned. Another window had been boarded up, and the church was dark inside. The lot had sprouted patches of weeds and unruly tufts of grass. Charlie left the headlights on and scrambled out of the Volvo into needles of rain. "I need to talk to you!" he shouted. "You got some explaining to do!"

As Charlie strode purposefully toward a confrontation, the figure turned and shielded his eyes. Another trick: Charlie was certain he'd seen Trouble, but this guy looked like Alice Cooper, with dark eyes and stringy hair. He gave Charlie a cruel, calculating look and stuck two fingers in his mouth, letting loose a piercing whistle.

Charlie stepped back. "My bad. I thought you were—"

His apology was short-circuited by a blow to the back of his head. Charlie staggered and turned to see a wiry man silhouetted in the headlights' glare, wielding a two-by-four embedded with nails.

The assailant, missing two front teeth, lisped, "You juth been thpiked, bith."

Charlie lunged and punched him in the face. A second later, the whistler jumped on Charlie's back and started choking him. Charlie cried out a garbled "Help!" and stumbled backward, crashing into the Hunger Palace's cement wall. He repeatedly pounded the guy against it. With a groan, his attacker fell off.

Two black men, also small and thin as whippets, rushed to join the fray. One held a length of chain, the other a brick. Charlie stepped forward. The four men closed in around him. "Let me go," Charlie said. "I'll give you my money."

"We'll get to that," the whistler grunted, grimacing and holding his side.

"We don't need you to give it," said the third. "We'll take it when we're through."

Charlie made a break for the car, laying a shoulder into the brick-wielding man, who struck him on the head. Charlie also took a shin-cracking blow from the chain just as the stringy-haired man again tackled him from behind. Charlie yelled as he stumbled. Another man piled on and the three of them crumpled into a pile a dozen feet from the Volvo.

Charlie managed to roll over and kick one attacker, who smashed the brick in his face, cracking his nose and breaking his glasses. He screamed when a nail on the spiked board punctured his right knee. As he struggled to his feet, the chain lashed the side on his head. Then somebody kicked him in the crotch, causing him to double over. His attackers took a moment to enjoy his discomfort. This gave him a chance to recover slightly. This time, Charlie saw the chain coming—though it was a blur—and grabbed it, jerking his attacker off balance. After he took a hard blow to the back of his head, Charlie no longer had a clear idea of what was happening.

He went down and the hits kept coming. A terrific blow set his left eye on fire with blinding pain. He put his hands over his face to shield it. Then came a kick in the ribs. Another and another and another and another. There was blood in his mouth. He couldn't see. Above him, they laughed and admired their work, but they weren't through yet.

"Got a message from your friend," said the stringy-haired scavenger. "He says, and I quote, 'Did you think I would let you live after you broke the deal? Forgiveness ain't my style.'"

"I don't even know what the deal is," Charlie whimpered.

"Keeping it all for yourself, you greedy-ass fool."

"Finish the motherfucker off!"

Blows rained down and Charlie gave up, thinking the end would be a blessing. He mumbled what Beck said when the Halloween candy bag was empty: "All gone."

Then he heard a child's voice from the deepest of distances. "Charlie, are you hurt again?"

There was a shuffling of feet around his head. Some great commotion and yelling. "Get her! She's the one!" Footsteps crunched on gravel.

Bang! A gunshot rang out, followed by a banshee scream. Then a woman's voice, also incredibly far off: "Get away from him." A board clattered to the ground.

"Bitch, we'll kill your infected ass if you don't give us the little one."

Bang! Someone fell beside Charlie and growled, "What the fuck you waitin' for? Get 'em!"

Bang!

"Get up, Charlie! Get up! Get up!"

Apparently, someone wanted him to get up. Charlie struggled to his feet. He heard a yelp of pain and squinted his right eye to see one of the thugs disappear behind the Hunger Palace. The others had retreated into the shadows, except for the one writhing on the ground, clutching his bleeding leg. As his attacker tried to rise, Charlie recovered his senses enough to grab the two-by-four. He clocked the guy with a clumsy swing. The man crumpled to the ground, hissing softly, like he was deflating. Charlie gave him a kick in the ribs, bringing a cry of pain, then followed with a kick to the head. The man fell silent. "I oughtta kill you," Charlie said, contenting himself with spitting blood on his assailant.

Charlie wiped his face with his forearm and turned toward the church. With his wits slowed and his vision blurred in one eye and gone in the other, it took him a moment to realize that Tawny was standing in front of him holding a pistol, braced against the corner of the building. Romy stood beside her. He shook his head to clear it, but whatever was stuck in there was stuck in there good. He staggered toward the two of them.

"My God, they fucked you up bad. We need to get out of here." She kept the gun pointed at the man lying on the ground. When Charlie didn't answer, she yelled, "Charlie. Charlie! We gotta get out of here! Can you drive?"

She was talking to him. He should say something. "I can try," he said, but it sounded like someone else talking.

Tawny turned her head and cried out, "Wyatt! Run to the car!"

Charlie thought he saw a pair of fiery eyes glinting at him from behind a junked washing machine by the abandoned laundromat next door. Then he heard a thump as a piece of brick hit the church wall near his head. The boy scampered out, holding a plastic bag. Tawny pushed both children toward the car and grabbed her backpack. "Hurry! Just keep moving!" She shoved her children into the back seat, climbed in after them, and slammed the door. "Go! Go!"

The man Tawny had shot in the leg was up, lurching toward the car. He stooped to pick up the chain, then continued his advance. Charlie started the engine and hit the gas, striking the man with the front bumper, knocking him away as the chain rained on the car's hood. Charlie slammed on the brakes and shifted into reverse, turning the Volvo around to face the street. A white man appeared from the shadows and ran toward the passenger side of the car, pointing a pistol. "Get down!" Tawny shouted.

A shot rang out as the Volvo's wheels went over the curb. The car careened into the street with a *thump* that jolted everyone inside. Car brakes squealed behind them and a horn honked. More shots were fired as Charlie raced away. Wyatt started crying loudly. Romy was eerily quiet.

"We're out of there!" Tawny told her kids. "We're never going back, I promise!"

A second later, Tawny stuck her head between the front seats, hyperventilating as she spoke. "The kids are OK, I think. Oh, God, Charlie. Those men took over the soup kitchen last week. I heard a woman screaming Saturday night, and then yesterday the police pulled a body out of the Dumpster. I'm sure it was her. It was horrible. That could have been me and the kids. They kept trying to get in. It was weird. They could have broken out a window, but they kept trying to unlock the door." She took a few breaths and swallowed. "I've been thinking of you. I prayed you'd come back for us. Sure took you long enough. I heard a brawl and before I knew it, Romy had slipped outside even though she knows not to. I grabbed the gun and chased after her, and I saw your car. Had to help you. You're a mess. Your eye looks real bad. You need a doctor."

"I'll be all right," Charlie mumbled, even though he had no idea what he was talking about. He was more than half-blind and could barely hold the road.

"Here. Keep this up there, away from the kids." She handed him the nickel-plated revolver, which was warm and smelled of shooting. He laid it on the passenger seat, then covered it with a plastic bag. She leaned back and buckled in the kids as best she could. "We need a place to stay."

"You can stay at my place," Charlie said, his voice heavy and dull.

"We've got a place to sleep," she said softly to her son. "So quit crying."

"I've got to move out in a couple of days, though."

"You can afford a new place, right?"

"Yeah."

"We need to call 911. Got a cellphone?"

Charlie reached into his pocket, then saw a convenience store ahead and pulled his hand out empty. *No cops.* "Use the pay phone. Don't mention my name. I'm already mixed up in one shooting," he said. "Maybe more." He pulled into the store's parking lot, which was bathed in fluorescent light, and parked near the pay phone, located near the end of the building.

"I'll tell them I know where the men are who killed that woman Saturday night," Tawny said.

Charlie dropped his forehead on the steering wheel. "Do that."

Tawny stepped out of the car. Charlie watched her walk away in her Daisy Dukes, pink tank top, and high-heeled sandals. He placed the gun in his lap and pulled the mirror down to check his face. It was a mess. An alien configuration of blood and pulp. His new rimless glasses were busted and had only stayed on because they'd been mashed into his face—now more like a monocle with antennae than specs.

And the pain was almost unbearable. To take his mind off it, he pivoted the mirror to check on the kids. Their watchful gazes met his. "You're hurt bad," Romy said.

"It's not as bad as it looks."

"It looks bad."

"Do you have any food?" Wyatt asked. "Do you have a TV?"

"Yes and yes." As he spoke, Charlie became aware of pain in new places.

Tawny returned. "We should get some food," she said. "They haven't eaten all day. I was afraid to go out with those men there."

"I'll feed them at my place," Charlie said. "Let's go."

He pulled out of the lot onto Memorial, barely avoiding getting T-boned by a pickup truck. Tawny muttered, "Don't kill us now, man."

"I've got it under control."

"You must have a concussion. Honestly, Charlie, I don't understand how you survived."

"I haven't survived yet."

"How can a human take a beating like that?"

"Don't know."

"Why you?"

Charlie felt a loose tooth with his tongue. "My turn, I reckon."

He watched the street move sideways in front of him. A pair of headlights shone directly in his eyes as a horn blared. He adjusted the car out of the way of oncoming traffic. "We'll be there soon," he said.

"If by there you mean the hospital, I believe it."

"Be a man. Answer the phone."

"I … didn't hear a phone," Tawny said.

Somehow, Charlie made it to Castlegate.

"Do you live in a hotel?" Romy asked as they pulled into the garage.

"No," Charlie said. "These are apartments."

He parked and limped toward the elevator as his passengers followed. He felt the pistol against the small of his back; he couldn't remember putting it there. When he glanced back at the car, he saw a bullet hole just above the gas cap door.

Tawny touched Charlie's back, where welts from his chain whipping were rising. He winced and pulled away. "Thank you for taking us in." Tawny stood on tiptoe and kissed his cheek. Unfortunately, there no longer seemed to be a place on his body that didn't hurt.

Charlie cleared his throat. "No. Thank *you.* They were going to kill me."

"They were doing a pretty good job, better than those guys that shot you."

When they got off the elevator, Charlie's hand trembled so badly he couldn't unlock the door. Tawny took the key and got them inside the apartment.

The kids walked gingerly across the concrete floor. "This is all one room," Wyatt said. "But it's a big room."

Charlie limped into the kitchen. He pulled off—or rather, extracted—his fancy spectacles and put them on the counter. Then he went to a corner by the bookcase and pulled out the kid-sized sleeping bags and mats he'd bought for Beck and Ben's stay. "Make yourselves at home."

Wyatt moved toward the TV. "You'll have to eat and take a bath before you watch that," his mother told him, then turned to Charlie. "Food?"

"Uh. Sure. Cheese sandwiches and apples."

"Thanks. You should clean up and assess the damage." She reached up to touch his face, but she winced at the sight of him under the kitchen lights and pulled back her hand.

"Are those nail holes? I think that's what got your eye. My God, can you see out of it? It's swollen shut. Try opening it."

"No."

"You should go to the hospital."

"I'll be all right," Charlie said, although he didn't see how. He didn't see much of anything, but there was a numbness coming over him that seemed to be killing part of the pain.

He realized that a beautiful woman had come to spend the night, and he was in the most pitiful shape of his life. His crotch ached up to his diaphragm. His brain was a cabbage. In his condition, he was more likely to piss blood than have sex. He wished he could just crawl into his cave and get well or die. Didn't matter which, as long as it happened quickly.

He pulled the pistol from his jeans and examined it. Amazing. A prostitute with a gun had saved his life. There were so many bad lessons to be learned here. He swallowed hard. Dragging his right leg, Charlie limped over to the bookcase and placed the revolver on a high shelf beyond the kids' reach, gasping in pain when he stretched. Now he knew what broken ribs felt like.

Tawny drew a bath while the children ate. Afterward she put them in the tub together.

Meanwhile, Charlie checked his face in the living-room mirror. One hell of a beating he'd taken. He looked like a boxer following a career-ending bout. He felt like he was trapped in a dim tunnel with a dull echo and a slow train coming. He was lucky he hadn't bled to death; instead, he'd coagulated nicely. There was dried blood where the tracks of tears should be. His left eye remained swollen shut and throbbed mercilessly. His cheekbone might be cracked. His nose, broken and disjointed, had stopped bleeding. He was pretty sure he would lose at least one of his teeth. His right knee, like his thighs, had been punctured several time. He suspected that the nails from that nasty two-by-four had pierced his skull. He was sure he had a major concussion and wondered if they'd damaged his brain—part of that small percentage he used. He also suspected some damage would be permanent. His overall assessment: He really should feel worse; in fact, he should be dead. Now he *really* knew what Lincoln Roberts had felt like.

He didn't want to sit down for fear he wouldn't get back up.

"Be a man. Put a Band-Aid on it," he muttered, and then took some Advil and washed his wounds in the kitchen sink, splashing water on his face. He plastered bandages on the lacerations he could see, even putting a large square Band-Aid over his left eye. His jeans were torn and bloody, so he slipped on a new pair behind the counter. With a single, loud cry of pain, he put his nose back in line—more or less.

Then he put on his old pair of industrial glasses, so he could see out of one eye, at least. He collapsed on the counter to take the weight off his legs. He coughed and spit blood into the sink, then wondered what part of his body it came from.

Tawny marched the towel-wrapped kids out of the bathroom. She pulled some clean clothes from her backpack while the kids danced around. They dressed in front of the TV. Charlie slipped *Toy Story* into the DVD player. Romy and Wyatt slipped into sleeping bags to watch the movie while their mother took a shower. Charlie thought they'd adjusted to their new surroundings quickly. Then again, this was a calm and secure place, unlike what they'd endured for the past ... actually, he had no idea how long they'd squatted in the church, or where they'd been before that.

Tawny emerged from the bathroom wrapped in a towel. "I feel better. But I'm exhausted. I need to lie down."

"You want one of my shirts?" Charlie limped to the armoire and pulled out a blue T-shirt.

When she put it on, it hung almost to her knees. She smiled and said, "You're a big man." The towel dropped to the floor and she picked it up, then tossed it toward the bathroom. She collapsed on the bed and gave Charlie a winsome smile. She could be a model, he thought. Why shouldn't he love her—that is, when he was able? She'd proved herself. She'd saved his life. There was no longer any need to judge. *I'm no better than her. All right, then. I'll do something about it just as soon as I quit pissing blood.*

He sat on the couch for a while, staring at the movie. Tawny fell asleep. Wyatt did, too. Then Charlie took a shower, washing away the blood and street grime. When he returned to the sofa in gym shorts and a T-shirt, Romy watched him with her all-seeing eyes.

"Don't you like the movie?" he asked.

"I've seen it before."

"Can I turn it off?"

"OK." She wriggled out of the sleeping bag and sat beside him.

"You should go to bed," he said.

"I will. Can I ask you something?"

"Go ahead."

"Can I play with your daughter sometime?"

"That would be nice. But I don't see her much."

"Did they take her away?"

"Yes."

"I hope they bring her back to you. Then I can play with her." She stood on the couch and hugged his neck. "That's what I'll pray for," she whispered. "Thank you for being good to us. I missed you not coming around. I'm glad you came back. I knew it was you, and you were in trouble. I went outside to help you."

"Well, thank you. That was very dangerous. You're very brave. How did you know it was me?"

"I know these things." She gazed into his good eye. "Don't cry, Charlie. Don't cry." She patted his face, managing to find a spot that didn't hurt.

"I can't help it. My eyes hurt. You go to bed now, sweetie."

"OK." She slipped off the couch and went to her sleeping bag, arranging it on the mat just so. "I like you. Are you going to take care of us?"

"I like you, too. I'll find you a place to stay, and ... things are going to be better."

"You can sleep with Mommy if you want to. That's what men do."

There was nothing he could say to that.

He sat still for a couple of minutes, then he remembered the prescription painkillers left over from January's shooting. He got up and swallowed a couple. He sat in the darkness and listened to the children's gentle breathing. Its familiarity was soothing. He felt a little better already.

He realized he'd survived only because a little girl thought he was worth saving. Otherwise, he would have ended up in the Dumpster like Shaundra. There was a word for what he'd experienced, but his enfeebled mind couldn't think of it right then. Something he'd received, a gift he'd done nothing to earn.

"Hey,"Tawny said, sounding groggy. "You need to rest. Come be with me. I won't bite. Unless ..."

Charlie limped to the bed, then fell beside her. He listened to her breathing, no longer afraid of anything she might give him now that she'd given him his life.

"Hold me," she said.

It took awhile to find a way to snuggle that didn't hurt. Tawny laid her arm across his chest and whispered, "I kept hoping you'd come back. I mean, I know we had a fight. But that doesn't matter anymore, does it?"

"No."

"Just promise me—"

She paused to look at his ruined face. The painkillers had kicked in. "We'll talk tomorrow."

"Tomorrow's good," he said.

Charlie stared at the ceiling and realized he'd be leaving this place soon. Moving to where, he didn't know. He would miss this ceiling. Of all the ones he'd stared at in his life, this one was the best, with its train shadows that danced in the middle of the night. Thinking of trains reminded him of that DVD out there by the tracks. He cleared his throat and mumbled drowsily, "I saw you before I ever met you. On my computer once. With a basketball team."

"A basketball team?" Tawny groaned. "Oh, *that*." She chuckled. "So ... what did you think of my performance?"

"Changed my life," he murmured, then drifted off to sleep.

Chapter Twenty-Eight

Charlie woke from a terrible nightmare—Beck was being crushed in a machine, and he was selling tickets for the event—to the sound of ear-splitting screams. Half the visible world was gone; his left eye, swollen and crusted shut, produced a ball of clarifying torment to match the piercing sound in his head. His body played a reveille of misery. For an instant, he didn't know where—or who—he was. He was a new man in a strange place, born of a grinder into a world of pain, awakened from lifelessness by blows from a baseball bat.

Endure, he told himself, and focused on the screaming: It came from a child in meltdown. The little one was at the door, trying to get out. Struggling to his feet, still in shorts and a T-shirt, Charlie staggered toward the brown girl with the mophead curls. Romy. That was her name.

"Mommy left us! Mommy's gone!" She turned to Charlie, sobbing violently, tears streaming down her face, hyperventilating. "I want Mommy!"

"When did she leave?" Charlie asked, his mind dulled by equal parts sleep and trauma.

Romy shook her head furiously and kept babbling.

"It's all right," he said. "I'll bet she went downstairs to the bakery to get you something to eat." He glanced toward the kitchen and noticed his wallet lying open on the counter. He limped over to check. He wouldn't begrudge her money for breakfast.

Two hundred-dollar bills were gone. *Whoops*. That was more than a couple of muffins and a quart of juice. His Visa card had vanished, too. His good eye darted about wildly. The Volvo keys? Not where he'd left them. He glanced at the hook by the door. The BMW and loft keys were still there. Then he saw a note on the legal pad. He rubbed his right eye, blinked several times, and read:

> Charlie,
>
> I can't take care of Romy and Wyatt anymore, so I'm going away. I don't plan to come back. I'm sorry for taking your things, but they're just things. Please let me use your card and don't call the police. I won't charge a bunch of stuff. I just need a new start. I know you'll take good care of the children. Wyatt is a great kid, and my girl is special. You'll see. You'll be better for her than I am. I'm leaving their documents with you. You're their only hope. Tell them I love them. This is a blessing for you. You'll see.
>
> —T
>
> P.S. You should go to a hospital. Maybe they can help you with that asshat problem of yours, too.

Beneath the pad, she'd left a manila envelope. He opened it and saw Social Security cards and birth certificates. Neither had a father's name written on them.

No. This can't be happening. "I'm going to check on your Mommy," he told Romy, who had fallen to the floor and was curled up, sobbing rhythmically. He grabbed his keys. Wyatt was still asleep. She popped up and held out her arms. "OK. OK. Come with me." He picked her up and walked out the door, locking it behind him. He wanted to run down the hall, but he was slowed by a punctured knee, broken toes, and a three-year-old around his neck, so he was reduced to hobbling to the elevator.

To his horror and dismay, the Volvo was, in fact, gone. He stomped the garage floor in anger and frustration, aggravating the pain in his foot where he'd been spiked. He limped over to the vacant space and gently lowered Romy to the floor. She sucked her thumb while he stooped like an Old West tracker, balancing himself upon fingertips on the oil-soaked concrete. He grunted. Each passing minute diminished the chance of her return. No way of telling when she'd left or which way she'd gone. He stood and sighed, brushing his hands together as he stared at the entrance.

"Can you find her?" Romy asked hopefully.

"Let's go back to the apartment." He scooped her up and limped to the elevator.

Wyatt was stirring when they returned.

"Mommy left us!" Romy shrieked with the door still open.

"Calm down," Charlie said, setting her on the floor. "It's going to be all right. I ..." He couldn't think of a proper ending for the sentence, however. "Go wash up for breakfast."

Wyatt took the news rather well. He told Romy, "Mommy goes away all the time."

Within a few minutes, he was slurping milk from his cereal bowl and Romy was doodling her finger in sugar that had spilled on the table. Then came a knock on the door. Charlie peered out the peephole and sighed. *Cops.* He opened the door a crack, bracing himself for bad news about his car and its driver.

"We had a complaint about a child in distress," said the black patrol officer. "May I come in?"

Charlie glanced around the loft to see if everything was in order. It wasn't. Some blood from his wounds had seeped onto the sheets.

"Hang on just a minute." Charlie rushed over and ripped off his bedding, tossing it in a pile by the washing machine, arranging it so the blood didn't show. He returned to the door after a suspicious interval. The officer entered, scowling at the mixture of brown kids and a white guy with a face so pulverized and swollen it was no longer recognizable as the property of Atlanta's most notorious writer.

"I'm taking care of them while their mother's out," Charlie offered.

"Their mother do that to your face?"

"No."

"What's your relationship to these children?"

And talking gets me where? Charlie stared at the officer and said nothing.

"May I see some ID?"

Charlie produced his driver's license. The cop glanced at it and hit a button on his radio: "This is Officer Pearson at Farm and Home Lofts. I'm gonna need backup."

Within minutes, Charlie's place was filled with black lawmen, seven in all, including a Fulton County deputy sheriff, a motorcycle officer, and a mounted policeman who had hitched his horse to a fire hydrant in front of La Patisserie. They milled about, talking amongst themselves, calling in on their radios, wondering aloud how a white guy ended up with two black kids. Worried that they would notice Tawny's gun, Charlie sidled over to the bookcase and surreptitiously felt for the weapon on the top shelf. He couldn't find it. As he groped around, Romy tapped his knee. When he bent down, she whispered, "Did they find Mommy?"

"No," Charlie whispered back.

"Are they going to take us away from you?"

The answer had to be yes, of course. The officers were waiting on the arrival of a caseworker from Family and Children Services. But he couldn't bear to tell her that. "I don't know."

"I don't want them to." She gazed into his good eye. "No one wants us. That's why Mommy ran away. 'Cause I'm different." She started crying again.

He picked up the abandoned child and without thinking, whispered, "I'll take care of you. I promise." He put her down and she ambled over to join Wyatt, who was engrossed in a cartoon on TV.

A cop put a hand on Charlie's shoulder. "You shouldn't have told her that," he said in a husky voice. "You know DFACS is gonna to take the kids. I know the mother. She's unfit. I bet you had a good time until her pimp got hold of you. I didn't even know she had one. She must be moving up in the world."

"Get away from me," Charlie said and pushed the cop in the chest. The officer pointed a finger in his face and gave a fierce warning look, but said nothing. When he stepped away, Charlie slumped against the kitchen counter. He hadn't meant to lie to Romy. He'd needed to say something, and that just seemed like the thing to say. He would take care of her if he could, of course, but that prospect seemed quite impossible.

When the DFACS caseworker arrived, Charlie did a double-take, certain that he'd seen her before. Wearing large spectacles and a wig, the stout African-American woman walked into the loft and appeared completely unsurprised to see Charlie there—as if she expected him to be at the center of this controversy. With a tiny smile, she glanced at the children, then looked over the assembled lawmen as she haphazardly swung her ID badge by its lanyard. "What seems to be the problem, officers?"

Pearson, the cop who had knocked on Charlie's door, drew himself to full height to make his report. The caseworker listened and nodded. When he finished, she turned to Charlie and gave him a schoolteacher's stare. "Mr. Sherman, are these your children?"

The question left Charlie speechless. Before he could answer, Romy marched over and planted herself in front of the caseworker. "Don't be a fool!" the little girl shouted. "Of course he's my Daddy!"

The cops broke out in shouts of disbelief and raucous laughter.

"*Child*, you best watch your tongue." The caseworker glared at Romy.

When the little girl returned the look, the woman flinched and stepped back. "I'm not messin' with you," she muttered. "You are *way above* my pay grade." She turned her attention to Wyatt. "Boy. Is that your father?"

Wyatt glanced up at Charlie. "I don't know. Maybe. I hope so."

"Well," said the caseworker. "Mr. Sherman? What say you?"

He remembered how much Trouble despised Tawny and her children. Just to spite the old trickster, then. "They're mine," he said, cringing at his stupid lie.

"That's a load of crap," Pearson said. "Their mother's white."

The caseworker stared at Charlie intently. "Did you adopt them, Mr. Sherman?"

"Uh—"

"Do you have their documents?"

Charlie pointed to the manila envelope on the kitchen counter. There had to be some truth in what he'd said, since he now held their paperwork. Yeah, that's the ticket. Tawny had made a trade: Volvo for kids, straight up. Registration's in the glove box.

The woman picked up the envelope while the cops stood by, shaking their heads and muttering in disbelief. Charlie wondered what crime he'd be charged with this time. Impersonating a parent? Or maybe just being a fool. People got arrested for that all the time.

"You would have saved us a lot of trouble if you'd just told the officers the truth from the beginning," the caseworker lectured.

"I—"

She held up her hand. "Enough." Clearing her throat, she turned to the lawmen. "They're his. His name's on the birth certificate. Shoulda known," she said, wagging a finger at the defiant little girl who stood with her hands on her hips. "She's just like him. Contrary."

Pearson snatched the documents out of her hand and scrutinized them. "I'll be damned," he muttered.

"I hope not," the caseworker said.

"But how? I don't get it."

"Now be a good cop and put the papers down."

Pearson, wearing a puzzled look on his face, did as he was told.

"All a misunderstanding," the woman said. "Move along. Show's over." She waved her arms and drove the surprised-looking cops toward the door. Overwhelmed by her ruthless shooing, they fled the scene. After they were gone, she stood in the open door and raised an eyebrow at Charlie as if to say *How about that?*

Charlie snapped his fingers. "I know you. You're a MARTA driver."

"Not today," she said with a wink. "You have a blessed day and good life with these gifts that have been given you, Mr. Sherman. If that's your real name. *Hmmph.*" She took off her glasses, put on a pair of shades, and slipped out the door. He thought he heard her mutter, "No cops," as it closed behind her.

With a question on the tip of his tongue, Charlie rushed after her, but he found the hall empty. A scent of lilac lingered. He returned to the kids, who embraced his knees as he walked double peg-legged to the counter. Intensely curious, he held Wyatt's birth certificate up to the light, then Romy's. His name—in crimson—was on both of them. "More red ink," he muttered.

"Wyatt, did you hear her say I'm just like Daddy? That means he's like me, right?"

"Dunno." Wyatt let go of Charlie and stepped back to appraise him. "She's special."

"I am," Romy agreed.

"Is that so?" Charlie asked.

"You'll see," the girl said.

The cellphone buzzed. Romy's specialness would have to wait. Bradley Roy was on the line. "Hey," Charlie said.

"You outta jail today?"

"So far."

"At least they got you downgraded from a suspect to a 'person of interest.' Or is it upgraded?"

"I feel downgraded. How's Susan?"

"Doctor just came in and said she was off the critical list. She's going to make it."

"Thank goodness." Charlie breathed a sigh of relief and glanced at the clock. "When did they take her off?"

"Just a couple of minutes ago. Doc came in and said it, just like that. He looked surprised, to tell the truth."

"Interesting." Charlie felt a tingle run up his spine. Strange and wonderful things were happening.

"*What*?" Bradley Roy asked, sounding irritated. "I guess you could call it that. Anyway, they been keepin' her asleep. Don't know how long that's gonna last. Sooner or later she gotta wake up and find out her back's broken. Maybe it's a mercy to be out cold, with the world crashing down the way it is. When you comin' by?"

"Uh. When nobody else is there, maybe."

"Well, look, there's somethin' I gotta tell you."

"Why don't you tell me now?"

Bradley Roy hesitated. "They don't know about operatin' yet. Don't know what good it will do. Doctors are still saying 'wait-and-see' about removing the bullet. At least she'll be able to use her arms, they say."

"She hasn't woken up at all?"

"Not while I've been around. I was here till midnight." He yawned. "Came back at seven."

"What about everybody else?"

"That's what I wanted to talk to you about. Susie's going to need you more than ever. No matter what happens or how you feel about everything right now, you can't desert her."

Had this been what he'd wanted all along? Charlie gulped. "I won't. But how things work out may not be up to me."

"You're the one that's got to help her. I know it's hard to see past your own hurt and pride. But get over it." He paused. "She never thought you'd make it. Always thought you'd come crawling back. Now she can't even walk, and you with two bestsellers, both of 'em carved out of Forsyth County's hide." He chuckled ruefully. "Can't say we didn't have it comin'."

"I never wanted a divorce."

"Hard to know what you wanted. You broke her heart when you left."

"Mine was broken already."

Bradley Roy scoffed. "Hell, I'm still waitin' to see if you got one."

"I've heard that before. So what you got to tell me?"

"All right." Bradley Roy's tone softened. "I got a phone call this morning from Jimmy Townsell. You know him?"

"Yeah," Charlie said, recalling the check he'd written to the political candidate. "He's running against Stanley Cutchins. Why's he calling you?"

"Probably because I donated to his campaign. And fed him information along the way. Jimmy told me that sheriff's deputies and the GBI are down at the property line between Pap's farm—what used to be Pap's farm—and the Owens farm next door."

"Yeah?"

"They're down at Long Creek, boy."

Silence.

"Hell, Charlie, I'm surprised you didn't do it yourself, knowing what you knew."

"I get shot at when I go up there. You sayin' they're looking for John Riggins?"

"No, I'm sayin' they *found* John Riggins. It's a crime scene now."

Charlie's pulse quickened. "He's there?"

"In a shallow grave. Of course, word about your book has been leaking out for months. I was hopin' Pap would have to answer for what he did ..."

"How'd the sheriff know where to look?"

"He was told. By someone who did some digging. That's all you need to know."

"OK. I won't go there."

"Nobody's left to hold accountable, except the estate. You know, Susie got a share of the money. Now she's paying for it."

"I didn't know. I guessed. And it looks like we're all paying."

Bradley Roy coughed. After a poignant silence, he said, "That woman you wrote about sounds like a good person."

"Minerva Doe? She is."

"And then her grandson does this to my daughter. His second cousin, turns out. Everybody up here thinks he did it 'cause he's black. But maybe it's because he's got some of Pap in him."

"That thought occurred to me, too."

"Any way you look at it, we got ourselves a mess. And then a detective talked to me last night. They don't think Pap killed himself, after all. They say there were signs of a struggle. And after that comes out, now there's a story that a black gang from Atlanta came up and killed him. For 'reparations,' that was the word," Bradley Roy said sarcastically. "Allegedly, the same crowd that hijacked Susie's car."

"The sheriff's not saying that, is he?"

"No. It's coming from Stanley. It's pretty fishy. Everything is unraveling. I know it started with you workin' on that first book. I just wonder when it's going to end. Lord, give me strength."

"I'll try to get by later today. But I have ... things to take care of. I have to move tomorrow. Don't even have a place yet."

"Susie needs you."

"I doubt she wants to hear that."

"She'll be hearing it from me when she wakes up. And until she's sick of hearing it. 'Cause I'm too old to be wheeling her around. You hear me, boy?"

Romy came over to Charlie with her shoes, wanting help to put them on.

"I hear you."

* * *

Charlie placed the birth certificates in a watertight (and hopefully blood-tight) container, then spent the rest of the day caring for his sudden family and packing for Friday's move. He took Wyatt and Romy shopping, but first he dropped by a storefront clinic for treatment. He received six stitches for a gash just beneath his rose scar. His cracked ribs and toes would heal on their own. Most significantly, his left eye was a ghastly mess, beyond the expertise of the staff doctor, who informed Charlie that he was lucky to be alive, referred him to an ophthalmologist, and told him to wear an eyepatch in the meantime. Charlie left with a handful of prescriptions for antibiotics, ointments, and painkillers. His two loose teeth would have to wait, since he had to find a dentist to replace Victor Blaga.

When he returned to Castlegate, Charlie sported an eyepatch but no glasses. The vision in his right eye was clear and needed no correction, an odd but welcome development. Apparently, his eyesight had been beaten back into alignment—that which hadn't been destroyed had been restored. He was disappointed that he'd been unable to visit Susan, but he vowed to do so the next day. Exhausted and loopy from painkillers, he wanted to lie down, but Wyatt and Romy insisted that he play the new Candy Land game he'd bought for them.

Looking up from the board, Wyatt asked, "If Mommy comes back, will you marry her?"

"I already have a wife. She's in the hospital."

"I want to see her," Romy said. "I'll make her feel better."

"That would be nice. Maybe we'll go tomorrow," Charlie said, grabbing her and pulling her onto his lap. Wyatt threw himself on Charlie alongside Romy. They rolled around on the floor, an activity that proved to be therapeutic for Charlie.

Later, Charlie played a CD of piano music while he packed. Romy interrupted him, pulling his hand to dance with her. He stood and swayed unsteadily to the music while she spun around like a dervish. The boy joined in the frolic. Playing with them reminded Charlie of old times at home and made him wish he could put together the missing pieces of his life. How would he ever find his way back to Beck and Ben with Romy and Wyatt eating his breadcrumbs?

Romy stopped dancing and stared straight at his eyepatch. "Are you going to love us?" she asked.

Charlie gave her a quirky smile. "Yes, I believe I will. And as your father, in accordance with state law. I'll take care of you, or die trying. That's the deal, the way I understand these things."

"You won't ever leave us?"

"No. Of course not."

"Just checkin'," she said, twirling away.

It is a strange and serious business, to make a lie the truth.

* * *

When Charlie checked his voicemails, he heard this: "Charlie, Muncie here. Wanted to let you know the divorce trial is postponed, by consent of all parties. I heard Susan is paralyzed from the waist down. That's terrible ... I'm so sorry. I hope it's not true. I do have some good news for you in the middle of all this. My guy spent the day on your case and found out a few things. Cops didn't tell us the dead guy's girlfriend was holding a ransom note that she was supposed to phone into Channel Six. The carjackers wanted a million dollars from you. But they got violent and screwed that plan, so they stole the car instead. Demetrious Warner claimed you took them to the bank. Which contradicts the ransom note story, of course. Then a MARTA driver came forward and told police they'd been on her bus and got off at Hanover. So there's some things that destroy your accuser's credibility. Who would have thought a bus driver would come to your rescue?"

Charlie looked up at the ceiling and blinked his right eye. "I have great faith in public transportation."

* * *

The kids were still awake when Charlie watched the eleven o'clock news. The top story on Channel Six: "Late Wednesday night, five men suspected in the murder of Shaundra Warner barricaded themselves in a warehouse on Memorial Drive when police arrived to arrest them. All five perished in an blazing inferno." There were few details, only footage of the fire.

Charlie was still staring at the screen open-mouthed when the anchor moved on to the next story and a camera cut to a familiar landscape. "Our Forsyth County saga continues," reporter Trent Brown solemnly intoned. "Earlier today, Sheriff Allan Burch announced the discovery of the skeletal remains of a man and either a horse or mule. Currently, GBI investigators are working to exhume the bodies, believed to have been there for several decades. While Burch says no positive identification is possible at this time, he told us that lawmen were acting on a tip from someone who had read the controversial bestseller, *American Monster*, which means it's possible that they have found the remains of John Riggins, a black farmer allegedly lynched by a mob in 1937. Isaac Cutchins, the man author Charles Sherman has accused of this crime, was found dead in his home a week ago. Cutchins's death, originally believed to be a suicide, is under investigation. More as it develops."

The newscast cut to a picture of the book's front cover, then the shallow grave and a section of an unearthed skeleton. Wyatt looked up at the TV and sang out, "Dinosaur bones!"

"Time for you to go to bed," Charlie declared. He turned off the TV and herded the kids to the bathroom to brush their teeth.

After they were tucked in, Charlie went out on the fire escape to be with the trains and that distant glimmer of Tawny. He tried to collect his mashed-up thoughts. Tomorrow he would leave this place, taking with him a laptop computer, an overpriced painting, his wardrobe, some books, two new kids, and not much else. What would happen after that, he hadn't a clue. Hopefully, each day would bring less pain. But no matter what, he had to endure, because people counted on him.

He heard a noise and turned to see Romy inside, comically splayed out against the plate glass, cross-eyed, nose bent up, nostrils flaring. He laughed and slid the patio door open.

"Sing to me," she said.

He scooped the girl up and carried her back to her mat. Wyatt was already asleep. Charlie knelt as she crawled into her sleeping bag, shifting his weight away from his right knee. When she was properly snug, he sang, though it came out as more of a croak:

> *There was a man in our town, and he was wondrous wise;*
> *He jumped into a bramble-bush, and scratched out both his eyes.*
> *But when he saw his eyes were out, with all his might and main,*
> *He jumped into another bush, and scratched them in again.*

Her dark eyes shining, Romy touched the bristly scar on his left cheek and brushed his black eyepatch. "You're Brambleman."

"I guess I am."

"I love you."

"I'm glad."

"Do you love us yet?"

"I suppose I do."

"It's about time. I've been waiting for *hours*."

Chapter Twenty-Nine

Loud, insistent rapping woke Charlie. He rolled out of bed and limped barefoot across the cool concrete floor. *Endure.* Before he reached the door, it opened and a surly, mannish-looking woman stepped inside, holding her key like a weapon. She froze him with a glower and dropped an orange five-gallon bucket filled with cleaning supplies at his feet.

"Your face is beat from shit," she declared.

Satalin's Eastern European cleaning woman. He knew her slightly, having declined her services in January after Satalin's next-door neighbor told Charlie, "We think she's ex-secret police." And now she returned triumphant and vengeful on this, the day of reckoning.

"Excuse me, but—"

"You must go now," she said, scouting the loft with narrowed, suspicious eyes. "And what are those?" she said, pointing at Wyatt and Romy, both now awake and blinking in fear at the strange and terrible creature. "Checkout time is ten o'clock." She gave Charlie an evil laugh.

He groaned, then looked at the clock. "Hey, it's not even—"

"I joke, I joke. Checkout time is *now*. Don't worry. I give you half-hour before I throw things out."

The effects of his concussion lingered. He had a headache and felt a heavy-handed stupidity controlling his thoughts. By Charlie's reckoning, he had fifteen hours left on his lease, but he was no match for the cleaning lady. Fortunately, he'd already packed up. Wyatt and Romy, accustomed to quick getaways, dressed and threw their stuff, virtually all of it new, in their sleeping bags. To honor the occasion, Charlie donned his monogrammed shipping department uniform, a gift from Barbara Asher—so he'd know who he was. Lately, he hadn't been so sure.

They fled her toxic brew of ammonia and bleach mixed together. Charlie packed the trunk and front seat of the BMW. (So little to show for being rich!) He threw the kids' backpacks on the rear floor, then walked them into La Patisserie for breakfast.

Charlie ate a Danish. Amy fretted over his ruined, swollen face and was surprised to hear Romy call Charlie "Daddy."

She whispered to Charlie, "Weren't your kids white last time?"

"Yes," he whispered back. "Go figure."

Amy turned away, then pivoted back toward Charlie, her pretty face a picture of puzzlement. "So you're their father?"

"Long lost," he said, nodding.

"But now you're found."

While the kids busied themselves with coloring books, Charlie got a refill on his coffee and pondered his changing fate. Realizing it might be a long time before he returned, he bought another Danish. Halfway through his second cup, Amy came hurtling out of her office and flopped her chest over the counter, urgently beckoning him. "Charlie! You need to see this! I heard them mention your book."

He stepped around the counter and squeezed into a tiny office decorated with clipboards hanging everywhere, positioning himself so he could watch the kids and the ceiling-mounted television at the same time. The set was tuned to Channel Six, with a "Breaking News" graphic running across the bottom of the screen. He heard helicopter rotors humming and saw the aerial shot of an upscale house by a lake.

Charlene Guy held a cellphone as she stared into the camera. "We're talking with a neighbor who says the house belongs to Marie Hastings. Apparently a family member is also in the house." Speaking into the phone, she said, "Mrs. Pilson, you're on air. Can you tell me if anyone else lives there?"

"Her son," the woman said in a slightly muffled, high-pitched voice. "They call him 'Momo.' He's in trouble with the law a lot. This may have something to do with him."

Momo's monster pickup sat in the drive. The heli-cam panned to show a black-helmeted deputy run in a crouch to take a position behind a stone wall. Other SWAT members advanced on the house like ants on a picnic basket.

"Thank you. Please hold a moment," the morning news anchor said, then addressed the camera: "According to the Forsyth County Sheriff's Office, deputies were attempting to deliver a murder warrant in the death of Isaac Cutchins this morning when they were fired upon. Since then, there's been a standoff, and our source reported that just a few minutes ago, a single shot was fired, apparently inside the house. SWAT members look like they're setting up to enter the house—"

"Charlene," said the reporter in the helicopter. "You can see smoke coming out under the eaves of the house." The camera zoomed in. "I see flames now. The house is on fire."

Then came a voiceover from Charlene Guy: "We're just had a report of another gunshot."

Charlie groaned. Amy touched his arm and said, "Do you know these people?"

"Yes."

"I'm so sorry."

"It's Judgment Day."

"That's harsh."

"Yes." He stared at the screen and watched flames quickly spread as black smoke roiled out from under the eaves. "Yes, it is."

He took a step back. "I can't watch this anymore."

After he said goodbye to Amy and promised to come back for Danish someday soon, Charlie slipped out with the kids. He buckled them into their safety seats and traveled down Memorial Drive, stopping at the Holy Way House to inspect the damage from Wednesday night's fire. Charlie had seen the news coverage of the inferno that wiped out the gang of cutthroats responsible for nearly killing him. Up close, the scene was terribly stark. The warehouse and other buildings on three sides of the church and the Hunger Palace had burned to the ground, and their ruins were now wrapped with ribbons of fluttering yellow tape. Redeemer's church and the Hunger Palace had escaped the flames unscathed and looked like they had risen from the ashes of the surrounding destruction. He briefly considered going inside to retrieve Romy's and Wyatt's things, then decided against the idea, especially since they didn't want to be there and neither one cried out for anything they'd left behind.

* * *

When Charlie exited the hospital's elevator with Romy and Wyatt, he sensed something was wrong. The ICU nurse's station was deserted. The floor seemed unnaturally quiet, even though he could hear unseen people talking and a far-off voice over an intercom speaker. A hard chill stronger than any air conditioning raised goose bumps on his arms, and the hallway was filled with static electricity. A glance through a window revealed storm clouds rolling in. He smelled deteriorating body functions vying with disinfectants, and to top it off, a whiff of the street. Trouble was near.

Wyatt frowned and said, "Something's wrong." Charlie glanced at Romy, who wore a serene expression. The poor little girl had no idea of the danger she was in. He hesitated, considering the threat to the children from the supernatural being who hated them. But Susan was in danger, too, and there was no safe place for the children or for him. At least here, they were in public—and close to an emergency room.

"No fear," Charlie muttered.

"No fear," Romy echoed.

Charlie scooped up the girl, grabbed Wyatt's hand, and quickened his pace. A shadow fell from Susan's room, forming a puddle of darkness on the hall floor. In Room 330, a man in a cleric's collar hugged an old woman, patting her back as she cried on his shoulder, both of them oblivious to the unearthly presence next door.

Charlie braced himself and walked into Room 332 with his new kids. Trouble was sitting in the aqua chair, wearing a battered tan jacket, reading a book Charlie recognized: *Dog Heaven*. The trickster was pallid, with dark circles under his eyes. The room smelled of rank sweat and decay. Well, the old death-dealer *had* been working overtime. What was it—ten people killed in the past week? Charlie couldn't keep track. The storm clouds were overhead now. There was a flash of lightning, followed by an understated *boom*—subtle, compared to what he'd seen and heard before.

Without taking his eyes off the book, Trouble said, "I love happy endings, don't you?" He pantomimed wiping a tear. When he glanced up, he recoiled in the chair like he'd been tased. "Oh no you didn't."

Wyatt whimpered and pulled on Charlie's hand. "Stand behind me," Charlie told him, and the boy stepped backward into the doorway. Romy stared at Trouble wide-eyed, unblinking.

"Well, that explains what happened the other night," Trouble said, shaking his head in sad amazement. "I thought maybe it was you, but I was giving you too much credit, as usual." He looked at the book in disgust and tossed it aside. "I was going to tell you I killed your dog, but we're a little beyond jokes, I see. Kill the dog, kill the bitch. Get it? No? Humph. I wondered why your wife—she is still your wife, no?—was so remarkably resilient. She was supposed to writhe in agony, then die. I was just getting ready to try again when you dropped in. Now I can see *that* ain't gonna happen. Everything makes perfect, horrible sense."

Not to Charlie. He glanced toward Susan, who wore a troubled expression in her sleep. He listened to her breathing, a wonderful sound, since she was off the respirator. Then he noticed that Trouble was tense, gripping the chair arms, looking like he would spring and attack.

"Yeah, I wondered why she wouldn't die," Trouble said, relaxing a bit. "Right when she was supposed to flatline yesterday, they took her off the critical list. Now I've heard about the miracle of modern medicine, but that was just contrary to nature. It was also a personal insult. So I had to see for myself, come in and—what's the opposite of jump start?"

He stared Charlie in the eye. "Now I know. You went and got yourself some kryptonite. Let me guess. You claimed her as your own." He glanced at his bare wrist. "I'm guessing you locked it down yesterday at nine-fifty-eight a.m., give or take."

Confused and unsettled, Charlie took a step back. He'd told the caseworker that Romy and Wyatt were his right around ten o'clock, of course. It was beyond belief to think—

"I've been trying to destroy her since she was born," Trouble said, pointing at Romy. "Always thought we had a shot, with no one to claim or protect her except the whore. And you, a fool of the major sort, latched onto her. I lost some of my best minions the other night." Trouble narrowed his eyes, then shouted, "Unlike you, they do as they're told! I said, NO COPS! And you had to change the locks. They couldn't get in ... well, too late now." He shrugged. "Then again, you never were a minion. More of a mistake, you ask me. But maybe I just don't get it anymore."

Seeing Trouble frustrated was quite amazing (and gratifying) to Charlie. Was it possible that he was now powerless? "I thought you'd be up in Forsyth County, supervising the mayhem," he said.

Trouble waved off the idea. "Oh, they didn't need me for that. The Cutchinses were bound to self-destruct once you exposed them like rats to light. Turned on each other. Tantie Marie informed on her brother and sister. Her son killed her and burned down the house while he was still inside. Tried to shoot himself, but he missed. Too bad. He burns. By the way, that firestarter trait is genetic. You can't teach it," Trouble said, sounding like a proud father.

"Are you saying the whole family was in the house that burned?" Charlie asked.

"Oh, no. Your mother-in-law will die in jail. I know *that* breaks your heart." Trouble let out a little chuckle. "By the way, in case there was even the tiniest bit of doubt in your mind, she's the one who paid to have you killed. Twice. And the man you call Uncle Stanley has embezzled just about all the family's money, abandoned his wife for his mistress, and boarded an airliner bound for parts unknown—to the authorities, that is."

Charlie's eyes narrowed. "You're not going to blow up the plane, are you?"

"You think I'm that clumsy?" Trouble held up his hands and twiddled his fingers. "I'm more of a surgeon. Or a maestro, I suppose. These things are orchestrated, more or less." He shrugged and wagged his head to the side. "You'll be interested to know what happened to Momo was an answer to Kathleen's prayer. Really unspeakable, what he did to his mother, even for my tastes. Again, it's a family thing." Trouble sighed. "Kathleen would have had her vengeance, too. But you had to set her up to die happy," he said with a sneer. "All because of that little piece of fluff you edited. And then you cut her and her heirs and assignees out of the real deal on the work in question! Unbelievable. You broke the deal—"

"Some deal. More like a trick."

"—and made your own worthless life forfeit. Yet there you are."

So he could have kept all the money from *Flight* and should have shared the royalties on *Monster*. What a bunch of hair-splitting nonsense. He suspected Trouble of running a rogue operation or just ad libbing everything.

"Here I am." Charlie shifted Romy to his left arm. "Though not exactly in one piece. What about Susan? What about Beck and Ben?"

"Well, you saved them, thanks to your dumb-luck stunt with the little whore-child. If it were up to me, well ... I shouldn't even say. I never could figure you out. Believe me, it was bothersome, watching you mess everything up. Takes a certain kind of ... well, it's not easy to do what you did and survive, let alone get in line for a promotion."

"A promotion? I almost died the other night."

"You still don't get it. And you may not get it." Trouble looked to the ceiling and held up his hands in exasperation. "That is what is so *amazing* about you. You stumble around, and ... somehow succeed. You were supposed to share that money for the Cutchins book, but *noooooo* ... you break a deal under penalty of death and go out and get yourself a bodyguard and a Beamer. Hardly original."

"The bodyguard was a fake."

"*Everything about you is fake*! From your footnotes to your industrial chic hairstyle, you're a fraud. How ya gonna teach the little whore-children to do right when you got no standards yourself, eh?"

"Watch your language," Charlie growled.

"Shut up. I'm tellin' a story."

"Don't you talk to my Daddy that way," Romy said.

Charlie thought he heard Susan say something and turned his head toward the bed just as Trouble charged forward, his fist raised, shouting, "Your mother is a worthless bitch, you insolent little whore-spawn!"

There was a *whump*, then a loud POP! Charlie was knocked backward. His legs buckled and he barely kept on his feet. Romy started to fly off his shoulder, and he tightened his grip to keep her from sailing away. A loud buzz filled the room, along with an acrid cloud of smoke that stank of ozone and burnt hair.

Charlie turned to look at Romy. Her eyes were on fire with anger. It took him a second to realize that Trouble was pinned between the top of the window and the ceiling. Whimpering, with his hair on fire. He tried to put it out with his hands as he slid down the glass and fell on his face. Charlie was awestruck. The girl had her smite on.

Trouble struggled to his feet, grabbed the water pitcher from the bedside stand, and poured its contents over his hair, raising a cloud of steam. He glared fiercely at the girl. If looks could kill, she would have left that room in a basket. But his didn't, not anymore. Trouble shook his head rapidly in an attempt to recover, then grinned maliciously. "I bet your name's on her birth certificate."

"In blood," Charlie said. "I guess you all ran out of ink."

"Don't blame that one on me. You're operating above my pay grade now."

"Oh, really?" This was the second time he'd heard that phrase recently. There was some kind of hierarchy in play. The idea that some other power was at work gave Charlie great hope.

"Yeah, I've seen this happen before. Don't like it much, but what can I do? That explains why the dump truck didn't run that red light yesterday afternoon when Raccoon-boy's wife was bringing her kids home from Bible boot camp." He shrugged. "They teach a lot of good Old Testament stuff there, by the way. Don't care what they say: The sequel is *not* as good as the original."

"Yeah, the First Church of Varmintville is heavy on the hell," Charlie said.

Trouble shifted his gaze to Romy, who continued to stare at him with unblinking eyes. "Went and got yourself a rich daddy, didn't you, you little—"

"Watch it," Charlie said.

"I can't touch you now. Oh, I can touch you." Trouble reached out and slapped Charlie's face, then jumped back as Romy swatted at him. "But I can't hurt you."

It *did* hurt, but there was no supernatural shock, just the pain from a garden-variety bitch slap to an injured face. Trouble gave him a sour smirk. "Like I said, you got kryptonite."

Romy reached out and tried again to hit Trouble, but he stayed just out of reach. Charlie stepped toward him, and Trouble found himself forced into the corner. "All right, I know I'm not wanted. And having failed to terminate you, I got to pay up as if you'd actually fulfilled your contract. Completely unfair. No vengeance or justice in that." Trouble grinned. "Sadly, you asked for the impossible."

"I didn't ask you for anything, you murderous lunatic."

"On the contrary." Trouble pulled out a tiny pad from the back pocket of his grimy jeans and scrutinized it, then rattled off a list. "There's the first one, with a note that says 'to discuss later,' then a million wishes, a go-kart, to see Jesus, to make the football team, getting in Annie Sutton's pants, passing the chemistry final, granting you the serenity—wait a minute, that's plagiarism—ah, this sounds more like you, not letting the check for your engagement ring bounce. Eww, sorry about that one. Baby number one born with all toes and fingers, Baby number two born with all toes and fingers. Now, that's just luck, by the way, I don't do toes and fingers. I mean I don't put them *on*. Quitting drinking. You're welcome."

Charlie laughed. "Most of those things I didn't get."

"Don't go Yoda on me. Ah, here it is: Wife down on both knees begging you to come back. Hmm, like I said, that's a problem. The second part, that is. I mean, who would want you back? Especially now that you've got the little whore-child."

"Sweetie. This is a bad … uh, man," Charlie said. "Don't listen to him."

"I'm not a man."

"Sorry. My bad. Demon."

Trouble gave him a hurt look. "I'm not a demon. I'm an angel. I thought you knew."

"You're an *angel*? I gave up on that idea a while back."

"I'm an *avenging* angel. People get us confused with demons, I admit. There's a little bit of overlap."

"A trickster," Charlie said. "That's what you are."

"Whatever. Distinction without a difference."

Romy reached out and swatted at Trouble's head. *Zzzt.*

"Stop burning my hair!" Trouble shrieked. "Mine doesn't grow as fast as yours, you know!"

"Get his nose," Charlie whispered to Romy as he advanced on Trouble, who backed away and ducked out of the little girl's reach.

"Truce! Truce! You win, dude. Just let me grant your prayer, and I'll be on my way."

"I don't want you to grant my prayer. I'm not working for an angry God anymore. I renounce you and your boss, if you have one."

Trouble stood up and stroked his chin. "Hmm. It *was* an impossible prayer," he mused, looking out the window at the storm clouds, which were dissipating as quickly as they'd formed. "I can't make her love him. That is *definitely* not my specialty." He looked up to the ceiling. "I mean, I can't get her to do it, if he can't get her to do it, see what I'm sayin'? No? I gotta try?" Trouble's face wrinkled in disappointment.

"You should leave now," Charlie said. "And don't come back." He feinted Romy toward Trouble, who danced backward. "You have no power here anymore. You can't even make it rain. Look! Your clouds are breaking up. I'm working for a new boss now. Be gone!"

"A new boss." Trouble glowered. "You're not out of the woods. And knowing you, you'll find a way to screw it up. But hey, no hard feelings, and congratulations on getting this far. Sorry I didn't consider your wretched life worth saving. But hey, what does it matter what I think, right? They say you live. Excuse me. She says you live." He gave Romy a sneer. "And that changes everything. If they want to deal with her, they gonna have to get a bigger boat."

"I find that comforting."

"You shouldn't. Try putting her in time-out, see what happens."

"Go."

"I will. But first, it is time to answer your prayer. I'd be remiss if I didn't try. Part of it I've done already. Actually, I may have done it a little too well. She's on her back, which is way beyond being on her knees. You'll give me that, right?"

"Just get out."

"Ut-ut." Trouble held up a hand. "Don't intervene in an intervention, newbie. You don't have any idea what this is all about."

"I renounce your judgment. Your vengeance. Your violence. Your hatred. I renounce you."

"All right. You do have some idea. Still," Trouble said, brightening. "Gotta let me try. I mean basically, you want to get back together with her. Save the kids, yours and hers. All that." He waved his hand nonchalantly. "I mean, last I heard she wasn't in a mood to ask you back. You can't make her ask you back. But you gotta admit I did a pretty good job of making her need you." Trouble's voice was filled with pride.

"I am so tired of you. Romy, swat him."

Trouble held up his arms as if fending off a stoning. Then he feinted toward the bed. Charlie held Romy out toward him like a chainsaw.

"Shame on you, hiding behind a little girl." Trouble scolded as he backed off. Then he switched to pleading. "Come on, let me do this. I'll perform a miracle." He rubbed his hands together vigorously.

"I don't like your miracles much," Charlie said, bobbing his head with every word. "They're nasty and cheap-hearted."

Trouble gave him a grin. "You should see me turn the blind lame."

"That's what I'm afraid of."

"Halfway there with you, dude."

"Tell him he's banished from this place," Charlie whispered to Romy. "Maybe that will work."

"No!" Trouble cried.

"You are banished from this place!" Romy shouted, waving her arm.

Trouble flew from the room over Wyatt's head like he'd been thrown out by an invisible bouncer, landing on his ass in the hall. He turned and looked daggers at Romy, then Wyatt, who now stared at him. Trouble made no attempt to reenter. Instead, he gave them a sly smile as he slowly got up.

"Forever!" Charlie whispered.

"Forever!" Romy declared, wiping the smile off Trouble's face.

"Well, my work here is done, whether I like it or not!" shouted Trouble as he slid out of sight, his shoes squealing on the floor. "Completely undeserved!"

Charlie looked out the window as sunshine broke through the clouds. He collapsed in the aqua chair with Romy on his lap. Wyatt joined them. They sat quietly while Charlie stroked the children's hair. He wondered if the nightmare was over—or if another one was about to begin.

A short while later, Susan showed signs of coming out of her coma and Charlie moved to her bedside. She opened her eyes and stared at the ceiling, then glanced at her estranged husband with a look of groggy puzzlement. She licked her lips, then dozed off for a minute. When she came to again, she gazed at his face and mumbled. "Charlic, is that you?"

"What's left of me."

"I barely recognize you. What happened?"

"I got poked in the eye with a sharp stick."

"Did Momo do that?"

"No."

"Anybody I know?"

"No."

"Looks bad."

"Well, I'm more concerned about you."

Susan's left hand was covered by Charlie's. She tried to move it, but it was strapped in a restraint. She glanced over and saw Charlie's wedding band. "Are we still married?"

"Yes."

"What day is it?"

This was the question doctors asked patients coming out of comas, so Charlie hesitated for a second, but he wanted her to score well on the test, so maybe some advance knowledge wouldn't hurt. "Friday. You've been out of it for a few days."

"What time is it?"

In the distance, church bells—the same ones he'd heard on Christmas Day—began chiming. Charlie savored the sound, believing somehow that the play clock was running out on their divorce. "Ten," she said when they fell silent. "The trial."

"You missed it. Under state law, you're stuck with me."

"That seems unfair."

"Hey, a deal's a deal."

"But I got shot." She stared at the ceiling. A tear trickled down her cheek. He reached for a tissue and dabbed her face. "Black guys," she said. "Just kids. One of them had a gun. I gave them the keys but they wanted me to get in the car. I wouldn't do it. I thought, God, let them kill me out in the street. I didn't want to die in a car trunk. Or worse."

"I understand. The police caught them both. The one who shot you is dead."

"It's terrible. I thought I was going to die."

"Well, you didn't. You're very strong."

"I'm very thirsty." There was a pitcher of ice water on the bedside stand, along with plastic cups and bendable straws. He poured a cup and positioned it for her to drink. She took a long sip, then tried to sit up, but she was bound to the bed. "Can you undo these?"

"I'll get a nurse." He reached over and hit the call button.

"I just want to get up and walk out of here. But something's not right. I feel a lot of pain in my back. My feet itch."

Charlie got up and looked out the door and fretted. "Where is that nurse?"

"Did I hear children's voices? I want to see the kids."

Wyatt and Romy, sitting together quietly in the aqua chair, took the cue to stir. Susan turned her head and stared wide-eyed at them, then at Charlie.

"Who are they? What are they doing here?"

"I was lonely, so I got some new kids," he said brightly. "I'll be happy to share."

Susan stared at him open-mouthed. "Get out," she said.

Charlie stood, feeling liked he'd been stabbed in the heart. "I'm sorry. Come on, kids."

"No. Wait. What are you doing?" Susan looked at him like he was crazy.

"I was—"

"I mean you can't be serious. Don't go. I don't want to be alone right now."

The boy stepped to her bedside, opposite Charlie. "I'm Wyatt."

Susan knitted her eyebrows. "Hello, Wyatt."

"I'm Romy," the girl said, scrambling up on a bedside chair and pressing her face close to Susan's, making the woman smile. "Brambleman can be silly."

"Brambleman?"

"He's my new daddy."

"Daddy?'

"Me," Charlie said with a modest shrug. "All these things and more."

"He can be very silly," Susan said. "And this is one of those times. Where's your mother?"

"She ran away. You can be my new mommy, if you want."

Susan looked completely shocked. "But—"

"Don't want to stress you too much right now," Charlie said. "We'll talk later."

Susan was sputtering about his mental health when a middle-aged nurse in flowered scrubs entered the room. "Are we up, then?" she asked in a pleasant Midwestern accent. "We're going to need some time alone with the doctor," she explained apologetically to Charlie. "Meanwhile, there's some things Susan needs to do."

Charlie was already pulling the kids toward the door.

"Charlie," Susan called out. "What the heck is going on?"

Charlie was never so happy in his life to have a door shut in his face.

As he trudged down the hall with his new kids, Romy asked, "Will she be our mommy?"

"Can't say."

He considered problems and issues as he waited for the elevator. All the spite and hatefulness. Harold, Bryan, and maybe even Scudder. A slow recovery of body and mind. Building a wheelchair ramp. No guarantee they'd ever join as man and woman again. Or want to.

But being an ascetic had prepared him for this. It seemed a perfect match otherwise, too: she with her broken body and her family from hell, and he with his ruined face and stray kids he'd picked up on the street.

Mainly though, a deal was a deal. He'd already broken a life-or-death contract, and only one thing had saved him. It wouldn't do to break another vow, especially the one that had been tattooed on his heart the day he'd stood hungover at the altar in Macon with his twenty-year-old bride. He would accept responsibility for Susan and what happened to her, whether she liked it or not.

All this would work out in time, one way or another. But first things first. He would do things right, beginning today. Eventually he would buy Susan a new ring. And this time, his check wouldn't bounce.

* * *

Friday afternoon, Charlie set up operations in a Residence Suites motel. While Romy and Wyatt bounced on the beds, he went online to see the damage Tawny had done to his Visa card. So far, she'd spent a paltry $543.39, made it to Biloxi, and checked into a Holiday Inn.

By the end of the day, Charlie had (A) checked on Beck and Ben and learned not only that were they safe and sound, but that Bible Camp was good for them (or so they claimed); (B) found a full-time babysitter; (C) been cleared in the carjacking; (D) learned from Muncie that Harold had retrieved his belongings from Thornbriar and requested a transfer to Charlotte; and (E) talked to Minerva, who had decided to accept his offer to pay for Shaundra's funeral.

"An act of contrition," she called it. Charlie, feeling contrite, didn't argue.

"Just curious," he said. "What made you change your mind?"

"I don't rightly know," she said. "I was just rocking on the porch the other morning around ten o'clock when the idea came to me."

* * *

When Charlie, Romy, and Wyatt visited the hospital Saturday morning, Bradley Roy was there, his face drawn and gray, watching over his sleeping daughter. He looked at Charlie like he was crazy. "I thought it was the drugs talking when Susie told me you showed up with two black kids," he said. "Where'd you find them?"

"In church," Charlie said.

Bradley Roy shook his head in puzzlement. "Last night, I told her about Momo and Tantie Marie. She didn't take it well. They drugged her to calm her down. They unplugged the TV because so much bad news is going on."

He took a deep breath. "And then I get a call from Vange, screaming at me to get her out of jail. Don't see how I can help. She's being held without bond. In addition to charging her along with the others with her father's murder, they got her for two counts of conspiracy to commit murder. That would be on you, of course."

"The Forsyth DA did that?" Charlie marveled. "I didn't think he cared."

"Apparently, they put their money in a pot to kill you, just like they used to do Pappy's taxes," Bradley Roy said. "I never saw such a bunch in all my life." He shook his head in disgust. "They can't find Stanley. I think he took Vange's money and went somewhere."

Romy stood by the bed, cooing softly to Susan and reaching up to pat her hand. Charlie brushed back the strand of hair that always seemed to find its way onto his wife's forehead.

"They're operating Tuesday," Bradley Roy said. "Going to take out the bullet, if they can. They're not sure it will do any good."

Charlie cleared his throat. "I'm thinking about picking up Beck and Ben and bringing them back to Atlanta. She wants to see them."

"There's another week of Bible Camp." Bradley Roy nodded at Wyatt, who was interested in where a loose wire on the floor would lead him. "Looks like you got your hands full, anyway." He scowled. "What were you thinking, adopting kids at a time like this?"

Charlie grabbed Wyatt to prevent him from getting electrocuted.

Romy looked over at Bradley Roy and said, "Are you mad at us?"

The old man's face softened. "I don't mean to be takin' it out on you. Come here, little girl." She came over to him. He picked her up, grunting as he sat her on his knee. He bounced her while she told him what it was like to be a three-year-old with supernatural powers. He chuckled indulgently.

"It only encourages her," Charlie warned.

Susan was showing no sign of waking. Wyatt grew bored and hungry, so Charlie decided it was time to go. Romy slid off Bradley Roy's lap, and the old man stood up wearing a surprised expression. He tested his leg and looked at Charlie. "My knee feels better. Arthritis has been giving me a devil of a time. I figured having a kid sitting on it would kill it, but it seems to have the opposite effect."

"How about that," Charlie said.

* * *

Sunday, Romy carried a vase with yellow and white daisies into Susan's room and struggled to place them on the stand alongside white mums and silver helium balloons. Charlie noticed that Scudder, that nasty pimp of a banker, had sent red roses. Bradley Roy had gone to eat lunch, and Susan was alone. She opened her eyes in response to all the clunking that was going on around her bed.

"Come here, you," Susan rasped. Romy stepped toward her. She smiled and gently brushed Romy's cheek. Tears filled the woman's eyes.

"Are you sad because you miss your children?" Romy asked.

Susan bit her lip and nodded, then sobbed.

"I miss my mommy," Romy said. "I cry sometimes, too." She gave the stricken woman a birdlike look, cocking her head this way and that. "You're sad because you think you can't walk."

Susan let out an agonized groan. Charlie looked away.

"Have you tried?" Romy asked, unblinking.

'No."

"When you try, maybe you can."

Susan reached out and grabbed her hand, still sobbing. "Thank you, sweetie. But you have no idea."

Charlie noticed that the kids seemed to cheer Susan up. She chatted with them for a few minutes, ignoring her estranged husband until she reached out and clasped his hand. "Thank you for coming by," she said. A minute later, she tossed it aside. "I want to be alone now."

"You sure?"

She gave him her argument-winning face. "Daddy will be back soon. So take the children and go now, please."

"All right."

"Oh, one other thing," she said.

"What's that?" he asked.

"I'm still mad at you."

"I know. Some things never change."

* * *

Monday afternoon, Bradley Roy followed Charlie from the hospital to Mason Brothers Funeral Home. Charlie, still amazed that his father-in-law wanted to attend Shaundra Warner's funeral, kept checking the mirror, half-expecting Bradley Roy to peel off and disappear. But the old man stuck on his tail, and they parked near the edge of the half-full parking lot shortly before two o'clock. A hearse sat under a dark green awning at the side door with a limousine and a half-dozen other cars lined up behind it. Their white flags hung limp in the still summer air.

"Hot day," Bradley Roy said, climbing out of his car. Charlie approached, wearing a black eyepatch and a thousand-dollar suit he'd bought for the book tour he'd cancelled that morning, thereby enraging his handlers. Bradley Roy glanced at the modest old bungalows across the street. "Never been to this part of town before." He gave Charlie's scarred face an appraising look, then turned toward the funeral home. "Reckon they'll run late? I don't want to be gone long. Susie's nervous about the operation tomorrow." He cleared his throat and said, "She says you been friendly as a dog lately. Thinks you're up to something. I told her I threatened to kill you if you didn't do right."

"There's always that to look forward to, I guess."

"You comin' back?"

"I'll be there for the operation. I've got to take care of the kids this afternoon. Babysitter has to go somewhere."

"You talkin' about the new ones, right?"

"Right."

"Damn quickest adoption I ever heard of," Bradley Roy muttered. "You sure they ain't yours?"

"They are mine," Charlie said.

"I know you're liberal, but I'm asking you a question, and I'd appreciate an honest answer."

"My name's on their birth certificates."

Bradley Roy tugged his belt with both hands. "I'm not sure exactly what that means, you sayin' it like you're dealin' with a car title."

"I'm their long-lost daddy."

"That's two things you're saying, ain't it? Maybe three."

Charlie looked away and whistled.

"I guess you'll have to forgive Susie her trespasses with that asshole."

"Ass*holes*," Charlie muttered under his breath.

"I'm still trying to get used to the fact that I got black grandkids. I mean, I'm from Forsyth County. Not that I'm proud of the history. It's just … a mixed-up world, that's all." He pointed at the funeral home. "This is gonna be awkward as hell."

"You wanted to come."

"Had to. Just keep me away from the one who did that to my girl." Anger filled his eyes.

"He won't be here. He's being held without bond."

"I might have a hard time being properly mournful, knowing—"

"She's your niece," Charlie said.

"By marriage!" Bradley Roy grumbled.

Charlie smiled and gently grabbed his arm.

"Can't get over the fact that Minerva Doe is my sister-in-law."

"Don't remind her of it. She's a lot more touchy about it than you are. I don't think I'll ever mention the fact that she's my aunt."

"Well, I don't blame her. If I woke up one morning and found out I was a Cutchins, I'd be pissed off, too. Bad enough waking up next to one for fifty years. Sorry."

Charlie gave him a weary laugh. "We are what we are."

"I wouldn't settle for that, if I was you." Bradley Roy swatted him on the back. "Come on. Let's do this thing."

At the door, they were directed down a hall to a visitation room half-filled with mourners, most of them Minerva's age. The carpet was worn, and the wood around the doorknobs had lost its finish. Some of the young black women standing around sported dyed blonde hair, gold teeth, and/or tattoos.

Charlie walked over to Minerva, who had just finished talking to a middle-aged couple and now stood by herself. She did a double take when she saw him. "Did someone try to kill you again?"

"Yup," Charlie said.

"Looks like they came close to doing it."

"Yup."

"How many times has it been now?"

"I quit counting."

"Are you a cat, or does this have something to do with the deal?"

"The deal's off. I broke it."

"That's good to know."

"Got a new deal."

She groaned.

Charlie changed the subject. "It looks very nice," he said, nodding toward the casket.

"Yes. Thank you for that." Glancing around, she said, "I'll be glad when this is over." She paused for a moment before continuing. "The Forsyth sheriff came to see me. Stood at my door Saturday morning with his hat in his hand and told me they'd found my father. I told him I'd seen it on TV. He said, 'That man has the rest of him.'"

"Meaning me."

Minerva nodded. "Then he said there wasn't a case anymore, since the man who murdered my father was killed by his own family. I told him there'd better be a case, and he'd better do right and tell the world what happened to John Riggins, or I'd sic you on him." Her expression was fierce and she wagged her finger as she spoke. "I told him, 'Charles Sherman will tear everything up, and you know it.'"

Charlie chuckled softly.

"He said, 'Yes ma'am.' This morning he called to tell me they'll issue a report. I asked him why that man Cutchins ... why his own family killed him. The sheriff claimed it was money. Then I asked if there was another reason and he said, 'You sure you want to know?' I told him nothing he said could hurt me. He said they were ashamed he'd fathered a black child. So that's what they couldn't live with."

"A drop of blood can be powerful stuff," Charlie said.

She gave a little *huff*. "The woman whose son killed her, she's the one that told the police."

"Tantie Marie."

"Maybe she had a conscience." Minerva buried her face in her hands. "I'm numb from all this, Charles. Just numb. When will it end? I'll be ninety years old when Takira's child gets out of high school, if I last that long. She wants to keep the baby but she doesn't have a home of her own. I told her she'd have to put it up for adoption." She shook her head. "Demetrious. I don't know that there's anything I can do for him. He is lost. I hate what happened to your wife. I don't think he would have done it on his own. I don't see why the district attorney is pushing the death penalty."

A woman in a black, form-fitting dress walked in and called out Minerva's name, then rushed to embrace her. Charlie broke away and went over to Takira, who was sitting on a cushioned chair. She gave him a tiny wave. "When is the baby due?" he asked.

She grimaced. "Any time."

"Good luck." He knew he should say more, but he couldn't think of anything right then.

"Thanks." She gave him a shy smile.

Charlie walked over to the closed casket, which was covered with roses. He ran his hand along the varnished maple. "My apologies," he whispered. "I'll try to make it up to you."

He never could, of course. Paying for the funeral was nothing more than pouring money in a hole in the ground. He'd have to do more. And it would never make up for his indifference to her fate. Some things are lost and stay lost forever. The only thing he could do was pay it forward, somehow.

After he inspected the wreath he'd ordered, he went over to Bradley Roy, who sat alone in a corner, looking very much like he didn't belong. The older man held a white envelope and tapped his thigh with it. Charlie was about to say something inconsequential when a dignified, middle-aged black man in a dark suit entered the room and announced the service would be starting soon in the chapel.

Two younger men in dark suits rolled the casket away and the crowd followed. Charlie and Bradley Roy accepted beige programs from the young, white-gloved attendants as they shuffled in behind other mourners, about two dozen in all, who spread out amongst the small chapel's pews behind Minerva and a few of her close relatives.

The Reverend Aaron Sapp of Campbell Chapel AME Church took the pulpit. Charlie, who knew so much and could say so little, shifted uncomfortably in his seat. When he looked over his shoulder, his head jerked back in a double-take. An old white woman was sitting alone on the back row. Arlene Cartier had come to pay her respects to her late niece.

"… If there is any solace in this tragedy, we can at least know that the people responsible for this horrendous death have been brought to justice," Sapp told the crowd, shaking his head. "Terrible justice."

Charlie listened as the stocky preacher spoke in a high-pitched voice about forgiveness and redemption. There was a prayer for Demetrious, a "young manchild caught in a moment." The minister gazed over the crowd, then rested his eyes on the one-eyed white man and spoke of "the mother in a hospital, shot in an act of madness, who we pray will recover fully and find forgiveness in her heart."

Charlie glanced over at Bradley Roy. His head was bowed, his eyes shut tight. After the preacher finished, a young girl took the stage and sang a gospel song to the accompaniment of an old cassette in a boombox. The tape's hiss reminded Charlie of the music of the spheres he'd heard between the words of Jasper Riggins the first time he played Professor Talton's twenty-year-old tape.

After that, mourners stood and sang the hymn printed on the back of the program. Bradley Roy sang quietly and off-key. Charlie mouthed the words.

Following the service, Minerva and Takira followed the pallbearers out of the chapel. As the other mourners trailed behind them, Bradley Roy bent toward Charlie and said, "I can't go to the grave. I need to get back to Susie."

"Did you see Shirlene—I mean Shirley … uh, Arlene?" Charlie asked. He turned to point her out, but the back pew was empty. Bradley Roy looked at him like he was crazy, then broke away from him and walked briskly out the chapel door.

Charlie followed and saw his father-in-law catch up with Minerva outside, by the limo. He handed her the envelope he'd clutched tightly during the service, patting her hand as he clasped it in his own. "My daughter wanted me to give you this," he said.

Minerva, teary-eyed, hugged him. "God bless her."

"God bless you, too." Bradley Roy turned and hurried away toward his car.

Charlie trotted after him and called out, "Wait up!"

"I ain't got time to explain to you, boy." Bradley Roy fumbled in his pocket. "Here." He handed Charlie a house key. "You take care of Sirius. He's your dog. And just remember, if you do wrong by Susie, I'll kill you." At least he smiled when he said that.

"I hear you," Charlie said.

"You take these death threats pretty well."

"I'm getting used to them. And I appreciate the warning. Usually I don't even get that."

Charlie watched him drive off, then went to his car and pulled it to the end of the line of cars behind the hearse.

* * *

Takira went into labor as Shaundra's casket was being lowered into the grave. Minerva and two other women surrounded the girl, encouraging her to breathe properly and "hold steady." After Takira had calmed down and the crowd was breaking up, Minerva opened the envelope Bradley Roy had given her.

Charlie, looking over her shoulder in an attempt to read the sympathy card, was there to catch her when her legs buckled and a slip of paper fell from the card. He helped her to the folding chair next to Takira. Both were soon engulfed by church ladies. Charlie stepped back and retrieved the paper as it fluttered away on the ground. It was a check from Susan for $250,000. Written on the memo line: "My share of your father's farm."

Chapter Thirty

No question about it: Taking care of Sirius meant moving back to Thornbriar, albeit surreptitiously. What else could Charlie do after Trouble's sinister reading of *Dog Heaven* in the hospital? The pooch needed a bodyguard, and that would be Romy, since Trouble feared her. When Charlie brought his new kids to the house, Sirius went immediately to the girl, not his old master. He whimpered and licked her face. She whispered something Charlie couldn't hear, but it comforted the old dog immensely.

And so they squatted. Monday night, Romy and Wyatt camped out in the family room while Charlie slept on the couch. Sirius spent the night curled up on Romy's sleeping bag.

Tuesday morning, Charlie left the kids with the babysitter and went to the hospital to wait out Susan's surgery. Sitting on a cushioned bench in the third-floor waiting room, Bradley Roy told him about the big check Susan had written. "I'll tell you what sparked it. The bank president, Scuzzer or Scudder, came to see her."

"Scuzzier," suggested Charlie.

"I thought he was bein' nice, then he started talking about the discrimination case, and I realized that's what he was there for. He was gonna hold her job for her and keep her on salary, then he switched gears to talk about her testimony, how important it was." Bradley Roy snorted in disgust. "Susie got angry and told him the bank had been discriminating not only in who they hired and promoted, but who they loaned to, and she wasn't going to be a part of it anymore. After he left, she told me she decided the money Vange gave her as her cut from the farm wasn't rightfully her mother's to give or hers to take."

"Minerva nearly fainted when she saw it."

"Susie nearly fainted when she wrote the check. She had to go into debt to do it."

Charlie's mouth dropped open.

"I told you she'd need your help," Bradley Roy said. "Susie hates her momma now that she knows she tried to have you killed. You actin' like you want to go on a date with her is the only thing that cheers her up. Still thinks you're a crazy fool."

Recovering slightly, Charlie said, "Some things never change."

"You know what really gets me? That Scuzzier guy, acting like he's part of the family, asking about Beck and Ben like they're his own kids. The nerve. Charlie. Charlie! Hey, where you goin'?"

* * *

Dr. Pennywell couldn't say if Susan would ever walk again. "Pray for a miracle," he suggested to Bradley Roy and Charlie. Susan had just been wheeled out of the operating room after three hours, and the surgeon declared the procedure a success, inasmuch as he'd removed the bullet. But by this time, Charlie was wary of any miracle a person had to pray for, since they came with all kinds of consequences and strings attached.

Charlie was sitting at her bedside when Susan woke from the anesthesia. "I'm taking care of Sirius now," he said, hoping to establish his new role in the household while she was too groggy to consider the implications.

"That's good." Susan gazed out the window. "He loves you more than anyone else."

Charlie saw no point in disagreeing, although he wasn't sure that this was true, now that the dog had met Romy.

* * *

Friday, Susan was transferred to Shepherd Spinal Center for rehabilitation. Since Bible Camp ended that day, Charlie left Romy and Wyatt with the sitter and drove in his brand-new minivan to Sheila's ranch house near Cumming. Beck and Ben jumped up and down when he walked in the door.

Phil McRae, still in his orange AutoParts polo shirt, was home early from the store. It had been two years since Charlie had seen his brother-in-law. He hugged Phil for the first time in their lives. Phil gave him a bemused grin when they broke apart. Charlie noticed that Phil's neck was crooked and furrowed his brow in concern.

"What's wrong?" Phil asked.

"Fuckin' raccoons."

"Fuckin' raccoons is right. I don't even hunt anymore. Little bastards are dangerous, I tell ya."

"You have no idea."

"Oh, I got an idea, all right." He gave a lopsided shrug of his shoulders for emphasis.

If Sheila harbored any ill will toward her brother-in-law, she did an excellent job of hiding it. For the first time in twenty years, Charlie and Sheila had a decent conversation, although it involved mostly bad news. She'd already heard about Romy and Wyatt and didn't know what to make of this new development, but she was good-natured about it, as well as Charlie's tentative reentry into family life. Charlie suspected Bradley Roy had laid down some law to her on the subject.

Charlie thanked Sheila profusely for taking care of Beck and Ben.

"It was like having two of my own for a while," she said, sounding wistful.

Charlie kissed her cheek and she hugged him. They packed up the kids' stuff and buckled them into the van seats. Beck and Ben found the new van much preferable to the old one, since it had a DVD player in it. As he pulled out of the driveway, Charlie said, "You know Mommy's hurt, right?"

"Yes. A robber shot her," Beck said.

Charlie was relieved to hear her put it that way after having spent time in Forsyth County. Perhaps the curse of racism had washed away with the fall of the House of Varmint.

"She's getting better," he said. "She should be home by the end of the month."

"Are you back at the house now?" Beck asked.

"Yes. I think so," Charlie said.

"Yay," said Ben.

"Don't you know?" Beck asked.

"For now I am. We'll see."

They were halfway back to Thornbriar before Charlie broke the news to them about their new siblings. Fearful of negative reactions, he was pleased to see that Ben was excited about the prospect of live-in playmates. "Romy and Wyatt are part African-American and part white," Charlie said.

"Which parts?" Ben asked.

"All of them."

"So they're mixed up?"

"Not as much as you."

* * *

The babysitter took Monday off. Charlie stayed home with all four kids, who played well together. Ben and Wyatt celebrated their newfound brotherhood with a wrestling match. Romy dressed up in an old Halloween costume of Beck's, a white lace gown with a fluffy skirt and wings on the back. Once Romy found a wand, she danced around the house, enchanting everything, taking extra care to charm Sirius, because he was old and beautiful.

That afternoon, the phone rang right after Romy "charmed" it. "You need to get down here to the Spinal Center," Bradley Roy said. "It's a miracle. It's happening! She can walk, I tell you! It's with a walker, but she's walking!"

Tears welled in Charlie's good eye, and he wadded up the plans he was drawing for a wheelchair ramp. Shortly after he hung up, he was enchanted by Romy for the third time that day.

"Hey, Romy. Enchant the phone again." Romy came over and pursed her lips as she touched the cordless receiver lightly with her wand. It rang immediately. "Hello?" Charlie said hopefully.

"This is Rachel with cardholder services. You may be eligible for more credit. Act now—"

Charlie banged the phone down, muttering, "Doesn't always work."

* * *

The next day, Charlie took all the kids to see Susan, who was still weary from the exertion and excitement of taking her first steps. She managed a smile for Charlie. "Proud of me?" she asked.

"You bet," he said, kissing her on the forehead.

"Taking advantage of my slow reaction time, I see," Susan said, giving him a look that was too severe to take seriously.

"Always. And I'm still taking care of the dog."

"You *are* the dog," she said.

He smiled, grateful for the promotion.

* * *

Susan stayed at the center for three weeks, learning how to walk again and building her strength. During this time, neither she nor Charlie mentioned their relationship. He tiptoed like a jewel thief around the issue, trying not to draw attention to his movement toward his goal. Besides taking care of the kids, he was also busy fending off increasingly hostile reporters, agents, and editors.

"I was trying to survive," Charlie explained to one insistent TV reporter who showed up at this door with a camera rolling and wanted to know why he hadn't gone to the police after the van bombing. *No cops* was such a simple rule, but so hard to explain.

"But that was nearly a year ago," the reporter insisted.

"And I'm still trying to survive," Charlie said, closing the door gently in the reporter's face.

By the time Susan was dismissed from Shepherd, Charlie's useless, painful left eye had been removed, along with two of his molars. He brought her back to Thornbriar in the minivan. She was still dependent on a walker, so he carried her up the steps and over the threshold. Sirius bounced around to greet them. Charlie took Susan into the family room and put her down gently on the sofa.

"Where are the kids?" she asked. "I thought the babysitter stayed here."

"They're down the street. All of them. Both sets."

"Yours and ours," she said.

He'd had something planned, but suddenly, it seemed like a bad idea. "I'll go get them."

"Go," she said.

Charlie stepped away from the couch. "Well, OK, then."

"Wait," she said. "I mean—"

She struggled to get up and took a tumble, managing to brace herself on the sofa arm as she landed on her knees. He knelt down to help lift her back up. "Wait," she said.

"OK."

"I mean, don't go."

"I'm confused."

"Don't go away again," she pleaded. "I couldn't stand it."

"I'm not back yet," he pointed out. And suddenly he felt like crying.

"All right. Charlie, please come back. I need you. God, I need you. Why'd you ever leave?" And then she started crying.

He was silent for a moment. Tears welled in his eyes. "I'm sorry."

"I left a light on for you for the longest time," she said, sobbing. "But it burned out."

"Me too," Charlie said.

"I have a confession to make."

Charlie braced himself. He didn't want to hear about Bryan or Harold, and he especially didn't want to hear about Scudder. But if she had to clear the air, so be it.

"I prayed," she said, then licked her lips. "It was kind of a mean prayer. I prayed ... that no other woman would have you."

"Well, it worked."

* * *

They bedded the kids down for the night, and then Charlie helped Susan to the couch. After hemming and hawing for a minute, he pulled the new engagement ring from the pocket of his cargo shorts. "I thought we could pretend to start over," he said.

"Oooh. I like to pretend," Susan said when she saw the diamond.

"So, will you stay married to me?"

She smiled. "I will."

"I should kiss you, I suppose."

"I suppose you should.'

Due to lack of practice—at least on his part—they embraced awkwardly and pecked each other on the lips. When they separated, Susan said, "You didn't have to do this, but I'm glad you thought you did." She slipped the ring on her finger. It was a perfect fit.

"I remember Betty Richards came over to me at the bank in Macon and told me your check to the jewelry store was non-sufficient funds. She said, 'Your fiancé got some money problems, hon.' I thought, God, what am I getting into?"

"Well, at least this time, you know."

"I'm still not sure. I don't think I ever will be, with you."

* * *

When Susan woke up the next morning, she scolded Charlie for sleeping on the couch. After that, they slept together. Just snoring, no sex. In the days that followed, Charlie and Susan were kind and civil to each other, but they remained somewhat wary, and reconciliation was not complete.

Life went on. Susan resigned her position from TransNationBank and started taking care of the kids full time (with Charlie's help), which was what she'd always wanted to do. In late August, she traded in the walker for a cane. By then, Romy had turned four and was enrolled in pre-K, so all the kids attended Gresham Elementary. Susan called Romy "my little angel."

Charlie said, "Don't. It will only encourage her." Being a wise one for her age, Romy understood the need to use her special powers discreetly. Susan joined the PTA board and became the Room Mom in Beck's class. Unfortunately, Charlie's fearsome visage often frightened small children—at least until they saw that his scar was a rose, complete with thorns (when he didn't shave). Charlie returned to writing with his one good eye and improved vision.

One evening in early September, after Wyatt and Ben had finished wrestling for the day and all the kids were tucked away in their bunk beds, Charlie was revising a chapter on one of his novels when he heard music playing. He got up to investigate, suspecting that Beck was breaking curfew. He found Susan in the family room, enthusiastically moving to a techno beat, holding her cane over her head like a tap dancer's prop. Charlie stood in front of her, hands on hips, marveling at her recovery.

"Romy enchanted me when I put her to bed, so I thought I'd check it out. Guess what? I'm healed!" she said, stumbling into his arms. "More or less. Dance with me, you fool!"

As he twirled her around, she said, "I want to love you forever, starting"—she kissed him—"right"—kiss—"now."

And so they made love for the first time in more than two years—he gently, she with her eyes closed. When they were finished, Susan said, "I want to adopt Romy and Wyatt. And I want to run in the Peachtree Road Race. And make love to you again. Soon. I want us to be happy."

"I'm glad," Charlie said.

* * *

After Susan gave a deposition for the plaintiff in the discrimination suit, TransNationBank offered to settle the case and change its personnel policy. Then Charlie helped Susan write an opinion piece about the bank's lending practices that got the attention of (who else?) Tyrus Bannister.

Charlie hadn't bothered to cancel the credit card Tawny had stolen, but when the October statement came in, he saw that the charges had stopped. The last one had been made on the day Susan and he first made love again. It was for tuition at a community college in California.

In October, Susan, with the help of Sandra Hughes, legally adopted Wyatt and Romy. Wyatt struggled to cope sometimes, but every day was better than the day before. As for Romy, she was, even at her tender age, a little bit beyond day-to-day struggles. Susan had worried about how her family would react to her two new kids, but by this time, only the opinions of her father and sister mattered, and they were happy for her. Bradley Roy insisted on taking his reconstituted family to the Forsyth County Fair. He carried Wyatt piggyback, and Charlie snapped a picture of Bradley Roy with the boy the old man now called, "my little man" underneath the Forsyth County banner. Bradley Roy introduced Romy and Wyatt to one of his old friends, a grand-nephew of a 1912 lyncher, by Charlie's reckoning. The man bought all the kids cotton candy and marveled at how the world had changed, then joked that Charlie Sherman was "the only person I know of in danger of getting run out of town these days."

* * *

The remains of John Riggins, reunited with his right middle finger, had been buried alongside those of his wife.

Minerva and Arlene, who had filed her own claim against the Cutchinses, dropped their lawsuits when they found out that the Cutchinses' vast wealth was gone with the windbag and that fighting the developer would also mean fighting the state Department of Transportation and attorney general, since highway easements were now involved.

There was one chunk of change remaining, however. Susan and Bradley Roy persuaded Phil and Sheila to give up what was left of their share of Pappy's ill-gotten gains. Minerva, having learned of Arlene's plight, split that money with her half-sister. Arlene would use her portion to buy a new double-wide and a pickup truck. During this process, Charlie had the opportunity to talk to Susan's hermetic aunt, and he asked her, "What really happened to your baby? Did you have an abortion, or was the child institutionalized?"

Arlene looked him in the eye and said, "Neither. I had a miscarriage."

Charlie was incredulous. "Then why ... why ... oh, I give up."

"Best that you do," she said.

Minerva used her money to set up a college fund for Takira and hire lawyers for Demetrious. His lawyers were able to negotiate a guilty plea in exchange for a ten-year sentence—a much better deal than the death penalty or even the two mandatory twenty-year sentences he faced if convicted. The deal went through after it received the victim's approval.

By that time, the old woman and young girl had decided it would be best for Baby Shaundra if she was put up for adoption. At John Riggins's funeral, Minerva had asked Charlie if he knew of any prospective parents,

Charlie mentioned Angela Talton and Sandra Hughes, who had told him at their commitment ceremony in August that they wanted to adopt. Minerva thought it was a grand idea for the girl to have two mommies. "I'm tired of men, anyhow," she said.

In November, news broke that fugitive politician Stanley Cutchins had perished of dysentery in Costa Rica. The money he'd taken was never recovered. Evangeline remained in jail awaiting trial and refused to allow her public defender to plea bargain. She believed that she'd be vindicated in a trial because, in her words, Charlie Sherman "needed killing."

* * *

While doing spring cleaning, Susan found Charlie's $12,000 painting in the garage. She insisted that he get rid of it immediately. Charlie hated the idea of throwing away something so expensive, even if it wasn't valuable, so he took it to Bay Street Coffeehouse to show it to Jean, whom he hadn't seen in nearly a year.

His favorite barista shook her head at the sight of him. "You've gone from lone wolf to pirate," she said, then quickly added, "I told you Dana was bad news."

Danger Girl had recently been sentenced to twenty years in federal prison. Charlie didn't want to talk about her. He just shook his head back at Jean.

"Whatcha got there?" She nodded at the painting, which he'd placed just inside the door.

"You want it?" he asked.

"Are you serious?" She came around the counter to view it more closely.

He groaned in embarrassment. "I know. Really. You can have it."

"How much you asking for it?"

"It's yours if you want it. In exchange for your many kindnesses."

"I don't remember being *that* kind."

"Consider it payback for that cranberry muffin."

"A muffin?" She squinted at him. "Your wife making you get rid of it?"

"Yup." He picked up the picture and peered over the top of its frame. For the first time, he saw it as the artist had intended. "Oh, my God! Is that … oh, definitely take it, then."

"Prude."

"Former ascetic, actually."

Her eyebrows perked up. "You really want me to have it?"

"Absolutely."

"In that case, I won't turn it down." She grabbed the painting. "You realize this is a Travinci? No? Oh. He was killed by terrorists a few months ago. And you know what happens when artists die."

"Hell, I just got *shot* and got rich. I hope you do as well. Without getting shot, that is."

She smiled and then gave him a kiss that reminded him what he'd missed while under his wife's prayer/curse. He left, glad to know he'd found a way to repay her for being his friend when he had no others.

He never found out how much the painting was worth, but the next time he dropped by and tinkled the doorbell, the place had been renamed *Jean's Bay Street Coffeehouse*. And while she wasn't working at the time, there was a laminated card taped to the counter that said *Free coffee for one-eyed writers*. The barista on duty looked up at Charlie and said, "You're the one."

Epilogue

Charlie was living a good life, loving his wife and children, giving away money, even donating time and effort to worthy causes. While *Flight from Forsyth* and *American Monster* had both been bestsellers, the issue of reparations died (again) without any concrete results, possession being more than nine-tenths of the law in this case. Charlie was disappointed that the books had not had a greater effect, even though he realized that some of the blame for this lamentable outcome fell on his shoulders. Still, he suspected that what had started that December night wasn't over yet. Something large was out there waiting for him, just over the horizon.

One day in May, Charlie felt a burning sensation on his thigh, like he'd struck a match in his pocket. After a blazing instant of pain, the feeling subsided. That evening, he heard the news that Redeemer Wilson had died, succumbing to cancer after a long battle. When Charlie read Crenshaw's article about the civil rights icon, he wanted to make another donation to the cause, but he couldn't even find anyone to take his money. The charity's finances were hopelessly tangled, and its prospects were beyond grim: The Hunger Palace had been closed for more than a year.

The old civil rights warrior was laid to rest on a Monday afternoon in overalls, with a bullhorn at his side, just in case. His pine box coffin was carried on a mule-drawn wagon to Eastside Cemetery, followed by thousands of marching mourners. He was laid to rest just a few feet away from John Riggins. As Charlie stood at the back of the huge crowd, he caught a whiff of that old familiar stench. He looked around but saw no bad angel lurking. Following the service, he slipped away unnoticed.

Redeemer's death reminded Charlie of something, and the next day, he started work in his home office on his long-delayed article about unrepentant racist Clint Brimmer. It was just after lunch, and he was by himself. The kids were at school, and Susan was also at Gresham, doing PTA work. As he picked up the phone to call Brimmer, Charlie heard the familiar rumble of a MARTA bus—odd, since Thornbriar had no service. With a sense of foreboding, he put the phone down and went to the front door, opening it just as the vehicle stopped directly in front of the house.

An emaciated old fellow stumbled down the steps, tripping on the curb and stepping awkwardly on the grass. It was Trouble, looking much more haggard and worn than Charlie had ever seen him before. As the bus pulled away, he shuffled slowly toward Charlie with tiny steps, then detoured to a concrete bench by the Japanese maple in the middle of the yard, where he collapsed. "Thirsty," Trouble croaked.

Instead of fear or anger, Charlie felt pity for the avenging angel. He ran inside and returned with a bottle of water. Trouble was slumped over on the bench. Fighting his aversion to the odor, Charlie gently grabbed Trouble's shoulder and pulled him up into a sitting position, then sat beside him to brace the old guy. He realized that Trouble's power was gone; not even a static charge was left. He opened the bottle and held it to the old being's lips. After a few sips, Trouble said, "Enough."

Charlie capped the container and set it on the bench.

"I always liked water," Trouble said. "Next to fire, it's my favorite element. How about you?"

"Earth," Charlie said.

"Ha. With you, I figured it would be wind."

They sat in silence for a while. A blue jay squawked. White butterflies flitted around the petunias the kids had planted in the flowerbed. Charlie smelled a neighbor's fresh-cut grass mingled with Trouble's stench. Finally, Trouble spoke. "It's over."

"Is it? I never know."

"That's your problem." Trouble wheezed a weak laugh, showing a few blackened teeth. Most were gone. "I meant for me, not you. Your trouble is just beginning."

"Why should I listen to you?" Charlie said. "Face it. You're not very nice."

"Niceness is overrated. Give me thunder and lightning any time."

"All you know to do is tear up and destroy."

Trouble twisted his neck until it popped. He grimaced and shook his head.

"You got me good with those rat traps. I knew something weird was going on then. I figured it was revenge for what happened to Raccoon boy. Your brother."

"My brother-in—yeah, my brother."

"The fact that he didn't die was a tip-off that this wasn't going to end well. From my perspective."

"I don't get it. Why kill him?"

"For the prevention of breeding more ... what do you call them? *Varmints*?"

Charlie looked at him in disgust. "Birth control? Sheila's forty-five years old."

Trouble shrugged. "They were talking."

"I don't believe this. I'm only sitting here because you've got connections. So what have you got to say? Spit it out."

Trouble appeared irked at Charlie's impudence. "*I've* got connections? You *are* a fool. But I knew that ever since the fakey suicide attempt you made just to get their attention. World's worst prayer," he muttered in distaste.

"I'm not proud of that," Charlie admitted. "But it wasn't a prayer."

"Was too."

"Was—"

Charlie was interrupted by the cawing of a crow overhead.

"Look, I'm doing better."

"That's what I hear," Trouble said. "And you ... you're too stupid to know this, but it's not just the little one. It's you. You must know you've been marked. That's how life on earth gets to us."

Caw!

Trouble winced. Looking to the sky, he said, "He's going to know in just a minute, anyway!" He leveled his gaze at Charlie. "Crows. Biggest assholes in the universe. This or any other."

Charlie looked up and saw the black birds approaching from all sides. Trouble waved a hand weakly. "You managed to save the Cutchins seed from extinction. Congratulations," he said sarcastically.

"It's my seed, too," Charlie reminded him.

"If you say so. Just don't let them compound—"

"Don't go there."

"I'm just sayin'. Recessive genes, you know. We don't need a comeback."

"They're not the only ones."

"You're talking about the carjacker's baby girl. Shaundra Talton-Hughes. Little kryptonite saved her, too. Umbrella effect." Trouble squinted at the early afternoon sun. Meanwhile, hundreds of crows circled in the sky. "This is where it ends for me."

Birds were landing in the surrounding trees, filling the air with raucous cawing.

"Don't have much time left. Just came to grant your prayer. As required."

Charlie stood up. "No more miracles. You've done enough already."

Trouble broke out laughing, then started coughing. Charlie slapped him on the back and felt the welts he'd seen under Trouble's T-shirt that night in the Pancake Hut. He had a few of his own from the chain beating he'd taken that night in the church parking lot, though his wounds weren't as prominent as the old timer's. They really knew how to lay on a whupping back in the day.

When he caught his breath, Trouble said, "You *are* a miracle. You *are* life after death. But you're more than that, you are—eh, I can't even say it. The new thing. But you're not indestructible, just lucky."

"That's funny," Charlie said. "But I'm leery of miracles you have to pray for. I prefer the everyday kind. You know, where the poor kid goes to med school and pulls the bullet out of a woman's back. Three-minute response times. Hookers with guns. That sort of thing."

"Your own reckless foolishness," Trouble added.

"Talk about reckless. Why'd you give the smite power to Kathleen?"

"That wasn't me. I just passed along the request … with a recommendation of approval," he added.

"OK. Why'd you pass along the request … with a recommendation of approval, then?"

Trouble shrugged. "Self-defense. She was worried, and I sure as hell didn't trust you to take care of her."

"Fair enough."

"Didn't work out. They took it away."

"I know. I was there. She could have used it later."

Trouble shook his head knowingly. "Timing is everything."

"So what kind of prayer were you going to grant me? World peace? A million dollars?"

"World peace is impossible, and you got the money, although it's probably gone."

"I got some left," Charlie said defensively.

"Your real prayer," Trouble said. "The first one. Your best one. They think you deserve it."

"Somebody up there likes me?" Charlie asked in amazement.

"I'd say *out* there." Trouble gave him a sly smile. "And I wouldn't go so far as to say they like you. Let's just say it was the kind of prayer they couldn't turn down—one of those ninety-eight foot shots at the buzzer they find so interesting. But you had to prove yourself. And somehow, in some stupid, dumbass way, you did. So—"

"I think it's selfish and greedy to pray for things. I've already got what I need. So, if you don't mind …"

Charlie started to get up. Trouble grabbed his arm. The angel's eyes lit up with angry fire, and his voice trembled with rage. "Shut up and listen, fool! Did you think we'd let you see all the things you saw and allow you to just walk away a free man when you're no longer either? What you thought was the curse is the miracle! Talk about making the blind see. *Sheesh.* With you, it's impossible."

Charlie gave him a glum look. "Great. Tell me what I won."

"What you *won.*" Trouble snorted. Again he looked to the skies, holding out his palms, as if to say *See what I got to work with here*?

"All right. What I prayed for."

Trouble addressed the sky. "He doesn't remember. That's how important it was to him." He shook his head and turned to Charlie. "When you were seven, you were outside your house, running up and down the sidewalk, flapping your arms, praying that you could be an angel so that you could find your father. We were never quite sure what you meant, but in any case, like I said, it was an interesting prayer. And the fact that we didn't know what you meant made it—and you—even more interesting. There are very few humans who are a mystery to us. By the way, your wife is the same way. We weren't sure what she meant by 'no woman would have you' so we treated it as 'no woman could have you.' I think." He shook his head in bewilderment. "Varmints. Varmints and fools. That's what they give me to work with."

Charlie thought for the moment. "Actually, I do remember what I prayed for. To be a bird."

"Nope. Angel."

"Pretty sure I wanted to be a bird."

"Too late now. Well, you'll be different, I'll say that much." Trouble glanced down at the water bottle. "Don't need that anymore." He stood and brushed back his stringy, greasy hair with both hands. Charlie heard a bus in the distance and stood, too.

"One last thing. I remembered what I was going to tell you."

"What's that?" Charlie asked.

"The night we met. I said I was going to tell you two things. I only told you one."

"What's the other?"

"Hell is overrated."

"That's good to know."

"Alrighty then. Time for the elaborate ceremony, replacement part," Trouble said, looking Charlie in the eye. "Here's to knowing who you are. You're it."

He touched Charlie's chest and disintegrated, clothes and all, falling into a neat, cone-shaped pile of grayish-black dust. In an instant, the huge flock of crows descended and began devouring Trouble's remains. Acting on instinct, Charlie reached into their midst and grabbed a handful of Trouble. Out of professional courtesy, not a single bird pecked his hand.

The birds kept coming, and Charlie backed away, his expression a mixture of wonder and horror. In less than a minute, they had finished and flown off in all different directions. The only thing left was a shiny piece of metal in the center of a bare ring of red earth pecked clean of grass. Charlie bent down and picked up the key. He reached into his pocket and felt the key Redeemer had refused to take from him that day he fixed the church door. It was warm to his touch. The one he'd just plucked from the ground, Trouble's key, was cold.

A horn honked. He turned and saw the MARTA bus in front of his house. With his fist clenched, he ran back to the house and locked the door. As he crossed the lawn, he looked up to the sun, which smiled down on his ravaged face.

The bus doors opened as he approached. The driver, a familiar-looking middle-aged black woman, wore a short wig and sunglasses. "Hey," Charlie said. "You got your job back!"

"I was only at Family and Children Services for a day," she said.

"Ah. Cool. So I need to go—"

"I know where you're going."

Charlie climbed aboard. The bus was full of passengers, all of them like him in one way or another. A man with long white hair was also missing an eye. A woman whose face had been badly burned smiled at him. A man's artificial leg stuck into the aisle. These were a bunch of hard cases—wingless, untrustworthy, scarred by life on earth, forced to ride the bus. And now he was one, marked by shotgun blasts, clubs, nails, and chains: Brambleman, born of Trouble, and as different from the other as day from night, new from old. He stood in the aisle, since he was the youngest one of all, this being his birthday. Now both a Thursday and a Tuesday child, he braced himself for the ride ahead.

The bus lurched forward. The others stared at their newest colleague expectantly as he stepped toward the rear. He held up his fist. "This is what's left of Trouble," he shouted above the diesel's roar. "I'm taking him with me to the holy place."

"You'll need to transfer to the Memorial Drive bus," the driver shouted back.

* * *

Trouble's key didn't work, but Charlie's did. After all, it was his door.

Redeemer Wilson once told Charlie, "It's not just what *they did* that matters. What *you* do matters more." Finally, he was ready to take those words to heart and act on them. With the money he'd earned from his books, he bought both the Holy Way House and the Hunger Palace from Redeemer's widow with the stipulation that the buildings' names and purpose would not change. He hired a social gospel preacher, since that's what the Holy Way House required, and persuaded Lucinda Persons, Redeemer's fierce black kitchen manager, to return to her old job.

Then he set about making repairs.

Early one summer morning—a Monday, just as Redeemer would have liked—Charlie was working alone, replacing the church's broken windows. He turned to his tool chest to get a pry bar, and when he looked up and squinted into the dawn, he saw someone hobbling toward him with the aid of a cane. Charlie stood and watched as a woman approached across the weedy, graveled lot, carrying a black garbage bag over her shoulder. She wore a dirty old tan coat and shapeless blue pants along with an oversized yellow sweater. She winced as she stepped on the rocks, for there were holes in her shoes. He realized that he had seen her before. Attached to the front of her coat was a name tag that said Lil Bit.

She started begging as she drew near. "Please, sir. I ain't got a place to stay and nuthin' to eat. I heard you was the one to come to. I lost my job."

"Where'd you work?" Charlie asked, already knowing the answer.

"Pancake Hut."

"What happened?"

"They got sued and went bankrupt. They didn't treat people right."

"Is that so," he said, pursing his lips.

"Yup. I came down here because I heard Redeemer had this place and maybe—"

"Redeemer passed on. Maybe I can help you get back on your feet."

"I was hopin' I could get *off* my feet. I been walkin' all night."

"Tell you what. I'm setting up the food kitchen, and I need people to work it."

Lil Bit brightened. "I been cooking and waitressin' for people all my life."

"Not all of them." He wagged a finger at her. "This time, you serve everyone."

"Yes sir." She looked up at him in surprise. "Do you know me?"

"Of course."

She stared at him like he'd performed a miracle.

"Meanwhile," he said, "you can have my brown-bag lunch and take a bed in the big building until you find a place of your own. You'll report to a lady named Lucinda. And if you have a problem with that, it will be your problem. I assure you."

"Thank you so much." She grabbed his right hand and kissed it. "You're an angel."

"Shhh. Don't tell anybody. I've got a reputation to uphold."

* * *

It took half of Charlie's earnings from both *Flight from Forsyth* and *American Monster* to get Redeemer's operation up and running again. Which was, he figured, as it should be, since a deal is, after all, a deal.

On Thanksgiving Day, the Hunger Palace was filled with people enjoying the bounty that Charlie and Susan had coerced and cajoled from Atlanta's wealthiest percentiles. Under Lucinda's watchful (and sometimes baleful) gaze, Lil Bit and the everyday people on the serving line dished out turkey and dressing, sweet potatoes, beans, pumpkin pie, and other hearty fare. Susan helped keep the line of hungry people moving, and Beck, Ben, and Wyatt wiped down tables. Romy did what she did best, moving through the crowd of homeless and poor, blessing everyone with her tattered old wand. All the news anchors had already finished work for the day, since Charlie had told them they could come in to volunteer at dawn or they'd be turned away at the door.

After conducting a contentious interview outside with a pack of reporters who wanted to rehash his sordid past of drug-dealing, international espionage, and footnote faking (Redeemer would have been so proud of him), the man in the shipping department uniform returned to the serving line. He leaned against the wall and watched with satisfaction as Lil Bit spooned a healthy dollop of mashed potatoes on a black man's plate.

Romy swung by, tapping him on his leg for the third time that day, singing a song about her daddy: "There was a man in my home town, and he was wondrous wise …"

There came a tapping on his shoulder. He turned to see Lucinda giving him her *storm's a comin'* look.

"We got some attitude back there in the kitchen," she said. "And you better get a new dish machine by Christmas."

"OK," Charlie said. "I'll take care of it."

He entered the kitchen, passing through the double doors Trouble had once electrified against him. He heard groaning coming from behind a mountain of pots and pans. The new dishwasher, a one-armed man hired last week, was overwhelmed by his work.

"How's it going back there?" Charlie shouted out.

The fellow—slight and ponytailed, wearing faded and frayed jeans—looked up at him through thick glasses. Without saying a word, he gestured helplessly with his arm at the six-foot-tall stack of cooking utensils. "I'll never be finished."

"True. But we can get these done."

And so Brambleman rolled up his sleeves past the scars, pushed the faucet to stop the drip, and started scrubbing pans alongside the poor fellow, having learned what Trouble could never admit: There is such a thing as Grace.

Acknowledgments

In more than one way, *Brambleman* is an outgrowth of my work on *The Way It Was in the South: The Black Experience in Georgia*, my father's award-winning magnum opus. Tragically, Donald L. Grant died without seeing his life's great work published. That task fell to me, his youngest son, due to the urging and assistance of my mother Mildred B. "Jeanne" Grant. (As it turned out, a history professor and a librarian make a pretty good combination.) Working on Dad's book was a life-changing experience for me, and I certainly wouldn't have written this book if I hadn't been involved with his. While both my parents are gone now, I think of this as their book, too. Thanks, Mom and Dad.

I'm also grateful to the members of my writers' group who helped me tweak my work in progress: Leslie Brown, Juanita McDowell, and peerless reader Ricky Jacobs. And I want to give a special shout out to Anthony Mattero, who believed in the book.

Writing the book turns out to be only half the fun, so I owe a debt of gratitude to my far-flung production team: proofreader/editor, Wendy Herlich, eBook formatter L.K. Campbell, designer Jerry Dorris at AuthorSupport, and photographer Matthew King (for taking such a cool cover picture). I can think of no higher praise for Wendy than to tell you that she skillfully handled extended dialogue between a Transylvanian and a man who'd just been shot in the mouth.

As always, thanks to my wife Judy, who bears with me. She's read *Brambleman* a few times already, and she may yet be surprised at the end result. My daughter, Laurel, was in first grade when I started writing this book full-time. As a college sophomore, she helped me finish it.

DeKalb County librarians at Embry Hills, Decatur, Dunwoody, and Tucker branches have always been helpful on this and other endeavors, including raising two children. And I would be remiss if I didn't express my appreciation to the Forsyth County Sheriff's Department for their hospitality and Forsyth County librarians for their assistance while I was researching the book.

Because the song had such a great influence on *Brambleman*, I must express my appreciation to Eric Bazilian for writing *One of Us*, and to Joan Osborne for her magnificent rendition of it.

Finally, a special note in memory of civil rights pioneer Hosea Williams (1926-2000), Unbought and Unbossed. His work lives on through the charity he founded forty years ago, Hosea Feed the Hungry and Homeless (HFTH). To learn more and see how you can help or to make a donation, visit http://www.hoseafeedthehungry.com.

About the Author

Jonathan Grant is an award-winning writer and editor (***The Way It Was in the South: The Black Experience in Georgia***), and ***Brambleman*** is his second novel. His previous novel, ***Chain Gang Elementary*** (also published by Thornbriar Press), tells the tragicomic story of a war between a reform-minded PTA president and an authoritarian principal. ***A Thousand Miles to Freedom***, his screenplay based on the real-life adventures of escaped slaves William and Ellen Craft, was recently optioned to Hollywood.

Grant grew up on a Midwestern farm and graduated from the University of Georgia with a degree in English. He is a former newspaper journalist and served for several years as a Georgia state government spokesman. He lives in suburban Atlanta with his wife and two children.

He may be contacted at info@thornbriarpress.com.

Made in the USA
Charleston, SC
12 August 2012